Knightfall

Book I of the CODM Prophecy

Natasha E Scholey

ISBN 978-0-9873894-0-4

Gwydion Books, PO Box 391, Stirling, SA, 5152, Australia

For Stephen

For your love and support, I thank you. When I stumble, you are there to pick me up. You are the strength that drives me ever onward and I am so grateful to have you in my life.

Acknowledgements

Many thanks to Valerie Grunitz for the original French translation and Margo Poirier for kindly assisting with the updated edition.

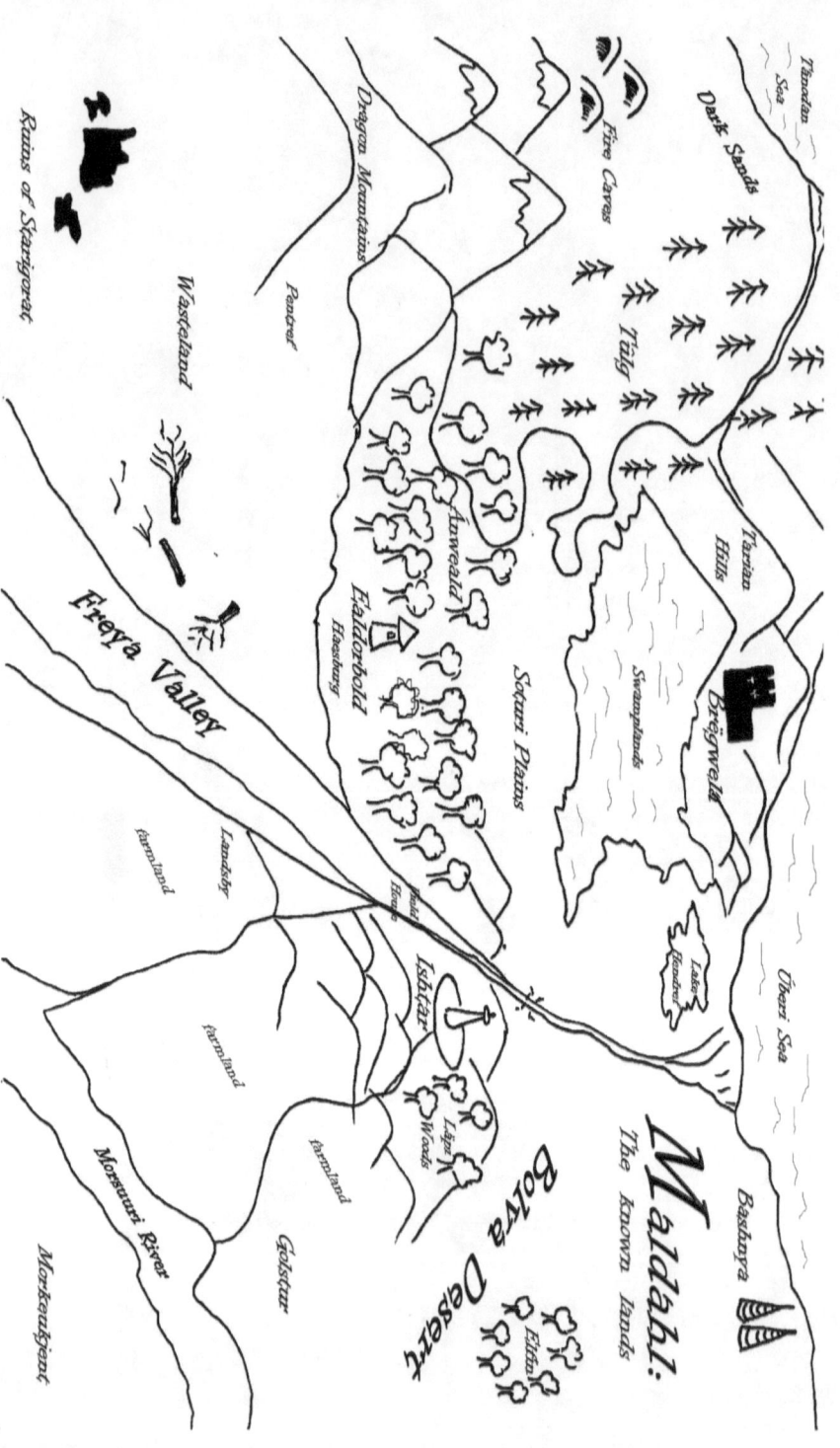

Knightfall

The board is set,

The Prize—the crown,

A dance begins of intricate steps,

Rules of movement and etiquette,

Clergy cross paths with knights,

As castles shift by hands of gods,

Mighty kingdoms laid low in boardom,

But the purity of thought and action cannot be questioned.

One thing above all else remains certain,

When the balance of power shifts,

Knight will fall

Prologue

It had been a magnificent day. The clear sky was dotted with dreamy clouds; the mild breeze refreshed the flora and fauna alike. From the palace gardens, came the sound of tinkering laughter as Exzalander freed herself from Katahl's embrace and ran swiftly away. He stood and watched as she danced about, the sunlight outlining her body through the shift in her dress. He smiled as she threw her head back, spinning, her long red hair flowing outward and falling wildly across her back.

She dashed off once more, Katahl following. Reaching out, he tried to grab her long robe as it streamed behind her, but every time he neared, her speed would increase and she would dodge gracefully out of reach. Realising he hadn't a chance, he settled on the grass. Exzalander continued until it became apparent that her fun was over. As she knelt beside him, he reached over, gently touching her silk-like skin. Her eyes shone in response to his touch and she leaned forward, holding his gaze. He moved his face instinctively toward hers, surprised when she pulled away.

'Something is wrong!' she said.

Katahl sat up, smiled and prepared to embrace her, but she jumped to her feet and began to run in the direction of the palace.

The great ancient building loomed ahead; black smoke encircled the turrets like carrion birds. The palace was ablaze. Exzalander came to an abrupt halt, gazing on her home in horror. Katahl caught up, catching his breath; his hand reached out for hers, and clenched it firmly.

'Come,' he said, 'let us go see if we can be of help.'

Exzalander nodded and resumed sprint. On reaching the palace, it became apparent that the cause of the fire was no accident. Dead bodies lay afoot, some with missing limbs which looked as though they had been simply torn off.

As fear seized Exzalander, she felt unable to turn away from the gruesome sight. It seemed unreal to her somehow. Her mind drifted back to her childhood and she recalled hiding herself in her father's private study—a simple game of hide and seek. Aware that the room was forbidden to all but the King, made it the perfect place for concealment; no-one would dare search for her there …

The room smelt musty. Exzalander traced her tiny fingers across several of the dust-covered volumes, and then set about finding something interesting to read in order to pass the time. She walked toward the back section of the study, being careful to keep her footsteps light, to escape discovery. A strange looking book sat on a pedestal to the corner of the room; its odd black cover had the appearance of carved ebony. Exzalander paused for a moment, her tiny hand hovering above the work, fearful to touch it and yet unable to resist. The weird carvings seemed to shift as she ran her fingers across them.

Footsteps sounded in the hallway and she heard her name being called. She watched the door fearfully, expecting discovery, but the footsteps receded. Obviously nobody considered that she might be brave or fool enough to incur the King's wrath, yet she was not afraid of the King; her father had never raised his voice to her, let alone his hand, so what possible punishment could he bestow that she need worry about?

Once the danger had departed, she turned her attention back to the book. Leaning over it, she peered at its peculiar design—a palace surrounded by trees, bending gently in a wind. It was not merely an image that depicted the motion; they were actually moving.

Her eager hand reached out to touch it once more, when she noticed the stains—red marks that were darkening by the second, like ageing blood. Aware that the only thing she had touched had been the book, she rubbed her index finger curiously along the edge of the cover, unwilling to disturb the odd design again. Fresh liquid oozed onto her skin and she gasped—certain that her supposition had been correct. Fear crept upon her and she backed away, wishing that she had never dared to touch it, regretting that she ever came into a place where nobody would think to look for her.

To her astonishment and fright, the book flicked open, its pages fluttering wildly, whispering her name. She cowered on the ground, unable to move or utter a sound as the book illuminated from within. Fragmented images leapt from the pages and she watched as great battles ensued and mighty warriors stood together, their capes blowing proudly in the wind. She saw a waterfall; one figure bent over another as if willing him back to life. Fear was replaced by wonder and she shifted forward, standing once more before the book, as the figure of a woman on a hill materialised before her inquisitive eyes.

The woman wore a long red dress and a dark cloak that seemed to change colours as the sunrays glinted off it; at her waist hung a belt, which carried an array of weapons. As the woman unsheathed her sword and held it high, the morning sun breathed light on her form, and the green stone in the pommel shone with a blinding radiance, swallowing up the image until only the sword remained.

Exzalander reached out, compelled and unable to stop herself. Her hands gripped the hilt and the golden light filled her being, bathing her in its brilliance. She stood rooted, staring, unable to breathe or even blink for fear that the darkness would come and she would never know such beauty again. The green stone began to liquefy and strands of the strange fluid reached out to form yet another link to her. A shock ran through her body; the sensation was no longer pleasant and she began to panic. Unable to remove her grasp from the phantom sword, she backed away, hoping to disrupt the image. However, the sword began to gain substance rather than lose it and she felt it solidify in her hand. The pain increased and the light grew brighter; the liquid gem held open her mouth and eyes, several tendrils entering her orifice, holding tight her vocal cords, clinging and crawling, until they wound tightly about her heart. Tears streamed from her open eyes and she wished the nightmare to end, that her Daddy would hold her and tell her it was all right; it was just a bad dream. The buzzing sound grew so loud in her head that she thought her teeth would shatter. Her body shook with the pressure, but she was not permitted to fall.

'Prepare yourself, Exzalander; the pain is yet to come. '

A searing heat ensued, which seemed to strip her very flesh and leave her bones exposed to such extreme cold, that they split and cracked. She heard a scream in her a mind—the sound she would have made had she been able. She could not tell whether the pain had lessened or if her body had adjusted to the torture by numbing her senses. The green gem seemed whole once more and the light began to dim. The scream she had envisioned in her mind found its voice, just seconds before she lost consciousness.

It had been her father who found her lying there, shivering in her unconscious state. He scolded her until she told him what had occurred. Before she could finish her story, he swept her up in his arms, holding her tightly. Removing her from the room, he locked the door behind them.

Once the court wizard had been dismissed, the King sat his daughter on his lap and attempted to explain the events of that day.

'You are a very special child, Exzalander. One day the north and south kingdoms will be yours to rule.'

'I know father,' she cut in.

'But first, my child, you must rid the land of the great evil that will befall it, for soon, and it will seem no time at all, the danger will come and you will be on your own. You must conquer this evil. Only then will Maldahl know peace and the love of its gods once more.'

The strange subject was never mentioned again. As time passed, Exzalander had dismissed his words as a method to scare her away from his room, recalling that night with little detail; the image of the sword and the words of her father that sometimes haunted her, she thought a forgotten dream.

That memory returned, sharp and painfully clear, filling Exzalander with fear. *What can I do?* she thought. *What is this evil? How do I confront it?*

'Exzalander, are you all right?'

The soothing and relatively calm voice of Katahl brought her wandering mind back to the present. She felt a tingling sensation inside her head and sensed a presence. Katahl felt it too and tried not to show his alarm as he grasped Exzalander's trembling hands.

A cry sounded from above and the couple glanced upwards towards the noise. Suspended above them were the King and Queen, around whom the air seemed to quiver. For a moment Exzalander froze, petrified by the disturbing sight.

With as clear a voice as she could muster, she shouted, 'LET THEM GO.'

There was a moment's silence before a deep laughter ensued, a terrible mocking sound—inhuman and hollow. Her father held her eyes and she saw only resignation there. She hated him then, hated him and loved him, wanted to scream her million regrets at him; she wanted him to fight back, but he was held fast. Better to face his fate resigned, than in terror as his queen.

Queen Shénnin sobbed for mercy, seeming unaware of her child. Exzalander's eyes searched for aid.

Where are the guards? Where are the archers? she thought ... *anyone?*

She watched helplessly as her parents were torn apart. She heard every tear and every scream, until finally their remains dropped to the ground, a mass of blood, bone and empty flesh. Tears brimmed in her terrified eyes, distorting the scene. She fancied that she could still hear the screams of her parents' last moments, echoing in her ears. She herself was unable to scream or cry out, her vocal cords as frozen as they had been as a child, when held captive by the mystical book of prophecy.

She blinked away her tears and tore her gaze from her parents' remains. Her eyes searched for Katahl, her hand no longer in his. Luminous mist surrounded him, the same foreboding phenomenon that held her immobile.

'What do you want with us?' Katahl cried, his voice fearful, yet defiant.

There came a metallic reply, whose lack of emotion chilled to the bone.

'We wish to teach you, Katahl; we will show you much. You Exzalander, we have no need of … yet. We therefore banish you from Maldahl. We will not meet again. Let the world know that one day you will return to reunite with Katahl and this will herald the coming of the new age that was foretold to you. Maldahl will know divine order once more.'

The words faded and Exzalander became aware of her own heartbeat thumping in her ears. The mist enveloped her; tangible it seemed, with a saline taste that made her retch. Consciousness was slipping away; darkness consumed her and she felt herself drifting, a mere spec through the vast immensity of time, passing through dimension after dimension in a dreamlike state close to death.

Drifting, drifting.

One

MONDAY:

Two girls clambered stickily across the fields, as the sun beat down and glinted off the ripples in the river.

'Look at that,' Geri said, 'it's a pterodactyl!'

'Don't be ridiculous, it's only a heron,' Kirsten replied, laughing at how silly her friend had been.

Insects buzzed in the haze and they tramped on merrily, the smell of cow parsley wafting up their nostrils. The land began steadily to rise and the girls knew that on reaching the summit of the hill, they would be able to see their houses. Kirsten felt a strange compulsion to look behind her before descending toward her home.

At the foot of the hill stood a man; his face was pale, accentuated by his jet-black hair. His eyes seemed to penetrate and burn, even at a distance. Kirsten stood watching him, until Geri hastened her away. She moved as if to go, but the feeling returned stronger than before, a pulling sensation that compelled her to glance back. The man held his hand toward her and she took several steps forward, drawn to him.

'Take my hand, do not be afraid.' His voice was like music, deep and rich in tone—mesmerising.

Geri gave a scream. 'No Kirsten, don't! He's evil.'

Kirsten saw the horror in her friend's eyes, and was afraid. She wanted to take the man's hand, but Geri's pleas prevented her. She floundered, unable to decide what to do. A ringing, which had been distant in her ears, now deafened her, filling her mind. Her eyes flickered open and her hand hit the alarm switch with annoyed force. Sitting up, she wiped the perspiration from her brow and reached for her slippers.

She slumped over her mug of coffee, crunching her toast, remaining lost in thought until a quick reminder from her father told her that she was running late.

'Oh bugger,' she said, grabbing her bag.

It was too cold for hockey and yet Miss Hacket, the P.E. teacher, still insisted on such a torture—probably out of spite. The fact that she had failed to make it as a professional athlete had made her determined that the girls should suffer, as compensation for her own torment in failure.

Breath hung in the air around the teams' shivering bodies. The ground was hard and the frost made it crunch underfoot. Running was the only way to keep warm, insisted the gym mistress, but they were too lethargic to try. Kirsten, whose limbs were numbing with the cold, dragged her body up and down the hockey pitch, trying to avoid the ball at all costs. When one was near the ball or stupid enough to dribble it, then bruised shins undoubtedly followed as a result of such folly. It was bad enough being made to participate in the sport, but to show any enthusiasm could prove fatal; in the eyes of the classmates, you were encouraging such a session and so deserved a hockey stick in the ankle, or worse, the nose. Safety rules were rarely adhered to at Bartholomew Hall.

Clack.

Looking down, Kirsten saw to her dismay, the ball resting beside her battered stick.

'Oh bugger,' she said.

Three sinewy girls charged straight for her. They were the annoying sporty types who liked to turn everything into a rugby scrum, just to show how tough they could be. Kirsten blindly struck the ball, in effort to avoid a head on collision with King Kong's sisters. Like puppy dogs, their direction instantly changed to match that of the ball.

'What the hell are you doing, Kirsten?' screeched one of her teammates. 'You've just passed to the other side!'

Kirsten shrugged, bewildered. 'Do you really care?' she asked.

'You stupid bitch,' the girl replied. She was the sort of student determined to win at any cost.

'Kirsten, do you actually know which side you're on?' Miss Hacket asked.

'When I'm about to be set upon by the gorilla triplets over there, I'm on *my* side. Am I the only one who begs the question, why are we here? We are told that exercise is beneficial to our health. How could traipsing about in a skirt short enough to give your grandad a heart attack, in the freezing cold, be seen as beneficial to one's health? It's barbaric that's what it is!'

The whistle blow that answered Kirsten's retaliation was so forceful, it was a miracle the pea did not shoot out and injure someone. Most of the class ceased play; the teacher signalled Kirsten to be sent off. One of the gorilla girls, whose senses were anaesthetised to the sound of the whistle, and would continue to play over a battle field most probably, swung her stick like a golf club and the ball shot through the air, hurtling toward Kirsten. Instinctively, she put up her arm to block the blow and caught the ball—one handed. If her teammates looked surprised, then she herself was more so, as she had not even seen it coming. Handing the ball to the teacher, she dropped her stick on the ground and walked confidently off the pitch. A few of the girls cheered, some glared and one said, 'I'll 'ave you!'

Communal showers were yet another thing that Kirsten failed to understand. Most of the girls ran through so quickly, in effort to avoid attention being drawn to their nakedness, that only a light spray of water ever made contact. Kirsten now had the luxury of the shower room to herself. She relished the touch of the hot water, as it thawed her freezing body; her only wish was for a scrub-mitt and a creamy shower gel. Steam rose in clouds and she inhaled deeply, each limb relaxing in its turn. She was reluctant to leave, but wished to do so before the hoard arrived on mass.

She was putting the finishing knot in her ankle boots when the windows shook slightly and the class began to clamber in. They started to strip and the contest began to see who could get through the shower with the least amount of water making contact.

'Detention Kirsten!'

The huge frame of the woman towered over her. The ironic thing was, she could have had a nice figure had she not ate and slept sport.

'So much for the freedom of speech,' Kirsten sneered.

'A WEEK!' Miss Hacket snapped back.

Kirsten decided to quit winding the woman up. *She's obviously not intelligent enough to appreciate my sense of humour,* she thought, *and not humanitarian enough to consider my point of view. If I continue to push this woman of stone, I'm likely to find myself in detention for the rest of the year.*

'Thank-you.' Kirsten gave a sarcastic smile, as she took the yellow slip from the massive hand before her.

In an instant the woman was gone, off to order about her minions. Kirsten gazed down at the slip in her hand, wondering what her father would say. *He is so going to freak,* she thought miserably.

Kirsten's mother had died during childbirth and she knew very little about her. Her father had removed every memory of her from the house, so not to be reminded; not even a photograph remained. Kirsten had even been considerate enough to look like her father, so she was unable to see her mother staring back at her in the mirror.

A few substitutes had been entertained, none of whom stayed very long. It had been years since her father had last let a woman into his life, and Kirsten was inclined to think that he would never do so again, at least not until she had moved out. There was something extremely off-putting about a man who had a teenager daughter she had discovered—often to her advantage.

'Come on Kirsten, we'll be late for French,' Geri said.

Kirsten's line of thought shifted back to the here and now.

'Okay I'm on my way.'

'Bonjour classe. Je vous emprie de rester calme! Merci.

Je lis les journaux de façon à vous tenir au courrant de ce qui pourrait vous interesser.

Hier à Saint Omer, deux personnes sont mortes aux mains d'un maniac.

Beaucoup de personnes ont été blessées même si la Police est arrivée sur place minutes après l'évenemment. La Police n'a pas pu appréhender le meutrier mais travaille de très prés avec Interpol car l'homme pourrait-être celui en route à Allemagne, et Le Luxembourg.

Aucune connection n'a encore été faite entre les deux victimes à Saint Omer et les onze autres qui ont été tuées dans les pays voisins. La possibilitée d'un meautrier sous contract n'a pas été exclus.

One of the things Kirsten hated most about French was the way Madame Whitlowe would gabble on, no-one understanding a word, and then choose her victim.

'Translation please, Kirsten.'

Kirsten slumped. 'Err, hello class … erm, you've been reading a newspaper, something about a man in Saint-Omer … the police and Interpol and something about Germany … Er …'

Madame Whitlowe peered over the rim of her spectacles, in disbelief. In her eyes, if she spoke in a different language often enough then the students would eventually pick it up. Nobody had ever suggested that she might progress more quickly if she attempted to actually *teach* the subject.

'Who is able to assist Kirsten? Anybody?'

When a question was thrown to the class, it was a race against each other for who could appear the most insignificant.

'Dawn, perhaps you could help fill in Kirsten's *many* gaps.'

A general sigh of relief shuddered across the classroom; Dawn was Madame Whitlowe's favourite pupil. Her father, being French, had enabled her to develop a fluent grasp of the language that the other students could only dream of possessing.

Dawn cleared her throat. 'You said how you read the French newspapers so that you can keep us informed about present events that might interest us. In Saint-Omer yesterday, two people died at the hands of a maniac. Many people were injured. Although the police arrived at the scene moments after the event, they did not manage to apprehend the killer. Police are now working closely with Interpol for fear that this could be the man who is wanted in Germany and Luxembourg. A connection has not been made between the two victims in Saint-Omer and the further eleven people who have died in neighbouring countries, but the possibility of professional hits has not been ruled out.

'Bravo Dawn, c'etait fabuleux,' Madame Whitlowe cried, as she clapped her hands.

One or two of the girls looked surprised, but mostly the reaction was that of apathy.

Kirsten was thoughtful for the remainder of the lesson. *How can a killer who has been seen by so many, be able to leave the country? Surely he'd be recognised. If he went through customs in disguise then he'd have to possess a fake passport—or many, as Interpol are likely to have a list of names of the people who travelled to those countries between each killing. Narrowing down should be a simple computer cross-reference search for the same name. The killer wouldn't be that stupid. But if he does possess counterfeit identification, he may have an accomplice. That makes the whole situation seem like it has a purpose—an objective.* Kirsten found herself wondering whether it might have been contract killing after all. *Perhaps he's a professional hit man with a huge backlog of work.*

'Hah!' A single sound of laughter erupted, quite unintentionally.

Madame Whitlowe peered down at Kirsten, who pretended to cough, placing her hand to her chest then holding it palm outwards toward the teacher, as if to thank her for her concern. Rapidly, she ducked her head and began to scribble, writing anything into her book before being able to sneak a look at Geri's work to see what she had missed. They were copying from a book— another one of the teaching mysteries; nobody learnt from copying, quite simply because they were able to allow their subconscious to take over while their mind was elsewhere.

Like now.

She turned the page to be confronted with a map of Europe. The task was to take the list of place names, mark their position on the map, give their French name and say a little about them. Kirsten gazed at the map and drew a cross in Germany, Luxembourg and France, then traced her finger from the French border up to Saint Omer. *The bastard's moving north.* A chill broke down Kirsten's spine. *Next stop, L'Angleterre,* she thought, and wondered whether Interpol had considered the possibility; she supposed that they had. *All major points into the country are probably on standby, awaiting the arrival of the killer with fortified security.*

The end of period bell made Kirsten jump; she had no idea that it was so late. She had study periods all afternoon, which usually meant that she would sneak home.

The fields were muddy and Kirsten found herself hopping over great puddles onto springy grass; she was an expert at keeping dirt off her shoes.

A frenzied barking echoed across the river. Glancing over, Kirsten saw Whiskey and Gemma, her two dogs. Whiskey spotted Kirsten and attempted to cross the water to reach her. Kirsten jumped behind the bushes, just in time to escape her father.

'What is it, boy? What have you found?' he said.

The autumn leaves had not yet begun to fall, so the bush still had thick and healthy foliage, perfect for remaining hidden, not so perfect for seeing when the coast was clear. Muddy water and sludge squelched over her feet, seeping over the top and into her shoes. She grimaced and pulled her feet out with a sucking sound. The dogs barking immediately began again and Kirsten risked a look behind the bush; Gemma was beside Whiskey, her tail wagging happily.

'Go away,' Kirsten hissed, making a shooing motion.

She stomped back to the path and attempted a hasty retreat. Her dogs began to follow on the opposite side of the bank.

'Kirsten?'

She stopped, hesitating before she turned to face her father. She said nothing, but shrugged a smile and risked a wave. The silence that followed increased her feelings of discomfort, becoming aware of the mud on her shoes and splashes up her legs and skirt.

He turned suddenly, walking on and whistled to the dogs. Kirsten's heart sank; she knew by his silence that she was in big trouble. *Not only am I bunking off school,* she thought, *but I've been caught walking across the fields, something which I'm strictly forbidden to do, and I still have to let him know about the detention. I am so busted!*

She turned the key in the lock, or at least tried to. A smile spread slowly across her lips. *The silly old bugger has left the door open,* she thought. *Now at least I have a card to play. Now, just to decide the best possible moment to play it … He's bound to begin with the lecture on personal safety and security. Oh it's perfect …*

'Oh! Hello. I'm sorry I wasn't expecting you, erm, anyone. I'm er, Lisa.'

Before Kirsten, stood a young woman with soft brown hair that fell neatly to her bare shoulders. A bath towel was held tightly to her bulging body, barely enough to cover her nakedness. Her brown eyes were warm and homely.

'You must be Kirsten,' Lisa ventured. She held out a hand, which Kirsten made no attempt to shake. Her towel slipped slightly and she made a grab for it, blushing. 'I'm a … friend of your fathers.'

Kirsten raised a stern eyebrow and brushing past the stranger, she headed for the stairs.

'Excuse me,' she said.

Kirsten's cold reception seemed to make Lisa's embarrassment reach severe proportions.

'It's strange though,' Kirsten said, turning slowly. 'I just met my dad and he didn't mention that *we* had a guest. Weird don't you think?'

On reaching her room, she threw herself onto her bed. She felt guilty for the way she had behaved, aware that it was a defence mechanism used to hide her own embarrassment, but she assumed that Lisa would think that she was a real bitch. *Dad is really is going to kill me now,* she sulked. The clock beside her bed read 13:40. He would not be long. She pulled off her dirty shoes, horrified to see pieces of dried mud in patches across the carpet and immediately set about clearing the mess up.

Yawning, she took her homework from the bag and lay back on the bed, hungry and thirsty. She began to scribble down the basic principles of glycolysis and the Krebs cycle.

He still wasn't home.

The complexities of the electron transport chain whizzed through her brain, the beginnings of an essay forming in her head. Her writing slowed and she yawned, her eyes blinked then closed. That blissful euphoria between waking and sleep followed. Her body relaxed, her breathing slowed, and she could feel the tension unwinding as her body melted into oblivion …

Mist swirling.

Kirsten found she could not fully open her eyes. Instinctively, her hands reached out to compensate for her blindness. The fog felt slimy, more than mere water particles. The air glowed, causing her to wince even more. She could not feel the ground beneath her feet and was far from sure whether she actually possessed feet any longer. Voices drifted to her mind, but she could not understand what was spoken. A tightening seemed to occur in her stomach, and a taste like seaweed invaded her mouth. She retched, and then quite clearly she heard a sound that made her freeze with terror.

Gun shots …

'Kirsten!'

She started out of the dream to see the return of her father. The stony features she had been expecting, absent.

'Kirsten, I'm not going to lecture you; you've heard it all before. I just want you to realise what danger you are placing yourself in.'

'I can look after myself.' *Ah, the most famous of all female phrases that in ninety-nine percent of cases proves to be utter bollocks,* she thought, not intending to admit as much.

His eyebrows peaked in the centre in a way that was both patronising and loving, a feat that he had down to an art; Kirsten assumed it was a parent thing.

Still, he isn't shouting which can only be a good thing, she thought. *Of course, his little lady friend. He has his secrets too …*

'I hate walking the long way home, Dad; it's so dreary. It's nice to get a little peace and quiet.'

'Kirsten, cut the crap okay. I thought that I could trust you … perhaps I should cancel my holiday …'

'What! No, don't be silly. Dad, you *can* trust me.' She had been counting the days until her father flew to Tunisia. He had never left her alone before and she had plans to take full advantage of that.

'You are not to walk home that way again, do I make myself clear?'

She nodded sheepishly.

'And what are you doing out of school?' he continued.

This is it, a chance for retaliation, she thought. *This is the moment for me to play my card.* 'I have a study afternoon, see?' she said, waving her textbook under his nose. 'When I got home the door was *open.* I thought we'd been burgled, and then your *friend* frightened the life out of me! I mean when did you intend on letting me know, before or after the wedding?'

'Cut the sarcasm, Kirsten; it doesn't become you. I was planning to tell you soon. I just wanted to see if it was likely to develop into anything serious.'

'Dad, she was practically naked! Call me old-fashioned if you will, but that sounds pretty serious to me.'

Her father laughed heartily. 'Yes I would call it a little old fashioned,' he said. 'Just who's supposed to be the parent here anyway? Anyhow poppet …'

She cringed.

'Do you often study in your sleep?'

Kirsten grinned. 'Absolutely,' she said. The smile on her face faded. *So far so good,* she thought. *He's been content to allow me to stew in my own fear; now for the biggie.*

'Dad, I got a week's detention.'

He looked at her disbelieving, not entirely sure he had heard her correctly.

'It's not my fault,' she said quickly. 'The woman hates me. She gave me detention just because I said that we shouldn't be playing hockey in the cold.'

'Kirsten, it doesn't matter what you think. You can't go forcing your opinions on people so pertly. You have to learn when to speak up for yourself and when to let something go, and back-chatting teachers is a big no, no, okay?'

She could scarcely believe it; he was actually smiling.

My God Lisa, you can stay!

Two

'The fucking bitch!' Kirsten stomped across the classroom and threw her bag so forcibly, that she knocked over a chair.

'What's wrong with you?' Geri asked. Kirsten's temper unperturbed her; she had seen it so many times before and was well aware that her friend flew off the handle at the least provocation.

'She's got me running 'round the sports field for an hour each detention. I can't believe it!'

There was a general laugh from those near at hand.

'Well you didn't think you'd get off easy, did you?' Geri said.

The nights had begun to draw in, consequently it was almost dark by the time Kirsten staggered back to the changing room after detention. She was wheezing and her limbs felt leaden as she began to undress.

'SHOWER!' barked Miss Hacket.

'Fuck you,' was what Kirsten really wanted to say, but managed to restrain herself. 'I'll have a bath when I get home, Miss.'

'So you want to walk home smelling, do you?'

Kirsten's jaw clenched. 'It might not be a bad idea. People are more likely to keep their distance, thereby decreasing my chances of being attacked.'

She continued to dress to prove that she was quite determined to have her own way. All the while, Miss Hacket stood over her. Kirsten felt sick, unsure whether it was due to her own lack of stamina, or the ogling presence of the P.E. teacher. Snatching up her belongings, she walked out, ignoring the woman's goodbyes.

Her cheeks burned and her body tingled as the cold hit it again; her breathing was almost back to normal. She had been a good runner as a child, winning gold in every event entered in the school sports day, but she had allowed her fitness to slip of late; it seemed irrelevant when there were exams to pass.

She paced her aching limbs down the dimly lit streets.

Rush hour.

Traffic beginning to multiply.

She felt miserable. Another four days of torture still remained and she wondered how she would survive. She passed by the gate to the fields, not stupid enough to go across them after dark. Gazing ahead, the street seemed endless—mile upon mile of dull, monotonous buildings and traffic building up beside her.

Her body trembled in protest on reaching her home; her chest felt tight and she was suffering from a severe case of stitch. Lisa was in the kitchen, clothed this time. She poured hot milk into a mug she had prepared. The familiar and inviting smell of cocoa wafted up Kirsten's nostrils, as she closed the door behind her.

Lisa smiled warmly. 'For you,' she said, holding the drink toward Kirsten.

Peace offering or bribe? Oh what the hell. 'Thanks, you're a life saver.' She cradled the steaming mug in her hands and made her way into the living room. In two expert movements, she dropped her bag to the floor then flipped her coat off, holding the mug in one hand then the other as her coat fell to the carpet. With a groan, she eased herself into the armchair and took a deep draught of the glorious treasure. A sigh of pure relief and pleasure escaped her lips.

'Are you ready for your dinner, Kirsten? It's about ready, but I could keep it cooking a little longer if you prefer.'

Kirsten sipped the cocoa again then inhaled deeply.

Stew.

'Bloody hell, he's got you well trained, hasn't he?' she said.

Lisa beamed. Her father entered and seemed instantly pleased at the fact that the two of them were not tearing a piece out of each other.

Kirsten could not help but like Lisa; the woman was so open and without pretension. In the past, her father's girlfriends had been very young with ample concern for their own appearance, but often in want of feeling. *She can cook too, which is always a bonus,* Kirsten thought. *It's nice to see the old codger looking so happy.*

'That was lovely thank-you, Lisa. Would you like me to do the washing up?' The words surprised Kirsten. *So very courteous, so unlike me,* she thought.

'No Kirsten, you go and make a start on your studies,' her father said, with a twinkle of laughter in his eyes.

She nodded and excused herself. Her muscles pulled tightly as she made her way up the stairs, her body stiffening with every step. She thought of the smug look that the teacher had worn, and snarled as she struggled to mount the final stretch.

Light from the landing flooded across the blackened room. Opening her top drawer, she removed an incense stick and a box of matches. Striking the match, she held it for a moment, allowing it to illuminate the darkness. The incense stick burned then glowed and the smell of sandalwood drifted across the room. She blew out the match before the flame scorched her fingers, and placed the smouldering stick in a holder resting on top of the drawers. Her hand scrambled about in the drawer once more, until she felt the coldness of glass. She threw her aching body onto the bed and pulled the light cord. Unscrewing the cap, she began to rub the tiger balm onto her swelling legs and feet. It took effect almost immediately and the cold sensation soothed away the pain. Crawling under the covers, she lay in foetal position—exhausted.

I'll have a nap, she thought. *Just for a while.*

Sinking.

The pillows and mattress seemed to envelop and drown her leaden body ...

A desert stretched on for miles; dunes loomed to her right, with odd scrubs of grass, fighting to exist in the blistering heat. Her feet sank deeply into the sand, as she began to climb the dune. Gunfire sounded and a great battle lay before her. Men rushed idly to their deaths against a race that were humanoid, but certainly not human. They were larger and stronger than an average male, their faces boar-like and hairless. Their stained teeth, like screwdrivers, disturbed Kirsten. It was plain that the creatures were not herbivores, and the glint in their eyes as they slew, convinced her that human flesh was a taste much to their liking.

'Stay back,' shouted a cloaked man, as he dashed past with several others.

Kirsten made her way down toward the fight, smoke and noxious fumes tearing at her nostrils and lungs. Warriors fell dead beside her; the battle was almost over and she was surrounded; the last of the men in her near vicinity, shot dead with an arrow of steel. Grinning fiendishly, the brutish creatures began to close; she turned to see them approaching from over the dune. A little way before her stood the man she had seen in her dreams so often of late and Geri's words refreshed themselves in her memory.

'Kirsten don't, he's evil.'

He held his hand toward her.

'Do not be afraid,' he said. 'Come to me; I will not let anyone harm you.'

What choice do I have? she considered. *I'll be destroyed for sure if I don't.*

The creatures cried out and began to close in. Kirsten sprinted toward the man; almost flying at him it seemed. Her hand grasped his and he pulled her into his embrace, just as the evil beings discharged their weapons.

She was safe. Somehow, the man had gotten her out of there and they seemed to be drifting in another existence. As she surrendered to him, she felt strangely comfortable; it seemed to her painful to fight him. Onward they drifted, their souls seeming to merge, as it grew darker and darker.

WEDNESDAY:

'Oh for crying out loud, Kirsten! Did you not hear your alarm?'

Her eyes shot open; disorientated for a moment, she failed to recognise her father standing over her. She yelled, convinced he was there to kill her. His brow furrowed with sudden concern for his daughter; her eyes seemed glassy and beads of sweat dripped from her reddened cheeks. Perching on the side of the bed, he put his hand to her forehead.

'Are you all right, Kirsten?'

She managed to focus again. Looking down at herself, she saw that she still wore her uniform, and it felt sticky. *Totally grim!* she thought.

Daylight flooded the room, serving as a reminder that she had overslept. She envisioned her tutor's face, as if prepared to lecture her for lack of punctuality. She remembered her detention and what was in store for her come three thirty.

OH GOD, PLEASE NOT AGAIN! she thought, and an idea formed instantly in her mind.

'D'dad?' she stammered. 'What time is it? I feel lousy.'

'You look it! Come on, let's get you up. I'll fix you some soup and you get yourself in a bath. If you still feel poorly after that, you'd better remain off for the rest of the day. I'll give your school a ring. Get yourself off to the bathroom.'

As he left the room, she did a little dance and whispered an excited, 'yesss!' before relieving herself of her dirty uniform.

The bath felt glorious as it unwound her tightened muscles. Submerging her head, her hair flowed about her mermaid-like. She lay for a while under the quiet of the water, before a distant sound forced her to emerge.

'Kirsten, are you all right in there?'

'Yeah Dad, I'm fine thanks,' she replied.

'Well don't fall asleep, will you. I'm going to make you one of my homemade soups now. Do you think that you could eat some?'

'That sounds grand. Thanks Dad.' *Oops, I should have sounded ill,* she thought, *but I can always play-up later on.*

The soup was extremely tasty, just the job for such a cold morning. As she ate, he talked about arrangements he had made for while he was away; the dogs were going into kennels; he was leaving her money in the biscuit tin for shopping, and the window cleaner was due on the Wednesday before he got back. Kirsten nodded, trying to take it all in whilst feigning illness.

'Any more soup, Kirsten?' he asked.

Kirsten would have welcomed seconds, but decided that she would rather have the afternoon off than an extra bowl of soup. Her eyes closed, as if involuntarily and then slowly opened. 'Oh, thank-you, no,' she said. 'I had enough trouble eating that one. I'm sure it tasted very nice, thanks.'

He stood for a moment watching her. She pretended not to notice, continuing to relax her face muscles, opening and closing her eyes. He seemed satisfied, rather than suspicious, about her condition. Clearing the crockery, he suggested that she return to bed, to which she readily agreed.

'Now I'll finish my essay for tomorrow, no problem,' she thought. She got her paperwork out and flicked on the television. If her father heard pages turning then she knew that he would check up on her; she did not want that.

'Kirsten, Geri's on the phone; says your mobile's switched off again,' yelled her father. 'Are you feeling up to talking to her?'

'Yeah, thanks Dad.'

She leaned over and snatched up the phone, waiting for the click as her father replaced the handset.

'Geri?'

'Kirsten, you soddin' wagger! How did you wangle that one?'

'Geri, I only crawled out of bed an hour or so ago,' Kirsten replied. 'I had a really shitty night, okay.'

'Detention a little tough on you, was it?'

'Fuck you, Geri.'

Geri giggled down the phone. Kirsten's eyes flashed at the television for a moment, her attention on Geri's taunting beginning to wane as her attention directed toward the screen.

'I've got to go now anyway, or I'll be late for history. Bye!'

'Bye,' Kirsten replied, without realising that she had replaced the handset.

She picked the remote up in order to increase the volume and waited to hear the report that had sparked her interest. The calm and emotionless voice of the reader offered complete detachment from the horrors that she related.

'In Calais today, a man has been arrested in connection with fifteen murders that have occurred across Europe in the past fortnight. He was apprehended by French authorities a few hours ago, and is said to be proclaiming his innocence.'

The picture showed a man being shoved into a French police van. He looked shaky and pale, hardly the criminal mastermind Kirsten had expected. She lay back, strangely relieved by the killer's capture.

'This news just in. Several witnesses have confirmed that the suspect was merely a bystander to the most recent incident and he has been released from custody. The man is being treated for shock in a Centre Hospitalier de Calais. The killer, who has eluded the authorities once again, is feared to attempt to cross over into Britain. Efforts are being made to increase security at Dover and Paddington, in hope of capturing him there. In the meantime, police are warning people to be on the look out for a man matching this description.'

A mock-up picture appeared on the screen, and Kirsten absorbed his features.

'The suspect is approximately six foot four, muscular build, light brown hair, eyes are possibly hazel or brown. More news at six, until then, goodbye.'

Kirsten was trembling, and the veins thumped in her temples; the whole sensation seemed without just cause, and yet she knew that the news report had disturbed her, as it had done in the classroom.

'I'm going to call a doctor; try talking to her again.'

'Kirsten, it's Lisa, can you hear me? Jason, I think she's coming 'round.'

She focused on Lisa and blinked; as she did so, water came instantly to her eyes. Her hands were still shaking when her father appeared at her bedside.

'Kirsten, are you all right?'

Why are they here? Kirsten thought. *Why did I not see them enter the room? Did I faint? No, if I had then I wouldn't be sitting up like this.* She struggled to focus, feeling disorientated.

'Kirsten, what the hell happened? We thought you were having some sort of epileptic episode.'

'Dad, what's going on?'

He sat beside her and lifting her face by the chin, he looked into her eyes. When he saw nothing obvious, he ruffled her hair.

'You were staring blankly at nothing and we couldn't even make you blink.'

Kirsten's eyes widened with concern, despite the stinging sensation that still afflicted them.

'I still think we should get you to a doctor.'

'I feel fine Dad, honest,' she protested. Honest was a word that Kirsten often used to disguise the fact that she was lying. She felt far from fine; for the first time in her mundane and ordinary life, she was afraid; she was actually scared. *How long was I sat in that zombie-like state and what caused such a reaction?* She looked at her clock.

15:10

The news report had finished about half past twelve, and that was the last thing she could remember, which left her with the burning question, *what happened in the two and half-hours that my mind was elsewhere?*

That evening, she dived downstairs.

'Where's Lisa?' she asked.

'She went home, flower. As I'm away from tomorrow, I thought that we could spend the evening together—just the two of us.'

Kirsten smiled knowingly, placing down her fork on her plate. 'Dad, I really like Lisa. You don't have to send her away because you think I disapprove.'

Her father's mouth twisted as if he was about to deny what she had thought.

'I just want to make sure that you're okay. You gave me quite a scare today. Humour your old man, will you?'

Kirsten frowned. She had been trying to forget about what had occurred. She did not understand it and neither did she want to. The entire situation freaked her out and she decided it was better to pretend that it had never happened. Her dad was still staring at her as if he expected to see her head spin around at any second.

'I'm okay!' she insisted.

He held her eyes for a moment longer then clapped his hands suddenly, as if to declare the subject closed.

He began to clear the table. 'In that case, *you* can do the washing-up,' he said.

Kirsten pulled a face, but knew that it was fruitless to try to get out if it.

As she rinsed the soapsuds off the plates, she stared at her reflection in the kitchen window; it seemed different somehow—a stranger. Suddenly, she snapped the blind shut, dripping water over the kitchen surface. The sound of the television drew her away from her brooding and she hurried the remainder of the washing-up before bidding her father goodnight.

'You're not going to bed already?' he complained. 'It's only seven o'clock!'

She glanced at the TV to see that the news had just started.

'I know,' she said. 'But I've an essay to finish and I'm tired. I don't want to be ill again tomorrow, if I can help it. Night Dad,' she kissed him. 'Have a lovely time.'

'Are you sure you're going to be all right on your own? Because I can …'

'I'll be fine. See you soon.'

She turned and dashed up the stairs, headlines fading as she closed her door with a sigh of relief.

THURSDAY:

'You okay Kirst'?' Geri asked. 'You look like crap.'

'Cheers big ears! Remind me to repay the compliment some time.'

'Hey, it's the way it goes, big nose.'

Kirsten punched her friend hard in the arm.

'Oww. Bitch!' Geri howled. 'Why did you come back for anyway? You should have taken the week off and got out of detention with Hacket.'

'Yeah well what can I say? I missed you!' Kirsten said, in a child-like voice and kissed Geri on the cheek.

'Get off, you les'.'

'Get a room!' shouted Dawn.

'Ya mother!' Kirsten said, brandishing a two-fingered salute.

'KIRSTEN!'

Kirsten's eyes shut in dismay, at the sound of Mr Brown's voice behind her. She turned, smiling sweetly.

'Sir?'

'Follow me. *NOW*.' he ordered.

She traipsed behind him to the staff room. It was empty. There was the sound of screaming and a crash from outside, followed by laughter.

'Wait here!' he said.

As he stormed off to meet the cause of the disturbance, Kirsten sat down and pawed through a discarded magazine. Her heart jumped when she replaced it, noticing the newspaper that lay on the table. Her hand shook, reaching out for it.

'Kirsten.'

Mr Brown had returned and she jumped immediately to her feet.

'The manner in which I have just witnessed you expressing yourself was extremely unladylike,' he lectured.

She bowed her head in pretended embarrassment.

'I wonder what your father would have to say if he heard you speaking like a common guttersnipe.'

Kirsten had no idea what a guttersnipe was, but knew that she would be in trouble if her father found out how she had behaved.

'Sorry sir,' she mumbled. 'We were just messing around.'

Mr Brown smiled, shaking his head. 'All right, off you go.'

Kirsten paused, hardly believing her ears. As she reached the door, she suddenly turned.

'Sir?'

Mr Brown looked back at her, without expression.

'Do you think it would be okay if I have that 'paper?'

He bent and picked the newspaper up, handing it to her.

'Of course, I believe it is finished with. Off you go now.'

I'm already late for first period; a few minutes more won't hurt, Kirsten told herself, as she read the front-page story. *The killer is in Britain, not only that but they've managed to get a photo of him taken from a CCTV camera.*

She felt the hairs on the back of her neck and her skin prickled. 'He's here,' she whispered. Running to class, she wondered why the story should strike such a chord with her, as she hated the news in general.

'You're late!' barked Mr Solomon

She took her seat next to Geri.

'Talk about stating the obvious,' Geri whispered to her friend.

Kirsten took out her rather crumpled essay and held it out to the formidable looking biology teacher.

'Let us hope, Miss Vái that *this* was worth the wait,' he said, as he took it from her.

Kirsten slumped on her stool, sulking. *My favourite teacher's angry with me,* she thought, *and my essay is going to fail because I couldn't concentrate on it.*

Just when things seemed as though they could not get any worse, it began to rain. It rained all day without pause and by the time Kirsten arrived for her detention, half an inch of water had sodden the track.

'Get changed!' barked Miss Hacket.

'You're not serious? I thought you would make me do lines or something. I'll drown out there!'

Miss Hacket grinned viciously, showing two gold caps on her upper premolars. 'You should have thought about that *before* you decided to cheek me,' she said. 'Perhaps now hockey in the cold does not seem so criminal, mmm?'

Kirsten breathed. She remembered what her father had told her about not retaliating. It was difficult not to when every fibre of her being told her to give as good as she got.

The house was dark and cold on her arrival home. Kirsten sighed, remembering that her father was away. She drew the curtains, locked the door and dashed upstairs to have a hot shower. Wrapping herself in her towelling dressing gown, she emptied her school bag onto her bed; her soaking P.E. kit was tossed onto her washing pile, her homework placed onto her desk. She picked up the rumpled, damp newspaper and flicked on the TV, greeted instantly by the face of the killer. There was footage of him, but the newsreader spoke over the top of whatever he was saying, warning people in greater London to be on their guard as the man had been spotted in Middlesex only hours before.

The phone rang and startled her.

'Hello petal, it's Dad. Just thought I'd let you know I landed safely.'

'Thanks Dad,' Kirsten replied. 'Have a nice time. Say hi to Lisa for me.'

Her father paused before answering, as if considering whether to deny that he was on holiday with his girlfriend or not. 'I will, little flower,' he said. 'Look after yourself.'

'Yeah, you too.'

'Bye then.'

'Bye.'

Then there was silence and the face of the killer staring back at her from the television set.

She found it difficult to sleep that night. The rain finally stopped about one a.m. and she drifted into an uneasy dream. She was looking for something, becoming agitated. Her father seemed scared and ran away screaming that he did not want anything to do with her.

FRIDAY:

A persistent ring sounded and Kirsten hit her alarm clock several times before realising that it was the telephone.

She tried, without success, to open her eyes.

'Mmm?' she grunted.

'Kirsten? It's Ger'. Don't you ever charge your mobile?' Geri said. She continued to talk without waiting for an answer. 'Dad's takin' us in the car today. Are you nearly ready?'

'Mmm.' Kirsten replied.

'Cool, see you at twenty past then.'

'Mmm.'

She replaced the handset and looked at the time, through half open eyes. It was just as well she was getting a lift, considering that her alarm had not gone off. She stumbled downstairs, made a coffee and waited for the world to begin to focus again.

'God, I feel lousy,' she said. She considered ringing Geri and telling her that she was phoning in sick. 'Nah. Hacket'd think she's got the better of me—cantankerous old cow.'

Kirsten winced as Geri slammed her father's car door. The sound of his electric window whirred and Geri's father leaned out, calling his daughter back.

'I'm going to pick you up tonight. I might be a bit late though. If I'm not here by four then you will have to walk, but I do *not* want you going across the fields, d'you hear?'

'Yes Dad,' Geri droned, and sloped off toward their form room.

'What's up with your dad?'

Geri threw her bag down on the floor, with a huff. 'He's just being paranoid, Kirst'. You know that psycho's supposed to be around here somewhere? He says he's had enough; wants us all to move up north. Mum and him had a massive barney last night, but he's adamant. Hopefully he'll have calmed down by tonight.'

'Hopefully,' Kirsten agreed.

'Yeah, as soon as he's checked out the drop in wages he'll see sense I bet.'

Kirsten nodded, no longer listening to her friend.

'Oh bugger,' she said.

'What?'

'I've forgotten my P.E. kit!'

Geri slapped her on the back with a laugh, as Mrs O'Connor entered to take the register.

'I'll bet Hacket'll have spares for you Kirst', never fear,' she said.

Kirsten put her head in her hands. 'Oh no, that stuff's never been washed!'

'HERE,' called Geri, as her name was read out. 'Oh well mate, it's skid marks and sweat patches for you tonight.'

Kirsten sneered at her, as she shouted, 'HERE.'

'I'll see you after lunch,' Mrs O'Connor said. 'Make sure you're not late for your classes, everyone; I have received complaints!'

By complaints, Kirsten assumed it was Mr Solomon and concluded that she must have graded *very* badly. He would not have complained if she had written an essay worthy of an A.

A paper ball hit her head and without thought, she picked it up and threw it back in the general direction from which it came. Chairs began to scrape as the girls left for their first lesson of the day. Kirsten sat for a moment in thought.

'Come on,' Geri muttered, 'you heard what O'Connor said.'

Kirsten got to her feet, aware suddenly of the noise of a helicopter flying low—very low, getting closer by the second, then quite clearly she heard it—a scream.

Jumping to her feet, her heart pounded. She could see the helicopter from the window, closing fast. Several of her friends had already left the building, to see what was going on. Without knowing why, she dashed out with the crowd, driven along by everyone else. The noise was incredible and the sight that met her eyes made her freeze as the fear and confusion set in, perhaps because she had not expected to behold it in her school of all places.

Armed police were posted about the courtyard; the chopper was hovering just above, and Kirsten could clearly see guns being aimed out of its side. Her friends were scattered about, seeming unbothered by the police presence, and not attempting to get away from the loaded weaponry. Ahead of her, stood Geri and a few more girls who had just left the classroom. Kirsten stared at the men with guns; all of which seemed aimed in her direction. One of them shouted something about putting the weapon down and as Geri stepped backward, Kirsten saw the man previously obscured from view, the person who the police were actually aiming at; a man with soft brown hair, *holding a sword of all things,* Kirsten thought, *not a gun, or even a knife, but a goddamned sword!* He wore a well-tailored black jacket that did not fit properly, as though he had borrowed it from someone with a much smaller frame. Seeming to sense her eyes upon him, he turned to face her.

Kirsten gasped on meeting the eyes of the killer. There was a moment's pause as they stared at one another; he seemed to recognise her. She grew more fearful on seeing the marksmen closing in. The helicopter chopping the air was deafening and it was hard to breathe. A voice over a megaphone warned the girls to clear out of the way. Kirsten looked about her at the dozen or so of her school friends, all of who had not moved; they appeared unaware of the voice and stared at the killer before them, drawn to him it seemed. There was a clicking sound, as the guns prepared to fire and she turned to flee; her legs trembled beneath her and she gasped for air—her last breath she assumed. The sound of the weapons firing caused a cry to escape her quivering lips, followed by a sensation she least expected; someone grabbed hold of her, shielded her, placing themselves between herself and the gunfire. She fought for breath; her body shuddered, as she heard the gunshots and she risked turning her head ever so slightly, enabling her to see.

It was him.

The murderer, who at last count had killed forty-two people, had just saved her life.

Kirsten saw with eyes unseeing, the bloody bodies of her classmates scattered about her; she found herself wondering whether they would be added to the killer's headcount. *The police are hardly likely to admit they shot them,* she thought. *But why did they? They're trained marksmen, how can they possibly have missed their target at such a short distance?*

Several cries of exclamation could be heard, as the armed police realised what they had done.

'Oh my God! But we aimed directly for him.'

The shooting had ceased. The man still stood and Kirsten assumed it must have been the force of the firing holding him up, but he stepped away from her to approach the marksmen—unharmed.

The spell was broken and she ran.

She ran back into the building, onward to the form room and out one of the windows that backed onto the sports field. Her body still trembled and there was a sickness in her stomach as she recalled her friends' lifeless bodies strewn about her. She stumbled on, finally breaking into a sprint, the end of the field growing nearer by the second; her breath started to come in deeper waves and her heart hammered in her chest.

BOOM.

An explosion.

She glanced back to see fire and wisps of smoke, dance into the grey sky.

Glad was she now for the detention she had served, as it had given her the opportunity to increase her stamina. On she ran, not daring to look back. Her lungs were bursting by the time she reached her own front door.

She was still fighting for breath when the police arrived at her house, almost an hour after the incident. The knocking startled her somewhat, and for a while she dare not move. It was only when she heard the voice of the officer explaining who he was, that she ventured to look through the spy hole. Two police cars were parked outside the house; three officers stood at the door and several PC's on guard about the area.

'What do you want?' she shouted nervously, from behind the door. She watched through the spy hole as she spoke, observing their reaction.

They seemed surprised.

'Miss Vái, I'm Inspector Stephenson. Are you all right?'

Why are they here? she thought. *Why do they have to draw so much attention to themselves and me?* She wanted to crawl into a ball and hide from the world until it became a saner place, not star in an episode of 'Lewis'.

'I'm fine, so you can leave me alone and go away!'

'I'm afraid we can't do that, Miss Vái. We need to ask you some questions, and I want to have a doctor check you out.'

Kirsten opened the door cautiously, peering around the edge. 'You mean a shrink,' she said curtly.

He gave her a brief, but none too convincing smile.

'If you like,' he said. As he spoke, he stared past her as if to check that she was alone.

'I see, so you're worried that seeing my friends being gunned down by *your men* might have damaging effects on my psychological well-being. Well you could have a point there.' She tried to be angry, but felt the choking sensation of tears. Turning quickly, she flounced over to the couch and settled, breathing deeply to prevent herself from crying. Three men stepped into the room and shut the door. The highest-ranking officer immediately sat besides her.

He's trying to display how supportive he can be, she thought. *He wants to gain my trust, to retrieve a coherent and useful statement from me.*

The second officer sat with a notepad on the opposite side of the room; the last stood with his back to the wall.

'You didn't catch him, did you?' her hoarse voice cracked.

'No, I'm afraid not. Do you feel up to answering some questions, Miss Vái, or would you like to speak to a doctor first?'

She did not know what she was feeling at that time. *Maybe it's shock,* she considered. *Is that why I have so little emotion where my dead schoolmates are concerned?*

'Perhaps Constable Walker could fix us all a nice cup of tea,' suggested the inspector, with a glance to the nearest man.

She saw a lot in that look. The whole action and words seemed slower somehow, slow enough to read what lay between.

'I suppose by tea, you mean for Constable Walker to search the house,' she said. 'He's not here, I can assure you, but please feel free to conduct your invasion of my privacy anyhow.'

'That's hardly constructive now is it, Miss Vái? We're simply concerned for your safety and well-being.'

'Like you were my *friends*?'

The inspector shifted uncomfortably in his seat. 'That was an unfortunate and regrettable accident.'

'Oh I see ... an *accident!*' she railed. 'So tell me, do they actually bother with firearms training these days, or do you just have to collect ten tokens from cereal boxes and they hand you a gun?'

'Walker, a cup of tea for me. How do you take your tea, Miss Vái?'

Not a flicker of emotion crossed his features, and she pondered. *Is it those years spent in the force perfecting the art, or does he simply not care? The latter would surely make him a monster.*

'Black, no sugar,' she said, directing her answer to Walker.

The man nodded to her, half-smiling as her eyes met his. She felt a shiver across her body; something about Walker unnerved her. As he left the room, Kirsten stared down at the floor, trying to overcome the sensation that was creeping up on her.

Fear.

Like an unstoppable disease, it spread through her limbs, seeming to stiffen them.

'Miss Vái?'

And it was gone.

She breathed.

'What is it, Miss Vái?'

The one thing she knew that it would be unwise to state was, "*Well actually that guy Walker, he freaked me out a bit. Scary chap isn't he?" It's not a good idea to taint another officer; they are a team and such teams stick together no matter what. They will no doubt attempt to pin the death of my friends on the mysterious killer, in order to protect their own.* She saw in her mind's eye, a cornered beast slavering, growling and baring its oversized jaws in effort to protect its young. *If I was to attack,* she thought, *it will kill.* She looked at him, fearful again. His grey eyes set hard, but within … behind that training and harsh life, she seemed to see a comparison; a loving father and husband. She found herself asking the question, whom would he put first, the force, or his family? If there were only one he could save, how deep would his loyalty go? She had no doubt that in any other circumstances, that he would protect any of his team with his life if he had to, but his family? Could he throw their lives away quite so frivolously for the sake of loyalty to his establishment?

No, was the answer she found. He would save his family, his flesh and blood offspring. *So, despite his rank,* she thought, *he's not one hundred percent loyal.* Relaxing a little, she felt more able to trust him. His face seemed older somehow and he looked weary.

'Why did he save my life?' she asked. 'The killer I mean. I was directly in their line of fire and yet, he saved me.'

'Miss Vái, do you know who this man is?'

'No.'

'Did he say anything to you, anything at all?'

'No.'

'Tell me what happened, Kirsten—all that you can remember.'

The man who was seated opposite flipped open his notepad.

Time for business, she thought, frowning. 'It all happened so quickly; I heard a noise and went out to see what was going on. The man was standing ahead of me. My friends were crowded around him. The helicopter flew in low. I remember the noise and how I couldn't focus properly, except when I saw his eyes. I couldn't move; I don't know why. I wanted to run, but I couldn't. I heard the guns click as they prepared to fire and it was like waking from a dream. I turned to run, not expecting to escape in time; there was a shower of bullets and he … saved me; he didn't kill anyone, not one single person, Inspector.'

She breathed for a moment to gauge his reaction. He seemed thoughtful.

'When he turned away, I ran.' she continued. 'I ran back here. That's it. That's all I can tell you.'

'Well for whatever reasons, Miss Vái, out of the thirty-two people involved in today's incident, you were the only person to come out of it unharmed. This worries me greatly. It seems that for reasons unknown, the man has singled you out. I'm going to leave you with protection for at least a few days, in case he turns up. Now I'll need to speak with your father, I'm sure he will agree with my suggestion.'

'He's in Tunisia,' Kirsten said. 'I haven't got a contact number for him, besides I don't see how leaving an officer or two around here is going to help much if he shows; he seems to have outmatched you all so far.'

Inspector Stevenson was silent for a moment and stared down at his intertwined fingers. 'Perhaps you are right. I shall place you in protective custody, instead.'

'NO WAY! I'm not leaving here,' she raved. 'I'll be no better off than a prisoner. He's not going to come after me, why should he?'

'Then you'll agree to have a couple of officers on guard; it's merely a precaution, Miss Vái.'

She stared stubbornly past him. The blue lights flashing through the windows made her think about what the neighbours were making of the commotion.

'Your tea, sir.'

'Thank-you Walker.'

'Miss, your tea.'

Walker did not bend to pass down the cup, but knelt, presenting it like a precious gift. Receiving the cup, she grunted a thank-you, refusing to meet his gaze. However, the sensation rose again; it began with a fluttering in her stomach where her adrenal glands began flooding her system in preparation for danger. He made no move, but leaned against the wall quite casually. She glanced at him, her trembling hands placing the tea beside her feet.

'Miss Vái, we're going now,' the inspector said. 'I'll leave a guard at the front and rear of the house, and a patrol vehicle in the street. Do you want a PC to stay with you?'

She glanced nervously to Walker.

'No, it really won't be necessary, thank-you.'

'We'll bid you good day then, Miss. Remember, if you need anything then let one of the guards know; if you need to speak to me then they'll put you through.'

After they had left, she had to speak with the doctor, to whom she could relate no more than she had to the inspector. The man concluded that she was suffering from mild shock and that she would need counselling once reality set in.

Alone at last, Kirsten lay down on the settee and found herself wondering silly things like, *did they evacuate the school? Are we on the news?* She hoped that she would not be named in any report, believing that it was best not to attract attention at such a time.

Will he really come after me? she thought. *Perhaps he already has. He could be out there right now ...*

She sprang to her feet, peering out of the small window of the front door. Across the street, a constable sat conspicuously in her car. Pacing through the house to the back door, she started with fright when she spotted Walker, stood in the back yard. His head turned and he looked directly at her, despite the fact that she stood in the shadows and the net curtains were restricting any vision. She froze, not daring to move. *He can't see me,* she reasoned, but knew that he could. He watched her, waiting for her to make her move.

She didn't.

Her eyes began to adjust to the obstruction from the net curtain. She knew that it was impossible to see into that room. Many times, she had tried to peer in when she had forgotten her key, to see if her father was about. However, even with her nose pressed to the glass, she had been unable to discern anything but the light flooding through from the living room, and yet she knew that he could see her; she saw it in his eyes.

Focusing on them in her fear, she suddenly realised why they petrified her so. They were that of the killer—the exact same eyes that she had faced earlier that day, but not for the way they looked, but rather, what lay behind them. She *knew* it was him.

He was there.

Somehow, somehow totally unexplainable, it was him.

Three

Her mouth opened to scream, but it was some time before any sound issued forth. As Walker stepped toward the door, she turned and fled into the living room, the sound of her terror trailing, merging with the rattle of the back door handle. She struggled with the lock on the front door; it felt oily and her fingers could not grasp it effectively. She saw the police officer moving toward her. The lock clicked, but she froze and her scream ended abruptly. Turning slowly, she saw Walker stood in the doorway, eyes shining. She backed away from the door, her body making contact with the armchair, obstructing her retreat.

'What do you want?' she screamed.

As he approached, her entire body seemed more alive than it had done in the whole course of her existence. She could actually feel her capillaries close as her blood raced to energise her limbs into action. The surge of adrenaline was so great, it gave the sensation of free falling; each hair on her head having a life of its own, as it lifted and swayed in a non-existent breeze. Each molecule in her body seemed to buzz and generate electricity that ran through her limbs, strengthening them on its journey to her fingertips. She felt it quite distinctly then, throbbing, as her fingers seemed filled with an unfamiliar sensation.

The front door shoved open and three police officers stormed in. Kirsten fell to her knees, the sensation dispersing and draining her as it did so. She could not help but look at her hands, expecting to find her fingers swollen. An officer ran to her side.

'What's the matter, Miss Vái?'

She looked at him sorrowfully; even though she felt normal again, a part of her seemed missing. She felt the tears trickling down her cheeks and she placed her hands to her face. A dull sensation radiated outwards from her fingertips, across her head and was gone; all that remained was the touch of her fingers, as cold as death.

'It's him,' she wept, no longer caring for any danger. 'It's him, he's the one!'

She pointed in the direction of Walker. It was some time before her eyes focused on the man. She became aware of the officer helping her to the chair. He was speaking to her, but she did not hear his words as she was concentrating on Walker; his unconscious form was pale and twitching. Kirsten sprang to her feet, but had not the energy to remain on them. As she swooned, the police officer caught her and helped her back to the chair. Her eyes seared into his, razor sharp was her glance as it travelled from one officer to another—searching.

'He's gone,' she whispered. Her eyes closed involuntarily and she was aware of a voice calling her name, but she could not return; her exhausted body demanded its rest, and she slipped deeper into unconsciousness …

The surrounding sea lapped gently about the rock on which she sat. She could feel the salt engrained in the roughness of its surface. The air was warm and filled with the sound of wailing gulls as they swooped to catch their dinner—the fishermen of the skies. The beach ahead was empty, but for two figures walking hand in hand. It was her father and Lisa, as happy as two people could be. They turned in to face each other and kissed. The sun glinted off the ring on Lisa's left hand and blinded Kirsten into waking. She found herself in unfamiliar surroundings and wondered for a moment whether or not she was still dreaming.

A drip protruded from her hand. She scowled and her anger rose. Reaching over, she peeled back the plaster and gently removed the needle, cringing. The other patients seemed too occupied with their own problems to be concerned at her rebellion. Gradually, she got to her feet, feeling stiff. She removed her belongings from the cabinet. It was her uniform. *The same clothes I was wearing when I ran from* … she could not quite remember. Dressing, she walked casually toward the exit, not a nurse in sight.

Once she was clear of the ward, she knew that the likelihood of being stopped was slim. Reaching the lobby, she recognised where she was; it was a few miles from home, consequently she had a long walk ahead, with no coat.

A prickling sensation crawled up her spine and without knowing why, she ducked behind a huge rubber plant, which marked the entrance. A man walked up to the front desk. Kirsten knew his face.

Inspector Stephenson.

The fog that hung over her memory, began to clear. As the inspector stepped into the lift, she slipped out of the building. The recollection of her dead friends flashed before her eyes like pictures in a flick book. She saw the killer, the killer when he and Walker were one and the same, and then she remembered Walker a twitching wreck. She hurried onward in the opposite direction to home, knowing that her absence would soon be discovered and had she taken *that* route, then so would she. She had nowhere to go, but did not care, her only desire to avoid discovery. She had done nothing wrong and did not want to explain her accusation towards Walker. Besides, judging the state of him when she had last laid eyes on him, she figured that they would try to pin the blame on her somehow. *I need time to focus, to think,* she thought. *Why was I in hospital? I can't remember.*

The sound of a siren startled her out of her thoughts. She was on an open stretch of road; there was no housing for at least another hundred metres. A church lay ahead; it sat on the edge of the fields that backed onto her route home from school. She jogged a little, aware of the siren growing louder. Running to the rear of the building, she peered around the side as the patrol vehicle whizzed past. The siren receded into the distance until it was lost from hearing. Kirsten walked cautiously toward the road and stopped, turning. The steeple loomed ahead of her, its megalithic power an effort to make a congregation feel humbled and insignificant in comparison to power and might of their Lord.

Without knowing what compulsion drove her, she approached the entrance. Her hand fully expected to meet resistance as she pushed against the door, but it opened, the age-old hinges creaking as she stepped in. The interior was dark and musty, like most churches she figured. Candles were lit, either for religious significance or in attempt to illuminate the gloom. The absence of stain glass, or window of any kind, was a quite noticeable. It was more like a crypt than a place of worship. Kirsten sat nervously on a pew; her hand caressed the smooth panel of oak, as she looked about her. The only other exit from the building was situated behind the altar, a simple wooden door, inconspicuous despite its prominent position.

She bent forward, her head resting on folded arms as they leaned on the row in front. It was peaceful there and, despite her lack of religious belief, she felt comfortable and safe.

Her eyes focused on one of the flickering candle flames and lost themselves in the shadows of memory. She became aware of her own heartbeat pounding in her ears. As it returned to a steady beat, her mind returned to recent events, reliving the shooting of her friends. Only now, in the peace of the church, was she able for the first time to discern the faces of the dead. *Geri was there … Geri's dead.* She had not the time to think at the time, the instinct to survive had driven feeling from her soul. She felt a wave of grief begin to choke her. Still the flame burned and she remembered more … the touch of the man, the killer who had saved her, how his hands offered warmth the like of which she had never known. His touch had filled an emptiness that she had not even realised existed.

'Are you all right?'

Kirsten heard the words, but was unable to reply. Her eyes remained focused on the flame as she tried to bring herself back, but it was not until the figure stepped in front of the candle, blotting out its light, that she could make any kind of reply. She blinked, her eyes watering slightly.

Before her stood a priest, so youthful in appearance that he could barely have been out of the seminary. He had startling pale blue eyes that Kirsten could discern even through the dimness, made paler still by the sweep of blonde hair. He was of large build and Kirsten could see that he was obsessed with physical fitness at least as much as more theological matters. Without his robes, she figured that he would look more like an athlete than a priest. His thin lips parted as he spoke again and Kirsten felt that time had not resumed its proper pace.

'We've never met before, have we?'

She wet her lips; her mouth felt dry and she wondered how long it had been since she had drunk anything.

'No, we've never met.' she replied. 'I'm not a particularly religious person … Do you want me to leave?'

He sat on the front pew and leaned on the back bar where her arms had rested a short time before.

'Of course not! I just thought I had better check on you. You've been sat there for hours.'

Her eyes flashed. 'And you've been watching me!'

He seemed to blush slightly and his eyes dropped.

'There was me thinking you're a priest,' she said, 'but you're nothing more than a Peeping Tom.'

His eyes met hers, appearing shocked by her words.

'Perhaps you were frightened I might take something.' She was prattling and she wondered if he realised that it was because she felt uncomfortable and embarrassed. 'I should go, I've taken up enough of your time,' she concluded.

He opened his mouth, as if to reply and stopped, his eyes quizzing her odd behaviour. She had turned in an instant from a floundering fool, to guarded, alert and ready for action. Her eyes darted, an ear directed toward the door and as the handle turned, she threw herself to the floor. The priest stood up, gazing for a moment at the crawling figure and then to the entrance in time to see the approach of a man in a taupe suit, accompanied by a WPC. The priest walked forward, as if to meet the man, but his true reason for doing so was to prevent them from discovering Kirsten.

'Hello Father, I'm Inspector Stephenson. I wonder if I might ask you a few questions.'

After the inspector had shown the priest his identification, they shook hands formerly. Inspector Stephenson drew out a photograph from his breast pocket. Kirsten hid in the shadows trying to think of a way to reach the back door without discovery.

The priest will alert them to my presence; I'll have to run for it, she decided.

'Have you seen this girl before, Father?'

She tensed, ready to spring. The priest leaned in to look at the picture.

'No, I'm afraid not, Inspector.'

Kirsten gaped. *The picture **has** to be me,* she thought. *Perhaps it isn't, or else it's such a dreadful photograph that I cannot possibly be identified by it. It would be just my luck for the police to be showing the worst photo ever taken to everyone. I'll have to come out of hiding just to prevent further humiliation.*

'What's her name?' the priest asked.

'Kirsten Vái; she went missing this afternoon from West Mid' Hospital.'

Well that's just great, Kirsten thought. *Make me sound like an escaped wackadoo loony. Still, the photo is me, which means that the priest is deliberately lying; he's good at it too—cool as a cucumber.*

Feeling more confident, she crawled to the centre isle and crouched there listening to every word spoken, until the police went to make their exit. The priest went before them and opened the door, his eye catching a glimpse of Kirsten as she slipped through the back entrance.

He stood in the doorway, the last remnants of daylight gracing the horizon. The police car drove off with a gentle growl and the birds chattered in their evening roost. Closing the door, he produced a key from his vestment. It was very large and of beautiful craftsmanship, from a time long gone by. As the key turned in the lock, a heavy clunk ensued; with such age-old artistry, padlocks were unnecessary; it would take a battering ram to take down the door. Smiling, he replaced key and turned to make his way toward the altar, extinguishing candles as he went, until the church fell into darkness.

Kirsten stood floundering as she entered; she had walked straight into the man's living room. A plush sofa was neatly juxtaposed to the enormous flat-screen television. There were a great many books and Blu-rays, all of which she would not have expected a priest to own. On the wall, an Elvis clock rocked his legs, as a pendulum, counting the time. A massive sound system lay beneath the dancing Elvis clock and speakers were conspicuously placed in each corner of the exceedingly modern room.

The priest strolled in, shutting out the gloom beyond, with a casual back kick of the door.

'I lied in a house of God; I shall burn in Hell for all eternity!'

Kirsten went rigid, not daring to move, feeling very much like an intruder. 'I'm sorry,' she stuttered. 'I didn't realise it was your home back here. I never would have presumed such an intrusion had I been aware …'

He grinned and kicked off his shoes, as her words trailed into silence.

'You don't exactly speak like an average teenager, that's for sure,' he said.

Kirsten's body seemed to relax and she faced him square on.

'And you're the most unlikely priest I've ever seen in my life! Besides, I've had a rough time of late, it was bound to have some adverse effect on my behaviour.'

Her eyes followed him suspiciously into the kitchen, watching for a moment as he poured some water. His image seemed blurred and then disappeared altogether, as she fell into a faint.

'Kirsten, Kirsten can you hear me?'

Her glazed eyes opened wearily.

'Thatta girl,' the priest said.

He held a glass of water to her mouth, which she sipped gratefully; her strength returned with each drop that passed her dry lips. Her hands reached up to take the glass from him, eager to consume the contents more quickly to relieve her extreme thirst.

'Whoa careful now, you'll make yourself sick,' the man said.

She paid no heed to his warning and gulped down the water as though it was the elixir of life.

'Why did you conceal my presence here?' she asked.

His eyebrows raised in mild disbelief. 'SANCTUARY,' he said, in the most Quasimodo-like voice he could muster.

She suddenly laughed at his clownish display, and it seemed to her that all the weight and burdens of late, momentarily lifted only to drop about her shoulders again, with painful collapse. *I have no right to laughter,* she thought, *not when my friends lie dead. Laughter is for the happy and carefree; I am neither.* More keenly did she sense the wall behind which she had bricked up her feelings of sadness and remorse. Her smile ended abruptly and she seemed to sag.

'God obviously thought you needed looking after,' the priest continued, 'or else He would not have guided you to me. I could not very well have allowed a stray lamb of the flock to wander into the jaws of a wolf, now could I?'

Kirsten's eyes hardened, surprised at his choice of analogy when she herself had been thinking along a similar vein. Self-pity flitted away and made no attempt to take hold again.

'What is your name, Father?' she asked.

'Troy.'

'Well, Father Troy, I can assure you that it was not your god that brought me here. I am not, nor never will be one of *His* fold!'

The corners of Troy's mouth tilted in amusement, as if he was party to some private joke.

'I expected you to appear shocked,' she said.

Troy crouched beside her, his jeans showing beneath his cassock.

'Sorry to disappoint, but whatever you believe or don't believe, you *are* in need of help.'

She bowed her head, having hoped to offend him and failed, she realised that she was in his hands; he had helped once and now extended the friendship for a second time. It worried her. *What price does he hold to his aid? I've certainly no desire to be converted,* she thought.

'You must be hungry, Kirsten. I'll make us some dinner, shall I?'

He smiled warmly and rising, he went to the kitchen. A clatter of pots and pans drifted amongst the darkness that clouded her mind.

Scream upon scream echoed in her ears. Fire rose and smoke choked her …

'Kirsten?' Father Troy waved a hand in front of her blank expression.

She blinked, his ice blue eyes coming into focus.

'They died and it's all my fault,' she said. 'It's all my fault.'

His hand rested on her arm.

'Kirsten, you feel guilty because you are the only one who survived; it's a perfectly normal reaction.'

Her eyes seemed glazed with both confusion and tears. 'I didn't mean them,' she murmured.

She blinked and the moment passed; looking at him with fresh eyes, she could not recall what she had said. Father Troy had changed clothes. He wore jeans and a sweatshirt. The smell of dinner took the place of burning that seemed to linger in her nostrils. His brow furrowed, but Kirsten could not think why.

'Come, you should eat something,' Troy suggested.

She scrambled to her feet and made her way to the table where a simple meal had been prepared.

'Thank-you,' she said.

Dinner conversation was polite and evasive to begin with. At all costs, the priest avoided talk of the massacre. Kirsten felt weary and her mind eventually refused to focus on small talk, choosing to revisit nightmares old and new.

'Do you believe in the existence of evil?'

'I wouldn't be much of a priest if I didn't, Kirsten.'

She gazed thoughtfully. 'Do you think *I'm* evil, Father?'

He laughed until the expression on her face convinced him that she was serious.

'Whatever makes you think that?' he asked.

Once again, she took on a far-away look, as though she imagined herself to be somewhere else. 'Bad, evil things seem to happen around me. That man, who's responsible for so many deaths, he saved me, why? *And* I have dreams,

dreams of death and destruction. Besides, you have to think I'm evil because I insulted your religion, your God.'

'Kirsten, you're *not* evil.' He leaned across the table, narrowly missing the glass. 'I know you're not a religious person, but I wish I could convince you how much I believe this to be destined. God has spared you for a reason and I think—no, I truly believe that you have some task ahead of you. The truth is that I've never felt this close to the Lord in my entire life. He has a particular plan for you I'm sure, and the fact that he has chosen an atheist is good, it shows that He has a sense of humour.'

As Troy withdrew, his hand struck the glass; water spread across the tablecloth like a chromatography experiment.

'Sorry Lord,' he shrugged, with a cheeky smile.

Kirsten shook her head in disbelief. She had never been that close to someone with such a strong faith before. It was a disconcerting for her to think that whatever she said would be seen as the will of god. She shifted in her seat, feeling suddenly uncomfortable with the entire situation.

'Well, I must thank you, Father, for your hospitality, but I really should be going. I've imposed on you long enough.' She rose to her feet and looked about for another exit.

'Kirsten, I couldn't possibly let you walk home now.' Troy said. 'It's pitch black out there, besides I thought you were trying to avoid the police. It's highly unlikely that you will make it back to your home, unnoticed. You may as well spend the night here and you can decide in the morning what's best to be done.'

Kirsten nodded, too tired to argue. *He's right,* she thought. *I have no wish to be questioned tonight. A new morning might give me a sense of focus that the long day has robbed.*

'Now, you go and relax while I do the washing up,' Troy said, 'then I'll bring you in a nice mug of cocoa. How does that sound?'

'As tempting as the devil in the desert … sorry.'

He laughed, to her surprise. She would like to have joined him, but her mirth had left her. The mention of cocoa had only served to remind her of her father and Lisa. *He doesn't know and will he really care?* She shook such negative thoughts from her head, assuming that drowsiness had settled upon her, dampening her spirits as well as weighting her limbs.

* * * * *

It seemed that Kirsten perceived the sun waking before it did so. She sat up, as the first rays seeped over the horizon and the dim light of dawn illuminated the room. Her head felt light and she yawned, reaching for her shoes. Quickly, she tied her laces and crept toward the back door. She paused on spying a memo pad next to the telephone, and scribbled a thank-you, placing the note on the table. The key turned in the lock with a loud click that made Kirsten gaze uneasily about her. She opened the door slowly, expecting some noise or resistance, but it opened with ease. The sun was riding higher, welcoming her with a blinding light as it peeped over the treetops. Stepping out into the chill morning, she closed the door behind her, able to discern little in the darkness beyond. She did not see, therefore, the shape in the shadows step forward to approach the window. Had she glanced back as she was walking away, she may have noticed the parted curtain, revealing the sombre face of Father Troy, watching her steal away like a thief in the night.

The world was silent as Kirsten headed home; only the odd car passed by, containing an unfortunate shift worker. She cut into the fields that took her almost the entire journey back, relishing the quiet calm of morning; the air had a freshness about it, left over from when nature is allowed to dominate over mankind for the duration of a few night-time hours. As she approached the last mile, terrific birdsong replaced the quiet. Her surroundings were familiar and she came to places that she associated with memories, mostly of times spent with Geri. Her whole existence as it was, seemed so distant to her that it was more like a dream whose memory is fleeting.

Two mallards passed over-head and came to land clumsily in the approaching river. Kirsten heard a twig snap and swivelled, her body rigid. A group of dense bushes lay beyond, but she saw nothing irregular. She resumed her journey, dismissing the sound as perhaps a fox returning from its nightly hunt. However, the disturbance was enough to put her on her guard and assess her danger.

How many times have I walked this way in the past? she thought. *How many times have I dismissed my father's warnings?* It seemed to make more sense to her at that moment. She had known of the danger, but had never really understood. She had crossed over a threshold of innocence and was only too aware that nobody could hear her scream, and she would have to run very fast to escape an attacker. Nobody would know. *I could be murdered and who would know? My father isn't due back for another week and a half. The police will assume that I'm in hiding, and even if my body were discovered, it would be of little consolation after I'm dead.*

Her pace quickened into a jog and home grew nearer, but all the while she remained convinced that she was being followed. Her breath was short by the time she cornered her street. She was unsure whether or not to expect a guest of the uniformed variety and so slipped silently around the back.

A couple of families were up, indicated by bathroom and bedroom lights, but the majority of the neighbourhood still lay in bed, unaware of Kirsten's attempt to sneak into her own house. They also would not have seen the figure who stepped out from the shadows, clamping one hand firmly across her mouth, restraining her with ease with his remaining hand.

Four

She could hear the scream quite clearly in her mind. She could picture the entire neighbourhood being woken by such a noise. Unfortunately, no such sound could be heard; the attacker's vice-like grip prevented any cry from escaping her lips. Her limbs refused to function, her stomach pumped full of adrenaline and she felt herself gag as the sickness of fear rose. The gate retreated from her sight and a new one appeared; her next-door neighbours. The only coherent thought that broke through her panic was,

Why is he taking me there? Her vision seemed abnormal. Time seemed to have no meaning and the events appeared to happen so quickly that she could make no reaction and yet so slowly that she wondered why she had not even attempted to break free.

Fear.

Fear had become a close companion of late—true fear; fear for what lay ahead and whether she would actually be alive long enough to find out.

The door slammed behind them. *The neighbours will call the police,* she thought. *They have to … where are they?*

Silence.

The kitchen was gone and the dining room filled her panic-warped vision. Furniture was strewn about the place. The hand left her mouth, but instead of an escape attempt, she stood rooted. It was the smell that made her freeze; the same odour that she had noticed when her friends had been shot.

Blood and death.

She sank to the floor, scanning the scene wide-eyed, breathing hard. It took some time before she was able to look up at the attacker. It came as little surprise that before her stood the man who had killed so many of late. The vision of him began to blur, as tears welled in her eyes. *This man is tearing my world apart piece by piece,* she thought. *Two days ago, I had a normal existence; now, my friends and neighbours are dead and I am wanted by the police. If my father had been here, would he be dead too?*

She blinked away the tears and his form came into view once more. He was staring down at her and seemed unsure how to react. Their eyes locked on each

other and Kirsten felt a shiver down her spine as she convinced herself that
somehow she knew the man, even though until two days ago she had never
laid eyes on him before.

There came a rap at the door, her eyes sharpened and darted toward the
sound. Through the netted window, she could make out the uniformed outline
of two constables. Her mouth opened, as if to scream, but before the sound
could leave her, the man had gagged her with his hand once more. He half
carried, half dragged her into the darkness of the pantry. There was another
knock. Kirsten breathed heavily through her nostrils; her eyes set on the killer,
whose look pierced her, as if by will alone he could silence her if he wished.

The smell of death in the pantry was so strong that Kirsten thought she
would vomit. Her eyes darted sideways towards the direction of the emanating
odour; the bodies of her neighbours—husband, wife and child—were stacked
in the corner. The woman's eyes were still open, a look of frozen horror on her
dead face. Kirsten felt herself heave, her eyes widened and she heard a squeak,
as her scream fought to escape. She struggled wildly to break free from the
killer. His hold on her increased, but she had one arm free to strike at him and
the door, hoping to create enough noise for the police to hear.

The hand that clamped her mouth, shot mechanically out to pin her other
hand. The beginnings of her scream were pushed back as his mouth closed
over her own. His entire body weight pressed her into the wall and she ceased
to struggle. She could not move; her whole body felt alive with electricity. She
had felt the sensation before, when he had saved her from being shot, but now,
with his lips pressed against her own, in what was the closest she had ever
come to being kissed, the feeling overwhelmed her. She felt giddy and
wonderful and fear slipped away. Her body buzzed with excitement and she
longed to turn the odd position into a lingering kiss.

The voice of an officer calling through the letterbox brought her reeling
mind back to the dangerous situation at hand.

*What am I thinking? This man is a psychotic killer. There are dead bodies
in here with me and I'm probably about to join them.*

But still the feeling was there, a sensation that made life before seem unreal
somehow, but she knew that whatever she felt was irrelevant. *He has to be
stopped,* she thought. *What he has done is wrong and someone has to stop him.*
Her leg lifted and she swiftly kneed him in the genitals.

Not even a flinch.

Surprised, she tried again and then kicked him in the leg. Her eyes looked lost and confused, not understanding how the man could fail to react to such a painful attack. But after all, the man had been shot at by expert marksmen and not received a scratch. She wondered if he were even human.

His eyes narrowed, as if he were listening intently, then his mouth drew away from hers and he released his hold. She stared incredulously at him.

His hazel eyes averted her gaze and he whispered,

'Forgive me.'

Kirsten felt her breath quicken. She did not understand; all she knew was that she had to escape from the madness. Shoving him, she made a dash for the front door, screaming as she went. The police had gone. She reached for the lock, hoping to gain the attention of someone—anyone. His arms were about her once more, and he dragged her backward. There he held her, bear-like, as she struggled in futility against his incredible strength.

Realisation set in, feeling like an icicle stabbed through the heart. *This man has killed dozens of people and evaded capture,* she thought. *He has been shot and remains unharmed. Somehow, he has managed to utterly change his appearance. Nobody can stop him, least of all me; I am powerless against him. He can kill me at a whim, and there is little point in pleading for my life. He has no remorse. Death is inevitable.*

She felt her body stop struggling and allowed herself to relax. The man gently lowered her to the ground and crouched beside her. She stared ahead, her eyes glazed, her lips quivering.

'You can kill me now.' Her voice was little more than a dream-like whisper.

She sensed him get to his feet and walk around her. He knelt before her, his head bowed, almost worshipful.

'I would never harm you, Milady,' he soothed. His voice was soft and cool, with an accent unfamiliar to Kirsten. 'I am sworn to protect you, even at cost to mine own life; a life which is now forfeit for my having dared to touch you in such a way.'

His words were insane, yet sincerely spoken. His head rose slightly, continuing to avoid her gaze, as if he had committed some deadly sin against her. Her mind span with confusion and she sat motionless, watching the man who knelt before her, not daring to move or speak.

When it became clear to him that she had no desire to converse, his eyes lifted toward her. He gazed in horror at her pale, trembling form, and his hand reached out, stopping before he touched her, as if he dare not make contact with her again.

'Milady, please allow me to make you more comfortable.' He gently lifted her and set her down on the sofa. Her eyes still stared ahead, unseeing.

'Please forgive me, Milady,' the man continued. 'I had no desire to offend you so. As I have said, for daring to touch you, my life is over, and yet I would not leave this existence willingly if I knew that you bore me ill will. Therefore, I beg you to forgive my indecent behaviour, so that I may face my executioner with an unburdened heart.'

Kirsten turned slowly to face him; her body shivered as the cold of shock set in her limbs.

She fought to keep the tears at bay and stuttered, 'Forgive you! You killed them all. You killed Geri and all my friends; Chris and Sheila lay dead in the pantry and little Simon is there; he's only five years old and he's dead because YOU KILLED HIM! How can I possibly forgive you? How can I be expected to unburden your heart when you so obviously don't possess one?'

Her body shook as she wept uncontrollably. He appeared wounded at her reaction to him.

'But their lives are irrelevant,' he said. 'Your safety is all that matters.'

Her tears ceased for a moment; blinking away the remainder, she stared, astonished. 'How can you say that a *life* is irrelevant? You've *taken* lives. They are people, they're living beings; how can you say that?'

'But they are not *your* people, Milady; they are hostiles. Such people are not to be tolerated in your presence. They have been trying to keep you from me and attempted to stop me gaining an audience with you.'

Kirsten failed to hear his words with any clarity; they were fragmented and she could only pick up on certain points, either that or she simply refused to hear anything else he was saying.

'How did Simon try to harm you? He's just a little boy.'

'The infant was armed with a weapon, Milady,' the man replied.

Kirsten gazed at him; disbelief was in her eyes.

'WHAT!' She was unsure that she had heard him correctly.

The man leapt to his feet and ran from the room. She stared at the front door ahead of her. It was less than three metres away, and yet she could not move. Her limbs felt stiff, almost frozen; her body continued to tremble, although the fear seemed to lessen. He returned in a matter of seconds, her chance of escape—lost.

'Here Milady, as I have said, the child was armed.'

She examined with dismay, the blue plastic toy in the killer's hands.

'That's a water pistol. How could he possibly have harmed you with that?'

The man did not seem to comprehend. Snatching the gun from his hands, she fired it at her palm. He moved swiftly in attempt to prevent her from hurting herself. As the jet of water struck, he flinched and then stared in disbelief as the water trickled off him.

'I did not know,' he murmured. 'How could I possibly have known?'

'It doesn't even look like a real gun!'

'Milady, I protest; all weapons here appear strange to me. On first arriving, I did not even realise that I was being threatened.'

Kirsten's mouth gaped, as she attempted to understand his meaning.

'Are you an alien?' She wondered what else he could possibly have meant by '*arriving here*'.

His confusion was plain to see. 'I do not understand your meaning, Milady.'

'Are you human? Are you from this planet?'

A chord of realisation struck the man and he backed away from her.

'Have you no recollection of me?' he asked. 'Do you not know who I am?'

Her eyes narrowed and she shook her head, as if trying to rid herself of a bad dream.

'I am Caitul, First Knight to Katahl, your betrothed. We knew each other of old. Do you not recall?'

Her cheek muscles contracted, causing her eyes to narrow further and her teeth to draw into a grimace. She seemed to have forgotten to breathe some time ago and had to force herself to ingest air, unsure whether her giddiness was due to shock or lack of oxygen. She could not speak. *That's it,* she thought. *No more … I have no desire to communicate further with this madman. If he's going to kill me, then I'd rather get it over with. I've no wish to prolong the inevitable. It's not that I want my life to end, but waiting for the event is proving to be so distressing that I just want it to be over. Death will be a release from the pain and misery I feel, the boredom of a mundane and average life. When I think about it, what is there really to live for? The best part of the day for the past fourteen years has been spent in a classroom learning countless reams of information that are going to prove utterly useless in the real world. Most of my life has been spent in the confines of the education system.*

What next?

Three years at university to put off for a while, joining the end of a dole queue, during which time I'll have accumulated so much debt, in student loans and overdrafts, that I will spend the rest of my life trying to pay them off. After all, it is a well-known fact that anyone foolish enough to opt for an arts degree is unlikely to earn a significant amount of money.

So why bother at all? To make Daddy proud. "My little girl's a Bachelor of Arts you know, with Honours of course."

Well so fucking what? It means nothing nowadays. Absolute zilch.

Perhaps if I went on to read for my Masters, or even PhD, that would be something. But how would I ever finance myself since the abolition of government grants? Twelve hours a day flipping burgers and accumulating more debt might get me through; after all, it's about all I will ever be qualified to do if I do a degree in music.

No that's unfair. There's always retail. They will take anyone.

So, seventeen years of hard work so that I can smile politely and ask, "Would you like to keep the hangers?"

A career in retail ... it's a blessing I'm going to die now. This man is actually my saviour, although I hadn't realised it at first.

She seemed remarkably calm once she lost herself in her own mind. However, she could not stay forever. It was time to go back—back to the dead that did not deserve to die and lay unburied, stacked like meat in a butcher shop window. She did not want to face them again, but knew that it was time to return, to go back—back to *him*.

She blinked, her eyes watering. She was back in her own home, lying on her sofa in her own living room. Sitting upright, she felt dizzy for a moment, her body ice-cold with shock and fear. Gazing about, she saw nothing unusual and her ears strained for a trace of sound.

Nothing.

'Did I dream it all?' she asked.

A knock at the door made her start so much, that her fear found a voice and she heard a cry escape her pallid lips. Her approach to the door seemed painfully slow, as her stiffened limbs refused to function properly. All the while, she expected strong arms about her, preventing her from reaching the door. She did not attempt to see who was calling; she did not care. Her weakened fingers struggled to turn the lock and she pulled desperately to open the door, but the wood had swollen in the damp and refused to budge.

Backing away, she collapsed back onto the sofa, shaking. Drawing her knees up to her chin, she hugged them to comfort her confused state. The door was forced open and Inspector Stevenson stumbled in, followed by two constables. She vaguely made out his features, as he crouched before her, examining her in turn.

He has not seen me since I was hospitalised, she thought. *For all he knows, I could have been in this state the entire time since our last meeting. Perhaps he will try to certify me. I'm not exactly behaving normally. I should speak— say something to convince him that I haven't cracked.*

'He was here,' she rasped.

His eyebrows raised and he turned his head, nodding to one of the other officers. Within seconds, the room was full of armed police who scurried through the house like an army of ants.

'Nothing Sir, all clear.'

Her mouth was dry, and she found it difficult to speak. She knew what she wanted to say, but the words just jumbled out from her parched lips.

'They're dead! He killed them … help but you didn't hear. Call out for … I tried.' Her voice broke off with a croak. She attempted to wet her lips, but her saliva glands seemed unable to comply.

'Get the Doctor,' the inspector ordered.

As he turned his attention back to Kirsten, she could sense his frustration. He had to be nice or he would land himself in trouble, and yet she knew that all he wanted to do at that moment in time was shake some sense into her, maybe even slap her in order to get the information he so desperately required.

Looking about her, she could see the room was full of subordinates, awaiting their next command. She fought to keep her mind off how thirsty and light-headed she felt.

Focus, focus, focus.

Her hands tightly gripped at her legs, until her knuckles strained white. Her teeth gritted as she attempted to establish in her mind whether the killer's abduction had been real or not. *If not, how did I get here? If so, then why am I here?*

She stared into the inspector's eyes, hoping to find even a tiny piece of compassion there. Her eyes begged him and deep within the swirl of his irises, he answered back. His anger was not directed at her; his frustration existed because of his own ineptitude at having lost the killer. It was what she needed to see to give her the strength she craved.

'Next door,' she said, almost in a whisper. 'He held me next door.'

Her head bowed, as the room began to empty.

'He killed them. They're in the pantry.'

The inspector held her shoulder, gently squeezing it as she rested her head against her knees. It was an action without meaning. It offered her no support, rather made her aware of his mounting excitement at the prospect of catching up with his quarry. He rose to his feet and paced toward the exit.

'How is Walker?' she asked.

It was an odd subject for her to bring up, but she was angry that he was about to abandon her. She did not look at him, but knew that he had frozen and turned to face her.

'He's on leave,' the inspector said coolly.

Kirsten heard so much more in his words. *Walker had broken down, was what they were calling 'mentally disturbed', and could not rejoin the force until he was given the okay. But the inspector knew that would never happen. He knew that whatever had happened to Walker meant that he was lost forever.*

'I see,' she said, her eyes half-closing.

The inspector left the building and the remaining officer offered to make her a cup of tea. She did not have the energy to say that all she really wanted was about ten gallons of water, but a cup of tea was better than nothing.

The doctor arrived before the tea had even been made; he established that she was dehydrated and still suffering from shock; he also drank the tea. He suggested that she be admitted back into hospital care, there to be given intravenous fluids until her levels returned to normal. Her heart sank at the thought of having to return.

While the doctor made arrangements for Kirsten's admittance, the remaining officer helped her to the bathroom. At his request, she kept the door unlocked. She was on the toilet for an embarrassing length of time, realising it must have been at least a day since she last relieved herself. After washing her hands, she scrubbed her face clean, followed by splashing on cold water, which managed to revive her a little. As she turned to reach for a towel, she caught sight of herself in the mirror. She looked pale and older—much older and no wonder; she had changed. The girl she had been did not exist any longer; everything she was and everything she might have been had been wrenched away from her, and as she gazed into her intense eyes she wondered if she would ever get her life back on a normal track again.

The sound of the front door slamming brought her back from her brooding. Footsteps thumped through the house and she reached for a towel, burying her face in it, dabbing it dry. There was a swish and a thud, as the door to the bathroom was thrown open. Kirsten removed the towel to face the stormy features of Inspector Stephenson, as he stood outlined like an angry bull in the doorway.

'Have you never heard of knocking?' she said.

As soon as she had spoken the words, she realised her mistake. He stepped in and closed the door behind him. In an instant, he was on her, his ageing hands getting a firm grip on her shoulders as he thrust her into the wall. There he held her, his eyes locked on her, his teeth gritted. She was too astonished by his behaviour to dare move.

'What game are you playing, young lady? Do you think that it's funny to waste police time?'

He shoved her again, causing her pain, yet she did not make a sound.

'Do you have any idea how much manpower like that is going to cost my department?'

He shook her and she began to see stars—or was it flying insects, lots of them buzzing around her skull and at the centre, his dark, angry eyes. She could bear it no longer. She was unwilling to give into the urge to collapse, and end the torment by letting consciousness slip away. What happened next, she had no intention to do; she acted merely on instinct to prevent him from hurting her again. Her hands lifted through the gap between his arms and with a swift jerk upwards and outwards, she broke his hold on her, then bringing her arms down, she swivelled slightly and dealt him a back-hand that sent him hurtling away from her. The door opened as the doctor and a police officer entered, catching the inspector before he struck the wall.

'Keep that maniac away from me!' Kirsten demanded.

The men looked from Kirsten to the inspector, trying to assess the situation.

'She hit me. The bitch actually hit me,' growled the inspector. 'Sergeant, place Miss Vái under arrest,'

'What's the charge, Sir?'

'Obstruction of justice, wasting police time and assault on a police officer.'

'Sir.' The constable nodded.

As he approached Kirsten, she shrank backward, unable to believe that he seriously meant to arrest her.

'He attacked *me*!' she stuttered. 'I was just protecting myself,'

The doctor budged past the officer and knelt before Kirsten where she had sunk down the wall.

'Stay away from her,' he said, 'look at this.'

He indicated to the red marks about her collar line, and with her permission revealed the damage about her shoulders where the inspector's pincer-like grip had bruised her.

'I hardly touched her,' the inspector protested.

The police constable turned back to his superior, his eyebrow raised in disbelief. Kirsten felt the pain from the bruising on her head where he had smacked her into the wall. She lifted her hand to feel if a bump had arisen. The doctor held her arm supportively, and his mouth opened in surprise when he saw blood on her fingertips where she had touched her skull. He tipped her head gently forward to observe the extent of the laceration.

'Sergeant, I believe that you are arresting the wrong person,' the doctor said. 'Your inspector here could have killed this young woman had she not struck out when she did. Now, if you'll excuse me, gentlemen, I need to get my patient to a hospital, that is if you have finished trying to bash her brain in.'

He helped Kirsten to her feet and the men parted to let them pass. Kirsten stopped, realisation sinking in.

'Did you not find the bodies?' she asked.

Inspector Stephenson challenged her; his face already beginning to swell from where she had struck him.

'Miss Vái, you know full well that there were no bodies there. We spoke to Mr Inglis ...'

'You can't have; he's dead,' she cut in.

'I assure you, Miss Vái, that he is very much alive, and didn't particularly appreciate us raiding his house. His wife has just left him, so he's feeling miserable enough, without us breaking down his front door and searching for bodies.'

'But didn't you check the pantry? Sheila and Simon are dead in there … so is Chris,' she ended, in confusion.

He leaned in so close that she could smell his anger.

'Miss Vái, there was nothing but what one would expect to find in a pantry, stores of food. All I can say is consider yourself lucky that you're going into hospital, young lady. Believe *me*, we'll have plenty of questions for you once you are discharged, starting with what the hell you did to Walker!'

It was pointless to try to explain or reason with him while his blood was up. He was angry and upset, and she did not blame him. As she stepped into the car, she noticed vanloads of police pulling away. She looked out of the window at her little house, wondering what her father would say if he came home to find their home teeming with police. As they drove away, she glanced toward a movement coming from the neighbours' house.

Chris gazed out of the window, his eyes following as they pulled away. His look made her shiver; he was so pale, almost blue.

I was wrong, she thought. *Chris is alive. I must have dreamt it after all. It just doesn't make sense. I remember arriving home from the church, that's when it all happened … unless none of it happened, and I arrived home from the hospital, catatonic and imagined it all. Something is niggling me though, something I can't quite put my finger on, but it has to do with Walker.*

'There's a bottle of water in the back, Kirsten,' the doctor said. 'Make sure that you sip it; you don't want to make yourself worse.'

She picked up the bottle and unscrewed the cap.

'It might be an idea for you to try and get some sleep; it's quite a drive.'

She pulled the bottle away from her mouth, with a pop. 'I don't understand. Are we not going to West Mid'?'

'No, I thought it best to put you somewhere which offers better security— for your own protection.'

'So does that mean that you believe me, doctor?'

The man glanced up at her in his rear view mirror.

'Miss Vái, all I know is that you did not get in this state spontaneously. It is of course possible that it could be posttraumatic stress as a result of the incident at the school, but I would rather be over cautious than to have you dead. Now try and get some rest if you can.'

She took a few more sips of water before leaning back, her eyes closing to the sound of Ezio's 'Saxon Street' on the doctor's CD player. She smiled and her body relaxed, as the gentle guitar rifts soothed her like a lullaby into a sound slumber …

Roads meandered onward, miles and miles of endless journey. Roads turned to rivers and they sailed on. Every moment her thirst grew; she was surrounded by water and yet could not stop to drink, for fear that the bogie man would get her; the bogie man, who wore masks to disguise how frightening he really was, *and if he catches me … what then?*

'I am Caitul, First Knight to Katahl … I am sworn to protect you.'

No.

He's here to drive me mad.

Or is that the doctor's job, to drive me to the madhouse?

No, it's a hospital.

How can a hospital offer more secure arrangements? It has to be an institution, surely.

Huge steel gates opened and closed behind their little boat, and they sailed up to the front entrance of a vast building as grey as the sky, with few too windows.

'Kirsten we're here. It's time to wake up.'

Her eyes felt reluctant to open. She yawned, her mouth drier than ever. The doctor assisted her out of the car and she stood gazing up in at the grey brick building looming above her. A man stood waiting with a wheel chair, as if he were expecting them. Helping Kirsten into it, he wheeled her through the entrance. She could not help but look back, trying to catch a glimpse of the tall steel gates from her dream.

She flinched as they inserted the drip. Various routine tests were performed, temperature, blood pressure, and blood—to her dismay. She felt tired and miserable; her room had no window and artificial light was no substitute for the sun. It was as if she was a prisoner awaiting execution. There was no television, anything to read, and nothing to look at except the bare magnolia walls; *prisoners are at least given something to divert themselves,* she thought miserably. She had only her mind to occupy her time of stay and her thoughts were dark, filled with the faces of the dead and the eyes of the man responsible for the catastrophe that was her life of late.

Hour upon hour passed in such a way. The nurse looked in on her, but seeing Kirsten's eyes closed, assumed that she was sleeping and so left her to her dark brooding. Then it happened; it seemed so sudden that she was not sure how the thought had popped in there. She supposed that she must have been thinking about Walker. It was so simple that she could not believe that she had not put two and two together before; perhaps it was because she was tired and weak. But just then, it seemed obvious.

My neighbours **are** *dead, including Chris,* she considered. *It was the killer they all saw. Just as he had been Walker, now he is Chris. Walker and Caitul had been one and the same, as though he was possessed somehow. But Chris is dead, which would explain why he looks so pale; there is a corpse walking around giving police statements. That's it, no doubt about it, but how can I tell the police that they have a member of the undead to arrest? How can I set about explaining what has happened to Walker and Chris when I fail to understand it myself? But I have to try; I don't want to face Caitul again if I can help it. I want him gone from my life and everything back to normal, or as near as it can be after all that has happened.*

'Nurse!' she yelled. Her body felt strong again and she would have walked out to fetch assistance had it not been for the drip. She peeled back the plaster and took hold of the needle, cringing.

'STOP!' The woman rushed in and checked the equipment, resealing the plaster after she was satisfied that the drip was still safely in place.

'What were you thinking?' she muttered.

It's all right, I'm becoming an expert at removing these things, Kirsten thought, but decided it was best not to mention her previous escape. 'I need to speak to Inspector Stephenson. It's urgent. I have information regarding the killer's whereabouts.'

Kirsten prayed that the woman had been briefed on her reason for being there; the last thing she wanted was to appear delusional. The nurse's eyebrows knitted together in concentration, as if trying to determine whether Kirsten had invented such information in order to get away from the hospital. However, the tension suddenly lifted and the woman smiled.

'Very well, I'll arrange for a mobile to be brought to your room, okay?'

Kirsten nodded and the nurse promptly left, seemingly not in the mood to chatter. Kirsten ran through her mind the least crazy way in which she was to explain herself, but no matter how she said it, she knew that she was going to sound insane.

The nurse re-entered, a phone in her hand, dialling the number off a card she was holding.

So the good inspector still thinks that I know more than I'm telling, Kirsten thought. *Oh boy is this a mistake, but it's too late to worry about it now.*

The phone was handed to her and the ringing tone stopped.

'Hello, Inspector Stephenson.' She held the phone tightly to her ear. Her mouth opened and in an instant, she forgot what she had prepared to say. 'It's me inspector … Kirsten … Kirsten Vái'

He said nothing, but she could sense his feeling of expectation.

'I have to talk to you about Walker. It's going to sound crazy, and you're probably not going to believe me, but I *have* to tell you.'

'Go on, Kirsten.'

She swallowed hard and tried to sound confident as she spoke. 'Somehow, the killer had … influenced Walker.'

'That's nonsense; Walker is one of the straightest coppers I know.'

'No, not like that, Inspector, more like … ' She could not say and so tried a different approach. 'It was as though Walker had no notion of what was happening.'

'You mean he'd been hypnotised, Miss Vái?'

'Perhaps, well sort of, except,' *here goes. This is when he's going to put the phone down,* 'except he was the killer, no, I mean the killer *became* Walker, just like he's now become Chris. I know it sounds crazy …'

'Crazy Miss Vái? Science fiction would be nearer the mark.'

'I knew you wouldn't believe me,' she mumbled.

She handed the mobile phone back to the nurse and could hear him shouting at the other end of the line, but she did not know what he was saying; nor did she want to.

The nurse spoke quietly. 'Hello Inspector Stephenson, this is Nurse Jones. Would you like me to put Miss Vái back on for you?'

He screamed a string of abuse down the phone then hung up.

The drip was removed later that evening and Kirsten was allowed to eat again, to her great relief.

'When am I going home?' she asked.

The nurses shot worried glances to each other and said nothing.

'Oh I see,' Kirsten said, 'so I *am* a prisoner.'

'We had a phone-call from Inspector Stephenson, earlier; he's coming up to see you tomorrow.'

Kirsten's heart sank low. *What could he possibly have to say to me now?*

Five

Inspector Stephenson slammed the telephone back onto the cradle. 'God that girl is so frustrating!' he fumed.

'Something the matter, Sir?'

He looked up, becoming aware of several of his officers as they watched him with mild amusement.

'Nothing's wrong, Sergeant. Go about your business.'

He stared at the case-file in front of him, his ears burning and his face flushed. A giggle sounded from behind and he threw an icy glare.

They're laughing at me, he thought. *I've failed to catch a killer who has not attempted to hide the fact. But perhaps most amusing of all is how a teenager is giving me the run-around.*

He thought of the look of horror on her face when he shoved her into the wall, and he felt suddenly ashamed. *Never in my thirty years on the force have I struck a woman.* Slamming the file shut, he snatched up his coat and paced moodily toward the door.

'Where are you off to, Sir?'

'Home,' he said, slamming the door behind him.

He stood at the bus stop, buttoning his coat and cursing the mechanic who said it would be another two days before he could pick up his car. The rain fell from the sky like tears from heaven. A van raced around the corner and hit a puddle, soaking the inspector to the knees.

'Bastard,' he shouted, shaking his legs.

Reaching for his pocket book, he proceeded to take down the car's registration. The bus pulled to a halt and the inspector tutted, screwing up the paper and throwing it into the gutter, deciding that it wasn't worth the paperwork to pursue such a matter.

'Isleworth please,' he droned to the driver.

The man proceeded to give a sarcastic comment regarding the state of his trousers and the inspector held the driver's gaze for a moment, far from amused. Removing the ticket, he faced the arduous task of trying to find a seat.

If I sit too far forward, then I might be obliged to give up my seat, he thought. *Otherwise, people will think I'm a complete git. I mustn't spend too long looking for a seat, because people could think I'm weird for staring at them all, and I can't take the first available seat next to someone in case there's a two-seater free further back and they know about it; they'll wonder why I chose to sit next to them.*

God I hate public transport!

The rain pelted down and pattered against the muddied windows. Two youngsters at the back were getting rowdy and people about him started to shift uneasily in their seats. The inspector observed, with interest, how easily people could be intimidated.

Not her though.

Not her.

As he stepped up to his front door and turned the key in the lock, he imagined bygone days when children would greet him with 'Daddy's home!' and the smell of his wife's cooking would waft through from the kitchen.

Simple joys.

However, the house was cold and empty, and the best the inspector could hope for was a meal for one. Catching criminals had always been his forte`, not cooking. *Anyway, since she left me, what's the point?* he thought. *Home-cooked meals are a thing to enjoyed with the family, not sat alone in the dark, thinking back on past mistakes; all the dinners that ended up in the bin, because I was too busy spending time with thieves and murderers, to spend time with the people I loved. Life as a policeman is hard,* he mused.

He opened the bills and placed them to the bottom of the pile that was building on the kitchen table. The last letter was from his wife's solicitor, stating that she was attempting to deny him access to his children. He screwed it up by making a fist, and then threw it toward the overflowing bin in the corner. It bounced upon the linoleum and landed in the cat dish. He found himself wondering why he had left the bowl there, considering that she had taken the cat with her as well.

He flipped the switch on the kettle and dropped a teabag into a mug, then sighing, he threw himself into a dining chair, which had been a wedding present from his in-laws, and listened with quiet contentment as the kettle began to boil.

* * * * *

Father Troy had felt unwell all day. There was a sense of relief, for his part, as the evening mass concluded and he ushered the congregation through the doors. As he went about extinguishing the candles, almost as ritualistic as the mass itself, he removed his cassock and sat for a moment at Christ's feet, issuing a silent prayer in hope of relief from the burning in his heart. The little sleep he had managed to obtain had been filled with Kirsten's dark eyes swallowing his soul, inviting him to relinquish his sacred vows. Her hair had brushed against his chest and her lips had lightly touched his cheek. He had awoken in a feverish sweat, fully expecting to find the young woman in his bedroom.

Peering around the door, he had spied her sleeping soundly where he left her, the blanket wrapped about her, exactly as he had placed when she fell into slumber. He closed the door, ashamed of his thoughts, and sat huddled in bed, unable to sleep again for fear of another visitation from the temptress who mocked his chastity.

He had heard her rise from her slumber, but made no attempt to greet her. Only on hearing the front door close as she made her exit, had he dared to venture out to read what she had written.

Thank-you Father Troy. I am most grateful for your assistance. I am sorry if I caused you any inconvenience.

Kirsten.

-x-

He held the letter to his nose as if he could scent its author. Letting it fall from his hand, he recalled watching her escape into the cold of dawn. He had wished silent luck to the girl, whether she was a devil or an angel to have awakened his sleeping senses so.

Inspector Stephenson finished his second cup of tea and removed his ready-made lasagne from the oven.

Walker was behaving strangely, it's true, especially around the girl, he considered. *He wasn't even supposed to have accompanied me back to her house.*

He volunteered.

The inspector twisted his fork into the lasagne and took a few mouthfuls, before realising that it was still frozen in the middle. Sulkily dropping his fork onto the table, he placed the food on top of the pile that used to be a bin. He listened hard; it had stopped raining. Grabbing his coat, he decided to pass by the chippy on his way to visit Walker.

The following morning, Kirsten lay on her front with her legs swinging like a child. She had lost all concept of time due to her lack of a window and had become so bored that she was attempting to recite the periodic table by heart. Hearing the door click open, she glanced up in dread anticipation, expecting her visit from the inspector to have arrived.

'Dad!' she cried.

He moved toward her and she jumped nimbly to her feet to meet his embrace. His tanned face smiled, but his eyes were clearly troubled. She did not care at that moment and clung to him as though with one hug he could alleviate the pain and suffering she felt. She had fully expected herself to cry in his presence, but she did not—could not.

'Dad, do you know everything that's happened? Did they tell you?'

'Yes flower, I know; I know everything. There's been a police guard on the house, and it's been suggested that I stay away from home for a while.' He sounded angry.

'It might be a good idea, Dad … just to be on the safe side. Anyway, you can stay with Lisa. It'll be good practice for when you're married.'

Her father stared, incredulous for a moment. 'Kirsten, I didn't want to tell you like this; it hardly seems appropriate, but since you've brought the subject up. Lisa and I …'

'Are engaged, yes I know. You bought her a diamond, surrounded by small sapphires; it's very pretty. I hope she appreciated the blood and sweat went into obtaining such a rock … er congratulations, Dad.'

'How could you possibly have known that, Kirsten?' her father asked, backing away.

She shrugged, unwilling to tell him how she had seen them on the beach together on the day that her friends were slaughtered.

'Will she be moving in with us, or did you want me to move out?'

'Don't be like that, Kirsten.'

'No I'm serious. I'm old enough to live on my own now. In fact, it seems like a pretty sensible idea at present, considering the amount of people who seem to get themselves killed in my company. Besides, I don't want to mess it up for you, Dad. You deserve a little happiness.'

He reached out his hand and pulled her into him, hugging her tightly.

'I'm sorry I wasn't here when you needed me, petal. It must have been so terrible,' he said.

He kissed her on the forehead, and she felt keenly the gulf that had come between them.

Is it my fault, or his? she pondered. *Perhaps neither. I'm simply not the little girl he left so short a time ago.*

'Ah, Mr Vái I presume.'

The inspector entered the room and extended his hand to her father. Kirsten noticed how much older he looked. Dark circles hung under his eyes, as though sleep had been but a brief visitor or had not bothered to show at all.

'I trust that you had a safe journey and I hope you can understand why I deemed it so important that you cut your trip short.'

Kirsten scowled, realising that Inspector Stephenson had been responsible for her father's premature return.

'Of course, Inspector. I only wish you had contacted me sooner.'

'Oh I would have done, had your daughter been more co-operative about your location, Mr Vái. Actually, Kirsten has been most *uncooperative* through this whole affair.'

Kirsten opened her mouth, as if to speak, but decided to glare instead.

'You see, the killer is directly connected to your daughter in some way and she would have you think that she is a complete innocent, ignorant of who this man is or why he is so focused on her.'

Her father's eyes bore into her, however she was too familiar with his facial expressions to feel intimidated.

'I've tried to co-operate with you, Inspector,' she protested. 'I've told you everything I know and even speculated a few things in attempt to help you, but you refuse to listen.'

The inspector smiled slowly and turned his attention to her father.

'There you see, she *speculated.* She's been fabricating events and giving me nothing factual to go on at all.'

Her father seemed unmoved and yet she knew he was deeply angry at having been placed in such an embarrassing situation.

'Is this true, Kirsten?' he asked. 'Do you know more than you are telling the inspector?'

Kirsten sighed, shaking her head, and sat back down on the bed, wondering why nobody would believe her.

'Ask her about Constable Walker,' the inspector said. 'Get her to tell you what she did to him.'

Her father raised a solitary eyebrow. Kirsten could not believe that he was taking Inspector Stephenson's side.

'Walker attacked *me*!' she retaliated. 'He was the killer. I did nothing to him; I simply screamed for help. By the time help came, the killer was gone.'

She risked a glance to her father, who was clearly confused.

'Just say for a moment that somehow the killer and Walker were one and the same,' the inspector said. 'How did you separate them again, Miss Vái?'

'Me? What makes you think it was me?'

'How did you feel, as he backed you into a corner? What went through your mind?'

She shuddered and her body went cold with the memories of that terrifying moment. 'I felt … scared,' she said, 'and then it was as though … my whole body was alive, like electricity. I don't know how to explain it …' She trailed off, feeling silly. It became clear to her how the inspector could cleverly manipulate his voice to force a confession from a suspect. She only hoped that she had not said something foolish.

He gazed back at her, his eyes shining and a thin smile upon his lips.

'It was discovered that Walker had suffered electrical burns when he was admitted into care,' he said. 'They thought he'd had a serious electric shock. Now, isn't that odd? What do you suppose could have caused such a thing, Miss Vái? Walker's in a coma! It is very possible that his current state is directly due to an electric shock received while in your living room on the day in question. You are in very serious trouble, young lady.'

Her father stepped forward and touched the inspector on the shoulder, trying to draw the man's brooding presence away from his daughter.

'You're not seriously suggesting that Kirsten attacked your officer, are you?' he asked.

The inspector continued to glower at Kirsten, as if to judge her reaction to his accusation.

'She, by her own admission, saw Walker as being the killer. She also admits to having used some form of electricity to protect herself from him.'

Kirsten felt crushed. *I didn't imagine Walker or Chris,* she insisted in her mind. *I was compos mentis at the time of the incidents ... well, the first one certainly.*

'May I speak to you outside, inspector?' her father requested, gesturing toward the door.

'No wait,' Kirsten tried to protest.

'It'll be all right, Kirsten; I promise,' her father said. He spoke as though he were soothing a wakeful child.

Inspector Stevenson smiled snidely at her.

'After you,' he said, and they disappeared into the hallway.

Father Troy felt his palms become clammy at the request made over the telephone. Even in a traditionalist diocese, it was almost unheard of to perform a Latin funeral mass, but the Morgan's were devout, not to mention generous parishioners and the bishop had been only too pleased to accommodate their wishes. Troy had agreed without hesitation to do the funeral, but now felt guilty for his reasons for accepting. *It's going to be a big affair, undoubtedly,* he thought, *child funerals always are. Half the school is bound to show, as well as the usual relatives and possibly her ...*

He was to perform funeral rites for a girl by the name of Geri Morgan. She met a tragic end in the recent shooting at the school, the same school that Kirsten attended; the incident in which she had been involved. *Had they been friends?* he wondered. *Very likely. So Kirsten has to attend and I will have the chance to speak to with her once more, to console her in her grief.*

The feeling was there again, like a washing machine in his stomach and tightness across his chest. He dashed to the bathroom and vomited several times; kneeling on the floor, he reached up and flushed the sick away.

'Dear God help me. Why is this happening to me? I thought that you sent her for a reason. Please say that she serves a higher purpose other than a temptation for me to test my faith. Oh Holy Father, relieve me of this suffering. I beg you ... I beg you.'

* * * * *

When Kirsten's father entered the room once more, his face was grave. Kirsten's gaze fell to the bed and she sighed, having no desire to hear what had transpired between them.

'The inspector's just taking a call from his office; he'll be back in a moment I expect. How are you feeling?'

Her eyes met his with stubborn indignation.

'Hurt, betrayed, used, a scapegoat; take your pick, Dad. How could you even consider that I would attack a policeman?'

'But Kirsten, you were seen attacking the inspector, so that's not a particularly sensible comment to make.'

She was furious, realising what the term 'stewing' meant as her temperature rose with her anger. 'He attacked me! I was protecting myself … This is insane! This man, whoever he is, was abroad until a few days ago. Do you think he's my fucking pen pal?'

'Don't you swear at me, young lady!'

'Well, don't be an idiot then! How can you possibly think that I would be involved in my best friend's death? How can you?'

The inspector stood framed in the doorway. 'Not directly perhaps,' he said, 'but inadvertently, yes; that is precisely what I believe. There is something that you are hiding and I *will* find out what.'

A senior nurse appeared behind the inspector.

'Will you kindly keep your voices down!' she snapped. 'This is a hospital not an interrogation room. Miss Vái needs her rest. You can talk to her again tomorrow, when you have had the chance to calm down. For now, I must ask you to leave … both of you.'

Her father did not look at Kirsten as he said goodbye. At that moment, she felt that she did not know him. She was no longer his little flower, and he had failed her worse than she ever believed possible.

The following morning, Kirsten's father visited her again. He was behaving in an overly cheerful manner, convincing her that he had gone into denial. He passed her some sweets, grapes and a newspaper, which she flicked immediately through, looking for news on the killer, whilst occasionally saying 'mm', as if listening to what he was saying.

Her eyes rested on a picture of Geri, attached to an article about her school. As she read, she felt her rage return.

'Why didn't you tell me about Geri's funeral?' Her voice flecked with anger.

'It was thought that the event would be too distressing for you, Kirsten. No-one wants to see you upset any more than you have been.'

'By no-one I can only assume that you mean the dear old inspector ... he wants to keep me under lock and key in case I try to make an escape, or contact the killer. That's if he even believes there is a killer any longer and it's not just me!'

'Kirsten, you're being foolish,' her father said. 'Nobody has accused you of killing anyone. You are here for your own protection. It is clear that this man has some personal interest in you, to have come after you again.'

He stared for a long while at his daughter's dejected state, before relenting.

'I'll have a word with the inspector and see what I can do. That is if you are sure that you want to go,' he said.

She looked at him with a hard stare, as if to say to him *'don't ask me stupid questions!'*

The organ stood silent, as the congregation entered the church for the funeral mass. Father Troy smoothed the front of his black chasuble and took a breath. As he reached the altar, he immediately scanned the crowd whilst they took their seats. *She's not here,* he thought. *No, I can't be sure; there are too many people ... No. I know she's not here.*

He kept his hands folded together, fighting the urge to mop the sweat that had formed on his forehead. The coffin was placed, feet first, before him, a black pal covering it. Crossing himself, he began.

'In nominee Patris, et filii, et Spiritus Sancti. Amen.' He joined his hands before his chest and spoke again. 'et introibo ad altare Dei Ad Deum qui laetificat juventutem meam.

The tears were overwhelming. Ordinarily, he would speak words of comfort on arrival at the church, but the family were strict traditionalists. It was just as well, as he could think of no such words to give; he was entirely unfocused on the task at hand. Swallowing hard, he crossed himself again, reaching for the words, the words that were meant to bring peace, and yet were in truth, unheard.

Kirsten felt an incomprehensible sense of foreboding on approaching the church. She considered that she might have been unsociable for too long and the thought of being surrounded by grieving people was a little too much to bear. She paused at the doors, listening.

'Lacrimosa dies illa,

qua resurget ex favilla.

iudicandus homo reus:

huic ergo parce Deus.'

She turned to look at the inspector, her eyes displaying the apprehension she felt. They were late; she knew they would be, despite the inspector's protestations that they could make up time on the motorway. Kirsten could not be angry; she felt many things, but anger was not amongst them. Pushing the door gently, she entered the gloom of the church. Hundreds of candles had been lit that omitted a welcoming glow. However, Kirsten felt far from welcome, as seven or eight-dozen people turned to scowl at them on their late arrival.

Father Troy stared at the open doorway, taking in the silhouette of Kirsten and her sombre companion-come-babysitter. He paused; the words took flight from his mind to be replaced by confusion and he closed his mouth again, unable to speak. A few members of the congregation tutted, believing that the priest's ever-lengthening pause was due to Kirsten's rude interruption.

Inspector Stephenson quietly closed the door and ushered Kirsten onto the back row, where she sat brooding in the shadows. She blinked a few times, forcing her eyes to adjust to the light, and recalled the night she had been a guest at the church, feeling ill at ease that she had to return there.

Father Troy cleared his throat uncomfortably, before delivering another prayer. As he spoke, the congregation's attention reverted to him, giving Kirsten the opportunity to look about her.

She saw many faces she recognised, mostly from school; it seemed an age since she had spoken to her friends and she found herself thinking about them, wondering what they had been doing and how they had been coping. School seemed so distant a memory, another life—another person even. The congregation sat in silent obedience and very few now seemed disgruntled at the interruption in proceedings.

The sound of Troy's words washed over her and she heard and saw the grief that surrounded from all directions; still she could not cry. She felt no grief at all for the passing of the friend who had been closer to her than her own flesh and blood. Her eyes found the casket and she was glad that she had been unable to attend the wake. To see Geri lying dead would be to truly admit that she was gone.

The crying voices about her seemed strained as they fought for decorum during the prayer. Drawing her eyes away from the coffin, she let them fall upon Father Troy who seemed to be looking her way. She felt distinctly uncomfortable under his gaze. It was though he was reprimanding her for not grieving for her friend.

Maybe he's annoyed because of the way I left his abode, without having thanked him in person, she considered. *Of course, he could simply be irked because I'm not praying* ... She put her hands together and closed her eyes for a moment, glancing occasionally in the priest's direction to see if his approval would draw his heavy gaze away from her. It didn't. He continued to stare until they said Amen and the company opened their eyes once more.

Kirsten ceased to listen to the service. She wished she had not attended. The whole thing seemed surreal. *Perhaps that's why I can't grieve; I'm still in shock.*

She felt the inspector fidget beside her, but did not look at him, not wanting to meet his disapproving gaze. She shivered, an odd sensation creeping up on her; it felt as though she was being watched. Gazing about her, she noticed the priest examining her again and answered his look with a scowl.

What is his fucking problem? she thought.

He looked away, seeming to redden slightly at her furious face. The sensation did not depart with his gaze; if anything, it grew stronger, a prickling feeling that spread from the side of her neck down the length of her spine. She moved her hand to the source of the irritation and rubbed at it, her eyes following the direction of her up-tilted arm.

She started.

Her father was at the funeral and faced her, his features adorning an intent expression. She smiled and nodded to him, wondering what he might be doing there. He continued to stare, making her feel uncomfortable.

The congregation began to stand for communion. *It's almost over,* she thought. The front rows moved first, their hands in prayer as they knelt at the alter rail.

'Dómini nostri Jesu Christi custódiat ánimam tuam in vitam ǽternam. Amen,' spoke Father Troy.

Kirsten lost sight of her father and in her mind questioned why he had not walked past her. The inspector nudged her to move and she looked back at him in confusion, the colour draining from her face.

'What is it?' he asked,

Her voice was barely more than a whisper as she replied, 'I don't know; I feel really odd.' The words were simply put, but barely explained her predicament. She felt out of phase. Her head was light and unfocused; fear gripped her beating heart and made an attempt to strangle it. She did not know what to do, but wanted to receive the Sacrament. It was not as though she believed, but rather her way of showing respect to her friend's beliefs. She staggered forward trying to remain calm. *I have to say goodbye to Geri,* she thought. *Then I can go back to hospital, where I obviously belong.*

The inspector steadied her, as she approached the altar. Passing the casket, she imagined the dead face within. She was aware of voices, but could not make out the words. Father Troy spoke to her father. Kirsten's stomach seemed to turn and she reeled forward. The two men moved instantly to her aid. The inspector gripped her firmly, but her eyes linked with her father's and she knew.

'Get everyone out of here,' she gasped. There seemed to be a huge pause before she turned to the inspector and said, 'Move … NOW!'

Her fear grew, but she seemed more focused. Unaware of her surroundings, she simply saw the danger and the lives of innocent people that she could save if she could just get them to …

'MOVE!'

She pushed at the inspector, as her father approached. He looked confused. There was no time to explain to them that she had to get them out of there before they were slaughtered like the others. She made a punch at her father screaming,

'IT'S HIM! Get out of here, all of you.' *What's wrong with them?* her mind raced. *Why don't they understand? It's not my father. It's Caitul.*

He made a grab for her and she tried to dodge backwards and slipped, colliding with the coffin. It crashed to the floor, a dead hand protruding from underneath. There were screams and people crowded around, oblivious to the danger.

A noise startled everyone present, even Caitul it seemed. It was as though hell itself had belched forth a cry to add to the chaos. The coffin began to tremble violently. More people screamed, but were wise enough to back away. Kirsten was sick with fear; it overwhelmed her and she was crippled by it, unable to move or speak. Father Troy retreated a few paces, mumbling something that could have been a prayer.

Suddenly, the coffin burst asunder and a noxious smell protruded forth, causing the further retreat of the crowd. Huge inhuman hands worked their way out of the splintered wreckage followed by a hideous body that could only be described as a monster.

The creature's jaws protruded and opened to allow greenish saliva to wash over rows of razor sharp canines; its mottled skin appeared more amphibian than mammalian; its massive bulk of a body was covered in shabby plates of armour; the chest plate bore an insignia, but it was faded beyond discerning. It trod on the body of Geri as it rose itself to full height, which was as high as, if not higher than the tallest of them. It seemed to be growling; at least if it *was* speaking, the sounds were indiscernible.

Kirsten no longer heard the cries and screams; she was not aware of anyone in the company other than the beast. The thing eyed her with cruel, reptilian eyes. It seemed as though time had slowed almost to a stop and she watched it sniff toward her, as though it recognised her scent rather than her face. Comprehension seemed to strike, its slit pupils narrowed further in a predatory gaze, and it made its move.

As the creature came for Kirsten, she scrambled backward; her eyes fixed on its claw-like hands, outstretched, ready to receive her in a deadly embrace. There was another sound of amazement, as before everyone's eyes, her father collapsed and a man stood beside him where before no man had stood. Furthermore, the face of the person was well known; it was the face of a murderer—the killer, Caitul. He lunged at lightning speed and with incredible strength, to tackle the beast to the floor. There they wrestled like two wild animals, Caitul bleeding from the many wounds that the brute inflicted upon him.

Kirsten felt herself being dragged up. She saw the priest and the inspector mouthing for her to come with them, to escape the madness. She was aware of attempting to tell them both to get her father out of there, but she did not hear the sound of her words. The men dragged her backward toward the exit; sirens sounded distantly. She reached out toward Caitul. The white noise in her ears seemed to clear until she heard herself screaming.

'Noooo. We can't leave him. It's killing him!'

She broke free of their hold and dashed toward the pair brawling murderously across the floor of the church. She ran past them, aware of the blood that spilled from both their wounds; the creature's was darker, almost black it seemed. Caitul screamed to her to get out, which proved to be his downfall; the creature took his distraction as an opportunity to sink its jaws into his throat. A tearing sound ensued, as Caitul's flesh was ripped open and there was a snap as something broke. The inspector and Father Troy approached the bloody pair from behind, attempting to coax Kirsten back to them before it was too late.

Unsteadily, the creature got to its feet; the damage Caitul had imposed on it, worse than at first thought. Kirsten screamed; it was not a scream of terror or grief, but a battle cry; a wild and maddening shriek that indicated that she too wanted to spill blood. *It sure as hell isn't going to be mine,* she thought.

She made a grab for the wooden lectern and swung it about with incredible ease into the monster's face; it howled as several of its teeth fell out. She attacked the creature repeatedly, seeming possessed by the strength of many as she brutally inflicted every injury possible with such a weapon. She was aware of the motionless form of her father and the siren sound from outside, as the squad vehicles pulled up. She was also aware of the men picking up large pieces of splintered coffin wood and approaching from behind. She was not aware, however, that the creature was still far from beaten; it had plenty of fight left in it. With lightening reflexes, it grabbed the lectern before Kirsten made another strike. It pulled hard and Kirsten fell forward catching a scent of its foul breath.

Its hand closed tightly about her throat and it rasped,

'For you, my lord Katahl'

Kirsten felt the blood drip down her fragile throat as the creature's claws pierced it. She thought of the sound that Caitul's neck had made when it snapped and wondered if hers would do the same. The pain seemed to dim, and darkness filled her eyes. She blinked and suddenly choked, gasping for breath. The creature lay before her—dead it seemed, two large pieces of wood protruding from its back. She scrambled over to Caitul, tears leaking uncontrollably from her eyes as she held him to her. She felt a hand on her shoulder and knew that it was time to go. Figures of police officers stood in the open doorway, a barrage of questions poised upon their lips to which she had no answers.

Her father was on his feet and being escorted to a waiting ambulance. She continued to cry, wishing Caitul had not died; he seemed more real, more in focus than the rest of her life had ever been. Her tears blinded her until she saw nothing else; the only thing she heard was her own gentle sobs as she finally found the grief she had been lacking.

Six

Father Troy yawned, his eyes refusing to open. He sat up and started when, instead of his sturdy mattress, he felt fine sand beneath him. He squinted painfully and looked about. The sun beat down on what appeared to be a desert. A few dunes and wild grasses dispersed amongst the vast expanse of sand. He wondered if he were dreaming, although he could not recall falling asleep and questioned whether he might be hallucinating after his bout of insomnia.

His eyes came to rest on a motionless body, some metres away. It seemed to be a man, clothed in a long mail shirt and chausses, which extended over a pair of huge weatherworn boots. A long sword protruded from underneath the man's leg, half covered over with the surrounding sand. Troy scrambled to his feet and over to the man, his head pounding, as though he had partaken in one too many glasses of communion wine.

With some effort, he rolled the unconscious man over; his limbs felt stiff and unwilling to respond. It took a few seconds for his mind to register who the person was. *The police inspector who came looking for Kirsten, the one who was with her at the funeral.* He started again, as he remembered … *the monster … the killer … Kirsten … Kirsten fighting … Kirsten weeping … Kirsten fading.*

His mind clouded over when he wanted it so desperately to focus. He failed to notice that the inspector was awake and yelled in fright when the man grabbed his arm.

'Did you see?' the inspector rasped, in an insane voice. 'Did you see what happened?'

Troy helped the man into a sitting position and held his arm, as if to calm him. He was unsure which part of his memory the man was referring to. He had seen a great deal, most of which he was unwilling to repeat for fear of being committed.

The inspector noticed their surroundings and looked back to the priest, wide-eyed.

'What's going on?' he demanded. 'Where are we?'

'I don't know.' The priest shrugged. 'The last thing I remember was trying to pull Kirsten away from that man in the church.'

'He wasn't a man, he was an animal!' spat the inspector.

A sickening sensation hit Troy in the pit of his stomach—the tight grip of jealousy. 'She seemed to know him quite well,' he said.

'Yes I agree. I knew it all along, but would anyone listen to me? I should have arrested that little tramp while I had the chance.'

'Inspector please, that isn't helping matters. We're stuck in a desert, with no comprehension of how we got here or where we are. We need to keep our heads don't you think? If we're ever to get out of this.'

'You're right of course,' the inspector conceded.

He held Troy for support, as he clambered to his feet. His eyes fell to the sword at his side and put a curious hand to the hilt. They looked hard at one another, pausing, as if not sure what to say. It was Inspector Stephenson who eventually broke the silence.

'Why do you suppose we're dressed like this?' he asked.

It was then that Troy realised that he too was wearing unusual attire. He was swathed in heavy black silk; his trousers were very tight, almost leggings, made from a fabric he was unfamiliar with; it felt like silk, yet seemed to stretch and move with him, almost like an extra layer of skin. He also wore boots, but they were shorter and made of softer leather than the inspector's. A jewelled hilted dagger hung from the thin belt at his waist and a long cloak was draped about his neck. It was of a supple leather and much too warm to be wearing in such sweltering conditions.

Both men decided to remove the heavier of their garments before proceeding. In the inspector's case, Troy had to assist in taking off the upper layers including the armour and gambeson beneath it. They wrapped the mail vestment and under padding in the cloak and formed a makeshift backpack. The inspector was unwilling to relinquish his armour to the desert, feeling that he would not have been given such an item without good reason.

As far as they could tell, they set off in a southerly direction. They talked little, thinking it best to conserve their energy, taking it in turns to shoulder the pack. The sun beat down, scorching their skin, and they struggled to remain in motion as their parched mouths complained soundlessly to their limbs.

They were staggering and moving slowly when the sun was on its westward course. The inspector repeatedly fell and Troy dragged him to his feet, urging him onward.

The sun was almost fully west when Troy gasped, 'Water.' He pointed. 'There ahead of us.'

They smiled at one another, their burnt faces creasing painfully and they stumbled toward the pool, as quickly as they could.

The inspector paused at its edge. 'Might be poisonous.' he said. His voice was nothing but a hoarse whisper.

Troy looked disheartened and gazed longingly at its smooth surface. 'But how can we tell?' he said. 'If we don't drink we're as good as dead anyway.'

'I'll drink first,' suggested the inspector. 'I'm weaker anyhow. If I die, you might be strong enough to make it to another waterhole.'

He collapsed at its edge and the priest fell beside him.

'We'll drink together, okay?' Troy said.

The inspector gave a half smile and nodded. He plunged his hands in; the water instantly eased the pain that afflicted them, and he splashed it on his face, opening his mouth to capture a few drops before following Troy's example and plunging his entire head in. They drank as much as their bodies would allow before coming up for air. Troy shook his head, feeling revived. The water was surprisingly cool considering the sun beating down onto it.

They continued to drink more sensibly, savouring the taste and its revitalising effect. The sun was beginning to sink and the sky glowed a rosy pink. Inspector Stephenson, feeling much more like his old practical self, suggested they make camp for the night. The priest agreed, and they set about trying to find anything that could be used to start a fire or burn. There was little choice and they decided the dunes would offer the best selection, as they contained the only signs of life the men had observed thus far. The small branches of the dunes' plants were prickly and Troy found himself nursing a cut finger on his return to the waterside.

A spectacular sunset streaked across the sky; hues of red and pink melded together with such elegance, it was as though the gods themselves had painted it. Both Tom and Troy were oblivious to such delights overhead; their attention focused wholly on the task of lighting a fire before the light failed completely. Already the temperature had begun to drop and they knew that they would be in danger of hypothermia if they remained without warmth.

The inspector selected the largest piece of dead wood and the strongest stick. He sprinkled dried grass about the stick that he held firmly with its point against the surface of the wood. He then began rolling it between his hands hoping that the friction would create sufficient heat to set light to the grass. He suggested that Troy unpacked their extra clothing, explaining that they would need the warmth whether or not he got a fire going.

Troy sat shivering, his cloak thrown about him. He could barely make out the inspector in the fading light. The sun fully set and the sky darkened; stars began to show themselves, twinkling in the darkness as if to mock their predicament. Troy wanted to offer to take over for a while, at least while the inspector put on his gambeson; but he dare not speak. He could hear the man's teeth chattering, but knew that if he as much as suggested that he help, then the inspector would scream at him, so obvious was the man's tension and frustration.

Over an hour later and the fire still had not been lit. Tom was freezing and could scarcely feel his hands as they continued to roll the stick. *I should at least put on the padded jacket,* he thought. *It will give me a chance of survival.* However, his stubbornness and melancholy got the better of him. *Just another failure … all those times when I was a scout leader, when I demonstrated how to make a fire the old fashioned way in the event of a crisis. Well, now is a crisis and I can't perform. Just like everything else in my miserable bloody life.*

He was about to give up when a small spark lit up beneath him. He heard Troy gasp with relief. He blew gently on the tiny flames, frightened of blowing them out, but he need not have worried. The flames spread quickly and the inspector left Troy to add more fuel, as his icy hands struggled to put on his gambeson.

It was not long before they had a roaring blaze going and the inspector basked in the heat, as though he were a boy on a camping trip.

The moon had come out and lit up the desert with an ethereal glow.

'I wonder where we are,' the inspector said. 'Look at the moon. It's not normal for it to be so big, is it? And the stars; do you know there's not one constellation up there that I recognise? Where the hell are we do you think?'

Troy's stomach rumbled and they looked at each other over the flame light.

'I've never been much of an astronomer myself,' he said. 'I do know this though; it doesn't matter where we are; if we don't find food soon, then we're done for.'

There was another long pause and the inspector settled down into a sleeping position. Troy remained staring at the firelight, reminding himself of Kirsten's face until he could almost see it in the dancing flames. He blinked, his eyes sore from having strained them.

'None of this makes any sense,' he sighed. How can we be in my church one minute and then here in a desert, in Lord knows what country?'

The inspector mumbled in agreement.

'It's so strange … impossible.'

The inspector leaned his head on his hand. 'This whole fortnight has been strange, if you ask me. Bloody weird! What the hell was that thing in the church? It wasn't human that's for sure. And that killer the girl was involved with … he just stepped out that man's body like he was walking through a door. It's insane! Kirsten said that the killer and Walker were one, but I didn't believe her. I mean, why would I? But she was right. What the hell was he?'

Troy did not answer. He was remembering Kirsten's face when she saw him again. She had seemed both embarrassed and annoyed. He clenched his fists.

'So you believe Kirsten was having a relationship with the killer, Inspector?' he asked.

Inspector Stephenson gave a long sigh. 'Oh I suppose not. She was genuinely terrified of him, certainly to begin with, but then, why the obsession with her? And why did she cry when he was killed? It doesn't make sense … any of this.'

Troy *could* make sense of why someone would obsess over the girl, but not why she had grieved over the death of the killer. He was glad the man was dead. He turned his ice blue eyes skyward and breathed heavily, silently asking God to forgive him.

Father Troy woke painfully; the sunburn stiffened his face muscles and his stomach ached with hunger. He groaned as he sat up, hoping it had all been a dream, or at least a very bad joke; nothing had changed, however; he remained in a desert with no notion of how or why he was there. The only difference he discovered was the absence of the inspector. The man's hauberk and gambeson were lying by the pool, but he was nowhere in sight.

A surge of panic struck the priest. *It's bad enough to be part of this crazy situation,* he thought, *but to have to face it by myself ... Inspector Stephenson may be sombre company, but he's better than being alone.*

Father Troy shifted over to the water and splashed his face before taking a drink. He then faced the arduous task of finding an opening from which to remove his penis so that he could urinate. The only fastenings that he could see, were leather straps pulled tightly at the hips. After struggling to loosen them, he decided that it was easier to take his trousers down. He watched with relief, as his urine hit the sand with a soft hiss.

'Good morning.'

Troy felt gratification at the sound of the inspector's voice. He pulled up his trousers, strangely not embarrassed by being caught with them down, knowing that the inspector had probably faced similar difficulty.

'I've got us some food.'

Troy shook himself, wondering if he had heard the man correctly. The inspector opened his arms to reveal a large rounded loaf of bread slightly flattened and a huge wedge of cheese.

Troy laughed. 'However did you manage it? Or are we sharing a mirage?'

'No, the food is real, my friend, and I have more good news. We are not more than a day's march to civilisation. I just met a native and he's given me directions to the nearest habitation.'

'And he *gave* you food?'

'Oh no,' said the inspector, 'I had to buy that.' He jingled the leather pouch at his waist.

Father Troy felt around his belt line, he discovered not only a moneybag but also a pouch containing ink, quill and parchment. He emptied the purse and eyed the contents curiously. The coins bore no figurehead at all; in fact, there was no writing or markings of any kind; they were as smooth as glass, appearing to be made of solid silver and copper.

They ate a good portion of bread and cheese and drank their fill of water before the inspector suggested setting off. The priest carefully packed up the food and clothes.

'As you seem to be so energetic this morning ... here!' He threw the pack to his companion and strode beside him, feeling ready to take on the world.

* * * * *

Once Kirsten had stopped crying, she was concerned that she had gone blind; she saw only white.

Everywhere white.

There was no sensation of feeling; it was as though her body was suspended in nothingness. She tried to speak, but there was no air through which sound could be carried. Her mind seemed to be functioning normally except for one thing; she was not afraid. She knew that she should be and yet she was not. She wasn't breathing, so far as she could tell, and yet she didn't fear for her life; some higher function seemed to have taken over her weightless form. Instinctively, she moved her hand to her body, to ensure that she was actually solid. Her surroundings seemed thick and the motion, slow. As her hand made contact with her own skin, she reasoned that she was alive.

She became accustomed to her surroundings, remaining patient, watching, waiting, and never blinking. Rather than resigning herself to the fact that she could be suspended there for eternity, she felt in her soul that someone she had long missed would greet her before long, and all would be well …

The second day's journeying was proving much easier than the first, despite the men's burns and exhaustion. They had a new purpose, their goal, a destination other than the seemingly endless desert—their silver lining. Neither considered their purpose for being there any longer. Having fought to survive and staring into the eyes of death, reaching their goal seemed far more important than debating.

Although they had drunk their fill before setting off, they soon became eager for more. Realising that they had nothing to carry water in, they hoped they would not collapse from dehydration before reaching their destination. The sun was beating down with a fierce heat. Both men decided to rest for a while and attempt to eat. Their mouths were so dry that it made it difficult to swallow and they were well aware that they could not manage another meal before reaching civilisation. It would be pointless to stop again, as the food would be of less use to them than water.

'I can't eat any more,' Inspector Stephenson said. 'My throat feels like sandpaper.'

'Let us get going then,' suggested Father Troy. 'The sooner we move, the sooner that we get out of this infernal heat. I for one am looking forward to a bath—a cool one. I don't suppose they will have such luxuries where we're headed; it's probably nothing more than a caravan of nomads.'

They packed up the remainder of their provisions and set off again, their legs becoming accustomed to the stomping walk that was necessary for travelling in the deep, soft sand.

'A few more days of this and I'd build leg muscles like yours,' the inspector remarked.

The priest grinned back at him; it was the least sombre thing he had ever heard the man say.

'It's just as well you aren't in your suit any longer, old man,' Troy said. 'Your trousers would probably be so loose, you'd have to hold them up.' To the priest's surprise, the inspector actually laughed.

The inspector had forgotten what it was to laugh. It felt good; it made him lighter somehow, and suddenly the burdens of his life seemed less. The stress of police life, the absence of his family seemed insignificant in the expanse of the wild outdoors. He felt free—truly free for the first time in years, perhaps ever. There was just him, the desert, and the fight for survival with his newfound companion at his side. Despite the fact that nothing made sense, he felt happy. He laughed again.

Troy paused. 'Are you okay, Inspector?'

The inspector laughed almost hysterically and punched the priest lightly in the arm before calming his spirits enough to talk.

'I feel fine,' he said. 'It's weird I know, but I haven't felt this young in years, and stop calling me inspector, I'm not an inspector here; I'm just a man and I have a name. It's Tom.'

The priest looked a little unnerved. He did not feel ready to give up his title of Father. He felt more than just a man. He had taken holy vows and was unwilling to relinquish his title because of their unfathomable circumstance. He looked hard at Inspector Tom Stephenson and smiled. It was indeed as if years had been lifted.

'Well Tom,' he said, clasping his strong arm about the man. 'We'd best get moving and give you the chance to make use of your newfound youth. What do you say?'

'Er yes of course.' Tom coughed. His face stiffened again, but his eyes sparkled and it was as though Inspector Stephenson was gone for good.

By late afternoon, their progress had begun to slow and their weary bodies stumbled as they staggered on. The swelling sun ahead of them, threatened its descent at any moment. They both thought the same thing, but neither had the energy to speak. *Where is it? Did the man lie? Should we set up camp? But without water, we're unlikely to survive.*

Huge dunes loomed ahead whose width seemed to stretch for miles in both directions. They clambered up awkwardly supporting one another. The sky was reddening as they reached the top, and their hearts sank when they viewed before them, an even higher bank of sand.

'Where is it, Tom?' Troy said hoarsely. His body was near to collapse and he knew that he would not manage another climb.

The inspector was unable to answer and lowered his head in despair. The settlement might have been just beyond the next dune, or they could have climbed that to find an endless row of hills. He did not feel so young any longer; he was ready to give up. His body ached and he fell to his knees. He would have wept, had his tear ducts contained enough water. The priest fell beside him.

'Come on,' Troy said. He tried to sound supportive; inside, he felt the same as the broken man beside him. But he had to believe that there were more than their present predicament; their purpose for being there had to be more than dying painfully in the wilderness.

He attempted, with little success, to drag the man to the bottom of the dune, until Tom moved of his own accord. They scrambled down and Tom tumbled the last part. There, they huddled together as the sun set behind the hill, the continuous outline of the dunes casting shadows until all the light was extinguished. Father Troy helped Tom into his gambeson and he covered their legs with sand. Wrapping the cloak about them both, he lay shivering, holding the inspector close to him to make best use of their body heat. Troy prayed, harder than he had ever prayed before, that they would survive the night.

Kirsten was aware of the increasing warmth on her back, followed by the tickling sensation of something in her nose and mouth. Gradually, she opened her eyes, coughing and spitting out the sand. The sun behind her was beginning to rise. Looking about, she saw the desolate land surrounding her, seemingly devoid of all life. Perched on a dune, she looked out towards the dawn as it warmed the cold expanse of sand. Her mind refused to focus properly and she could not remember how she had come to be there.

The sun warmed her and she threw open her cloak. The red, velvety folds of fabric that made up her dress, starkly contrasted against the weapons that clung to her belt. She gazed in puzzlement for a moment before pulling a dagger free. It was a cruelly curved blade, its hilt shaped realistically into the head of a dragon, whose eyes seemed to watch her as she moved it. Carefully replacing the weapon into its scabbard, she felt the cold steel of the star shaped discs that were packed together in a half pouch of tough leather. She stretched and yawned, the movement spreading through her, all the way down to her booted feet, enough to allow her dress to reveal her leg through a high split. She covered herself over, amused by her own modesty.

Excitement oozed from every pore, and she jumped energetically to her feet. A sensation spread across her physical self and awakened a sleeping thought in her brain. She turned full about, as if sensing its presence; the item she had been missing—the sword, half buried at the summit of the sand dune, its hilt glittering in the rising sun and a huge green gem embedded its rounded pommel.

She approached ceremoniously, her fingers twitching with anticipation. Her hand reached out and eagerly grasped the ancient weapon. It was at one with its claimant; the moment she had been waiting for, though she had not known it, had arrived. She swung the weapon and held it high. The thought found words at last and she said,

'I'm home.'

Seven

Light peeped over the summit of the facing dune. Troy could not tell if it was getting warmer or not. His limbs had long since stopped registering temperature. As the night had grown colder, he and the inspector had shivered so much that had anyone been able to witness them both, they would have appeared to be convulsing. The pain from the cold had felt like a thousand knives stabbing simultaneously, again and again.

He tried to move, his first attempt to no avail. Trying to speak, he managed a weak sound, barely a whisper.

'Tom? Tom, are you still with me?'

The inspector gave a quiet groan.

At least he's still alive, that's something, Troy thought. *My prayers have been answered after all. Now we have to wait until the sun is a little higher and can thaw out our limbs enough to struggle on.* He gazed despairingly as the sky lightened, wondering whether either of them would be able to move again. *Perhaps it would have been a mercy to die in the night.*

The light hit the outline of something on the hill. His heart jumped at the shape of a cross. *Here in the desert—a sign from God. Perhaps it has been a test after all, in which case, I've failed; Jesus survived forty days and nights, and I less than two. Does this mean it's all over?* He fidgeted and tried to nudge the inspector into waking. The man's eyes half opened, but remained bleary and unseeing.

'Look,' he managed to whisper.

The sun rose over the hill and the silhouette of a woman came into view. She pulled the object from the ground where it protruded, and Troy saw that it was not a cross at all, but a sword. As the woman held it high, the sun glinted of it like beams of fire. The sunlight encircled her halo-like, and they heard her clearly say,

'I'm home.'

Neither man could speak loudly enough, but the mere excitement of seeing another human being seemed to warm them into action more than the sun ever could. They lifted their limbs, as best they were able, waving frantically in hope of catching the woman's attention.

'Down here. Help us.'

It was enough to draw her away from her own thoughts. She peered down into the shadows between the dunes. Two men were struggling to remove a large black cloak from their bodies and flap their arms like demented birds. She sheathed the weapon before going down to meet them, feeling a tug of regret at having put it away.

As she approached, a chord of recognition struck and she gasped. *I know those men*, she thought. A life she had forgotten flooded back and she stumbled, overwhelmed by confusion. Before, she had been ignorant of who she was and had experienced a blissful waking in the knowledge that she was meant to be where she was. Such feelings were torn away mere minutes later by the two men before her, whom she had last seen thrusting wooden stakes into the back of some grotesque creature. She found herself longing for ignorance once more.

The two men's appearance had changed drastically since she had last encountered them. Their faces were red and blistered, their hair dry and greyed by the sand, their clothes too were strange.

'Water,' Father Troy gasped. 'He needs water; he's dying.'

She looked to the inspector and then returned to Troy. *Ever the man of God,* she thought. *So full of humility and so damned polite.*

'You appear a little worse for wear yourself, Father.' She felt around her belt, hoping to find a flask, yet there were nothing but weapons. 'Damn!' she said, 'I don't appear to have any.'

The inspector sagged into unconsciousness.

'How did you know?' Troy asked.

'Know what?'

'That I'm a priest.'

Kirsten expelled air with a huff. 'I think the sun has affected your memory, Father Troy.'

He backed away slightly. 'You know me?'

Kirsten didn't know how to feel that he did not recall her—relieved that the attention of a man of god was not drawn to her, or annoyed because she was not considered important enough to remember, especially as she had spent a night at his home.

'It's me, Kirsten. Do you not remember me?'

He drew further away from her, as if she had said something highly offensive. She made no move to follow him, keeping a cautious distance.

'Father, do not distress yourself,' she said. 'You've obviously had a memory lapse. We *have* met though; you were kind enough to allow me to stay with you when I was in trouble. You helped me …'

'I know who Kirsten is!' he hissed.

His voice filled with venom and Kirsten was slightly shocked, unable to understand his reaction and how he had the energy for such an outburst.

'If you can't help us then I suggest you leave and let us die in peace!' he said.

Kirsten could not believe what she was hearing. *What's his problem?*

Father Troy stared in disgust, amazed that he had mustered the energy to fend off one of Satan's messengers. He considered that the thought of her must have been plucked from his mind, as a woman of ultimate beauty, and the woman before him was without a doubt the most beautiful woman he had ever seen. Her long red hair hung silkily past her waist and her perfect ivory skin blushed slightly at the cheeks. She had large green eyes that gazed at him quizzically. Yes, she was exceptionally lovely, but she was not Kirsten and Kirsten was whom he desired.

'You're an abomination!' Troy spat. 'Go back to the pit from which you crawled!'

Kirsten edged away from his anger. She spoke in a soothing voice that seemed clearer and more moving than the most passionate song.

'Father, please try to calm yourself. I fear that you may be hallucinating. You're exhausted.'

He growled at her savagely. 'The devil has sent you to test me in the desert. I will not listen to you, TEMPTRESS! Go back to hell and tell him that I will not listen. I *will* pass this test, and if I am to die … SO BE IT!'

Kirsten shook her head, not knowing how to deal with the ranting priest.

'You're delirious!' she said.

'LEAVE, NOW!'

Inspector Stephenson regained consciousness. 'What's going on?' he asked.

'Inspector, I'm going to try and find help,' Kirsten replied. 'You must look after Troy.' She ignored Troy's insults, glad to turn away from the hatred in his eyes.

Tom told her to head west, as he had been informed. He threw his purse at her, to which Troy spouted another string of abuse.

'Both of you keep to this side,' she suggested. 'You should be reasonably well shaded until about midday. I'll be as quick as I can.' She tied the purse to her belt and turned to meet the eyes of Troy. 'I promise.' With that, she was gone, half-running up the taller dune and out of sight.

Father Troy felt a shiver down the length of his spine. Her eyes had changed shape and colour when she had looked at him; they were brown and the lashes shorter; eyes that he recognised as those belonging to Kirsten. He crawled wearily over to where Tom lay; his sudden outburst had cost him dearly in energy. He lay back, silently praying that the girl, whoever she was, would keep to her promise.

It was several hours before Kirsten returned. She still wore her cloak, as if shielding her skin from the effects of the sun. She ran so fast toward the dying pair that she seemed to be flying down the hill on a cloud of sand. Both men were unconscious and her heart leapt, fearing that she might have been too late. Opening her newly purchased pack, she removed a large flask and uncorked it. She gently tipped back the inspector's head, pouring only a little water in, remembering what it was like to be dehydrated. As she shifted over to Troy, she felt her apprehension grow. Cautiously, she opened his mouth; his skin felt dry and sore, and his lips were cracked. He, unlike the inspector seemed to revive a little at the first few drops of water. His eyes opened and she withdrew, expecting another attack. His hand reached weakly to her face and brushed her hair back behind her ear. He smiled, closing his eyes again.

Returning to the inspector, she removed a cloth from her pack, soaking it in both water and a blue tinted liquid from an oddly shaped bottle. She gently dabbed his face, then did the same with the priest. She waited, recalling in her mind what the old woman had said.

'Depending on how bad they are of course, the reviving effect should work almost immediately.'

The old woman had sold Kirsten a variety of goods that she had placed in her pack. She had spent longer than she had intended, discussing the various virtues of healing plants. The old woman seemed impressed about how much she already knew. When Kirsten explained that she did not know or recognise anything that she was shown, and had merely guessed what she would need and what to mix it with, the woman knowingly nodded her head and held Kirsten's hand. Kirsten remembered how her impatience had turned to intrigue and allowed her to stay and talk with the woman longer than she should. She was brought back to sudden reality when a hand seized her throat.

Tom was awake.

'You!' he exclaimed.

He seemed full of his old vigour, leaving Kirsten wondering why she had bothered to help at all. Father Troy, seeming much revived, gently removed the inspector's hand. Kirsten waited for the priest to set upon her with more of the abuse he had thrown at her previously. However, he did not.

She held the bottle to them with uncertain hands.

'You must drink,' she said.

The inspector drunk first, eyeing her suspiciously while she dabbed the poultice on the Troy's blistered face. She was as gentle as she could be and was sure that it must hurt, but he did not so much as flinch; his shining eyes locked on hers until she could bear it no longer.

'So, you don't think I'm a devil any more?' she said.

Realisation struck his features and he faltered for a second, unsure how to proceed.

'I must have been hallucinating,' he said. 'Please allow me to apologise.'

Kirsten took the bottle from the inspector and sprinkled some more water on the poultice before handing the water to the priest and treating Tom.

'You're both weird,' she muttered. 'One of you wants me dead and the other is all politeness, then the next thing I know is that you've changed roles and are working vice versa.'

It was the inspector who spoke as Troy drank.

'How come you're here? Where's that other woman gone?'

Troy looked from Tom to Kirsten, seeming distrustful of his own eyes. He described the woman he remembered and Tom corroborated his description. Kirsten's head bowed as she attempted to disguise her flushing face. She seemed unwilling to explain her miraculous change of appearance and insisted with a note of authority that they were both to rest while she prepared some food for them. There was silence for a few short moments before they bombarded her with questions.

'Where are we?'

'What happened?'

'Why are we here?'

Kirsten faced them sombrely. 'I don't know,' she said. 'I know that *I'm* supposed to be here, but as to your presence ... I don't know. I'm sorry. The town down there is called Golstur, but I discovered very little apart from that. I was too busy getting provisions to stay and ask questions.' It was a lie, she realised. She had stayed to question the wise woman, only the questions she had asked were not relevant to what the men wanted to know.

'Might I suggest that we eat then see if you feel strong enough to travel to town. It's not very far. I'm sure we'll be able to find some things out there.'

Tom eyed her suspiciously; he seemed convinced that however they had arrived at their present predicament, somehow it was her fault. Reluctantly, he agreed to her course of action and they placed the provisions into the pack that she had purchased. Kirsten, seeming the healthiest of the three, carried it with no objection from the two men.

As they scrambled up the high dune facing them, the two men gasped on realising just how close to their goal they had come the previous night. They could see the town in the near distance and both noted the dramatic change in the landscape as they drew closer. Grass sprouted in odd tufts at first and then sprang up into a luscious green carpet on approaching the Golstur's gates. The temperature too dropped by several degrees, being more comparable to a warm summer day rather than a blistering heat.

Kirsten drew her cloak over her head, almost completely shielding her face. She nodded stiffly at the gate wardens, as they approached. The wardens eyed them strangely, but perhaps no more than they returned the gaze. The men were dark skinned with streaked fair hair, which appeared bleached by prolonged exposure to the sun. Both men were short and stocky with small, piggy eyes. One of the guards leaned forward on his large war hammer, trying to catch a glimpse of Kirsten's face as she passed. Sensing his eyes upon her, she bowed her head.

The town was bustling with colour and life; various musicians played about the approaching marketplace, and a couple of gypsy-looking girls danced among the crowd, collecting money as they went.

The two strangers were more than a little overwhelmed by the contrast between Golstur and the desert from which they had just escaped. Kirsten turned to them and suggested that they find an inn in which to stay for the night, but their health seemed to have suddenly improved, and they were eager to explore their surroundings. Ignoring her advice, they moved through the marketplace, savouring the sights and smells.

Kirsten's eyes searched for the wise-woman once more, feeling that she might be able to provide them with answers to their many questions. When she arrived at the stall, the woman was no longer there. Kirsten asked a neighbouring horse seller where the woman had gone. He seemed unwilling to tell her and she soon caught on that he wanted her to purchase information. She had no wish to needlessly give away money, but she could not shake the feeling that she *must* speak to the woman.

She still had the inspector's purse and knew that he would be furious if she spent his money. Gazing back to where she had left the men, she saw that the two gypsy girls seemed rather interested in the newcomers and the men were having the devil of a time fending them off. Kirsten smiled to herself.

She pointed to the end horses; a bay coloured packhorse and a piebald that looked very much like a shire, only slightly smaller and more nimble in appearance.

'How much for those two?' she asked.

The man grinned, revealing a gap where his front teeth should have been.

'For you, twenty silver.'

Kirsten had already spent a good portion of Tom's money and had no idea how they would go about obtaining more. She knew that the purse did not contain nearly that amount of silver and she wondered if it would be possible to haggle with him. She emptied the contents of the purse into her hand.

There were six very large gold coins, ten silver and a handful of bronze. She was at a loss to how many silver coins there were to one of the medallion-looking gold coins, and she was not keen on being cheated. Handing him a gold coin, she hoped for the best. The man's eyes lit up and her insides churned as she suddenly felt she had made a huge mistake. The horse seller made it obvious that he did not receive many gold coins.

'A pleasure doing business with you,' he said. 'Please be waiting while I fetch you the leftover.'

By this, Kirsten assumed that he meant her change. He seemed to be bustling around for a long time before returning, his face looking flustered and worried. He had a handful of silver coins, but shook his head, mumbling.

'I am most regretting that I am short of coins. Please accept my apologies. I may be able to offer some extras to meet your needs. A good saddle and halters for both, extra pack ... nosebags.' He looked anxiously about him for inspiration to prevent him losing the sale.

Kirsten observed his flustered state and saw it as a chance to gain the upper hand. She looked about for anything that might prove useful.

'Make it three saddles, *two* packs, three of those blankets,' she said, 'two water-skins, do you have any tinder? And of course the information I require.'

The man appeared delighted and left Kirsten wondering just how much profit he had actually made. She counted out the silver in her hand and found sixteen pieces; that made at least thirty-six to a gold and considering the amount of accessories she had purchased, she was willing to bet that there were more than forty pieces to one gold. She tried to determine how much the extras would have come to and asked for how much he would ordinarily sell one of his saddles. The man saddled the horses and packed the accessories neatly and securely. He looked uncomfortable with the question and immediately began offering more extras. She got a good travelling cloak that would do nicely for Tom and more packs suited specifically for the horses, before she discovered that one saddle would fetch up to three silver pieces.

Kirsten guessed at about sixty or more pieces of silver to one of the large gold coins, possibly less, but she did not think the man would have been so pleased were that the case.

He informed Kirsten that the old woman had left for home and he gave her directions, heading northwest from Golstur, explaining that it was a good half a day's ride. She thanked him and made her way toward the square, leading the horses carefully through the crowd. Father Troy approached her, having finally escaped from the scantily clad dancers. His face seemed flushed with embarrassment, despite the sunburn.

'Where did you get these?' he asked.

'I bought them. I thought that we might be needing them if we're planning on leaving here at some point.'

She glanced around and saw the inspector still dancing with the two girls, seeming most unwilling to part from them. He giggled like a carefree fool, as he put copper coins into the bra-top of the taller girl.

'Where did he get that money?' Kirsten asked.

'*I* gave it to him—just a few copper coins. He didn't have his purse, as you have not returned it yet.'

Kirsten shot a threatening glance to the priest.

'So, you think it's fine for him to be throwing away your money, do you? What will you do once it has run out? Tell me that!'

Father Troy backed away, seeming hurt by the harshness of her tone.

'He's just having a little fun. I think he deserves it, don't you? We nearly died out there you know.'

Kirsten remained unsympathetic and strode away, the horses following in tow.

'Well when you've both quite finished *having fun*,' she said, calling over her shoulder, 'perhaps you would care to join me at the inn.'

The priest turned and waved impatiently at Tom who, taking the hint, broke away from the charms of the gypsies and jogged up to him.

'What's wrong?' he asked.

'Kirsten's bought us horses and has gone to find stabling and a room for us. I think we should join her.'

'Do you indeed?' Tom said. 'And whose money did she use to pay for horses, eh?' He spoke as if the Police Inspector was back to stay.

The priest sighed, feeling caught between their dislike for each other. He walked after Kirsten, hoping rather than expecting that Tom would follow.

Kirsten waited outside a battered looking building whose creaking sign hung off his hinges.

'What's your game now, Miss Vái?' the inspector stormed. 'Who said you could spend my money on these?'

Kirsten faced him, raising her head so that he could see her venomous eyes from within the folds of her cloak.

'Here's your money!' she spat. 'And may I remind you that it was *you* who gave it to me in order to save *your* lives! How you expect to travel on foot at your age, I don't know.'

The inspector seemed a little humbled, realising she had indeed saved his life.

'Well, you obviously expect one of us to be on foot,' he said. 'You only bought two horses.'

'I know,' she paused. 'I'll be fine. Now shall we go in, or did you wish to stand and argue with me all day?'

She tethered the horses and pulled her hood forward a little further. The early shadows of evening were beginning to appear, as they entered the inn. At once, a short, skinny fellow with large blonde side-burns approached them, greeting them coolly.

It was Tom who spoke. 'A room for the night please and we have two horses out front that will need shelter as well,' he said.

The landlord nodded and signalled to a man who Tom suspected to be his son, so alike in appearance were they.

'It'll be five copper, payment up front,' he said. 'That includes two meals and hot water.'

The inspector gave him the sum requested and the man instantly seemed warmer, developing a set of manners and offering to take the baggage to their room.

It was not a particularly large room, but was clean and seemed comfortable enough. The innkeeper explained that he would have an extra bed put in directly and offered to bring up hot water so that they might wash before supper. Tom and Troy thanked him in unison while Kirsten remained silent, staring out of the window at the setting sun. A few moments later, the innkeeper's son was at the door with a couple of lit candles, and a woman entered with a pail of hot water that she poured clumsily into a white basin on the table. She gave an equally clumsy curtsey on her way out and the son informed them to ask for Cal if they needed anything (they assumed that Cal was he).

Kirsten continued to watch as the last rays of sun disappeared from sight. Father Troy used the lit candles to light several others that were already present. Tom decided that one bowl of water was insufficient to cleanse away the desert grime and went after Cal to see about the possibility of getting a proper bath. Removing her cloak, Kirsten sat on the nearest bed. Father Troy watched as she removed her boots and aired her feet. Sitting beside her, he spoke softly.

'Are you all right?'

She met his eyes, seeming to focus again.

'Yes I guess so,' she replied. 'How about you?'

'All things considered, I'm okay. So what's this plan of action you have then?'

There was a knock at the door and Troy answered it. Cal and an older man entered carrying an extra bed; they set it down next to Kirsten and the older man glanced at her before looking back to Troy, grinning wolfishly. Cal ushered the man from the room, nodded to Troy and left.

Kirsten got to her feet and rummaged through her backpack.

'Come on; get yourself washed,' she ordered. 'I want to treat your face again.'

Troy removed his upper garments, seeming unabashed. Kirsten's initial assessment of his physique had been correct. Every muscle had been worked on and toned.

He splashed the water on his face and scrubbed the upper half. A cloth had been laid beside the basin and he used it to pat his body dry. The smooth, pale torso appeared odd against his red face with its dry, cracked and blistered skin.

Kirsten motioned him to sit beside her, while she applied more of the herbal solution she had purchased from the old woman. A pungent fragrance lingered in the air similar to chamomile and lavender. The priest kept his eyes on Kirsten as she gently dabbed his face with the poultice. His breathing grew steadily heavier, either because he was relaxing or due to her proximity.

'Does that feel any better at all?' she asked.

He did not know how to answer. He *wanted* her, more than ever before. With every touch, he felt his desire grow.

The door opened with a slam and Tom hobbled in, wrapped in a small sheet. With a groan, he threw his shirt onto the floor and lay back onto the bed. It was then that Kirsten noticed the extent of his burns, where he had walked in the desert without any protection.

She jumped to her feet, asking Troy to fetch her some clean water. He was slow to rise for fear of his erection being noticed and walked awkwardly from the room.

'I'm going to make you better,' she said.

Despite the sympathy in her voice, he growled back at her.

'Leave me alone!'

He rolled on his side so that his back was to her and she could see the burns as low down as his belt line, before he haughtily pulled the sheet up. When Troy returned, Kirsten prepared a new solution. Finally, Tom agreed to treatment only if she would leave the room and he apply it himself. Reluctantly, she did as she was bid, pulled on her boots and glanced back with worried eyes to Troy. Wrapping her cloak about her once more, she made her way downstairs.

A crowd of people seemed to be in once it was dark, and she supposed that there were locals present as well as guests. Walking over to the bar, she ordered a drink. The tankard seemed to be filled with ale, but she could not be entirely sure having never drunk such a substance before. As the landlord did not ask for payment, she assumed that he would prepare another bill on their departure. She sipped the brew and found it to have a pleasant buttery texture with a slightly bitter aftertaste.

She wondered how long she should stay away while the inspector tended his wounds, feeling reluctant to be away for long considering her present company—an intoxicated rabble. She tried to lean casually against the bar to view the scene. The people of Golstur were easily distinguished from outsiders; they were all of a similar stature, being squat and heavily muscular, and sharing the same small eyes and flaxen hair.

As she surveyed it, the scene became more rowdy. A group of travellers were borderline paralytic and yet continued to shout drinks orders to the bar. One fair-haired man reached out and slapped the serving girl across the backside, as she set the tray down. The woman blushed and rushed away. Kirsten tutted.

'What's your problem then?'

It took a second or two for Kirsten to realise that the man was addressing her. She peeped up at him, careful not to reveal her face. He was almost seven feet tall and more animal than man in appearance. His huge, hairy ape-like arms rested eagerly on a club so large, that most men would have had a job lifting it off the ground.

'No problem,' Kirsten muttered in a gruff voice. All the while, her legs felt weaker.

The man's companion stepped beside him to get a look at Kirsten. He was a slender, weasely-looking man, the paleness of his skin accentuated by his wearing bright green. He held a golden dagger that he played with in his hands threateningly, before placing it into his belt. His orange, brown eyes narrowed, snake-like and he smiled thinly.

'It seems as though our friend here has something against a beautiful woman, Garth.'

The ape-like man toyed with the handle of his club for a moment. Kirsten's heart beat faster, realising she was in danger and uncertain how to avoid it.

Why was I so foolish, to come to the bar alone? she thought.

'Oi Brenda, come 'ere!' Garth shouted.

The barmaid looked uneasy, as she approached the colossal sized man. She smiled nervously.

'What can I get you?' she asked.

He grabbed her with his huge arms, pulling her into him. She squealed and struggled, asking him to behave. He bent down and slobbered on, rather than kissed, her bulging breasts. The landlord was nowhere in sight and the girl was growing increasingly upset, realising that Garth was having more than a little fun. He began pulling up the woman's skirt. Tears stung her face and she pleaded with him to stop.

Kirsten was aware of two sounds at once. The first, her sword being unsheathed as she pointed it at the Garth's throat, and the next, a similar but higher pitched sound, as the weasel-looking man removed his dagger and poked it into her back.

'I'll take that from you if you don't mind,' the man sneered.

Kirsten's hands were steady as she handed over the sword, but her insides were as turbulent as an ocean storm. Garth thrust Brenda away, eager for new sport. The woman fell to the floor, whimpering, where she gazed up at Kirsten, wide eyed and tearful, one of her breasts exposed through her torn blouse. Garth drew himself to full height; Kirsten's head barely reached his chest. She felt the dagger dig deeper, yet did not draw blood.

The booming voice of Garth spoke again. 'Don't go anywhere, Brenda, this won't take long.'

Kirsten breathed a sigh of relief when the landlord came rushing over.

'Stop this at once!' He ushered Brenda away and stormed over to Garth, appearing unafraid. 'I will not tolerate brawling in my inn; now leave. Both of you!'

For a moment, Kirsten thought that they would obey him, then she realised that the knife at her back had not moved. Garth raised one of his massive hands and shoved the innkeeper. The man flew across the room and landed amongst the drunken party in the corner, unconscious. A few of them seemed annoyed as drinks went flying, but most found it hilarious when the funny little man landed with a crash.

The weasel-looking man violently pulled back Kirsten's hood.

'What are you trying to hide then?' he asked.

There were a few gasps of astonishment when they saw that it was a woman before them. The only woman Kirsten had seen in the whole inn had been Brenda, and she guessed that it was a rarity for females to stay in such places. The man pulled his dagger back as he half stroked half grabbed her hair. Garth ripped her cloak off with one swift movement and Kirsten understood what it meant when she watched him whetting his lips.

Eight

A sense of complete calm came over Kirsten and she seemed to see events in slow motion. Firstly, her elbow swung full strength into the weasel-looking man's face. She saw, rather than felt, the tug on her hair as he fell away from her, his nose bloodied. She ducked and rolled as one of Garth's enormous fists swung at her. Looking about for her sword, she spotted it some metres away, lying beneath a barstool, where the injured man must have dropped it. Garth swung about to meet her and she sprung nimbly to her feet, backing away. At his bulldozer advance, her hand moved swiftly to her belt, feeling at once something cold and sharp. She saw the madness in his eyes and envisioned the metal star embedded between them.

With a rapid jerk of her hand, she threw. He was almost upon her when the shuriken struck, exactly how she had imagined it. Droplets of blood spattered her and she watched with morbid fascination as the giant toppled to ground with a crash.

Dead.

Sound returned with normal time and she saw a crowd had gathered about the scene. Her eyes searched and observed the weasel-looking man darting for the exit. Too many people blocked her path for her to be able to reach him. Stepping over the body of Garth, she walked over to the bar; a fair-haired man stepped out from the crowd in the corner, his hand moving to his belt, sneering. Kirsten did not wait for him to draw a weapon; she sprang up and hitch-kicked him in the face. He fell back, his head cracking on the bar. A few of his companions rushed forward to tackle Kirsten together. She ducked again and swung her leg out so fast that they all tripped. She heard the landlord's voice as he came back to consciousness, but nobody paid him any heed; they seemed far too entertained by the spectacle.

A bottle shattered as it hit the back of Kirsten's head, and she reeled forward, feeling sick. She removed the dagger from her belt, trying to ignore the red wine that stung her eyes, and she saw, as if from above, a crowd of men kicking and stomping. *I have to move*, she thought.

Now.

She sprang in the air, cat-like, her dagger drawn like a long claw as it tore into the flesh of the nearest attacker, gutting him. The cruel blade was wet with blood when she ripped it away and turned to face the crowd, wide-eyed. The blood covered her hand and arm and splashes of it accentuated the murder in her eyes.

They backed away from the fresh body, deciding enough was enough, that it was best to leave the crazy woman alone. They parted on her approach. She picked up her sword and sheathed it, but kept hold of her dagger. Bending over the body of Garth, she plucked the shuriken from his forehead, allowing the blood to ooze from the wound. She gazed for a moment into his lifeless eyes, the pupils like gaping holes waiting to swallow her in their darkness.

Kirsten was unsure whether it was wine, sweat or blood that she could taste, as she headed toward the stair door. There was silence in the bar except for the shrill voice of the landlord.

She did not feel her feet touching the steps on her ascent. Her body began to numb with the horror of what she had done. At the head of the stairs, Cal greeted her, his face faltering on seeing the bloodied weapons about her person.

'I would very much appreciate it if you could prepare me a bath, Cal.'

'Certainly miss', he said.

He ran as fast as his legs would carry him to what Kirsten supposed was the bathroom. Steam clouds escaped into the coolness of the hall, as he opened the door.

'You can take this one if you like,' he offered. 'I'm sure your friend won't mind waiting a little longer.'

By friend, she assumed that he meant Troy. She followed Cal into the steam filled room, her hands beginning to shake and a sickness rising in her stomach.

'Thank you, Cal. Would you be so kind as to tell your father that I am very sorry for the disturbance and we will of course compensate him for any breakages or cleaning that will need to be paid for.'

Cal nodded, fear still in his eyes. She closed the door behind him and stood leaning against it, heaving air into her lungs, trying to stop herself from vomiting.

As her stomach calmed, her eyes worked upwards to the bloody weapons in her hand and threw them aside with a cry, backing away from the door. Sitting on the edge of the tub of steaming water, her body shook uncontrollably as shock set in. She became vaguely aware of raised voices in the passageway, and as a knock came suddenly at the door, she was unable to move and could only squeak a reply.

Another knock came, followed by the voice of Troy telling her that he was coming in.

'Dear Lord,' was all he said, as he gazed at her bloodied form. He turned and bolted the door, his eyes falling on the discarded weapons on the floor. Kneeling before her, he was unsure how to proceed.

'Come on, Kirsten,' he said. 'We need to get you cleaned up.'

Her eyes remained unfocused, as she obeyed him. Standing, she removed her belt and pulled off her boots. Her breath came in short sharp gasps, as if she was weeping, yet no tears leaked from her wild eyes. Troy turned flushing, realising she was going to strip. He did not turn back until he heard a quiet splash of water, as she settled in the bath. At first, he could not make out her form through the clouds of steam that enveloped her.

'I killed them,' she said. Her voice sounded distant and she rested her head on her knees.

Troy was relieved that he could only see her head, shoulders and the tops of her knees, as they alone had begun to arouse him again, despite his shock.

'I know, Kirsten; it's all right,' he soothed. 'The landlord told us what happened. Everything's all right.'

She looked up at her hands; the blood washed away and she turned them before her eyes, as if she was unsure that they would ever truly be clean.

'No, it's not all right,' she said. 'I've just killed two people! They're dead. There's no bringing them back. I've just committed murder.'

Troy found it hard to believe that the fragile and delicate girl before him could even have been capable. He wanted to cradle her in his arms and make the pain and remorse go away. Dipping a sponge into the water, he was careful not to make contact with her flesh, wringing it out and beginning to wipe the blood from her face. The water thinned the blood and it dripped from her face like tears. He withdrew sharply, a hundred or so images of Christ at the crucifixion stabbing his eyes.

What am I doing? his mind questioned. *I'm locked in a room with a naked girl; a girl that I have already admitted to myself that I have feelings about.*

Sinful thoughts.

I've given myself to Christ and that means certain sacrifices. He bowed his head in shame, praying for forgiveness.

His mutterings were enough to draw Kirsten away from her darkness. She became aware of her nakedness and drew one of the sheets about her, it growing heavy as it drank the water.

'Father Troy?' she said.

He seemed lost in prayer. The concentration on his face made him look much older, as it emphasised creases that she had been unaware of before. She felt suddenly ashamed.

'I am sorry,' she whispered.

Father Troy heard her voice; it seemed much older and clearer, yet familiar. He ceased praying and raised his head, already guessing what would meet his eyes. He had heard the woman's voice before and remembered the exquisite face that accompanied it. He wondered for a moment if he was dreaming, as the beautiful woman gazed down upon him through the vapour, seeming luminescent in form.

Kirsten's mind was clearer and she held out her hand to Troy. He took it, unsure why.

'Forgive me Father,' she said. 'Twice you have come to my aid, allowing me to compromise your position. I had not considered the mortification this might have caused you. I have not even thanked you. I do so now, and I say this. I will not forget such support as you have offered. I am in your debt.'

Troy gazed in awe and wonderment; it was as though the room filled with goodness and his heart with song. He felt small before her, but he was not afraid. Her touch and the clarity of her voice made him feel that he could fight a war for her if she requested it. The visiting angel had answered his prayers.

It's not wrong to be so devoted to this woman, he decided. *I always felt that she served some higher purpose. It's not wrong to love ... for god is love.* He felt alive, his whole body buzzing with electricity. She had said very little, but had meant so much. She inspired him. *I must repress my desires, but allow myself to love as I am permitted.*

There was a loud knock at the door and Tom's gruff voice followed. The moment passed in an instant and Troy found that he was holding the hand of Kirsten, her familiar features smiling warmly at him. He smiled back, before proceeding to answer the door.

Kirsten caught the fury in the inspector's face, before the priest pushed him back and they left her alone. She found that she was still smiling, but could not fathom why considering the circumstances. It was as though for a moment she had found herself, a traveller lost in darkness who finds a light to guide them.

She immersed herself in the bath and lay in silence, holding her breath, allowing the still warm water to wash away the blood and guilt. A few bubbles of air escaped her lips to break the silence beneath the surface. Her entire body seemed to relax and she felt her mind wander. She saw the outside corridor and the door to the bathroom approaching ever nearer. She heard arguing from their room, as she walked by—the bathroom mere doors away. Passing a mirror to her right, she glanced briefly at her reflection. It was at that moment that everything seemed to happen at once.

First, the panic hit her when she saw the face of the weasel-looking man in the mirror. She knew that she could not reach the door before he did, and could not even scream as she was still beneath the water. She allowed herself to calm and concentrated on the latch, picturing it in her mind's eye, clamping down the bolt just as the handle turned. Next, she sat up out of the water, gasping for air. She looked to the door and realised the bolt was down. Her heart jumped and her mind raced.

I must have done it, there's nobody else in the room, she thought. The door was secure and she was safe. *But how can I be sure that I had been in danger to begin with? I didn't actually see man's approach; it was so vivid, though. It was as if I was there in his mind, watching from behind his eyes.* A noise at the door startled her from her thoughts. She gazed with anticipation, as a thin blade slipped in the tiny gap between the door and wall. With horror, she realised that the intruder intended to lift the latch and enter.

Scrambling out of the bath, she became caught up in the sheet and fell awkwardly to the floor. As the latch lifted, she reached over for her sword, realising it was too far away to reach in time. Instead of struggling over to where it lay, she felt the need to make it come to her; it was an odd sensation, like a bending in her mind. As the door began to open, the sword was in her hand and she was struggling to her feet. She did not have time to wonder how she had managed to get it there, for she was too busy covering her nakedness and preparing to fight.

Shouts ensued from the corridor and she saw a flash of green as the intruder sped away. The door opened and Inspector Tom Stephenson entered, broadsword in hand.

'You all right?' he asked gruffly.

She nodded and acknowledged Troy, as he entered.

'He got away through the window,' he said.

The inspector raised a single eyebrow at the scene, the discarded and bloody weapons, the water soaked floor and the drenched, half-naked form of Kirsten as her lithe arms clutched at both sword and sheet.

The two men waited in the corridor while Kirsten dried and dressed herself. She did not put her belt back on and was loath to touch the soiled weapons, feeling a sharp pang of guilt whenever she spied the ugly, dark red patches.

They ushered her back to the room, where a fire had been lit. A strong smell of stew invaded Kirsten's nostrils, as she slumped on the bed nearest the window. Cal served her a bowl, offering a weak smile whilst urging her to eat. She assumed that the only reason that they were permitted to dine in their room was a precaution to avoid further mishap.

She relished the food; it was unlike any stew that she had ever tasted before. It had a beefy taste, but the vegetables that she chewed on were unfamiliar and the herbs seemed to magically blend the flavours together in a way that no two mouthfuls were alike. Breaking off some bread, she wiped her bowl clean. The portion had been small, yet extremely filling. Cal returned shortly after, handing Kirsten her weapons, gleaming clean. Fear was in his eyes and his hand trembled, as he set down the dagger. He removed the bowls and wished them a peaceful night.

Kirsten wondered how late it was, guessing that it could be no later than nine. She assumed that the landlord had requested that they remain confined to their room for the remainder of their stay. Wrapping the top blanket about herself, she gazed out at the swollen moon.

It was Tom who broke the silence, his voice softened slightly by the crackling of the fire.

'So, are you still going to deny that you had anything to do with all those murders back on earth?'

Kirsten turned slowly and met his accusing eyes with calm.

'Inspector Stephenson, it would be rather hard for me to kill someone when I was in a different country now, would it not? I was at school for *most* of the killings.'

'It could prove difficult for me to corroborate that, considering our circumstances,' he sneered.

Father Troy got up to stoke the fire, unwilling to get involved.

'Are you trying to blame me for *you* being here now as well?' she challenged.

Tom's nostrils flared slightly and he fidgeted. 'Well I don't see who else's fault it could be,' he said.

'Can you explain to me exactly how you propose I brought you here?' Her eyes gazed into nothingness, as she lost herself in thought. *What if it is my fault? I made the sword appear in my hand. I made the door lock ... but the wind from the open window could have blown the bolt down and I could have been so distressed after what happened, that I might not have been aware of scrambling over to pick up the sword.* She shook herself and came back to the inspector's angered voice once more.

'You said that you didn't know the killer and yet you used his name. You even cried over his body,' Tom accused.

That hurt. A sharp pang of emotion stabbed at her and she remembered Caitul's lifeless body, more real somehow than the carnage after her friend's destruction.

Father Troy turned his attention to the conversation, it seeming to hold a little more interest for him.

'He told me his name, when he held me captive; I already informed you of that,' she explained. 'I can't tell you why I cried. I was in shock and upset, and it seemed as if he was the only one who had any answers to what had been happening. He had been so gentle with me; it was hard to believe that he was a killer.' She swallowed, knowing that was how Troy thought about her at that time.

'He was like a lost child, not trusting anything he saw; everything was new to him,' she continued. 'He was as lost and alone there, as we are here. Most, if not all of the deaths had been accidents, or rather they were the victims of circumstance rather than cold-bloodied slaughter. He didn't understand that killing was wrong, but perhaps more importantly, he said he only killed in self-defence.'

Tom swung his legs over the bed and leaned forward, challenging her.

'Miss Vái, I saw the bodies of your neighbours after they had been pulled out of the river. I would like to know just how a wife and child could have been any threat to him.'

Kirsten stared at the fire, clearly seeing an image of the inspector in the leaping flames. He was weeping in an empty house, a note left by his wife clutched in his snot-covered fingers. She felt the pain in his heart when his daughter told him that she didn't want to see Daddy any more. Kirsten met his eyes and could not prevent herself from saying,

'You of all people should understand how dangerous a wife and child can be, considering yours almost destroyed you.'

The inspector seemed astounded for a moment, wondering what she had meant or how she knew.

'You bitch!' he exclaimed.

Kirsten half expected him to spring at her, but he bowed his head in self-pity. She was sorry for what she had said, yet did not bring herself to apologise.

'There were circumstances of which you are not aware,' she said. 'In Caitul's eyes, the boy was a threat. He made a mistake that's all. I'm not saying that it excuses what he did, but at least it explains it.'

It was Father Troy who spoke, as the inspector continued to brood.

'Kirsten, you seem to be trivialising death. The fact remains that the man was a killer and you are defending him.'

Kirsten reeled on the priest, annoyed by his interruption.

'It is not your place to judge him or anyone else, Father,' she spat, 'so I suggest that you remain silent!'

His eyes blazed with the anger he felt, but he kept quiet, believing her to be right, despite the insensitive manner in which she had expressed herself.

'Perhaps you would rather bring up the subject of myself as a killer,' she said. 'Indeed I am surprised it has taken as long as this. Two men lie dead by my hand. I killed them with as much regard for my action, as I might purchase a pair of shoes. What have you to say to that?'

Kirsten was shocked to hear the inspector speak, his voice not filled with the malice and scorn that she would have expected.

'We understand that you saved a girl and were attacked yourself,' he said. 'If you had failed to use every method at your disposal in order to defend yourself, you might now be defiled and/or dead. I myself am not saying that I agree with your killing those men, but I am satisfied that you did so for the right reasons, and am relieved that you came to no harm.' He mumbled the last sentiment, as if embarrassed at having said a kind word to her.

'I too am pleased that you were able to defend yourself so effectively,' Troy said.

Kirsten sagged, her mind confused. *They have forgiven me murder, feeling I was justified and yet I committed the worst crime imaginable.* 'So why do you still issue venom upon Caitul?' she asked. 'Our situations differ little. He killed to defend himself, as did I.'

The priest gave a scornful laugh. 'Are you telling me an angry mob tried to rape him? I doubt it ...'

'No, but he *was* defending himself ... and me,' she ended quietly. She was aware of both their eyes upon her; her cheeks felt hot and she was unsure whether it was because she was sat too close to the fire or if she was merely flustered.

'So now we get to it,' the inspector said. 'So you *did* know him!'

'No,' she protested, facing them. 'But he seemed to know me. I didn't believe anything he said at the time. I thought that he was crazy and about to kill me, but he didn't. He looked after me and after I collapsed, he returned me home so that I could be cared for properly. I don't remember exactly what he said, but I know that it was the truth. We're here, I'm home.'

Their faces were blank and she supposed that they did not believe her. She climbed beneath the covers of her bed and laid the blanket on top, ignoring their comments, making it clear that she intended to sleep. She felt tired and drifted off almost immediately, their voices washing over her like waves, the pain in her heart lessening as sleep took her.

The two men discussed the possibility of Kirsten having been drugged for her to fall asleep so quickly. They thought it likely, considering the commotion she had caused. It was a couple of hours before they decided to blow out the candles and attempt to sleep themselves. The fire was dying and the remaining embers omitted a warm glow.

Kirsten awoke in the dead of night. It had cooled somewhat once the fire had gone out. Pale shafts of moonlight beamed through the window and cast shadows throughout the room. She could hear the heavy breathing of her slumbering companions. Closing her eyes again, she attempted to sleep, when a noise from outside the window startled her. She strained her eyes to see two hands working nimbly on the latch. Sliding silently out of her bed and collecting her sword, she hid in the shadows to await the visitor.

A shadowy shape crawled quietly into the room. Neither man stirred. The figure was short and thin, not much bigger than a child. He moved soundlessly toward the bedside table, seeming to know his way. He searched stealthily through Tom's hauberk until a jingle of coins told Kirsten that he had found what he sought.

She watched him amused, as he expertly explored the room, failing to notice his audience. As the thief arrived at Kirsten's bedside table, he started, realising that she was not in bed. Cautiously, he slid his hand beneath the sheets to check if they were warm and Kirsten stepped out from the shadows, her sword held out. The thief snatched up her dagger and pointed it toward her threateningly.

She could see that he was a boy, no more than fifteen years old. His eyes were fearful, but his hands remained steady.

'Keep away. I warn you!' he said.

It was enough to wake Tom, and he sat up.

'What the devil?'

That in turn awakened Troy, and so the boy found that he had three to contend with instead of one. Kirsten, who was smiling to herself, put out her other hand and lowered the sword to the ground, in a gesture of peace.

'Now come on, put down the knife. You're no killer,' she said.

Her words seemed to make the lad more determined and he swiped the air toward Kirsten. He yelped suddenly and dropped the dagger. Blood dripped from his fingers and tears welled in his eyes.

'It bit me!' he cried.

The inspector grabbed the boy by the scruff of the neck, to Troy's protests, seeming set on giving him a thrashing. Placing her dagger back onto the cabinet, Kirsten noticed spots of blood on the carved hilt. Troy wrenched the boy free and both men retrieved their property. Tom planned to fetch the landlord before Kirsten prevented him.

'You're hurt boy. Let me see your hand,' she said.

Apprehensively, the boy approached her. His face looked pale in the moonlight. He held out his injured hand and Kirsten noted his long fingers and slender wrists. She made the boy sit while she applied one of the herb mixtures from her pack, much to the protest of Tom who felt they should turn the boy in. Firmly holding a compress against his delicate hand, she stared into the depth of his sad eyes.

'Do you think that we should turn you in?' she asked.

He shrugged pathetically. 'Do what you will, Miss.'

She stared deeper still and the boy shifted uncomfortably under her penetrating gaze.

'If I let you go, what would you then do, boy?'

His eyes lit up at the possibility of freedom. 'I would go straight home, Miss,' he promised.

'Tell me. Why do you steal?'

He looked around at the staring faces, feeling that they were looking down on him, thinking that they were better than he was. He struggled pointlessly, as Kirsten's grip tightened.

'I'm hungry and I've tried getting a job,' he said. 'But nobody wants to hire me because of who my da was. He was killed for being a fief, and we is not well liked 'round these parts. But we're too poor to move and me ma's too old to work, so I steal like me da before me.'

Kirsten's heart filled with pity, but Inspector Stephenson was scornful. He told Kirsten how many such protestations he had been made to endure in interview rooms. He got to his feet and stormed from the room in search of the landlord.

Kirsten moved quickly. 'What is your name, boy?'

The thief's frightened eyes met hers tearfully.

'Jeb,' he sniffed.

'Well tell me, Jeb,' she continued. 'If you had money, would you steal any longer?'

Jeb shook his head, his tattered black hood falling to his shoulders, revealing a mane of matted golden hair. Kirsten still held his arm and concentrated on his pulse as the boy made his reply. She saw an image flicker in her mind for a moment and was gone. She gave a wry smile, unsure of what she had seen. Footsteps could be heard below and Kirsten knew they were running out of time. She pressed a large gold coin into Jeb's hand and ushered him to the window.

'Now go! Quickly,' she urged.

The boy's eyes were wide with surprise and excitement, as he sped out of the window and clambered catlike across the surrounding rooftops, before she could change her mind. By the time the door opened again, Jeb had disappeared from sight.

The landlord seemed upset that there had been such an incident and was hinting at the fact that such bad luck seemed to be a companion to their party. Troy was quick to usher the man from the room, and there were a general sigh of relief when the flustered innkeeper departed. Each of them made their way back to bed. The moonlight was dimming and the sky turned deep purple.

'So you let him go!' the inspector said vehemently.

'He didn't harm any of us, Tom,' Troy said. 'Why put him or his family through further distress? We frightened him enough.'

'A crime is a crime. Thou shall not steal … I'm surprised I should have to remind you of all people.'

Kirsten interrupted viciously. 'So let me get this straight, I kill two people and you can show understanding, but a starving kid who hasn't had a fair chance in life, deserves to have the book thrown at him?'

'Stop it the pair of you. I am so sick of this bickering,' Troy said. 'Kirsten, we *understand* why you did what you did; we do not condone it. And stop quoting my beliefs back at me all the time. Yes, I am a priest and am well aware of the commandments; I do not need both of you rubbing my face in it and treating my beliefs with contempt. You would do well to take on a few Christian virtues, starting with forgiveness. We can't go on if we're to constantly be at each other's throats night and day. We have to stick together.' He turned to Tom. 'The boy was in the wrong, but Kirsten *forgave* him; this was a good thing. I am pleased that she did. You are not a policeman any longer. If the boy steals again, what concern is it of yours?'

Kirsten's eyes shone, impressed with Troy's sermon. Tom shrugged.

'Now we have to learn to get along with one another, and *trust* each other. Is that clear?'

They both agreed, somewhat reluctantly, but Troy thought that it was better than nothing.

Nine

They managed to get at least a few more hours sleep, before the dawn light flooded through the window and the sound of a cockerel awoke them. The inspector had insisted on setting a trap in case of Jeb's, or any other undesirables' return. He had also slept with his purse under his pillow, oblivious to the fact that Kirsten had removed another gold coin from it. Both she and Troy felt it unwise to mention it, for fear of arousing his temper yet again.

Tom stretched, asking Troy where the nearest toilet was. Troy pointed to the pot in the corner. They glanced over at Kirsten, whose eyes refused to open properly. She yawned and sat up, her hair settling like a bird's nest, jutting out at odd angles. Taking the hint, she pulled across the bedclothes and made for the door, catching Troy's worried glance as she passed.

'Don't worry,' she assured him. 'I'll stay out of trouble.'

She crept up the corridor to the bathroom she had used the previous night; it was empty and the sheet-come towels were piled neatly on a chair. She spied a chamber pot beneath the chair and made good use of it, wondering where they disposed of the waste. Before returning to the room, she tried brushing her knotted hair with her fingers, to minimum success.

Kirsten knocked before entering and found that the inspector was trying to treat his sunburn with the wrong salve. After much arguing, she convinced him to allow her to apply the correct mixture. The burns looked as though they had almost healed and their faces were no longer blistered, but had tanned. They both looked as though had not been on holiday, rather than perishing in the desert.

Troy sent for Cal to arrange for breakfast and have the horses prepared. The meal was simple, consisting of several rounds of what appeared to be pikelets, but much larger than they were used to, with unhealthy helpings of creamy butter. They were served a jug of fresh water and a tea-like beverage that Troy described as having a woody taste to it.

While Troy and Tom settled the rest of the bill, Kirsten stepped out into the fresh air of morning. A cool breeze greeted her from the west and she breathed in deeply. She gave a warm greeting to the stablehand, as he led the horses over to her. The boy nodded and persisted in looking at her belt. She noticed that the extra saddle had been securely packed on the stouter of the two horses and the remaining luggage had been put on the packhorse. She patted the latter on the neck and it responded by shaking its head. The stable lad still waited and Kirsten hoped that she was not expected to tip him, as she had no money.

'What are you looking at?' she asked, in mild annoyance.

He looked slightly embarrassed at having been caught staring at her.

'I just wanted to know if it was true.'

'What are you talking about?'

'Your dragon; is it real?'

Kirsten remained none the wiser and did not have time to question him further, as he darted off as soon at her companions' approach.

'So where are we headed?' Tom asked.

His bright manner left Kirsten distrustful.

'Northwest,' she replied, 'to meet the wise-woman that I saw yesterday.'

She handed the inspector the reins to the piebald horse and the bay to Troy.

'What are you going to ride?' Troy asked.

'I'm not. I'm going to walk. It won't take more than a day to get there, and the conditions are not treacherous like they were in the desert, so I will be fine.'

Troy tried to give up his steed, refusing to let her be on foot. Kirsten shook her head, as she loaded her pack onto his horse.

'I'll have my own soon enough and I will be fine until then.' She had no idea why she had said such a thing and silently cursed herself for not purchasing three horses while she had the chance. *Yeah, sure, I'll be fine,* she thought. *I have no money and nothing with which to barter for the price of a horse, everything peachy here ... bloody idiot!* Despite her silent misgivings, she remained adamant that she would walk and so considered the debate over.

Tom mounted expertly, seeming undaunted by the size of the animal. Troy, however, seemed nervous at the mere proximity of his horse, let alone having to actually mount and ride it. Kirsten held the reins steady while he clambered awkwardly on.

Tom laughed. 'Now we see why you were so eager to be a gentlemen and walk. You've never ridden in your life, have you?'

He trotted over to the priest and gave him a brief lesson, leaving Kirsten to walk ahead, to save delay.

She kept to the main path leading through and out of town. It was a marvel to her how early people were out and about, setting up market stalls and going about their business. The street grew narrow and the buildings taller, before Kirsten heard the sound of hooves behind her. She turned and smiled up at them, as they slowed their pace to match her own. It took less than an hour to reach the town gate on the west side and they could see that it was used to receiving more traffic than the desert entrance.

There were guards at the gate and they looked more alert than those previously encountered. Kirsten drew her cloak over her head and suggested that she go ahead, worried at being stopped after the previous night's events at the inn. She was correct in her assumption. The guards crossed their pikes and pulled her aside. She tried to calm her breathing when she saw a hand reach to a lethal looking broad bladed axe.

Removing her hood, she gave them a pleasant smile. They appeared immediately shocked and whispered excitedly to one another.

'Sorry to have troubled you,' one of them said. 'You should be very careful if you are planning to travel alone, Miss.'

'Thank you for your concern, but some friends will be meeting me on the road, and I assure you that they are not men with whom I would wish to trifle,' she lied.

Her voice was clear and strong, yet charming as a summer breeze. The guard actually smiled and bowed his head, as he opened the gates for her.

Her companions watched in wonderment as she pulled her hood over her long red hair, gleaming like fire in the morning sun. They rode toward the gate, neither wanting to mention what they had just witnessed, what they had both seen before. Kirsten seemed to be able to change her appearance at will and it had been this she had used to fool the guards, knowing them to be on the look out for a woman of athletic build with dark brown shoulder length hair and dark eyes. The guards having seen a flash of a red dress beneath her cloak had assumed that they had found the killer, but on seeing the vision of loveliness before them, realised their mistake at once.

The men passed through the gate with ease, the guards barely glancing their way. As they approached, they saw that Kirsten had replaced her hood; her oddly coloured cloak shimmered in the morning light, like a peacock feather.

It was difficult to believe that they were only an hour or so away from the edge of a cruel desert. The vegetation there was rich, and soft carpets of lush grass lay on either side of the road, stretching out into fields on one side joining with farmland. The fields were well ordered and crops grew healthily in the pleasant climate. To their right, the pastures were meadows filled with wild flowers and wooded areas. The trees were in blossom and they caught the sweet fragrance every time a breeze blew their way.

They talked little while still in sight of Golstur. It was not until Kirsten removed her hood once more, that conversation began.

'Are you planning to explain any time soon, how it is that you seem to mysteriously transform into someone else,' Tom asked, 'or did you intend to keep us guessing?'

Kirsten looked up at him. His eyes were fixed sternly on the road ahead.

'I don't know how to explain it,' she began. 'It's like this face is a mask, one that I am finding increasingly difficult to wear. It's easy for me to change, but it's a lot harder for me to remain looking like this. I know it sounds crazy …'

'On the contrary, Kirsten, three days ago I would have you certified, but now…' He looked about him, highlighting their situation. 'It's a lot easier to believe in the unbelievable. So tell me, is this the same trick that Caitul used, do you think?'

'No,' she replied. 'He seemed to be able to occupy the bodies of others. I don't know how he did it, although I'm equally unsure how I am doing what I do. Like our entire situation at present, it remains a mystery.'

'Do you know why you change, Kirsten?' Troy asked earnestly.

She gave a heavy sigh. 'I have a suspicion, but I'm not sure. It is one of the reasons that I am so keen to speak to this woman. She hinted at things yesterday, but I didn't have time to prise information out of her.'

After a few hours, the road narrowed into little more than a dirt track, making it necessary for them to proceed single file. They started to climb, as the land rose steeply before them. Kirsten pointed to a small house on the hillside in the distance, still some miles away. Their stomachs were growling by the time they arrived, having been unwilling to rest once their goal were in sight. They dismounted before leaving the track, and led the horses across the field toward the tiny abode, which appeared nothing more than a hut once they were up close.

A short, grey-haired old woman came striding toward them, her arms full of dried flowers and fresh herbs. Kirsten stepped forward to greet her.

'Hello there,' she said. 'Do you remember me? We met yesterday. You sold me some potions to help my friends.'

The woman's steel coloured eyes briefly flicked to the men before returning their attention to Kirsten.

'Worked didn't it?' She sniffed. 'Told ye it would do the job. Here, hol' these laddie!' She thrust the bundle into Troy's unsuspecting arms.

'Suppose you'll be wantin' some vittles before yer on yer way again,' she said, her beady eyes fixing on Tom.

'That's very kind of you to offer,' he said.

'Yes, yes, come on then all of ye.'

She grabbed Kirsten's arm and hobbled toward the hut. The chimney was smoking and as they entered, they saw a large fire ablaze. The hut seemed quite roomy once inside. There was only one window in the front, where the woman had large bundles of flowers hanging from the roof. The place smelled mostly of freshly baked bread, but after a while, more subtle scents became apparent; the herbs and flowers she had hanging and lying in baskets, and an odd woody odour of something bubbling in a small cauldron over the fire.

'Set them down here, lad.' She patted a large wooden table dimly lit by the firelight. Tottering over to the fire, she removed the bubbling mixture, replacing it with a huge pot of water. She then picked up a large loaf of bread that had been cooling on the window ledge and placed it on the table.

'Sit down, sit down,' she said.

They watched as she bustled about, collecting cups, knives, butter, cheese and what appeared to be a large ham. Kirsten offered to help and was sharply put in her place by the woman. As the water boiled, the woman poured it into what looked like a huge coffeepot. However, Tom thought it too much to ask that he was about to receive his well-missed dose of caffeine. His hopes were dashed when a scent of herbs filled the air, as she passed the pot around.

'Well tuck in, tuck in,' she said.

She took a slice of bread and cheese and sat herself in the armchair beside the fire. They ate and drank with as much ease as they would if they had been invited guests of a friend. The place had a homely feel to it and the woman herself felt to each of them like a grandmother who likes nothing better than to spoil her young relatives. Tom seemed most satisfied after eating his fill and they were surprised on seeing him rise and re-fill the woman's cup. She smiled a toothy grin that accentuated her lined face.

'That was most gratifying,' the inspector said. 'You have our thanks, but pray tell us to whom are we indebted.'

The woman chuckled to herself, as if flattered by Tom's words.

'Meggan is my name, if ye wish to use it. Now, what is it that yer want for me to tell ye?'

The companions glanced briefly at one another, wondering why she would arrive at such a conclusion even though she was correct.

'Come now, do not look so surprised,' she said. 'The sense of expectation coming from ye is easy to interpret y'know. You should all try and hide your intention a little more if ye wish for them to remain un-read.'

'Meggan,' Kirsten ventured. 'We have come from … far away. But we do not know how we got here. Yesterday, you seemed to know more than you were saying. Will you not let us hear your thoughts on our situation?'

The woman's old eyebrows rose sharply. She signalled them over to her and ushered them to sit. Kirsten felt like a child at school, listening to stories told by the teacher before home time.

'What is yer name, child?' she asked.

'Kirsten,' replied Kirsten, shifting position in attempt to get comfortable.

The woman's eyes narrowed slightly. 'Is that the only name by which ye call yerself? Might there not be another name, an unspoken name that ye might use? Yer true name?'

Kirsten was aware of all eyes upon her and she felt her face beginning to burn.

'Come now,' Meggan said. 'Either ye are or ye're not; if the latter be true, then I must warn ye of the great danger that ye place yerself in. For whomsoever falsely claims to be her, will be struck dead.'

Kirsten displayed the same confusion as her companions and Meggan sighed at their blank faces.

'Yer sword, girl!' she said. 'It was yer sword that I did recognise, not yer face, for I saw a picture of it once that my mother did show me. It is an ancient blade of long lost past—a sword of legend more so than reality. It was said to have existed only in dream since its making in the forge of Taiohãhn. In legend, there is only one hand that could bring the blade from the Underworld to Maldahl and that is Exzalander, the only child from the line of Tuâth and Shénnin.'

Kirsten's eyes widened at the name, as she remembered Caitul's words.

'Caitul called me Exzalander,' she said.

Meggan blanched and crouched toward them conspiratorially, as if she were afraid that the walls would hear her.

'He mentioned Maldahl,' Kirsten continued, 'but it all meant nothing to me. My name is Kirsten and I have no memory of the person of whom you speak.'

Meggan's hand moved swiftly toward Kirsten, the heel of her palm pressing tightly against her head. Kirsten flinched as she saw visions from her dreams.

Fighting in a desert ... flames, as they leapt from a burning castle ... the chiselled features of a man from her dream whom Geri had told her was not to be trusted, and her hand, as it reached out to him ...

The woman hissed and drew away from her.

'Ye fool, what are ye doing?' she said.

Kirsten's eyes refused to refocus at first.

'Are you trying to get yerself killed?'

'I don't understand,' Kirsten muttered.

'Such foolishness will only draw him to ye. He is not the man ye knew. He is yer enemy; ye must accept that!'

Kirsten gave a pleading glance to Troy. She felt her body trembling and wondered whether the room had turned chill.

'Meggan, you think that Kirsten is this Exzalander person,' Troy said, 'but she has been living in England her entire life. She cannot be the woman you say she is.'

Meggan spat, annoyed by the priest's interruption.

'Who was she before that?' she hissed. 'Where did she come from? Tell me that!'

Troy huffed; he had no time for people with notions of past life experience. 'She didn't exist then,' he said. 'She was born in England and has lived there her whole life.'

'Exzalander was banished from Maldahl over three hundred years ago,' Meggan explained. 'Who knows where she has travelled in that time before reaching this Ing-land of which you speak. After such travels, is it any wonder that she has no memory of her origin?'

Tom felt that they were getting answers without knowing the questions. 'Meggan, this makes very little sense to me,' he said. 'Would you be so kind as to explain from the beginning who this Exzalander is?'

The old woman's eyes were bright in the firelight and a smile touched her aged lips.

'So it *is* ye,' she said. 'The time has come at last and not one of ye knows why it is that yer here.' She cleared her throat, as if making ready for a long speech and wishing to sound as eloquent as possible.

'Exzalander was the daughter of King Tuâth and Queen Shénnin, and she was as beautiful it is said, as a spring morn'. Many at that time scorned the naming of the child, thinking it presumptuous to assume her to be the one, but Tuâth insisted, explaining that the name had been ordained and he had been commanded to name her thus. Many people felt that the king was a fool to tempt fate, saying that such a deed would be their undoing and the kingdom's downfall. Nevertheless, Tuâth was unmoved, explaining that the choice was not his.

'At the Ceremony of Naming, Shénnin wept in fear for her child's life; for it is said that if an impostor takes the name of Exzalander, they will die a painful death. Many there believed the child would not last the ceremony once the name had been given. When nothing drastic occurred, most began to forget, deeming the prophecy to be a foolish story to allow people to enjoy the good times.

'There were only few who objected to Exzalander's betrothal to Katahl, reminding Tuâth of the prophecy and the predicted darkness that would befall them if he allowed such a match. But Tuâth, who had no wish to see his only child unhappy, allowed their love to grow.

'The day of their union had been planned, but never came to be. As foretold, a great evil attacked Brëgwela Castle in the north, and many of the household were slain. Shénnin and Tuâth both suffered terrible deaths and Exzalander was exiled from this world. It is said that she would return so that she may be joined to Katahl after he had received his conditioning, and so make his power absolute, although that is but one version of the prophecy.

'Exzalander was never seen again and many assumed that she had been killed along with her parents to make way for Katahl's rule. Before they left our world, the Dark Ones tutored Katahl, and he is now a powerful force who has mastery over much of Maldahl. He has many servants, some of whom followed him during the old time. His most powerful allies are his knights; Dahal, Aarnon and Nimrïn, who in the old time were courageous, bold, and loved by all. But now they are as dark as he, twisted by his evil influence and more powerful than any of his servants or slaves.'

'But what about Caitul?' Kirsten heard herself ask.

'Caitul was First Knight to Katahl and they were close friends before the darkness fell. He was the most powerful of his guard and undefeated in battle. We are perhaps fortunate that he is no longer with us, for what a terrible enemy he would have made. For it is said that soon after the princess disappeared, Katahl's lessons in the majick arts began. But it was a long while before he gave in to evil. He learned much, but remained uncorrupted and panged for the loss of his love, ever searching for a means of escape. And so it was that he came across an incantation that would allow a man to travel beyond. He sent immediately for Caitul, whom he trusted above all others, begging him to be the one to search for Exzalander and bring her back to him.

'Katahl had not realised that the Dark Ones observed his spell working so closely. They lay in wait until the spell rendered him most vulnerable, and they used it to saturate him with evil. Thus was the prophecy to that point fulfilled. For Katahl had changed and set in motion a search to bring his betrothed back to him. It was his love for Exzalander that was at last his downfall.'

To her amazement, Kirsten had tears in her eyes. She felt pain in her chest, as she recalled Caitul who had indeed found her and met his death because of her.

'It has been two hundred and seventy years since the Dark Ones departed, ne'er to return,' Meggan continued. 'Katahl in that time learned of the CODM prophecy and found it not at all to his liking. The elders of the Vampire Ælves wrote it; of all Maldahl's creations, Taiohãhn most revered them, trusting them with the knowledge to write the great work. It tells of how his betrothed would indeed return and would be the means of his destruction. Katahl decided that he erred in sending Caitul and dispatched one of his warriors to find and destroy Exzalander before she had a chance to come back.

'That is the last I know of the story of Exzalander and Katahl. In the meantime, Lord Katahl has plundered the land. Many civilisations fell and much of Maldahl has become a wasteland. It grows ever difficult to keep the borders of his domain from spreading and polluting the land with his evil.'

There was a silence for a while where none of them seemed to breathe. The fire cracked and popped, as the wood was consumed by flame.

Tom cleared his throat uncomfortably. 'So, you actually believe that Kirsten is this Exzalander?' he asked.

'I see all the signs,' Meggan replied, 'besides, if Caitul found her, as she says, then there can be little doubt.'

'Why do you suppose that *we* are here, Meggan?' Troy asked. 'Our home is the place where Kirsten has been residing. Why would we suddenly have been brought here too?'

'That, I know not. There might be one who could help ye that I know of; he passed through only days ago and I know which direction he was headed. His name is Gailon, and he knows much that has been, what is passing and it is said what may be. Ye would be wise to seek his help. He is very old and I have heard it said that he was actually a member of Shénnin and Tuâth's household, before its destruction and the coming of the dark times.'

She smiled at their puzzled expressions and chuckled to herself.

'Yes, that makes him very old, does it not? But he has learnt the art of prolonging life by use of majick. There are few now that possess such knowledge. Seek him out. He will know if ye are indeed Exzalander and he will be able to guide ye—all of ye. But let me give ye this warning. Do not tell *anyone* what ye know or believe; such an admission could place ye in great danger. If the Lord Katahl suspects yer return, he will muster all his power in order to bring about yer destruction, lest he should be destroyed himself. It will matter not that ye have no memory; he will be unwilling to take the risk. He kills at a whim—man, woman or child. His wrath would be great indeed toward one who has hinted to be his mortal enemy. Therefore, be wary. Trust nobody. Find Gailon; he will know what is best to be done.'

Kirsten's mind was awash with confusion. *This can't be happening,* she thought. She suspected that she had actually been dreaming, that she had been in an accident and had a brain haemorrhage. *It must have occurred when I collapsed during the news forecast,* she reasoned. *I didn't actually wake up and I'm lying in a hospital somewhere, my father and perhaps even Geri at my side. That would mean that Tom and Troy are figments of my imagination, along with Meggan and Katahl and the creature that killed Caitul, who incidentally, is not Caitul but a psychotic killer who is being tracked down by Interpol.*

So what has happened? A coma is a serious thing. Am I going to die? My condition probably isn't stable; so much has been reflected in my dreams ... Caitul's attack ... the inspector's attack ... the monster ... the men at the inn ... So much violence. All signs that my body is destabilising as I struggle to fight, just as the medical staff are fighting not to lose me. That could explain the lights, the place where I floated and felt peaceful. I had a near-death experience and they pulled me back, but my condition has deteriorated, because now my mind has brought me here.

Maldahl—a fictional world created by my own brain, as it struggles against the bleed on the brain that has led to my prolonged sleep.

So, what should I do now? Is it right to play along with these images? Will acting out my dreams help me to find a way home or will they push me deeper into my subconscious until I am lost forever? Perhaps I should simply ignore events, listen for the voice of my father, and try to get back to him—back to reality. It's odd though, that despite my confusion, I do feel more at home here, but then I suppose that I should, if this place is part of my own mind.

'Kirsten?' Troy raised his voice, as if he was repeating himself, touching her shoulder to draw her attention.

'Leave me alone,' she replied, pushing his hand away. 'You're not real—any of you, and I refuse to play this game any longer.' She jumped to her feet and made for the door, thinking such a rejection of her companions might bring her a step closer to getting back.

She was wrong. Troy and Tom were at her side in an instant. The sun seemed brighter than ever, after their spell indoors. Kirsten fell to her knees and clasped her hands over her ears, blocking out their words. She called out with her mind to her father.

Nothing.

Refocusing her energy, she tried again, attempting to open her eyes and see him, to contact him and let him know not to switch off the machine.

It was not a hospital bed that she saw. Her father was at home; Lisa was by his side and comforted him while he wept. Kirsten urged him to return to the hospital, to be there when she woke. A police officer stepped into view and sat beside them, shaking his head. They were talking, but she could not hear what was said. Her focus fell on a small pile of discarded newspapers on the coffee table.

LOCAL PRIEST SUSPECTED OF BLACK MAGIC, AS THREE MYSTERIOUSLY DISAPPEAR IN CHURCH.

Another read, POOF THE MAGIC DEMON, and another, MIRACLE OR VANISHING ACT?

The print began to blur and the scene faded, until Kirsten saw only grass before her overhung head. She reeled forward, struggling to breathe. Troy rubbed her back and spoke in a soothing tone.

Well, I tried to wake up, she thought, *and I caught a glance of the world without my being in it. What does it mean? Probably nothing. I'm simply not strong enough to wake up yet.*

'Come on, Kirsten, snap out of it,' Tom said.

He shook her by the shoulders, none too gently.

'The first explanation we get and you flip out on us. Now pull yourself together!' he ordered.

'None of this is real,' she snapped. 'You, him, her, this whole place; it's not real. I refuse to believe it any longer. I'm going to sit here and wait until it's time to go home.'

The inspector huffed. 'Well that's just bloody wonderful that is! Do you hear that, Troy? She thinks we're not real. Gee great, so will you just wake up then *Alice* so I can go *fucking home!*'

She winced, as his anger hit her like a wave. Troy immediately stepped up in effort to calm the inspector down.

'Please Tom; losing your temper with her is not going to help matters. She's confused; it's a lot to take in. I myself am having difficulty believing the situation, but until we can find any reason or other explanation I suggest that we take things as they come, and that means continuing under the premise that Kirsten is this person who was banished from here three centuries ago.'

Meggan approached and bent stiffly before Kirsten, holding out a steaming infusion to her.

'Here, drink this. It will calm ye.'

Kirsten accepted the mug with a weary nod.

'You must not distress yerself, child; it will do ye or yer friends no good. Ye must learn to accept yer situation or else ye will be lost, belonging neither in the other world or Maldahl.'

Kirsten felt instantly lighter on sipping the tea and wondered if it had been drugged. She supposed that it had; it was the woman's trade after all, creating medicines for all ailments. Kirsten looked up into Meggan's bright eyes and found strength there. Meggan believed that she belonged in Maldahl and there seemed little else she could do but go along with the illusion. Her companions were unwilling to allow her simply to give up.

'Where are we most likely to find this Gailon?' she asked. Her voice sounded drained.

The woman got unsteadily to her feet; Tom helped her as she tottered slightly.

'Thank ye laddie,' she said, holding his arm. 'Gailon did not tell me where he was going, but he took a path northwest. There is an inn beyond the hills in Freya Valley, about two days march from here; ye may find him there. If not, then ask the innkeeper's wife, Sally. I treated her baby a while back. Mention my name and she will assist ye, if she can.'

'But what will we do if we cannot find Gailon?' Tom asked.

Meggan seemed to stand suddenly tall. Her face seemed younger and slightly menacing and the companions wondered whether it was a trick of the light, as the sun passed behind the clouds.

'My dear, that ye must do, for what do ye expect? That ye will live out yer lives in Golstur or even Ishtar? If ye wish to go home then find him ye will, for apart from Katahl himself, Gailon may be the only man left in Maldahl, powerful enough to send ye back.'

Her words seemed to be all the encouragement the inspector needed and he immediately went to fetch the horses, which were happily grazing in the field to the rear of the house.

'Northwest you say? Then I think we had better get moving. This Gailon already has a head start on us and he knows the country whereas we do not.'

Troy helped Kirsten to her feet. She looked tired and older; her eyes were sunken, as though she had not slept, and her face was pale.

'Thank you Meggan, how may we repay you?' Troy said, trying to sound cheerful.

She looked at the weakened form of the girl who was supposed to destroy Katahl.

'Fulfil yer destiny,' she whispered, and with that, turned back to the house.

Kirsten put up little objection to riding Troy's horse, and he watched with increasing worry as she mounted the beast, a far away look upon her weary face. He led the horse in tow of Tom, glancing up frequently to determine if her fragile form made any improvement.

With every mile that passed, Kirsten became more distant, as if her mind had no wish to return. Troy let go of the reins and strode up to Tom. The horse followed obediently behind its leader.

'Tom,' he said, 'I'm worried about Kirsten. She's not herself.'

The inspector gave an ironic glance and resisted the temptation to say *'no shit, Sherlock, where have you been for the past couple of days?'*

'Probably in shock,' he huffed. 'It'll wear off I expect. Then she'll be back to her annoying, troublesome self again. I shouldn't worry.'

He glanced back over his shoulder. Kirsten's face looked almost grey and her body seemed shrunken. The inspector feared that she was ill, but he was so eager to press on that he was unwilling to rest. *The sooner we find Gailon, the better,* he decided.

Troy attempted to get Kirsten to eat while they journeyed, but she refused. After a while, the hills were no longer pleasant to climb; they grew steep and rocky. The horses began to tire and they decided it was best to take a break. Tethering the beasts next to a stream at the bottom of a hill, they sat beneath the boughs of the trees.

Kirsten remained silent as she ate and drank. The men left her to brood while they discussed their journey and refilled the water bottles.

'By George, did you see the size of that fish?' Tom said. 'I wish I had my rod and tackle with me; we could be eating fresh fish for supper rather than bread and cheese.'

'Oh stop it! You're making me hungry too.' Troy said. 'Will you listen to us ... we go from dying in the desert to complaining because we want a change of diet.' He looked over his shoulder to see if Kirsten had smiled; she seemed not to hear.

Troy's supposition was incorrect; she had taken in the entire conversation, only failed to find any amusement. She wondered why she had bothered to eat at all, when the food was not real. Her stomach had rumbled so she appeased it the only way that she knew how. She missed food as well, and found she craved a huge plate of chips, swimming in vinegar topped with lethal amounts of salt and lightly decorated with a strong brown sauce

Gazing up at the men, Kirsten discovered that they were trying to lance the fish with small branches. She sighed and looked about her. The place in which they had settled was picturesque, the different greens of trees and grass as vibrant as an artist's paints. A patch of what looked like bluebells lay to her left, but they were literally as their name suggests, a deep royal blue that glistened as the sunlight hit them from where it sifted through the branches overhead. The grass beneath was soft and springy, smelling of summer.

Kirsten watched their clumsy attempts as they stabbed at the water, the fishes darting with ease, away from their oncoming blows. She got to her feet and fixed nosebags to the horses, which munched gratefully. Patting them, she felt the urge to hurry the men along. She wondered if they planned to spend the entire day fishing in such a crude manner. Her body twitched and she heard the horses neigh, as they backed away from her. Marching over to the water, she plunged a hand into its refreshing depths.

'Good Lord! Tom exclaimed.

The water fizzed briefly and several fish floated to the surface—dead.

Troy felt his hairs on end and was unsure whether it was the current in the water or the event itself that had caused it.

'You wanted fish?' Kirsten said blankly. 'I suggest that you collect them before they float away.' She felt weak and drained and cupped her hand to take draughts of the water.

'I *knew* it!' spat Tom. 'I knew it was you who electrocuted Walker.'

Kirsten backed away and lay on the bank, feeling dizzy. 'I don't know what you're talking about,' she muttered.

Watching the sun, as it glittered in small beams through the leaves above, she felt an urge to doze in the peaceful setting. She was vaguely aware of Tom's angry face over her, before she drifted into slumber.

Ten

Kirsten awoke to the smell of fish in her nostrils and an ache in her head. The day seemed to approach late afternoon and she felt disorientated, neither remembering why she had fallen asleep nor understanding why she had been permitted to remain so during valuable travelling time. Her bleary eyes settled on the nearby fire, where a makeshift spit had been made and the two men were busy cooking and eating fish. She removed Troy's cloak, which had been wrapped about her, and approached the company, her limbs feeling tired and stiff. The men were deep in conversation and failed to notice her approach, until she stood directly over them.

'Kirsten you're awake,' Troy said happily. 'Come, sit with us and have something to eat.'

Kirsten cautiously eyed Tom, judging his mood before sitting between them. The inspector stared at the flames, refusing to acknowledge her. She accepted the fish on a stick and munched it thoughtfully.

'I didn't mean to harm Walker,' she said. 'I didn't realise that it was *me* who hurt him.'

'And that's supposed to make it okay, is it?' Tom growled.

'No, I guess not, I'm sorry.'

'Don't be sorry to me, be sorry for Walker. The last time I saw him, he was in a coma and had lost the ability to breathe for himself.'

Kirsten put down the food and walked away from the fire. She petted the horses, wondering why she felt so guilty when she believed none of it to be real anyhow. She felt light-headed and sleepy and wondered whether that was a good thing. *Perhaps I am closer to waking because of the incident,* she thought. *Perhaps it signifies some sort of treatment is being administered.*

Stroking the piebald horse, she loosened the reins with her other hand, aware that Troy was watching her. She assumed that Tom had told him what had happened to Walker. *I don't care,* she thought bitterly. *I just want to be away from this madness.*

Without warning, she sprang onto the horse's back, kicking him into motion. Before her companions could reach her, she sped off up the path through the woods, the shout of Troy and Tom ever diminishing behind her.

Kirsten was out of sight by the time they had un-tethered the remaining horse.

'How are we going to catch her?' Troy said. 'The horse won't take both our weight.'

'I'll ride ahead and you pack our things and follow. If the road splits, I'll leave a sign to indicate which path I took.'

The priest nodded in agreement, standing back as Tom mounted, speeding off after Kirsten. He hastily packed their things and stamped out the fire, and then swinging the bag over his shoulder, he rushed down the path after his friends.

The wood through which she rode, grew on a large hill and the path climbed ever upward. Kirsten failed to notice; she urged the horse on, as if she could ride forever if that is what it took to get back to reality.

Tom reached a dilemma; he had not expected Kirsten to be such a good rider. She had sped off like a lightning bolt, leaving him unsure which path she had taken. He dismounted and looked carefully for tracks. One path wound left seeming to lead out of the wood back into the smaller hills, westward. The other path led north, straight up and odd-looking hill whose soil was like fine ash. He could see no horse tracks on either path and so reasoned that she had headed north, as tracks dispersed as soon as made in the fine earth. He looked about him for a way of signalling to Troy, aware that every second that passed was precious. He saw a fallen branch, brittle and dead. Picking it up, he pushed it deep into the grey soil in the centre of the path, hoping it would not fall from its position before Troy saw it. He mounted his horse once more and began to trot forward gazing back to check his marker, before he broke into a canter. It remained unmoved and stood like a deformed sapling in the strange ground.

Kirsten brought the horse to a sudden halt and it spluttered at her in a bad tempered manner. She blinked, unable to believe her eyes, and then worried again that she had slipped further into her subconscious and would be unable to wake from the dream.

Before her lay a huge crater, spreading miles in each direction to the centre of which, lay a vast city with tall beautiful buildings, some of which glittered in the sunset; several actually reflecting the sunlight, as if mirrored panels had been placed on the outer walls.

At first, she failed to hear galloping hooves coming up the path behind her, so lost in wonderment was she.

Troy trudged on, wishing that he had been proficient enough on horseback to ride after Kirsten. The sun was beginning to set and he was struck by a sudden fear of losing his companions. He had no desire to be left alone in the bizarre world.

'Good Lord!' Tom exclaimed, when he realised what had caused Kirsten to stop.

She faced him, not caring if he was angry.

'None of this is real,' she said.

Tom's voice softened and he touched Kirsten lightly on the arm. His change of temperament disconcerted rather than soothed her.

'Do you not think, Kirsten, that we have considered the same possibilities? Thinking any time now, I'll wake up, or I've been involved in an accident. Maybe I'm dead and there is no heaven, or perhaps this is purgatory, to be stuck here with you.'

He gave a sly smile and to his surprise, she let out a single ironic laugh.

'But how do I know that I'm not in hospital?' she replied. 'I *was* ill. I did collapse. Maybe I didn't wake up. You can't prove that you're real.'

'No, and neither can you. I had a thought similar to yours, that when I wake up, my family will be at my side and I'll discover that their leaving was part of my illness. But Kirsten, it's not going to happen. My arm is bruised from the amount of times I've pinched it and I haven't woken up. You've got to pull yourself together. It's a lot for us all to take in but it's like Troy said—we're in this together.'

She could feel the warmth of the horse beneath her, its silky hair; she could smell the evening air and hear the birds in their roost. It felt more real than any dream, and yet she still doubted its actuality.

'Kirsten, retain your doubts if you must, but you cannot allow them to endanger yourself, or us. Because if Maldahl is real then you may find it hard to forgive yourself, or you may find yourself dead.'

Kirsten nodded, wishing the man could be that reasonable with her all the time.

The moon shone pale on the path ahead, making it glisten in a most unnatural fashion. Troy stepped up to the peculiar marker in the road, threw the branch aside and headed upwards. The air grew colder, but he failed to notice. All about him seemed unreal. The strange grey earth glowed and shimmered, unnerving him. He continued on, trance-like, believing that he could hear his name on the breeze, yet there was no wind. He felt as though he had wandered for hours—lost.

The branches grew thicker and spiny, until movement became difficult. Thorns tore into his flesh at thigh and arm, which was enough to bring his focus back. Looking about him, he realised that he had strayed from the path. He plucked himself free from the thorny bush and winced at the pain from his wounds. Turning one hundred and eighty degrees, he decided that direction should lead him back to where he was meant to be.

The voices that he thought he had imagined, grew clearer and he hurried through the thick tree and bushes, feeling sure that he did not want to meet their maker. The sounds of tramping feet and snapping twigs came to his ears, followed by a high-pitched laughter that burst suddenly forth into a strange song. He felt drawn again and his fear was forgotten as he headed toward the singing.

Kirsten had agreed to ride back down the path with both horses while Tom waited at the top of the crater overlooking the magnificent city. A growing sense of unease came upon her; the path before her was bathed in peculiar light, and a sudden cry confirmed her need for caution.

Troy yelled, as an unseen throng swept him up. He heard muttering voices all about him and the trees seemed to part at the host's coming. He shouted again, when what felt like fingernails raked his skin, tearing into him. He struggled to break free, but that only made them hurt him more.

As Troy yelled for a second time, Kirsten galloped toward the sound. An immense ball of light was before her eyes and she saw a mass of tiny humanoid beings with small wicked faces, whose eyes glinted in the luminescent light that seemed to surround their company. Some were naked, others wrapped in leaves and twigs, which appeared to grow from their delicate bodies rather than adorn them. Kirsten spied the struggling form of Troy, as he was carried above their heads. A wind seemed to gather about them and they began to lift off the ground.

'STOP!' Kirsten heard herself shout.

The host came to a halt, more out of surprise than obedience.

'Who dares delay our cavalcade?' The voice belonged to a larger one of the beings, who wore a crown of leaves and twigs.

'My name is Kirsten, and you hold there my friend. I would wish that you free him.'

The little man planted his feet and spat. 'YOU WOULD *WISH*, WOULD YOU? What do you think we are, for you to make wishes of us? Away with you or sure enough, you will join our cavalcade and we will feast upon you *and* your friend at journey's end.

Kirsten was unsure whether she had heard him correctly. He said that he meant to *eat* them. She drew her sword and many of the small folk backed away.

'I have no wish to harm you,' she said, 'but I cannot allow you to take my friend.'

A small green faerie hissed at the leader, 'My king, see her sword. Surely it is the blade ...'

'Silence!' the king interrupted, then directed his attention back to her. '*You*, go now, but leave the horses; they will be part of our banquet at the end of our procession. Now go, child!'

'My king she is no child,' said the faerie. 'Surely, you can see that she is older than many of us. She is surrounded by ...'

'ENOUGH I SAY!' the king yelled at his subject.

Kirsten moved forward a step and several faeries hid themselves, surrounding her in whispers. She seemed herself bathed in the strange light, and yet no faerie touched her.

'Why would you take *him* and not me, Lord?' she asked.

The faerie king was impressed at the respect in her address, although such appreciation was not displayed in his reply.

'I have no desire to talk with you; begone,' he ordered.

The air blew cold and Kirsten feared that Troy would be whisked away on the faerie wind. She made a grab for the king, but instead caught the green spritely-looking faerie who dived in front of his liege. The host halted its retreat and silence fell amongst the crowd, making Kirsten acutely aware that she had committed a great taboo. She heard Troy's entreaty, figuring he had probably been praying the entire time of his captivity.

'Take heed, human; you do not want this one back,' the king warned. 'He will bring great danger; *that* I can foresee. He has some power with him, a perilous power. This I have witnessed before and many of my people were exiled or destroyed as it swept across one of our most beloved homes, like a pestilence. Listen now, as he chants in attempt to aid him. Let us have him and the luck of this cavalcade will go with you.'

'I thank you, Lord King for your concern, but he is my friend and I have need of him, just as I am sure that you have need for this fellow. She hoisted up the struggling form of the faerie, who seemed to grow more fearful as she held him to her face.

'What do you know of my sword?' she asked.

The king fidgeted and made the answer for his subject.

'It is the blade forged in Taiohãhn's kingdom. It is not of this world, but this you already know; now let him go.'

Troy had stopped praying and noticed Kirsten, as if a spell had been lifted from his eyes.

'Kirsten, what's going on?' he asked. 'What are all those voices?'

Kirsten frowned in confusion and looked to the king.

'He cannot see us,' explained the faerie king. 'None of his kind can.'

'So how comes it that I may see you?'

He laughed. It was a shrill sound, painful to her ears. 'You think yourself human?' he said. 'You travel further than our clan ever could and have practised such majicks unknown to our kind and you ask me that? Go. Take your friend. I have lost my appetite. Release Cob and go now. I have no desire to converse with you further.'

Kirsten's head swam. It was as though he had opened a floodgate in her mind that shut tight almost immediately. Carefully, she placed Cob on the ground and Troy scrambled over to her, bleeding and bruised. Cob approached his people, but they kept their distance from him.

'You are the Macara Shee,' she said thoughtfully.

The faeries looked to her, expectant. The king nodded.

'Long time has it been since I heard us called thus. It seems our majick helps to free your mind. There is more in there than you know. One of my kind has put a lock on your memory; for what reason, I know not. Now, we must depart.'

'One thing more before you go, king,' Kirsten said. 'When we leave the cavalcade, will we have been infected by faerie time?'

There were several shouts of indignation.

'Please forgive the reference, I meant no disrespect by the use of such a word, but it is vital that we return to the exact moment that we left.'

'PAH!'

The king clapped his hands and the Macara Shee disappeared on the wind. Kirsten blinked for a moment, wondering why their surroundings seemed suddenly brighter when she had expected quite the reverse.

Troy felt cold and fought back chattering teeth. 'Have they gone?' he asked weakly.

'Yes,' Kirsten replied. She turned sharply to see if they had left them the horses.

'What did you mean by faerie time?'

Kirsten helped Troy to his feet and ran over to the horses.

'The passage of time in the realm of faerie differs from our own,' she explained. 'It is said that hundreds of our years may pass in the space of a few hours in their domain. So, you can understand my concern. We were about an hour with the Macara Shee and so fifty or sixty years may have passed. Tom would most likely be dead and Gailon too, knowing our luck. Katahl would have probably conquered the entire world and where does that leave us?'

Troy's form sagged on his horse, hoping beyond hope that the faeries would have shown mercy on them.

'How is that you know so much about faeries, anyhow?'

Kirsten shrugged. 'I don't know, Troy. Their king said that there is some kind of lock in my mind. All I know is, for a moment back there I had the strongest feeling that I had met them before.'

Nothing much seemed to have changed, except that it was a lot lighter. Kirsten's concern grew when she realised the sun was setting, proving that a discontinuity in time had indeed occurred. When they reached the edge of the crater, it was no surprise to Kirsten, to discover that Tom was not there. She felt tired and Troy looked ready to drop. Small stains of dry blood stuck to his black shirt.

As he sat looking down at the city below them, Kirsten fetched her pack of medicine and applied a marmite looking ointment and a few drops of the purple lavender smelling oil to treat Troy's scratches and bruising. She sensed, before she heard, a horse coming up the trail behind and jumped to her feet, dragging their horses off the path.

'What's wrong?' Troy asked, as he followed her under cover.

'Sshh!' she hissed back at him.

Troy let out a gasp of astonishment when he saw Kirsten ride to the rim of the crater and pause. Kirsten turned to Troy and whispered.

'Don't panic. We're in the past. The faerie king sent us back a little too early. All we have to do is wait until I ride off to find *you*.' Although she had said not to panic, the reality of the situation seeped in and she could feel her hands trembling with fright at having to watch herself in such a way. She fought to get a grip on her fear, and began to imagine what would happen if she changed history.

Troy felt claustrophobic in their hiding place. The horses too became restless and he wondered what would happen if they were discovered. Kirsten, on the other hand, had a growing desire to communicate with herself.

If I can only give me warning about the Macara Shee, then perhaps I might find out more information from them, she thought. *Perhaps I can take my place and ride down again to question the host.*

She made a movement and Troy stopped her.

'What are you doing?' he whispered. 'Anything you do now, might prevent my rescue. You must let history play out.'

He was right, but she wished that she could risk it anyhow. They watched as Tom rode up and spoke to her. Troy nudged her and smiled when he saw how nice Tom was being. It seemed like an age since they hid there and willed Kirsten to make her move. They watched in anticipation as Tom dismounted and took down the food pack and Kirsten rode off down the trail.

'Finally,' Troy whispered.

They emerged from the bushes, eager for a share in the vittles. Tom's reaction was swift and unexpected, as his huge double-edged sword was unsheathed and pointed toward them. He appeared puzzled and kept the weapon pointed their way.

'How did you get up here so fast? It's not possible.'

Troy took on his most priest-like voice. 'Tom, Tom, calm yourself. There is a perfectly good explanation, if somewhat fantastic.'

Tom looked at the patches of goo covering the priest's many wounds.

'Well out with it!' he barked, 'How did you manage to arrive just after me when you were on foot, and what the hell happened to you? You look dreadful.'

'I was attacked by faeries,' Troy said.

Kirsten smiled, thinking that the explanation had not been as complicated as she had envisioned it.

'I think we should move on,' she suggested. 'We don't want to risk running into ourselves.'

Tom shook his head, clearly confused.

'As long as we don't go down that path then we should be fine,' reasoned Troy. 'I don't know about you guys but I'd like a nice warm bed for the night' He stifled a yawn. 'What say we go down into the city and find an inn?'

It was Tom who seemed in doubt. 'Meggan said that we were to head to the valley to find Gailon. What would be the point in staying here?'

Kirsten gazed back down the moonlit path, considering what might happen if they ran into the faerie horde again.

'We can head for the hills again first thing tomorrow. I think it may be wise to get out of these woods until daylight. Troy barely escaped with his life, and I am convinced that he only did so because he is a priest and they felt it would influence the way he tastes. I doubt they would have any qualms about eating *you*.'

Smiling, she handed the horses to Troy and began her descent. Tom grunted and snatched the reins from Troy, leading his horse down to the glittering city below.

Eleven

As in Golstur, Kirsten was careful to swathe herself in her cloak to avoid the curiosity of onlookers. At Tom's suggestion, they chose an inn on the westward side of the city, to enable them an easier route come morning. The establishment he chose was so battered, that Troy found himself wondering if it was safe to sleep there, for fear of the building collapsing before the night was out.

Tom made arrangements with the innkeeper and soon they were all settling down to a late meal. Kirsten was wary of the meat; part of its ribcage was still attached; she had always been a bit hypocritical when it came to eating meat. She liked it, but did not like to be reminded where it came from, and that meant avoiding eating meat still attached to the bone. She ate the vegetables and was delighted to find that although yellow, the large mango-shaped vegetable tasted much like potato. She smiled, thinking she might be able to have chips in Maldahl after all.

The innkeeper apologised for the delay in seeing them to their rooms, explaining they were very busy and had no room free with three beds in. After waffling on for a good few minutes, he offered them a round of drinks on the house to compensate for the inconvenience. Tom and Troy seemed most gratified, but due to her previous experience, Kirsten remained wary. She pulled the hood of her cloak so far over her face that all she could see were feet. The atmosphere was hot and smoky and the room echoed with merry speech and laughter.

The companions sat at a table to the rear, around a corner. Kirsten became aware of the different voices about the room; her companions as they chatted about Troy's brush with death, and the barmaids as they bustled around collecting tankards and taking new orders. A new party seated themselves close by and Kirsten found herself peaking from beneath her cloak to see what manner of man would have such a sweet voice.

The newcomers were four in total; two had their backs to her and spoke to a young man who sat opposite them. Kirsten listened intently, trying to determine which one had caught her attention. A younger man with large eyes seemed a good candidate, until he spoke and Kirsten realised that his voice did not match his features; it was deep and almost jarring—the complete opposite to his child-like features. Next to him, sat a raven-haired man with a peculiarly, yet comely, long angular face, wearing a dark green leather doublet. The other taller man was elderly with long grey hair that fell neatly across his cloaked back. Beside him, sat a shorter brown-haired man who was carrying the main thread of their conversation; it was plain to Kirsten that it was not his voice that had caught her notice.

A joke was made, to which they all laughed and Kirsten felt her cautiousness slip away. The voice had sounded again, so melodious that it made her want to dance. She looked at them each in turn, discerning it was the man in green who had peeked her interest. She could not help but stare at him, wondering if he were really man at all; it was then that she noticed his ears, wondering if it was a trick of the light, for they seemed to be pointed. As she stared, she noticed that the man beside him stared curiously back in her direction and she suddenly bowed her head, to avoid his gaze.

From the four of them, he alone was silent, his soulful eyes lost somewhere where his direction of thoughts roamed. Kirsten realised that she could see him quite clearly in her mind; she had no need for her eyes. He stared in her direction, appearing to look through the cloak until at last they faced one another. Their surroundings faded along with the noise, leaving only Kirsten and the strange young man, gazing at each other, neither daring to blink for fear of losing the image before them.

It was a while before Kirsten did anything, so lost in wonderment was she. When she finally tried to speak, she found it difficult. They were locked in each other's minds; merely opening her mouth to communicate was not enough; she had to reach out with her thoughts and let her words find him.

'Hello,' she ventured.

It was too much for the man. Daydreaming was one thing, but visions were quite another. He jumped back to reality, knocking a tankard of ale as he did so.

'Is everything all right, Ioan?'

'Yes Gailon, I am sorry; I think that I may have drifted off there,' the young man said.

'Indeed? It has been a long day. We shall retire in a while, my friend.'

Ioan made no reply. He was staring into the shadowed face of Kirsten, as she relinquished her caution in order to spy on the old man.

Can it be, that this is the man we seek? she considered. *He is in the wrong place if it is, for this is not the inn in the valley that Meggan directed us to.*

She listened intently, but a sudden burst of noise from her companions drowned out their voices. She felt her body trembling, wondering if she should approach the table. However, with such a need for secrecy, she was unsure how she would she explain herself. *Besides,* 'she thought, *who is to say the old man is **the** Gailon? Meggan did not say that he had travelling companions. For all I know, the name Gailon could be as common here as John is back home.*

Ioan continued to stare, convinced that within the folds of the cloak was the woman who had spoken to him. Despite the shadows, her eyes continued to speak, whenever she glanced his way. Kirsten, aware of his attention let her guard down and held his gaze, trying once more to let their thoughts meet.

'Do not be afraid, Ioan. I am a friend. I have need of your help if you are willing.'

'What is it you wish of me, lady?' he replied, no longer startled.

'Answer my question, if you can. The old man in your party, is he the same Gailon that lived at the court of Shénnin and Tuâth?'

Ioan paused before his answer. 'I know not,' he said. 'It is true that Gailon is indeed very old and he has seen much of history that we hear of only in tales. I am sorry that I cannot be more help to you, fair lady.'

His troubled voice seemed to fill her with courage and she immediately brightened at his apology. The effect was strange, as though they were somehow connected—bonded. She was unsure how she knew, but she felt certain that she could trust the stranger implicitly. However, she did not throw all caution to the wind, on her reply.

'I thank you, sir, for your concern. Perhaps I should explain myself. I was told to seek a wise man by the name of Gailon. It is said that this man is powerful in wizardry. I do not seek his majick though, merely advice that his length of years can offer.'

'I am sure, Milady, that Gailon will be willing to speak with you. But why do you not approach him yourself?'

'I have need for … caution. I would have spoken to him thus, had this not been a completely new experience for me. I thought that it might have been yourself who had connected our minds.'

Ioan laughed at her suggestion and his deep voice enriched—a joyous sound that warmed her to the core.

'I have no majick in me, lady; you tease me surely.'

The clarity of his face began to fade until she was looking at him once more across the smoky room.

'I think you had best retire, my friend,' Gailon suggested. 'You're falling asleep where you sit. Come, I will see you to the room. I am feeling a tad sleepy myself.'

The two men rose from their seats and bade their companions, goodnight; as they passed, Ioan shot a glance her way.

Kristen's heart was jumping. *Now's my chance to speak to Gailon,* she decided. She stood up, informing Tom and Troy she was going to check on the room situation and slipped out after Gailon and Ioan. Her attention remained fixed on the two ahead of her, oblivious to their remaining companions, who had noticed her follow their friends and also observed the sword protruding from the back of her cloak.

Kirsten crept up the stairs and watched which door the men entered, before striding after them and knocking lightly. She felt foolish, thinking it most likely that she was mistaken and they would dismiss her as a mad woman. The door opened and Ioan stood there, smiling pleasantly up at her.

'Who is it?' the gruff voice of Gailon stabbed in their direction.

Something sharp touched her back and prodded her forward.

'Yes, I am sure we would all like to know that, sir. Come, reveal yourself and explain why you have followed our friends to their room—armed as heavily as you are.'

The raven-haired man pushed her forward and the shorter, stout companion stood firmly with his sword drawn, fire burning in his brown eyes.

If Kirsten felt foolish before, she felt even more so at that moment; she had not intended to reveal her identity to an audience. Feeling a surge of panic, she realised that it was four against one. She was alone in their room and once again, blood might be shed.

Gailon faced her and Ioan desperately tugged at his sleeve.

'Gailon, she's a friend,' he urged. 'She wishes to speak with you.'

'She?' The man with the exquisite voice released the pressure from the blade.

Kirsten did not know what to do. Slowly, she removed the hood from her face and looked at Gailon. The blade was pulled away altogether and Kirsten found herself intrigued by the expression on Gailon's face; if she had not known better, she would have said that he knew her.

'I was sent by Meggan to seek Gailon,' she stuttered. 'I am in need of help … I … Do you know me, sir? I cannot help but notice the strangeness of your manner.'

'It cannot be …' Gailon muttered in astonishment.

All the party moved to see her fully and she felt her face blush at their scrutiny. Both Gailon and the raven-haired man had recognition in their eyes and she could not help it; she opened her mouth and the words poured out of her. She had not planned to say them; it was as though someone else was speaking and although she heard the words, she had no control over their making.

'My name is Exzalander,' she said. 'I have returned. I am in need of counsel and so turn to you, for I do not know where to go or what I am to do. I remember … nothing.'

The raven-haired man spoke first. 'If there was any doubt of the truth of her words, as she has not been struck dead, see Gailon, she has the sword of Taiohãhn.'

'I have looked upon it, Cröedaw, but had I not, then I would still know her to be the princess, for she looks the same as she did in the weeks before her banishment.'

Ioan's amazement switched from Kirsten to Gailon.

'You were actually there?' he asked.

Gailon stepped toward her trembling form. He was indeed the man she had sought. She felt overwhelmed and sinking to her knees, she wept. Gailon held out his aged hand, a large silver ring was upon it and a magnificent green gem set in a steel cage, sparkled in welcome.

'Come my child, you are not alone. We are here to help you in any way that we can.'

Kirsten rose to her feet and without warning, threw her arms around the old man, grateful for his support. She drew away from him and noticed a look of surprise, as he backed away. Kirsten knew why he had done so and put on her most reassuring tone.

'This is the appearance of the person I have been on another world. Her name is Kirsten. I have been travelling thus and will continue to do so, for if you can recognise me then so too can the enemy. Besides, I am more accustomed to this visage; Exzalander is still a stranger to me.'

Gailon gave a wry smile. 'My dear, I think it a wise move on your part; not only to avoid detection, but also with every day that passes that you manage to hold this form, your power will increase. I foresee a time when your disguise will prove most valuable to you and our cause.'

Kirsten's mind considered his words regarding power. She thought of her mind reading and second sight, the electrical charge and the metamorphosis. She had pushed such feats from her head, but it occurred to her then that she was meant to be able to perform them. She glanced up at Ioan whose large brown eyes continued to stare. He blushed suddenly.

'Thank you my friend,' her mind whispered to his.

The shortest of the companions, seemed a lot less in awe of her than the rest of the party. He scowled suspiciously up at her, as if suspecting her of bewitching his friend with some evil spell.

Ioan's voice spoke softly, as he introduced them. 'This is Tehd. We are friends from the village of Landsby.'

'It's nice to meet you, Tehd.' Kirsten ventured.

'Likewise I'm sure,' he replied, making it very plain that he disliked her.

The other man stepped forward and took Kirsten's hand, kissing it.

'Forgive me, Milady, for my harsh treatment of you. I am Cröedaw, a forest dweller of the Elfin in the east; I am honoured to be here at the time of your return.'

So he isn't human after all, considered Kirsten. 'I too am honoured to meet you, all of you. I have so many questions, I hardly know where to begin.'

'I suggest then that we begin with sleep and leave all the questions until the light of day,' Gailon said. 'In the morning, we shall be travelling westward into Freya Valley, to meet with a friend of ours. There we will discuss what is the best course of action. Now Kirsten, do you have a room?'

Kirsten's thoughts returned to her companions and she realised that she had not informed them where she was going. 'I do and I should return to it at once,' she said, making toward the door. 'I will see you all tomorrow. Goodnight.' She beamed and skipped off before any of them could form an objection.

Once she had discovered which room they were to occupy, she entered, removing her belt and boots. Climbing into bed, she found herself longing for a nightgown. She was aware of the odour beginning to saturate her dress and considered how long it might be before she could get a change of clothing.

Her mind was buzzing with all manner of inconsequential thoughts before drifting back to Gailon and his party. She tried to avoid the thought of them, as her excitement kept sleep at bay.

It was some time later before her companions returned from their night's merry-making. They staggered through the door like a couple of old drunks, loudly shushing one another. Kirsten ignored them, deciding it was not the most suitable time to inform them about Gailon—far better to allow them to pass out and leave her to the peace of the night.

At sunrise, a cock crowed loudly. Kirsten awoke with a start from what seemed like the shortest and lightest sleep of her life; her companions slept on. She washed and readied herself while they snored away, none too quietly. Breakfast was brought to the room and still they slumbered. She shook Tom first, who seemed to be sleeping a little lighter than Troy. He awoke with a grunt; the smell of stale alcohol and other bodily odours caused Kirsten to step back from him in disgust.

'What the devil is it?' Tom grumbled. 'Why are you waking me this early, woman? … Is that bacon I can smell?'

He was up more quickly than Kirsten could have imagined possible, and tucking into the mammoth breakfast prepared for them. In the meantime, Kirsten's attempts to awaken Troy were proving unsuccessful. He merely snorted and shifted position.

'Why don't you leave him?' Tom spoke with a mouthful of food. 'He'll be a wreck if you wake him now. I don't understand why you wanted to get up this early anyhow.'

Kirsten huffed and stole a slice off bacon from the plate. 'I have met someone that we are to rendezvous with after breakfast. That is, what I mean to say is … Gailon,' she stammered. 'He's here, in this inn. I met with him last night.'

Kirsten had not even finished her sentence before Tom was on his feet and reaching for the water jug.

'Are you sure it was Gailon?'

'Yes, we spoke. He knows me.'

SPLASH.

Tom tipped the water over Troy, who groaned into waking, immediately clutching his head.

'Come on, Father. Grub's up,' Tom said.

'Leave me alone,' Troy groaned. He made a few inaudible sounds and put the pillow over his head.

Tom snatched it away and began coaxing him up, while Kirsten seated herself and continued to eat her fill. By the time the knock came at the door, Tom had managed to get Troy into a sitting position, but he was threatening to vomit. Kirsten answered the door and smiled nervously up at the bright face of Gailon.

'Good morning, Kirsten. I trust that you slept well.'

She greeted them all and ushered them in.

'These are my friends,' she ventured, frowning at the sickly dishevelled form of Troy. The two parties of men stared blankly at one another.

'Thomn-the-Cleaverhand!' Gailon exclaimed. 'So you made it after all!'

Tom stood at the strange greeting.

'No, it's *Tom*,' he corrected.

Kirsten felt as if a burden had suddenly lifted. 'So Tom is also from Maldahl!' she cried. 'He has been blaming me for his having been brought here.'

Gailon smiled, his age-old eyes glinting mischievously in the morning light. 'Well strictly speaking that is true of course, or perhaps it is more precise to say that Thomn would never have *left* Maldahl had it not been for you. However, it was his choice. He was the highest ranking Royal Guard left alive and insisted that it was his duty. And you, you must be the messenger, although I don't remember you looking in quite that sorry state when you embarked on your journey.'

There was a tinkering laugh from Cröedaw that send pleasant shivers down the length of Kirsten's spine, making her glad that he wasn't too chatty.

Troy's mind felt clouded over. He kept hearing snatches of strange conversation. The man with a beard had called him a messenger, stating that he too was from Maldahl. *How is that possible? I'm a priest on Earth,* he thought. He shook his head, as if it would clear the cobwebs.

Kirsten looked at Troy's grey features and watched him shaking his head. Sitting beside his sunken form, she put her arm around him, aware of several comments about her derogatory behaviour, but when she glanced up, she realised that they had been thoughts rather than voiced opinions. She knew she should be terrified at the realisation, but along with everything else that had occurred, mind reading seemed quite trivial.

'Troy, it's all right. We're all in this together. We all feel a little lost and we don't understand how this happened. But you have to try and keep it together, okay?'

He seemed barely to acknowledge her, but stared trance-like at the floor. He knew that she was speaking to him, as he could hear the soothing sound of her voice, yet no words. A heat spread rapidly from her fingers across his entire body, each part feeling instantly more alive. He thought that he heard a voice in his mind.

'Let's sort you out, shall we? You don't want to be a laughing stock, now do you?'

His head was tingling, as the fog cleared from his mind. Not only was his hangover gone, he felt so energetic that he could face the desert again with a smile if he had to. He looked up and immediately Kirsten released him, hoping that he would not mention what she had done; she had acted on instinct and did not want everyone to make a big deal out of the fact that she could cure hangovers. The party seated themselves, as it became apparent that they would not be going quite as soon as planned.

'So, I too am from Maldahl,' Troy said. 'You said that I was a messenger. What was my name?'

'That I do not know,' Gailon replied. 'You were just a messenger and a messenger would have no need of any name. You were sent to gather news and bring it back. After several years when you did not return, you were assumed dead. You see, you were to map the journey of Thomn, and it was planned that we might send more help if we could but establish a nearer location.'

'But how were we supposed to get back, Gailon?' Tom asked.

'Your mission was to find the princess and guard her, at all costs. There was no way for you to return unless the princess had found the power to do so. The messenger however, had been equipped with a powerful spell, cast by my master; he could have returned whenever he chose. It was thought that your memory had been lost, therefore you had forgot your mission, or that having found nothing you were too ashamed to return. In any case, after Katahl had turned, the people mostly forgot about you and resigned themselves to thinking that you would never come back.'

'But why were they sent at all,' Kirsten asked, 'if Katahl had sent Caitul to protect me?'

Gailon grunted. 'Caitul's mission was to bring you back to his master; we could not allow that to happen. Caitul, unaware of his Lord's alteration, would have surrendered you to Katahl, as was his duty; you would have been lost, as would we all. Even if Caitul had realised in time, the change in his master, he would still have relinquished the princess. For he was honour bound by an oath to Katahl and an oath is a sacred thing, being among the simplest of majicks and among the most powerful. To break an oath is perilous and even the strongest willed man would not dare.

'Before my master sent the captain and messenger, he recovered an ancient book of whose origin he said, was the forest of Tûlg. The book had been gathering dust in Tuâth's library at Ealdorbold. It was not until after the two of you had been sent, that he consulted it and realised his error. He hoped, for all our sakes, that you did not succeed too quickly, for if the princess was returned before passing through Taiohãhn's and Anarkhane's realms, then we would have lost our chance to defeat Katahl.'

'Who are they?' Kirsten asked.

'Anarkhane, is the deity of light, whose power over Maldahl was held in a stone, the gem of creation.'

Troy stood and walked abruptly toward the door. 'I'm not listening to this blasphemy,' he said. 'I worship the Almighty of which there is one and I will not hear tell of your heathen gods whom you proclaim to exist. I'll be readying the horses when you decide that you are ready to leave.'

Gailon's party stared in bewilderment to Kirsten and Tom, who shrugged uncomfortably.

Gailon cleared his throat and continued. 'Taiohãhn, as you may already know, is the deity of the Underworld. His influence over Maldahl was more suggestive and at its most powerful during the hours of darkness. He envied Anarkhane's stone and He quarrelled with Her saying that they should rule Maldahl equally. Taiohãhn's wrath caused great fireballs to fall from the sky in the east and much of the land was scorched into the great Bölva desert you see today. Anarkhane wept and rains fell for years in the west, which is why great marshes lie about your father's domain. During the battle, the stone shattered and the god's power over Maldahl was lost. Anarkhane cast the shards away, deeming them useless and in sorrow for what had occurred, She became a hermit in Her kingdom and was never seen again.

'Taiohãhn was sorely troubled for what He had done and He cast a spell that used much of His power in its making so that they were finally equal being able to exist in Maldahl on the edge of dreams. He gathered the remains of the great gem and set each of them in metal forged by His hand. It is believed that all items, but the sword, were sent to Maldahl in the hands of the ancient wizards, who held light and dark in balance. Each hid the stones, as ordered. The pendant and the ring, we already have in our possession.

'We know that one of the stones was set in a crown that belonged to an ancient Mo-Rye king, another is believed to reside with the Clan of the Dark Moon. The greatest of all the remains of course, you already know about; Taiohãhn set it in a sword of His making, claiming that Anarkhane would be sent a warrior whom She must train in the healing and majick arts. Only the warrior, who had been blessed by Anarkhane, would be received into His kingdom and presented the blade.

'With Maldahl lacking divine rule, the Dark Ones came and so put into motion a chain of events that would lead to its destruction, unless Taiohãhn's warrior prevents it.'

'So are you saying that I passed through these other kingdoms before I arrived here?' Kirsten asked.

'Yes, you would have had to in order for Taiohãhn to relinquish His sword to you. Besides, where do you think that you learned to wield it? Exzalander, apart from being the daughter of a king, was not very different from anyone else. It was through the Dark Ones' banishment of you that the prophecy was being fulfilled.'

'But why was I banished at all? I don't understand. Why did they not just kill me?'

'They would have lost Katahl. It was his hope that he might see you again that kept him from destroying himself, and it was his attempt to bring you back that allowed them to take control over him at last.

'You were also banished to ensure that you retrieve the sword of Taiohãhn, for they could not take it themselves. Their power existed in the chaos remaining from the fall of Anarkhane and Taiohãhn. Although losing His influence over Maldahl, Taiohãhn remains in control of the Underworld and they would not have dared invade there. Therefore, in order that the gem be restored, the sword would need to come back.'

'But why? Cröedaw cut in. If the Dark Ones had control, why would they need the gem of creation?'

'I cannot say for certain, but my master thought that the reasons the Dark Ones invaded and then left, was to ensure Maldahl found order once more. They had no desire for rule. They sought balance ensued from creating a new order. They set about recreating darkness by using Katahl, and light by sending Exzalander to train with the gods of old. Together, you would restore balance—for one cannot exist without the other. However, that is but one strand of the prophecy. As my master researched more deeply, he concluded that you were destined to *defeat* the darkness and only when you had obtained *divine* power would you be able to restore balance. Either way, it is the reunification of the stone that will ensure the future of Maldahl. Whomsoever possesses the stone will rule, absolute.

'You see, that is why Katahl did not conquer all. He is powerful yes, but without the stone, there will always be an army who is willing to stand against him.'

'Then it's the sword that's important and not *me,* at all,' Kirsten mumbled.

'No Kirsten, it was through your training that you were given the sword. The weapon is powerful and if it fell into the enemy's hands, it would go ill for us. However, while you live, there should not be a warrior alive able to take it from you. It is your duty to protect the part of the stone in your possession above all else; it is ours to seek the stones that are still missing, so that I may perform the ritual of reunification and Maldahl may be at peace once more.

'Our quest had already begun and is to take us to the Sealands, Dragon Mountains and Tûlg. It was decided that possessing four out of the five stones would be enough power to keep Katahl at bay, should he decide to order another attack on the outer-lands. It has been an age since he last did so and that attack cost us dear. Many tribes from The Tarian Hills came under his power and those peoples that did not submit were wiped out. But for the most he has seemed content to keep his domain small and well protected, although he did lay claim to Ishtar and Golstur, he never enforced any law or formed any government of his own, and the people there continue to follow the principles laid down by the Council of Shénnin.

'But he will attack again. He has not been idle. His army has taken long to create and he will use it and other means to take us piece by piece; day by day we grow closer to enslavement and most realise it not. Nobody cared when the peoples of Maldahl were captured or killed; they looked strange to each other and spoke differently. Nobody was willing to stand and fight with a stranger and so it will go ill for all of us I fear, unless we can stand together. He will take us a little at a time until there is nothing left to take, and growing bored with domination, he will destroy.

'But there, I feel I have talked long enough. I fear the messenger will be growing impatient. Come, we must depart. We will head west and meet with Thaniel, as originally planned. He will be so pleased to make your acquaintance. He will no doubt think that your arrival here more than a coincidence, considering our present mission.'

Gailon readied himself to depart. Tom and Kirsten grabbed their luggage, assisted by Cröedaw.

'But Gailon, how *did* we get here?' Kirsten asked. 'The last thing that I remember was some sort of monster trying to kill me; Caitul died protecting me.'

'Caitul? He reached you then.' Gailon stopped, seeming lost in thought.

'Yes, a week or so ago; I met Tom and Troy about the same time. But Caitul died, so how could *he* have sent us back?'

Gailon frowned. 'I wonder … he was not sent in the same way as you. He … no, if you saw him die, then dead he must be. At least let us hope so, for our sakes. It may have been the messenger who brought you back, although the spell he was equipped with should not have been powerful enough to bring three of you home. I doubt at least that it was the monster, which I think was the Trolg that Katahl sent to kill you, after the darkness took him. He had heard rumours of the CODM prophecy you see. It is meant to be the original text, dictated by Taiohãhn himself to one of the Vampire Ælf clans.

'After hearing of the prophecy, Katahl felt that he could not take the risk of your return. He would not have equipped the beast to bring you back; the thing's mission likely had been to find you and kill you. It is strange, however, that you all met within such a short space of time. I wonder if Taiohãhn or Anarkhane may have had a hand in that; it seems more than likely.' Gailon trailed off, and turning, he made his way down the stairs, lost in thought.

Tom sorted their bill while Kirsten found Troy sitting on a milking stool, around the back of the inn. The horses were with him. She approached him brightly, hoping his dejected mood would have subsided.

'Come on, Troy. Don't be gloomy,' she said. 'Gailon did not say that they *worshipped* Anarkhane and Taiohãhn. Think of them as two powerful beings, different from ourselves.'

He appeared unmoved by her words. 'These people are godless, then? Is that supposed to make me feel better?'

'Troy, look around you. Have you seen anyone here that looks like an average human being? They're all different. We are not on Earth any longer. You can't think of everyone as Christian children because they are not. You have to accept them and their customs and beliefs, whether you agree with them or not. It's not as if you can't be used to it anyhow. Let's face it, you lived in London ... need I say more?'

He looked up, his eyes sorrowful. 'Am I alone? The only Christian on Maldahl, then?'

'It looks that way,' Kirsten said sympathetically. 'Unless Tom has some religious belief we are unaware of.'

'That makes me feel kind of lonely,' he mumbled.

He looked down again and Kirsten grabbed his hands.

'That's pretty much the gist of what Gailon's been saying. We're all alone—divided. Now we have to bring people back together; we have to unite them in order to save them from the darkness that would seek to conquer them.'

'Princess?'

The voice was in her mind; Ioan had established the link.

'Everyone is waiting. Are you all right?'

'We're on our way, Ioan, thank-you.'

'Come on, Troy; everyone is waiting. We have to go.' She squeezed his hands, got up and led the horses around, meeting with their new companions once more.

Twelve

The march to the inn at Freya Valley was a pleasant one. The sun was warm, but a mild breeze kept them alert and awake. Gailon gave a knowing look from beneath his heavy brows, when Kirsten appeared to have no horse. Cröedaw insisted on her riding his horse, saying that it was unheard of for her to be on foot. After a while, she gave up arguing and mounted the strange steed. It was sleek, almost spindly-looking, but she could tell as soon as she seated herself that it was very powerful. Its coat was so soft that it felt more like fur than hair and it was grey green in colour, reminding her of shade beneath the trees.

It felt good to be away from Ishtar and back into the hills again. Kirsten felt that her home must have been green, rather than a city such as that. It was nearing noon and Tom was complaining that it was time to stop and eat. Troy was silent; he had been so for the entire journey and Kirsten figured that he too must have been hungry, not having eaten breakfast. Ignoring Tom's complaints, Gailon insisted that they keep moving, explaining that they had not much farther to go and they could eat on their arrival.

Tom appeared put out at first, but at the promise of a heartier, much nicer, meal at journey's end, he seemed to mellow. He trotted up front with Gailon and while they conversed, Kirsten watched with fascination. She had never noticed before how easily Tom seemed to fit with his surroundings. She had been seeing him as the police inspector, but that man was gone. He had adapted a lot better than she had it seemed. Troy, on the other hand, had appeared calm and collected until he discovered that instead of finding a way home, he *was* home. He seemed to be having a crisis of faith. Everything he believed in was gone. He had not even a bible to console himself in, no congregation to listen to his teachings; gone from a position of power, in religious terms, to a messenger whose name was never considered important enough to ask. He looked sullen and lost in thought. Kirsten wondered if she could communicate with him in the same way as she had done with Ioan. She focused on him, trusting the horse to follow the others. His thoughts were like pictures with no words and it took a while for her to adjust before making sense of them. He *did* feel lost. Gailon's treatment of him had been taken extremely badly.

*'You **are** important, Troy. Gailon meant no disrespect. You were selected for a very important mission. How many do you think would have been considered? But it was you who was chosen.'*

Troy reined his horse, waiting for Kirsten to catch up. She focused once more, the images in her mind failing to make sense; they were darkness and confusion, her semblance ever present midst them. She blinked and found Troy beside her.

Leaning over he hissed, 'Stay out of my mind!'

His face was stone and his eyes, venomous. As he rode on, Kirsten remained, shaken by his reaction to her. Cröedaw ushered her on again, seeming not to have noticed what had just passed between them.

'So tell me Gailon, what were you doing in Ishtar when we were told that you would be in the hills?' Tom asked politely.

'That is a good question, my friend and there is a strange answer for it. It was Ioan. He had an overwhelming desire to see a big city. He practically begged to stay a night or two in Ishtar. As we were not due to meet with Thaniel until today, I decided to indulge him. I know not why. I suspected danger, especially as Tehd informed me that Ioan hates crowds, had visited Golstur once and despised the place. It led me to believe that some other force was luring him there.

'Cröedaw would hear none of it and prompted us to hasten to Freya valley and leave word there for Thaniel while we ride on. Despite all his urging toward caution, though, my own curiosity was peaked. Now it appears that we were fated to meet with you.'

'Is Ioan a soothsayer then?' Tom asked. He realised that only weeks before, he would not have even entertained such a notion.

'No, not at all, Thomn,' Gailon answered. 'His people are farmers and carpenters, a simple, homely people. I have never known one of their kin to possess second sight. I think Ioan was *drawn* to Kirsten. Already they seemed to have formed bond of which they think that I am unaware. But as to the reason, that we shall discuss another time. Anyhow, here we are. I believe you were eager for a feast; well, Sally is one of the greatest cooks I have ever known, and if it's vittles you value, Thomn-the-Cleaverhand, then I think that you will be reluctant to leave Field House once you have tasted the delights that her table has to offer. Come my friend, I have worked myself into appetite. Let us waste no more time. YAH!'

He urged his horse into a gallop and Tom followed at his heels, ravenous at Gailon's words, and eager to see if the landlady was the culinary genius he claimed her to be.

Kirsten dismounted, deciding to arrive at Field House on foot. She thanked Cröedaw for the use of his horse and reluctantly, he rode on ahead leaving her to slow her descent into the valley. She failed to notice the exquisite house they were to stay at or the rolling fields, magnificent trees and a lake that shone mirror-like, reflecting the sky with perfect clarity. It was the image of the fury in Troy's eyes that plagued her sight, the darkness in his mind when he realised that she had been there. *It was wrong of me to look,* she reasoned. *I just wanted to reassure him, away from prying eyes.*

By the time Kirsten arrived, the party had already started eating. She felt dejected. Ioan had saved her a seat, but that was not enough to lighten her mood. She smiled mildly, thanking him, but explained that she was not hungry. Walking away, she met with the landlord, Jack, who showed her to her room. She tried to make small talk, aiming to keep her mind off her annoyance, asking after Sally and the baby. Jack seemed pleased by her attention and when she mentioned that she was a friend of Meggan's, he made it very clear that if she needed anything at all, then she was to ask for him directly and not the servants. She thanked him, feeling a little better for his kind hospitality, but a surge of relief flowed through her as she shut the door behind him.

Peace.

Nothing but birds in the gardens.

Bliss.

She looked about her. The room was large, beautifully decorated with a double bed made of sturdy wood. There were table, chairs, a pretty rug, which covered much of the floor space, and a bath. The curtains reminded her of hand-woven cloth that she had seen made at craft fairs when she was a child. Looking out of the window, she saw the lake in the distance. She sighed, feeling some of the tension disperse into the sweet country air. She could not decide what she wanted more ... sleep, a bath, or to visit the lake, its mirror quality, hypnotic.

Removing her cloak and weapons, she lay on the bed for a while, hoping for sleep to come, perhaps to wipe away the memory of Troy's look of hatred, or the lack of etiquette of her companions. No sooner had she closed her eyes than there came a knock at the door. She wanted to ignore it, but her manners got the better of her.

'Come in,' she said.

A pretty woman of average height entered, holding a tray. Her wavy, blonde hair bounced, framing her beaming face.

'You must be Sally,' Kirsten said, smiling politely and getting reluctantly to her feet.

'Yes miss, that's right. And you're Kirsten, or so your friends tell me. I thought I'd come and see if you was all right. Jack thought that you might be hungry.' She held out the tray of food. 'So I brought you up some vittles, thinking you might want to eat away from the men; get a bit o' peace.

Kirsten felt a grin forming. She could not help but like the woman. She was so open and warm that it seemed to flow from her, infecting anyone near.

'Thank-you Sally, that was most thoughtful,' she said, taking the tray. 'There is something that I crave more than food, though. I was wondering if I might borrow some clothes during my stay. I only have that which you see and I fear my dress, as well as myself, are in serious need of a wash.'

Sally nodded, laughing. 'Come with me, Kirsten. I'll see what I can do. When you've picked out a few things, you can give me your dress. It's washday tomorrow, so I'll have it back to you clean and dry before you go. How does that sound?'

'My thanks, Sally. That is most gracious of you.'

'Not at all,' she said, opening a door to what Kirsten assumed to be her and Jack's room. 'Any friend of Meggan's is a friend of mine. She saved my baby's life you know.'

'Yes, I had heard.'

Sally opened two huge trunks. 'You have the look of a healer yourself. Is that what you do?'

Kirsten was a little taken aback at the suggestion. 'No, I'm a warrior.' As she said it, the word sounded ridiculous and she felt suddenly foolish. 'But I have started to study the art of healing.'

Sally smiled warmly. 'Have a look in these and see if there's anything that takes your fancy.'

Kirsten rummaged carefully through, picking out a couple of country frocks. She held up an odd-looking garment, a vest and trousers all in one. Sally chuckled taking it from Kirsten.

'Dear me, I forgot I had that thing,' she explained. 'Jack's ol' ma made it for me, saying that I could go bathing in the lake. What a notion!'

Kirsten smiled cheekily and taking it from Sally, folded it and put it on her selection pile. They laughed. Kirsten had not realised how much she missed female company, to laugh at something frivolous; she had not done so since Geri was alive. Her smile broadened when she spotted the final items that she thought she would like to borrow.

'These are nice. But they look a little long in the leg for yourself.'

'Oh dear, look at those. Jack used to wear those. He was a prize-fighter when I met him. Hard to believe, I know.'

Kirsten smiled. 'Not at all. Could I make them my final choice, Sally?'

The landlady looked oddly at Kirsten for a moment, but agreed, gathering the rest of the outfits and helping her carry them to her room. She thanked Sally who offered to get the bath filled for her. Kirsten explained there was no need, and holding up the all-in-one garment explained that she was going swimming. They howled with laughter. Sally wiped a tear from her eye and said that she would send someone to collect the dress. Kirsten thanked her again.

It was a relief when she removed her dress, which reeked. She slipped on the odd-looking bathing costume and laid the dress on the bed. With one look at the lake, she headed out from her room. The men were still eating, but seemed to be slowing pace. She felt a little embarrassed having to walk past, wondering how absurd she looked. Conversation at the table stopped dead at her approach and she tried not to meet anyone's eye.

'Gentlemen.' She nodded and was through the door in a flash, skipping barefoot down to the lake, before any comment could be made.

She had never swum in anything but a swimming pool before, but that did not deter her. The sun was very warm and she craved the coolness of the water. Wading in, she was surprised at how deep it was, and swam gracefully out, basking under the clear sky.

Hearing Troy's voice calling her name, she glanced up and saw him approaching through the trees. Without thinking, she gulped a breath and surface dived. Down she stayed, not wanting to speak to him. She had never been a particularly good swimmer, but she had always been able to stay under water longer than most. She was glad of the ability at that moment. Her eyes firmly closed, she tried to see through the priest's eyes. The image was fuzzy at first, and then she saw the glassy surface of the lake. He stared for what seemed an age before turning to head back to the house. When she re-focused again, she found her eyes were open and her lungs were beginning to ache.

The lake, although dark, was extremely clear and she could see huge fish as they passed her by. She looked upward as she swam, realising that she had dived quite a depth in order to avoid the priest. As she broke the surface, she gasped for breath and bobbed there, treading water for a while before returning to the bank. There she lay, drying off in the sun, drinking in the clear air.

'God, I could stay here forever,' she sighed, closing her eyes.

Kirsten awoke with a start, worried that she had slept the day away. However, the sun was still quite high in the sky. Her stomach grumbled and remembering the food that Sally had left in her room, she dashed off to feed her appetite. On opening the door, she almost bumped into a man who was conversing with Gailon. He was tall with brown hair that seemed as wild as his penetrating aqua coloured eyes.

'Ah Kirsten,' Gailon greeted. 'This is Thaniel, he's been waiting to meet you.'

Kirsten was suddenly most conscious of her damp, dishevelled appearance, also that most of the party were still present to witness her obvious embarrassment.

'Thaniel.' She bobbed her head in greeting, avoided his eyes, and ran upstairs to be away from them all.

Swiftly closing the door, she placed the key on the windowsill. A pretty, embroidered nightdress had been placed on the bed for her, but she did not put it on. She lay naked for a while, tucking into the food at her bedside before slipping on a simple, grey cotton work-dress and a pair of pantaloons. She put her boots back on and thought how silly she must look. It was obvious that Sally had a bigger bust, as the dress sagged at the chest.

Sitting on the windowsill, she pondered how ridiculous it was that she was supposed to be a princess and yet she had borrowed clothes from an innkeeper, and that nobody showed the slightest respect for her concerning whom she was. They were all hungry,' she said to herself. 'Who am I that they should wait on my account?'

A crow sounded in the tree next to her window and she watched as it hopped nearer.

Opening her window a little wider, she spoke softly, 'Well my fine friend, you may not sing as well as the other birds and I'm sure many would say you're not as pretty, but I think you're handsome enough, and I thank you for the company.'

She felt suddenly silly, talking to a bird. As soon as her back was turned, she heard a gentle flap of wings and assumed it had taken flight, no doubt startled by her movement. However, when she glanced back, she discovered it on the windowsill, where it croaked with confidence.

She dare not move at first, frightened that it would scare into panic and perhaps injure itself as it tried to escape. However, it seemed unconcerned with her proximity and eyed her as carefully as she eyed it.

She approached it slowly; still it did not move. Holding out her hand, she was amazed when the bird allowed her to stroke it. It was Tom knocking at the door, which startled the crow back to the tree. She stared after it then flounced over to the bed.

'I'm resting,' she said. 'I shall see you later.'

Her words seemed to have a touch of finality to them and Tom went away without another word. Lying back again, she huffed, wondering what he had wanted. She closed her eyes trying to sense what Ioan was doing. She had not noticed him at the table on her return and found it difficult to connect to his mind. It was as though he himself was not quite there, and so there was little to tune in to. Her eyes snapped open.

Something's wrong, she realised.

Jumping to her feet, she grabbed the key and paused, deciding that she did not want to see the party again. Scrutinizing the large tree outside the window, she considered how proficient she might be at climbing. It was then that she saw Ioan outside, heading toward the lake. He was walking awkwardly and stumbling. The crow watched her curiously from the higher boughs, as she slipped out of the window and onto the nearest branch. Seeing no easy way down, she jumped. It was quite a drop and she was fortunate to have bent her knees as she landed. She sprinted off after Ioan as fast as her feet would carry her while the crow continued to observe her from the boughs of the tree.

Kirsten found Ioan lying with his back to a tree, his face pale and his eyes glazed.

'Ioan, what's wrong? What happened?'

He smiled up at her. 'It is nothing … just needed some air and sunshine.'

She knelt beside him and felt his forehead; beads of sweat had formed, but he was cold to the touch.

'Ioan, you're ill. I'm going to get you help.'

'No!' He clutched at her sleeve and looked up at her, his lids heavy. 'Nobody can do anything. It happens from time to time. I just have to suffer it.'

'It's an illness that you have had for a while, then?' she ventured.

He looked darkly into the water. 'It's not an illness; it's an honour. I am the bearer of the pendant of Anarkhane, one of the gems that we seek to reunite. The trouble is, as I told you yesterday, I have no majick in me, and so cannot protect myself in the way that you can. It drains me from time to time. There is nothing that can be done.'

Kirsten drew away from him slightly.

'It is a thing not of this world,' he continued. 'It is not for the likes of me to control. I was merely chosen to hold it for a while, to protect it because I am,' he laughed grimly, 'pure of heart, and so would fail to be corrupted by it.'

Kirsten stroked his hair back and he smiled, his eyes closing as she soothed him.

'Why not give it to Gailon?' she suggested. 'He surely has enough power to withstand its influence,'

He nodded weakly and opened his eyes once more. 'That is true, Milady, but he already carries one of the stones. Two could well be his undoing and I am certain that he would not take the risk.'

'The ring!' Kirsten recalled.

He nodded again. 'Yes, the ring that he wears carries the smallest of the Anarkhane gem shards.'

He reached out for her hand, smiling.

'Be not troubled; I chose this danger and I do not regret it. It is essential that I wear the pendant for it is believed that the enemy is able to detect its presence, if left unprotected. The stone has been worn by the eldest son of my family for generations and I hope that I may have the honour of being the last who has to carry it.'

Kirsten gently squeezed his hand.

'But surely there must be something that can be done for your condition,' she said. 'Has Gailon not attempted anything?'

'Gailon does not know and neither will you tell him, Milady. I knew what would happen when I accepted my duty. It would bring dishonour to my family should the pendant be taken from my keeping now, due to my weakness.'

His breath was short and he fell silent, seeming to have slipped into unconsciousness. Kirsten held her breath, reaching forward and opening his shirt. There, hanging about his neck was a simple chain with the green quartz shaped crystal, embedded in a flattened oval of metal. It was a crude looking, yet strangely alluring object.

Kirsten held it in her hand and felt at once, its mastery over Ioan. Gripping it tightly, she felt it tame to her, but Ioan slept on, his pale face looking deathly under the early evening sky. Placing a hand to his heart, she closed her eyes, concentrating on his pulse; it was weak and his life force seemed clouded over. She reached out for him in the fog, but he could not find his way. Her hand gripped more tightly about the pendant, as if to shield him from its influence and she burned like a flame in the fog to light his way back to her. There she held him, filling him with light, until his eyes opened. Colour was back in his cheeks and he looked up, smiling.

High in the trees, a solitary bird watched with interest as a girl changed before his eyes, gripping an object that glowed brightly in her hand and bringing a man back from darkness. The bird bobbed his head as the girl leaned forward delicately kissing the man as she replaced the odd looking pendant beneath his shirt, and with a smile sent him back up to the house, happy as a playful child.

The crow flew down to a lower branch and noted how pale the maiden looked, how she had not changed back to her former appearance, and how she struggled to get to her feet. He followed her staggering form back to the house, where she paused at the tree, cursing herself for leaving the key on the windowsill.

She was too weak to climb the tree and had no desire for the others to see the state that she was in, least of all Ioan. Dropping wearily to her knees, she struggled to focus. A croaking noise from above brought her back, and she glanced up weakly to see a crow clasp the key in its talons and fly down, depositing it in front of her. She was too feeble to show her amazement, but accepted the key with a weary nod of thanks and struggled to her feet again. The crow immediately flew away.

Exzalander stumbled through the door, barely noticing that her party had dispersed. She could only vaguely make out the stairs and pulled herself heavily up, one at a time; resigned to the fact that if she could just make it to her room, then all would be well.

A voice on the landing echoed in her ears and she turned to see Thaniel, as if fading in and out of existence, and then she saw no more.

Thirteen

She could not feel the clouds as they drifted past. In fact, she could not feel anything. She seemed to be suspended in the heavens, as the world rode onwards far below. Why she was there or how she came to be in the clouds, she could not remember. Gazing down, she saw in the distance an ancient palace. It was night and lights shone, twinkling though the windows. She seemed to know the place. A sound directly below drew her attention away from the stronghold, whose stones shone ghostly pale in the moonlight.

A magnificent horse was approaching fast; its black coat shimmered, as it stamped before the gates, whinnying and neighing so loudly that men came out to view it, but it was *she* who heard the horse as it called her name.

'Exzalander.' It nodded and shook its mane, as it heard on the wind, her reply to his call. She descended to meet him, as guards from the castle held ropes at the ready to capture him. A great crowd had gathered at the gates and there seemed to be much debate, but she could not hear. The horse approached her; even then, the people seemed unaware of her presence. She warned the horse of the approaching men and he asked her to mount and ride with him. They were away before the ropes hit.

The forest and hills sped quickly by and were a mere blur to her eyes. She grew tired and snuggling into the horse's mane, she slept; no dream came to replace that one.

Troy approached Kirsten's door for the second time that morning. *She can't still be asleep,* he thought. *She must simply be ignoring me.* He walked away again, almost banging into Cröedaw.

'Is she up yet?' the Elfin asked pleasantly.

'No,' was Troy's only reply. He wandered up the corridor and turned the corner, heading for his room.

Cröedaw waited until his keen hearing informed him that Troy's door was opened and then shut, before tapping gently at Kirsten's door.

'Thaniel, it's me; open up,' he whispered.

The door gave a quiet squeak and Cröedaw slipped in, locking it behind him. Thaniel looked tired and the dark rings about his eyes would inform any onlooker that he had slept little.

He eyed the motionless form of Exzalander.

'Any change?' Cröedaw asked.

'None,' Thaniel said. 'She hasn't moved all night.'

'Do you not think that we should inform Gailon? He may be able to do something.'

'No,' was Thaniel's sharp reply. 'She will be fine; she just needs rest. You know how angry Gailon will be if discovers what has happened.'

Cröedaw nodded thoughtfully. 'Yes, but if she does not wake soon, then Gailon will find out anyhow.' He seated himself next to Exzalander. 'Go get some rest, my friend. I will wake you as soon as there is any change.'

Thaniel gave the ghost of a smile and walked heavily from the room, wondering if his fatigue was due to lack of sleep, or worry. He had experienced many sleepless nights before and they had never taken their toll on him thus.

'Good morning Thaniel,' came Gailon's voice. 'We missed you at breakfast. Is everything all right?'

The old man's door was ajar and he could not possibly have seen that it was Thaniel. Wearily, Thaniel popped his head around the door.

'Dear me,' Gailon exclaimed. 'You're looking a little worse for wear.'

'I did not sleep well last night. I'm going to have some down time now. I will see you at supper.' With that, Thaniel made his way to his room, knowing in his heart of hearts that Gailon suspected something.

Cröedaw noticed that Kirsten had many visitors since Thaniel had carried her into bed the evening before; Troy had visited three times in all, Ioan twice and Sally, also twice. He gazed down to the sleeping form that was still that of Exzalander and not Kirsten. Whatever she had done had drained her incredibly.

'Kirsten?' It was Troy rapping loudly on the door. 'I need to speak to you. I know you can hear me. I'm sorry for what happened yesterday ... Kirsten?'

Cröedaw heard Troy's footsteps as they stomped down the stairs and wondered what had passed between them to warrant an apology. He watched through a gap in the curtains as Troy strode off toward the lake. It was then that a flash of movement caught his eye. Gazing across the fields, he saw a horse crossing at great speed, heading directly toward the house.

Thaniel could not sleep. He headed downstairs to get some breakfast and returned to Kirsten's room. Cröedaw quickly opened the door and ushered him in to look at the approaching horse, as it came to a halt before Field House and stamped impatiently upon the ground.

The Elfin excused himself, saying that he wanted to take a closer look at the animal. Thaniel locked the door and munched on cold toast, too tired to care about wild horses at the threshold. He slumped in the chair next to Kirsten's bed and listened as the horse began to neigh loudly.

Kirsten heard the sound in the darkness—the calling of her true name. Her eyes flickered open and she gasped for air, as if she was taking a breath for the first time. Thaniel dropped his toast in surprise.

'Princess!' he exclaimed.

She turned her head to see a face that she recognised as the man she had met briefly and had hurried away from. She gave a weary smile, the action taking the greatest of effort.

'I do not think you are supposed to address me, thus,' she said.

Thaniel's face beamed, happy to see her awake.

'That is true,' he agreed. 'But I do not think that you are supposed to look as you do, if you are to be disguised.'

Kirsten glimpsed down to see red hair lying sprawled across the bed-sheets. She concentrated until her hair shortened and darkened. The metamorphosis took more effort than before, leaving her breathless. Thaniel stayed her, as she attempted to sit up.

'Kirsten, be still. You're unwell. You must not exert yourself.'

Her mind raced. She remembered Ioan and the effect that helping him had on her, and recalled seeing Thaniel just before she collapsed.

'Thank-you for helping me, Thaniel.'

He smiled down at her, the bags under his eyes, protruding.

'My pleasure,' he said. 'Now, if you can pace yourself, I think that you should get some breakfast and show your face. Gailon could already be suspicious by your prolonged absence.'

She eased herself into sitting position, wondering how long she had slept. 'Thaniel, I would like to get washed and dressed before going down. Would you please excuse me?'

Immediately, Thaniel rose to his feet and made for the door.

'You look as though you need some sleep,' she suggested.

He nodded, smiling and was gone. Rising unsteadily to her feet, she poured some water and had a hasty wash. The noise of people running down the stairs caught her attention. She slipped into the leather trousers and vest, tightly fastened the weapon belt and slicked her hair back with water. Using some lose braiding from the bedspread, she tied her hair into a ponytail. She felt light-headed, as she descended the stairs.

The front door was open and she stepped out into the morning sunshine, recoiling as it stabbed at her eyeballs. Gailon was talking animatedly to Cröedaw, and a small crowd gathered about a huge black horse, whose sleek coat shimmered purple and blue in the sunlight. Cröedaw spied and warmly acknowledged her. Gailon smiled, but his eyes appeared troubled on noticing how pale she was. The horse trotted over to her and began nuzzling her hand, reminding her of strange dreams of castles, clouds, and riding bareback.

'Ravenwing?' she ventured; the horse sounded to her voice and she gently stroked his coat.

'You know him?' Gailon queried, his bright eyes shining.

'No. He *told* me his name,' she replied.

There was a murmur from the small crowd and Gailon laughed.

'Yes, of course he did. Would this have been when you overdid the ale?'

Kirsten let out an uneasy laugh to appease the curious crowd, many of whom ventured back into the house, convinced there was nothing particularly amazing about a horse that returns to its master. She whispered in Ravenwing's ear and he trotted off toward the fields to graze. Gailon approached her and led her indoors.

'You look extremely pale, my dear. Are you unwell?'

She sat at the nearest table and reached for the pitcher of water. 'I am a little tired, Gailon, that is all. This has been a lot for me to take in, as I'm sure you can appreciate,' she suggested as an excuse.

Gailon's lips thinned into a line and leaned in toward her, so that others could not hear what he had to say.

'Ravenwing could only have been summoned by majick,' he hissed. 'You should have consulted me if you planned to make use of such powers. You have to be very careful.'

'But I didn't summon him,' Kirsten protested.

Gailon's eyebrows raised in an unimpressed manner. 'Then perhaps you would not mind telling me how it is that you are finding it difficult to hold form today?'

She grabbed her ponytail; it was dark brown.

'Your *eyes,* Kirsten, they are green!' he said, in a patronising tone.

She corrected the mistake at once, but again found herself weakened. She drank a tankard of water in one and wiped her mouth.

'Perhaps it was something that I managed to perform while I slept,' she said innocently. 'Is that possible?'

The suggestion seemed to appease him and he agreed that it was not unheard of for powerful sorcerers to do such things.

Jack brought over a small plate of food and Gailon left her to eat in peace. When the landlord returned to take the plate away, he commented on how good his old outfit looked on her, making a gift of it. Kirsten thanked him, secretly wishing that she did not have to leave his house at all, or ever have need for such a gift.

As the food settled, she felt her energy return a little; she decided that a spell by the lake might further rejuvenate her. Sitting beneath the first tree she came to, she closed her eyes, basking in the warmth of the sun.

Troy saw her approach, thinking that she had come to talk to him. He watched as she sat a little away from him, smiling as the breeze hit her. She looked deathly pale and her eyes were slightly sunken.

Did I upset her that much? he wondered. *And look at her all in black. Is she hoping that by dressing that way she can somehow harden her heart?*

He approached stealthily, careful not to make a sound, and knelt beside her. She seemed to be sleeping, appearing so fragile despite her outfit and array of weapons.

So beautiful in her frailty.

So kissable.

Leaning a little closer, he was startled by a squawking from above. Kirsten's eyes shot open and she was surprised to see Troy bending over her.

'Troy!' she cried. 'What do you think you're doing sneaking up on me like that?' Glancing up, she saw a large black crow making its way to the upper branches. She watched it curiously, it stirring a memory.

'I was just making sure that you were okay,' Troy lied, and distanced himself. 'Why didn't you answer the door? I kept calling.'

'Did you? I was asleep. I guess I didn't hear you, and to be honest I'm glad. The last thing I want right now is for you to have another go at me, so I would appreciate it if you would just leave me alone.'

Troy knelt up toward her so quickly that it startled her.

'I never meant to do this to you,' he said. 'I was shocked and embarrassed I guess, wondering how often before you may have read my mind without me knowing.'

Kirsten shook her head, finding it ironic that she had been in trouble for reading his mind and yet he was so way off the mark when it came to her.

'You had nothing to do with my being ill, Troy; I don't know why you even thought that you would, and you needn't worry about me invading your privacy. I was only concerned for you. It won't happen again.'

Troy's eyes fixed on the ground; he could feel his face burning. *How can she be so cruel? She must know by now how I feel and yet treats me like this,* he thought. He got to his feet and stormed away, leaving her feeling confused regarding his odd behaviour. The crow flew down and sat beside her and she stroked it thoughtfully.

It was not until the evening meal that Thaniel returned from his slumber, where Cröedaw proceeded to tell him about the events of the day. Gailon and Thaniel decided, after much debate, that they should continue west to Ealdorbold, the birthplace of Exzalander's mother, Shénnin. Ealdorbold housed the Council of Shénnin, who had ruled since the demise of the monarchy. It was the Council who had ordered the quest for the missing shards and Gailon thought it best to revisit, making them aware of new developments.

Thaniel, however, was against telling the Council of Exzalander's return, explaining that they would not care and would refuse to believe it. His argument was that after so many years in power, squandering the wealth of the people, they would be reluctant to hand over leadership to a mere girl who is little more than a myth in the present day.

Kirsten found the discussion discomforting. She had not considered that she would be expected to rule Maldahl. She felt suddenly very small, not knowing the first thing about leadership or indeed even the politics of the kingdom. She found herself missing Earth, her father, her own bed, even school, but most of all a life without the responsibilities Maldahl seemed intent on thrusting upon her.

Troy remained silent throughout the meal, as did Tehd, who continued his suspicious looks in her direction. Most of Tom's conversation was about the excellent meals they had received. Kirsten noted how the group listened with utter respect as he talked, especially Thaniel, who fell silent each time Tom spoke. As dessert was served, Tom shifted the subject to that of money, explaining that he did not know what each piece was worth. Cröedaw explained that there were fifty silver pieces to one gold and ten bronze nuggets to every silver.

'What about the larger gold coins?' Tom asked. He produced the large, gold coaster size coins from his purse and laid them before him.

A hush fell upon the company.

'My dear Thomn, these are beyond price!' Gailon said. 'They are the tokens of Tuâth and Shénnin, only the very highest members of the household would ever have possessed them; they were presented for honour and bravery, and very few were ever made. To show one of the coins was to receive the respect and love of the people, including free food and board wherever you graced with your presence. Katahl was thought to have destroyed the last remaining, yet here we find that you have four. *Four tokens,* Thomn! This probably makes you one of the richest men in Maldahl.'

Kirsten suddenly choked and took a sip of wine. She had given two of the tokens away, thinking them to be mere money. *The horse seller and the thief, Jeb, must be very happy,* she thought.

Gailon handed the token back to Tom. 'Put them away, Thomn,' he said. 'It could prove very dangerous for us if anyone saw them.'

Kirsten felt suddenly hot. 'Why?' she asked.

'Why? Because their very existence is a sign of your return. Word would spread quickly; let me assure you. It would take little time for Katahl's army to hunt us down and we are unprepared to face him.'

Kirsten swallowed hard and shot a worried glance to Troy, whose pale blue eyes held hers in silence. She had no appetite for dessert and excused herself, with apologies to the company.

She paced about her room. 'How could I have been so foolish?' she thought, aloud.

Opening the window and without thinking, she climbed down the tree and ran off into the night.

Troy excused himself, explaining that he needed some air. As he walked down the path, he saw what appeared to be Kirsten dashing into the trees. He glanced back at her window, finding it open.

She stood looking up at the moon shining between the branches, asking it silently what to do, when a noise from behind startled her.

'It's me,' Troy said.

He stepped from the shadows and Kirsten ran to him. For a moment, Troy thought that she meant to embrace him.

'What shall I do, Troy?' she cried. 'Gailon's going to kill me when he finds out.'

'So don't tell him.'

She began pacing again. 'You heard what he said. Katahl will find me. It will all be over.'

Troy grabbed her to stop her pacing and pulled her about to face him.

'You think that scared little kid is going to tell anyone how he came by it? Stop worrying.'

Kirsten's eyes brimmed with tears and she threw herself into Troy's arms. He needed no reason to hold her to him.

'You don't understand,' she wailed. 'That's how I paid for the horses!'

She pulled away and looked up at him and he stroked her face tenderly.

'I still think that he's making a big deal out of nothing. They could have *found* the coins, Kirsten. Just because Tom returned, doesn't mean that you did too.'

'Yes it does,' she wailed. ' Because Tom couldn't come back without me. That's what Gailon said.'

He held her to him again, cradling her gently and resting his chin on top of her head.

'Well if you ask me, this Gailon knows a lot less than you think. After all, he was only a kid when you were banished.'

'Why do you say that?'

'Because he talks about his Master; he was an apprentice.'

Kirsten drew away from him, digesting his words.

'Kirsten?' It was Thaniel's voice, as he ran toward them. 'Is everything all right?' he asked.

'Er yes,' Kirsten said. 'I just wanted some air, that's all.'

'Most people use the stairs. Especially when they are still weak and should be resting,' Thaniel said. His manner was light-hearted, but his face was hard as flint

Kirsten nodded and bade goodnight to Troy, whose face reflected Thaniel's coldness back at him.

Thaniel decided that it would be best that they climb back up the tree to avoid detection. As he came through the window, he drew the curtains across sharply.

'Just what in Taiohãhn's kingdom do you think you are playing at?' he hissed.

His abruptness took her aback.

'You are not behaving in a manner fitting to your birth!'

'What are you talking about?' she said, flouncing over to the bed and removing her weapon belt.

'I am talking about the messenger, as well you know. You climb out of your window in the middle of the night and I find you in his arms.'

'It's not what it looks like. I was upset. Troy was just being a friend, that is all.'

'Well friends like that, Your Highness, could damage your reputation.'

She sat down, a wave of tiredness hitting her. Thaniel approached and knelt before her.

'You are to stand before the Council in a few days,' he explained. 'Your honour must be intact and unstained. If there is but a hint of a blemish on your reputation, then they could cast you out, and without the support of the Council of Shénnin, Princess, our cause is as good as lost. They control the army that could stand against Katahl's troops, and as I said at dinner, I think that it is going to be very difficult to convince them of your heritage. It will be nigh on impossible if they discovered that you have been consorting with a messenger of the realm, in the middle of the night.'

Kirsten's cheeks felt hot with embarrassment and anger. She stood suddenly, ignoring the stars of dizziness in her eyes.

'And what would the Council have to say to *your* presence here, Thaniel? You spent a night in my room and I find you here a second time, climbing through my window no less.'

Thaniel's proud face faltered. He bowed swiftly and walked from the room, understanding her meaning all too well. She let out an exasperated sigh and put her head in her hands.

'This is crazy,' she whispered. '*Consorting with a messenger of the realm,*' she mimicked Thaniel's stern words and shook her head in despair. Undressing and slipping on her nightclothes, she heaved another sigh.

Opening the curtains slightly, she gazed out at Ravenwing dancing in the moonlight, and thought over Gailon's words to try to drive Thaniel's cold manner from her mind. *Ravenwing can only be summoned by majick. I suppose it makes sense. If he is Exzalander's, I mean **my** horse, then he would be over three hundred years old and no horse can live that long.*

As if in answer to her thoughts, the horse trotted over to the window, his mane shone like moonbeams as he shook it.

'Hello Ravenwing. I hope you've been resting. We've got a long journey ahead of us.'

He nodded in reply.

A squawk from the tree made Kirsten start. The crow had returned.

'Good evening my friend. I never had the chance to thank you for retrieving my key for me. I do so now.'

The bird croaked a reply and flew down, sitting on Ravenwing's back. Kirsten smiled and closed the curtains. It was a strange sight, and made her think of distant faerie tales.

She lay for what seemed like hours. Slowly the noise below died down, as one by one the guests went to their rest. A tapping at the window caused her to stir some time later. It was quiet at first, but became more insistent. Kirsten got to her feet, the cold of the night stabbing at her tired limbs. She opened the curtain and screamed, coming face to face with a bull, its nostrils flaring, and its eyes intent on her.

She sat up in bed, relieved that the nightmare had passed. Her skin felt clammy and her breath froze in the air. It was cold.

Very cold.

The curtains blew wildly and Kirsten realised that she had left the window open. Getting to her feet, she crossed the floor and swiftly closed the window, her heart thumping with memories of the floating face of the ferocious bull. She shivered and turned to retreat to the warmth of her bed and screamed again.

Before her, stood a woman so hideous that Kirsten felt herself retch. The woman reeked of death, of putrefying flesh and decay, yet there was a familiarity. She froze with horror when she realised who it was.

By god it's me, she thought.

I'm three hundred years old; what should I look like other than this hag—this thing. My face is a mask created by majick that's all.

Kirsten awoke again and sat bolt upright. *Just another dream.* She shook herself, trying to determine if she was still asleep and would have to face another hideous apparition. Remaining sitting up, she rocked gently to the echo of distant laughter, until the sun rose and she heard the sound of the house coming into waking. *Have I been haunted? Or was I dreaming?* she wondered. *At any rate, I've been awake for hours and as a result am really tired.*

She dressed herself in her old clothes, clean and dry as Sally had promised. Clambering down the stairs she slumped onto a bench, ready for breakfast. Only Ioan and Tehd were at the table that early.

'Good morning,' she muttered.

Tehd grunted a reply.

Ioan took note of the dark rings beneath her eyes. 'Kirsten, you look very tired. Are you quite well?' he asked.

'YES!' she snapped, 'I'm fine.'

She was aware of Tehd's eyebrows, rising at her short temper, and she did not have to be mind reader to know his thoughts at that moment,

'Typical woman!'

Jack greeted them, and began to lay the table; Tom was next to arrive.

'Good morning, good morning,' he said heartily.

Kirsten suddenly wished that she had worn her cloak, so scrutinising were the looks of her companions as they each joined the table. Tom poured a hot beverage while the others grabbed sausages, bacon, eggs and toast.

'For someone who went to bed so early, you do not appear to have had very much sleep,' Gailon remarked.

Kirsten wondered just how bad she looked and shivered, as she remembered the rotting old hag.

There was tension at the table, which made her feel worse. Only Tom did not seem to feel it. Her mind briefly swept over each of them, hoping to stay one step ahead of any trouble brewing. Ioan was worried; Tehd was annoyed and feeling negative toward her; Troy was so closed off that she was unable to read him, but there were oppressive vibes, and Gailon showed clear thoughts of suspicion. Cröedaw's mind was too different to read and she skipped past it; finally, there was Thaniel, who was brooding because she had upset him.

She looked despondently down at the red berry liquid before her and sighed, wishing it to be coffee. Holding the cup to her lips, she paused, concentrating hard, until the aroma of a smooth dark roast wafted up her nostrils. Gratified, she drank the contents down in one, before anyone could question what she had done. She yawned and stretched, feeling more human again as the caffeine surged through her system.

'Gailon, is this place haunted do you know?' she asked.

Gailon looked at her quizzically. 'What do you mean by haunted?'

'You know, by dead people, coming back to frighten the living.'

The entire table stared strangely at her, as if she had said something distasteful.

'It's just that I thought there was something in my room last night; that is why I did not sleep.'

Gailon faced her, his stern expression making his face almost frightening.

'And you did not think to wake any of us?' he asked.

She shrugged. 'Well, no.'

'It might have been the enemy,' Gailon whispered. He gazed about suspiciously, as if the very walls were against them.

'No,' Kirsten said, with confidence. 'I think they would have just come in and lopped my head off, don't you? This was like something playing with me, trying to frighten me and, well, inconvenience me. By keeping me awake, whatever it was knew that I would be tired and bad tempered in the daytime.'

The faces of her companions drew a blank.

'Oh never mind!' she said irritably, shovelling a forkful of mushrooms into her mouth.

Only Gailon seemed to take what she had said with any seriousness, and he continued to stare at her long after the others.

Fourteen

When it came time to bid farewell to their hosts at Field House, Kirsten hugged Sally and thanked her for making her stay a happy one. The landlady held her tight and whispered in her ear,

'Don't give up on the healing. You have the gift, that much I have seen during your stay with us.'

Kirsten thanked her again smiling, thinking that Sally was more aware about the goings on at Field House than Gailon could ever hope to be. She mounted Ravenwing, who had been fitted with her saddle and some of the luggage. Waving farewell, she joined the company, as they rode north and out of Freya Valley.

Kirsten fought the urge to sleep, until Ravenwing assured her that he would not let her fall if she wished to rest. She gently patted him and drifted off into peaceful slumber, much to the amazement of her companions.

'What a truly magnificent horse,' Cröedaw remarked. 'They are made for each other. Surely this will show in her favour when presenting her at council.'

Thaniel slowly shook his head. 'I do not think any evidence will get them to relinquish power. However, we shall see. Gailon is convinced that this is the best course of action and I trust his judgement.'

When Kirsten awoke, she found that they were descending a steep hill. She stroked Ravenwing's mane in greeting. Cröedaw informed her that she had slept most of the day and they would be stopping as soon as they found a suitable camp for the night. Gailon decided that they would need no shelter as the night promised to be warm and clear. As evening set in, they found a reasonably level patch of ground within easy distance of a stream, which ran down from the hills they had descended that day.

Gailon sent Tehd and Thaniel to gather firewood and Tom and Troy to fetch water, while he unpacked the blankets. Kirsten suspected that the reason that she and Ioan were not sent on errands were because they each bore a shard of the Anarkhane stone and he did not wish them out of his sight. That led her to thinking just how much protection the old man would serve if an attack were to occur while they were alone.

Gailon arranged the kindling and the company stood back as, with a wave of his hands, the wood burst into flame. Kirsten smiled and wondered if she might get him to teach her how such a thing was done.

Tehd placed pans to boil while he chopped vegetables and herbs, placing them into the pot. Kirsten watched him for a while.

'Are you a cook, Tehd?' she asked. 'You seem to prepare food most expertly if you are not.'

Tehd's scowl lessened slightly. 'No ma'am,' he replied. 'I am a farmer, like my father before me. But my ma' taught us all to cook so's we'd never stave.'

Kirsten smiled. 'That was very wise.'

Tehd did not look at her, but continued emptying the herbs into the water.

'Yes ma'am it was. But then my ma was a wise woman in all things, except one.'

'And what was that?'

'Trusting strangers. Faces of the enemy come in many guises. My mother was too gullible; I am not so foolish as to let a handsome face lull me into a trap as she did.'

His face remained stern and Kirsten drew away in silence, understanding why he disliked her so.

The aroma from the pot, although in the early stages of cooking, made her stomach rumble and she longed for it to be ready. The others gathered to talk, as the birds sang evensong and came to roost. It was during the pre-dinner conversation that it became apparent why Thaniel was in such awe of Tom. He was it seemed, his descendant.

Thomn-the-Cleaverhand had left behind his wife and remaining son to fulfil his sacred duty and seventeen generations of offspring had chosen to serve the realm, as Thomn had before them, in honour of his memory. Thaniel had quit the royal guard though, saying that it was nothing more than pomposity and ritual, and he had done more good since he abandoned his post as Captain of the Guard, than he ever did while in the service of the Council.

Tom seemed most proud of newfound grandson and made him sit next to him for the evening.

Kirsten spoke mostly to Ioan, finding his company the most tolerable, since Troy had become so brooding. They spoke of his land and his family. She learned that Tehd owned a great deal of land adjoining his own, which he inherited after his parents' demise. Although Ioan did not tell Kirsten how they had come to meet their deaths, Kirsten surmised that it had something to do with the stranger whom Tehd had previously mentioned to her.

'And what about you, Ioan? Have you a sweetheart back at home?'

He blushed badly and could scarcely meet her gaze. 'No Milady, I have not. Although it is my duty to ensure the continuation of my line, I have not yet considered taking a wife.'

Kirsten dropped the subject, having no desire to embarrass him further, besides which, Tehd had heard every word and his eyes were like daggers on the back of her neck. She got the distinct impression that there was more to their relationship than either of them were saying. She had no idea how homosexuality was viewed by the people of Maldahl and decided it was a subject best left alone; it was none of her business and if there was something to know and they wanted to tell her, then they would do so in their own time, she figured.

With relief, dinner was served and Kirsten gratefully held out her bowl to Tehd. She saw Father Troy saying grace and took note of the odd looks that he received for doing so. She felt sorry for him. He was not happy and she blamed herself.

If I hadn't been banished then he would never had left Maldahl in the first place, she considered. *Then Tom and Troy would have lived out their lives and died, as would I.* She dipped her bread into her broth and ate with morbid thoughts in her mind.

After dinner, Kirsten approached Gailon and asked him whether he would teach her how to light a fire. He was sombre in his reply.

'Why? Do you think that lighting a fire will help you defeat the enemy? You wish to learn an impressive trick; it serves no purpose in your destiny. Besides, you would not need my help in such a simple task; you have already gained the correct state of thought. Or did you think me ignorant of your little feat at breakfast this morning?'

Kirsten bowed her head, staring into the flames. He had put her in her place and she felt the eyes of the company upon her. Having no desire to look up and see their faces, she continued to stare into the heat of the flames until the image consumed her vision …

She could smell burning, as the palace was engulfed in flame. She was aware of a man shouting her name and screaming, as people ran from the burning building, pointing up at the sky. Following the frightened eyes, she caught her breath. A dark shape was before her, an ugly cloud of oily blackness from which came a voice without emotion, without expression, a metallic voice that chilled her to the bone, and all about her was smoke, screams, and death.

'Are you all right?'

She jumped back, screaming as Ioan shook her from her vision. Her eyes stung with tears and she felt a sickness in her stomach. Gailon eyed her knowingly, as she walked away from the campfire. Ioan, Troy and Thaniel moved to follow her.

'Leave her be,' Gailon's voice commanded. 'She was fire-gazing and no doubt saw something not to her liking.

Kirsten sat by the stream, the moon, only a quarter full, gave out very little light; only on the surface of the water, as it trickled across the stones, was she aware of its presence. She continued to see the vision, the moonbeams in the water animating it once more.

She saw the face of Shénnin and Tuâth, fearful and pale. As she looked into her father's eyes, she knew that he expected death. She wished it to be quick and painless.

It was not.

She watched helplessly, as they were torn limb from limb. The screams broke her heart, and through the tears and smoke, she could still see.

She heard her own voice, begging not to have to witness any more—pleading. However, once she had opened a floodgate, she knew not how to close it. She tried calling out to her companions, yet knew that her voice made no sound.

Blood spattered the courtyard and she could no longer hear the screams over her own cries. She reached the moment she had been dreading, perhaps most of all.

Facing Katahl.

As she looked into the eyes of a man she recognised, she felt her breath stop. Katahl stood beside her, his blue-black hair, jet eyes and pale skin, all familiar, for she had been dreaming about him as long as she could remember—the phantom of her slumber, who of late had played a more active role; a figure that she had been unable to resist, even at the warning of her best friend.

His eyes met hers and they saw each other for only a moment, before she found that she was gasping for breath, struggling to break away from the hands that held her down.

Slowly, she became aware of the voice of Troy chanting in Latin. Her eyes struggled to focus; she saw the hazy outline of Thaniel and Tom pinning her; Gailon knelt over her and Ioan sat away, fearful. She broke free of their hold and plunged her hands into the cold water of the stream, bathing her face and drinking to try to clear the horrors from her head. She was shivering and welcomed the cloak that Gailon wrapped about her.

'Gailon, I saw them die. I saw what happened,' she wept.

Gailon placed his ancient hand to her head, his long fingers outstretched on her pallid skin. She felt herself instantly calming under his influence and her breath returned to normal.

'I saw him. I saw Katahl.'

Gailon's eyes widened. 'Did he see you?' he asked.

She looked back at the water. 'Yes, but it was in the past,' she replied.

'Kirsten, if you can visit another time, then I assure you so can he. If he *was* there, we just have to hope that he did not realise that your presence was anything more than a shadow of the past.'

She ran her hands through her hair, breathing hard. Unable to shake the violent images from her mind, she contemplated what she had been doing to warrant them restraining her. Gailon helped her to her feet and led her back to the camp. She lay down, wrapping the cloak about her, chilled by the wetness of her hair and face as a cold breeze blew their way. She closed her eyes, but did not sleep, too fearful of another nightly visitation of some horror or other. She heard whispers as the companions talked next to the fire. The tears ran freely from her eyes, as she saw the death of her parents over and over again.

It was the first time she had felt grief since Caitul died, and that was short-lived in comparison, lasting mere minutes in actuality. Now, she felt as though her heart was breaking. She could not remember her parents, but had seen them die, knew that they died because of her. She wondered if their death might have been prevented if Tuâth had but named her something else. She felt a fresh stream of tears, hot on her cheeks at first, but after a while, they felt like droplets of ice leaking from her eyes. She could see her breath on the air and shivering, she sat up.

The fire had died down and the company slept. Over by the trees, the horses stamped uneasily and Ravenwing was like a shadow in the darkness. Her tears stopped, as her sense of foreboding grew. She had attributed the occurrences of the previous night to a ghost or some such entity occupying Field House, but her supposition seemed to have been incorrect as a new apparition manifested from the dying embers.

A huge serpent appeared, whose deadly jaws presented its venomous fangs, and its slit eyes fixed upon her. She drew her sword, hoping that the noise would alert her companions.

'Gailon,' she hissed.

The snake slithered toward her and Gailon did not stir. As it made its move, she swung the blade of Taiohãhn and found herself stopping within an inch of Gailon's throat. The serpent was gone and the old man looked none too amused by the disturbance. Immediately, she lowered the weapon. The party demanded explanations for her attack and Tehd suggested that she be restrained, proclaiming that she was mad. She also heard, quietly at first and then so loud that it drowned out the others, a laugh.

'Can you not hear it?' she protested.

Yet, it seemed that they were ignorant to the sound. The laughter rung in her ears and she could see the others debating what was to be done with her; clearly some of them believed that she was insane.

Perhaps I am mad, she thought. *I'm hearing voices now.* Yet as she listened, it occurred to her how familiar the sound was. 'The laugh', she said. 'I recognise it. There's majick afoot, Gailon; can you not feel it? It's one of the Macara Shee, whom Troy and I recently encountered.'

Gailon's eyes darted about, surveying every shadow in turn.

'Don't be a fool, girl,' Tehd spouted. 'The tramping folk don't travel alone. They go about in clans.'

Kirsten ignored him and focused on everything but her companions. It was like opening her eyes after a long sleep; they seemed filled with light. As she looked about her, she spied amidst the trees, the being she sought.

'There!' She pointed. 'There's the culprit.'

The others turned to the patch in the trees, but saw only darkness.

'She's mad!' shouted Tehd.

Gailon stepped up, seeming less sure of madness than Tehd would have them believe. He raised his hands and muttered under his breath. There came a gasp from some, as a faint glow appeared, surrounding a tiny man, wearing an assortment of leaves to cover his modesty.

'Cob!' she exclaimed. 'What are you doing here?'

The faerie appeared annoyed at the staring eyes and merely pouted.

Gailon laughed aloud, and sitting down he said, 'Well my little fellow, what seems to be the trouble? Why do you issue your threats at my good friend here?'

His back was to the faerie and the companions watched with astonishment, as the little man stomped across the grass and stood before Gailon, shouting,

'That *woman* was stupid enough to handle me! King Noch has banished me, saying that I am unclean and no longer fit to be among his people. I came for revenge! I vowed that I would not let her rest. She will rue the day she chose to abuse poor Cob.'

The others gathered again. Tom stoked the fire and added more wood; the faerie seemed glad of the heat and stood warming himself. Gailon's fierce eyes set upon Kirsten.

'What explanation have you for such an act of cruelty?' he asked.

Kirsten coughed uncomfortably. 'His clan were going to kill Troy' she explained. 'I tried to reason with them, but they refused to listen.'

Gailon's eyes softened, as if satisfied that it had not been a malicious act.

'Well my little friend, since your presence here is now known, I think that you had better come along with us.'

Cob stopped rubbing his hands and placed them firmly on his hips. 'Travel with *you?* Never! Do you not think that I have suffered enough of an indignity?'

Gailon shrugged and lay back down, as if going to sleep. 'Suit yourself,' he yawned, 'but I tell you this; if anyone will be able to reunite you with the Macara Shee, it will be the one who got you banished to begin with. She has powers that she has only just begun to realise. If anyone can set things to rights, it will be her.' With that, he closed his eyes and seemed to sleep.

The others gawped at the faerie before following Gailon's example. Cob's eyes blazed at Kirsten. She returned the stare, angered by Gailon's promise.

Why should I help the rude fellow, who has seen fit to terrorise me so? she thought. Baring her teeth, she put her hand to her sword and Cob ran behind the slumbering form of Gailon, sticking his tongue out at her.

Dawn came too early for Kirsten, although she did feel more rested than she had for days, which came as a surprise considering that she had slept on the ground for the first time in her life. Looking about her, she was relieved to see no sign of Cob. She went off to the stream to wash and prepare for breakfast.

'How are you feeling this morning?'

She was startled by Thaniel's silent approach. He smiled warmly and she decided to let her grudge go.

'I'm fine,' she replied. 'Sorry to have shocked everyone.'

Thaniel filled the water pot, supporting it with both hands. 'There is no need for apologies,' he said. 'Gailon explained what you saw. If it had been me, I probably would have killed someone.' Setting down the water on the bank, he faced her head on.

'Kirsten, what happened back then was terrible, that is why it is so important for you to focus on the task at hand. Through the re-unification, the land will know peace, and so will you. You will have avenged the murder of your parents and fulfilled your destiny.'

Kirsten smiled wryly. It was not quite how she would have wished to be cheered up, but she figured that it was nice of him to make the effort.

Breakfast was a simple affair and Gailon was quick to hurry them along.

At least it appears that I've got rid of Cob, Kirsten thought. *After all, it isn't really my fault that he's homeless.* She glanced up at Ravenwing, who gave her a knowing look and blew out air between his lips.

'Don't look at me like that!' she muttered to the horse. 'Cob could have stuck around—he didn't. So stop trying to make me feel guilty!'

She heard a laugh from Tom.

'Sounds to me like your doing a pretty good job of that all on your own,' he said. 'Poor thing is in the same position as you are. I would have thought that you'd show a little sympathy.'

Kirsten sneered as she mounted Ravenwing.

'Okay, okay. If he comes back, I'll be nice. But I bet you wouldn't be so supportive if it had been your ass they were going to roast!'

Tom laughed again, pleased to see she at least had her sense of humour back. He kicked his horse into action and joined the file, as they set a steady pace toward the forest path.

Kirsten noticed that the nearer they came to Ealdorbold, the cooler it became. The sun remained bright, but there was a chill in the air that reminded her of early spring. By evening, Kirsten found herself cursing for not wearing leather. She wrapped her cloak tightly about her shivering form and longed for a huge mug of cocoa. The landscape too began to change; trees were taller and imposing, their huge trunks jutting out of the surrounding landscape, like huge gateways into the forest beyond.

In the day that followed, the scenery changed little. The road was easy and well trod, and they met with few complications. Thaniel trotted up to Gailon, and reined in beside him.

'Do you not think that I should ride ahead to announce our coming?'

Gailon shook his head. 'No,' he said. 'The lookouts should spy us as we approach and that is all the herald I want or need.'

Thaniel gave a stiff nod. 'How do you think the Council will react to our coming?'

The old man's eyes seemed clouded over, as if he were trying to gaze into the future. 'I do not know,' he said, 'but we must take her there. It is not for us to decide her fate. She is the rightful ruler after all.' He reined his great dapple-grey horse, bringing it to a halt so that he could address them all.

'On reflection,' he said, 'I think that we shall steer a path through Ánweald. I do not wish a welcoming committee that might be spied from other sources. No, I think it best that we come out of the forest approaching Ealdorbold from the west rather than take the main road. Although it will put another day on our journey time, they will have only minutes to prepare for our arrival. I deem it better that way.'

Kirsten barely heard Gailon's words. She gazed about her in wonder, as the land became increasingly familiar to her. She had been there in a dream where she rode Ravenwing swiftly to safety. She wondered if the individuals in the dream were her people—the worried faces in the firelight whose eyes glistened at the prospect of capturing such a magnificent animal. *The castle in the pale moonlight … that must have been Ealdorbold, the birthplace of my mother,* she thought. *But how could she have been my mother? Shénnin died hundreds of years ago. Am I the reincarnation of Shénnin's daughter? If so, what happened to my body? Is my rotting corpse lying somewhere unknown? What happened during those years between my banishment and return?*

'Milady?'

Kirsten returned from her brooding thoughts and found Ioan smiling down at her from his horse.

'We're heading into the trees now.'

Kirsten nodded, smiling. Ravenwing disliked their choice of path immediately and began to shake his head and snort loudly. Kirsten gently patted him.

'Apologies my friend, but this is the way that has been chosen.'

She turned to see a brilliant smile from Cröedaw, who seemingly approved of her conversing with her horse.

The path was ill–trod; in many places, branches grew over it, forcing the party to dismount and carefully wind their way through the maze of obstacles. The evening was drawing late when Gailon decided to stop and make camp. They had marched all day without rest, as Gailon deemed it necessary to place as much distance between themselves and the main road as possible. They found a small clearing carpeted with soft moss, which made a tempting mattress for the night.

Thaniel set about building a fire, whilst Tehd began preparing food for everyone. Cröedaw informed Gailon that he was going to scout the area and Kirsten wondered what he could mean. She removed Ravenwing's saddle, unpacked her water-skin and followed Tom to the stream to fill it. She felt uncomfortable in the silence of evening. The forest was noiseless; not a single bird settled down to roost. Helping Tom carry water back to Thaniel, she said nothing of her growing unease. He smiled his thanks to them, setting it above the fire.

'Thaniel, is it normally this quiet here?' Kirsten whispered. Her voice seemed to thunder out of her, as if for the whole forest to hear and she fell into silence, unwilling to say more.

Thaniel shook his head. 'No,' he said. 'Something is wrong. Cröedaw is having a look. We do not travel these paths often; there is no need when we have a perfectly good road, but … well, no this just isn't right.'

As he spoke, the last shafts of evening sunlight disappeared completely and the forest was engulfed in darkness; only the fire provided them a way to see one another.

'You are quite correct. This is not right. You should be enchanted by now.' The voice was Cob's; he came into view as the darkness fell.

Kirsten rolled her eyes and stormed to the edge of the clearing, preferring to sit in darkness and cold, than abide the faerie's company.

Cob strode to the centre, his tiny legs covering only inches at a time.

'You have gone and set up camp in a faerie ring. You should all be under its spell.'

'Thanks for the warning,' Tom huffed.

'I tried, but I could not get you to hear me,' Cob protested. 'My powers are lessened by sunlight and you all seem unwilling to believe in my kind in the brightness of day.'

'Our apologies, Cob,' Gailon chimed. 'You need not have troubled yourself, however. I heard your warning, but I could see for myself that your people have long abandoned this ring. Look, even the markers are gone.'

The faerie stood centre and ceremoniously raised his arms. A faint glow appeared at several points about the circle. A purple toadstool-like shape formed and then vanished. Cob's face strained and he sighed sadly, dropping his arms.

'You are correct, Master Gailon,' he said. 'The markers have been destroyed. I wonder what happened here. To destruct our circles, takes a powerful spell. I am not sure I would like to meet the bearer of such majick.'

Kirsten watched, hawk-like from the darkness. She silently questioned what the function of the faerie ring would have been, and came to the conclusion that it served the same purpose as a web to a spider; she was glad that it had been destroyed.

Cob was deep in counsel with Thaniel and Gailon. He seemed to respect Gailon, having called him *Master,* she observed. Gailon knew his ways, his majick. *She* had not heard him that day. *He was unlikely to have spoken to me though,* she figured.

Tom sat with Tehd helping him to prepare food; Kirsten smiled at his clumsiness; he obviously let his wife do all the cooking at home, when they had still been together. Ioan talked to Troy, telling him the purpose and role of the messenger. Kirsten watched as Troy nodded politely at intervals during the conversation. The food began to smell wonderful and the group mingled.

Cröedaw still had not returned.

They all seemed at ease, not caring that their voices boomed and echoed through the trees like a sound wave across the silent forest.

Kirsten shivered and stood stiffly, having sat on twigs and stones rather than the mossy growth in the circle. She wondered what Cröedaw might have discovered, if anything, and felt a desperate urge to find him rather than return to the circle where the sound was increasing.

Slipping into the velvet darkness of the forest, she walked ever further away from the firelight, feeling safer once she had put some distance between herself and the beacon of sound and light. Even her breathing sounded too loud to her and she held her breath for a moment, attempting to relieve her fear.

She was afraid—afraid of the prevailing darkness, but afraid of the light more. She found herself wishing that Gailon had let them stay on the road. Without knowing why, her body sprang into action, scrambling up the nearest tree, where she sat awkwardly in the boughs, watching the firelight from a distance. It seemed brilliant against the backdrop of night, and the noise they made, carried. Kirsten clung tightly to the branch.

It was a trap.

A faerie ring no longer, but in principle the same. They had not even noticed her absence. *Whatever broke the faerie majick could still be here,* she thought. Trying to shake off her creeping paranoia, she told herself it was the darkness that had brought upon her fears.

A motion to her right caused her to gasp and the sound bellowed in her ears. *It must be an animal of some kind surely, but I can't see,* she thought. She sat motionless, poised with fear, until she heard a flutter of wings and a croak.

'Is that you?' Her fear was such that she remained unsure whether she had voiced the words or if they were in her mind. She concentrated hard on the sound and tried to focus in the same way that she had in order to reveal Cob.

It was like opening her eyes and seeing for the first time; the darkness lifted, replaced by a purple iridescence, enabling her to see clearly. A large black crow bobbed its head up and down beside her. She reached out her hand and it nuzzled against her. Smiling, her fear lessened on realising that her friend from Field House had followed them. The bird seemed to eye her strangely, as if she herself was an oddity. Suddenly, he took flight and she was alone, wondering why she had left the camp.

'Ioan?' her mind reached out to him.

Nothing.

She could still hear the party in the distance, but she could not reach Ioan's thoughts. *Something is wrong after all,* she thought. She jumped down and gasped as she came face to face with Cröedaw.

'Your eyes! How do you make them do that?' he asked.

Kirsten looked at him quizzically, before realising that her newfound sight must have affected the way her eyes appeared.

'We have to get back. There's something wrong,' he continued.

'I know,' Kirsten agreed. 'They all seem to have forgotten us and the silence…'

'Yes. Something is drawing nearer; I can hear it.'

Kirsten listened carefully, cocking her head to one side; she heard nothing but her companions.

Cröedaw smiled. 'You may be able to see in the dark, Milady, but you'll need to grow ears like these before you can hear as well as my people.'

Kirsten smiled back at him, a smile that faded when she felt her skin prickle.

'Can you feel it?' she asked

'Come on, we've got to get them out of there, and fast.'

They ran. Kirsten's breathing sounded so loud, that she could hear nothing else. Cröedaw stopped suddenly at the edge of the clearing.

'Thaniel! Gailon!' he shouted.

The companions continued to talk and eat without so much as a glance in their direction.

Kirsten stepped forward, but Cröedaw held her back.

'No!' he protested. 'Whatever has enchanted them, will be here soon. If you go to them, you could fall under the same spell. I need you with me if we are going to fight it. Come, arm yourself.'

With that, he strung his bow and remained at the ready. Kirsten unsheathed the sword of Taiohähn and planted her feet firmly apart.

'If whatever it is was strong enough to create this trap, should we not be using majick against it?' she asked.

'Milady, my majick is not a weapon, and Gailon is under the spell. If you have ought that you can use then do so, but be careful; do not weaken yourself with the use of majick and make it impossible for you to defend yourself.'

Kirsten found it difficult to focus; the air seemed thick with fear and despair. She wondered whether she would be able to use the power she had to any effect.

Her sense of foreboding grew when the purple outline of the trees faded a little, as if the air itself was darkness. A stench of decay increased until she thought that she would vomit.

'KIRSTEN!'

It was the voice of Cröedaw. He had reached out from the darkness and touched her shoulder; immediately, she re-focused again. A dark oily cloud was enveloping the clearing; an invisible barrier had surrounded it. Cröedaw let lose an arrow at the top; the slivering shell shuddered, yet did not relent. He tried again, but to no avail. They watched in horror as out of the oily mass, a long serpentine tail dropped and coiled itself around Thaniel, lifting him out of the circle, whilst the others remained oblivious to the attack.

Cröedaw climbed a tree as nimbly as a squirrel, taking another shot.

'What are you doing? You might hurt Thaniel!' Kirsten yelled.

Cröedaw seemed past caring and he continued to shoot, his only goal to destroy the hideous thing. His arrows, however, sank into the goo and were lost without any sign of injury. Kirsten felt helpless, aware that the longer she remained where she was, the nearer Thaniel was to death. She heard a shout of protest from Cröedaw, as she entered the circle.

The first thing that she noticed was how bright it was. She looked up and saw Thaniel's worried face as the features of a woman slithered nearer, her strong serpentine body squeezing him so tightly that he wheezed and gasped for breath. From her tail issued the inky cover that protected her while she prepared to feed. Kirsten began to feel the effects of the spell and a sense of euphoria threatened to overwhelm her. She shook herself and fought back, trying to block off her mind.

'Gailon!' she shouted.

'Ah Kirsten, are you joining us for dinner?'

'Gailon, look up.' Her voice strained with the urgency that she felt. She *needed* him to see. His strength would give *her* strength.

Removing a shuriken from her belt, she aimed for the coils that were suffocating Thaniel. His straining face was deep purple, as he struggled to hold onto life. The throwing star sank deep into the scaly flesh, as an arrow whizzed overhead and pierced the tail tip. The tail shuddered and the serpent relinquished its grip on Thaniel, dropping him to the ground. Gailon was by the fire, chanting loudly as the spell broke. The snake woman fell into the clearing with an outraged hiss.

Kirsten ran to Thaniel, who was coughing and straining for air. There was a sound of swords being drawn and the companions stood rooted; the woman's exquisite face surprised them, making them forget a while, her monstrous form. Her beautiful eyes widened at the thought of her destruction and she gazed at each of them, hoping to find mercy.

'Cröedaw?' Her voice was cold, yet charming.

Cröedaw lowered his bow. His face betrayed no emotion, but his feelings were like a beacon to Kirsten and she sensed the writhing turmoil within him, as if his very soul had been dealt a blow.

As the creature did not seem intent on further attack, Kirsten knelt by Thaniel, helping him into a sitting position. The purple pallor had all but gone and his eyes were no longer bulging, but as he smiled up at her, she heard him wheeze. He opened his mouth to speak and Kirsten prevented him.

'Just rest for a moment,' she suggested.

The bruising had begun to form and she noted the dark patches about his neck. Loosening the buckles on his jerkin, she pulled open his doublet to observe similar patterns across the top of his chest. He did not wince or cry out when she touched his broken ribs, but focused on her eyes as they changed from brown to green.

No longer aware of the dangerous situation, she seemed elsewhere, in the tranquil plane where she had first met Ioan in their silent speaking. There, Thaniel crouched over in pain and Exzalander tapped him lightly on the shoulder. He looked up and saw her hand as it was offered to him.

At first, he was so dazzled by her that he did not move, afraid that the vision would end. However, things were happening far away, back in the darkness of the forest, and he knew that such a moment could not last. Forgetting his pain, he touched her pale, slender fingers and she tightly gripped him, pulling him to his feet, and they ran. He felt his bones knitting back together; his body seemed to buzz with light and energy as they ran like the wind, back into reality.

She smiled at him as his breathing returned to normal, a smile that faded on seeing Troy's face.

'Come on, Thaniel, on your feet,' Troy barked. His voice was so authoritarian that the order was not questioned.

His glance shot briefly back at Kirsten, before returning to the scene that lay behind her. Turning, she saw that circumstances had changed since she knelt to aid Thaniel. Most of the party were under the influence of the spell again and stood like waxworks, staring into nothingness. Gailon held his staff high, chanting in attempt to break the majick that held them. Cröedaw was nowhere to be seen and Kirsten assumed that he was with their attacker, behind the black cloud, which had formed in her absence. She could hear voices distantly, masked by Gailon's incantation.

Thaniel attempted to break through the cloud and got a nasty shock for his trouble. Kirsten felt weak and sat down; the majick on the air appeared draining to her and the counter majick gave her the sensation of being pulled in two directions at once. As the party fell from the spell, Cob stood with Gailon, attempting to remove the creature's shield.

Kirsten closed her eyes, listening to the sound of Cröedaw's voice beyond, allowing her senses to home in and blot out all else …

'You have no-one to blame but yourself,'

So he does know her, Kirsten thought.

'It was during my attempt at his destruction that I was made like this. I did not ask for such dishonour; I did not beg to be loathed and detested, to be forced away from my home and the society of anything other than foul beasts. I am not remembered heroically, as I made my stand; I was hated and hunted. Can you find no pity for me, Cröedaw, even you?'

Cröedaw was silent for a moment and when he spoke, his voice was wavering.

'I pity what happened to you, but it was *you* who gorged yourself. *You* created a monster, not the darkness.'

The creature howled with rage and the whole forest seemed to shudder. 'And so you would destroy me then? Even as you escort the princess home.'

Kirsten's skin prickled, concerned as to what the creature had to do with her.

'It could take years before she confronts Katahl,' Cröedaw said. 'And even then, there is no guarantee of victory. If we lose, then you, Shénär would be a darkness among darkness, yet another evil to be defeated lest we be consumed by your corruption.'

She seemed to Kirsten to be weeping, and yet she made no sound to indicate as much.

Cröedaw's voice softened as he spoke again. 'Do you honestly believe that you could live as one of us after having been tainted for so long? You would be a wild thing, craving ever the taste of blood and desiring not to heal, but enslave and destroy. How many would die before the spell is lifted? And how many more once you are reborn? Shénär of Elfín is already dead. Nothing and nobody can bring her back. I can only hope that she will forgive me when we meet in the next world.'

The feeling of grief and pain emanating from them both overwhelmed Kirsten. She heard herself cry, and as the darkness of unconscious took her, a scream from Shénär rang out that seemed to embody the anguish of Cröedaw, but containing also Shénär's shame, self disgust, and a deep longing for that which could never be.

When Kirsten finally came to, she found herself weeping. Her companions gathered about her, all except for one.

'Where's Cröedaw?' she asked. Sitting up too quickly caused stars to dance before her eyes. 'He's not dead, is he?' The link between them was completely severed and she felt nothing more than her own concern for his well-being.

Tom helped her to her feet and steadied her while she gathered her wits.

'Cröedaw is to travel alone for a while,' Gailon said. 'He will join us again soon I hope.'

'What happened? Is he all right?'

Gailon's bright eyes bore down on her. 'You know better than any of us what occurred, Kirsten. As for his well-being … he needs space; he will mend in time. The folk of Elfín are made of sterner stuff than most. We will see him again and no doubt sooner than we expect.'

His riddling manner puzzled her, but she was at least satisfied that Cröedaw was no longer in danger.

The sun had fully risen and Kirsten wondered if their encounter had lasted so long as her own unconsciousness. She allowed a shaft of sunlight to warm her face and remarked at how less threatening the forest seemed in the light of day.

'The forest will not appear as threatening in the hours of darkness now, I deem,' Thaniel said.

They ate a large breakfast before continuing on their way. Little was said and Kirsten remained haunted by the sound of the scream, which still echoed in her ears, leaving her wondering whether it had been Shénär who had made the sound, or Cröedaw's tortured soul.

The journey through the forest was slow and they often found themselves scrambling down steep banks, hacking back undergrowth that threatened to entangle them. They forced their way through thorny bushes that lay beneath every gap in the canopy, drinking the light as the sun passed overhead. Kirsten eased Ravenwing when he grumbled at another scrape across his flank.

As before, Cob was not with them in daylight hours, leaving Kirsten looking about her, seeing if she could sense him travelling with them through the denseness of the trees.

By midday, their path was easier. Although the trees were tightly packed, the thorny bushes could not survive under the wall of foliage overhead; each tree entwined with the next so that the canopy was like a huge blanket, roofing softly the quiet of the forest floor below.

'I never thanked you for what you did last night, Kirsten,' Thaniel said, as he joined her.

Kirsten had all but forgotten that he had been injured, so busy had she been worrying about Cröedaw.

'Don't mention it,' she said, 'it was nothing.'

She glanced in his direction; even in the dark beneath the trees, his eyes burned brightly.

'You saved my life,' he said. 'I would not call that nothing, unless you value my existence thus.'

Kirsten paused to face him. 'I did not mean that,' she stuttered. She did not want him to feel that she was being impolite. 'I meant that it was what anyone would have done.'

Thaniel frowned and walked away.

Despite the denseness of the forest, Kirsten still felt a chill in the air as they approached their destination. Everyone wrapped their cloaks about them, even Tom in his long hauberk. Kirsten's thoughts returned to Cröedaw and wondered if *he* was cold. He had left his pack and his horse and was travelling on foot, without provisions.

Tom was soon complaining for want of his lunch and Gailon led them south to meet the river. Kirsten was not hungry, but felt the need of a bath. She sat and scrubbed her face and neck in the freezing water, while the others ate. Across the water, she spied a flash of wings fluttering. A large black crow was bathing in the shallows on the opposite bank. It hopped and ruffled its feathers to dry, as she watched.

'Are you going to eat anything, Milady?' Ioan asked.

She looked up at him, bread in hand.

'Thank you, Ioan,' she said.

Taking the bread, she rejoined the party. Tehd scowled at her, as she seated herself and sat silently watching her companions. Troy still appeared solitary, having not bonded with the group; he sat alone and silent. Kirsten pondered his behaviour. He had seemed content with their situation *before* he discovered his heritage. As if he sensed her looking at him, he glanced up; his eyes appeared slightly sunken and his brow was so tense that it darkened his entire face.

How different he seems from the happy-go-lucky young priest I met in what seemed an age ago, she considered.

He suddenly smiled and she saw again a glimpse of Father Troy, except he seemed older somehow. She smiled back, until the sound of the crow drew her attention away. Ravenwing blew air from his lips and stamped his foot at the noise.

When they set off once more, Kirsten chose to walk beside Troy.

'You're not happy,' she affirmed.

He seemed surprised by her approach.

'I suppose,' Troy agreed. 'My whole life has been taken away from me. I feel like an actor whose character dies in the first act and just wants to go home to bed, but the director insists that he stay for the curtain call.'

'So if we can find a way, you're going to return to Earth?' she asked.

He looked at her, as if trying to read some deeper meaning in her question.

His shoulders sagged. 'I guess so,' he said. 'There's nothing for me here. I've served my purpose.'

He quickened his pace, leaving Kirsten to deliberate over his words.

By early evening, the trees were thinning and had Kirsten not felt so tired, she may have enjoyed the scenery, with its little hillocks, wild flowers and sparkling streams. The greatest advantage the change had afforded was that they were able to ride once more. Her legs still ached on horseback, but the pressure in her feet lessened.

As they grew nearer their destination, they saw the tallest turrets of Ealdorbold, and by the time they came to the edge of the forest, Kirsten caught her breath, as the most beautiful castle she had ever seen, was bathed in a perfect sunset, making it seem like something from a dream.

As they approached the gate, a bugle sounded above and people came out to meet their advance. Kirsten felt the points and stares of the crowd, finding them disconcerting.

'Halt!' boomed a commanding voice.

A man of considerable years had come out to meet them. His robe of deep red velvet made him appear majestic; his grey beard, although as long as Gailon's, was well kept. Four guards accompanied him, two on either side, armed with poleaxes, and the remaining two with drawn swords also held upright in front of them in what Kirsten assumed was a salutation.

'Greetings Gailon. We would have expected prior news of your arrival in order that we might prepare a more fitting welcome for you.' Despite the politeness of the man's words, his voice remained emotionless.

'Greetings to you, Counsellor Genargh,' returned Gailon. 'We apologise for our arriving during the evening banquet. We travelled by way of the forest and that is why your herald did not see us.'

The company dismounted, following Thaniel's example, and removed their packs. Stable hands led the horses away, seeming extremely wary of Ravenwing. Genargh watched the horse, then turned and rested his gaze upon Kirsten. He continued to stare while he addressed Gailon.

'Come Master Gailon, you and your companions must join the banquet tonight, and then you may rest.' He clapped his hands and several servants appeared. 'The servants will take your belongings and prepare your quarters, but now to the feast. Tomorrow shall we hold counsel.'

Gailon nodded and followed the small procession back to the banquet hall, where the feast had already begun. The largest table Kirsten had ever seen was before her, laden with a banquet fit for a king. All manner of dishes were served, some of which appeared familiar and others that did not. More servants removed their cloaks and yet more seated them.

Kirsten felt once again, the sensation of many eyes upon her. She saw faces of well-groomed ladies as they scorned her weather beaten dress, with its high splits on each side. Promptly, she seated herself, forgetting her fatigue and no longer feeling hungry. All she wanted to do was run from the hall, away from the palace and never return.

Her companions seemed oblivious to the observations of the guests, and ate the many courses with vigour no different from their first day at Field House.

It felt like an age before the gossip finally subsided and people tired of looking their way. She placed some food onto her plate and began nibbling. *My turn to have a look about,* she thought.

At the far end of the table, a group of men each wearing velvet robes sat and talked, seeming oblivious to the newcomers. At the head of the table sat an ancient looking man with a long, wispy white beard, wearing a gold robe with fine embroidery He sat in conference with Genargh, who was seated to the man's right. The man to the left of the table head was of a younger age, whose black hair matched the colour of his robes; the only hint of colour was a simple gold trim.

Further down the table seemed to be other members of the household of Ealdorbold; elegant females in long flowing dresses and men in richly coloured and expertly embroidered doublets. In a dimly lit corner, musicians played, the sound almost drowned out by the diners as they laughed, talked and drank too much wine. As guests gorged themselves, yet more food was brought in and the servants bustled about the table, cleaning, clearing and serving.

Kirsten was home, but she never felt less at home in her life. Overwhelmed by the scene, she felt alienated from everyone and everything around her.

'Are you not eating, Miss? If there is nought here that pleases you, then I could fetch something else.'

She turned and saw a young man, not much more than a boy, smiling pleasantly. He had a mass of ash blonde hair that was pushed back neatly behind his ears. Kirsten decided that he was the first person that she liked since her arrival that evening.

'No, thank you,' she replied. 'I am simply not hungry. I wonder, if I might retire to my room.'

The young man gave her a slightly worried look as she rose from her chair. She heard Thaniel speak, yet paid no attention to his words as she followed the servant from the hall. Outside, the young man called over one of the serving girls and asked her to show Kirsten to her chamber.

'Thank you again,' Kirsten said.

He bobbed his head, seeming unsure how to react to her.

'What's your name?' she asked.

It was impossible for the man to conceal how odd he found her behaviour.

'Richard,' he stammered.

'Well, goodnight Richard. I hope that you do not find the guests as rude and annoying as I did.'

Richard and the maid exchanged a look that was both shock and amusement. He bowed low, bade her goodnight and returned swiftly to the revellers.

Kirsten decided that it was going to be impossible for her to remember her way about the palace. She felt that she walked about half a mile before finally reaching her room, by which time she had hiked up so many stairs and turned so many corners, that she imagined herself starving to death before finding a way out.

The maid entered the room first and lit the candles. Kirsten followed, discovering that there was no fireplace and the air chilled her to the core.

'Will there be anything else, Milady?'

Kirsten thought herself rude for asking, but she felt so cold and dirty.

'I would be really grateful if I could have a nice hot bath,' she said. 'It's freezing in here.'

'Certainly Milady. I will fetch the water.' The girl nodded and left.

Kirsten laid her weapons on the side and put her cloak over the sword, in case anyone realised what it was. Removing her dress, she wrapped a blanket about her.

It was some time before the girl returned with four others to fill her bath. When they were done, Kirsten tried to politely dismiss them.

'Would you not like us to bathe you?' asked one.

Kirsten was shocked at the thought and then envisioned one of the women at the banquet demanding such a thing.

'No, thank you so much for your trouble.'

They gave half smiles and left the strange woman to her odd ways. Kirsten let the blanket fall and stepped into the tub, sighing loudly.

Her room was sparse compared with Field House. Even the bath was uninviting, made from iron and wood. The one difference that it had was a lid that closed over her body to keep the heat in. She lay back and let the water and steam ease her sore feet and aching limbs.

'You have not made a very good impression so far, have you?'

Cob's voice startled her and had the lid not been down then she would have flooded the floor.

'Cob, get out of my room!' she demanded.

The faerie was perched on the end of her bed, his lips tightened stubbornly and he crossed his legs in defiance.

'Gailon would not allow me to join the feast,' he sulked. 'He said that my presence there might raise too many questions. Where am I supposed to sleep, tell me that?'

'I don't know, Cob, but you can't sleep in *my* room!'

There was a knock at the door and Cob vanished. Kirsten huffed.

'Come in!' she snapped, wondering if she was going to get a moment's peace.

Thaniel stepped in, closing the door behind him. On seeing her in the bath, he immediately turned his back and spoke to the wall.

'What do you think you were doing leaving the feast like that?' he said.

'I was tired.'

'Kirsten, nobody is permitted to quit the table unless dismissed by Head Counsellor Daihron. You have insulted your host in the worst possible way.'

'I can think of better ways to insult someone,' she said.

'Kirsten, you do not seem to comprehend my meaning; to leave the table in such a way shows a lack of respect and contempt for the Council that will damage our chances of gaining their support.'

She felt foolish. Asking to be excused was a basic courtesy and she knew that well, yet she was too stubborn to admit it.

'Well, if you wanted me to obey such a silly rule,' she snapped, 'then perhaps you should have made me aware of it in the first place!'

There was a moment's silence and she wondered what his face might be saying, as he continued to keep his back to her for the sake of propriety.

'Goodnight Kirsten,' he said. Without another word, he walked from the room.

Kirsten tutted to herself and ducked her head under the water, feeling instantly refreshed.

'He is right you know. If you want to be accepted as the princess, then you are going to have to start acting like one.'

'Why are you still here, Cob? I thought I told you to leave.'

'What are you planning to wear when you are introduced as Princess Exzalander? Your dirty red dress perhaps, or those leather trousers of yours? Yes, dress like a man; that will be sure to convince them of your birthright.'

Kirsten scowled and he hopped off the bed and jumped nimbly onto the bath lid.

'These people live on pomp and ceremony,' he explained. 'Riches and grandeur impress them. You are more likely to convince them who you really are if you at least look the part.'

Kirsten's frown uplifted slightly. 'Very well, Cob, what do you suggest? I have nothing else to wear.'

He jumped to the ground laughing, as if she had said something foolish.

'Have you forgotten, Princess, that I am one of the Fair Folk? I can create you the most beautiful gown imaginable, all by the use of a little Shee majick.'

She smiled broadly, feeling suddenly like Cinderella. 'But why would you want to help me? I'll probably walk in and all my clothes will disappear.'

Cob shook his head in protest to her accusation.

'If you fail to conquer Katahl, then you will not be powerful enough to reinstate me in the Macara Shee,' he said. 'I can assure you that it is for purely selfish reasons that I wish to help you.'

Kirsten laughed. 'Well that's all right then. But how are you going to help, if you vanish as soon as the sun rises?'

'Just because you do not see me, does not mean that I am not here. I will create the gown whilst you sleep and in the morning, it will be a simple matter of fitting it. Now, might I suggest that you take your rest and leave me to work on my masterpiece.'

Kirsten lifted the lid and stepped out of the bath. The room felt warm, as soon as Cob began weaving his majick. She dried herself and climbed into bed, no doubt in her mind that she would sleep that night.

Fifteen

If Kirsten had any more visitors, then she was unaware of them; so soundly did she sleep. Thaniel met with Gailon to discuss her behaviour to which she was seemingly oblivious. Gailon was calm, explaining that there was little need to be angry, as what was done could not be undone and they should have taken greater care to teach her the rudiments of court etiquette.

Later that night, Gailon visited her in the view of informing her what to expect at the Council meeting, but on she slept, not hearing Cob as he chatted to the wizard about the gown fit for a queen of old. Gailon seemed both pleased and amused, leaving the faerie to work in peace and Kirsten to slumber.

He himself could not sleep. Despite what he had told Thaniel, he was deeply troubled. He could not shake the thought that he should have taken greater care of her and tutored her in what to expect. *Now, I am to let her loose into a den of rapacious predators,* he thought, *and I hope beyond hope that she will not let me down.*

When Kirsten first opened her eyes, she breathed in deeply, quite forgetting where she was or what had happened, but simply drank in the morning. Sitting up, she blinked, her eyes trying to focus on the most beautiful dress that she had ever seen, floating before her as if worn by an invisible woman.

'Oh Cob it's wonderful!' she gasped. Gazing on the intricate detailing of the lace and beading, her eyes were dazzled by the stormy blue, as it peeped from beneath the lace like waves ebbing and flowing, revealing treasure after treasure.

She stepped out of bed and washed her naked body in cold bath water.

'Shall we?' she said, with a smile.

The gown slipped smoothly onto her form, tightening about her. It was not until Cob allowed it to fall that Kirsten realised just how heavy it was. Cob had made her a masterpiece, however, she wondered if she would be able to walk in it. She slipped her feet into the blue satin slippers, as her hair wove up, over and under and a pearl headdress was fixed in place. She had no mirror in her room, but she felt magnificent.

A swift knock came at the door.

'Milady, I am to escort you to the Council Chamber,' a female voice called. 'Are you up yet?'

'I am ready,' Kirsten said regally.

Opening the door, she was gratified by the look of astonishment that greeted her. She had transformed overnight from a dirty weather-beaten hobo, into the most elegant of ladies.

She turned to close the door before the maid could object.

'Thank you Cob, ' she whispered, and readied herself for the Council.

Huge doors loomed before her, decorated with ornate carvings of eagles, wolves, along with beasts that she did not recognise. She was asked to wait until she was called. The dress seemed weighty and she sighed, suddenly feeling foolish and wondering why she had allowed Cob to talk her into such a farce. She listened as voices rose and fell within the Great Hall and edged closer so that she might hear better.

'You dare even suggest that that ill-mannered brat be of Shénnin? One would not even be sure if she was female from her appearance last night. What proof do you offer to support such a preposterous claim?'

Gailon answered. 'She has the Sword of Taiohãhn, if my word is not enough for you, Counsellor Gohrn.'

A hush seemed to follow, until interrupted by a quiet, deliberate voice, apparently undaunted by Gailon's air of superiority.

'And how do you know that it is truly the Sword of Taiohãhn, Gailon? It may have been forged to its likeness. That is no proof!'

The voices rose to a crescendo until Daihron hushed them.

'Bring in the girl!' he ordered. 'Let us see what account she can give of herself.'

Kirsten stood away from the door, not wanting to make it obvious that she had been eavesdropping. She no longer felt regal, but scared and very small.

The doors swung open and she heard herself summoned. Standing up straight, she walked in. Some of her companions and the twelve counsellors were seated in a ring and she observed, with mild amusement, the look of surprise at her change in appearance from all present.

'Ah, Kirsten is it not? Come, be seated.'

Daihron seemed polite, but Kirsten remained wary. She glanced to the vacant chair, as if it might bite. Two Counsellors sat either side of her appointed space, one of whom was entirely bald and wore a scarlet robe of much tighter fit than his associates; the other was older with a matted grey beard and a faded yellow robe. As she sat, Kirsten looked over to her companions, not daring to risk a smile at their gawping expressions.

'As you may already be aware, Kirsten, Gailon has told us of your claims and has asked us for aid,' Genargh spoke evenly.

Kirsten acknowledged his words with a slight dip of her head, as though it was of little importance to her. She felt sick.

'What proof can you offer that you are indeed the princess?' asked another Counsellor.

Kirsten turned to face the man who appeared to be the youngest of the twelve. He did not wear a full robe, as the others did, but a sleeveless, velvet overcoat, which covered his sky blue tights and tunic.

'What proof do you wish me to produce, *Counsellor?*' Her voice was as smooth as honey and her question served to indicate his lack of manners.

'It is Whil, Counsellor Whil,' the man said.

Kirsten assumed that the only reason that formal introductions had been neglected was because they had proclaimed her *'an ill-mannered brat'*.

'Perhaps we might begin with taking a look at your sword,' Whil suggested.

Kirsten nodded. 'Certainly,' she said. 'It is in my room.'

A man with a heavy voice, wearing a lime green robe that accentuated his auburn hair, spluttered, 'You left what you claim to be the Sword of Taiohãhn, in your room … foolishness!'

Kirsten appeared unperturbed by his outburst.

'And you are?' she asked.

'*Counsellor* Ryan,' he snorted.

'The room is protected and is quite secure, let me assure you.'

There was a general murmur amongst the Council, wherein she risked a glance to her friends and raised her eyebrows with half a smile. She was beginning to enjoy herself thinking, *these silly little men seem to pose no threat at present.*

Thaniel respectfully bowed his head before speaking. 'Counsellors, ask Genargh of the horse on which Kirsten rode in. It is the mighty Ravenwing, returned from legend to be at her side as was foretold.'

Genargh shifted in his seat. *'That horse* was here five nights ago, *without* its present rider I might add. Congratulations on its capture, but a horse proves nothing!'

His voice, for the first time, betrayed his emotion. It was hinting at anger, but mostly what Kirsten sensed was fear. She stood slowly, feeling all eyes upon her.

'Gentlemen, we could argue for days on this subject and still reach no resolve,' she said. 'We can present you with evidence, and yet no matter what I do, you will refuse to believe in me, because you made up your minds before I even entered the room. Is that not so? What, no answer?

'You welcome me here as you might welcome a plague. Well let me tell you, I did not know until a short time ago that I was anyone other than Kirsten. I have lived on another world from this one and had no knowledge of this place before my return, yet do you know what the first words were that I spoke on my arrival? Do you?'

'I'm home.' Troy said beaming.

Kirsten turned to him, her eyes shining back.

'This is Troy; he was the messenger sent to bring back word of me. And he,' she pointed to Tom, 'He is Thomn-the-Cleaverhand, Captain of the Shénnin Guard, sent to protect me. These things sound incredible to you, but let me assure you that they are even more so to me.'

'Eloquently put, Lady.'

It was the smarmy voice that she had heard condemn her earlier. It belonged to the bald headed man beside her.

'Pray take a seat,' he said. 'If the Council will indulge me, I have a test to perform that will prove that such a claim *cannot* be proven.'

Kirsten felt unnerved again, as the man signalled to the doorman.

'Yes Counsellor Gohrn?'

'A serving girl ... quickly!' he ordered.

Kirsten observed the look of horror from a Counsellor who had remained silent throughout the meeting. His robes were a less colourful muddy brown, and he wore a skullcap over his dark brown hair. Kirsten watched him intently, trying to determine why he was suddenly so distressed.

A servant was beckoned into the circle and both doormen were ordered to leave. As the doors banged shut, Gohrn summoned the girl before him.

'What is your name, woman?'

The girl was nervous and Kirsten hated Gohrn at that moment for subjecting her to such an ordeal.

'Marin, Counsellor Gohrn.' She curtseyed clumsily before him.

'By the power of the Counsel of Shénnin, I rename you Exzalander.'

Her eyes widened in fear and she dropped to her knees, trembling violently. Kirsten moved to help her and Gohrn snapped.

'REMAIN SEATED!'

'No Gohrn, I forbid you to do this!' said the man in brown, as he stood from his seat.

'Be quiet, Jaden. I will prove that her existence cannot be proved and the legends are nothing more than superstition, so you will be silent if you do not wish to be struck from our order.'

Jaden looked about him, his eyes appealing for support, but all gazed fixedly at the serving girl with growing curiosity.

'What is your name, woman?' Gohrn demanded.

The girl was crying and shaking her head. Kirsten looked helplessly to her companions, not understanding what was happening. Gailon's face was grey, but he remained silent.

Gohrn slapped the woman hard across the face.

'YOUR NAME WOMAN, OR I KILL YOU WHERE YOU STAND!' he screeched.

'Exzalander,' she snivelled. 'My name is Exzalander.'

Gohrn gave a triumphant smile and seated himself, seeming completely composed once more.

'There, fellow Counsellors, there you see how in these modern times, we are plagued with folk tale and legend. She is not harmed you se ...'

He was cut off suddenly by a guttural sound coming from the girl, as she reeled forward, struggling for breath. Gohrn kicked her away as she reached for the hem of his robe, hatred in her dying eyes.

Jaden sprang toward her, but he could do nothing to comfort her as she died in his arms. Gohrn paled, his plan having backfired. Kirsten shook her head in disbelief at the lifeless body of the girl.

'I don't understand,' she whispered.

Gailon spoke sombrely. 'The name was given by Taiohãhn Himself to signify His chosen. It is written that one who falsely proclaims to be Exzalander will suffer a painful death.'

Kirsten felt tears in her eyes as she recalled the words of Meggan, who had warned her of the possibility of such an occurrence.

'*Why?* Why would you do such a thing?' she half whispered, half sobbed at Gohrn. 'Why did you not ask me to tell you *my* name?'

She fell to her knees as Jaden gently laid the girl on the floor. Her hand reached out and checked for a pulse, but there was nothing. Marin's horror-struck eyes already held the look of death. Kirsten cried freely and held the girl to her. She no longer heard the voices around her and was oblivious to the exclamations, as before their eyes she began to change.

She was searching, searching in the plane of light; searching for Marin, knowing that if she could find her, then there was a chance that she might bring her back. She tried calling Marin's name, but no sound escaped her lips. Looking about her, she saw nothing but white. It was no use; Marin was gone.

Through her tears, the body of the girl came into focus. *One more dead because of me,* she thought bitterly. Then it came to her suddenly, *Walker and the fish ...*

She placed her hands on Marin's chest and watched it jump repeatedly as the electricity flowed into her. Marin's dilated pupils shrank back and the girl suddenly blinked. She was alive.

Kirsten dismissed the buzzing sensation that remained at the tips of her fingers, crying as Marin smiled at her and sat up. She did not need to look about her to know that there were a lot of shocked and scared Council members. Slowly, she rose to her feet, composing herself once more.

'My name is Exzalander,' she said, 'Daughter of Tuâth and Shénnin and if any one of you tries something like that again, your own death will follow swiftly!'

The double doors opened on her approach and slammed behind her, leaving Gailon smiling at the room of distressed Counsellors.

Kirsten wandered, but her subconscious found the way back to her chamber. She slammed the door behind her, tore off the pearl headdress and shook out her long red hair, with a huff. Her fingers still had a faint electrical buzz and her hair floated with static.

'I take it that my idea did not work,' whispered the disappointed voice of Cob, in her ear.

She gave a heavy sigh, fiddling with the headdress. 'It took them by surprise, which was a good thing, as it caught them off guard—most of them anyway. Cob, would you be so kind as to leave me now. I just want to be alone for a while.'

The faerie left soundlessly, the door closing behind him. She lay back on the bed, the scene with Marin and Gohrn replaying repeatedly in her mind. By the time her companions arrived to speak to her, she was gone.

Despite being sworn to secrecy by the Council, word spread quickly of Marin's resurrection. She no longer feared them, not since being witness to Exzalander's threat. The household was abuzz with excitement at the rumour of Exzalander's return.

Richard retold the tale of how she had left the banquet and treated him with such courtesy, which was received with almost as much excitement as the miracle of Marin.

Kirsten drifted aimlessly away from noise and people, into the darker places of the palace, eventually coming to areas that had long since been abandoned and forgotten, figuring no-one would find her in the blackness of the corridors. She used her night vision so that she could see, but all looked the same—dank, dirty, endless hallways and steps that delved deeper into the heart of Ealdorbold.

No thought was given to how long she had been gone or whether she would be missed. She forgot all that had occurred, allowing herself to be simply a child, exploring in hope of discovering something wonderful.

High above, the search had begun for Kirsten. The gatekeepers assured Thaniel that she had not left the palace. Troy questioned some servants, but they seemed more interested in discovering if Marin's tale was true. Troy found the whole subject uncomfortable. He was not sure what he had witnessed, but he refused to believe that it was a miracle. *Kirsten electrocuted Marin,* he thought. *It was science that brought her back ...*

Tehd refused to help in the search. 'I won't go!' he said. 'It be a lot o' fuss over nothin'. She's probably wandered off and got herself lost. She'll turn up eventually, and if she doesn't, good riddance I say!'

Ioan's face was horrified. Nevertheless, Tehd remained adamant.

Cob had seen which direction Kirsten had gone in, but was having difficulty getting anyone's attention. The best response he had was when he followed Tom down to the kitchen area and knocked over some plates.

As one of the cooks picked up the pieces of broken crockery, she tutted, 'Faeries!'

Unfortunately, Tom did not make the connection.

The deeper Kirsten explored, the lighter it seemed to become. A peculiar sensation came upon her, an air of familiarity. Breaking a wall of cobwebs was like crossing over a bridge of time. *I know this place,* she realised. The smell, which had been damp and stale, filled with exciting odours. She paused, her mind recalling perfectly the way it was … *the toys and inventions, the explosions and curses, the funny looking books that I was not allowed to touch and the bald-headed bird whose eyes followed my every move.*

Pausing, she looked suddenly to her right, where a painting hung on the wall. Carefully, she cleared the cobwebs.

'It cannot be!' she said aloud.

It was a painting of a woman on a sandy hill; she wore a crimson dress and her long red hair fell below her waist. In her hand, she held aloft the Sword of Taiohãhn, which shone as the sun rose behind her. It was the moment she had arrived on Maldahl, portrayed in an old painting in a lost part of an ancient palace.

For a long time she stared, observing new details such as the weapons that hung at her belt, depicted accurately. She moved on toward a heavy door before her, the point to which she had been drawn. Stepping up, she lifted the latch, and pushed.

It was late afternoon before the Council was *officially* informed of Kirsten's absence. They for the most part, did not seem particularly concerned for her well-being; some said that she had disappeared again and perhaps they would have to wait another few hundred years for her to grace them with her presence once more.

Gohrn ordered a room-by-room search, using all soldiers on duty, other than the gatekeepers and herald. Tom and Thaniel were immediately suspicious of his sudden willingness to help and decided to keep a close eye on him.

It was not until Gailon was alone that Cob managed to get his attention and finally let him know where Kirsten had gone. Gailon called off the search and reported that Kirsten was safe and well, in her room. Taking a torch, he set off down the corridor where Cob had seen her go.

'Master Gailon?' called Richard the serving boy. 'It is not safe to go down there. The tunnels go on for miles, it is said. Nobody who has gone down there has ever come out.'

'Thank you for your concern, lad, but these tunnels hold no fear for me,' Gailon replied. 'It has been many a year since I last ventured down them, but I believe I still know the way.' With that, he was gone, swallowed by the darkness.

Muttering a light spell under his breath, the torches on the walls illuminated fiercely. He felt hot, being well aware how dangerous the catacombs of Ealdorbold were. Majick maintained them and they had a life of their own, often moving and shifting so that the maze of corridors would confound all who tried to retreat from them.

However, Gailon knew the way; he knew where she had gone…

It was locked.

Kirsten pushed again and to her frustration, the door refused to budge. She tried looking through the keyhole, considering that the contents of the room might not be so special after all. *If that is so, why bother to lock it?* she thought.

Darkness.

All she could see was darkness. Her eyes strained, but it was blacker in there than Ánweald forest had ever been. *If only I thought to bring the sword, at least I might have been able to prise it open,* she reasoned.

Suddenly, the torches in the corridor ignited and she gasped in fright, expecting something dreadful to happen. When nothing did, she sighed in frustration and sat with her back to the door, her dress filthy. A noise from behind the door startled her and she shuffled back, peering cautiously through the keyhole. The room had filled with light and despite the cobwebs and dust that covered everything; it was all she had hoped for. There were piles of books, desks, flasks, jars, but the strangest thing of all, daylight. She could clearly see the light of day as if it was flooding through a window of some kind.

'It's not possible,' she murmured. 'It wasn't there a moment ago and I've been travelling down; I must surely be underground by now.'

More than anything, she wanted to get into the room and tried the lock again.

'Oh please let me in,' she said pathetically, her voice childlike in its plea. The wood itself shuddered, as if responding to her voice, and the door creaked open.

'Thank-you,' she whispered.

Both apprehensive and excited, she stepped in. She had been correct; there was indeed a window, and if that was not strange enough, when she looked out, she could see the whole of the palace below. The room was in a very tall tower.

'Impossible,' she said.

Behind her, lay a vast amount of books and equipment. She spied a perch and recalled again as if from a dream, the vulture-like bird as it silently watched her. Sniffing at one of the jars, she recoiled, as a whiff of sulphur offended her nostrils. Blowing a heavy layer of dust off a nearby volume, she sneezed. The title was written in letters unfamiliar to her, but the pictures told her all she needed to know, graphically depicting dissection, the removal of organs and the uses thereof. She put the book down in disgust, deciding not to look too closely at the jars on the shelves. Dust and dirt covered her dress, but she no longer paid any heed.

She sat at the main desk and unravelled scrolls of parchment that appeared not to have aged in the least. Her heart jumped when she realised what she had found.

'Yes … it is the spell.'

Kirsten jumped at a voice other than her own. The scroll snapped shut and fell to the floor. Gailon entered the room and Kirsten's eyes were drawn to him. He seemed younger—much younger. He lifted a hand and the scroll levitated back onto the desk. The room seemed alive at his presence; she could almost see the latent majick, as it greeted an old friend.

'Gailon!' She wanted to say more, but was unable to find the words.

The old wizard's eyes surveyed the room, seeming both excited and sad.

'We were worried about you, Kirsten,' he said.

She was still looking at him in wonderment, as he seemed to rejuvenate by the second.

'It is forbidden to walk these passageways,' he continued. 'If the Council were to learn of where you have gone, it would give them every excuse to criticise—or worse.'

He stared at her silent form, her eyes watching him with a child's wonder.

'Come, we must return before anyone realises that I lied about your whereabouts.'

It was as though he had thrown a glass of water in her face and she snapped back at him.

'No!'

He sighed, but amusement was in his eyes. 'You were ever like this,' he said. 'My master was begged not to indulge you so, but … come, let us return you to your room and I will tell you what you desire to know.'

Kirsten gazed longingly about her and then snatched up the scroll with a nod of agreement.

'Take nothing from the room, Kirsten. There must be no evidence of your being here.'

'But Gailon it's …'

'I know what it is. It will be safe here. Nobody can enter this room except myself and it seems, you. Now come.'

He held out his hand, his long fingers adorned by the ring of Anarkhane. Reluctantly, she placed back the scroll and got to her feet. Gailon led her by the arm from the room.

'Look at the state of you,' he remarked. 'We had better return by the short route. What will Cob say when he sees what has become of his night's work?'

Kirsten sagged, feeling a tug of regret as he closed and locked the door behind him. They were in the corridor again and Kirsten stood before her picture.

'Gailon, how is this possible?'

He smiled. 'That was painted by a young apprentice who was keen to depict future events.'

She watched as he touched the wall behind the painting and saw it dissolve before her eyes. He urged her forward, but she did not move.

'Come Kirsten, this is the quicker route back. It will not harm you.'

She stepped forward into the unknown. Her stomach turned over and she felt as though she was falling. About her, objects and people seemed to pass at incredible speed, like pictures on a spinning top, which distorts the faster it turns. They stopped with a jerk, and it took a while before her stomach let gravity catch up with it once more.

Gailon pushed gently forward and she found that she was in the corridor just outside her chamber. She felt too disorientated to exclaim her amazement, simply allowing Gailon to lead her to the room and dispel the majick that sealed it.

She walked over to her bed then had second thoughts to lying on it, for fear of soiling the sheets with the grime of her adventure.

'Now I will leave you to get cleaned up. I will send the servants to bring you fresh water, but do not let them see you in that state.'

'Gailon, you said that you would tell me about the room,' Kirsten protested.

He turned back smiling. 'And I will,' he said, 'just as soon as you are in a fit state to receive company, and that includes having eaten. You've hardly touched a bite since you arrived. I will return before the feast and escort you down.'

He was gone before she could offer another objection. With difficulty, she removed her gown, understanding why maids dressed the ladies. She had only just managed to remove the heavy garment, when there was a knock at the door. Kicking the dress under the bed, she hastily wrapped a blanket about herself, hoping that her face was clean.

'Enter,' she called. She was looking forward to soaking the day away.

To her surprise, it was not the servants carrying bath water who entered her bedchamber, but Counsellor Gohrn. His eyebrow rose slightly at the sight of her and he smiled thinly as he closed the door. Her heart pounded and she cursed herself for not having enquired who it was.

'Expecting someone else?' he scorned,

'Counsellor Gohrn, I am about to take a bath, so if you ...'

'Yes, I would say that is a good idea,' he said as he walked over to her. 'Whatever have you been doing to lend yourself in such a state? You look positively wild.' Reaching out, he wiped some of the dirt from her cheek.

She drew back, horrified that he had dared to touch her. She wanted to order him from the room, but could not find the words.

A second knock came at the door and she spoke with difficulty and growing relief at the interruption.

'Enter.'

The servants sounded excited until they saw Gohrn was present; he made no move to leave and continued to leer at her semi-nakedness. The women filled the bath in silence and Kirsten observed their knowing glances, imagining the rumours that would be born at that moment. *I have to do something,* she thought. *Now.*

'As I was saying, Counsellor, I am about to take a bath. I am sure whatever you came to discuss with me can wait for a more convenient time.' She quickly checked the girl's expressions and felt a surge of relief as they changed.

'Please do not mind me, Milady,' Gohrn said. 'It does not offend me if we hold our meeting why you bathe. I will stay.'

Kirsten breathed heavily, feeling humiliated and wishing that she had more experience in dealing with men. She mustered up all her courage and her reply was far more insulting than the polite dismissal that she had intended.

'No Sir, you shall not! My bathing may not offend you, but your presence here *does* offend me most greatly. You will leave here at once, and may seek an audience with me only when your manners have improved. Good day, Sir.'

She did not need to look at the servants to know that no rumours would spread regarding Gohrn and herself, other than that she detested him. His face revealed nothing as he walked from the room, but Kirsten could not help but sense on his anger.

The servants filled the bath and seemed to be waiting for the opportunity to address her. However, her confrontation with Gohrn had left her in no mood for conversation with strangers and she harshly dismissed them.

Sixteen

The maid who took the food to Kirsten's room, had been forewarned of her foul mood and told not to speak with her. Kirsten, having soaked away her troubles for a while, greeted the girl warmly. She wore the nightdress that Sally had given to her and lay back on the bed.

'Where would you like me to put the tray, Milady?' the girl asked.

'Over here is fine. Thank-you.'

The girl was apprehensive, as she drew near.

'Would you do me a favour? I'm sorry what's your name?'

The girl placed the food down. 'Chana,' she replied.

'Would you send my apologies to the women who filled my bath earlier. Tell them that it was not my intention to take my problems out on them. Can you do that for me, Chana?'

'Certainly Milady, but I am sure that they understand.' She curtseyed and walked toward the door. 'Is it true?' Her voice wavered with emotion as she turned back to Kirsten. 'Are you really Exzalander?' she whispered.

Kirsten grimaced. 'I thought our assembly was supposed to be a secret,' she said.

Chana ventured forward a little, her excitement overcoming her conditioning to follow orders. 'Milady, how could you expect to keep such news a secret? Especially after what you did.'

'And what was that?' Kirsten asked dismissively. She began to eat, suddenly feeling very hungry.

'You brought Marin back from the other side. Is it not true, Milady? *And* the way you spoke to the Counsellors. Nobody has dared threaten them before, and you rejected Counsellor Gohrn. If you are not Exzalander, then at the very least you must be a powerful wizard to achieve such feats.'

Kirsten found Chana a little hard to follow; the girl spoke quickly and seemed to get carried away. She signalled for Chana to sit on the bed; the girl was hesitant, until Kirsten insisted.

'Now listen to me, Chana; I don't know what has been said, but I do know one thing, if this rumour of my presence here persists, then we are all putting ourselves in danger. Sooner or later such gossip will leave the palace walls and then we'll have Katahl's army at out gate with no time to prepare. You do understand, don't you? My presence must not be known. So I am begging you, please ensure that your friends see sense. I am not to be treated any differently from the other ladies in the palace. Will you do that for me?'

Chana nodded. 'I will try, but *all* of us know.'

'Thank-you,' Kirsten said, 'now tell me what did you mean by, resisted Counsellor Gohrn?'

'Well, he has a lot of women, as far as I know, no woman has ever said no to him, until today that is. He must be furious.'

Kirsten remembered how dominated and defenceless she had felt when she had been alone with him.

'Is he a wizard, Chana?' she asked.

Chana shifted forward and whispered conspiratorially, seeming completely at ease with Kirsten.

'Majick is outlawed here,' she said. 'But it is rumoured that Counsellor Gohrn has practised it to achieve his own ends. I doubt it can be true though, as there is nobody who could have tutored him. There is no Master in these parts, except Gailon and he's never had an apprentice, to my knowledge.'

There was a sharp rap on the door and Chana jumped immediately to her feet in alarm. She collected the plate and made for the door.

'Master Gailon.' She curtseyed.

'Thank-you, Chana,' Kirsten called after her.

'You're welcome, Milady,' Chana said. She gave Kirsten a winning smile as she closed the door behind her.

'You are becoming quite popular with the servants, I see,' Gailon grunted. 'It is a shame that you could not have made such an impression on the Council.'

Kirsten gave him a knowing stare.

'It would not have made one bit of difference how I behaved,' she said. 'They would disapprove of me whatever I had done.

'Perhaps, but threatening to kill them was a little extreme I feel, Kirsten.'

Her eyes dipped in shame. 'I was angry. It was Gohrn, what he did to that poor woman …'

'I know,' Gailon said. 'But he is dangerous. You must try not to upset him if you can.'

Kirsten's eyes fell to her lap and she felt her cheeks growing hot. 'I think it may be a little late for that.'

She sensed Gailon stiffen.

'What have you done?' he asked, straining to keep calm.

'I threw him out of my room and in none too nice a manner.'

She looked up at Gailon whose eyes appeared horrified.

'He wanted to stay while I took a bath,' she protested. 'He even had the nerve to touch me—only on my face, but he made it feel indecent. I am sorry Gailon, truly I am. It was not my intention to cause more trouble.'

Gailon seethed, seeming unable to speak. Kirsten moved forward, as if preparing for the lecture that she was expecting.

'He can think himself lucky that I did not witness such behaviour,' Gailon said. 'I would have whipped him from here to Bashnya for such an insult. It is not to be borne. I am going to place a formal complaint to Daihron himself for such offensive behaviour. You were quite right to throw him out; I would have thrown a chair at him as well.'

Kirsten was too caught up with dread to react in the way that she wanted, which was to laugh. 'I thought that you would be angry at me,' she said.

Gailon shook his head and smiled. 'No my dear, quite the contrary. Today you have made me very proud. Apart from the threat of death, you conducted yourself like a true leader. Well done.'

Kirsten felt good. Praise from Gailon was praise indeed.

'Thank you Gailon, that means a lot to me,' she said.

'Now, you wanted to know about the room that you discovered …'

Kirsten found herself fidgeting to get into a more comfortable position, with child-like eagerness.

'The room belonged to the great wizard Ardahl,' Gailon explained. 'It was his workplace, his library and his home. The room is situated in the highest tower of Ealdorbold, but there are no stairs or entrance of any kind to the tower. It is by descent into the catacombs that one ascends to the tower. Ardahl created a maze of majick in order to protect his spells and his work from falling into the wrong hands, although back in the early days of your parents' rule, a few people knew how to reach the tower; they needed to, for Ardahl was apt to disappear for weeks. If not checked from time to time the delay might result in the spell asked for, no longer being required.

'It became easier for him, I think, when he took on an apprentice. It was then that he had no real need to leave the tower and his apprentice became his only connection with the world outside.

'You have been to the tower before, but that I believe you already guessed. You would often play there as a child. I do not know how you came to find your way in, but Ardahl welcomed your presence there and even encouraged it. You would read, watch and listen. Sometimes you would simply play with his inventions, but all the while, you were learning.

'After your move north, your visits became less frequent, but luckily by then Ardahl had taken on his apprentice. I sometimes think that the only reason that he did so was because he missed your company.'

'*You* were the apprentice, Gailon!'

'Yes, you are correct. We have met before; I would be studying or preparing compounds when your final visits came. I remember listening to you telling Ardahl about Katahl and his knights and how in love you were. I think you must have been oblivious to my even being there.'

Kirsten frowned, wishing that she could remember more than flashes. 'What happened to Ardahl?' she asked.

Gailon stood and walked a little. 'He died. The spell you found was too powerful and it killed him. I warned him, but he was determined to send you help and perhaps even bring you home. Silly old fool; I told him that it would not work. I showed him the visions that I had painted, but he insisted that even if it did not go to plan, that his spell would play its part, as would the two who were sent, and that it was beyond my comprehension to realise how.

'The spell killed him instantly, and the Council who by then had formed our controlling government, decided to seal off the catacombs and punish all those who tried to gain access to the tower.

'All my Master's work was lost and I was forbidden to attempt to retrieve it. The Counsellors were establishing themselves in firm positions of power and saw Ardahl as a threat. When he died, it was easy for them to win the loyalty of the people. Majick was a threat to them and any further attempt to retrieve you, a treacherous offence. The spell that you grasped was last in the hands of my Master on the day of his death.'

'Does that mean that it is not possible to sent Troy back?' Kirsten asked. 'The spell is too dangerous?'

Gailon nodded. 'Yes it is—at present anyhow. So, Troy has told you that he wishes to leave?'

She shrugged. 'No, but he seems very unhappy ... and bitter.'

'Yes, but I do not think his going back will help him any. He has touched the face of love and it has filled him with only emptiness and despair. He must find another cure, I deem.' Gailon smiled. 'Now you look much puzzled. Come, you must dress yourself. It will not do for us to be late for the evening feast two nights together.'

'My dresses are both dirty,' Kirsten grumbled. 'I only have my leather.'

Gailon shrugged. 'Then tonight you will wear that and show them the warrior that you are. Tomorrow, we shall arrange for a new wardrobe for you. I will await you outside.'

He nodded to her and left the room. After Gailon's history lesson, she found herself disliking the Counsellors even more. It seemed to her that they had used the demise of her parents and of Ardahl, simply as an opportunity to seize power, and from what she had witnessed of their behaviour thus far, she could not imagine Katahl himself being much worse.

Once again, all heads turned as Kirsten entered the banquet hall. This time, however, she held her head up high, unconcerned that she was not dressed as finely as they were. She was well groomed and the sword of Taiohãhn gleamed like the sun, daring eyes of disapproval.

To her dismay, she had been seated amongst the Counsellors, between Whil and Borin. Borin, from what she could gather, was the third most powerful counsellor; he sat on Daihron's left, opposite Genargh. Whereas it was Genargh's task to deal directly with the High Counsellor Daihron, Borin's position allowed him greater interaction with the other Council members.

Whil stood from his chair at her approach, as did a few others Kirsten noted, but they were most assuredly in the minority. She nodded to them in greeting.

'Good evening gentlemen,' she said formally. She wished, more than anything, that she had been permitted to sit with her friends.

The banquet had not yet begun and the guests at the table talked.

As the tip of her sword brushed against his knee, Borin grumbled, 'Lady Kirsten, it is a little inappropriate to wear weapons to the table.'

Kirsten smiled demurely, stating loudly, 'No more inappropriate than seeking an audience with me whilst I bathe!'

Borin appeared shocked. 'I would never …' he protested.

'No, but Gohrn would. So you will excuse me, gentlemen, if his obscene behaviour places me on my guard and deprives you of the lady at dinner, as it is my belief that the warrior would never be abused so.'

Gohrn's face reddened.

'Is this true, Gohrn?' Daihron seethed.

Gohrn did not answer; his lips twisted tighter and his eyes were all daggers. Kirsten appeared unperturbed by his reaction to her, taking the opportunity to glance at her party. The others chattered among themselves, but Gailon watched events with avid interest, ready to intervene if necessary.

'Your silence speaks volumes, Gohrn,' said the High Counsellor. 'You will leave our company and dine alone. I will hold counsel with you on the 'morrow, when you had better produce a valid reason for insulting a lady so.'

Gohrn's face sneered and he retorted, 'She is no more a lady than you are, Daihron!' He stormed from the hall before further words could be spoken.

Kirsten was surprised at Daihron's reaction and hoped that she had not done the wrong thing. Risking a glance at Gailon, her worries quelled as she observed his gratified look to all that had occurred

'Ah, food!' Ryan said loudly.

As they began to help themselves to dishes placed on the table, Whil began to chuckle.

'Something amuses you, Counsellor Whil?' Kirsten asked.

He turned to her while munching on what appeared to be a piece of poultry.

'It is just that, I have never seen Gohrn so angry,' he replied. 'And to be put down by a woman, meaning no disrespect to you, Lady Kirsten, but it is simply delicious!'

'Well I did not mean to upset anyone,' Kirsten said. 'I simply want him to treat me with the respect that he thinks he deserves.'

Whil laughed louder. 'Oh you are a gem. "With the respect he *thinks* he deserves"; you really have it in for him, have you not? Tell me, was the death threat really extended to all of us, or did you have eyes for him in particular?'

Kirsten swallowed her mouthful of food before it was ready and it made her choke. 'I simply meant that I would protect anyone who was preyed upon in such a way,' she said.

'Whil, our counsel was supposed to be secret, or had you forgotten?' Genargh interrupted. 'Hardly a fitting subject for the table!'

Whil's smile faded and he bowed his head in respect of Genargh's words.

'I should not worry about *that*, Counsellors,' said a husky voice. 'From what I hear, all the interesting parts of the meeting have been told and retold all day.'

It sounded as though the man smoked too much. Kirsten recognised him as one of the Counsellors who sat next to her that morning.

'That is Jonah,' Whil whispered in her ear. 'He is a direct descendant of Danah, the original High Counsellor of Ealdorbold. He is a little eccentric and seems to have no regard for what people say or think about him.'

Kirsten leaned in a little, delighted by Whil's gossiping nature.

'He did not have much to say this morning,' she whispered back.

Whil's eyes sparkled with mischief. 'Yes well, this morning he was recovering from last night, if you take my meaning.'

Kirsten smiled cheekily.

'Ah, you do have a smile after all.'

She stopped smiling, hoping she had not acted inappropriately.

'You *are* permitted to smile you know,' Whil said. 'Unless it is your intention to *scare* us all into submission. I certainly will think no less of you for doing so.'

Kirsten smirked. 'For smiling or scaring you into submission?' she asked.

'Both I imagine,' he replied.

She poured herself a goblet of wine.

'I have to admit that I found your arrival to be rather exciting news,' Whil continued.

Kirsten's face remained without emotion. 'Is that so, Counsellor Whil?' she said.

'Of course. You are renowned as a great warrior and I was happy to find a new challenge.'

She felt uncomfortable in the extreme, wondering who might have told him that she was a 'great warrior' when all she had managed to do was get herself into a bar room brawl and kill a couple of thugs.

'I am not sure that I understand your meaning, Sir,' she replied.

'Why, the archery contest of course! It is to be held in nine days time. You will take part, will you not?'

'I … I am afraid that I have not the skill in archery,' she stuttered. 'To hold truth, I have never held a bow in my life. I would therefore be a most poor competitor.'

All eyes were once again on her. Whil had issued her a challenge and she was trying to refuse him. Her status as a warrior would diminish unless she accepted. She knew that she should not care, but her vanity got the better of her.

'I will of course compete if it be your wish. It seems to mean such a lot to you.'

Whil beamed at her, and she sighed, wondering how she was going to learn to shoot in just nine days. *If only Cröedaw was here,* she thought. *He would be a proficient tutor.*

'Tell me Whil, are you the youngest Counsellor?' she asked, eager for a change of subject.

'Yes,' he said, with a smile. 'Callarn over there in the purple, he is the second youngest, but he is still five years my senior and never says anything. The only time you get any kind of response is when we have to vote on something.' He lowered his voice further due to the close proximity of his subject of conversation. 'Next to me is Ryan. As you probably gathered, he is a bit of an act first, think later person. He was actually a member of the guard who rose in the ranks—do not ask me how. The rest of us were born to take our rightful place, but when Counsellor Haden died, he left no heir of any kind and a replacement had to be chosen. I think they voted for Ryan because they believed him so dense that he could be easily manipulated. The man is an oaf, with all the leadership ability of a horse!

'The man in yellow is Torhn, he will always follow the majority and so you never know where his loyalties lie. Opposite him is Vahrn; he has hopes of becoming High Counsellor. He is a man of sensible judgement, but will not stand against Genargh or Daihron whether he agrees with them or no'. He would not dare risk losing his chance of promotion.

'And opposite you is Jaden. He is an odd one, quiet for the most part. He tends to try to pass laws regarding the welfare of the people. He believes that the poor should, for the most part, be left to their own devices and be able to sort out their own troubles.'

'Ah, laissez-faire,' Kirsten remarked. 'Yes I am familiar with that policy of 'non interference', but in the history of the place where I have been living, it proved problematic to the tax payer, who wondered why he had to pay money for nothing.'

Kirsten sipped her wine thoughtfully, failing to notice that Jaden was listening intently to her words. Genargh broke in, eager not to have to listen to the rights of the poor it seemed, and was quick to change the subject.

'Tell us, Lady Kirsten. Where did you get to today? You had us searching high and low,' he said.

His voice sounded concerned, but Kirsten knew better than believe such a thing.

'I apologise to have caused any trouble. I was simply exploring the palace. Had I known there had been concern for my whereabouts, I would have returned at once.'

Genargh smiled pleasantly. 'You should be careful, Lady Kirsten; there are parts of the palace that it is forbidden to go. We would hate for you to become stranded or land yourself into trouble. Next time you wish to explore, might I suggest that you tell someone where you are likely to be found or perhaps take a guide, thereby avoiding any … mishap.'

'I thank you for your concern, Counsellor Genargh and will take your advice into consideration, if choosing to explore again.'

Genargh winced slightly. Despite her charming manner, her words flecked with defiance. This time, Whil did not laugh.

Kirsten ate and drank her fill, but avoided more than one glass of wine, feeling that it would not do to become intoxicated. Each time a new goblet was poured, she drew on her majick to reverse the wine making process, thus turning wine into harmless juice without anyone being any the wiser. Later, she asked Richard if a servant could take up a selection of food to her room in case she got hungry later. He nodded, smiling.

They were three hours at the banquet table and Kirsten had sampled more food than she had thought possible. After Daihron bade them all goodnight, the company rose and departed to the Great Hall; Kirsten joined them, feeling as though she was rolling from the room rather than walking; her leather trousers were uncomfortably tight and she felt a little sick. In the accompanying hall, music and dancing had begun. Kirsten assumed that it followed dinner every night and the reason that she had not been party to it previously, was due to her early retirement.

She joined her company with a sigh of relief. They all seemed merry with too much wine; even Troy was laughing, as she approached.

'I'm glad to see that you're enjoying yourselves,' she commented.

'Well are you not?' Thaniel asked, a little too loudly. 'Counsellor Daihron served a most exceptional wine this evening.'

'I wouldn't know,' she said. Looking about her, she saw the revellers grow increasingly intoxicated, as even more wine was served.

'What do you mean you wouldn't know?' Troy said merrily. 'You've been drinking all night!'

Tom laughed. 'I know why,' he slurred, as he wagged his finger. 'She's been up to her tricks again, changing wine into water no doubt. Heh Troy, does that make her the antichrist, do you think?' he said, hugging the priest.

Troy seemed horror-stricken for the briefest of moments, before he laughed hysterically and clashed goblets with Tom.

Kirsten felt even more uncomfortable, realising how drunk her party were. She made a move to retire, but found herself being pulled into the arms of Whil, as he dragged her amongst the dancing couples.

'How about a dance, Lady Kirsten?'

'No Counsellor Whil,' she replied. 'Thank you, but I am hardly attired appropriately for such an activity.'

'Nonsense! If you can move enough to fight in that get-up, then you can certainly dance!'

He hauled her unwillingly, further into the crowd. She had no idea how to dance and more pressing considerations than a desire to learn. She concluded how once again, the evening had turned into a mess. Whil grabbed her around the waist and she allowed him to lead her in a polka-like dance.

'I really think I should retire,' she protested. 'I have to be up early. I've to find myself an archery instructor.'

Whil laughed. 'Hah! I shall teach you.'

'I hardly think it a good idea to be taught by the opposition. If I did win, you would *still* get the praise.'

After a while, she resisted escape and found dancing to be a pleasant, even fun experience, and Whil was a merry companion.

'Are you not afraid of the Counsellors' scorn at you dancing with me, Whil?'

His face was serious; the music stopped and he led her from the floor through the midst of polite applause.

'Not all of us are against you, Milady. I think, when we put it to the vote tomorrow, the power to rule will be given back voluntarily. You scared them witless this morning. I do not think that they would dare stand against you again. Now, I am not saying that they like you because I know that most of them do not. However, you have to put yourself in their position; you are a thing of legend and not of law. Even were your claim proved true, and I for one believe you, there is no law that states that control of the kingdom should be relinquished to you. Maldahl was in chaos when you left and the new system of government brought order. It is a way of life that the people know and accept. They have no concept of monarchical rule. The only people I know of who would, are Gailon and Katahl.

'We have lived all our lives with a group deciding what is best, with different counsellors in charge of different aspects of our society, such as roads, taxes, land and law. The accused have us all as a judge not a single figurehead dictating all. It will be a strange and difficult transition for us all I think.'

Kirsten's face was grave. She had not given the matter any thought before that moment. She had not considered what it would mean to rule, or how the people themselves might resist such a change. Her knees buckled suddenly and Whil caught her.

'Are you quite well?' he asked.

'Yes, too much wine perhaps. I think that I shall retire. Thank you for your insights, Counsellor Whil; they have been most illuminating,'

Whil took her hand and kissed it, watching her intently as she walked away.

On the main stairwell from the hall, she was surprised to meet with Gohrn, as he oiled his way over to her.

'Lady Kirsten,' he said. 'I feel that we have got off to a rather unfortunate beginning. I would like to apologise for my behaviour this afternoon. I realise now that I was wrong, but you must understand that you were half-naked when you invited me into your room. I regrettably picked up on the wrong signal.'

And there it is, Kirsten thought. *That is how Gohrn plans to worm his way out of trouble with the High Council. He is going to twist the situation into being my fault because I invited him in.* 'That's clever Gohrn. I like it! Goodnight.'

'Wait!' He strode after her. 'Are you unwilling to accept my apology? That is rather ungracious of you.'

Kirsten wheeled around on him.

'Don't play games with me, Gohrn!' she said. 'I'm not in the mood.'

He grabbed her roughly by the arm and pulled her over into the shadows.

'You are the one playing games, and I will be sure to tell the High Council as much. If you decide to protest, then I will inform them where you really were today.'

Kirsten yanked her arm free. 'What are you talking about?' she raged.

'Do you think me a fool? After Gailon called off the search, I saw him enter the catacombs. I waited there and yet he did not return. Later, as a servant passed, she said that he had just ordered her to prepare a bath for you.

'It is against our law to enter the catacombs, woman. How do you think it will fair with Daihron when I tell him how pleasant and peaceful you are to his face, but all the while you and Gailon plot and plan, using forbidden majick to bring about our downfall.'

'You're crazy, Gohrn. Tell Daihron what you like. I'm going to bed.'

With that, she strode away, leaving Gohrn feeling triumphant, his eyes gleaming after her like a hawk on its prey.

When she arrived at her room, she was too flustered to break the majick seal.

'Cob!' she ordered. 'Open up!'

The door swung open and she stormed in, slamming it behind her. Cob sat on her table eating the food that she had sent up.

'The servants left this outside your room. I assumed it was for me,' he said, his mouth full.

She nodded, removing her weapons. Approaching the bed, she stopped.

'Are these for me?'

Cob nodded, still munching away. 'Gailon said that you need new clothes and considering the fact that I made such an expert job last night, he suggested that I tailor for you. So I did.'

The beautiful colours and fabrics overwhelmed Kirsten. She ran over to Cob and kissed him.

'Get off!' he protested. 'Am I not contaminated enough, woman?'

Kirsten laid the dresses over a chair, thanking Cob again. Despite his complaint, the faerie seemed pleased by her reaction to his handiwork.

'Cob, will you guard my room again? There's somewhere I have to be. I'll be back by sunrise, I promise.'

He eyed her strangely.

'Is it no longer customary for your kind to sleep in the hours after twilight then?' he asked.

'Yes, but one night won't kill me. Besides, I'm used to sleepless nights after your antics.'

'Go on then! But you owe me. I do not plan to remain cooped up in your room forever, you know.'

Kirsten turned to him, smiling.

'Trust me,' she said. 'If tonight goes well, I'll be that much closer to sending you home.'

Making regular checks to ensure that nobody followed her, she headed toward the forbidden passageways. Even with her night vision, the tunnels were eerie and the cold of that uninhabited part of the palace, made her shiver. She found herself cursing for not thinking to bring her cloak.

It took a lot less time for her to reach the tower, as if the maze permitted her access sooner. Pale moonlight beamed through the window and the blanket of dust seemed to glow. She did not dare risk lighting the torches or even candles, for fear of the light be spied from below and it becoming known that Ardahl's Tower was in use again.

She positioned herself at the centre of the room; closing her eyes, she imagined the dust and the room as separate entities. *The dust simply forms a cover. It is not part of the room,* she thought. She concentrated on lifting and dispersing it out of the window, to be lost on the night breeze. When she opened her eyes, she found the room was clean. Majick was so much easier to perform there; it surrounded her at all times and it was simply for her to reach out and make use of it, rather than having to create from nothing. She smiled.

Sitting at the desk again, she contemplated the spell that had destroyed Ardahl. After a while, she placed it to one side and allowed her hand to guide her to a book for study. The contents seemed familiar and many of the spells came like second nature to her. She covered locks and seals, paralysis, sleep spells, and power of suggestion, before tiredness got the better of her and she sank into weary slumber.

Her dreams were vibrant, as she recalled Ardahl in his faded robes and his ancient loveable face, with white hair that seemed to have a life of its own, growing out in all directions. She heard Beaky squawk and flutter his great wings, as he watched her practising a light spell with a candle and set fire to a bookshelf. Ardahl laughed and it was like music to her. A boy entered with wood for the fire and Ardahl cursed him.

'Boy, just because you have mastered how to break a majick lock, does not give the right to barge in unannounced. Now get out and stay out until you learn some manners!'

Ardahl's voice was rich and warm as Christmas pudding despite his scolding the boy, and she laughed at him.

'Now what are you doing here, Exzalander? You have to go. You'll be late. Go on now!'

Her eyes flickered open and a squawking noise made her jump into alertness. Her friend the crow sat on Beaky's perch, seeming determined to wake her. She walked over to him and stroked him gently.

'What's all that noise about, eh? And how did you know that I was up here?'

He croaked again, and it was then that Kirsten realised that the sky was getting lighter. The servants would be up and she was in a forbidden part of the palace.

'Oh no! I've got to go, my friend. Come see me tonight, I shall be glad of the company.' With that, she ran from the room. The door clicked shut and the bird flew away to greet the dawn.

Standing before the picture, she wondered how Gailon had made the strange shortcut appear. She concentrated, but nothing happened; the wall remained solid and the picture, in focus. Breathing deeply, she tried not to panic. *I can still make it back by taking the long route,* she considered. *I just have to be cautious.* She stood a while in thought, yet could not remember the way. The tower had been easy for her to find, because it was like a beacon, drawing her in. Now, she was lost, trapped in a forbidden area with no hope of escape until Gailon realised where she had gone.

'I'm going to be in so much trouble,' she muttered.

Ioan seemed to be her best hope; he was susceptible to her thoughts and could let Gailon know where she had gone, before anyone noticed her disappearance and raised the alarm. Still, she knew how angry Gailon would be with her for having gone there again and wondered if there was a way back without using the wizard's device for transportation.

She returned to the Ardahl's Tower and sat cross-legged, meditating, breathing in the majick air, hoping it might inspire a solution to her predicament. Then it came to her, like a doorway in her mind, once tightly locked that now opened, and a piece of the past revealed itself. She heard Ardahl's voice as he praised her for what she had achieved, but warning her of the consequences.

It seemed her mother had disliked the idea of her only child entering the majick parts of the palace and so had placed a warden at the entrance to the catacombs, forbidding Exzalander's entry. Exzalander had counteracted this by doing something that Ardahl explained could not be taught. She had simply appeared where she wanted to be, but once she had done it, she became so tired that she had fallen asleep, only to be caught anyhow. It had been one of the reasons why the family had moved north to the birthplace of her father. The appointed Council handled the upkeep and local affairs, receiving orders from Tuâth. *We moved because of my mother's fear for her child,* Kirsten thought. *Yet, Shénnin didn't manage to put a stop to my visits to Ardahl's tower. She simply made it impossible for me to be caught.*

Kirsten trembled as the memories flooded back. She was breathing too deeply and felt the need for air not saturated with majick. *So, I practised majick as a child. It's not new to me.* Concentrating on her room, the stone floor, the hard bed, the clothes draped over the chair, the table with Cob's empty dishes on, she sustained a perfect mental picture, then placed herself in the image.

When she opened her eyes, she found that she was back in her room. She heard Cob's excitable exclamations at her miraculous appearance, but she ignored them. Undressing, she climbed into bed, no longer able to function.

'Cob,' she said, 'protect the sword, but open the door, and have a nice day.' With that, she fell asleep.

Seventeen

The counsellors met soon after breakfast, debating whether they stand against Kirsten or she should be allowed to take leadership. There was and equal split and nobody could be persuaded to swap their vote to make a majority.

Thaniel sent Marin to fetch Kirsten for breakfast, who returned soon after reporting that she had been unable to wake her. Thaniel exchanged looks with Gailon and they sprang to their feet, heading towards Kirsten's chamber.

She slept peacefully and all their urging could not bring her to waking.

'Cob!' Gailon's voice was angry, and had Cob been there he may have feared it, however, he was prancing in the fields south of Ealdorbold.

Thaniel asked Marin to sit with Kirsten and let them know the moment she awoke. He led Gailon away, who appeared too angry to speak.

'What do you suppose ails her, Gailon?' Thaniel asked, as they reached his room.

'Majick. Is that not obvious? Majick!' Gailon replied. 'Cob was supposed to be guarding her. If I find that he is responsible for this, then he will wish that his clan would have hanged him,' he fumed.

'Might it not be a spell that Kirsten herself performed?'

Gailon paced erratically. 'Would she have been that foolish? That, on the most important day of her life, she performs majick that prevents her representing herself? She would not dare!'

Thaniel felt uneasy. He had never seen Gailon so upset and he had a feeling that *that* was precisely what Kirsten had done.

The order came for her to attend the Council, and the Great Hall was in uproar on being informed that the Lady Kirsten was unable to attend, as she was still asleep. It was suggested that they adjourn for lunch and that Kirsten *'grace them with her presence'* when she was ready.

It was mid-afternoon before Kirsten finally awoke, and Marin jumped up in excitement.

'Oh thank goodness you are all right. I thought that you had been enchanted. I will go and let your friends know that you are up.'

Kirsten heard little of Marin's words. She felt disorientated and she lay still for a while, trying to clear her head. Slowly sitting up, the door burst open and she realised that she was naked. Snatching up the sheet, she covered her modesty just in time.

'What have you been doing?' Tom said. 'Gailon is furious. You had better get down there.'

'I will, if you allow me to get dressed.'

Tom coughed, embarrassed. 'Of course,' he said.

He stepped back, as Thaniel rushed in.

'Are you all right?'

'Thaniel, I overslept. Why did you not wake me, if it was a problem?'

He gave her a look before leaving, and she knew only too well what it had meant; no-one had been able to wake her.

She chose a simple cut dress of royal blue silk. It was light and flowing because of its lack of petticoats. Slipping on matching shoes, she brushed her hair before dashing from the chamber, ignoring her friends' well wishing comments behind her.

Her sleep had not been dreamless and the majick, which she had utilised, had opened her mind to visions of possible futures. She mulled over all that Whil had said the previous night and by the time she reached the hall, she knew what she had to do.

The great double doors opened for her and she was announced. As she entered, she saw Gailon with Daihron; his face was slightly reddened and he appeared to have been arguing. He did not leave as he should, and was not bidden to do so.

Kirsten took a breath before she spoke. She could feel all eyes on her, expectant.

'Counsellors, I must apologise for keeping you. I come to you now with an announcement.'

The tension in the room increased ten-fold and Kirsten found herself coughing to clear her throat.

'My father was king, my mother queen. Does it then follow that I should rule? Should I now dissolve this government and take power, as is my birthright?'

There was silence in the hall.

'I do not wish to know the outcome of your vote,' she continued. 'I came before you to tell you this. I travelled to Ealdorbold in search of aid in defeating Katahl. I request the strength of your army and I would like us to try to recruit people from the towns and villages, make them see that this is *their* battle. They fight for their freedom. I would also ask that I be permitted to join Gailon's quest for the shards of the Anarkhane stone.

'But as for leadership ...' She breathed heavily. 'I reject it utterly. I move that the Council remain in power and I be freed from my duties as queen.'

There was a gasp among the Council; clearly none of them had expected such an outcome.

'I know nothing about being a ruler, and I fail to see how my taking the position helps us in our fight against the enemy. It is through secrecy that we will defeat him. By setting me up as queen, we would only encourage our downfall, as we are not yet ready to fight. I offer my services to the realm as a warrior. Will you accept this?'

High Counsellor Daihron walked over to Kirsten and took her hands.

'My dear, we cannot force you to be queen. Of course we accept your terms. It is only for me to say that this is your home; you may come and go as you please. You will have all the help you require to defeat Katahl; you have only to ask.'

He squeezed her hands and Kirsten felt the relief flowing from him. She turned to walk from the hall and caught sight of Gailon, his features livid as the reality set in. He did not speak to her and looked as though he had been stabbed through the heart.

Drinks were offered around, as the counsellors felt the need for celebration. Kirsten watched with dismay as Gailon retreated from the hall.

'Why did you do that?' Counsellor Jaden asked. He spoke quietly, as he handed her a goblet of wine.

'I think that Whil made me see sense. He convinced me that the people would not accept me as their ruler, even if I did win the vote here. This way at least I can be defeated graciously.'

'Fine advice coming from a man who voted against you, Milady.'

Kirsten backed away. 'What?'

'Strange, but you did not strike me as a woman to be taken in so easily by a young man's charms; now I see that I was wrong.'

Kirsten wanted to explain that he *was* wrong, but she felt weak. Placing down the goblet, she swept from the hall, breaking into a run towards Gailon's chamber.

Her hands were shaking by the time she rapped the old man's door. All the companions were present, with the exception of Cob.

Gailon's eyes burned. 'Do not speak to me!' he ordered.

She felt the fury of his words penetrate the very core of her being.

'Gailon, we've obtained their aid,' she pleaded. 'That is what you wanted. I have no desire to be queen.'

'It is not a question of desire, Kirsten,' Thaniel ventured carefully. 'It is a matter of duty.'

'DUTY!' she cried, in disbelief. 'I did not ask for any of this. I have agreed to try to find the Anarkhane stones and confront Katahl; nobody said anything about my having to rule!

'I have the support of their armies, but you're angry because I don't want to sit on a throne all day listening to problems and barking orders. Well if that is my duty, you can stick it! I'm going back to Earth. I'd rather be in *P.E.* detention than put up with this crap!'

She turned to leave, but her temper had something else it wished to express. 'You're only mad, Gailon, because you knew that you would be appointed my advisor and basically rule Maldahl for me. I don't know how to rule, but you do, don't you? You were trying to use me to overthrow the political system and seize control for yourself. Well be angry. I don't care any more. I'm going home!'

She slammed the door and headed for Ardahl's Tower, past caring if anyone saw her. As the temperature of the dank corridors cooled her fury, the guilt set in, and she winced when she recalled how she had spoken to Gailon. *I've wounded him deeply and he will never forgive me,* she thought. *I got upset with him when all I really wanted was to vent my anger on Whil, the man who charmed me with his smile and gentle attentions and then voted against me. He convinced me that we shared a friendship and manipulated me into thinking that it was an unwise decision to be queen.*

'Bastard!' she said.

On reaching Ardahl's tower, Kirsten found that the door would not open. She tried a simple lock spell, but still it would not budge. Finally, she decided that she would have to make herself appear in the room and the door clicked open. She felt a little unnerved at the coincidence in timing. It was as if the room had a consciousness of its own and sensed her dangerous mood. *But I would not damage the tower; I love it here,* she considered. *But I intend to attempt the spell to send me back to earth, the spell that destroyed Ardahl …*

She ran over to the desk. The scroll had gone. It was as though the tower would not allow her to attempt the spell in case it failed, or worse, succeeded.

'Okay, okay, I get the message. I'm not allowed to try the spell.'

She slumped at the desk, holding her head in her hands, wanting to cry, but no tears would come.

Back in Gailon's chamber, the others were trying to convince him to go after Kirsten, once he revealed to them the spell that she had found.

'She will not perform the spell.'

'But how can you be sure of that, Gailon?' Thaniel said, 'Your anger could result in her death if you do not stop her.'

He paced back and forth and Troy got to his feet; Gailon's words stopped him before he could leave the room.

'You would not find her. Nobody can reach the tower, but I. I tell you she will not use the spell. The tower will not permit her.'

They appeared puzzled by his words.

'There remains there, a part of my master's consciousness, mingled with the majick that he created,' Gailon explained. 'He will not allow harm to befall her when he can prevent it; she means too much to him.'

Ioan touched Gailon on the arm, fearful at the old man's reaction.

'Gailon, she did not mean the things that she said, She was upset; she feels lost and relies on us to guide her. When that support was taken away she was scared, that is all.' His eyes were full of sympathy and understanding for the old man's pain.

Gailon seemed visibly calmer, as the sentiment of Ioan's words soothed him.

'I do not see why she should be a queen anyway,' Tehd retorted. 'She has done nothing to deserve the title. She is supposed to defeat the enemy, well I say let her get on with it! She can't very well do that sat on her behind being all noble, which if you ask me she aint cut out for anyhow. She can't do both, and so far she's done neither!'

'He is right, Gailon,' Thaniel said. 'To be queen, she would still have to leave control to the Council if she went to war. For the fight will be on the battlefield and it will go better for us if she leads the assault. If she succeeds, the respect and the admiration of the people will demand that she take leadership. It is too soon for her at present. She is still coming to terms with who she is. It is not right that we thrust so much responsibility on her at this stage.'

Gailon sat, seeming frail beyond measure. 'I would have hoped for her to have enough respect to tell me of her intention before I fought her case before the Council. She made me look a fool.'

Tom placed a supportive hand on his shoulder.

'So you don't mind that she rejected leadership; she bruised your pride. Let me tell you, Gailon, she made me look an idiot in front of a whole department of officers on more than one occasion. At the time, I thought that she was being manipulative and cocky. Now I see that she is headstrong. She does not mean disrespect, but needs guidance. She needs to calm down and grow up, for her offences are merely the disregard of youth.'

Gailon patted Tom's hand and they were relieved when they realised that he had finally seen sense.

Kirsten stood after a while, venturing a look out of the high window; the view was magnificent. She could see beyond Ánweald forest to the hills that they had crossed. Leaning forward, she spied the courtyard, where the guard were training, the gardens, where ladies walked and sat while musicians played. The groomsmen were out with Cröedaw's horse, who seemed to enjoy being pampered and preened in his master's absence.

She leaned forward with her head on her hands taking in more sights, momentarily forgetting the guilt and anger that she felt. She breathed deeply the late afternoon air and time seemed to have no meaning. More, and still more could be seen from her new found haven; to the west lay treacherous ice-capped mountains, moving north beyond the dense trees of Ánweald, lay a great plain. She spied the sea twinkling in the distance, as the sun approached the horizon. Almost directly north of the Ardahl's tower, she saw remotely, another tower; hidden in mist, so that she could not be sure if it was truly a tower, or a trick that her eyes played, as they reached into the far distance. Continuing to strain her focus, she convinced herself that it was indeed the top most part of a tower smiling back at her from the many leagues that lay between them.

As the sun sank, she stood once more, stretching the stiffness from her limbs. She knew that people would be gathering for the banquet and expected her to be there. The tower felt more like home than any other part of the palace and she found herself reluctant to leave it. Closing her eyes, she began to imagine her room, but the sound of the door opening startled her before she could leave. Gailon entered and seemed at first more interested in the transformation of the room than he did of her.

'You have been busy,' he said gruffly.

She did not know what to say, so shocked was she to see him there and speaking to her.

'Gailon,' she stuttered. 'I did not mean what I said. I am very sorry that I got angry and I am sorry that I let you down. I … I don't know what I can do to make amends.'

His features did not soften. 'I have come to take you down to the feast. Tonight it is to be even grander than usual, apparently in honour of you.'

Kirsten followed him solemnly, thinking, *he'll never forgive me. I've probably turned the others against me too. What is there to go back for?*

They arrived as everyone was filing in. Kirsten found that she had been placed opposite Daihron at the very end of the table, a singular honour, as the seat normally remained empty.

She felt dejected; she did not want to eat and could not smile when a toast was raised to her, choosing rather to sit staring into her cup. Tehd sat to her right; he never spoke to her, having made it perfectly clear that he thought that she was a fraud. Gailon sat to her left, and he remained silent, merely picking at bits the table had to offer. The remainder of her companions felt it wise not to say anything in earshot of other guests, and so while the rest of the hall made merry, they sat in silence, brooding over the events of the day.

Kirsten dare not look up, in case a comment was passed from one of the Council; she was in no mood for pleasantries.

'Milady, do not be sad. Master Gailon is angrier at himself than he is with you.'

The voice was Ioan's as he spoke directly to her mind. She risked a glance in his direction.

'*You can hear me?*' he asked, in surprise.

'*Yes, perhaps I am growing more receptive to your thoughts.*'

'*I am pleased.*' he said. '*It is a comfort to know that you are there.*'

'*I fear there would be few who would share your view, Ioan.*'

'Kirsten, you must eat something,' Troy urged, trying not to draw too much attention.

She picked a piece of fruit, with a wavering hand, and ate it slowly as a token effort to appease the priest's concern.

The hours dragged and little was said, as they all felt too exposed. When the meal was over, Genargh announced that he hoped very much to hear the Lady Kirsten sing. She appeared despondent at his words. *The last thing on my mind is singing,* she mused, *even if I did know any of their music.*

The company sat in a corner, all except Tehd and Ioan, who slipped out as soon as the meal had ended. The musicians pestered Kirsten, asking which song she would be performing. Other parties entertained them and Kirsten thought that at any other time she might have found a medieval karaoke amusing, but not now.

Eventually, Troy took up the challenge. He did not sing at first, but played on a lute-like instrument, strumming it like a guitar. He sounded excellent to Kirsten, but the company frowned at the strange sound. Finally, he asked Kirsten to join in.

Without thinking, she sang and Troy seemed pleasantly surprised, as her rich rock voice worked with his own, to a song that she knew well. She failed to notice the look of horror on several faces in response to the sound that she was producing. She sang from the heart, the lyrics about living a thousand years, seemed ironic considering recent discoveries.

When they finished, Troy's eyes were gleaming. The applause was slow to start and quick to finish. Thaniel however, seemed delighted.

'That was wonderful,' he said. 'I've never heard anything like it.'

Troy handed the instrument back to the ensemble and sat in silent pride. Kirsten tried desperately to pluck up enough courage to excuse herself.

'Ah, Lady Kirsten; your very presence is music itself.'

At the sound of Whil's voice, she silently cursed herself for having been so gullible.

'Have you found yourself a teacher yet?' he asked. 'You have only eight days remaining before the tournament.'

Kirsten wanted to hit him, to wipe the smug look off his smiling face. The attention grew from those around her and she cringed. She had not informed her companions of the challenge that she had accepted, and tried to appear composed as they listened with mounting curiosity.

'I am sure you can appreciate that today has been a little too important to be concerned with a foolish contest,' she said, 'however, tomorrow I will give the matter my complete attention, I assure you. Perhaps once the tournament is over we might arrange another, such as say fencing or hand-to-hand combat, so that I may return the challenge. That is if you are not frightened of having to fight a woman.'

She smiled demurely, taking the moment as a perfect cue to depart the throng, leaving Whil wondering at how she had managed to insult him so pleasantly.

Eighteen

Kirsten did not return to her room, but headed out into the night, toward the stables. The air refreshed and revived her after the horrendous day that had passed. She patted Ravenwing fondly, burying her head in his mane for a while.

'What am I to do, Ravenwing?' she sighed.

A croak and a flutter of wings told her that her other friend from the animal kingdom had arrived. Her head flicked up suddenly.

'I've got it!' she said to the bird. '*You* could find Cröedaw; he cannot be far away. You could find him and show me where he is and I will fetch him back. He can't stay away forever. Do you think that he understands me, Ravenwing?'

The horse nodded.

'Oh, what am I saying? I'm busy being selfish *again*. Cröedaw wants to be alone. He's grieving, and all I'm concerned about is winning a stupid tournament. Forget I said anything, my friend. I just hope that he is all right; you could find that much out. I promise that I'll respect his wishes and leave him alone.'

The bird flew to her arm, taking her by surprise. She walked out into the moonlight and held him up so that he was silhouetted against its papery whiteness, then with a quick movement, she urged him to fly.

Heading back to the warmth of the palace, a movement to her right caught her attention. Tehd was sprinting as fast as his short legs would carry him.

'Out of my way!' he gasped, ' I need Master Gailon.'

The urgency in his voice filled her with fear and she knew that something must have happened to Ioan.

'I will go to him.' she said. Ignoring Tehd's protests, she ran toward the gardens and found Ioan lying motionless under the trees of a starlit orchard.

'Ioan?' she urged.

His eyes remained firmly shut. She spoke to him with her mind and got no reply, knowing what ailed him only too well. Removing his pendant, she held it tightly in one hand, the other she placed on his heart.

Tehd screamed as he approached her, demanding she leave Ioan alone. He struck at her twice with his fists, yet she did not move or heed him, but rather, remained in the odd embrace with his friend.

Tehd took to flight again, searching desperately for Gailon, only to be informed that he had already retired for the night.

'What is it Tehd? Can I help?' Thaniel asked, placing down his mug of ale.

Tehd was hysterical and could not relate clearly what was wrong. 'He's hurt. She's killing him. Oh help.'

Thaniel was on his feet in an instant and sprinting in the direction Tehd indicated.

Beads of perspiration formed on Kirsten's brow, as she fought to restore her friend. Had anyone seen the faintly glowing figures at that moment, they might have thought themselves in the presence of ghosts. The light from the stone was blinding, its rays escaping through the cracks in her clenched fist. Kneeling, she appeared to kiss Ioan, her breath visible as it permeated life back into him. Suddenly, she was thrown back, as if the stone fought against her interference.

Ioan's eyes opened and he looked no worse than if he had had a troubled sleep.

'Princess?'

'How do you feel?' She tried to keep from wheezing.

'Fine. But how did you …?'

'No time,' Kirsten gasped, 'Tehd has gone to find Gailon. If you are still determined that your problem remain secret, you had better stop him. Now.'

She managed to return his smile, before he dashed away.

'Ioan, are you all right?' Thaniel said, slightly out of breath. 'Tehd's beside himself, 'says that someone's trying to kill you.'

Ioan laughed nervously and patted Thaniel on the arm.

'He's pulling your leg. I am fine as you can see.' He walked toward the house, hoping that Thaniel would follow.

'Tehd, is it true? Were you playing a prank?' Thaniel asked.

Tehd's face was white as Ioan passed him.

'He was dying I tell you,' he insisted, scratching his head.

Thaniel sighed with relief, his heart returning to normal and he followed Ioan back indoors. Tehd scowled and stomped off in the direction of the orchard. The sight that met his eyes filled him with cold fear. A man knelt over the unconscious body of Exzalander trying to urge it back to life.

'Cröedaw, is that you?'

The man's head snapped up and Tehd could see it was indeed their missing companion, though his face was drawn and pale.

'Tehd, fetch Thaniel … quickly!' Cröedaw ordered.

'Wha, what's the matter with her?' Tehd muttered, moving closer.

'She tried to help Ioan and it has nearly killed her; you must fetch help.'

Tehd was in turmoil as he dashed back into the banquet hall, believing she was dying because of him; he had hit her and if she died, it would be his fault.

Tears ran down his cheeks as he found Thaniel once more, standing quietly by the fire, watching the dancing.

'What is it?' Thaniel said. 'Not another joke I hope.'

But he saw the tears and distress and followed Tehd outside.

'She's dyin' and it's my fault. Cröedaw asked me to fetch you.'

'Cröedaw?' Thaniel said incredulously. He ran like the wind. In his mind, he had already pictured what had happened.

'Help me, Thaniel. I am too weak to lift her.' Cröedaw's voice was frail and rasping, as though he had made no use of it of late.

Thaniel took the woman in his arms; her face was deathly white, and he feared that she would not last the night.

'Tehd quick now,' Thaniel said, 'find Richard the serving boy. Say that Kirsten is sick and is to be relocated to a room with a fireplace, somewhere out of the way. He is not to discuss the matter with anybody, and see that the fire is lit by the time we arrive.'

'Yes sir,' Tehd said. He ran. Despite feeling as though his lungs would burst, he was glad to be given a task to distract his mind.

Thaniel walked steadily, wishing he had his cloak to cover her.

'You do not look too well yourself, old friend,' he said.

'You know very well what ails me, Thaniel. A few days back in society and you will see me fully restored … in body at least.'

'I hope so, because we could use an extra ally at the moment.'

Despite Tehd and Richard's orders not to apprise anyone of the situation, Ioan overheard Tehd's pleas and soon got from him that Kirsten had been taken ill. He immediately ran to fetch Gailon, telling him only that Kirsten was sick and that he was needed. By the time Thaniel managed to get up to her newly prepared quarters, a fire was blazing as requested, but they were not expecting the presence of Ioan and Gailon.

Thaniel gently placed her into bed, covering her tightly with blankets.

'What happened?' Gailon asked, as he examined her.

Silence was his answer; each present had a different version of events in his mind and each seemed unwilling to relate them.

'She was helping *me*,' Ioan said at last. 'She knows about the pendant and that sometimes it makes me ill. It's been getting worse, especially since she joined us. But she took the pain away. I did not know that this would happen. She was fine the last time that she helped me.' He sniffed and began to cry.

'Actually she wasn't,' Cröedaw said sombrely. 'She allowed you to think that, but she was unconscious for over half a day.'

'Field House,' Gailon said, pronouncing each word slowly and clearly, as realisation dawned. 'And you thought to keep this from me?' he said, emotion mounting.

'We thought that you would be angry,' Thaniel protested.

'AND YOU WOULD BE RIGHT!' He held Exzalander's hand, looking grave. 'How could you all be so foolish?'

'She's not going to die, is she, Gailon?' Ioan's voice was so fearful that he could only have been pitied at that moment.

'I do not think that she will die,' the wizard replied. 'But she will be weakened by the experience. Tell me all of you, if she had come to Ioan's aid and then had to face Katahl, how do you think that she would fare?'

The room appeared humbled.

'She would die,' Gailon continued. 'We would lose everything. I have known her long enough now to see how passionate that she is. She will not consider the consequences of such an action; she will help a friend in need or in the case of the Marin, a complete stranger. In her effort to be good and do what she thinks is right, she could destroy herself.

'Powerful healing majick takes its toll on even the most accomplished wizard, and you expected a mere child to be able to cope with its repercussions. Foolishness! She must never put herself at risk, even for us. She is too important.

'Remove your pendant, Ioan.'

Ioan's eyes were bloodshot with weeping. 'You're not taking it from my keeping, Gailon?' His hands trembled at the thought of his disgrace.

'No I am not taking charge of it; I simply wish to see why it has made you ill.'

Ioan removed the pendant and handed it carefully to Gailon.

'There is no reason, Gailon. My family has endured the pain for centuries; it is an honour.'

Gailon raised an eyebrow. 'Foolishness!' he said again. 'You mean to tell me that nobody has spoken of this before? The pendant is cracked, you idiot! That is the problem. The outer casing protects you from the power of the stone only so long as it is not damaged, a simple tinkering in the forge would have saved you from the pain.'

Ioan reclaimed the pendant, feeling utterly silly.

'I suggest that you report to the smithy tomorrow and do not allow him to replace the metal. He simply needs to mend the crack. Now leave me, all of you. I will sit with her tonight. It is good to see you back, Cröedaw. I am glad that you decided to watch over things here.'

Cröedaw nodded, but could not manage a smile as he left.

Kirsten's prolonged sleep meant that a statement had to be issued to the Council, who had requested her presence on more than one occasion. All the companions took turns at sitting with her in the hope of coaxing her into waking. Tehd attended her more than any, night and day, until Gailon sent him away to get some rest.

Ioan had his pendant mended and wondered how cross Kirsten would be when she discovered that she had suffered for nothing. Gailon explained to him how all the stones had been set in metal only found in the kingdom of Taiohãhn and that is what protected Kirsten, not her majick.

It was a few nights before Cröedaw would allow himself to join the company at dinner. He sat alone in his quarters or singing sad songs to Kirsten, hoping that she would wake and tell him to sing something merry. Gailon sealed the sword of Taiohãhn in a chest in his room, aiming to protect it against theft or curious eyes.

Cob seemed to have tired of human company and had not been seen at all.

At dinner on the fifth day of Kirsten's ailment, Counsellor Whil commented that the great warrior was pretending to be sick in order to avoid being humiliated when he beat her in the tournament. The hall laughed and clapped, but the company shook their heads at his display. Cröedaw hoped that she would wake in time to make him humble.

That night, Tehd sat with Kirsten until soon after midnight, when Chana the servant girl pleaded with him to get some sleep. He was tired and had been nodding off for hours, and so he agreed on the condition that she run and fetch him if there was any change. She smiled warmly, assuring him that she would.

Chana sat telling the sleeping princess stories for a while, her voice echoing against the stone walls as she spoke the version of the Exzalander prophecy that she had been taught as a child.

In her darkness, Kirsten heard a noise form slowly into words. She shivered and felt a coldness creep upon her. Her heart tried to race to get her blood pumping so that she might move. She was afraid, although she knew not why, or even where or who she was. The only clear thought in her muddled mind was that it was time to move before it was too late.

The woman's voice had stopped, but there was another sound, further away. Kirsten's eyes prised themselves open and the firelight burned at her retina. She moved her head stiffly.

She was alone.

The door was open, and she was alone.

Her cold limbs shuddered as she strained to get to her feet. She recognised the walls of Ealdorbold, but she was not in her room. She could not recall what had happened and did not struggle to remember. Her stinging eyes scanned unsuccessfully for her weapons and she felt cold sweat as it oozed from every pore and her fear grew.

She heard a scream and forced herself to run. Her body refused to obey her to sprint like a cheetah, but rather she half jogged, half staggered away from the awful sound in her ears—the scream, the growling and the tearing.

Not recognising where she was, she searched for a door—any door, figuring that someone had to help her. Someone had to make the madness go away. Her mind screamed out to Ioan asking him to send aid. She fell against a door, limply banging her hand against the wood. Her eyes were losing focus again and her body trembled violently, both weak and afraid. The only thing that she was certain of was that she did want whatever had made the tearing sound to find her.

The door opened and Kirsten fell into the arms of Counsellor Jaden. She no longer cared for pride or propriety. She was in danger and she was scared.

'Help me, please,' she begged. Her voice was little more than a whisper. 'It's coming and I cannot find my sword.' She lost consciousness again.

An inhuman screech drifted closer and Jaden pulled her inside. Holding her in one arm, he lowered a heavy wooden bar across the door and locked it. A growling sound grew nearer. Kirsten came to, her eyes wide with fright. Counsellor Jaden feared that she would cry out, as her breathing grew louder at the beast's proximity. He grabbed her, holding her face to his, trying to calm her with his eyes, and mouthing that everything would be all right.

When the bang came at the door, he tightly held her trembling body, her closeness giving him as much strength as he gave her. He watched with horror, as the bar across the door began to split. Kirsten clung tightly to Jaden, welcoming the darkness of his heavy robes. Then the noise ceased and shouts sounded; help had arrived.

Men clambered past, in pursuit of whatever foul thing had seen fit to attack them. Now the danger was not so immediate, Kirsten slipped in and out of consciousness. Jaden carried her frail form over to his bed and wrapped her in blankets.

'You really *are* unwell,' he murmured.

'Is it over?' she asked weakly.

Jaden smiled, but his face was troubled. 'Yes, you are safe now. Rest. Sleep.'

She needed no further encouragement and slipped once more into heavy slumber, leaving Jaden to wonder how she had managed to rouse herself at all.

There were shouts of dismay and more footsteps rushing down the passageway. Jaden lifted the splintered bar and unlocked the door. Thaniel ran past and Jaden called him back.

'No time Counsellor,' Thaniel said. 'It appears that Kirsten may have been taken.'

'No Thaniel, she is here.'

Thaniel's face was both shocked and relieved at the sight of her sleeping in Jaden's bed.

'Do not trouble yourself, Thaniel. She managed to escape whatever that was and made her way here. Why was she placed in such a remote part of the palace and without a guard? That thing almost broke down the door.'

'One of the servants was with her, but she is dead. It ripped her to pieces. It was terrible … oh to think if it had got to Exzalander …' His face went pale, as he watched her peaceful form.

The Counsellor poured him a drink, which he gulped down in one swallow, thanking his host. Jaden poured another drink for Thaniel and one for himself.

'What was it?' he asked.

'A Trolg scout. It killed both gate wardens. I warned Genargh to have guards posted on the walls and draw the bridge up at night, but he said that it was unnecessary. Now three people are dead. Thank goodness you were here or who knows where we would be'. He swigged back his second shot, seeming to calm.

'Well, for propriety's sake, I shall relocate myself for this evening,' Jaden said. 'I trust that you will assign an armed guard to watch the princess for the remainder of her convalescence.'

'I shall remain myself, and Anarkhane help anyone who tries to harm her while *I* am here.'

The Counsellor nodded and bade him goodnight. Thaniel closed the door behind him and rushed over to Exzalander's side, holding her hand tightly to his chest, kissing it with relief.

The following morning the palace was in uproar about the lack of security, and Thaniel argued his case along with several angry household members including Chana's husband, who was distraught over the violent death of his wife.

Gailon was interested to know how Ioan had identified that there was any danger when he had been in a different wing at the time, but he was unwilling to enter into detail.

'I heard her asking for help. It was as though she was in the same room,' he said, as if it had been a freak occurrence.

Gailon watched him closely and he fidgeted under the wizard's scrutinising gaze.

'But how could you be sure that you were not dreaming?'

'Because I was awake, Gailon,' he said innocently.

By early afternoon, Kirsten awoke again. She stretched and yawned, as though waking from a normal night's sleep.

'Well well,' Tom said, with a smile, ' I was beginning to think you would sleep all year.'

Kirsten sat up and looked about her.

'Where am I?' she asked.

Tom frowned. 'I think that I should fetch Gailon before I tell you anything—just to check you out.'

He dashed from the room and Kirsten stretched again, swinging her legs out of bed. The room was like a study, with books and scrolls neatly shelved on every spare piece of wall. She noticed a large cracked piece of wood on the floor and recalled suddenly, a loud banging, as if something had been pounding on the door. Slowly, the events of the previous night sharpened to focus and she remembered the sounds and her fear, also Counsellor Jaden, who had saved her from whatever awful thing had been roaming the corridors.

As her disorientation began to fade, she recalled the face of Ioan, pale in the moonlight, and she realised that she must have collapsed again. She eased herself out of bed, wondering who might have dressed her in her nightgown.

News of her waking spread quickly and Gailon asked Thaniel to keep everyone away. He escorted her back, remaining silent until he closed the door and settled her into her new room. He spent hours explaining and lecturing her on responsibilities and how she was never to do anything of that sort again. He explained why Ioan had been having problems with the pendant and how, if he or she had been forthright about the situation, it would have been sorted without trouble or harm coming to either of them.

Kirsten was so pleased that he was talking to her again, that she found it difficult not to smile as he spoke of serious things. He went on to apologise for having pressurised her, and although he was still adamant that she should be queen, he agreed that it was best to wait until she was ready for such a responsibility.

When the lecture was finished, Gailon said that he would send for her clothes so that she might dress and face the world once more.

'You need some air. You're still very pale.'

'But Gailon,' she stopped him. 'You have not said what attacked me.'

His age-old face was troubled, as if debating whether he should tell her.

'You may as well know sooner rather than later I suppose,' he said. 'A Trolg scout broke through the palace defences last night and went on a rampage. We do not know why it tried to infiltrate Ealdorbold, but there was an obvious concern at its proximity to you. Might it have been a coincidence? Well, let us hope so. Let us suppose that it was merely a stray from the pack that found its way here and decided to do what its kind does best.'

'And what is that?' asked Kirsten apprehensively.

'Wreak havoc. Servants and masons have been at work all day, clearing and rebuilding.'

'Was anyone hurt?'

Gailon averted his gaze and she already knew the answer to her question.

'How many died, Gailon?'

'Only three. Believe me that is what I would consider minimal casualties where one of these creatures are concerned. Their sole purpose in life is to kill and destroy.'

'Who was killed? I remember a woman's scream. Who was it?'

'Chana, the serving girl; it appears that she left you and went to investigate the noise and put herself in the path of one of the deadliest killers that our enemy has to offer.'

Kirsten was dumbstruck by the news.

'The delay that Chana caused when facing the creature probably saved your life.'

His words did not make her feel any better.

'Someone else died because of me ...'

Gailon seated himself beside her.

'Not because of you, Kirsten; she *chose* to investigate the noise.'

'Yes, but she would not have been here, but for me.'

'Kirsten, life is cause and effect, if you were to consider the consequences of every different action then you would drive yourself to madness. Think rather that it was meant to happen. You cannot blame yourself.'

'I was almost killed.' The thought stuck her like an icy hand at her throat.

'No,' Gailon disagreed, 'you have an incredible survival instinct. Even though you were trapped in sleep while your body mended, part of you remained alert. That was what managed to get you to safety. Come now, try not to dwell on this at present; we need you to get well again.'

A maid entered Kirsten's chamber, carrying a selection of clothes. Her eyes were red and it was clear that she had been crying. Kirsten grabbed the woman by the hands.

'I am sorry about Chana,' she said. 'I wish that there was something I could do.'

The woman burst into a fresh flood of tears. 'Not even you could help her,' she spluttered, 'there was only bits of her—just bits,' she wailed.

Kirsten held her close in effort to calm her. She felt weakened by the memory of the terrible tearing sound and tried to push the thought from her mind. The woman drew away suddenly, wiping her eyes.

'Forgive me, Milady, you do not want to listen to me when you've enough troubles of your own.'

'No wait!' Kirsten cried, but the servant ran from the room, her wailing descending the hallway.

She washed then dressed herself in the only black garb that Cob had made for her. It was not a fitted gown except about the throat, and it flowed triangular from that point. She slipped on a comfortable pair of flat leather shoes and draped herself in a magnificent black velvet cape. Pulling the hood up, she walked solemnly from the room; her thoughts paused on poor Chana.

Gailon showed her down to the main wing of the palace, where she saw the last remaining workers, as they lay new marble flooring. Kirsten wondered how the Trolg had got so far without waking anyone with its clamour. Gailon tried to lead her on to the kitchens, but she refused.

'I'm going to take your previous advice and get some air,' she said.

'But you have not eaten in days, girl!' he shouted after her.

The afternoon air did more to revive her than food ever could, although she did feel famished. She strolled about the gardens for a while; receiving strange looks from the courtiers as she passed them, the hood hiding her troubled face. A voice that she recognised caught her attention and she looked up from her brooding to see Troy. He stood with a group of people who she did not recognise, and seemed to be speaking funeral rites.

She approached slowly, keeping to the rear of his vision, so not to distract him.

He was not just performing rites, she realised; he was preaching, talking of a better place and telling them about god and how He is love and would receive their fallen friends with open arms into the kingdom of heaven. A man embraced him after the ceremony and Kirsten suspected that it was Chana's husband.

She walked away from the scene, unwilling for thoughts of the woman's death to creep back into her mind. Approaching the orchard, she hurried to be away from the sound of Troy's reassuring voice.

She picked an apple, and sitting with her back to a tree, she ate it. Closing her eyes, she relished the taste of the juices in her mouth and the feeling of food, fighting back the pain in her empty stomach. She breathed in the wholesome air then opened her eyes and savoured the rich green of her surroundings. The beginnings of a smile touched her lips, until she saw Tehd's approach. She frowned, feeling a sudden compulsion to walk away, but his face seemed changed; he no longer wore the usual scowl he reserved only for her. He seemed thinner and dark rings circled his sunken eyes.

'Lady Kirsten, I hope that you are feeling better,' he said humbly. 'I picked these for you.' He blushed and thrust an assortment of wild flowers at her. Kirsten was unsure how to react to his offering and thought for a moment that he may have poisoned them.

'Thank you,' she said.

Cautiously, she took them from his trembling hands. He bowed low and when he returned to an upright position, Kirsten could see that he was crying.

'I am sorry that I hurt you,' he said. 'I thought that you were killing Ioan. It's my fault you were ill and it's my fault that Chana died. *I* was supposed to be on watch last night.'

Kirsten knelt up and took his hands, touched by the change in him.

'Tehd, you had nothing to do with my being ill or Chana's death. *I* made myself ill and Chana put herself in danger rather than bolting and barricading the door, as she should have. You cannot blame yourself.'

He sniffed his tears away. 'I'm sorry for doubting you. I thought you were a spy; I was a fool.'

Kirsten smiled at his words. 'Please Tehd; stop apologising to me,' she said. 'How could I expect you to believe who I am when I was unsure of that myself? Thank you for the flowers.' She headed back to find the kitchen, leaving Tehd thinking that he had gotten off rather lightly.

She sat in a corner out of everyone's way, as the evening meal was being prepared. Len, the head cook, gave her a plate of meats, bread and cheese and a glass of something that he said would set her to rights. Its herbal taste was not very palatable, but she drank it anyway, feeling invisible as people bustled around her.

As she finished her meal, she felt a peculiar sensation come over her entire body; her eyes seeing more, her nose taking in new smells, her ears sharpening to different sounds and her mind reaching a sense of calm and clarity.

Len collected her plate as he passed by, barking orders to the crew.

'Ah that's good, drank the lot. Gailon will be pleased,' he said.

She thanked him and decided to search for her companions, feeling so awake, that she hardly knew what to do first.

In the main hall, Tom was deep in conversation with Counsellors Vahrn and Borin about the level of destruction. He appeared suspicious about the attack and voiced his reason for concern with detective expertise.

'Kirsten!' The voice was that of Cröedaw, as he descended the stairs with Thaniel at his side.

She sprang toward him, her hood falling from her head, and before he could prevent it, she threw her arms around him.

'Cröedaw, I'm so pleased that you are with us again. How do you fare?' she asked.

The Elfin stepped away, glancing quickly about him. 'I am well thank you, Milady.'

'Lady Kirsten, it appears that you know this man, intimately well,' came the voice of Counsellor Whil. 'It is good to see you up and about. I thought that you might sleep through the contest, and now there is a wager, it would be a pity if you were to deny us your participation.'

Kirsten cringed at the voice and silently cursed herself for her lack of propriety. 'Counsellor Whil,' she said, 'I am sure that you can appreciate that something very serious occurred here last night. The people are shaken by what has happened. Do you not think that it would be in poor taste to hold the contest at this time?'

'Nonsense.' Whil laughed. 'All the more reason to allow it to continue; it will give people something to look forward to. I do hope, Lady Kirsten that you are not trying to back out of my challenge, which I might add, you already accepted.'

Cröedaw laughed, and the sound was like rain upon water, immediately raising Kirsten's spirits.

'Of course she's not backing out,' he said, 'Lady Kirsten merely wishes to save you from the humiliation of being beaten, after your many boasts about court.'

Kirsten smiled weakly. It was not what she felt at all. Whil had been correct; she did not want to shoot. Whil seemed most disgruntled by the Elfin's speech and took it as his cue to leave.

'Well I shall look forward to the challenge,' he said. 'Good day Lady Kirsten. Gentlemen.' He bowed and strode away, his blue overcoat swishing behind him like a velvet wave.

Kirsten swung about to face Cröedaw.

'Why did you have to tell him *that* for? All you've done is provoked him into not allowing me to lose with any dignity!'

Cröedaw frowned. 'Kirsten, you are not going to lose; you have been trained by Taiohähn himself.'

She let out a sigh of exasperation. 'Yes, but not in archery!'

The Elfin's face faltered.

'Well that does it,' she said. 'You've just volunteered yourself. At least we have a week to prepare.'

Thaniel winced in good humour. 'You were asleep for five days,' he explained. 'You have just over two days until the contest.'

Cröedaw smiled, shrugging and she hit her palm against her forehead.

'Typical! Well we had better make a start.'

'But it is almost time to eat,' Cröedaw protested.

'You should have thought about that *before* boasting about abilities that I do not have. Come on.'

Thaniel shrugged at Cröedaw as Kirsten dragged him away.

'But it will be dark soon …'

'And you and I can see perfectly well in the dark. Stop making excuses. I am sure that Thaniel will have us some food sent out.'

She sat looking up at the sky as the first stars began to appear, while Cröedaw fetched bows and arrows from the armoury and set a target. Kirsten watched with fascination as he shot bullseye in the dark.

'That was amazing!' she said.

'Now you.'

He helped her into the correct stance, placing her left shoulder toward the target and her feet hip width apart. As he demonstrated how to nock the arrow and draw, she had hoped that it would suddenly feel second nature to her. It seemed a reasonable assumption considering she had not been aware that she could use a sword or shuriken until she had actually gotten into a fight.

The first attempt at release resulted in the arrow falling to the ground, as did many attempts after that. When she finally managed to loose an arrow, it missed the target completely and struck a wall some twenty paces off to the right.

The feast was well underway and food was sent out to them. Kirsten had still not managed to hit the target, and Cröedaw urged her to sit down to eat with him.

'Thank you for doing this, Cröedaw,' she said, feeling guilty at how she had forced him into it.

'No thanks are necessary, really. It is good to give me something to focus on.'

Kirsten was silent as she ate, but her mind was racing, desperately wanting to question him. Cröedaw watched her for a while before breaking the silence.

'You wish to learn of Shénär, do you not?'

She looked up, surprised.

'It is obvious,' he said. 'Your face told all,'

'I may want to know, but I know how painful the whole situation is ...'

'She was my beloved.'

Kirsten's eyes widened.

'She was not always as you saw,' he continued. 'She was young and carefree when we met; the most beautiful sight that I ever beheld and I was proud to have her at my side. Our happiness was brief, however, as the Dark Ones came and seized Brëgwela and the Elfin were called to the aid of your people. The castle became a dark, impenetrable fortress and the evil of Katahl grew. After Starigorat fell, we took it upon ourselves to attempt to defeat him before he became unstoppable.

'A siege was laid to the castle that was to last many long years. Good men were lost without so much as seeing Katahl; the Dark Ones majick was too powerful. Finally, it was debated whether the attack be postponed until after the Dark Ones had departed. A great Counsel was held and it was argued that Katahl grew in power for each moment we delayed; it was concluded that it could be impossible to defeat him if we did not plan a way sooner rather than later.

'And so it was that in the fiftieth and final year of Katahl's tutelage, my people conceived a plan. It is not unheard of for the higher houses of Elfín to have the ability to change form. Shénär was of pure blood and she could transform herself into a snake at will. It was she who was chosen along with her sisters who could change to mouse and sparrow. The three daughters of Ârgrïn were keepers of the high majick and would be able to defend themselves if the occasion arose.

'They were sent to infiltrate Brëgwela, entering in animal form, watching and hiding until their target was sighted and vulnerable, then they were to kill him. Once within, they decided to separate thus decreasing their chance of being caught. Three days I watched and waited for them and on the evening of the third day, Shénär was released.

'Her sisters had been captured and were chained and tortured to death in the throne room, for Katahl's amusement. Shénär, unaware that they had betrayed her presence there in hope of a quick and painless death, found Katahl waiting for her. As she was in the process of taking human form again, he cast a powerful spell that fixed her, neither Elfín nor serpent.

'This spell was the suspected cause of the Dark Ones departure after their occupation. They perhaps felt that Katahl was ready to claim his birthright.

'I carried Shénär's tiny form for many days, back to our forest in the east, but nothing could be done. The most powerful of our healers could not cure her. I proclaimed that I loved her despite the spell and I took her home with me. She remained only a few weeks before disappearing forever.

'I searched for days uncounted, but found no trace of her. Years later, I heard tell of a snake-like creature residing in the Forest of Tûlg, where the Vampire Ælves dwell. I wondered if it may have been her, perhaps seeking their aid, as their majick is darker than our own and perhaps they are familiar with her predicament.

'I never sought her there; I know not why. I suppose I was fearful of what I might find, scared of having to make the choice that I made in the glade that night.

'She had indeed gone to Tûlg and they had welcomed her and taught her well. She fed, as they do, on the warm blood of the living, and she grew. She learned of dark majicks to trick prey and hold them. I do not know why it was that she left Tûlg after all those years.' He sighed and fell silent, his eyes filled with sadness.

'Did you kill her?' Kirsten asked. 'I heard a scream.'

'Yes. I cut her head from her body and burned the carcass. It was well that you lost consciousness when you did, so that you did not have to witness the pyre.'

Kirsten touched him gently on the arm.

'You feel that you made the wrong choice,' she said, 'that you should have waited to see if defeating Katahl would break the spell.'

Cröedaw bowed his head. 'Come, you're not learning how to shoot sitting here, are you?'

She held him down and his eyes met hers. No tears were in them, but they were like pools of sorrow.

'She would have killed you, Cröedaw; she would have killed all of us if you had given her the chance. She blamed you for what she had become and her love for you twisted to hate. She wanted you to kill her the moment that you realised the spell could not be broken. She returned home with you, thinking that you would do it quickly—painlessly, while she slept. But when day after day passed and it became apparent that you had no intention of putting her out of her misery, she went away; bitter at you for expecting her to exist in torment; believing that aimless travel would bring her doom in her fragile state, but she was wrong. The wild served her, not as executioner, but caused her to become hard and strong—a survivor.'

'What made you say that?' Cröedaw asked.

'I read it all in you. You know in your heart that you had no choice. If you had not slain her, then we may not have made it out of the forest alive.'

She got to her feet and picking up the bow, she shot an arrow. It hit the edge of the target, just outside the markers. Cröedaw jumped to his feet, smiling.

'Well it's a start.'

Nineteen

The following day, Kirsten and Cröedaw worked from dawn, well into the night, practising her aim. By afternoon of the next day, she was hitting the target every time and on occasion had even hit the bullseye.

Cröedaw was amazed at her progress, but she knew that it would not be enough. The contest was to begin mid-morning and she only had the night remaining. If she allowed herself to practise all night, she would be too weak to even lift a bow, let alone shoot it; already her arms ached with the strain of having held them up for so long.

'There is nothing more that we can do,' Cröedaw said. 'You are tired and to speak truth, so am I. You will do well enough tomorrow.'

'But I won't *win*,' Kirsten sulked, as she collected her arrows. 'I want to show Counsellor Whil that I am not a woman to be crossed and make him think twice before he tries to make a fool out of me again.'

'Kirsten, I want you to use my bow tomorrow. It is far superior to any of these, and my arrows are faster and stronger; they will give you an advantage.'

Kirsten received them, smiling. 'Thank you, Cröedaw. I don't suppose it would be possible to get you to shoot for me as well …'

He laughed, but Kirsten's face was suddenly serious.

'That's it,' she cried. 'You *can* shoot for me. I can make everyone think that you're me. It's so perfect, why did I not think of it before?'

'Kirsten, that would be cheating!'

She sagged. 'I know. Sorry. I just hope that I don't make a fool of myself that's all. You should enter anyway, make Whil look like an even bigger idiot than he already is.'

On retiring, she found that she could not sleep. Despite Cröedaw's objections against cheating, she continued to think of underhand ways of winning. *I could levitate the arrows or enchant the bow,* she considered. *Or stop being foolish and get some sleep.* However, she was too wound up to sleep.

She considered going to Ardahl's Tower, but remembered that she if she transported back, then she might not be able to wake herself in time for the contest. Throwing her cloak about her shoulders, she decided to take a walk.

Counsellor Jaden's door was open and he sat at his desk, pawing over several scrolls.

'Lady Kirsten,' he said, 'it is late. Should you not be sleeping?'

She turned, startled, forgetting that his room was so close to her own.

'I could not sleep. May I sit and talk with you a while?' she asked.'

He nodded and gestured for her to take a seat.

'I have not had the chance to thank you for saving my life.'

'No thanks are necessary I can assure you,' he mumbled.

'Yes they are. Had it been any other Counsellor here that night, then I fear I would be dead. You put yourself at risk to help me and I shall not forget it.'

Jaden gave her an uncomfortable smile.

'What are you studying?' she asked curiously.

'They are my notes on a new law that I am trying to get cleared with the other Council members, giving everyone the right to a fair trial and making it illegal to hold or execute a man without this.'

'Habeas Corpus,' Kirsten mused.

Jaden looked at her with a puzzled expression, having clearly not understood what she had said.

'It is an old law, where I'm … in the place where I have been living,' she explained.

'It was passed?'

She nodded.

'And it works?'

'Yes, it has been in place there for hundreds of years. It is difficult to imagine a society without such a law, although I know they exist.'

'This world that you speak of sounds just and fair.'

'I would not go as far as to say that, Counsellor. But it certainly is different.'

'There is something that I do not understand. I was led to believe that you rejected your duty through lack of understanding, and yet you appear to have a good grasp of law.'

'Not really,' she replied. 'Besides, do you think that I would want to mould Maldahl into an image of the world I know? I cannot imagine anything more terrible.' She hugged her knees up to her chest, wrapping her cloak about her. 'It was not only Whil that prompted me to turn down the throne. Whatever his motives for doing so, his words were true. It is not my time to rule.'

'But you could have done such a lot of good,' Jaden said. 'I have seen this already. The respect that you show for the servants and the help that you lend to any in need.'

'And yet I am ill-disciplined and cannot control my temper. For me to be given so much power now might lead to my abuse of it. I *will* do good, but as *me*, not as queen. Now, I should leave you to your study. I have to be up early for a last minute practise.'

He nodded, smiling. 'Ah yes, the archery contest. The odds are fifty to one against you.'

Kirsten groaned, realising that the odds had increased because people had seen her practice. 'Thanks for letting me know *that*,' she said, getting to her feet.

'I think it is marvellous,' the Counsellor said. 'You are going to make me a rich man tomorrow.'

It took a moment for what he had said to sink in. He had taken the odds and bet on her. She wondered if he had seen her shoot and decided that it did not matter. Someone believed in her. Someone other than her friends was actually willing her to win. It made all the difference to her confidence, but unfortunately, not to her sleeping.

She lay in bed listening to the faint tapping of rain as it began to fall, a plan formulating in her mind. *I can't enchant my bow; that would be outright cheating. But if it were to rain … Whil is such a dandy that I doubt he would normally dip his toe in so much as a puddle. Imagine what he'll be like trying to shoot during a rainstorm so bad, that the mud is up to his ankles!'*

She grinned and concentrated on the tapping until she heard thunder overhead and the heavens opened, pouring forth her chance of victory.

By morning, the rain had lessened and she meditated, allowing her majick to create a fresh downpour. After breakfast, she slipped into her leather gear and slicked back her hair into a ponytail. She wrapped her cloak about her and lovingly picked up Cröedaw's beautifully crafted bow and quiver.

The spectators huddled together at the courtyard entrance and the competitors argued over whether they should continue.

'I really do feel that it would be best to postpone the event until fairer weather,' Counsellor Whil ventured.

Kirsten smiled to herself, as she approached. 'Really Counsellor Whil,' she said. 'I am surprised at you being deterred by a little rain.'

Looking about her, she saw that many her fellow competitors seemed to agree with her.

'It appears that the majority has no objection,' Whil said, 'then I suppose that we should proceed.'

He was clearly uncomfortable with the idea and Kirsten smiled, realising how unsuitably dressed he was for the weather. He was wearing his usual royal blue velvet Counsellor's garb, minus the overcoat.

Kirsten's companions went out to meet her. They were all cloaked up, having no intention of observing from inside. There were twenty archers in total, some of whom she recognised from court. Richard the serving boy was present, seeming untroubled by the weather.

'Shall we?' Kirsten asked. She gave a mischievous grin as she stepped out into the rain. Her feet immediately sank into the mud and her path to the targets was slippery and difficult. The rain fell in sheets and had she not trained her eyes so well, she would barely have been able to make out the targets.

The competitors shot their first arrow in sets of fours. After each shot, the servants at the target end waved a coloured flag. White indicated a miss, blue the outer ring, yellow the inner ring and black the bullseye. A white flag indicated immediate disqualification.

As the rain fell harder and the wind made it difficult to open their eyes, many of the archers complained After the first round, over half of the contestants had already been eliminated; they consisted of gentry, for whom archery was simply a pastime and were not accustomed to extreme weather conditions, having lived their lives in luxury. They left the field immediately, protesting at such an outrage in allowing the contest to continue, and sought out the nearest warm fire. Those that remained seemed hardier to Kirsten—woodsmen and hunters. Richard was still in, although he only had a blue flag and like Kirsten, Counsellor Whil went onto the next round with a yellow flag, leaving her disappointed. She had hoped that she would defeat him in the first round.

Eight competitors remained and it was announced that because of the heavy rainfall the rules were to change. Ordinarily, only those who hit the centre could now continue, but from the next round, they would disqualify white and blue flags only. Kirsten considered if such a decision was reached because Whil had hit off mark and was the favourite to win. She watched him nock an arrow and focused on sending an icy blast of wind in his direction. He winced as he shot, his eyes almost closed. Kirsten smiled, sure that he would miss.

There came a distant cheer from the archways and a black flag was waved above Whil's target. Everyone else in his group was out. She caught his smug look, as she approached the shooting area, making her determined that she too would hit bullseye

The cold was beginning to set in and the rain seeped through the opening in her cloak. She thought for a moment whether it would appear suspicious if she allowed the sunshine to glint through while she took her second shot, but decided not to risk it. Allowing the rain to ease off a little and the wind to drop, she aimed the arrow, the bow feeling smooth in her hand. Aligning her sight to the centre of the target, she checked her string alignment then allowed the bowstring to slip off her fingers, releasing the arrow.

As the arrow flew, a cheer went up. With shock, she realised that she had hit the bullseye. Even if she did not win, she knew *that* would be remembered at least.

More cheers were heard, as three of the four in her set remained in the competition. She was one, as well as Richard, and a man whom she did not recognise.

For the third round, they split into groups of two, the best shot eliminated the partner, and so two could carry through to the final round.

Their names were announced and Kirsten learned that the other man's name was John and he was a hunter from the village of Haesburg. His family cheered and Kirsten saw his wife and four children wrapped in battered cloaks, which barely kept off the rain. Their faces beamed proudly in his direction.

Although Richard's shot was good, John's was better. Both were in the yellow, but John's was touching centre. Richard shook the man's hand and stayed to watch the outcome of the contest.

As she approached, Kirsten looked at Whil; his clothes were saturated with rain and his hair stuck to his face; water streamed down each chilled and reddened cheek so that he had to constantly blow it away to avoid further obscuring his vision. She reached her marker, glancing at Cröedaw with a wolfish grin as she took her place. *This is it!* she thought. *The stand off between me and the smug Counsellor.*

Thunder bellowed and lightning flashed overhead. John waved at his family, signalling them to take cover. Rain did not simply fall from the sky; it spewed forth in waves. Kirsten steadied her balance as the mud made her slip. Positioning herself, she could not help but glance to Whil. He was unable to aim; the rain distressed him, his balance was faltering and he looked as though he were crying as he took his aim.

Lowering her weapon, she slid over to him and removed her cloak, wrapping it about his pitiable form. He smiled through chattering teeth, gratefully receiving it, but so cold and lost was he, that he did not realise to whom he was indebted.

The sky darkened and the lightening drew nearer. The cold was like a thousand knives piercing Kirsten's exposed skin. She focused completely on the job at hand, her eyes seeing beyond the curtain of water between her and the target. Her bow bent further, giving her arrow enough force to break through the gale. The rain was so bad that she could not hear the screams as Whil was disqualified with a white flag and she went through to the final round with her arrow in the black; not only was she given a black flag, but her arrow had struck with such force, that it could not be removed from the target.

Whil slipped over in the mud as he made his way to safety. Kirsten found that she pitied, rather than jibed at him, as the amused faces stared at his mud-covered body. She allowed the rain to ease to a shower, having accomplished what she had set out to do, which was humiliate Whil.

John and Kirsten were called to their marks and it was announced that it was the deciding round, the winner of which would receive the prize. Kirsten sagged as a hundred silver pieces were held up in an embroidered moneybag. She looked back at John's family; they watched eagerly, their hands blue with cold, clenching in the hope of their father's victory.

She waited until he had taken his shot: In the black, two fingers left of centre. She took aim, focused on the yellow ring and let loose her arrow. There was a cheer from John's family as he was announced the winner. Walking over to him, she shook his hand, offering her congratulations. His eyes were a little glazed as he accepted the prize, his family hugging him.

Kirsten backed away, catching sight of Counsellor Jaden at an upper level window; he seemed to be smiling. Cröedaw ran over to her, unaffected by the mud. She hugged him tightly, thanking him for all his help. Gailon hobbled carefully over, taking care not to slip; his brow was stern as he congratulated her.

John was led indoors, invited to luncheon with the court in honour of his victory. Kirsten however, chose to sit alone in her room, where a fire had been lit in time for her return. The knock at her door was so quiet that she almost missed it.

'Enter,' she said. Her voice sounded awkward with her head upside down, as she dried her hair.

Jaden timidly announced his presence. 'Milady.'

She stood immediately on realising that it was not one of her companions. 'I am sorry that I lost your money, Counsellor,' she offered.

He waved his hand as if it were nothing. 'What I just saw was worth more to me than any wager, Lady Kirsten,' he said. 'I have just witnessed you deliberately lose, have I not?'

Kirsten felt like a child who fidgets when being questioned about its guilt. She shrugged.

'You allowed that man to win because you knew what the winnings would mean to a poor man and his family,' continued Jaden. 'I came to tell you how proud I am.'

Kirsten felt instantly guilty for having doctored the weather. Many good archers lost their chance to win because of her childish pride and she did not feel good about herself at all.

After the midday meal, John took the opportunity to thank her for what she had done, it seeming common knowledge, and it did not make any difference when she insisted that he had won on his own merits.

Counsellor Whil was not seen for the remainder of the day and Kirsten assumed that he was licking his wounds, far from the sight of mocking eyes. It was not until the evening's feast that he made an appearance once more, wearing slightly different robes. Kirsten, however, did not see him there. She sent her apologies to the Council for being unable to attend. Her miserable morning had brought on a craving that needed to be met, and she sent an invitation to Tom and Troy, hoping that they would appreciate the gesture.

They met in one of the empty parlours and Tom lit a fire. Their stomachs ached with hunger and anticipation as she handed them traditional fish and chips, complete with paper wrapping, lots of salt and vinegar and cans of soft drinks; or in Tom's case, a bottle of English Ale. They talked as old friends about Earth; things that they missed, as well as things that they did not. They laughed as the food filled their bellies and the fire warmed their limbs, until it was late into the night and Tom excused himself, explaining that he was training with the guard at dawn.

As they sat talking, Troy seemed happier than he had been for a while and he did not seem to care when she told him about the spell she had found that could send him back to Earth.

'I really enjoyed this evening, Kirsten,' he said. 'It has been too long since we had a good talk.'

Kirsten shrugged dismissively, whilst moving closer to the fire.

'Your skill in majick is increasing I see.'

She froze, wondering how he could possibly have known about the rainstorm.

'I don't think I've tasted chips better,' he affirmed.

Relaxing once more, she threw the empty bags into the fire to destroy all evidence of their ever being there.

'Well I'm going to call it a night too I think,' she said. 'I've got to be up early tomorrow. I'm going for a dawn ride.'

'Outside the palace?'

She nodded. 'Yes, but there's nothing to worry about. I'm taking Richard with me for a guide, so I shan't get lost.'

Troy's eyebrow rose sharply. 'But are you not concerned about what people will say?'

She got to her feet and brushed herself down. 'I'm surprised at you saying something like that, Troy. But in answer to your question, no, it does not bother me what people say. I will keep company with whomever I choose. If the court want to be ruled by an antiquated class structure—let them.'

'What would happen if you fell in love with a servant of the realm? What then? You would be thrown out of the palace—disgraced.'

Kirsten laughed. 'I am not in love with Richard, Troy; I barely know him. But if I were to fall in love with a servant, I would not let the court dissuade me. Anyway, this is hypothetical talk. I am not in love with anyone. In fact, nothing could be further from my mind at present.'

She bade him good night, leaving him alone with the bitter truth at last.

As Kirsten approached the far landing, she saw Whil in the distance, as he waved to her.

'Counsellor Whil.' She nodded genteelly.

He bowed low, taking her by surprise.

'Lady Kirsten,' he said. 'I want to thank you for your kindness in lending me your cloak. It was a most gracious gesture.'

He handed her the cloak reverently and a pang of guilt stabbed her as she accepted it.

'I would like to apologise to you, Milady,' he continued. 'I underestimated your skill. To shoot in such horrendous conditions, you must be a master bowman. It was an honour to have competed with you.' He bowed again, leaving her to wallow in her guilt.

I cheated, she thought. *No matter how that I try to justify my actions, it still comes back to the same thing. I deceived them. I chose to relinquish my honour for the sake of revenge.* A bitter taste was in her mouth as she laid down the cloak.

'Ah there you are!' came a cheerful voice.

She looked tired as her eyes met with Cob.

'Cob! Where did you disappear to?' she asked.

He hopped onto the end of her bed and eyed her curiously, as she slumped into her chair.

'I went back to the faerie ring. I wanted to see if any of the clans would return now that *thing* has been destroyed. I waited, but nobody came,' he said sadly. 'Still, the birds have come back and I suppose that my people will revisit soon.'

The news only seemed to make Kirsten feel worse. *She* had been the one who had gotten Cob banished to begin with and if it had not been for her, Cröedaw would not have been in the forest at all and would not have been forced to kill Shénär. Despite his sorrow, he had helped her prepare for the contest, believing her to be true and honest and to have taken second place on her own merits.

'Cob, how powerful is your majick? Could you for instance, make everyone start the day over?'

'Perhaps,' he mused, 'but even if I did so, they would still remember today unless we put a charm of forgetting on them and that would not affect Gailon. He would still know that you deliberately made it rain in order to beat that pompous Counsellor.'

She looked at him, incredulous.

'What?' he said. 'You think that I do not hear things? I am invisible for the most part—not deaf! I hear and see a lot that goes on behind closed doors. I was with Gailon when he told Thaniel what you had been up to.'

She put her head into her hands with a groan. 'He must be so mad with me,' she said, wondering how she would ever face him again.

Cob jumped off the end of the bed and walked over to her, his tiny head reached only to her knees.

'Gailon is angry certainly; I would not want to be in your shoes when he catches up with you. However, Thaniel seemed amused by what you had done. He said he admired your idea, as it gave the poorer contestants who are used to bad weather, a greater chance of winning the purse. But Gailon, he is definitely not happy.'

He reached up and sympathetically tapped her arm, before leaving her for the night.

She slept little and continued to ask how she could have behaved so foolishly. Dressing and quietly arming herself, she made her way down to the stables. The sky was beginning to lighten as dawn drew ever closer.

Gently stroking Ravenwing's mane, she leaned her head against his velvety neck; the warmth of him soothed her in the cold before morning. A mist was rising and swept eerily about the palace grounds as people slept, making it appear otherworldly in the fading moments of moonlight.

Saddling Ravenwing, she led him out to the gate. The wardens looked tired after their night's watch and barely stirred at her approach. She asked them to pass a message to the next watch to inform Richard that she had rode on ahead. They let down the bridge and allowed her to pass, without argument; she was after all, free to come and go as she pleased.

Mounting Ravenwing, she trotted out. The top most tip of the sun revealed itself in the eastern sky; the dew sparkled and her breath hung in the air as she made her way through Haesburg and on toward the forest, eager to put some distance between herself and Ealdorbold.

As the sky brightened, birds began to sing and the forest was calm with the serenity that she craved. She rode on, wanting to find peace, to leave behind for a while the responsibility, duty and the guilt. Breathing the fresh morning air, she rode ever deeper into Ánweald.

Richard arrived at the stables a little after sunrise and was quick to discover Ravenwing's absence. As the night guard passed by on their way to bed, they informed him where she had been heading. Without a second thought, he followed her path, fearing for the safety of a woman who chooses to ride alone.

Many hours passed before he discovered Kirsten sleeping peacefully near the river, while Ravenwing happily grazed. He sat some distance away and watched the sky overhead, as it grew steely with the threat of rain.

In her dreams, Kirsten soared over the palace walls and saw Tom joining the guard for their morning practice. He was graceful as any of the soldiers, despite the disadvantage of his years. She watched him from above as he thrust and parried in time with the others, like a well-ordered dance.

Troy was also outside and people of the court gathered eagerly about to hear him speak, but she had not the time to stop and listen. On she soared, past Ardahl's Tower and toward mountains that climbed ever onward.

In her dreams, she felt free, away from the pressures of having to fit in and do the right thing. She wished that she were really breathing the cool air and seeing with her own eyes, the untamed beauty of the mountains, their jagged snow-capped summits reaching up toward the darkening sky.

Richard whispered her name, trying to coax her into waking and she turned from the peaks looking out across Maldahl for a moment, before she found herself returning unwillingly into consciousness.

'Richard?' She yawned. 'I'm glad that you could join me.'

The serving boy smiled with uncertainty. 'I thought it best to wake you,' he said. 'You have been sleeping for a while now. I feared that you might have fallen ill again.'

She jumped to her feet and stretched. 'No. I failed to get any sleep last night, that is all.'

'Lady Kirsten, you should not have left the palace without an escort,' he chastised. 'What would happen if you ran into trouble?'

Kirsten stretched again and laughed. 'You worry too much, my friend. I was fine. Besides, there was nobody but the night guard up at that hour and I needed to get away for a while. I find life at court oppressive.'

Richard handed her his water flask and she drank long draughts.

'From what I hear,' he said, 'you will not remain at Ealdorbold much longer anyhow.'

She pulled the flask away from her lips with a pop. 'Why? What do you know?' she asked.

'I heard the Council say that they were to send you away, to quest for the shards of the Anarkhane stone.'

She handed the flask back to him and looked about for Ravenwing. The horse was further down the bank, basking in a patch of sunlight, which had appeared through the murk overhead.

'Excellent,' she said. 'The sooner we achieve our goal, the better. All this waiting about is getting us nowhere.'

Richard fidgeted uncomfortably and opened his mouth, as if to speak.

'What's the matter, Richard?'

'Nothing Milady. I was going to ask if ... what I mean to say is ...'

Kirsten smiled as he stuttered into silence. He seemed offended by her reaction and his shoulders stiffened.

'I want to ask to be one of the party,' he said indignantly. 'I am faithful and loyal and I can fight. I know that I am not a soldier or a wizard, but I want to do what I can.'

Her smile faded and she drew her sword. Richard backed away, his eyes wide. It was not the reaction he had been expecting or hoping for.

'Something's here!' Kirsten hissed, as the fear prickled down her spine. 'Draw your weapon.'

Richard did not need to be told a second time and he stood back to back with her, awaiting their hunter's arrival.

She focused on the landscape before them and cursed her foolishness for having left the safety of Ealdorbold.

'Trolgs!' she whispered. The familiar feeling of terror was upon her, as they drew close to her presence. 'Do you think that you could make it back to the palace?'

Richard stood firm. 'I am not running,' he said.

'Richard, this is no time for bravery. One of those things can tear out your lungs before you can even think about screaming for help and there are at least three of them heading this way.'

Escape, however, was not an option, as the Trolgs descended upon them. Kirsten screamed to Ravenwing to run and fetch help and the horse sped off in the direction of the palace. She readied herself, planting her feet firmly and circling her sword to loosen her wrist as her body had stiffened with trepidation.

'Richard, stay behind me!' she ordered.

'No I will not,' he protested, his face pale.

'Do as you're told, boy!' Her tone demanded nothing but obedience.

He stepped back and watched the onslaught. The river to his back, his dagger remaining drawn in wait for one of the creatures to break Kirsten's defence. He soon forgot his fear and watched her fight back each of them, all of which were much larger in stature, yet she beat them back as if they were equal; a kick there, parry, thrust, sidestep, swing, thrust and swipe. She removed one of their heads, yet the remainder continued their onslaught.

More joined the fight and Kirsten was beginning to tire, the fight feeling less effortless than it appeared to her onlooker.

Richard stabbed madly at a Trolg as it fell near him. The blood smeared across his hands and spattered his face. His dagger, he had thrust so deep that he had to stand and use his leg for leverage to remove the blade from the dead creature's flesh.

Three Trolgs lay dead; one be-headed, another its neck broken and the last with stab wounds. Two of the terrible killers remained and they seemed not to tire as they thrust and clawed at the warrior woman before them. Hearing further noise, Richard looked beyond the immediate danger to see more of the creatures approach. The newcomers ignored the fight and made straight for Richard's horse; it whinnied and neighed, pulling desperately at its tether in effort to escape the foul beasts.

Without thinking, Richard ran screaming at them to draw away their attention from his horse. Kirsten, hearing his cries, cursed at him for breaking her rear defence. Richard soon discovered that fighting a Trolg was not as easy as Kirsten had made it appear. The first shove knocked him off his feet, so strong was the beast. Next, he felt a burning heat as the Trolg tore open his chest with its terrible claws. The pain was too intense to bear and the last thing he thought before darkness took him, was that the creature would eat his heart.

Kirsten had no intention of allowing that to happen. She attacked them with brutal force in order to protect her fallen comrade. However, she had performed a trance spell on the two Trolgs that she had been fighting; with Richard so close to death, she had taken the risk, knowing that it was a dangerous and foolish thing to have done. It was a simple spell that she had learnt in the tower, but it was majick nevertheless; if their fight was observed by spies of Katahl, then she knew word would reach him and his suspicions might be raised as to her identity.

Every second that passed, she was aware that Richard was bleeding heavily. *If I don't get him to safety soon, then he will die,* she realised. The newcomers seemed stronger than ever and she found it difficult to concentrate as she was looking for somewhere to conceal Richard so that she might heal him.

A tiny groan ensued from him and she decided that she had wasted enough time with fighting. She performed the trance spell once more and slit her enemies' throats. A sharp spasm of shame swept over her, knowing that she had killed the enemy in unfair combat while they had been unable to defend themselves. She cut Richard's horse loose and it ran wildly away.

Lifting Richard, Kirsten scrambled up-river to the waterfall, feeling the strain on her fatigued body. She hoped that the two remaining Trolgs did not revive and see her, or that reinforcements did not arrive too soon to avenge the blood spill, the latter of which being her greatest concern, as she could sense the presence of more of the vile creatures, each of them like a cold stab of alarm in her body.

The waterfall was not very large and spilled forth into a small lake some twenty metres below. She searched for an easy path down, but found that she would have to carry Richard over her shoulder. Timing was critical; placing him thus would cause his wound to gape and she realised that he might bleed to death before they reached safety. Scrambling down, it seemed to take an age to reach the bottom. She set Richard down close to the bank that they had just descended, hoping to provide him with adequate cover should the enemy peer over the edge.

He was pale and blood covered everything. Tearing open his tunic, she poured water over his chest so that she might discern the wound. The water revived him slightly and he spied a fading image of her bending over him. He smiled up at her; she seemed to glow faintly, warming him a little.

Kirsten worked hard on knitting the flesh back together and breathing life back into him, aware that healing him would tire her, but the extent of the wound was such that if she did not help, then Richard would die before aid arrived from Ealdorbold.

A cry overhead informed Kirsten that the Trolgs had come 'round. Her mind raced with fear, realising that they must be killed; if they escaped then Katahl would surely discover what she had done. Releasing her hold on Richard, she observed that he was still deathly white, but his wounds had almost closed.

She felt the Trolgs heading toward her and she moved quickly away to intercede them before they had a chance to discover Richard. Running alongside the river, she scrambled up the muddy slope. They turned, catching sight or scent of her, their cruel eyes glittering as they ran to face her once more.

Her body and mind felt drained and her spirits sank lower when four more Trolgs attacked from the rear. She drop kicked with a circling action, setting them all off balance, and then somersaulted over the newcomers' heads so that all six Trolgs were in front of her. As she fought, she tried to keep her back to a large tree to cover her rear.

Her throwing stars proved useless at such short a distance and although she used both sword and dagger to strike out with, she found herself wishing for a shield to protect her from the numerous blows. It was perhaps lucky most of the Trolgs were unarmed and used their claws as weapons, fighting like wild animals.

The blood ran down her arms where she had failed to block their attack. She stabbed forward, spying an opening and skewered one of the beasts, ducking whilst trying to retrieve her weapon from its hulk of a body and narrowly missing a stab from the side. Her hand shot out swiftly and tore at leg flesh with her cruel shaped dagger. The Trolg roared loudly as the blood began to ooze and he backed away. Kirsten did not have chance to wonder at his retreat and continued to fight for her life. She threw a shuriken after it and it fell dead several metres away from the fray.

Four Trolgs remained and as her blood loss grew, her body felt beyond fatigue. She concentrated her sword on the Trolg holding the hammer while leaving her left hand to fight off the claws of the others. She blocked and struck automatically and her mind began to drift, wondering how long she had been fighting and whether Ravenwing had reached Ealdorbold.

Her dagger blocked another swipe and cut so deep into the wrist of her attacker that it lodged there. The Trolg grinned with its screwdriver teeth, realising it had broken down part of her defence. With a growl, it pulled out the dagger from its partly severed wrist and swiped at her with her own bloodstained weapon.

To her surprise, the dagger swung straight past her face and lodged in the throat of another Trolg. The creature holding her dagger howled as it removed the weapon from its murdered comrade and Kirsten took the break as an opportunity to literally disarm the Trolg holding the hammer, before removing its head. The move cost her dear when the remaining beast managed to get a hold on her and tore into her flesh.

The pain seemed remote and she broke free from its hold, lashing out blindly. The Trolg backed away with a hiss. The end was near, her movement clumsy as the blood poured from her shoulder. The other Trolg had rejoined the fight and raised her dagger as if to strike her down, then collapsed to the ground, squealing. It rolled about, seemingly in agony.

Kirsten gained fresh hope from the strange occurrence and her eyes burned with fury, swinging the Sword of Taiohãhn in a figure of eight causing the last of the attackers to take a step back.

Despite her rising temperature, the sword felt cool in her bleeding hand. The Trolg ducked and retrieved the fallen hammer, swinging it fiercely before letting it fly.

She raised her sword to block its deadly blow and the force of the impact sent her off balance. The Trolg wasted no time and dived at her, pinning her to the ground.

The Sword of Taiohãhn fell from her grasp and she wrestled desperately with the creature with death in its eyes, knowing that if she let go of its arms, then it was all over; the Trolg would tear her apart. She remained locked in the embrace, the Trolg frustrated by the woman's strength as she clung to his wrists with a pincer grip. It snarled, snapping its jaws, and she fought to keep its teeth away from her straining face.

As the last ounce of her strength left her and the creature broke free, Kirsten felt a simple resignation.

I'm going to die.

The Trolg pulled upward ready to make its final blow. She was vaguely aware of a whistling sound before the creature collapsed on top of her, its weight crushing the breath out of her. Her eyes were losing focus, but she thought that she could make out the form of Tom and Thaniel as they wrenched the body of the Trolg from her own, four of Cröedaw's arrows protruding from its back.

Cröedaw dismounted Ravenwing and led him over to where his mistress lay. Kirsten heard a familiar voice and her ashen face managed a weak smile, realising that help had arrived at last.

'Richard …' her voice was no more than a whisper, 'the waterfall …' She spoke no more, but allowed herself to slip into the comfort of darkness.

Twenty

Several members of the guard retrieved Richard. He was conscious and his blood loss had stopped, making the soldiers question why he had been hiding at all, when a woman had been in need of aid. Thaniel attempted to staunch Kirsten's bleeding and placed a makeshift dressing on the worst of her wounds. Ravenwing bore her back to the palace in the arms of Thaniel. She felt weightless and cold in his grasp and he worried that life might be leaving her, even as they rushed to safety.

The healers were already on standby at the party's approach, and they carried Kirsten on a litter to their house on the far side of the palace gardens. Thaniel moved to follow, but was told that it was forbidden and they would keep him informed of her progress.

Richard was released later that evening and Breh, the Master healer, held counsel with Genargh and Gailon to discuss his recovery.

'He must have amazing healing power,' Breh said. 'I have never seen such a thing happen; there is not even a scar to show that he was ever injured. It is simply not possible.' The healer paced up and down seeming both fearful and full of wonder.

'It was the girl who healed him, not himself,' Gailon explained. 'It is a pity that she did not leave herself enough strength so she might administer to her own wounds. How does she fare?'

'We have stopped the bleeding and dressed her wounds and yet she does not wake. She remains pale and lost in another world from this one, I fear. I know not what ails her.'

The healer was dismissed and the Second Counsellor argued with Gailon.

'If she weakens so easily, what use is she against the enemy? We should give the Sword of Taiohähn to a warrior more worthy I deem.'

Gailon stood suddenly, his temper clear in the swiftness of his movements. 'A more worthy warrior?' he said incredulous. 'Twelve Trolgs lay dead! Trolgs Genargh—not men! Show me one such warrior in the realm who could achieve such a feat and in the process bring a man back from the brink of death to full recovery. A more worthy warrior you will not find.

'It is true that she has not yet tamed and matured the power that is in her, but it grows stronger by the day. Besides, the sword is hers by right and I dare not think what would happen if you tried to take it from Taiohãhn's chosen champion.'

The counsellor fidgeted uncomfortably. 'Let the servant be brought before us all in our chamber, so that we might learn what occurred today.'

As he related events, Richard was clearly distressed, seeming more concerned with being permitted to go back and sit with Kirsten, than doing as he was ordered. Gailon seemed impressed by Richard's bravery in attempting to tackle two Trolgs in order to save his horse. He had a glint in his eye on suggesting that Richard be one of the company to quest for the lost shards.

At Gailon's suggestion, Richard's face brightened, until the counsellors abruptly dismissed him without expressing any opinion on the matter. Dinner was announced and the High Council rose, signalling that their conversation was over.

Throughout the feast, the companions discussed whether Kirsten would be well enough to go join the quest.

'Do not even question that,' Gailon said. 'Her presence will be vital if reunification is to be achieved, unless she is to relinquish her duty and surrender the sword.'

'Where are we to go, Gailon? Do you know where the other pieces are hidden?' Ioan murmured.

'I know nothing for certain, but I suspect that they lie in the North Kingdom, Tûlg is most likely, and that of course will bring us dangerously close to him.'

'When are we to start, Master Gailon?'

The old wizard's eyebrows knitted together into a frown. 'As soon as Kirsten is well again. Our company is likely to be divided, and it has not yet been decided who will journey and where.'

'But surely Tom and I will be going!' said Troy.

Gailon's frown deepened further. 'Thomn perhaps might be sent to protect the Princess, but I fear you may not be permitted to go, unless a messenger be required. Already your welcome as a guest here has been more than I expected. It will not last long. You are a messenger of the realm and although the two palaces no longer communicate, I am certain that the Council will find some duty for you to perform. You are sworn to serve and that is your place, unless you turn traitor and dismiss your oaths.'

Troy's face was pale at the thought of servitude. 'If I made oaths, they were in another life,' he said. 'How can they bind me now? I have no desire to be a servant, unless of God. I am a priest, that is my calling and if Maldahl cannot accommodate me, then I will find a way to return home, where I am a respected member of a community.' He was swift to depart the evening's activities, walking off into the dark.

'Our friend is upset,' Gailon observed. 'His passions cloud his mind and judgement. Let us hope it will not prove his undoing.'

'Is there no way that you could convince the Council to allow him to come, Gailon?' Ioan asked, as they settled away from the musicians.

'Even if I could, I would not ask. Troy needs to focus on himself for a while and find his place. It would not be healthy for his state of mind to join us. A little distance will make him stronger.'

Thomn-the-Cleaverhand, Inspector Tom Stevenson as was, guzzled down a frothy mug of beer. As he put down his empty tankard, the foam clung to the beginnings of a beard. 'It's all nonsense, Gailon,' he said. 'You say I can go, but Troy isn't allowed. You seem to have a particular reason, but you speak in vague riddles.'

Thaniel laughed and bowed his head. 'That is his way, my friend,' he said, although his eyes revealed that he knew exactly what Gailon had meant.

Troy stood for a while outside the white columned building in which Kirsten was housed. He went down on his knees and prayed to the unfamiliar heavens. The stars were different, but he liked to believe that God was still listening to one of His flock, one who felt lost and alone.

'Forgive me Father for I have sinned. I have had unclean thoughts about the girl, Kirsten. I thought that you had sent her on a mission but I used this to disguise my true feelings.

'I pray for guidance and forgiveness and the strength to do your bidding. I pray that I might find my path in life again and serve you to the best of my ability.

'Amen.' He crossed himself and returned swiftly to the palace.

Thaniel watched from the shadows, as Troy crossed himself and re-entered the main building, then he made for the healer's abode himself. The house reflected the moonlight with an almost spectral light. The healer that came running out in her white robe, appeared equally ghost-like. She yelped as Thaniel caught hold of her.

'What is it? What is wrong?' he demanded.

'The Lady Kirsten, she's screaming,' the woman replied. 'We know not what ails her. Master Breh sent me to fetch Gailon.' She wrenched herself free and dashed off toward the palace.

Thaniel entered the house. Nobody prevented his admission, as all were attempting to calm the hysterical woman. Following the sound of her cries, he quickened into a run when she screamed, the noise piercing his heart. He found the chamber in which she was housed, but could not see her through the wall of healers who gathered. Breaking through the crowd, he confronted her pale, copious form. Kirsten's visage banished, it was Exzalander's features that writhed in anguish.

'You should not be here, Thaniel. Leave at once!' Breh ordered.

Thaniel ignored the Master of the house and gathered the princess in his arms, holding her to him. Screaming again, she pushed him away, seeming only partially awake. Her breathing was heavy and eyes wide as she attempted to focus on her surroundings. The strange people in white were unknown to her, but among them was Thaniel. She threw herself into his arms and clutched him tightly.

He forgot the presence of the healers and gently stoked her head in attempt to calm her trembling form. Her breathing began to slow and he felt her hold on him release as her body relaxed and she fell asleep in his arms. Her mind seemed at peace from whatever torment had set upon her and he gently laid her back onto the bed

'You should stay with her tonight. She appears to trust you, Thaniel.'

Thaniel felt a jolt, realising how his actions might appear and he wondered how long Gailon had been stood there.

'I will relieve you later tonight so that you may get some rest,' Gailon continued. 'I know Master Breh, that it is not usual for you to allow such a thing, but I think that you will agree that these a far from normal circumstances.'

The Master nodded in agreement.

'But what ails her, Gailon?' Thaniel asked.

'I am surprised that you need to ask. She fought for her life against a terrible enemy. There was no help, simply herself and more Trolgs. I am already aware that she fears them. I shudder to think what distress she underwent, pitted against so many. Her body is exhausted and the use of majick has drained her, but much worse than that, her mind is locked in torment.

'Master Breh here has cured her body, but cannot ease the suffering in her mind. She will need the support of her friends for that. We must be here when she needs us and soon I hope, she will return.'

The healers went back to other tasks, and Gailon spoke for a while with Breh. Thaniel held Exzalander's hand and stroked her hair from her face. He mopped her brow and whispered to her that he was there and everything would be all right. But in her mind, Trolgs surrounded her, and it was Katahl who offered such promises.

Several days passed and Kirsten remained in her unconscious prison, trapped by fear and desperation. There were only moments of reprieve when she caught sight of Thaniel or Cröedaw, but their images were so distant and brief that she could not be sure if they were real.

She wandered in dark woods, ever pursued by the enemy, not daring to pause for rest as she sensed them drawing closer; she heard their breath heaving as they closed in for the kill. It seemed to her that she had been days on her feet and the trees never came to an end. At times, Cob would flit besides her telling her to return, but she refused to listen to him, so fearful was she of confronting the Trolgs.

'We cannot delay any longer, Gailon,' Daihron said. 'Already the enemy is at our door. Never have Trolgs passed over the threshold to defile our cherished halls. We are all in danger and the longer we delay, the more likely will it be that the Lord Katahl will seize the stones we already possess. The sooner Ioan puts some distance between himself and Ealdorbold, the safer it will be for all of us.'

'But to send him off alone ... it is too dangerous,' Gailon protested. 'If Katahl has Trolgs posted in Ánweald, then I would imagine that he has spies watching our every move.'

'Gailon, that is precisely why I am not sending the lad on his way with an armed escort of guards. Katahl is much less likely to be suspicious of a handful of foreign travellers.'

Gailon shook his head. He seemed much aged over the past few days. 'It is a dangerous assumption to make, Counsellor Daihron,' he said. 'I will go with Ioan and Tehd, and will take Thomn-the-Cleaverhand as a guard. We will head north-west to Tûlg and I hope beyond hope that we will evade capture so close to Katahl's domain.'

Gohrn rose from his chair and slithered before the High Council.

'But what of the woman?' he questioned. 'Is she to remain here to endanger us all? If the enemy comes now, what use will she be to prevent it? We should have the healers remove her from the palace at once.'

Gailon's face reddened. 'That you must not do! At least here, we may offer a little protection, and if we lose our lives in attempt to save her, then so be it. She is too important to risk capture. Counsellor Gohrn, might I suggest that it is time you discard personal differences. For if we are to go to war, there will be but two sides.'

Gohrn bowed his head respectfully in acknowledgment of the sentiment, but his eyes remained as ice.

'How fares she?' Cröedaw asked, as he stood before the ashen-faced girl.

'No change my friend,' Thaniel replied. 'Cob tried to use his majick, but still could not aid her.'

Cröedaw seated himself on the end of the bed. 'Gailon and Ioan leave tonight,' he said. 'If the Lady awakes, then we are to escort her to the Sea-lands. If she does not wake, then the Council has decreed that you shall take the Sword of Taiohãhn and continue the journey without her.'

Thaniel stared for a moment at the fragile form of Exzalander and then walked over to the window and stared out at the moonless night.

'I should go and say my farewells.' His voice was distant and dutiful.

Cröedaw watched his friend leave, knowing in his heart that Thaniel did not want the burden of carrying the sword.

The stars began to peep out, but Kirsten was unaware of them; it was forever dark in her prison. Already that night she had fought ruthlessly with

Trolgs. She was running now, running in the only direction from which they did not approach. She ran ever north with the enemy moments behind her.

Ahead, she saw four figures on horseback. They appeared strangely illuminated despite the deep darkness; their cold faces noble and their armour, black. The central figure remained hooded until she drew closer.

It was Caitul.

She stared in wonderment at his death-like features and was no longer afraid. The Trolgs had reached their target and surrounded her on mass, ready to tear her apart with their glistening claws. It was only the will of the knights that prevented them; as Meggan had said, they were the most powerful of all Katahl's servants. Yet, they were her salvation in the madness. She took a few steps toward Caitul, her eyes locked on his, remembering both times that he had saved her life. A screeching noise from the trees drew her attention. A crow swooped down and her eyes followed it. There was a murmur amongst the Trolgs and their weapons raised against it.

'No!' she shouted,

They hurled stones at the crow and she drew her sword; fear forgotten, she charged the host, prepared to slay every last one of them in attempt to save the bird.

'Kirsten?' Thaniel asked tentatively.

Her eyelids flickered and a croak from the bird on her bedpost caused her eyes to open. The blurred outline of the crow came into view and the bird bobbed its head at her arrival back to consciousness.

'Hello my friend,' she whispered. 'Thaniel?' She smiled and it was like a breath of fresh air in the nighttime gloom. She reached up weakly and touched the crow that had once again settled. 'I was unsure whether it was real or no'. Glad am I to be back ... Richard!' she recalled, panicking, 'Is he?'

'He is well,' assured Thaniel. 'You saved his life.'

She fidgeted, attempting to gain a sitting position.

'No. Try not to stir yourself. You are weak and you need rest.'

The crow flew out of the window and off into the darkness. Kirsten did not feel like resting. She feared to sleep and face again, the darkness of her dreams.

Thaniel waited until morning before seeking an audience with the Council. He informed them of Kirsten's progress and Counsellor Callarn requested that she be brought before them, so that it might be established if she was fit enough to begin the quest.

She followed Master Breh up to the palace; the morning air was chill about her, and her limbs tight. Feeling dirty and dishevelled, she entered the Council Chamber and as their eyes rested upon her, she longed for a bath and any gown other than the flimsy white robe in which the healers had placed her.

'Counsellors.' She respectfully bowed her head and a general murmur of greeting ensued.

'It is time, Lady Kirsten, for you to begin your quest,' Daihron said. 'We have only to be assured by Master Breh that your health has returned.'

Breh stepped forward, uncomfortable under the heavy stares of the Council.

'It is my opinion that she should remain with us a few more days, to be sure that she does not relapse.'

'Yes, yes, yes,' said Vahrn shortly, 'but you feel at present that she has made a full recovery?'

'It would seem so,' Breh replied. He felt that whatever he said would have been manipulated into the answer that they wished to hear.

'Very well,' Genargh announced. 'Your quest will begin as soon as you have packed and eaten. May the luck of Ealdorbold go with you.'

They were dismissed and the large doors closed behind them. Kirsten thanked Master Breh for taking care of her and then returned to her room in order to pack. Feeling weak and disorientated, she wondered how long she had been in the healers' care.

She packed very little, aware that she had neither the room nor the need, for the host of beautiful gowns that had been made for her. She armed herself fully; her blades were gleaming, cleaned since the fight, but a ghostly reminder of the terrible struggle with the Trolgs.

Picking up her pack and cloak, she left the room, wondering if she would ever return.

Thaniel and Cröedaw awaited her at the foot of the main stairwell to escort her for a final meal at Ealdorbold.

'Where are the others?' she asked. She began to wolf down a plate of food, but observing the silent exchange between them, she stopped eating.

'Thaniel and I are to escort you to Lake Hendref,' Cröedaw said. 'If nought is to be found there, we shall continue onto the Úberi sea. In addition, the serving boy, Richard had been permitted to accompany us, Milady.

'But what about the others?'

'Everyone but Troy has already set off in the direction of Tûlg.'

Kirsten pushed her plate aside, her stomach confirming her loss of appetite. Without Gailon, she considered who would guide her and realising that she was left with no-one else from Earth to talk to made her feel as though part of her had been torn away. She felt helpless and began to suspect that the quest would be a fruitless one.

Outside, the packs had been prepared. Nobody had gathered for a farewell. Kirsten's pallor was grey in the daylight and her silence projected her solemn mood.

'Milady, there is something that Gailon wished us to do when we are on the road,' Cröedaw said. 'He told me that we should be wary of discussing our quest for fear of being overheard and above all that we should treat you as an equal of birth and address you only as Kirsten.'

'That is wise advice,' Thaniel said, 'and we shall heed it.' He gave a stern and warning glance toward Richard.

Kirsten remained silent and checked her bridle.

'One thing more,' Cröedaw announced. 'Gailon gave this unto my keeping, to present to you. He said that a friend had suggested it.'

Kirsten watched as the Elfín pulled a strange object from beneath his cloak. It was oddly wrought metal with faceted glass-like panels on either side. She realised suddenly what it was for and, taking the object from Cröedaw, she unsheathed her sword, holding it to the weapon. All jumped when the thing moved by itself, closing tightly about the hilt until it became part of the sword. No longer did the weapon look like the Sword of Taiohãhn; it had silver and gold gilding and seemed strangely smaller; the Anarkhane stone appeared a deep blood red.

'Amazing,' Cröedaw said. 'It looks like a completely different blade. Truly Gailon is a master of majick.'

Kirsten glanced up at Ardahl's tower and smiled wryly, guessing all too well who had aided Gailon in creating the miraculous contraption.

Twenty-One

For their travelling that day, they followed the road on the outskirts of Ánweald forest, Thaniel's reasons being twofold; He hoped to evade suspicion and keep Kirsten away from the scene of the attack, concerned for her state of mind.

By evening, they set up camp at the side of the road, just at the eaves of the forest. There were signs of a recent encampment and Kirsten felt a pang, wondering if it could have been Gailon's party, who were a full day ahead.

Thaniel cooked the evening meal while Cröedaw and Richard refilled the water-skins. Kirsten sparred with an invisible partner a little away from the fire and Thaniel marvelled at how well she handled a sword; he had never seen a woman fight before and felt eager to test her skill. He threw a stone toward her and smiled as she parried with her blade.

'Amazing!' he said.

'That would have hurt!' she exclaimed.

'It is well that you did not miss then.'

Thaniel returned to his cooking, leaving Kirsten to mull over the meaning behind his statement, considering that his stern manner was perhaps to teach her that their quest was no game.

Kirsten ate little that evening, feeling neither the need nor want of sustenance. 'What happened to Cob?' she asked, while the others ate their fill.

Richard placed down his bowl as he replied. 'He said that he liked the palace food so much, that he would remain at the kitchens for a while.' He returned to his meal, but gave a worried glance to Thaniel.

'You should eat.' Thaniel said.

Her mind seemed to be far away and she made no reply.

The night was clear and the stars twinkled brightly above as the party took their rest. Cröedaw took first watch, allowing his keen hearing to pick up every movement about them. After a time, he let his glance settle among the stars and he watched the heavens, allowing them to comfort him like a familiar blanket.

Kirsten awoke a little before dawn and found Richard on watch, his eyelids heavy. She told him to sleep and she prepared breakfast for her companions. Having only a vague idea of how to cook without the convenience of a kitchen, she searched the food pack in hope of inspiration. There was bread, so she could make toast; but no butter, jam or honey.

She looked cautiously about her for any signs of life, considering that none of them would know what *her* pack contained. She smiled, feeling like a magician pulling a rabbit from a hat, laying the honey and butter proudly on her cloak. She stoked what remained of the fire. The embers glowed. *It might be enough,* she thought as she skewered a chunk of bread on the toasting fork and held it toward the dying fire.

Cröedaw stirred as the first piece of toast was prepared and smiled broadly when she passed him his breakfast.

'I have not tasted as good as this since Field House,' he affirmed.

Thaniel woke at the sound of Cröedaw's voice, but Richard slept on.

'You should have been resting, Kirsten,' he said, 'I left Richard on watch.'

Her smile faded at his manner.

'I was awake anyway,' she protested. 'I told Richard to rest. Why should I not be put on watch? Do you think me incapable?'

Thaniel yawned, his eyes lighting up as he spied the toast. 'It is not that we do not trust you, as well you know. You have been ill and would still be in the healers' care had I my way.' He stopped to take a mouthful of toast and his eyes widened at the taste of it. 'Delicious!' he said, with his mouth half full.

Kirsten placed the items she had conjured back into her pack and woke Richard. His eyelids were heavy, but he seemed glad not to have missed out on breakfast. Cröedaw and Thaniel went off to gather supplies and take a wash. Kirsten followed their example, hoping to avoid more questions about honey the like of which none of them had ever tasted.

Hearing a splashing sound on approaching the river, she caught sight of Thaniel, stripped to the waist in the cold morning air. She watched for a while, captivated. She was sure that she must have seen men in that way before, but perhaps had never really noticed. Observing his muscles ripple as he dunked his head and shook his hair, she felt a quiver in the pit of her stomach.

'Kirsten?'

She jumped, her face blushing at having been caught a voyeur.

'Cröedaw!' she exclaimed. 'I was just waiting for Thaniel to finish, so that I might bathe.'

Her mouth twisted awkwardly and her eyes fixed on his blue-black boots. When she risked a glance upwards, she saw quite clearly that there was laughter in his eyes. She blushed again and spoke stubbornly, trying to change the subject.

'Is this not the river that flows past Field House?'

Cröedaw nodded and the mischief was gone from his glance, so severe was her gaze.

'Yes it is. It also leads west and Gailon will follow it until he sees the Dragon Mountains, then he will take a path north to the Forest of Tûlg.'

Thaniel approached, his shirt covering his torso, seeming oblivious to his previous audience.

'Will we pass through Freya Valley?' Kirsten asked hopefully.

'No, we're going up and 'round. Ishtar will give us a good road for travelling north and will be better for gaining news and supplies.'

The men strode back to camp, leaving her to wash alone. She scarcely noticed the ice-cold water against her skin, recalling the hospitality of Sally and Jack. She wished that she could have remained at Field House rather than having to traipse about the country in the freezing cold, searching for something she had never even seen, in a land so totally unfamiliar to her.

'Are you ready?'

It was Thaniel's voice behind her. She had not even heard his approach. Jumping to her feet, she returned to the party, leaving her brooding beside the gentle trickle of the river that led to Field House.

The grey morning grew colder, and by noon, a heavy rain fell to dampen Kirsten's spirits even further. Thaniel failed to light a fire that evening, which led to Richard's suggestion that, despite their fatigue, they should continue the last few miles to the city so they might rest in warmth and comfort.

Kirsten sympathetically patted her horse and felt the cool wetness of his neck.

'Sorry boy,' she whispered in his ear, and he blew air through his lips in reply.

Keeping her hood up and head down, she allowed Ravenwing to lead her toward the city.

Ishtar was a welcoming sight and the companions hurried to the gates thinking only of food and warmth. It was not until the wardens asked them to state their business that they were on their guard once more.

'We are travellers,' Thaniel replied. 'Just passing through, looking for shelter for the night.'

'Where have you come from and where are you headed?'

Thaniel stiffened slightly at the man's probing. His voice replied calmly and Kirsten was amazed at the ease of his dishonesty.

'We are making for the city of Bashnya,' he said. 'We have passed through many places and I am sure that you realise that we still have a long journey ahead of us.'

Another voice ventured forth from the warden's tower. It was laconic and low in pitch, making Kirsten's skin prickle when she heard it.

'Huh! You are none of you from Dokee-Gavan and they do not permit strangers to enter, or residents to leave. What is your purpose in travelling so far, only to be turned away?'

Kirsten's skin felt like ice. She pulled her cloak tight about her and wished more than anything that they would turn back and head for Field House.

'We seek wisdom and a new way of life,' said Thaniel. 'It is said that the City of the Towers is advanced beyond our imagining. We wish to learn from them if we can. I am sure if we reason with them that we will be permitted to stay.'

Kirsten only distantly heard Thaniel's words. She felt as though arms were reaching toward her, peeling back her cloak and revealing her secrets. Cröedaw and Richard remained silent and Kirsten wondered if they were feeling in a similar way afflicted. If Thaniel felt unease with the stranger, then he showed no signs of it and he continued to talk about the wonders that he had heard rumoured.

'You are now entering the north gate,' grated the voice above them. 'Tell me, did you pass through Ánweald?'

Although she could not see the stranger's face, Kirsten could sense his eyes upon them, feeling as though he were staring into her soul.

'Yes, via the main road,' Thaniel replied. 'We came from Ealdorbold, where I might say, sir, that we rather outstayed our welcome. People there will not stand to hear of new things. Change to them is not to be borne, and so we were sent on our way.'

Silence followed Thaniel's words and Kirsten felt less probing, sensing rather, ironic amusement, which frightened her. She saw quite clearly, the stranger's malice toward the people of Ealdorbold. Before she could reach further to look into his mind, the stranger spoke and she felt his thoughts shielded against her.

'Let them pass,' he hissed. 'Strangers, you may find that you do not need to travel so far as Dokee-Gavan to discover the change you seek.'

Smiling, Thaniel bowed his head, but the others hurried through in effort to be away from the voice at the gate.

It was not until they were safely in their room at the Brown Bottle Inn, warming themselves in front of the fire, that they spoke about the events at the gate.

'What is going on, Thaniel?' Cröedaw asked. 'Ishtarians are never that cautious. They *like* receiving travellers,'

Thaniel stared into the flames. Kirsten watched his eyes as the flickering reflected hypnotically in them.

'I know and I do not like it,' agreed Thaniel. 'That was no gate warden back there. For one thing, he knew the ancient name for Bashnya. Few now would have such knowledge. I myself know only because Gailon told me once.' He began to pace the room.

'Yes, *I* had forgotten the name until I heard it uttered this evening,' Cröedaw said. 'And why was he asking about the forest? I fear that he was a servant of Katahl, in which case the question was aimed to discover what happened to the patrol of Trolgs.'

Kirsten shivered suddenly, remembering the vicious creatures, which she and Richard had destroyed.

'Whoever it was had a power that made me anxious,' she said. 'His mind pressed against mine so hard that I wanted to scream, "yes it's me. I am Exzalander." I hid my thoughts, but it was a strain. If all the servants of Katahl are that powerful, how can we ever hope to defeat him?'

Cröedaw sat by the fire, his worried eyes meeting Thaniel's. Richard shook his head, seeming confused.

'I do not understand any of this,' he said. 'I did not feel anything other than a desire to get out of the cold. I did not know why you were lying, Thaniel; I assumed that you were merely being cautious in front of strangers.'

'But I thought that you were *all* affected by him!' Kirsten exclaimed.

'I myself felt a chill when he spoke, but nothing more.' Cröedaw said. 'This however was enough to put me on my guard.' He warmed his hands as he spoke again. 'I think that he probed you because he realised that you are female. In which case, they know that a woman was responsible for the death of the Trolgs. They are probably looking for you.'

Kirsten jumped to her feet. 'Then what are we doing?' she said. 'We should get out of here!'

'Calm yourself, Kirsten. If we were to leave now, then there would be little doubt as to who you are. If you shielded your thoughts as you say, we need not fear. He will not suspect that it was you.'

'You're lying, Thaniel,' she replied. 'We're in danger; I can feel it. Who was it? You and Cröedaw know, don't you?'

Thaniel released a drawn out sigh and did not meet her gaze.

'Only the knights of Katahl can do as you described, Kirsten. The enemy is here.'

'And you *knew*, or at least suspected, and still you allowed us to enter. I don't believe this!' she complained.

'Kirsten, if we had retreated, then he would have known for certain; we had no choice. In hindsight, two of us should have rode ahead. We should have been more cautious. However, it is now too late; we just have to remain calm.'

She slumped on her bed, feeling drained. *How can I stay calm,* she thought, *when I may have to face one of the most powerful warriors in Maldahl?*

There was a knock at the door and a servant brought in their evening meal, which they ate in silence. Later, Cröedaw suggested that he scout the area to see what he could find out. Kirsten and Richard tried to dissuade him, saying that it was too dangerous, but Thaniel remained silent.

Outside, a clock chimed nine and Kirsten peaked cautiously behind the curtain into the street below, in search of Cröedaw.

'You need not worry for him,' Thaniel remarked. 'When Cröedaw does not want to be seen, he will not be seen. When Cröedaw does not want to be heard, then he will be silent.'

Richard retired to bed and Thaniel sat drinking. Kirsten watched him for a while; his proud profile, kingly in its solemnity.

'You find my face interesting, Kirsten?'

She jumped slightly. 'No! No of course not ... I mean, erm ...' she fell into awkward silence,

Turning from the fire, he smiled, his bright eyes observing her blush. He laughed suddenly and the sound was like music to her heart, strong and pure, a wonderful stranger to her. His features appeared even more chiselled as the firelight shadows danced across his face. Realising that she was staring again, she turned uncomfortably away, but she could feel his eyes upon her, burning. She tried to stop her heart from racing, endeavouring to think of anything other than his eyes, his voice, his smile, his strong arms that had held her close, and the gentleness that broke occasionally through his austere exterior.

She felt hot and tried to think of cold water, lots of it, but such thoughts only made her recall the sight of Thaniel as he had bathed in the river. She remembered the contours of his body with perfect clarity and felt a squirming sensation in the pit of her stomach and lower still. Breathing hard, the rain outside poured suddenly heavier and she wondered if it might have been her fault, for having thought about all that water.

'Are you all right, Kirsten?' Thaniel's voice said, breaking her thoughts.

'Yes,' she snapped, jumping to her feet. 'I think I shall see if I can take a bath.' *A cold one at that,* she thought as she strode from the room. She silently cursed herself for entertaining an attraction to Thaniel, realising how inappropriate it was to have feelings for anyone in her present situation.

At the bottom of the stairs, she heard voices speaking in whispers; instinctively, she flattened herself against the wall and focused on what was said.

'Yes, I know who you mean. They're on the top floor. Only paid for the night.'

Kirsten heard a chink of coins being passed into the innkeeper's hands; her blood went cold. **We're** *staying on the top floor and have only paid for the night,* she considered. *Of course, it was not necessarily our party being discussed ... still, only one way to find out ...*

She shoved open the door and came face to face with a startled looking innkeeper. The other party had gone.

'A word if I may, landlord,' she demanded.

As she beckoned him out the back, he looked desperately behind him, in hope that someone might have observed his encounter with the woman who had an insane look in her eyes. She pulled him suddenly, impatient for his obedience.

'Talk or die,' she threatened.

'Wwwhat?' he stuttered, his body beginning to tremble pathetically.

'Who were you talking to just now?'

His eyes widened. 'The north gatekeeper,' he replied. 'He was asking about your party. Wanted to know how long you were staying for.'

She lifted him off the ground by the collar, pinning him against the wall.

'Now, why would anyone be interested in us?'

The man winced with pain, as she pushed him harder.

'Not the others, just you,' he said. 'There's been people here for days, strangers asking questions about a warrior woman. I don't know why, I swear.'

She let him down and he coughed, his breath heaving.

'I hope I've done you no wrong, miss, but I *had* to tell the truth. You don't know what they're capable of,' he whimpered.

She leaned over him menacingly. 'You obviously don't know what *I'm* capable of!' she hissed.

The man closed his eyes, expecting death. When he dared to open them again, she was gone.

When she crashed through the door, she was surprised to see Cröedaw back, and wondered how he had managed to return to the room before her, when she had been stood on the only stairwell back up.

Richard was awake again and Kirsten realised that somehow they already knew what she had been about to tell them.

'They'll be expecting us to leave by the northern gate,' Richard said, with a yawn.

'That is as may be,' said Cröedaw, 'but all the gates will be guarded.'

Kirsten was at a loss how he had managed to discover such information. She looked to Thaniel, his stern features discomforting.

'The inn is probably already being watched,' he said.

Kirsten's mind sprang suddenly back to her meeting with the thief, Jeb, and she smiled. 'The entrance perhaps, but not the rooftops,' she suggested.

'We are not cats.' Richard said, with a worried glance to the men. 'We would surely fall to our deaths.'

'Excellent idea,' Cröedaw said. He did not seem to share Richard's view. 'I will go ahead and release the horses and meet you in the next street.'

'Yes, but we have still the small matter of getting out of Ishtar,' Richard grumbled.

'We will worry about that later,' Thaniel said, in a manner that convinced them he had already formulated an escape plan.

Cröedaw slipped out again and Kirsten gave a puzzled look to Thaniel who winked at her, as if he knew something that she did not. Hastily, she helped Richard pack their things and changed into her leather, which she felt more suitable for scaling rooftops than her red dress. They blew out all the candles and smothered the fire. Kirsten's eyes stabbed the darkness for signs of life down below. Slipping feline-like onto the window ledge, she scampered agilely onto the next building. Thaniel followed close behind, but Richard paused. Even in the darkness, Kirsten could see the fear in his eyes. She considered a levitation spell, but decided against it, knowing that if Katahl's knights *were* about, then it was possible that they could sense majick. She locked her eyes on his, trying to give him strength.

He sat on the ledge, silently cursing himself for his fear. *I insisted that I could be of use on the quest,* he thought, *now I am proving to be nothing more than a hindrance.* In the end, it was his anger at himself that got him across. Kirsten smiled and squeezed his arm, knowing he had found the courage to continue.

They carefully scaled up the steep roof and slid uneasily down the other side. The street below was in complete darkness and Kirsten could see no sign of Cröedaw with the horses.

'How do we get down?' Richard whispered.

Kirsten could not see anything that resembled a drainpipe. She calculated that they would have the best part of a fifteen-metre drop, if they decided to jump. She sighed with relief when Thaniel produced a length of rope from his pack and set to tying it about the chimney.

'Richard, you first,' Thaniel said, presenting him the rope.

The serving boy nodded, seeming composed as he lowered himself over the edge.

'We will get through this, Kirsten. Trust me.'

She turned to Thaniel, his face shrouded by the night.

Her voice held a note of finality as she replied. 'I do trust you,' she said, holding his eyes for as long as she dare, before slipping over the edge to meet Richard at the bottom.

'No sign of Cröedaw yet,' Richard muttered, gazing uneasily into the surrounding darkness.

Thaniel abseiled expertly down to meet them and noticing that Cröedaw was absent, decided to change the plan.

'Let's go,' he said. 'Cröedaw will join us later.'

Kirsten grabbed him by the shoulder.

'No, we'll leave together or not at all,' she hissed.

Thaniel smiled. 'Cröedaw knows where I am headed. He *will* join us.'

Kirsten remained unconvinced. 'He might be in trouble. He may need our help.'

Thaniel shook his head in seeming amusement. 'Trust me, he will join us when he can.' He pulled her along with him and they moved in the deepest shadows towards the centre of Ishtar, keeping to the back streets.

Kirsten marvelled at how he could remember his way through the maze of buildings, especially in the dark. Richard struggled to keep up, his fear that they were being followed causing him to constantly glance over his shoulder to ensure they were alone. Thaniel, however, kept a constant pace, not pandering to his companion's trepidation. He knew where he was going and how unlikely it was for them to be caught on their present route, yet he did not see need in informing Richard, feeling that if the boy were going to be of any use to the quest, he would need to toughen up.

It seemed well over an hour before Thaniel stopped outside a huge building, which reminded Kirsten of a casino. Thousands of mirrors and glittering beads were encrusted in its exterior, which caught and reflected the street lamps, much to the same effect as electric lights would do in Las Vegas, she figured. Kirsten marvelled at it, until a movement off to her left caught her attention; Cröedaw stepped out of the shadows to greet them.

'Horses are on their way,' he said. 'Rook will hide them as soon as they arrive.'

'Excellent,' Thaniel said. 'Shall we go in?'

Richard and Kirsten exchanged puzzled looks, following the men around to a back entrance, where Rook awaited them. He hurried them into what appeared to be a secret passageway inside the huge building. They climbed for a while and Kirsten thought they had made so many twists and turns that she would never be able to find her own way back out again. The passageway widened into a well-lit room with satin drapes and cushions aplenty.

It was clear that their host was of Elfin blood, seeming older than Cröedaw and much more weathered. Embracing Cröedaw and Thaniel, he then introduced himself to both Richard and Kirsten.

'So, you are the one causing all the trouble, are you?' Rook said. There was a twinkle in his eyes as he kissed her hand.

She made no response other than to pull her hand away. Rook turned back to the men when it became apparent that Kirsten was not going to be as friendly as he had hoped.

'So what is it that you need, my friends?' he asked.

'A place to stay and a way out of Ishtar.'

'Well, you know that you are always welcome here, but as for getting you out … *that* may be difficult. However, let me see what I can do. Meanwhile, enjoy my hospitality. Stay on this floor and none of the guests will see you. You can trust my staff not to give you away.' He bowed low.

Richard decided to go back to sleep and wandered off into an adjoining bedroom. Cröedaw urged Kirsten to follow Richard's example, making her instantly suspicious as to what their plans were. She waited for a while until she was sure that they had left, and then slipped out of the door in search of them.

The building was filled with music and laughter; after observing several scantily clad women pass by, Kirsten began to suspect that she might be a guest in a brothel.

'Can I help you t'all?' a busty young woman asked.

'Er yes. I'm looking for some friends of mine. I wonder if you might have seen them?'

'Thaniel?'

Kirsten felt her skin prickle. *She knows him by name*, she thought.

'I saw him talking to Bobby in the bar, that way.' The woman pointed.

Kirsten thanked the woman and headed for the bar, trying to calm herself. *Rook is a friend,* she reasoned. *Just because the woman knows Thaniel's name does not mean that he has been a client of hers.*

The bar was more brightly lit than she had expected, with a casual atmosphere fitting for those taking a break from their duties. Kirsten spotted Cröedaw and Thaniel, noting that Bobby was a busty woman with straight blonde hair. She stared in disbelief as the woman touched Thaniel in an incredibly friendly manner. Looking up, he caught sight of her horror-stricken face just before she turned and stormed away.

She wanted to leave—walk up to a knight and say, "Hey, I heard you're looking for me", in a real Al Pacino type of way. Pacing over to her bed, she removed her boots and tossed them aside, pulling the covers over her head. Jealousy burned inside her for the first time in her life, and she found that she had no liking for the experience. She knew that she had no right to feel the way she did, but could not help it. Once the spark of feeling for Thaniel had been ignited, it was difficult to suppress.

The door opened and she snapped her eyes shut.

'Kirsten?' Thaniel whispered.

She made no reply, but relaxed her breathing in attempt to convince him that she was asleep. *Why does he want to talk to me anyway?* she thought.

After a while, the door closed. She huffed and opened her eyes, startled to see Thaniel staring down at her.

'I knew that you were not sleeping.'

'Leave me alone,' she said.

'We were just talking, Kirsten.'

'What you get up to with that *whore*, is not my concern, Thaniel. Now if you don't mind, I would very much like to sleep.'

She tightly scrunched up her eyes and when she opened them again, Thaniel was gone.

When Kirsten awoke, she was astonished that she had managed to sleep at all. Her companions were already out of bed and she stared at the shafts of sunlight gleaming across the empty room. Washing and changing into her red dress, she firmly fastened the Sword of Taiohãhn to her belt and began to think about Gailon and Ioan.

'Good morning,'

The cheerful voice of Rook was at the door. Cröedaw was with him and it was only as they stood together that Kirsten saw the striking resemblance. Rook was much larger in both height and stature, but their faces had only lines to differentiate between them.

Their host seemed humbled somehow and Kirsten took one look at Cröedaw to realise what had changed.

'You *told* him!'

'There are no secrets between my brethren, Kirsten,' Cröedaw said. 'Besides, if Rook is going to put himself at risk, then he at least has the right to know why.'

Rook stepped up to her and bowed his head.

'Do not be too hard on Cröedaw; I knew that he would not be protecting you without a very good reason; it's just that I felt it necessary to know what that reason was. Now once you have packed, meet us at the bar and I will tell you all of my plan.'

To Kirsten's dismay, she found Thaniel seated with Bobby once again. She forced her face to remain emotionless, despite the fact that her insides were screaming with jealousy.

'Now listen,' Rook said, 'there is no way to get you out through the gates. There is a knight posted at all four and you will not be able to fool them a second time, not now that they know what to look for. There is a horse-seller setting out later today for Golstur. We have paid him to take your horses and he will meet with you before sun down, at the hill north of the Läpi woods. You four will be leaving Ishtar through smugglers' tunnels that I have access to, but I want no questions asked. Do we have an understanding?'

The company nodded.

'You have a few hours before we need to leave, so might I suggest that you eat and rest while you can. The journey across the town will be the most dangerous. The nearest tunnel entrance is close to the eastern gate and I am told that area is the most heavily guarded. I will send for you when it is time. Until then.' He bowed his head and walked away.

A feast was brought to them to assist in passing the time more enjoyably. Richard seemed overwhelmed by the attention of so many females and his face reddened at each girl's approach. Kirsten sat in infuriated silence and ate her fill, not daring to glance in Thaniel's direction for fear of what she might see. She felt uneasy about the plan, but why, she could not tell. *It seems sound enough,* she thought. *But there is something that Rook said that troubles me ... I just can't figure out what it is.*

As they made ready to leave, Kirsten ignored Thaniel, walking closely to Rook. What the Elfin had said before suddenly made sense and she stopped in the corridor so abruptly, that Richard walked into the back of her.

'How can there be a knight at each gate?' she asked.

It was Cröedaw who understood what she had meant. 'Caitul must have returned,' he said.

Kirsten shook her head. 'But I saw him die! He can't be back.'

Rook urged them on, but she refused to move.

'You fail to understand. If somehow Caitul is here, then he will recognise me. He knows who I am, not only that, but he can somehow sense me. If he does, then Katahl will soon discover that I have returned. All will be lost.'

'Kirsten, that is all the more reason for us to get as far away from the city as possible. We have to keep moving.'

She did as they had urged and walked dreamlike through the streets of Ishtar recalling ever, how Caitul had met his end whilst trying to protect her.

'Almost there,' Rook ventured. 'Be careful now; we are nearing the eastern gate.'

Kirsten risked a glance from beneath her hood and came face to face with someone she recognised. Her heart jumped, as it was clear that the weasel-faced man had recalled her too and he sped off in the direction of the gate.

'We have to get out of here *now*,' she hissed. 'That man knows who I am. I killed his friend while I was in Golstur. He is going to betray us!'

'This way!' Rook said. He broke into a run down a nearby alley. Pressing a notch in the wall revealed a passageway and they clambered in, closing the opening.

'We must move swiftly. I do not trust that a knight of Katahl not to be able to discover this place, if he puts his mind to the task. Quickly now!'

He lit a torch and ran down the tunnel, which became gradually steeper and narrow. Kirsten felt stifled in the darkness and her fear of discovery grew. It seemed as though the minutes turned into hours and the sound of their breathing was unbearable. She wanted to stop, to dig her way out, wanted to say something, anything, to break the silent tension that hung in the stagnant air.

After what felt like days to Kirsten, the passageway forked and Rook stopped.

'Here is where I leave you, my friends,' he said. 'I will take this path to the other side of town. You will carry on straight and come out in the eastern woods; from there, head north and meet the horse-seller beyond the hill. He will be using the road, but I suggest you stay well hidden until you see him. Good fortune go with you.'

Cröedaw embraced him and Thaniel held his arms and said his thanks. Rook bowed low to Kirsten and taking the torch, he disappeared down the right-hand fork, leaving them to clamber on in complete darkness. Her night vision only revealed her companions and the confined space of the seemingly never-ending tunnel.

When Thaniel thrust open a door and the light of the setting sun fell on the ground before them, Kirsten gasped greedily for air and freedom from her confinement. Thaniel expertly camouflaged the entrance once more and they made their way to the edge of the woods anxious to rendezvous with the horse-seller.

In Ishtar, a short lithe man, dressed in green, had betrayed them to the guards at the gate. A search of the area was ordered and all traffic from the gates, stopped. A horse-seller on his way to Golstur found himself and his stock detained and he grumbled, explaining that he would not get a decent night's sleep before market tomorrow. The warden, however, was unsympathetic. The horses too grew restless; a large black stallion impatiently stomped his feet at the delay.

The sun had long since hidden its face and there was still no sign of the horse-seller.

Cröedaw gazed down toward the city. 'Something is wrong,' he said.

Thaniel got to his feet at last. 'We should go. Ravenwing knows where we are headed; he and the other horses will join us. We should tarry here no longer.'

'No!' Kirsten protested. 'I am not leaving my horse!'

She closed her eyes and blocked out Thaniel's arguing, reaching out to Ravenwing's mind. The horse was worried. The horse-seller was being questioned and the knight was no longer at the gate. The man in green was close, eyeing Ravenwing as if he was prize to be taken in reward for his recognising the girl. Kirsten watched through her horse's eyes, as the man approached and reached out toward him then screamed in pain, when Ravenwing kicked at him. She laughed and looked up, the others eyeing her strangely.

Her mind was wracked with ideas for creating a diversion. 'I need to get closer,' she said. 'I'll get them out of there.'

Thaniel's temper rose and was calmed out of shouting at her by a look from Cröedaw.

'I will come with you,' the Elfin said. 'I have no desire to lose Träkehnér. He is my friend.'

'No Cröedaw, you scout ahead,' Thaniel said. 'Richard, wait here with the supplies and I will go with Kirsten.'

Kirsten stamped on ahead, having no desire to be anywhere near him.

'What are you so angry about?' he asked.

'Leave me alone. I never asked you to come.'

'Bobby's an old friend. I do not understand why you should be so upset.'

She stopped suddenly, realising she had placed herself in a difficult position. The only cause for her to be upset was the fact that she had feelings for him. Now, she was too angry to ever think of expressing as much.

'I am not upset,' she said. 'Why should I care who you sleep with? You can ride the entire whorehouse; it makes little difference to me. It was simply an embarrassment seeing you with a woman like that!' She coughed awkwardly. 'After all, you used to be Captain of the Royal guard. You should have greater restraint and demonstrate more decorum!'

Turning, she paced away, feeling utterly foolish. Thaniel stormed after her and yanked her about to face him. She looked up at him, shocked and feeling again the butterfly sensation in her stomach, thinking that he meant to kiss her.

'How dare you!' he said.

It was not the response she had wished for.

'How dare you talk about my friends as though they are beneath you. You are right, it *is* none of your business whom I bed and I trust that you will remember that and stop behaving like one of those spoilt court brats!'

She walked away from him in silence, forcing herself not to cry. *Don't say anything, Kirsten,* she told herself. *You'll only make matters worse.* She knelt down when she found a clear view of the city, aware of Thaniel behind her. The city lights blurred as the tears flowed from her eyes. Carelessly, she wiped them away, cursing her stupidity and concentrating on the illusion to be created.

She shaped a picture in her mind of a small group of travellers from Golstur approaching the gates, and then made it so. They talked to the gatekeeper about their need to find a knight, explaining they had urgent news for their ears only.

'They've all gone,' the gatekeeper said. 'Three of em left hours ago, t'other a little while back.'

Kirsten breathed hard, trying to stem the tide of panic she felt, in order that she might hold the illusion.

'That being so, perhaps we might come in and wait upon their return. Can you suggest a good inn for the night?'

As soon as the gates opened, Kirsten gave Ravenwing the signal to move. The horse-seller's entire stock bolted through the gate, four of which headed north toward their masters in wait.

Kirsten's breathing came in gasps and she reeled forward, feeling sick.

'You did it!' Thaniel cried.

Approaching her, he saw that she had been crying. He reached out to her, but she drew back.

'Kirsten?' he ventured.

'Do not touch me!' she hissed.

He appeared hurt by her response, but had not the chance to retaliate, as Cröedaw appeared with urgent news.

'Richard has been taken!'

'What!' Thaniel uttered, in disbelief.

'They must have been watching us all along.'

Kirsten heard her heart pounding in her ears, as the blood fought to pump harder to help cope with her sudden distress. The pounding of her heart mingled with the pounding of hooves and she knew in an instant what she must do. *Richard has been taken because I neglected his safety,* she thought.

As Ravenwing approached, far ahead of the others, she sprang onto his back and urged him swiftly on, leaving the screams of dismay from the two warriors to fade behind her.

Twenty-Two

Having sensed her dangerous mood, Ravenwing made no attempt to dissuade Kirsten from her course. She kicked at him, none too gently, and he hurried on toward the main bridge, which crossed the river that ran the length of Freya Valley. Miles passed swiftly, too swift for even Cröedaw's horse to match.

'I did not even give her their message,' the Elfin said. 'She went to him anyway. What is to be done, Thaniel? She will ride to him and all will be lost.'

'*You* could follow her, Cröedaw.'

'No. Ravenwing is too swift and will not tire as quickly as I. We are all doomed.'

Thaniel held his head in his hands and cursed himself for having upset her, feeling that she would never have been so rash had he not incurred her anger.

'How many did you see?'

'Two only, carried the lad off,' Cröedaw replied. 'They said that Katahl wishes to see her and she must go to him or her friend will die in slow torment. I could do nothing; they put a paralysis spell on me.'

Thaniel looked up, tears were in his worried eyes. 'Find Gailon; tell him what has happened. Fly like the wind, my friend. I will ride toward Brëgwela to get her back, or die in the attempt.'

Cröedaw knew that his only way of saving Thaniel was for Gailon to stop him before he reached his goal. He held him tightly, before slipping into the shadows. Thaniel quickly loaded the supplies and tied the horses together so that he might swap between them as soon as one tired, and so travel further without being forced to rest.

Vast plains stretched out before Kirsten and she galloped on, wondering why she had not at least caught sight of them. She figured they could not have had more than half an hour start on her and one of them was carrying the burden of a prisoner. Her eyes searched the plains, knowing that even in the dark, she should have been able to spot them on the vast flats before her, but spying only emptiness, she supposed that Katahl had made use of majick of some kind to enable the escape of her quarry. Half-heartedly, she considered giving up and turning back, knowing that Richard was lost and would not have the strength to resist Katahl. *He will betray my identity,* she thought, *and I ride, therefore, to my end.*

Nevertheless, she did not stop or turn back; she did not fear death and in a way, was relieved to be approaching release from the strange existence thrust upon her. Maldahl was no utopia and her Earthly life, even less so. She had long since ceased her belief in Maldahl being a dream, realising that the fleeting vision she had seen of her father had revealed to her events following their mysterious disappearance. She wrestled with her thoughts as she sped ever onward. *Maldahl may be different to Earth, but the problems are the same; love, hate, power, jealousy, dishonesty. My transition, like many others, into adulthood is difficult enough, without a complete change of existence that includes my having committing murder.*

In the short hours before dawn, she decided to rest. Ravenwing was sweating and she poured the contents of her water skin down his throat, hoping that they would find a water source before they reached the ancient home of her father.

Lying back, she slept. In her dreams, she floated calm and centred in the white place of healing, allowing a voice to guide her into how to elude Katahl as to her identity.

She awoke only a few hours later and continued without breakfast, much to the complaint of Ravenwing.

As the sun rose, Thaniel yawned. He was riding slower, he and the horses craving sleep. It was only the discovery of a recent track made by a speeding horse that forced him to clamber onward. There was a chance that Kirsten would rest and he might find her before it was too late and she was caught like a fly in Katahl's web of majick.

He cursed himself when he found signs of her resting, but she was nowhere to be seen, only a trail that led off, beyond his line of sight.

Cröedaw was ready to drop, when his keen hearing picked up Gailon's voice ahead. Stepping out from behind an old oak tree, he collapsed, wheezing, much to the surprise of his former companions. Tehd ran to aid him, immediately handing the Elfin his water flask. Gailon was impatient, his face growing paler every moment that passed as Cröedaw caught his breath.

'Gailon,' Cröedaw gasped. 'Thaniel asks that you come quickly. Richard has been taken by the enemy and Kirsten rides to save him.'

Gailon gripped at the nearest tree to steady his balance. '*Why* did you not stop her?' He silenced himself, knowing that Cröedaw and Thaniel would have, if they could. 'Rest my friend. Thomn, look after him. When he is ready you should all continue on to Tûlg; Cröedaw will be an able negotiator if you run into trouble there.' He mounted his great horse and sped off through the trees, without so much as a farewell.

As the day ended, Ravenwing dragged himself, with the little energy he had remaining, through heavy swampland. Kirsten was fearful that they might sink and Ravenwing would drown. She dismounted and sank up to her thighs in the sludgy bog water, dragging the exhausted animal on. Seeing trees ahead, she trudged toward them, hoping to discover a little land so they might rest, away from the cold water of the marsh, which seemed to chill to the bone.

Thaniel thought he caught a glimpse of Kirsten in the distance, as she guided Ravenwing through the huge prehistoric looking trees, which clung to life throughout the swampland ahead. He called to her, but his voice was answered by a battle cry that seemed to tear forth from the very earth itself.

With dismay, he turned to see two knights in ancient armour, both bearing the emblem of Starigorat upon their shields. Thaniel released Cröedaw's horse with a swipe of his sword and it ran screaming westward, as if it knew that his master lay in that direction. His own horse stamped uneasily and Thaniel steadied him, readying himself for the oncoming attack.

Katahl's knights were exceptional warriors and had lost none of their vigour for the kill since they had succumbed to the darkness of their master's spell. As he parried another blow, Thaniel found that he was grateful only two had been following. They did not seem to tire and their relentless attacks wore him down. As hope began to leave him, a flash of light and a familiar voice replenished his waning spirit.

Gailon had arrived. Cröedaw had achieved the impossible and all was not yet lost.

There stood wizard and warrior together, ready to make their stand against the dark foe before them.

'Out of our way, old man,' said the larger of the two knights.

'Has it been so long, Nimrïn, that you forget my name?' the wizard asked. The knights glanced briefly at one another.

'With such insolence, I would suspect that you are Ardahl's brat, old man.'

'Very good, Dahal, perhaps your master has not quite destroyed you yet.'

Nimrïn swung his sword and Gailon raised his staff. A burst of white light knocked the blade from the knight's hand and he hissed in frustration.

'Should you not be dead by now, old man?' the knight asked.

'Only so much as you should, Dahal.'

As Thaniel heard Dahal speak, he realised that he had been the voice at the gate when they had entered Ishtar.

The knight edged forward and Gailon raised his staff once more.

'Enough Dahal,' said his companion. He seemed more wary of Gailon. 'We are expected.'

They turned, galloping off in the direction of the swamp.

Thaniel gave a weak smile. 'Glad to see you,' he said.

Kirsten heard the sounds of battle ahead and hoped to find that Richard had attacked his captors. She struggled on through the swamp, toward the shrill inhuman cries, the water reaching to her breasts.

The sight that met her eyes was not what she had hoped to see. In the shallower water near the trees, there was a great deal of splashing, as four or five creatures fought. Several goblin-like creatures battled against a man with a huge demonic looking head. She drew her sword, unsure as to whose side she might be on—if indeed she was on either.

Turning suddenly, the small goblinoid creatures saw her and shrieked, combining for attack. Their last victim lay bleeding and motionless against an ugly set of tree roots. Kirsten felt sickened by the hideous little creatures with their cruel piggy eyes and large snotty noses.

Despite their size, they were ferocious fighters; unlike Trolgs, they worked together and attacked as one. She took several wounds before adapting to their style of attack, using her sword like a fishing spear, lancing them one by one, until the water was filled with their strange coloured blood.

She dragged her body over to the other creature. He was much larger than she had first thought, at least two feet taller than herself, she figured. She spoke gently to him, but received no response; his wounds were still bleeding and she tore lengths off her dress to bind them. He was warm to the touch, but she could feel no breath coming from his horned head. A movement in the water startled her to her feet and she saw that the beast had a long tail that began to lash about beneath him.

Ravenwing gave a warning snort, and looking up, Kirsten saw two black knights heading her way.

'Ravenwing go!' she ordered. 'Get out of here! When I need you, I will call.'

The horse trod awkwardly away and Kirsten turned back to the creature she had saved.

'That is all I can do for you,' she whispered. 'I'll draw them away from you if I can. But I am afraid that you are on your own now.'

She jumped back into the water and waded toward the oncoming knights. They stopped before the sodden female, their horses' breath hanging heavy in the air. One of the knights lifted his visor and surveyed the scene, noticing the bloodied water.

'You have been busy it seems,' he said.

His voice was like a whisper and yet loud and clear. His face was deathly pale, and Kirsten was far from sure whether he was even real; he seemed to have an unnerving transparency to him.

He approached, giving no warning as he lifted her into the saddle behind him. As they sped away, she held him tightly about the waist, a backward glance revealing that the body of the swamp man had gone.

In Ánweald, Tom lit a fire and Tehd busied himself with making supper. Cröedaw sat in silence and despite their prompting, would say nothing. He had a faraway look and seemed unable to see them.

'Will you not eat, Cröedaw?' Tehd urged. 'You look done in if I may say so, sir. You'll be no good to no-one dead.'

He wafted the broth under his sombre friend's nose. Cröedaw blinked and looked down at Tehd.

'You are right. Thank you,' he said. 'I should eat; I will need my strength. We all shall.'

Ioan and Tehd's eyes met in a worried glance.

'What happened, Cröedaw?' Ioan asked anxiously.

'She left us, my friends. She rides to her ruin and it is only a matter of time before she dooms us all, for how can she hope to conceal herself from *him*?'

Ioan laid a comforting hand on his arm.

'She has a power that grows by the day. We have all seen the things she is capable of. I think that if it *is* possible, then Kirsten will do it. We should have faith.'

Tom and Tehd nodded in agreement, but Cröedaw remained unconvinced.

Gailon insisted that Thaniel rest, despite his arguments. There seemed to be a sort of inevitability in the air and he nodded slowly at the sight of Ravenwing approaching, dishevelled and riderless.

'We must make for Ealdorbold and raise an army. We need to prepare for the worst. It may be that she will defeat him. She has grown powerful. We will have to live in hope. It is my thought though, that Katahl does not realise who he invites into his domain. That might prove to be his undoing. Let us at least have trust in that, Thaniel.'

The knight was cold against Kirsten—not simply cold; it was as if he drained heat from her. As they rode on, she drifted into troubled sleep, her body so chilled that she could not remain conscious. She fell forward and dreamed once more of Anarkhane's kingdom, a sweet voice filling her head.

Nimrïn rode on towards his master's castle, the girl he was to deliver clutching him as they journeyed on. She seemed so warm to him, radiating with heat. He had not felt warmth in as long as he could remember, and now he remembered much.

Dark hues washed into greens and yellows before his eyes as he recalled the senses of touch and smell, longing for the girl to grip him tighter. He had been emotionless and senseless for so long, that the touch of the girl, the warmth that she gave him, was like a drug and he wanted more.

By the time they reached the abode of his master, Nimrïn recalled in perfect detail the splendour of the grounds during Tuâth's rule. He remembered himself back then and his friends Katahl, Dahal, Aarnon and Caitul. *We were knights of Starigorat, but it was Katahl who was destined to be more. He ...*

The bang of the drawbridge as it closed behind them, caused his vision to waver, and as Kirsten slipped off the back of his horse, he watched in dismay as colours bled back into grey and he felt no more. He looked down at the dirty, dishevelled woman and wondered why he wanted to be near her again;

He found himself thinking that she was important to him, but could not remember why.

Kirsten's tired eyes glanced up at Nimrïn and she shivered, glad to be away from him. She looked about the enormous courtyard and to the castle, which lay beyond it, feeling sure that it must have been magnificent in the days of her father. It seemed larger than Ealdorbold and far more ornate with its carvings in the walls and statues scattered about, most of which were blackened and fire damaged.

Swallowing hard, she realised that her parents had died in that very courtyard. She breathed, trying to remember to keep control, repressing her thoughts, as instructed by the voice in her dream.

Several goblinoid creatures ran over, cringing and bowing before leading away Nimrïn and Dahal's horses. Kirsten was pleased on realising that she had killed three more of Katahl's servants. As though some ancient memory of etiquette had remained, the knights nodded to Kirsten, before striding away into the shadows.

A taller goblin approached and she caught her breath; its ugly and twisted features made it look like a failed crossbreed experiment.

'This way,' the thing rasped.

He led her into the castle towards the throne room, carrying a green glowing lantern that illuminated only a few feet in front of him. She considered whether to simply kill him and attempt to find Richard on her own. Hearing voices ahead, she decided that her plan was unwise, at least for the present. As the creature opened the door ahead, a foul stench made her heave. She followed onto a rising platform with a banister on the left and wall to the right. They were in an enormous cavern-like hall. Below them lay the source of the noise and presumably the smell.

Trolgs.

Hundreds of them.

Kirsten felt her legs weaken, imagining Katahl throwing her among the creatures, laughing as they tore her apart. She exhaled and hurried after the green light, several paces ahead.

As the creature closed the door behind them and continued on his way, she breathed more steadily, the tension easing. She caught sight of many paintings and repressed the desire to wonder who the subjects might be. *Why do I care? I am simply a warrior, nothing more,* she told herself.

A huge marble hallway was suddenly before her. It was well lit and the goblin-like creature extinguished its own light and trotted on toward the ornately carved doors, guarded by the biggest and most well behaved Trolgs that Kirsten had ever seen. The doors opened and she followed the creature in.

The throne room was not what she had expected; a huge fire roared to her left and her body welcomed the warmth it gave; candles burned softly, giving the room a homely feel, despite the marble floors and stone walls. She noticed grooves in the floor as if weapons had struck it. *Probably Katahl has people kill each other for his own amusement,* she considered. She primed herself for what he might do, feeling that if she prepared herself for the worst, then at least she might die with a little dignity.

The goblin-like creature bowed low and a wave from darkness about the throne was enough to tell him that he was dismissed. He grovelled again and rattled out; the doors shut behind him and Kirsten strained to see the silent figure sat in the shadows.

'I have come for my friend!' she said. Her voice was strong and displayed nothing of the fear that she felt. 'I would ask that you release him.'

Then he spoke, and his voice was like a lullaby that soothes the fearful child. 'Indeed, and if I were to release him, what would you give me in return?'

Kirsten surveyed the room again, realising that there was no guard and she had been left fully armed. A cold surge of excitement coursed through her at the possibility of so easy a victory.

'What could I offer, Lord Katahl, that you could possibly want?'

His presence was like electricity and she had to remind herself to breathe. He stood slowly from his throne and stepped out from the shadows. She had seen his face in dream and vision, but its original was far more becoming. His shoulder-length blue, black hair with flecks of white framed his perfect skin. His eyes were as black as midnight and yet seemed to shimmer different colours in the flicker of the firelight. He was not a tall man, barely an inch more in height than herself. He had an iridescent quality about him that convinced Kirsten that she could actually *see* his majick. *But then he would have no cause to hide it,* she considered. As he approached, she fought for words, anything to say that might help her fight his hold over her.

Observing her dirty face all the way down to her mud-crusted clothes, he shook his head with obvious distain.

'I can assure you, woman, that the only thing you have worth the offering, is your sword-ship. You will bow before me and swear your allegiance.'

Kirsten attempted to stay calm at his affront to her womanhood.

'Why should you want a mere female as a soldier, Lord?' she asked.

He walked over to the fire, staring into the flames. 'Because you show some skill with the blade and are a cold hearted killer, both are things that I can appreciate. Or did you think me ignorant of what you have done, woman?'

She wondered whether he was speaking of the Trolgs she had killed or the men in Golstur, then decided it was probably both.

'What I would very much like to know is, how you became so strong? I assume that Gohrn has been up to his tricks again. He must think me a fool.'

Her eyes flashed and she fought the desire to question him further about the Counsellor.

'And now he has found a way up to Ardahl's Tower; I know, for I saw the majick. He thinks I can be defeated by parlour tricks! He bewitches one of my Trolgs, no doubt thinking that he could create his *own* army, and now I discover *you*. You are most likely one of his harlots that he has bored of in the bedroom and has decided to put to more *interesting* use.'

Her face was burning and she took a chance while his back was turned; she took a chance now her anger had overcome her fear. Drawing the Sword of Taiohãhn, she threw it at his back. It struck the wall and lay embedded there, protruding from his cloak; the sword wobbled slightly and the cloak caught fire.

Katahl laughed softly in her ear. She gasped and found that he had materialised behind her. Raising his hand, the fire extinguished. The action was languid, as though he found so obvious an attempt, tedious. As he appeared so indifferent to her attack, seeming not to take it as a serious attempt on his life, Kirsten decided to play along with the premise.

'I am no creation of Gohrn's and I would sooner sleep with a rat!' she said, as though the very mention of the man's name was deeply offensive. 'Counsellor Gohrn is nothing but a fool and I would rather kill him than converse with him.'

Katahl's responding laugh was slow and deep, sending a tingling sensation along the length of her spine.

'I find your lack of respect for one of Shénnin's Counsellors, most pleasing … but your apparel is offensive.' He sniffed the air, as if it was not only her looks but also her smell that displeased him. 'We will talk again when you are fit to be in our presence.'

The doors opened and two chained slaves entered, beckoning her away. She wanted to demand to see Richard, but thought better of it. She bowed—a gesture that noticeably pleased him, and followed the scrawny children to one of the upper chambers.

'In here, Miss,' the girl squeaked. The restraints about her wrists had worn through the skin, causing horrific sores.

Kirsten was appalled. 'How long have you been here?' she asked.

They looked at each other fearfully, as if not knowing whether they were permitted to answer. Kirsten closed the door.

'It's all right. I will not harm you.' She tried to sound as soothing as possible.

The boy shrugged. 'A long time.'

'Where are you from?'

More shrugs.

The door opened and another slave entered carrying buckets of hot water and clothes. They urged Kirsten to take off her clothes and get into the bath. She felt herself blush as her naked body was scrubbed clean by the doughy-faced woman.

'What is your name?' she asked.

The woman's face remained as stone. 'Lilith,' she answered.

'What are you all doing here?' As soon as the words left Kirsten's lips, she realised how ridiculous they were.

Lilith waited for the children to pack up the dirty clothes and leave before she answered. Her voice was scornful, as if she wished to invite the anger of Katahl's guest—as if she invited death.

'I would have thought that was obvious,' she said. 'We're slaves. Some of us are caught and imprisoned; others have been bred here. We serve the Lord Katahl by cleaning, cooking and fighting, or amusement and food for his Trolgs.'

'What!' Kirsten could not believe her ears.

'I do not know why you are acting so surprised. You must have known, and even if you didn't, why should you care? I heard tell that you are here by invitation because of the killin's you done.'

'Of course I care,' Kirsten retorted. 'I am only here because a friend of mine has been captured and I came to rescue him. The only people I ever killed were trying to rape me. I took out a dozen or so Trolgs; if that makes me a blood-thirsty killer well, then I guess I'm guilty as charged.'

Lilith seemed taken aback and hushed Kirsten, as if she feared who might be listening.

'He has seen something in you, that much is plain. Otherwise why would he have gone to so much trouble to get you here?'

Kirsten stood and the woman rubbed her dry.

'Do you know where they took my friend?'

Lilith shrugged. 'No. Slave pens probably, possibly the dungeons.'

'Can you take me there?'

The woman stood back. 'You are touched by a madness surely. Do you know what the Lord would do to me if I betrayed him?'

Kirsten nodded solemnly. 'I understand', she said. 'Sorry'. She looked down and saw that two outfits had been laid out. One was a set of black mail, the other a deep aqua coloured gown with as much beauty and elegance as any of the dresses that Cob had produced for her. 'The dress methinks, do you not?' she said. 'I am not his warrior, nor will I agree to any such thing unless he first releases my friend.'

Kirsten stared at her reflection, pondering her situation, as Lilith brushed her hair.

'I should have chosen the other if I were you,' Lilith said. The worried tone in her voice extended to her eyes, as she gazed at Kirsten in the mirror.

Before Kirsten had time to ask Lilith what she had meant, the door opened and the cretinous butler entered, instantly ogling Kirsten's transformation.

'I trust that you are here to take me to Richard,' Kirsten snapped.

The butler grinned. 'OUT!' he barked to Lilith.

The woman hurriedly gathered the armour and left, all the while keeping her head down, to avert the gaze of Katahl's servant. Kirsten heard Katahl's voice outside and the goblin bowed low.

'So you chose the attire of a lady,' he said. 'I find that both disappointing and amusi …' He stopped short on entering the room and catching sight of her.

The butler left swiftly, closing the door behind him. Kirsten felt her fear begin to rise; she had not expected Katahl to visit her there. He circled her, his eyes upon every part of her form. With each moment that passed, she felt increasingly uncomfortable and was in secret agreement with Lilith, wishing she had chosen to dress like a man.

'Amazing,' he said. 'You could pass for a lady.'

She was instantly on her guard. He had bruised her ego, but her foolish retaliation was leading him dangerously close to the truth of the matter. She wanted to demand that she see Richard, to call for his release, but she could no longer move or speak. Her heart pounded with fear of discovery and she fought to create a wall between them.

Katahl watched, as she grew more timid, sensing her fear and secrecy; he moved closer, trying to taste what she was hiding.

Then it was gone.

She seemed composed once more; her eyes were cold and held nought but anger.

'Shall we go?' he said. The ghost of a smile touched his lips. 'I believe that you wished to see your friend.'

The journey to Katahl's dungeon seemed to take no time at all and Kirsten was convinced that they had moved by majick. Although Katahl gazed ahead as they walked, she could feel his eyes upon her. His scrutiny was such that she dare not think of anything other than the sound of her dress as she moved and the corridors ahead, knowing that if she felt anything more then he would be aware.

The dungeons were not as she had expected. At first, they were dank and dark; water dripped from an unseen source and slime covered the walls. Further in, the chambers were so well lit that they caused her to wince. Produced by majick, the light shone brighter than any spotlight. As her eyes fought to adjust to the dazzle, she saw the figure of a man chained to the wall; his head drooped to his chest as if sleeping.

'Richard!' she cried, running over to her friend.

He raised his head slowly and smiled. 'Is it really you?' he rasped. His smile faded suddenly and he sobbed. 'You should not be here. You should not have come.'

Kirsten placed a hand on his shoulder to calm him, hoping all the while, that he would not say anything that might place either of them in more danger than they already were. She sprang towards her enemy and her eyes blazed with fury.

'You have me here, Katahl, now let him go!'

She saw his hand move to strike her and blocked it with ease, holding his arm tightly for a moment. His touch was like extremes of both fire and ice. Her eyes locked on his and saw nothing, only two pools of emptiness. It unnerved her into letting him go, however, he too was startled by the strength of *her* reaction, and he backed away.

'You agree then, to stay here?' he asked.

She nodded. 'If I have your guarantee that Richard is safely escorted back to the plains, there to be set at liberty; I shall remain here without argument.'

Katahl's eyes narrowed and he gestured toward the boy. The manacles fell from Richard's wrists and ankles and he dropped to the floor. Kirsten moved to help him, but a pincer-like grip held her back. It was Nimrïn. She looked about her and realised that Katahl had disappeared. Dahal dragged Richard to his feet and began to lead him away.

'Richard!' she shouted after him, 'tell them … tell them that I am sorry.'

A cold sensation was spreading down her arm from where Nimrïn gripped her. *I saved Richard, but all is lost,* she thought, as realisation hit her. *It's only a matter of time before Katahl discovers who I really am.*

'Come.' Nimrïn said, as he led her away.

They began to climb again, leaving Kirsten certain that Katahl had made use of majick in order for them to gain access to the dungeon, as the ascent was wholly unfamiliar.

Her arm felt numb with cold. 'You do not need to hold me so tightly,' she complained.

Nimrïn stopped, briefly letting go; his eyes darkened and he grabbed her once more, using both hands. She watched as his face lost its grey pallor and appeared almost human again.

'Show me more,' he breathed, his body trembling.

Kirsten could no longer sense Katahl's mind upon her and hoped that he would have better things to do with his time than constantly survey her thoughts. Closing her eyes, she concentrated on the knight, sensing his joy as his feelings grew, his wonder as the colours returned along with his memory and he recalled what she could not—the distant past during the rule of her parents.

She saw meadows filled with flowers and sweet smelling grass. She heard the sound of hoof beats, as Brëgwela grew ever closer. Ladies waved and turning, she saw Caitul grinning; he was in full armour and looked handsome and carefree.

As they rode into the courtyard and dismounted, Nimrïn's exhilaration increased. Beautiful statues of beasts and men decorated the area, and the castle seemed to generate life and splendour. She watched Caitul stride over to greet someone and felt a shiver as she realised that she was looking at Katahl—Katahl, before the evil took him. She watched as Katahl smiled on Nimrïn's approach, ready to embrace him. Caitul bowed low to the woman who had been on Katahl's arm.

It was *her.*

Princess Exzalander, beautiful and delicate, as if a cross word might make her run for cover. Kirsten continued to watch Caitul, as he conversed with the princess, his eyes ever shining.

She blinked and tried to pull away from Nimrïn's grasp. They were both breathing hard and the knight refused to relinquish his hold on her.

'Who are you?' he demanded. 'How have you made me remember what I had thought easier to forget?'

She felt his pain and his own self-loathing when he recalled what he was and saw what he had become. She pitied him, but knew not how to help him.

'Will Katahl not be angry at you for conversing with me?' she said, hoping to distract him. 'Is there not somewhere that you were meant to take me?'

'The tower,' he murmured. 'Katahl is to prove your friend has been safely released so that he may get you to swear your allegiance, *but you must not!'* Nimrïn insisted and as he did so, he released his grip on her.

His face lost its colour and appeared momentarily pained. 'Come,' he said. Leading her silently, he was lost in thought, having retained some of the colours and memory that the warrior woman had bestowed upon him.

As Kirsten entered the tower, the first thing she noticed was how similar it was to Ardahl's old home. She walked over to the window. The day was clear and she could see for many hundreds of leagues. Far in the south, she spied Ardahl's tower as it rose above the confines of Ealdorbold. At that moment, she realised it had been Katahl's tower that she had caught a glimpse of while she had stared from the south. *It was probably my activity in Ardahl's tower that Katahl observed and not Gohrn's,* she realised. *Gohrn has probably sought a way up to the tower and as yet has been unsuccessful.*

'Do you approve?'

Kirsten turned to see Katahl watching her from the corner.

'It is beautiful,' she said, without thinking.

He held her eyes for a moment and she felt again the pressure of his majick, easily ten times stronger than the knight's had been. He beckoned to her and watched as her graceful form approached, the long gown accentuating her magnificent figure.

'You wanted proof, here it is,' he said. 'This is a forelócian glæs; I use it to see what is happening in my domain. You may use it now if you wish, to witness the boy's return south.'

She wanted him to back away, but it was clear that he had no intention of doing so. Approaching carefully, she spied a convex lens of over a foot in diameter. The surrounding rock appeared so interwoven that the crystal lens seemed to be growing out of it. Involuntarily, she reached out and touched it, and it seemed to her that the very tower was alive.

'Look and you will see your friend,' Katahl's voice breathed next to her.

She leaned closer and saw Dahal as he pointed out a path to Richard and turned back toward Brëgwela. Richard rode in the direction of the swamp, as if Death himself was at his heels. She observed his struggle through the muddy water and as darkness fell, he staggered on. She watched, as the last remnant of the life she had come to know slipped away into the darkness.

'Enough!' Katahl said. 'It is time to eat.'

As the forelócian glæs dimmed, Kirsten turned away. Candles had been lit and slaves stood by ready to lead her to throne room. Katahl stood before her and the blackness of his eyes seemed so enlarged, that the whites were scarcely to be seen. She felt a shudder down the length of her spine at his gaze, and forced herself to look away. When she looked up again, he was gone and the slaves beckoned her to follow. As she passed the window, she glanced out toward Ealdorbold, silently cursing herself for having been so headstrong.

Twenty-Three

By the time Kirsten returned to the throne room, she found that it had changed somewhat. The throne itself had been moved backward and a small banqueting table had been laid out before it.

'Eat!' Katahl ordered.

Kirsten sat in the chair that had been placed for her and any appetite she might have had, fled as she recoiled in horror from the meat selections, which were clearly human. She watched Katahl as he tore the crisped skin off an arm and sank his teeth into the flesh, allowing the juices to dribble down his chin. Her stomach heaved and bile rose to her throat, leaving her fighting for composure.

Since her arrival, she had found Katahl to be almost charming, but now it was clear that she was catching a glimpse of his darker side. She supposed that he desired to break her spirit, to drag her down to such levels of depravity that she would submit to his will without question.

'I said eat!' Katahl hissed, and tossed a half-eaten arm into her lap.

She hurled her weight backwards and the chair scraped loudly. Her eyes flashed and her nostrils flared with anger as she wished him dead at that moment. He gave a slow smile, observing her attention toward her sword, where it still protruded from the wall. Katahl nodded to one of the goblin-like creatures, who in turn was forced to delegate the blade's retrieval to a slave, when he discovered the weapon was out of his reach. Kirsten's anger turned to cold fear as Katahl toyed with the Sword of Taiohãhn, examining it from every angle.

'You want this?' His voice mocked, as if he dared her to take it from him.

She watched patiently as a spider until he seemed tired of teasing her and returned to his meal. Making a grab for the sword, she swung it toward him. Her entire body shook, cymbal-like, as her blade was met by an enormous broadsword mere inches away from Katahl's head.

Kirsten sprang back, swinging her weapon. A knight had prevented her attack. He was taller even than Nimrïn and wore his helm with the visor down.

His armour was black and reflected nothing but his own menacing presence as he loomed portentously before her.

'The woman is insolent and it bores me. Kill her,' Katahl ordered.

Kirsten felt her heart jump on his command, considering that the only reason for her presence was to provide worthy entertainment, a toy to distract from the boredom of so long an existence. However, there were more pressing concerns to draw her attention away from such thoughts. The terrible warrior stood patient and still, making her wish more than ever that she had chosen to array herself in armour, rather than the pretty dress.

She was vaguely aware that both Katahl and his throne were being moved back, for a better view rather being placed out of harm's way. She waited in dread anticipation, as several nervous slaves removed the table, which stood between the two warriors.

Despite his heavy armour, the knight's speed was phenomenal, and she felt the weight of his sword drive her back. His sheer strength was his greatest advantage, as each time Kirsten blocked the heavy broadsword, she feared that her own weapon would break and she would be dead. Her blade remained true, however, and despite *feeling* clumsy in her attack, to the onlookers she appeared to be coping well.

She managed to get in a few kicks, in effort to throw him off balance, but her heavy skirts inhibited to such an extent that she was thrown to the floor. Quickly dodging his great sword, it narrowly missed her ear but succeeded in removing a chunk of her hair. She used her low position to her advantage and teddy bear rolled catching him between her legs as they swung and pulled him down. There was a crash as the knight hit the floor. Kirsten flipped to a standing position and had her sword at his throat before he had so much as reached for his own weapon, where it lay some feet away.

A cold silence ensued, as if each there present held their breath, waiting for her to strike. Now that she held her enemy's life in her hands, her mind allowed itself to think. *Katahl has ordered my death. If I can gain his favour once again, then there is still hope.* She took the blade away from the knight's throat and offered him her hand. He hesitated before seizing it and getting to his feet. There was a murmur about the throne room as the puzzlement grew.

'Lord Katahl, I apologise if I appeared ill-mannered,' she said with care. 'I am unaccustomed to your diet, and I admit that you angered me. I was rash and for that I am sorry. If you still desire my service … I would rather be living than dead. But of course, it is your decision. If I am to die, then your knight may kill me now. I will fight no more tonight.'

It seemed an eternity before Katahl spoke and Kirsten knew that he was reading her sincerity. She centred herself completely, keeping the sword of Taiohāhn at the ready, should her bluff fail.

Katahl slowly nodded and his shadow flickered ominously in the firelight. 'You fought well,' he said. 'I *will* let you live—for the present. Caitul here will begin your training tomorrow.'

Her body went cold as the goose pimples shot up her legs and arms. *Caitul ... he's alive and he hasn't betrayed me.* She struggled to re-centre herself, lest her shock be read by Katahl's prying mind.

'I had thought the mighty Caitul to be dead, Lord,' she said.

Katahl rose from his throne and walked over to them, his eyes seeming more hypnotic than ever. 'No, not dead. He was on a mission to bring back my betrothed, but he failed. Now he has returned.'

Caitul bowed his head and Kirsten wished that she could see his face. She was finding it difficult to believe that it was really him.

'Take her away now,' Katahl said. 'I will send for her when I have need of her.'

Kirsten followed the towering form of Caitul out of the throne room and breathed a sigh of relief as the doors clanged shut behind them. She walked silently beside him, pondering on what she might say. If he indeed knew who she was, he had given no indication. She was confused. *He was so kind to me, so gentle*, she remembered. *But now that he is back with his master, he could have changed. The other knights are barely living, why should he be an exception?*

As Caitul reached the door to her chamber, he turned to go. Kirsten wanted to say something to him, anything, to keep him there. She needed to know.

He turned back suddenly. 'I have never known defeat in armed combat before,' he said. His voice was a little hollow as it reverberated off his helmet, but it was unmistakably Caitul.

'Take off your helmet, Caitul. Let me see your face,' she murmured.

He remained unmoved. 'I will meet you tomorrow. Be ready.'

He began to walk away and Kirsten grabbed him by the arm, *willing* him to see that to which he had become blinded. He paused, as if contemplating her action and then slowly his hands went to his helm and removed it. He turned, his eyes wide with sudden realisation and his pale face met hers in silence. Kirsten became suddenly nervous, aware that she was in the corridor where the scene could be observed by passers by. She urged him into her chamber and closed the door.

'Your Highness, you are here! I thought that you were dead. How could I not see you before?'

'I am glad that you did not, lest you betray me to your master.'

His eyes dropped suddenly to the floor. 'He has changed, and I change too. The world is not what it was. Yet, I am sworn to do my lord's bidding. *That* oath, I took long ago.'

'I am glad that you did not die,' she said, 'although I know not how you came to survive.'

Caitul's eyes met hers and he seemed to be smiling. 'The protection majick I had been given, lifted, allowing the spell that was to take you home, to cast itself. My Lord saved me. I thought the Trolg had killed you, and it was when I informed Lord Katahl of your death, that I realised that something was not right. Rather than weeping for his loss, he seemed pleased. It was then that I learned, it had been *he* who sent the beast to destroy you.'

Caitul's eyes locked onto her hands as she pulled away his gauntlet and took his hand in her own. He was ice-cold to the touch and it was clear that he was falling under the same spell as the other knights.

'Caitul, will you help me to escape? I need to get to Ealdorbold.'

He pulled his hand away and walked toward the window, gazing out at the night sky; it was grey with fog and the air was cool.

'You know not what you ask. If I aid you, then my oath to Katahl will have been broken. My very soul will be in peril.'

'Caitul *please*, you are my only hope. Katahl ordered you to bring me home and you know now that he does not want me. He will kill me if he discovers who I am. Do you wish that to happen?'

He swung suddenly to face her and to her astonishment, she saw that there were tears in his eyes.

'Princess, I would wish that my allegiance was sworn to your house; ever since I met you I have wished it. I would want nothing more than to serve *you*. I know not what to do. I could not live with myself if you died, knowing that I might save you.'

'Then help me. Please.'

'I cannot,' he said quietly. Snatching up his gauntlet, he made for the door. As he reached for the latch, he paused, his back to the princess. 'I will keep your secret, but I cannot help you to escape. Please do not ask me again.'

Kirsten was left alone in the quiet of her room. All about her, the night seemed too close and chilled her frightened form to the bone. It seemed to her that Caitul was blinded by his loyalty. He was in peril to stay and yet he would not leave the service of his master. She believed that he would not intentionally reveal her presence, but her danger increased ten-fold with his knowing. It was merely a matter of time before Katahl discovered her identity and she shuddered when she thought what he might do to her at such a time.

Wondering if she were to attempt to transport herself beyond the castle whether she would be detected, she closed her eyes and let her mind search Brëgwela's boundaries, but her subconscious discovered a flaw in her plan. There was a majick barrier that besieged them; all that would happen were she to make the attempt, is that she would be detected sooner.

Richard abandoned his horse, as he reached the plains. The feeling that he was being watched, subsided and he sat next to a patch of waterlogged grass, bathing himself as the horse sped back to Katahl's fortress.

He was hungry beyond measure, and tired, but he did not dare search for food; he did not trust Katahl's word and he feared his return to Ealdorbold. He had begged them to become a member of the party and felt that he had dishonoured them. The quest had failed and he believed it was because of him. He rose painfully to his feet and continued in an easterly direction, wanting to put as much distance between his failure and Ealdorbold as possible.

Despite her exhaustion, Kirsten slept uneasily that night, and her troubled mind gave her disturbing dreams. She saw Brëgwela engulfed in flame; she heard the screams of the dying people of Tuâth's fortress. The burning smell increased in her nostrils and she floated above the chaos. Below her, Katahl's knights fought to aid him and as she drifted away, she saw Caitul's tear-streaked face and heard his cry of anguish as she was expelled from Maldahl.

She awoke in the early hours of the morning, feeling at once disorientated in her unfamiliar surroundings. A suit of mail had been laid out for her, making her uneasy; someone had entered the room while she slept and she had failed to awaken. She sat up and gazed suspiciously about her, sensing a presence in the room. Someone, or something, was watching her from an opening in the curtains, which hung on the west side of the wall.

She reached for her weapon belt and felt the cold steel of the throwing stars. 'Show yourself or die.' she ordered, taking aim.

One of the short goblin-like creatures stepped out in an oily fashion, grinning a razor smile. 'You were dreaming,' he said. His voice strained, as if human speech was a struggle for him.

His hideous form and way of expressing himself made her feel sick.

'What are you doing in my room?' she demanded.

'The Master sent me to watch over you. I am to escort you to Nimrïn for training.'

She got to her feet with the sheet wrapped about her, insisting that he leave the room while she dress. The creature was adamant that he was to stay and she attempted to get the odious thing to turn its back to allow her a little privacy. To her horror, he rang a bell and a dozen or so of the creatures entered the room and began tearing at the bedclothes. She attempted one-handed to fend them off, but within moments, the sheet was in tatters and she was left naked before their ogling eyes. Turning to reach for her armour, she discovered that it had been removed. Several of the creatures made grabs for her bare flesh, and to her disgust, she saw that some were playing with themselves as they delighted in her helplessness.

She still clutched the throwing star in her hand and in a fit of rage at such an indignity, she let it fly at the 'Peeping Tom' who had instigated the attack. He fell dead and in an instant, the groping hands left her person. There was a murmur amongst them and Kirsten was unable to determine whether it was of fear or pleasure that had been the source. Her eyes searched for something to cover her modesty and she felt a sudden surge of pain as an armoured fist struck her in the face.

She fell to the floor, blood seeping from the wounds, which the cruel looking gauntlet had caused. One of Katahl's knights had been sent to fetch her and seemed unimpressed by her tardiness. He wrenched her up by the hair, thrusting the pile of clothes at her.

Kirsten's vision was blurred at first and by the time she focused properly again, she found the filthy little creatures had gone. Without a word, she slipped on the rough woollen undergarments. The wounds on her face continued to bleed and she wondered if they would leave a scar. The knight was examining her weapons while she readied herself and seemed to pause longest on the dagger, as if it were familiar to him.

'I am ready,' she said. She tried not to sound unnerved by her treatment, but inside she felt frightened and sick.

He handed her the weapon belt and she affixed it over her hauberk, following the knight silently toward the courtyard. When she arrived, she saw Nimrïn training Trolgs, but no Caitul. Her face pained her and she could feel it beginning to swell and tighten as the blood dried on her skin.

The courtyard was cold and damp and Kirsten started to think that if rain could get in, then there must be a way out. Nimrïn greeted her with a nod, staring briefly at her wounded cheek. He led her across the courtyard and paired her with a squat Trolg, armed with a nasty looking halberd several feet taller than him. She could feel the eyes of other Trolgs as they scrutinised her and she assumed that her reputation for being a Trolg killer would not make her popular in the ranks.

Her opponent swung the halberd and she jumped backward, drawing her sword. Glancing about her, she saw that the training had ceased and all took a sudden interest in the fight. The Trolg, although smaller, was well trained and familiar with his weapon. Kirsten had not been given instruction and was unsure whether she was supposed to be merely training or fighting for her life.

Her face had swollen so much that her vision was impaired and between the pain and distraction of not being able to see properly, her skills were unimpressive. The Trolg found it easy to disarm her, although broke his halberd in the process. She could hear the cries of the Trolgs as they urged their comrade in for the kill. She let the shuriken fly, but to her disappointment, the Trolg blocked with the remainder of his weapon and swung straight back at her. The throwing star lodged into the splintered end of the halberd, catching on her wounded face as he struck back. She fell to her knees, screaming in agony and a cheer went up from the Trolgs.

It was over. The pain was so great that all she wanted was to lie down and die. The cheers echoed in her ears; between the swelling and the blood that ran into her eyes, her sight was almost gone. She fought to get to her feet and as she did so, the pain lessened slightly. Whether or not through her body's endorphins kicking in, or because she had blocked out the pain through sheer determination, she did not care. The only thing she was aware of was their laughter. They were laughing at *her*. She had let the foul, stinking beast get the better of her because she had underestimated his skill. She felt the hilt of her dagger in her hand, strangely hot against her skin. There was a warning cry from the onlookers and the butt of the halberd swung at speed into her stomach. She was knocked backward and the Trolg stood over her. Annoyed by her defiance, it decided to add the ultimate insult. As a final humiliation, the Trolg removed his genitalia and made ready to urinate over her. It did not take training from Taiohãhn to make her do what she did next. Girls of any age are taught as much in self-defence.

Thunk.

Her foot sped upward finding its target. The Trolg toppled, groaning and did not get up. She struggled to her feet and spat on him; to her amazement the cheers were now for her. The underhand attack had gained respect in the legion. Baring her bloody teeth, she gave a savage smile and let the cheers bathe her wounds better than water ever could.

Twenty-Four

Gailon and Thaniel sped on toward Ealdorbold, but their horses were exhausted despite Gailon's use of majick to increase their stamina. By sundown, they finally admitted defeat, allowing the beasts to eat and drink their fill while they slouched miserably by the fire.

'Even if we were to raise an army, Gailon, what use would it be? No-one can enter Brëgwela unless he wishes it; we do not stand a chance.'

'It has been many years now since majick has been attempted and I have made use of that time, adapting and perfecting all my master's spells that I could recall. I may have enough power to penetrate. We shall just have to see, my friend. You will have to excuse me now; I am weary and feel the need for sleep like I never thought I would. For the first time in my long life, I feel old. I held so much hope when she returned and now, that hope is gone.'

He lay back and closed his eyes. Thaniel remained awake, watching the stars as they peeped out one by one. Tears distorted his vision, as his despair grew. *We have lost the war before any weapon has been drawn,* he thought. *My foolishness in provoking a headstrong girl will result in our doom.* His heart ached at her parting and at the thought of her all alone with a gulf of darkness between them.

Kirsten watched as a goblin approached Aarnon and whispered to him. She felt her skin prickle as the knight paced over to her and gripped her about the wrist, dragging her from the courtyard. The goblin creature smiled wickedly at her departure and she guessed that she was to be punished for having killed the butler. She was too weary to consider retaliation; her adrenaline levels dropped and the pain had returned. Her arm was like ice where the knight gripped her, and she felt dread at the thought that he might beat her again. She was chained in the darkness, but to her relief, he did not hit her, seeming in haste to be away from her. She did not wonder at this, but rather, let the pain and despair wash over her like a blanket, lulling her into fitful sleep.

* * * * *

Caitul left the castle at his master's bidding. He was glad to do so, lest Katahl read in him emotion with regard to their new guest. He had tried to forget her presence there, yet knew that it could not be long before she was discovered.

Tûlg was thicker and darker than any forest Ioan had seen; he and the companions felt a chill as they stepped over the threshold from one forest to the other. Dark majick hung in the air and there was a smell both familiar and sickening to the companions.

Cröedaw had spoken little since Kirsten had been taken. He seemed to be led in his despair by the quest that had been set, but his mind still dwelt on another point, that there must be something he could do.

There had been no word from Gailon, and Cröedaw expected that the rescue attempt had therefore failed. His heart told him that she was still alive, but whether that was a good thing, remained to be seen.

'I do not like this place at all,' Tehd complained. 'It gives me the shivers.'

Ioan drew his cloak about him and nodded back to his friend.

'It feels as though we are being watched,' Tom said sternly.

Cröedaw turned to them, momentarily abandoning his brooding. He seemed like a shadow in the shade beneath the trees. 'Do not concern yourselves,' he said. 'It is the trees that are watchful. They are the only living things near us at present. However, be vigilant. We must stay close together. It would not do for us to be killed before at least having the opportunity to explain our presence here.'

Tehd's eyes widened and he felt his legs tremble. Ioan stared ahead into the gloom, letting his mind reach out to Kirsten.

Nothing.

All attempts had failed. It was as though her mind had ceased to exist and yet he, like Cröedaw, had no doubt that she was still alive. He could feel her. She had given part of herself when she had cured him and it lingered, a tiny spark of warmth, deep inside. He kept trying—refusing to give in while hope remained.

Katahl was uneasy, but knew not what troubled him so. He considered that Gohrn had entered Ardahl's tower and had managed to control one of his Trolgs. Shénnin's people had defied him. The warrior woman had wreaked havoc amongst his troops and he wanted to know where she had come from. *She is magnificent—a true warrior,* he mused. *But all warriors must train somewhere ... She has denied Gohrn's involvement, but I do not believe her; it is clear that she hides something. Why was she in both Ishtar and Golstur?*

In response to his suspicion, Katahl ordered troops to be sent to both cities. All traffic between Golstur and Ishtar was to be tightly controlled and tolls charged to merchants and traders. Although both cities were officially under the Council of Shénnin's rule, anyone failing to acknowledge Katahl's supreme authority was to be put to death. Those were the orders Katahl had made clear to his First Knight, and Caitul intended to follow them to the letter, needing to convince himself of his own loyalty.

As the troops began to arrive, many families gathered their belongings and headed for Ealdorbold. They had heard rumours of a possible attack from the dark one's domain and were unwilling to wait to see if such rumours proved true. And so it was, as days passed, many hundreds of people gathered at the palace, in search of food and shelter. Those who remained had to ration, after food supplies were cut indefinitely.

Kirsten found it impossible to tell how long she had been a prisoner in the darkness. The days seemed to bleed into each other; she would train, fight, and on occasion, kill during the hours of daylight. At night, they would lock her away in the damp hole with only bread and water. At such times, she had learnt to free her mind from her body. She no longer felt the torture or saw her abusers. In the beginning, she had wandered in the light in search of Anarkhane, whom she had hoped would help to free her. But after a while, she had stopped searching and let her mind sleep in darkness.

Each morning, she dragged herself down to training, having endured nightly beatings, torture and occasionally violation. She thought less and less about her friends and simply fought to survive, no longer seeing her treatment as atrocities, but as a fact of life. She felt little, other than the thrill of the kill and would have to be dragged from an opponent to prevent the death of yet another of Katahl's soldiers.

Gailon argued for almost a day with the Council, whose decision was to prepare for a siege and wait for the enemy to come to *them*.

'Counsellors, this is madness! We must advance now to the aid of the cities. If we do not unite forces and bring the people back to us then rest assured, Ealdorbold will fall. He will take what remains of Maldahl, one piece at a time and when his attention turns to us there will be nobody left to come to our aid. Do not make the same mistake that your predecessors made.'

'You speak out of line, Gailon. My word is final, so I suggest that you remove yourself from our presence.'

Gailon stormed from the room, angered by Daihron's threatening inflection.

'UPSTART!' he fumed, as he entered Thaniel's chamber.

Thaniel sat sadly staring into the firelight. 'They refused to help? We knew that they would. Now I must return to Brëgwela.'

'What's this?' Gailon said, his eyes burning.

'I cannot abandon her, Gailon. I must go back, even if it is only to die by her side.'

Gailon felt his temper subside as he observed his friend's sunken eyes and sagging clothes.

'Come my friend, sit by me. I know that you blame yourself in all this, but you riding to your death will not help matters any. Besides, your skills will be needed here ere the end.'

Thaniel sat with a sigh; tears stung his eyes as he imagined what might be happening to the girl whom he had cradled in his arms, the beautiful woman who had seemed so frail for the most part. He began to cry and Gailon rested a hand on his shoulder. His brow furrowed deeply in concern for his friend, for never in the whole time that he had known him, had he seen the man weep.

'You care a great deal for her, that much is plain. I too feel the emptiness now that she is gone. But war is at hand and we must put aside such feelings, lest they destroy us before the enemy is able. There is nothing that you can do at present anyhow. Counsellor Daihron has ordered siege conditions. Nobody is permitted to enter or *leave* the palace now. If we did so then he would charge us with treason; we would be outlawed and hunted for the rest of our days.'

Thaniel's face hardened and he wiped away his tears. 'So we are to sit here and wait for the end? Never!'

'I know how you feel, Thaniel, and I for one am willing to risk being branded a traitor, but we must think up a suitable plan.'

* * * * *

It had been many days since a Trolg had been able to get a strike on Kirsten, so skilled a fighter had she become. She no longer felt pain and her attack was even more relentless than her opponents'.

There was excitement among the legions that evening. They were to be deployed to Ishtar to strengthen the garrison already stationed there. All about her, Trolgs' eyes gleamed and they whetted their lips at the thought of being permitted to do what they do best. Kirsten felt no such joy. She sat quietly sharpening her blade, making it ready to receive warm blood.

A murmur rose across the courtyard and the legions stood to attention as Lord Katahl's presence was announced. Kirsten stood at his approach, her clouded mind holding only a vague recollection of him. He stared at her and smiled at the scars that streaked across her cheek—cold reminders of the violence inflicted upon her.

'The company leaves before dawn for Ishtar. Do you wish to be one of the party?' he asked.

'I will do as my Lord commands,' she replied. Her voice croaked, sounding strange to her ears, so long it had been since she had used it for anything other than a battle cry.

Katahl continued to smile. The woman's former strength of mind had gone. She was empty. Whereas before he had tried and failed to read her, now there was nothing to read except her bloodlust; her desire to kill was all that remained. He had known of the tortures of course; it had been he who had ordered them, viewing many nights' sessions of violation and pain for his amusement. The result was glorious to his eyes. He had created a new warrior, a new terror to kill in his name.

Cröedaw and the companions roamed through the realm of the Vampire Ælves, the darkness choking and hindering their steps. Days and nights merged into one in the never-ending blackness. They had seen no sign of any inhabitants, but remained convinced that their presence was known. Glancing about them as they stumbled through the gloom, they persuaded themselves that a watchful malice haunted their steps.

As the company made camp that night, they sat in their usual reticence, none of them willing to speak for fear of what lay behind the trees. They all started in fear as Ioan jumped up and broke the silence, convinced for a moment that they were under attack.

'She *is* alive. She is coming back to us.'

Tom relaxed the hold on his sword. Cröedaw 's eyes narrowed.

'What do you mean?' he asked.

Ioan paced impatiently. 'The princess and I can communicate without words. Since she entered the dark domain, I have heard nothing, but now I can feel her presence again.'

Cröedaw jumped to his feet, needing no more encouragement. 'Thomn you are in charge,' he said. 'You should escort Tehd and Ioan back to the safety of Ánweald Forest and wait for me there. I must go.'

Tom shook his head in confusion. 'I don't understand,' he grumbled.

Cröedaw's eyes held their old twinkle and he smiled grimly. 'Brëgwela is protected by a powerful majick. The barrier is so strong that even time passes differently there. That is why Ioan, has been unable to speak to her. If, as Ioan says, he can reach her mind once more, then she must be outside the castle walls. I may be able to rescue her. But you must get out of Tûlg for the present; it will not be safe for you once I am gone.'

The great gates opened and Katahl's army poured forth—thousands of Trolgs led by Aarnon and Nimrïn. Among the host there was something else though; what looked as though it may once have been a woman, horribly scarred and such emptiness in her eyes, that she was to be feared rather than pitied.

As Kirsten rode over the threshold, the darkness in her mind's eye lessened and she became vaguely aware of a cool wind as it blew her hair backward like a dark banner. All about her, the war chant began and she shivered, forcing her mind to darken deeper, having no desire for her senses to function, not now that battle might be close at hand.

As night turned into dawn, they descended into the bog. The chanting had long since ceased and a dreary quiet settled upon the host. The few horses there were, blew air from their lips as if complaining about the desolate swamp before them and the cold water, which squelched up their legs.

A fog lay heavy in the early morning air and the swamp smelt stagnant. The Trolg army gazed about them in the gloom, expectant. A squawk from above caused a shudder to spread throughout the ranks and each Trolg kept a hand to its weapon. Kirsten too had heard the crow and gazed up into the gloom.

Twisted branches jutted eerily out toward her through the mist, as if suspended in nothingness. She heard the croak again and felt a shiver down the length of her spine as she saw a large black crow hopping down a branch toward her. Gasping for air, she moved on, wanting to forget about the bird and the feelings that its simple song brought. There was a squawk once more and she glanced back, her heart pounding. Her eyes widened when she spied through the gloom, a raven-haired man crouching in the branches above.

She drew her sword and the surrounding warriors gazed uneasily at her, following her example, believing her to have seen a danger of some kind. Her stomach heaved as the memories came flooding back, memories from so long ago.

She was Kirsten of Earth, Taiohãhn's warrior, Princess Exzalander of Maldahl.

She saw about her, Trolg upon Trolg—her enemy. Her heart pounded in her ears as she remembered how she had come to be there, remembering how hope was lost as the weeks passed by. Separating herself from the pain had been the only way to face the horrors she had been made to endure, but perhaps worst of all, was facing the fact that nobody was coming for her. Her hand reached up to her face finding the jagged scars, and she screamed. It was a cry of despair, pain and anger. Spurring her horse forward, she brandished her sword.

There were other cries about the swamp as the army fell under attack. She failed to notice as Trolgs fell dead about her, their blood spilling into the mire. She rode on, still screaming, outraged at the abuse she had suffered and the humiliation that she had repressed.

Aarnon heard her cry and turned, only in time to see the murder in her eyes. His sword met with hers and broke; for the first time in centuries, he felt fear.

Since he had struck the woman, he tried to avoid her, but found unable to stay away for long. She was strange to him. Firstly, she had brought the light, the warmth, and he sat with her after the first torture, holding her in his arms, letting her bring back memories long forgotten. Each time she was beaten, he would wait for the Trolgs to depart and then go to her. Each time he felt more human and her less so.

He began to wear his visor down, as his appearance changed and he experienced more sensations, each seeming rich and colourful. Still it was not enough. He was like a child beside a sweet stall, leaning in to touch, yet restrained by its mother. He wanted to be whole again and she would make him whole.

He had expected a struggle as he stripped her bare, but she gave none; as he entered her, he realised why; she was gone; her body was cold, as if dead, and her glassy eyes saw nothing. He withdrew, knowing that he would never be whole again, his only hope, that he might slip back into the darkness and forget again that he was once a man.

She bared her teeth at him and howled with pleasure as she removed the despoiler's head.

Nimrïn had not seen the knight fall. He sounded the retreat as the army fought in chaos. Kirsten continued to slay everyone who lay in her path; madness was upon her and she laughed as she spilled a river of Trolg blood.

Cröedaw called to her, but she could not hear him over the battle cries. As the army made for the plains, he jumped down to a lower branch, shouting her name. Her horse reared up in fright and she fell into the cold swamp, aware of the many hands dragging her into its slimy depths. Cröedaw found no sign of her and cursed himself for losing her again.

Cob alerted Gailon to the trouble at the gate. Ravenwing had broken free from the stable and fought to escape the palace. The stablehands could not calm him, neither could Gailon. Cob spoke quietly to the angry stallion who informed him that he needed to return to his mistress, as she had need of him. Gailon convinced the guards to lower the bridge, explaining that the horse was likely to damage their defences should they not let it go. The old man watched as Ravenwing seemed to fly north.

Counsellor Gohrn scowled at the scene down below, his eyes narrowing as the great black horse disappeared from sight.

Nimrïn lost many of his troops by the time he finally escaped the swampland to the safety of the Soturi Plains. He rallied the Trolgs together and stared curiously toward the bogs behind them. The swamp-devils had never attacked such a large group before; they had never been considered a threat. He knew that his Lord would be displeased when he discovered the rebellion, especially when he was to learn of Aarnon's death, and that of the warrior woman. Nimrïn continued south, his regret at having lost the woman, fading with each step toward their goal.

* * * * *

After almost a day's march, it seemed clear to Tom that they had gotten lost. He had been sure that they were heading the right way, now everything looked exactly the same and each direction felt dangerous.

'Why did Cröedaw have to leave us?' Tehd complained. 'We'll never get out of here.'

'There is a chance that he may be able to save Kirsten; he had to go.'

'Well tha's all very well and good, but what does that make us? Expendable! Nobody cares what happens to us, do they?'

Tehd's words were met by silence and as he turned to observe his companions' reaction, he saw that they were no longer there.

'Ioan? Thomn?' he said quietly. His legs trembled once more and the darkness closed in.

Kirsten struggled against the force that pulled her down, her rage began to cool in the darkness of the swamp and she concentrated on holding her breath, hoping that her attackers would think she had drowned and leave her for dead. To her surprise, she felt air once more and cautiously opened her eyes. She was alone in a chamber made entirely out of crystal. A bed stood at one end of the room; it had been covered with sheets like fishes scales, as smooth as silk. A crystal bath had been filled and clothes had been laid out. There did not appear to be any doorway.

It was a while before Kirsten dared to move. She stared about her in wonderment, her body began to quiver and she fell to her knees and wept. It was too much for her to bear; she could not cope with a new torture, not having recalled so much. Catching sight of her reflection in the glass, she sobbed loudly, her voice seeming to resonate out and off the walls.

There was a high-pitched ring and an unseen door opened. Kirsten struggled to her feet, sword in hand, barely able to see the newcomer through her tears.

'You have no need of Taiohãhn's blade. We will not harm you.'

The beast's voice was strange; it reverberated slightly as he spoke. Kirsten blinked away her tears and caught sight of the swamp man who she had saved before being taken to Katahl. A fresh flood of tears fell as he approached, his huge bony head tilted as if puzzled by her behaviour. She swung her sword and it clanged against his head. Watching in disbelief, the swamp-devil removed, what she now realised was a helmet, and revealed his true face.

The man had golden hair and large eyes of the same colour, whose pupils were horizontally elongated. The only clothing that he wore barely covered his manhood. He approached with his palms up. Clumsily, she swung the sword again and he caught hold of her hand, swiftly removing the blade from her weakened grasp. She did not resist when he unbuckled her weapon belt and vestment, but continued to weep, expecting molestation from this new danger.

He gently lifted her naked body and lowered her into the crystal bath. The water refreshed and as he bathed her, the tears began to slow.

'There,' he said, in his strange voice. 'Are you feeling a little better?'

She nodded slowly, her bloodshot eyes gazing into his pure gold ones.

'Who are you?' she asked.

Standing, he offered her his hand. She took it and stepped from the bath, allowing him to dry her aching body.

'I am Prince Bydand and I want to thank you for saving my life. Your intervention that day did more than prevent my death. You gave my people hope that we will soon return to our mother Anarkhane.'

Blinking in disbelief, she wondered if she was dreaming. She felt strange; everything about the place seemed too serene, too tranquil and she supposed it to be unreal. Stepping into the gown he held, she allowed him to fasten it. His touch was neither sensual nor passionate. Despite the fact that he had undressed and bathed her, had touched her naked body, she felt no embarrassment, repulsion or arousal; it simply felt normal to her.

'Your mother is Anarkhane?' she asked matter-of-factly.

He smiled as he combed her wet hair.

'When Anarkhane wept, her tears fell on Maldahl,' he explained. 'From the pool of our Goddess' tears, a consciousness developed, which evolved into us. We are of majick, yet can use none. Katahl's people call us swamp-devils. They hunt us for food and sport, realising not, that we are higher beings.'

'Do you know who I am?' Kirsten asked.

Prince Bydand smiled, and it was as though he was emulating the action from having observed it in others.

'Of course. I knew from the moment that you saved me, for you placed me momentarily back with my mistress. I saw Her and spoke to her; She told me to care for you and cleanse the darkness that contaminated your being.

'The mask you wear is tainted with depravity, therefore, cast off your disguise, for you have no need of it here. Here you will stay until your hurt is healed.'

'But I cannot stay here,' she protested. 'An army marches to Ishtar; it has to be stopped.'

'Perhaps Princess, but not by you. We have brought you back from the brink of insanity, but the darkness lies on you still and you must be healed.'

She stepped away from Bydand, her eyes flashing dangerously.

'You wish to take from me, all that I have learnt? My skill, my discipline …'

'Your hatred and your pain will taint you, unless you purge yourself of it.'

'I have become far more powerful in Katahl's care than I ever could whilst free. I am stronger than ever I was, and soon I will be ready to face him again.'

'You must let go of your hate, Exzalander. The extra strength of which you speak is only physical. It was through your hardship that your body strengthened. Your power is as it has always been. You are simply able to utilise it more effectively. You have to understand that you were non-corporal when tutored by Anarkhane and the power you possess needs to adjust to your physical form. It is your hate that prevents your majick self from returning.'

'No,' she snapped. 'Closing my mind has only made me able to see more, as I have learnt how to let it wander without me. If I close my eyes, I can clearly picture Ealdorbold. I see the Counsellors in debate; I see Katahl's army as it makes for the city of Ishtar; I see my horse, Ravenwing, as he rushes to meet me; I see Troy preaching to the people; I see …' She stopped suddenly, her feeling of freedom and elation transforming to fear with what she discovered. 'I have to go,' she said.

Snatching up her weapon belt, she made a grab for her sword, but Bydand was there before her.

'Do not delay me,' she said. 'My friends are in danger and need my help.'

Prince Bydand spoke calmly. 'Exzalander, Anarkhane wishes you to stay. She would not want you to rush into trouble while you are not yet healed.'

Kirsten raised her hand and the sword flew from the prince's grasp to its mistress, where she quickly sheathed it. Approaching the prince, she embraced him.

'I am glad to have saved you,' she said. 'You should not worry yourself; you have helped me more than you realise. I will not let Anarkhane down.'

With that, she kissed him lightly on the cheek and disappeared before his eyes.

She appeared in the darkness of a cave, the only illumination the precious stones glittering in the walls, which reflected phosphorescence. Struggling against the fatigue such majick produced, she released her disguise, in effort to prevent her power draining completely. Having held the image of Kirsten for so long, she found it difficult to let go, but as she released her true form, it was as though the weight of years had been lifted from her mind and she felt free.

Ioan and Tehd were sleeping in a corner; Tom was nowhere to be seen. She dashed over to her friends and attempted to wake them.

'It is pointless, Lady. They will only stir if I bid them to do so.'

Kirsten held her sword ready and turned about, seeing nobody. She remained motionless, her eyes piercing the darkness; nothing but the sound of her breathing met her ears. Without warning, a Vampire Ælf dropped from the ceiling in front of her.

'Your sword has no use here, Milady.'

His eyes were hypnotic, violet in colour; facially, he bore a similarity to Cröedaw, but he was at least a foot taller.

'What may I do for you, fair one?' the Ælf asked. His voice was rich with majick.

'Release my friends,' she ordered.

Other Vampire Ælves seemed to appear from the shadows, until she found herself surrounded.

'I am afraid that will not be possible, fair one. They travel with Thomn-the-Cleaverhand and their lives are therefore, forfeit, besides … we are hungry.'

Kirsten could feel, rather than see, them closing. Swinging the Sword of Taiohãhn bought a hiss from them, which sounded a lot like laughter. She focused on the blade, imagining it at one with her body and mind. Remembering the peace of Anarkhane's realm, she centred her thoughts on bringing that light to the cave of the Vampire Ælves. When she swung the sword again, they did not laugh. The blade seemed made from pure light that sent a beam to all who stood between her and her companions, and they fell back screaming.

Their leader remained, however. He did not back away, and as he raised his arm, Kirsten felt the blade removed from her grasp as if by an invisible hand.

'Interesting toy,' he said.

Before the sword reached him, she stopped it with her will. It hung in the air between them, each of them battling for mastery. When it was clear that neither was weakening, they both relinquished their hold. Kirsten stepped forward to recover her weapon, but the Vampire Ælf moved quicker than the eye and grabbed her hand,

'Who are you?' he asked smoothly.

She had expected his touch to be similar to Katahl's knights, cold and death-like. She was wrong. Her skin prickled with sensuality; his gaze attempted to lure and she fought it, unknowing if they were allied with her enemy and unwilling to discover too late.

'I am the sword keeper and the Trolg killer. I have been in the company of Katahl and yet serve him not. Whom do you serve?'

The Ælf hissed, and in doing so revealed his long canines, gleaming coldly in the darkness.

'I serve nobody. We live only for ourselves and leave your people to your petty wars and alliances.'

Kirsten could feel the eyes of the clan upon her, but as yet, no move was made against her.

'Come, why speak in riddles?' he said. 'Tell me your name and purpose here.'

'My purpose is to aid my friends, whom you have taken captive,' she said. 'Their purpose was to seek your counsel.'

The Vampire Ælf's eyes narrowed into a frown and he beckoned her to sit with him.

'You say that they sought counsel and yet they travelled with Thomn-the-Cleaverhand. He is our deadly enemy, and had we known that he was yet living, we would have sent assassins to bring about his most deserved downfall.'

Kirsten shifted uncomfortably and leaned in, wanting to avoid the ears of the clan. 'What crime has Thomn committed, that you would speak of him so?'

The Vampire Ælf raised his eyebrows in disbelief, making a guttural sound in his throat. 'Do you not know how he got his name? Those he butchered were my brethren. By order of King Tuâth, the forest was purged of our kind. Many of my kinsman were slain in the attack led by Thomn-the-Cleaverhand.'

As Kirsten listened to him, she could clearly picture the slaughtered and wondered if it was the Vampire Ælf's attempt to trick her with his dark arts.

'But it was so long ago,' she protested. 'Tom is not the same person of whom you speak; he has travelled to different worlds and has no memory of the person that he was. He does not recall these crimes. Is it fair to punish him for a crime he cannot even remember? Is it fair to punish a soldier for following orders?'

The Vampire Ælf sighed, his eyes glinting. 'Tuâth is dead and what care I for orders? It was Thomn's hand that stretched forth and killed my clan, *his* hand that murdered my family. There are no women left in the Clan of the Dark Moon, because he executed them *all*. Tuâth said that if vermin could not breed, then vermin would not spread. We were his allies; we were no threat to his crown and he destroyed us. The few of us that are left live a lonely existence, many of who lost a mate during the attack. I care not that he has no memory. He must be made to pay for what he has done.'

Kirsten's stomach turned at his words; she had liked to picture her father as a good man, yet here was an account of his attempt to annihilate an entire race. Feeling both dizzy and sick, she reeled forward trying to catch her breath. Her body and mind were more exhausted than she cared to admit. She wanted to force herself to fight, but sorrow consumed her.

'Why do you weep, Milady? Why should you care? You came here to kill us.'

She shook her head and the tears streaked her face. 'No,' she said. 'I came to save my companions, nothing more. I wish ... I wish that I could make it all better, but I can't. Please, release my friends and *I* will be your prisoner.'

'Noble words, fair one, but you are already our prisoner.'

She wiped her eyes dry, trying to harden her heart. 'You have a choice,' she said. 'Either you release my friends, who came in peace for your guidance, or you will join your Clan in death. But know this ... I am the daughter of the man who sent Thomn to kill you. So if you *will* have your revenge, then take it upon me.'

The Vampire Ælf stared long at her, his eyes wide, either in disbelief or he was trying to read the truth in her words.

'You are the daughter of Tuâth? You are Princess Exzalander? That explains why you have resisted our majick. Fair Lady, it is a gracious gesture you make, but you are blameless for the crimes of your father. Your bloodline alone cannot condemn you. I am Jared, chief of the Clan of the Dark Moon. It was my Grandmother who was charged with the protection of one of the Anarkhane stone shards. However, if it is on this subject that your friends sought counsel, then I am afraid that they wasted their time. My forefathers, who were great sorcerers, foretold the prophecy of your line. In the book of prophecy was set the stone and long it remained in our keeping. During the attack, the book was removed and its whereabouts is now a mystery to us.'

Kirsten failed to notice how hard that she had been biting on her lip until she tasted blood upon her tongue. She sighed, looking up at Jared. His appearance had changed as his pupils narrowed and all focus fell upon her mouth. Realising the distraction, she sucked at the wound, willing it to close, removing temptation from him.

All eyes watched as her shimmering form glided through the blackness, cautiously approaching her unconscious companions.

'*Ioan, can you hear me? Wake up!*' her mind called to his, but she saw that he was dreaming.

It was a heavy sleep that held him, nothing more, and as she reached into his mind, she saw him walking through the fields of his home, hand in hand with Tehd, feelings of contentment emanating from him.

'We are not cruel, Princess, no matter what tales might tell. We drink the blood of the living, that much is true, but our prey feels no pain or fear; we do not let them suffer.'

Kirsten gently stroked Ioan's fringe. He was smiling as he slept.

'Is this the skill that you taught to Shénär?'

'You know of Shénär?' Jared said, taken aback.

'Yes I knew her and her history.'

'Knew? Is she dead then?' he asked.

'Yes. She was killed in Ánweald Forest, close to Ealdorbold.'

'She is at peace then. I am glad.' Jared walked from the cave and sat staring up at the stars. 'Ealdorbold you say? It seems that she went to seek revenge for her hardships, as she vowed that she would.'

'Did none of you ever try to … I mean did she …?'

He looked up at Kirsten, and a sad smile danced upon his lips.

'Breed? No. She was like ice. Nothing would warm her heart, not even *our* majick. We took her in and offered our aid as we would any of the Elfin. But she became more distant as her strength grew.'

'Are you related to the Elfín then?'

Jared wrapped his cloak about him and as he sat there on a rock, seeming more shadow than man.

'Not exactly,' he said. 'The folk of Elfín are of Anarkhane. She sent them to Maldahl to help create light and harmony in honour of Taiohãhn, who had given Her a gift beyond price. Taiohãhn is *our* master. With the help of His power channelled through our great sorcerers we once travelled between worlds. Once the great stone was shattered, we were stranded here. There lies still, a way to Taiohãhn's kingdom right here in Tûlg, but we do not risk using such a path, lest we lose ourselves in the Forest of Forgetfulness; we may no longer be impervious to its majick, since the gem of Creation was shattered. There are so few of us left, that it would not do to lose more. But as for the Elfín, we honour them, as it was Taiohãhn's will that we should.

'One of our great sorcerers was an advisor to your father for a while, reminding him of the CODM prophecy. It was perhaps this that increased his fear of my people. It was my clan who had predicted his death and your banishment. Perhaps he thought that by eliminating us, somehow he might prevent the CODM prophecy. I also suspect that in his mind, he came to see *us* as the great darkness of which had been spoken. In fact, the court began to fear majick more by the year, and the only person permitted to practice it, was Ardahl, yet even *he* was locked away from society. It was after the downfall of our wise ones and your father's death, that Ardahl the wizard sought our help. He knew that of old, we had travelled and we gave him a spell, of which none of us remaining were powerful enough to perform. It was this, I have been told, that destroyed him.'

'Yes, I have seen the spell of which you speak. It still exists in Ardahl's Tower,' she said. 'If I succeed in my quest and manage to reunite the stones of Anarkhane, I will have the power to send you to another world. You could find other clans and unite with them, be whole once more.'

Jared jumped to his feet, his eyes lamp-like in the starlight. 'You would do that for us, fair one?'

Kirsten placed her hands lightly on his arms. 'I promise I will; it would be a small recompense for what my family did to you and your clan.'

A dark shape appeared suddenly before them. 'Excuse my interruption, Jared, I was told to inform you that an Elfín has arrived. He is not conscious.

He was brought here by ...' The Vampire Ælf fell silent, as if unsure how to say what needed to be said.

'Yes?' Jared asked impatiently.

'A great black horse,' he replied, his eyes wide.

'Ravenwing? Here?' Jared said incredulously.

Kirsten's tried to catch her breath, wondering how they knew about Ravenwing. *But if Ravenwing is here then the Elfin must be ...*

'Cröedaw!' she cried. 'Please I must go to him.'

Jared stared at her for what seemed like an age.

'We will take you to your friend,' he said. 'But you must excuse me for a while. I wish to hold counsel on what has been spoken between us.'

Kirsten was led to an area of complete darkness and she used her night vision to pinpoint Cröedaw. Running to him, she cradled him in her arms. He opened his weary eyes, his face both gaunt and pale.

'Milady, I have found you at last!'

'Shh, rest now my friend,' she soothed. 'Sleep and mend your pains.' She rocked him gently back into slumber. A cough some distance away drew her attention away from the Elfin.

'Tom, is that you?' she whispered.

'Good Lord! I never though to hear your voice again,' came the man's reply.

It was indeed Tom, but his voice slurred and it was not until Kirsten approached that she realised why. He has been badly beaten and his lips were too swollen to speak coherently. Blood had dried from several cuts and what appeared to be bites. Kirsten felt her heart racing; the Vampire Ælves were in discussion and yet she feared that they would never release Tom; their malice toward him was too great. She gripped him by the shoulder.

'I am sorry that I cannot heal your wounds, Tom. I am going to need every ounce of my strength to get you out of here. The healers at Ealdorbold will tend you. Be sure to tell Gailon that Ioan and Tehd are under some kind trance or sleep spell, and Cröedaw needs rest.'

Tom stared blankly into the darkness, unable to see his companions. 'What about you?' he rasped.

'I will be fine. Don't worry.'

She backed away, closing her eyes. The sound of voices rose and fell and then there was nothing but the wind rushing in her ears. She pictured the courtyard of Ealdorbold and placed Tom in the image. Cröedaw's eyes snapped open, sensing her majick. He saw the light before him, but before he could protest, he found himself lying in the grounds of Ealdorbold; Tehd, Ioan and Tom at his side.

Jared ran to catch Kirsten as she fell. 'What have you done?' he screeched.

'What I had to,' she whispered, as her life slipped away.

Twenty-Five

Tom stared in painful amazement as a host of guards surrounded them, swords and spears pointed in their direction.

'What the devil?' he said.

Cröedaw screamed in anguish and fell silent, slumped forward on the ground, seeming not to notice or care about the spearhead that was touching his back. The guards glanced uneasily at each other, but stood their ground until the arrival of Genargh.

'What form of trickery is this?' Genargh demanded. 'Who sent you here, dark spirit? What is your purpose?'

Tom coughed awkwardly at the counsellor. 'Counsellor Genargh, it is I, Thomn-the-Cleaverhand. Surely you recognise us.'

'Silence foul thing and begone to the darkness from whence thou came!'

The voice, which had spoken, was hauntingly familiar and as Tom turned to face the new speaker, he was stunned to see Troy before him. The priest's eyes were sunken, his face pale, and he was dressed in long heavy black robes. Beside him stood Gohrn, a thin mocking smile upon his lips.

'Troy, don't be an idiot!' Tom said. 'Kirsten sent us here … I don't know how.'

'Counsellor Genargh, that t'would be impossible, even for Ardahl of old,' Gohrn asserted. 'These are evil sprites sent to test our faith, to confuse us in our already troubled state. See how the others do not speak. They are not real I deem, for if they were our friends, surely they would stand and greet us as such. I suggest that we lock them up until we decide how best to execute them.'

'They might prove useful hostages in the days to come,' Genargh agreed.

'Nay Counsellors, we should destroy evil as we find it, lest it poison us all,' preached Troy.

Tom took a step toward him and Troy cringed back, fingering a crude wooden cross that hung about his neck.

'Troy, what the hell is wrong with you?' he asked.

Counsellor Jaden arrived with Gailon and Thaniel, pushing past Troy with little regard.

'Counsellors, we have spoken at length about this,' Jaden said. 'These men have a right to a fair trial before judgement is passed.'

'Yes Jaden, and we are considering your proposal most carefully. Until such a time, however, our current law stands firm and if we deem it fit that these men be executed then it shall be so.'

'Strange,' Jaden replied, 'I thought that the decision fell upon all of us. Is that not the point of our system of government? No one person holds power; or is that simply a fallacy to keep public opinion on our side?'

'Counsellor Jaden, you will silence your tongue, or you will be cast from the Council.'

Jaden's face was red with anger and Gailon patted his arm in effort to calm him.

'Gentlemen please,' he interceded. 'Do we wish such a spectacle in front of the court?' Stepping forward, he held Tom's gaze for a moment. 'This is indeed Thomn-the-Cleaverhand. He knelt before Cröedaw and took his hand. 'What happened, my friend?'

Cröedaw slowly lifted his head, his tear-streaked face seeming not to recognise the wizard.

'She is dead,' was all the reply that he would make, and he wept again.

Gailon backed away seeming stricken; his wide eyes fell upon Tehd and Ioan.

'She said to tell you that they are in a trance, and Cröedaw needs rest,' Tom said, his voice beginning to waver. 'She said she would be all right.'

'I was a fool to return to here,' Gailon whispered.

He stumbled and Thaniel caught him, holding him steady. The guards' weapons lowered. They had all heard the rumours that the princess had returned and discovered the disguise she held. Parents had told them stories taken from the prophecy, and despite troubled times there had been a sense of hope about the palace that the evil in the north would be vanquished at last.

Silence followed, as each person present digested what had been said. Suddenly, Troy shrieked and fell to his knees, roughly shaking Cröedaw.

'You lie! You filthy, lying outsider. Tell them! Tell them that you're lying.'

With a movement quicker than the eye, Cröedaw had a dagger to Troy's throat.

'Take your hands from me, messenger of Shénnin, or I will slit your throat. The only outsider here is *you*. It has always been you.'

Troy's hands shook as he let them drop to his sides. He got to his feet and walked away, seeming shrunken. Cröedaw rose unsteadily, his voice beyond despair.

'Will you help me carry them inside,' he directed at Thaniel, who allowed Jaden to lead the distraught Gailon away through the silent crowd.

Thaniel placed Ioan and Tehd in the hands of the healers and assisted Breh in getting Cröedaw into bed. The Elfín had no strength left to resist, allowing them to tuck him in. Thaniel rested his hand on Cröedaw's shoulder and his glassy eyes looked up and met his friends.

'For one brief, shining moment, she sprang up out of legend and we were making history. We were all part of a much larger plan. Life will never be the same again, will it Thaniel?' He closed his eyes at last and welcomed oblivion.

Thaniel felt his chest tightening as he went back out into the morning sun. The emptiness inside him swelled, until he knew that life would indeed never be the same again. She had become so much a part of his being that now she had been taken from him, it felt as though there was nothing left but pain and growing despair.

The Clan of the Dark Moon gathered about the altar, with Jared at its head; the lifeless body of a woman lay before them, her dead eyes gazing upward, but seeing nothing, her pale skin like wax.

'Lord Taiohãhn, hear our plea. Return your warrior to us from the lonely path upon which she walks. Give us the power to renew her.'

He began to chant in their ancient tongue. Hour upon hour passed and none could turn away from the path to which they had committed themselves. A ripple of energy broke the silent air and each in turn felt the suggestion of their master as they stood in dream-like state. Each bared his fangs and sank their teeth into Kirsten's flesh at Taiohãhn's bidding. Each was surprised at the taste of warm blood, and as they drank, Jared continued his chant, his voice soaring into the sky, which was forever night in his domain.

Lifting on high his dagger of willow bark, Jared slit his wrist, allowing his blood to drain into a plain silver chalice at his side. He passed both dagger and chalice left about the circle, before gently sweeping away the hair at Kirsten's neck and biting into her throat. His eyes closed in ecstasy, fighting to stay in control of his actions as her latent power connected with his own. Each of the clan added their blood to the chalice and he continued to feed while it was filled. She tasted strange, yet sweet to him—inhuman. Despite her incapacity, he could feel the power that he and his clan were instilling in her and wondered if it was wise that their perspective strengths should merge.

Standing tall, the chalice was returned to him and taking it in both hands, he raised it above his head.

'Accept her as one of your children, O' Taiohãhn. As she has given, so do *we* now instil in her, all the power of our clan.'

He painted the dark moon on her forehead, then tipped her head back and poured the remaining contents of the chalice down her throat. They waited. Her dilated pupils narrowed into slits and she saw with perfect clarity, the night sky gaping before her. The wounds about her body closed and she shivered, her limbs feeling ice-cold, as she attempted to manoeuvre into a sitting position.

Vampire Ælves surrounded her, appearing as shocked as she felt. Her senses began to function and she became aware of the coldness of stone beneath her, the smell of majick and blood, the brightness of the moon above as it welcomed her. She slid off the altar, wondering what had happened.

'How do you feel?' Jared asked.

'Strong,' she said without thinking, as her memory began to return. 'Did I die?' she asked. Her body began to tremble with shock.

'Welcome back,' Jared said. Reaching out, he took her hands in his. 'You are now a member of our clan and pleased are we that we have been able to assist you.'

Kirsten sat on the altar, overwhelmed and shivering with cold. Jared removed his cloak and wrapped it tightly about her.

'Take this cloak and may it serve you well; all members of the Clan wear such attire and I would be proud for you to wear mine.'

She nodded as if she had not been wholly listening, and gripped at the cloak, the beginnings of fear reaching her at last. 'Am I dead then? Did you make me into a Vampire?'

His violet eyes met hers and he smiled wryly.

'Truly, we do not know what it is that we have done. The incantation was incomplete and we allowed Taiohãhn Himself to guide us while we were in our trance. You are not dead and I am not sure whether you were to begin with, else we may have been unable to bring you back as anything other than a one of us. It was a ritual almost forgotten by our clan.'

'Thank-you,' she said, clapping her hands on Jared's shoulders. 'I will not forget what I have promised you.'

'You are not leaving?'

She walked away, summoning Ravenwing to her. 'I must. Katahl's army marches and time is running short. If I am to fight them, then it must be soon.'

'You are one of us,' Jared said, 'we cannot force you to remain, but I would beg you to do so. I would at least have you rest before your journey. Our blood now flows with yours, as yours with ours; there are many things that I need to tell you.'

'One day, I may sit with you at leisure, Jared, but this is not that day. Farewell.' She kicked Ravenwing on, wishing that she could have transported herself to Ealdorbold, but knew that the risk was too high.

Jared watched as she sped away, wondering if she knew that the horse that bore her was not of Maldahl.

On the night of the second day from Tûlg, Kirsten saw the turrets of Ealdorbold above the treetops and it made her glad. It was not until she drew closer, that she noticed the gates were firmly shut; hundreds of people camped outside the palace walls. Dismounting, she sent Ravenwing back into the safety of Ánweald and drew Jared's cloak tight about her. Staying to the shadows, she moved throughout the crowd, unseen.

She spied a great many refugees from Golstur, their skin and hair colour being distinctive enough to recognise.

'Friend. Come warm yourself by the fire. Tis a cold night to be a wandering.'

Kirsten turned, spying a short woman with glistening white hair, beckoning her to sit. This had been the first person to notice her presence whist wearing her shadow cloak. She sat uneasily and stared about her. A baby cried nearby and she watched the mother's silent tears as the woman cradled her screaming child.

'What happened here?' Kirsten asked.

'Ah! I was right. 'Thought you weren't from the camp. Something different about ya. Katahl's army arrived at the cities, but I know nothin' 'bout that.

You'll find most of us here left on the mere rumour of his coming. We came to beg for the Council's aid.'

'And?'

The woman cackled and dished a cup of watery broth into a mug, holding it to Kirsten, who sipped it cringing; it tasted of nothing more than vegetable water.

'They won't see us; left us out here to starve. We can't go home. For all we know, there may not even be a home to go back to. They send us the holy messenger. He gives the people hope. If we have faith then anything is possible, he says.' She lowered her voice to avoid the ears of others. 'Have faith says he, and most believe it. Them's that don't, know better than to speak out now. There was killin' a few nights back. We sit here and starve and fight amongst ourselves. Who is this Lord of whom he speaks? I've ne'er heard of him before.'

Kirsten saw a gleam as a blade was drawn and in an instant she stood, her dagger unsheathed.

'You speak not the Word, but lies and blasphemy, mother,' the man spat.

Kirsten did not strike, but looked into his eyes, searching his mind; what she found there sent a chill down her body and anger rose within her.

'Stay your hand, son of Golstur,' she said. 'Better use I will find for your blade when my army rides to defend your city.'

The man's sword dropped away from the old woman and faced his new threat.

'What are you talking about, you fool?' he said. 'What army? Begone. Our city will not be saved, and only through our sacrifice may we join Him in His blessed kingdom.'

'Do you forget the prophecies so quickly then? You would turn your back on Exzalander's return and offer yourselves as lambs to the slaughter for Lord Katahl?'

Several people laughed as she mentioned herself and the man smiled viciously, as if prompted by the crowd.

'You speak of myths and I, the Living Word. Where was Exzalander when my house burned to the ground, when my wife and sons' screams from within were finally drowned by my own? The only solace I have found since, is that I will see them again in heaven, if I hold my faith.'

Kirsten felt sick, sick with guilt, sick with anger. 'That may be so,' she said. 'But you would rather run idly to your death before theirs may be avenged?'

'No. I will do as the messenger asks of me. I will pray and I will spread the Word.'

Kirsten sighed. Many people had turned to watch—confused faces, lost and hopeful faces, leaving her mind a whirl with anger. *What can I tell them?* she thought. *How can I make them see?*

There came a shout from the far side of the camp as the two smaller beacons were lit. A murmur spread quickly amongst the people and Troy stepped onto the battlements and began to preach. The argument was forgot as people shoved each other to be near to him.

Kirsten looked back at the woman by the fire; she had not moved, but chose to remain seated whilst she stared strangely in Kirsten's direction, as if waiting for some great change in events. Kirsten turned away, weaving her way through the crowd; her face was burning with anger and she did not take her eyes off Father Troy for even an instant. She watched, she listened and she waited.

'It is our faith that will defeat our enemy, not strength of arms,' Troy cried.

His voice rang out across the crowd and Kirsten cringed, cursing the day that she had walked into his life.

She shouted back in a gruff voice, so as not to be recognised. 'What of Exzalander? Will she not defeat the enemy?' Moving through the crowd, she watched his reaction carefully.

He lowered his eyes and gripped his cross. 'Do not allow yourself to be led astray by false prophecies, my children,' he cried.

She raised her voice again, this time high-pitched and feminine. 'I heard tell that she'd returned. She was seen in Golstur!'

Many people shouted at her words and Troy looked down into the crowd, dismayed.

'My children. MY CHILDREN!' he shouted.

A hush fell once more upon the crowd.

'She is dead,' Troy affirmed. He stopped for a moment, allowing the news to sink in, and Kirsten could plainly see the torment in his eyes.

'She was a warrior, brave and true and now she is departed. How can the dead defeat an army?' He turned to go, as if unable to speak further on the subject.

'Why do you walk away, *priest?'* Kirsten hissed at him.

He stopped, as if he had received a blow. 'Wh … who called me that?' he stuttered. His face was white as he turned back to the crowd.

'Why do you not walk among us?' Kirsten said. 'What are you afraid of?'

People surrounding her were shouting, their voices angry, nothing but hate and fear in their eyes. Troy was silent, his eyes scanning the sea of faces.

'My children,' he placated. 'I came out to you tonight to give you hope, to …'

'And yet you have taken hope away!' Kirsten shouted back, too irate to disguise her voice.

She felt a shove from her right, yet did not retaliate. Throwing back her cloak, her sword gleamed against her silver dress, shimmering like a reflection in clear water. People backed away at the sight of her and whispers began to spread across the camp. Troy's eyes widened, seeming both affeared and delighted.

'It cannot be!' he said.

'Let me in, Troy.'

He shook his head like a child in denial.

'Very well,' she said. 'I will let myself in.' She raised her arms, focusing her majick; the creaking of the portcullis was heard and the gates burst asunder.

The crowd was still for a moment and then, as a tide, they swept into the palace courtyard, screaming for food as they went. Kirsten summoned Ravenwing to enter during the chaos and allowed herself to be swept along by the masses as they pushed forward. By the time Troy had climbed down the battlements, she could no longer be seen. He turned, as if to run for help. Guards had spears pointed at the refugees, attempting to round them up.

'What have you done, Troy?'

She swung the priest around and he was so overwhelmed by the sight of her, that he could barely speak.

'You … you're alive!'

'How dare you preach to these people. *How dare you!*' she screeched at him, and many of the refugees calmed enough to listen.

'These people have no God, not one church,' Troy explained. 'They are heathens. Unless I spread the Word of the Almighty, they will burn in hell.'

'What gives you the right to dictate their lives? It's always *your* god. These people are suffering *now*, they don't need to be told about eternal damnation. If you have no help or good news for them in *this* world when they are in dire need, then keep your sermons to yourself. Too often in the past have cultures been destroyed by your religion, and I say I'll not have you hurt these good people by your forcing your fantasies upon them.'

'You cannot prevent me from spreading the Word of ...'

'*Spreading*, yes what an apt choice of word. Spreading, like a disease, and that is what it will be; a disease, eating away at the core of this society until there is nothing left.'

'Change does not mean destroying, Kirsten,' Troy attempted to explain. 'These people are soulless; they *need* spiritual guidance. I just want the chance to save them. To fill their lives with purpose and meaning.'

'Why don't you try filling their bellies first, for that is their primary need. These people are *starving,* Father; I can see that well enough. You are willing to preach to them, but when have you actually tried to help them? Not once have I seen you make the effort to feed the hungry. Stop trying to gain power over others by using your religion. Listen to yourself. *You* want to save them. *You* want to fill their lives with purpose and meaning! What *you* want is to rule them, control them; you want to gain power and recognition. I understand, even if I do not condone it. Everyone feels a little lost and in need of attention and I know you have found it difficult adjusting to being here, but that is not an excuse to hurt them.

'I tell you, Father, that these people lead simple lives; they have simple joys. I beg you not to take the little that they have away from them ... I demand that you leave them alone.'

'You *demand*? By what right can you demand anything of me?'

'I am rightful ruler of this land, Troy. I have every right ...'

'And yet you waived your right to the throne. You have no authority to command anyone!'

She slumped, her energy depleting and the crowd watched in amazement unable to believe their ears.

'I am just a child. What was I supposed to do? I have no concept of what it is to govern a kingdom and command an army. What choice did I have?'

He smiled ruthlessly, closing in on her.

'Either way, *Your Highness,* I am answerable to my Lord God Almighty and no-one else.'

He was close now, so close that she could smell the faint odour of musk. He smelt like Gohrn. Her jaw clenched suddenly as she began to see the game that was being played.

'If you do not heed the commands and desires of others,' she said. 'If you ignore the laws and rules of a land, whether you consider it your native land or no', then you are a renegade; heedless to the feelings of others; cold, heartless and you *will* suffer for it!'

'And now you threaten me,' spat Troy. 'I am not afraid of you. I have the power of God on my side.'

'*LISTEN TO YOURSELF!* The power of god? You make it sound as though you can summon lightening bolts from the sky by the use of a simple prayer. You are not god! You do not hold His power in your hand. Remember how many priests and holy men that there are on Earth and then realise *please,* that you are not some special profit; not singled out by Him to become a missionary on Maldahl … Please,' she touched his shoulder and his body went rigid. 'Do you not see how much damage that you can do? We have wars enough here. Such battles are easily understood—a simple choice between good and evil. I beg you think before you create a *holy* war. Think about the future, when others are translating the word of god and nobody can agree. The stronger will lead the weak and the different factions will battle for a hopeless cause, each believing themselves to be just because they have god on their side. Good people, misguided people; their blood staining the field that they had tilled so happily, when their efforts and use of force could have been united against the true evil—Katahl. He will laugh so long when he sees that we have completed his task more effectively than he ever could.'

'Take your hands from me, *woman*!' Troy hissed and walked away.

Kirsten screamed and sent a lightening bolt crashing into his path barely ten feet away. He halted and turned to face her, fear in his eyes.

'Do not walk away from me!' she commanded.

Gohrn oiled into the courtyard, drawing himself to full height. 'That is quite enough,' he said.

Once again, Troy stood with him and Kirsten felt a cold stab as she envisioned the ramifications of the new partnership.

'Is this all the greeting that you have for me, then? Armed guards.' Kirsten said. 'Where is Gailon? Perhaps I will get more sense from him.'

'Hold your tongue, woman! You forget who we are!' Gohrn said. If he felt fear, then he did not show it.

'I have not forgotten who you are. You are thieves and murderers all!'

'Guards,' Gohrn screeched, 'arrest this traitor!'

The guards edged closer, becoming bolder when it was clear that she would not attempt to resist them.

'You speak of traitors, Gohrn and yet it was *you* who let a Trolg into the palace,' Kirsten shouted. 'Your foolishness in consorting with the enemy resulted in the death of three people. You allowed Gailon to be sent to Tûlg, knowing full well that what he sought there is in *your* keeping!'

The guards had stopped and seemed to be waiting for a reply to her accusation. The Counsellor shifted uncomfortably and sweat glistened on his brow.

'There is no truth in what she says, my Lords. Are we to believe a traitor who gave herself up to the enemy? Are we to allow his greatest weapon to roam freely among us, to poison our minds before the final attack? She has already attempted to murder our holy messenger and has let rebels into the grounds. How much more damage will you allow, before we put a stop to her?'

Kirsten saw the guards' approach. She looked into their hearts and read the hope that they held at her return.

'Remove her weapons!' Daihron ordered.

'I am unarmed, my Lords,' Kirsten said. 'Do you honestly think that I would allow you to take the Sword of Taiohãhn from me?'

'She is lying. It's a trick.' Gohrn pushed forward. 'She had the sword when she arrived. I saw it!'

'See Counsellors, how eager Gohrn is to possess the blade? Be wary of him. Search his room and you will see that I speak the truth.'

She allowed herself to be led away and her eyes searched ever for a face that she knew.

Jaden.

He stood agape and her eyes flashed at his approach, warning him not to intercede. He watched for a moment as she was led off toward the dungeon, then ran in search of Thaniel.

Twenty-Six

The sun beat down on Richard and he felt his limbs weakening from exhaustion. He had travelled for days, fearful of recapture. Above all, he felt that such a thing must be avoided, lest his rescue prove to have been in vain. He collapsed in the sand, his legs no longer functioning. Beyond caring about his failure, he welcomed death, hoping for it to come swiftly. His mouth opened to gasp as he hit the ground, but his parched throat made no sound. As his eyes closed painfully, sand blew into his face. He was unconscious when they lifted him and carried him across the threshold into the shining white city. While they bathed and dressed him, he slept on, plagued in his dreams by Trolgs and dark knights.

A young blonde woman in a pleated white robe smoothed over the crisp sheet that covered Richard and leaned in close to look at him.

'Where do you suppose that he has come from?'

'I know not, Clara, but I believe it best not to ask such a question. That is for our emperor to determine and only when he deems it time to discover such things.'

The man took Clara by the arm and they left Richard to his dreaming. Closing the door, they walked down a narrow well-lit corridor with large glass panels on either side, which looked down on the vast shining city.

When Richard awoke, he found himself blinking up at the sky. He fought his way from the covers and to his feet, his eyes darting about the room in search of danger. He was alone, alone in a strange room unlike any he had ever seen. The walls and floor consisted of highly polished white granite, but the ceiling was the most amazing—a window to the heavens. He did not stop to wonder for very long. Wherever he was, he had not chosen to be there and therefore considered himself a prisoner. Shuffling over to the door, he tried the handle. It was open. He dashed outside, expecting a fight. There was no guard, however, and he stood for a moment, his nose pressed to the glass and stared at the glittering city below him.

He had been heading east from Katahl's castle and there was little doubt in his mind to his whereabouts, the city that Thaniel had called Bashnya. *But he said that they suffer no trespassers,* Richard considered. *So, what am I doing here?* He fought back in his memory and could only recall sun, sand and the approaching oblivion of death.

He felt a chill as he made his way down the stairs. There were no windows, yet it remained well lit, reminding him sharply of the dungeon of Katahl. Nobody paid any heed to him, as he stepped out into the street. He was dressed as they were and his hair was blonde, but they were all much taller and their skin had a blue tint to it, making him think immediately of the sea. Hoping to find a way out, he walked toward what he thought to be the edge of the great city. He was careful to make no eye contact and ensured that his attention did not stray too long from the path ahead.

Stalls formed part of the surrounding buildings and opened out into the street, many of which were selling crystals, charms and books. He had never known books to be available to any other than the wise and certainly never to be sold in the street.

Struggling on, he could feel his thirst grow and wondered how long he could go on without food or water. To his relief, he came to a small queue standing before a water fountain in a plaza. People sat and talked, ate and drank. Richard's hands were shaking as he joined the queue, hoping that nobody would attempt to converse with him. The water cooled his mouth and throat; his entire being felt immediately revived. He stepped aside, breathing deeply, and his gaze fell upon two towers, rising up before him.

He gasped, sure that he had been heading away from them. He was in the centre of the city and therefore precisely the opposite direction to where he wanted to be. He turned, knowing that if he walked in a straight line away from the towers that he was sure to reach the edge of the city—before nightfall if he was lucky.

Two appearingly identical men stood in his path.

'Greetings stranger,' one said. 'We have been waiting for you.'

Richard stiffened. 'But how did you know that I would be here?'

The men smiled. 'All roads lead here, unless we direct you otherwise. Please follow us.'

Although they did not appear to be armed, Richard decided to follow. They had offered no threat and he did not wish to cause possible hostility unless entirely necessary. He walked behind the odd pair into one of the great towers, following them into a very small empty room. The doors closed behind them and Richard turned panicking.

'Do not be alarmed,' one of the men said, 'we use this device to take us up the tower. It will not harm you.'

Richard felt a bump as the tiny room moved and he gripped the wall, trembling. There was another jolt and the doors opened and he stumbled out, looking pale.

'Here is the man we were bidden to escort to you.'

'Excellent. You may go now.'

Richard turned to face the Emperor, unsure what to expect. Unlike the others, his hair was brown and he was slightly shorter in stature. In his presence were others who seemed equally curious of Richard. The emperor smiled and asked Richard to take a seat. He approached with caution, sitting in a high white leather chair.

'What is your name, boy?'

'Richard, Sir.' His mouth felt dry again.

'Tell me Richard, what is happening in the western lands? Why are forces gathering and why did you flee to our gates?'

Richard's eyes widened, unaware of Katahl's move against the cities until now. He did not speak, could not speak, but his mind told all as he recalled the dungeon of Katahl and his rescue by the princess. It was as though he could see it clearly before him, until he realised that *that* was exactly what was happening. His thoughts were being projected for all to see.

'I know that girl!' the emperor cried. 'She's not from Maldahl. She's the one who sent me here.'

There was a murmur amongst the group and Richard fought to think of anything other than the princess, but his thoughts betrayed her.

'It cannot be! Surely this is some kind of trick.'

'No Iseren, our princess has returned. Now we see why our emperor was sent to us. Exzalander herself sent him from another world so that we might prepare for her return. We have stayed too long, isolated from Maldahl and its problems. It is time for us to take what we have learnt to the aid of our princess.'

'H ... h ... how did you know?' Richard stuttered.

The man smiled down upon Richard and touched his shoulder.

'We are old. We knew Exzalander long before she was banished, but we were not on hand to prevent it, as our kind were long ago driven away as the Council drove fear into the hearts of men. Long we have lived here with the Mariners and now our features are indistinguishable from them. We read; we create.

'One day we sensed the presence of Macara Shee as they passed by in preparation for a great feast. We would have let them pass without incident, but for the tormented spirit they had enslaved.'

Richard looked at the emperor, noticing his translucence.

'We brought him back and made him our guide, our architect, and the Mariners' ruler. We read such magnificent things in him and from his mind we created this great city. He told us of the girl that had sent his spirit here and in doing so released him from the hold of a great force that bound him. We felt that he was our connection to higher beings.'

'Does this mean that I might be able to return home now, Fahl?' Walker asked eagerly.

'Yes, if you so wish; I am sure that Her Highness will be able to accommodate you.'

'But the princess has been captured by Katahl; it may already be too late!' Richard protested, growing more agitated.

'No. It was foretold that they would meet and that he would not know her. This is all written in the book of CODM. Has it not yet been consulted?'

Richard gazed blankly at them, clearly not having understood what they talking about.

'This is grave indeed. What could have happened to it? Surely the Council would not have destroyed it, despite their rejection of our ways. We should go.'

'But where, Brother Fahl?' Iseren asked. 'The attack has already begun on Ishtar and Golstur. Should we not go to their aid?'

'Let me think, and here decide a course that will benefit the greater good. We could attack the stronghold of Katahl. All of us together might be a match for his majick and hopefully he we will divert his attentions away from the cities. We might also hope to weaken his defences while others seek the reunification and Exzalander gathers her forces in the south.

'What say you to this action?'

'Fahl, I believe that you speak rashly. Surely, we should gather news before rushing blindly into peril. For all we know, Exzalander may have already been defeated, if what the boy says is true and she had not the stone of Anarkhane in her keeping.'

Fahl tossed his hands up and paced about, muttering, 'Have you no faith in the prophecy? Here is the one who will lead us to our destiny as was foreseen and you now doubt the meaning of his arrival. For over three centuries we have waited the fair-haired stranger who would not seek and yet find the land of the Mariners, Bashnya, where the twin towers gleam like the sun. We did not even abide here when these things were foretold. Let us not come so far only to turn away from our path now.'

Richard felt a sudden chill. His legs were shaking with fright at the wizard's words. He questioned why Gailon had thought that his joining the quest was a good idea, wondering if the wizard knew about the CODM Prophecy. He shook himself, thinking it all an elaborate mistake. *I am not meant for great things,* he thought. *I am simply Richard, the serving boy who managed to get himself captured by the enemy and lived to tell the tale.* He smiled grimly, as he came to comprehend that such a feat was great indeed.

Twenty-Seven

The door to the dungeon opened and a dim light from the corridor pierced the gloom in a narrow shaft. Kirsten looked up, squinting.

'Thaniel!'

The door clanked shut and they were left in darkness. She watched as his eyes narrowed, straining to see.

'Is it really you?' he asked. 'Cröedaw said that you were dead.'

Reaching out with her mind, she felt his pain and confusion along with a growing sense of hope. It was all the encouragement that she needed and she ran into his arms, clinging to him.

'Thaniel,' she wept, gripping him tighter. 'I never thought I would see you again.'

His arms wrapped about her and he stroked her hair, weeping softly. Her mind remained locked on his, feeling the surge of his love and desire for her, intensifying her own emotions. Free from past inhibition, she allowed her lips to find his, willing and wanting. The kiss lasted only a moment before he drew away from her.

'I cannot,' he whispered, his breathing heavy. 'You are the princess, whether you choose to embrace your sovereignty or no'. This is forbidden. You can only be with someone of noble birth.'

Kirsten's head was swimming; her lips still tingled from his touch.

'But you, I thought that you are of a noble line,' she said.

As he turned away, her own turmoil prevented her from being able to read him.

'Thomn was honoured with a title long ago and I am of his line. But his title is linked to position of Captain, which I rejected. I turned my back on Ealdorbold. I am little more than a vagabond; my presence here is only tolerated because of my ability to discreetly gather information. I would be put to the sword for daring to presume such a match.'

Kirsten ran her fingers through her hair and sighed, 'I am a princess and I say that I can choose to love who I damn well please. I don't care what anyone else thinks or says. Besides, do really think that any such rule applies? They threw me in the dungeon!'

Thaniel turned slowly, cursing the darkness. 'Love?' he asked.

She took his hand and kissed it and he embraced her once again, knowing that whatever occurred thereafter that he would always have that moment.

Once the burning anger had subsided, Troy cursed himself for his foolishness. *Where is Kirsten?* he thought. *If there is such a need for secrecy, why has she returned in Exzalander's visage?* He wandered aimlessly at first, thinking over all that had been said. His feet eventually led him to the dungeon where the princess was being held. He nodded to the guard as he passed, his hands sweating as he advanced toward the iron door. *I'll demand to speak with Kirsten,* he thought on his approach, but stopped short of the door, hearing Thaniel's voice speaking in little more than a whisper.

And so it was that Troy overheard what passed between Exzalander and Thaniel. He slipped away, his body trembling with sheer hate.

'How is Cröedaw?'

Thaniel smiled as he held her to him, breathing in the scent of her as though trying to convince himself that she was actually real, that such a thing was truly happening and it was not some sweet dream that would torment him in the waking.

'He is recovering, but Ioan and Tehd are still under a spell. Gailon has been forbidden to use majick and he himself is weak. News of your death took its toll on him, I fear.'

'I should not have come back, Thaniel. If everyone believed me to be dead, then I might have used it to my advantage. If Katahl has heard rumour of my return it might force him to premature action. I have to get out of here. Can you tell Gailon that I have returned? I have to escape from Ealdorbold. Gohrn will push to have me executed and I have not the time to prove myself. I am going to the Dragon Mountains; I know Gailon planned to go there after searching Tûlg. One of the stones he seeks is in a book that Gohrn is hiding, in his chamber most probably. It is a book of prophecy written by the Tûlg-dweller elders. Do you think that you can get it back?'

'You are not planning to travel alone, are you?'

'Yes. I don't want anyone else in trouble with the Council, if I can help it.'

He smiled wryly. 'I think that it may be a little late for that.'

'I will take Cob then. The extra majick may prove useful if I run into trouble. Does that appease you?'

'Hardly, besides I have not seen Cob since my return. I am not even sure that he is in the palace grounds any longer.'

She smiled, a glint of mischief shone in her eyes. 'Oh he's here all right. I saw him just before my arrest. He was the one who gave me the idea of enchanting my weapons, and it is well that he did so, otherwise things may have gone differently. I would have been forced to defend myself to avoid them taking the sword. I should have struck Gohrn down, that snake!'

There was a knock at the door and Thaniel drew away from her, feeling suddenly cold.

'Sorry sir, it's time.'

Thaniel gripped her hands tightly in his own, before he walked away. She held the guard's gaze for a moment, seeing only sympathy there, before he too turned from her. Waiting for the door to clang shut, she listened as the footsteps diminished. As soon as the hall was silent once more, she drew her cloak about her and cast a simple lock spell on the door, moving as shadow, unseen and unheard.

Gohrn slapped the servant across the face with a gloved hand.

'What do you mean, she's gone?'

'The dungeon was searched. Her cell is empty. She's vanished. Troy the messenger was seen leaving the dungeon just before her disappearance and he too cannot be found. Perhaps they are together.'

The servant backed away, expecting another blow. Gohrn's eyes narrowed in fury, and he began to pace.

'Inform the Council at once!'

The servant bowed quickly and dashed away. Gohrn strode up the stairs to his chamber and flung open the door.

'*I KNEW IT!*' he screamed, dagger in hand.

Thaniel dodged out of the way, as the red-faced Counsellor flew at him.

'Where is it Gohrn? Where's the book?'

'You will die for this outrage, Thaniel. Now get out!'

Thaniel drew his sword and approached slowly as though stalking.

'Guards, murder. GUARDS!' Gohrn yelled.

His dagger swiped the air between them and Thaniel parried with his sword, its edge cutting into Gohrn's wrist causing him to drop his weapon, screaming with fear and rage. In moments, Thaniel was on him, his knees pinning the Counsellor down while he held the sword over him like a sacrificial dagger, its point breaking the skin of the Counsellor's neck.

'Where is it?' he asked.

Gohrn cried, the blood pouring from his wounded wrist less worrying to him than the possibility of losing his head.

'Over there,' he wept, 'the panel behind the bed.'

Thaniel drew away the sword with one hand and punched him in the face with the other.

'You know not how long I have wanted to do that,' he said.

Moving over to the bed, he pressed carefully about the carved ridges of the panel until he felt it give. Reaching inside, he touched what felt like dried skin and he shuddered, withdrawing the age-old book from its hiding place.

Gohrn struggled to his feet, touching his battered nose with a shaking hand. Thaniel stared for a moment at the ornate cover, absorbed by the complexity of its design, seeing something more as his eyes searched. The Counsellor watched in silence, carefully backing away to the door as the book held Thaniel's attention long enough for him to flee.

While the remaining members of the Council gathered to discuss Kirsten's escape, she slipped unseen across the courtyard and fetched Ravenwing. The horse muttered angrily at having been disturbed from his rest.

'Sorry my friend,' she said. 'But we're off again.'

He spluttered and shook his head in greeting as Cob entered the stable.

'Why did you summon me?' the faerie demanded.

Kirsten tightened the saddle strap and began adjusting the stirrups.

'I am going to Dragon Mountains and you are to be my guide.'

'No! Why should I?' Cob stamped his feet and began to walk away. 'You had me banished from my clan and now you want me to go traipsing off with you when you have made no effort to reunite me with my people.' He turned on reaching the door, his tiny face, scowling. 'I like it here. The food is good and I am not leaving.'

Kirsten raised her hand; a sudden wind knocked Cob back into the barn and the door slammed in his face. He stood, enraged, and Kirsten thought that she might have felt fear, had he been larger.

'How dare you use your majick on me, woman!'

He raised his hands as if he was going to retaliate, but Ravenwing snorted loudly in protest.

'Cob stop this. I need your help,' Kirsten said. 'The time is fast approaching. If Katahl wins then the Macara Shee might be lucky enough to leave Maldahl, but *you* won't be with them. Alone, you are not powerful enough to escape. You need my help, and I promise that when the time is right, I will reunite you with your people.'

Cob pursed his lips for a moment then nodded slowly. 'Very well,' he relented, 'but we should hurry. Your escape is already known and it will not be long before you are discovered. I am surprised that you do not take time to help your friends. They are not well.'

Kirsten mounted the great black stallion and lifted Cob up into the saddle before her.

'I know,' she said, 'but I cannot risk weakening myself in any way—not now. I got them out of mortal danger, that will have to be enough.'

Kirsten kicked Ravenwing, who burst through the door and toward the portcullis. Guards shouted and ran toward her. The refugees in the courtyard stood and cheered. Kirsten reined Ravenwing and faced their oncoming approach.

'Behold, soldiers of Ealdorbold. I am Exzalander; I have returned. While the Council sit in their dark hall and wait for the end to come, I go to seek a weapon that will defeat our enemy. With that weapon, I will ride out to face the army of Katahl and I hope there may be those among you who will wish to join me. But until then …'

The portcullis rose so suddenly that sparks flew and Kirsten galloped off to the delight of the onlookers.

Gailon stood at the window hearing raised voices once more. His tired eyes closed and he seemed to doze whilst standing. His head bowed involuntarily and he moved away, his curiosity passing into despair once more. Shouts came again and he lay back on his bed, closing his eyes. In his dreams, he heard

Exzalander's voice as she ordered the guards at the gates to stand down. He awoke some time later to Thaniel persistently shaking him.

'What is it, Thaniel?' he asked wearily.

Thaniel unwrapped The CODM Prophecy from his cloak and saw Gailon's eyes widen.

'Where?' was all that he could utter.

'In Gohrn's chamber, and that is not all, Gailon … she's alive!'

The old wizard began to tremble as his gaze tore away from the book to his friend.

'Exzalander?'

Thaniel nodded, smiling. 'She said to prepare, as she is going to bring the final piece of the stone here, the other missing stone is contained within this book.'

Gailon ran his hand across the cover and its texture rippled and changed beneath his touch.

'But where does she hope to find the final piece? Surely she does not ride all the way to the Sea-lands.'

'No, the Dragon Mountains; it is not a long journey and she has taken Cob as a guide.'

Gailon stood, all weariness seeming to fall from him. '*Why* should she think to go there?' he hissed.

'Part of our quest was to search there. Why should she not?'

Gailon looked out of the window again, a flame rekindled in his gaze. 'Yes, we need to visit there. But it was not a stone we sought and *she* was never to be permitted to go, because that which she bears will cost her life should she meet Morlech.'

'The dragon? I imagine any of us would be in peril should we meet with him.'

Gailon shook his head as he started to undress from the robes of the healers into his old attire.

'You do not understand, Thaniel. We have to stop her!'

Cröedaw stood in the doorway, his face drawn and his body seeming misshapen somehow. 'I shall go,' he offered.

'You need your rest, Cröedaw; we cannot possibly expect you to fly.'

The Elfin hobbled into the room and perched on the end of the bed. 'If not me, then who? There is no-one else who could reach her in time.'

'Ioan!' Gailon suggested. 'We need to wake him. He and Kirsten have a link. He could warn her if we could but rouse him.'

Thaniel sighed. 'They are under close guard. Gohrn said that anyone who attempted to use majick to wake them, would be charged with treason and face execution without imprisonment.'

'Gohrn's threats do not frighten me,' Gailon huffed.

'That may be so, old friend, but without Kirsten I do not deem it wise to face a host of the Shénnin Guard. You are not at full strength whether you think it or no'.'

'Counsellor Jaden,' Cröedaw suggested hopefully.

Thaniel nodded. 'Yes, he was always sympathetic to our cause. I think if we are going to convince him to help us though, then we should move quickly. If Gohrn gets to him first, he may not be so willing to ally himself with us. I attacked him when he refused to hand over the book.' He bowed his head like a guilty child.

'He would not dare make a move against you,' Gailon said. 'It would be as good as an admitting his guilt. This book was thought to be lost and Gohrn could be burned for having it in his possession. This is the CODM Prophecy. It is a very powerful book, which is said to be a gateway to another world. If Kirsten has been led to believe that one of the stones is contained within it, then it may not be in Maldahl at all. Keep it safe, Thaniel, whilst I go to see Jaden. Find Thomn if you can; we may have need of him.'

Thaniel nodded and ran off in search of the age-old warrior.

As Gailon approached the Council chamber, he heard raised voices. The great doors stood open and he could clearly hear the debate that ensued. Genargh argued that the princess *'if indeed it was really her'* had returned to Katahl, and it seemed that she had taken their holy messenger with her. Whil stood in protest and defended her, to the surprise of all present. Gailon slipped in and spied Jaden sat quietly in the corner.

'Gailon, what brings you here? We have not sent for you,' Daihron crooned.

'I am aware of my intrusion, my Lords, but I have been informed that Exzalander is still alive and I wished to verify the truth of this.'

His eyes flashed at Jaden, who shifted in his seat.

'I think that I speak for many present,' said Daihron, 'when I say that you have outstayed your welcome at Ealdorbold. You brought that woman here, since which time you and your companions have created anarchy in our fair kingdom. Now begone from our sight!'

Gailon bowed, again meeting Jaden's eyes before leaving them to debate further.

'High Counsellor,' Vahrn said, 'might I suggest that we imprison and question the girl's companions, and let us send an armed escort after the woman, before she can return to Katahl'

Borin shrugged. 'Why waste guards? They will not catch her on that abomination of a horse of hers.'

'But should we not at least attempt the rescue of our holy messenger?'

'Do not be so naïve, Vahrn. You do not honestly believe in this god of whom he speaks? It was a notion devised by Gohrn in order to control the masses. You are a fool if you think otherwise.'

'Speaking of Gohrn, where is he?' Whil chimed. 'Surely he should be present. It was he that called us to council after all.'

Jaden stood suddenly. 'I will go and look for him,' he offered. He crossed the room, an insatiable desire to speak with Gailon growing by the second.

Outside the Great Hall, a servant greeted Jaden and asked that he follow him. They moved past the kitchens into an old storage room. Tom, Thaniel, Cröedaw and Gailon awaited him there in the darkness. The servant bowed and left.

'Jaden, thank you for coming. I would not have asked if there was any other way.'

'What can I do, Gailon?' the counsellor asked.

'Ioan and Tehd, we need to get to them. Will you help us?'

The Counsellor sat slowly, in heavy thought. 'Gailon, they are under a spell. What would be the point?'

'Come now, Jaden, please do not pretend to forget what I am. You all tolerate me because I do not openly use my power and have proved useful to you in the past. But that time I fear is rapidly drawing to a close, is it not?'

Jaden said nothing, but his eyes told all.

'I need to wake them both and get us all to safety before it is too late.'

'You know the penalty if we are caught?' Jaden asked.

Gailon nodded gravely. 'I do not ask this lightly, but Exzalander rides into great danger and Ioan is the only one who can save her.'

The counsellor was silent, a thousand thoughts running through his head. 'I accepted my position on the Council in the hope of doing some good. Perhaps in rejecting that honour now, I will achieve something great.'

Gailon smiled. 'Let us hope so. Let us hope so.'

Jaden approached apprehensively, his palms sweating and his head pounding as part of his conscience battled to change his mind. The guard opened the doors at his approach and he stepped into the room where Ioan and Tehd were being held. He gently moved Ioan into a lying position and shouted to the guard.

'Quickly. Run and fetch Master Breh. One of them is stirring.'

The guard ran off in search of the healer and as soon the man was out of sight, Gailon stepped out of the shadows and went to their side. He held a hand to each of their foreheads for a moment. Jaden watched for the guard's return, willing Gailon to hurry. A small cough ensued and a very long yawn; Jaden breathed a sigh of relief, hurrying Gailon from the room only just in time for the guard's arrival.

'Master Breh, I release these two into your care,' Jaden said. 'Now if you will excuse me … Guard, you are released from this charge and I request that you help me search for Counsellor Gohrn and Troy the messenger, who are both missing.'

The man stood to attention and marched off down the corridor.

Tehd yawned. 'What's going on?' he asked.

'Follow Master Breh,' Jaden said. 'He will take you to Gailon. I must leave you now.'

Ioan stared sleepily after the Counsellor, wondering how he had come to be back at Ealdorbold, when the last thing he remembered was being in the Forest of Tûlg.

As the sun sank low in the sky, Ravenwing demanded a rest and despite her eagerness to press, on Kirsten was forced to stop. Cob watched with fascination, as she created them a meal by majick.

'I wish my people could do that,' he muttered.

Kirsten shivered as she remembered that their delicacy had been human flesh and was instantly accosted with memories of Katahl's dinner table. Remembering the half-eaten human arm did little for her appetite. She dipped her bread into her stew and forced herself to eat, trying to put thoughts of cannibalism from her mind.

The evening was mild and she lay back, looking up at the heavens. She started suddenly as she saw quite clearly Katahl's face, mocking her. Shivering at the memory, she drew her cloak about her for comfort. Cob was some metres away, basking in the twilight as some might in the sun.

'Milady?'

Kirsten sat upright, her eyes darting about her.

'Milady. It is I, Ioan. Can you hear me?'

She smiled broadly. *'You're awake! Are you well?'*

'Yes. Thanks to you. Gailon wants you to return. He says that you are not to go to the Dragon Mountains.'

'Will he say why?'

'No, only that if you go, then you will die.'

'Ioan, we're resting for the night. I will think over what you have said and speak to you again in the morning.'

Ioan turned to Gailon, his expression betraying his thoughts.

'Fool of a woman!' Gailon said. 'Why would she not listen to reason?'

Thaniel sprang to his feet and began to arm himself.

Ioan shrugged 'I do not think that she will return without a better cause than I gave her, Gailon.'

The old man's face darkened, as if haunted by some terrible memory.

'If I ride all night, I may reach her by morning,' Thaniel said, slamming his sword into its scabbard.

Gailon nodded for him to go and there came a thump at the door.

'Open up, in the name of the Council of Shénnin!'

Tehd and Ioan exchanged worried glances and the door was shoved open.

'What is the meaning of this?' Gailon demanded.

'You are all under arrest, by order of the Council.'

Tom stood up, spluttering. 'This is preposterous! What's the charge?'

The guards looked grimly back at the man who they had heard stories of since they were children, a man who had trained with them and shared their ale in friendship.

'High treason, Thomn-the-Cleaverhand.'

Thaniel drew his sword and it gleamed like a tiger's eye in the firelight. 'Out of our way!' he demanded.

The guards stood their ground, seeming to pale somewhat, as their quarry armed themselves.

'Gentlemen,' Gailon said, 'we do not have time for this delay.'

He approached slowly, his body looking old and bent as he leaned on his staff. With the sudden speed of a fox Gailon swung his staff and took them by surprise, flicking right then left knocking the guards to the floor with bloody noses and pulling back he thrust forward and knocked the final guard unconscious.

'Need any of us tarry? The Council has declared war on Exzalander and all those who stand with her. Here, take the book of CODM and guard it well, Thaniel. We must be gone from here at once. Tehd, run and fetch Cröedaw, quickly now!'

They gathered cautiously in the corridor and heard a scuffling noise to their right.

'Tehd?' Gailon hissed, but there was no reply.

Dashing down the corridor, they discovered Tehd, sword in hand, standing over a dead guard.

'I had no choice, Master Gailon. He was going to kill me.'

Gailon nodded and squeezed Tehd's shoulder.

'Come, clean your blade, wipe your tears. We must hope that Cröedaw finds *us*.

'Where would he be, Gailon?' Ioan asked.

'I do not know, but I fear that danger presses near.'

They ran toward the gate, not stopping to wonder how they might get past the guards without the shedding of more blood.

'THAT IS FAR ENOUGH!' Gohrn yelled.

In the courtyard, the Council had gathered. Guards held back the crowds from Ishtar and more soldiers protected the Council. Gohrn held a cruel looking dagger to Jaden's throat and spittle ran down the Counsellor's face as Gohrn hissed.

'See my Lords, it is as I said. They have the book of CODM. I caught Thaniel trying to hide it in my room and I fought him off.'

Blood still seeped from the now bandaged wrist of the crazed counsellor, where Thaniel's blade had cut deep.

'You are charged with conspiracy to overthrow the Council, the practice of forbidden majicks, consorting with the enemy and the murder of our holy messenger. You are all found guilty of treason and are to be executed along with this traitor here.'

Thaniel moved to attack and Gohrn's eyes glistened with mad rage.

'Light the pyre!' he screamed.

The companions saw Cröedaw tightly bound to a stake; about him, the flames began to grow.

Gohrn's eyes glittered with triumph. 'Die Elfin brat!' he cried. 'Be cleansed of the evil you brought upon us all.'

As the flames leapt higher, there was a gasp of astonishment from the crowd. Amongst the flame and smoke, the Elfin disappeared and a large black crow flew away to safety.

Jaden used the distraction as an opportunity for escape, elbowing the shocked Counsellor and dashing toward the oncoming company. The soldiers did not attack at first and the delay cost Gohrn his life. Thaniel's sword sliced across his chest before he could even bend down to retrieve his knife.

'Follow me,' Gailon shouted.

He ran back toward the palace with guards at their heels, the screams for vengeance over the death of Gohrn, diminishing with every step.

'I thought that we are trying to escape, Gailon,' Ioan panted. 'What is the point of taking us into the palace? We'll be trapped here.'

'Less talking, Ioan—more running,' Gailon said. 'The Council will skin us alive if we are caught, especially after Thaniel killed that upstart, Gohrn. But I have no intention of dying yet, worry not on that score.'

The corridors darkened and they entered the catacombs. Shouts and cries were heard behind, becoming more distant as the palace guards refused to enter the darkness of the forbidden part of the palace. Instead, they posted watch at the entrance.

'There is no way out,' Genargh said slyly. 'They will surrender or they will starve. Either way, they are all dead men.'

Twenty-Eight

Troy struggled on into the darkness, cursing the day he had met the girl. He knew not which direction he was heading; he let his hate guide him through the night and drive him on, until his pain quenched at last, blanketed into oblivion by the abhorrence that infested his soul.

In Bashnya, preparations were being made for the Mariners to depart. Fahl gazed into the throne room fountain, whispering an almost forgotten language. His face was like stone as he watched the images unfold before him. Shaking his head at what he saw, he turned to Walker.

'We must change our plan of attack. The enemy must be left defenceless in his stronghold. We must draw those who remain to us. Let us approach Golstur and attack his legions there. If we can defeat his forces at the cities then he will be forced to send his remaining troops to counter us.'

'Why change the plan, Fahl?' Walker asked, eyeing his friend intently in attempt to read his face.

'I have seen something that disturbs me; an enemy that Exzalander has not foreseen moves against her. If we attack Katahl directly, then I fear that he will be waiting for us. This way is at least a little less hopeless, although the Trolgs are formidable fighters and we are few. I think that we could convince the Elfin to join us.'

Walker nodded, but his mind was drifting, remembering days when he was a man, recalling the face of his wife and wondering if she might still be alive and if he would ever be able to hold her again.

The door to Ardahl's Tower creaked open and the companions clambered in, sighing at the sight of the night sky and failing to see a figure step from the shadows.

'I wondered when you would get here.'

'Cröedaw!'

Thaniel embraced his friend briefly, before turning his attention back to Gailon.

Jaden panted, as he struggled to regain his breath after their long descent. 'What are we going to do, Gailon? Can they find us here?'

'No. We are safe for the time being. Nobody will be able to reach the tower and we have the advantage, because they believe that we are trapped.'

Tehd brushed himself down and dust filled the air. 'Is that not the case then, Gailon? Is there another way out?'

'Of course my dear fellow. My master was not fond of company it is true, but at times, he liked to walk among the trees or sit in the sun. He built a portal that opens in many places, one of which leads deep into Ánweald. We can escape without them even knowing.'

The company smiled, but Gailon's face remained grave.

'My only concern is that there are seven of us. Never have so many attempted to use the gateway at once. We may come out in different places, or not at all. Cröedaw of course could meet us in the forest, but I would prefer not to be separated if we can help it.'

Ioan stood gazing out of the window, thinking he saw in the distance, a tower rising above the clouds.

'Be wary, Ioan,' Gailon warned. 'If Katahl stands in his tower he could spy you stationed there, for his eye is keen and sees much that is hidden from ordinary sight.'

Ioan backed away in alarm, imagining Katahl's gaze upon him.

Kirsten slept dreamlessly as Cob sat on a stone singing softly to himself, remembering times when the cavalcade reached its end and the before dawn feast that followed until cock crow. He sighed and hung his head, feeling an emptiness, which was growing by the day. The snap of a twig brought him swiftly back from his brooding. His sharp eyes searched the blackness of the forest, but saw nothing. His nose, however, picked up a scent nearby. He waited, poised for attack, yet nothing more was heard and the princess slept on.

Gailon insisted that he use his time well while in the Tower of Ardahl. He conjured supplies from the air itself, much to the astonishment of the onlookers.

'Shoulder your packs, my friends,' Gailon said. 'We must be gone from this place. Ioan how goes it?'

'I think that she is sleeping.'

Thaniel swung the largest pack over his shoulder, smiling grimly. 'At least we shall have a chance to close the gap. That is if we are all willing to travel by night without rest.'

'I am willing,' Tom said, 'but what of the horses? Surely we will not catch her on foot.'

'We cannot possibly get them out of the palace. Even if I were to use majick to open the gate for them, it would be too much an indication of where we were; the hunt would be hard on our heels I fear. This is the only way.'

Cröedaw sighed sadly. The thought of leaving his beloved Träkehnér clearly troubled him.

They clambered into the hallway and the torches lit at Gailon's approach. Standing before the painting of Exzalander's return, they watched in silent fascination, as it seemed to dissolve before their eyes.

'Enter all. I will hold the doorway open from this side. Let us hope that we all make it through. If not, stay where you are if you can and I will attempt to reverse the portal from here. Once I pass through, I will be able to do nothing. Most of my power is bound up in this tower. Once I leave it, I will be limited to more simple majicks.'

Gailon ushered Tehd and Ioan through first; Tehd felt as though he were falling so far that he might drop straight through Maldahl.

Gailon's eyes were like steel as they gazed unblinking into the light. Jaden stepped through next, followed by Tom and Thaniel. The wizard's face strained with immense concentration and effort.

'All is well, Cröedaw,' he panted, 'off you go.'

As Cröedaw stepped through, Gailon fell in after him. They landed awkwardly in the thickness of the trees. The sun had just set and the sky was a rosy glow, darkening by the second. Gailon remained on his hands and knees, catching his breath.

'Are we all here?' he wheezed.

Thaniel patted him on the back and helped him to his feet.

'Yes Gailon, you were concerned without cause.'

'No my friend, luck played its part I deem, but it was a struggle. I am quite weary now. But there is nothing for it. We head southwest. Lead on Thaniel.'

* * * * *

In the morning, Kirsten awoke, stretching and yawning loudly. 'I think that was the best night's sleep I have ever had,' she said, smiling at Cob. 'Good morning my little friend.'

Cob spat. 'I am no friend of yours! If you were my friend, then you would not have got me banished.'

Kirsten raised her eyebrows, beaming as the early morning light sifted through the trees, bringing a golden haze.

'I do not know why you dragged me away on this excursion,' Cob continued. 'You have no real need of my help. You are more powerful than ever. You can even see me by light of day. I will tell what I am, shall I? Your watchdog. You took me away from the food and warmth and fine wine to sit here all night, cold and alone while you sleep like there is no tomorrow. You did not even stir to see our attacker. You left *me* to defend our camp. Obviously too menial a task for you to soil your hands with …'

'That is enough, Cob! What attacked our camp? And why did you not wake me?'

Cob sulked and his mouth twisted awkwardly. 'Nothing. I heard a noise that is all,' he muttered, with reluctance. 'But we might have been attacked. I could smell something and it remained all night. Not that you would care!'

'Can you smell it now?' Kirsten's eyes darted among the trees as if expecting a monster to jump out.

'No. But my powers diminish in daylight, woman, or had you forgotten that?'

She gathered her pack and loaded it onto Ravenwing. 'Did you see anything boy?' she whispered to the horse.

He stamped and nodded back. She drew her sword and marched through the trees.

'I know you're there, so you may as well show yourself!'

She swung about as a swishing noise came from behind and she saw what appeared to be a man jump nimbly down from the tree.

'Milady,' he said and bowed low. He was clothed in black leather and his face swathed in a wrap of black silk. 'May I present meself to you as a protector? I 'ave travelled for many days in search of you and so it was when I arrived at Ealdorbold, I saw you save the people there. I waited near at hand and followed you as you ventured forth again, for I was unsure who to trust at the palace, other than yourself and the other warrior woman.'

Kirsten frowned. His voice sounded familiar to her. She assumed by warrior woman that he did not realise that Exzalander and Kirsten were one and the same.

'Let me see your face,' she commanded, keeping a steady grip on her sword, should she still have need of it.

He unwrapped a little of his trappings and although it looked older than it had, Kirsten recognised his face at once.

'Jeb!' she cried.

The boy knelt before her, his head bowed low. 'Your Highness honours me. But how do you know who I am?'

She sheathed the Sword of Taiohãhn and pulled Jeb to his feet, smiling.

'Because it was I who let you go in the tavern, and I who gave you the token.'

'Truly, your majick must be great,' Jeb marvelled.

Kirsten beckoned to him, leading him back to camp where she lit a new fire and began to cook breakfast, to the amazement of the former thief.

'Jeb, what brings you here?'

He bowed his head as he spoke. 'As you know, Golstur fell under attack; many people was killed. I urged me ma to leave with the others, but she refused. She stood in the crowd and shouted at them to go 'ome, then spat in the face of one of the knights and he … he killed her; cut her down like wheat, and the troops trampled over her as they advanced into the city. By the time they 'ad passed through, she was unrecognisable. I buried her remains and left.'

He sighed and Kirsten thought that he might weep, but no tears came.

'I am sorry, Jeb,' she offered. 'I am sorry that I was not able to stop it.' Her thoughts were dark as she recalled that she would have been one of Katahl's troops, had the children of Anarkhane not saved her.

Cob stood to the left of the princess; his hands on his tiny hips, pouting like a spoilt child.

'Who is this brat? Kill him and let us be on our way.'

'Cob, this is Jeb of Golstur. He has skill as a thief and may prove useful.'

Jeb looked about him, seeming puzzled.

'Cob is a faerie, Jeb,' she continued, over Cob's screams of outrage at her choice of title. 'You will not see him by light of day, by night either, unless he has a mind to reveal himself to you.'

'You travel with the fair folk? That is strange indeed, why not warriors? Why has no guard been sent to accompany you?'

'The Council have turned against me. Indeed, I believe that they were against me all along. My capture gave them the excuse that they needed to publicly denounce me. I am on my own.'

'No Milady, *I* will not abandon you,' Jeb promised. 'Ever since I learned of the token of Tuâth and Shénnin I have sworn my allegiance to you and your cause. I 'ave not been idle.'

A shadow passed over Kirsten's face and her heart began to race. 'You knew what it was when I presented it to you?' she asked.

'No Your Highness, it was me ma who knew. She beat me, thinking that I had stolen it. When I told her what had 'appened, she cried for joy, making me hide the token and promise not to show it to anyone. For weeks, she was a changed woman, talking about little else but your return. I took to finding any news that I could, to the delight of me ma.

'After her death, I travelled to Ishtar and there I heard tell of you, although I did not know at the time that you and the warrior was the same person. Soldiers were searching the city for you. I was by the east gate the night that they claimed to have seen you. A horse-seller was detained and the knights rode out of Ishtar. The horses broke free and out of the open gate and the horse-seller was beaten and searched. If I 'ad realised what he had been carrying I would have tried to save him. Incredulous to me it seemed that he was also a bearer of a token of Tuâth and Shénnin.'

Kirsten could feel her hands trembling. 'So he knows, or very soon will,' she whispered. 'The knights will present the token to Katahl and he will scour the land in search of me. It is an irony indeed that the knights did not discover it sooner, as they were setting a trap for me in the hills.

'We must find the missing parts of the stone of Anarkhane; I will have the power then to defeat Katahl when the time comes.'

Jeb ate as one who had fasted for many days and then they were on their way, much to the protest of Cob who felt more superfluous than ever.

Kirsten, Jeb and Cob came to the edge of the forest. The bright sun blazed to their left and directly ahead, mountains loomed. As they drew nearer, Kirsten was relieved to spy a path winding its way up into the grey peaks. She was struck with recognition by the ground underfoot and stooped to touch the silver grey sand.

'It is like the rise around Ishtar,' she observed.

'Yes Milady and I don't like it,' said Jeb. 'Something 'appened to Ishtar, long ago—something terrible; I don't know what it was. I may have been told in stories when I was young, but if so then I don't remember. All I know is that the land was devastated and the city of Ishtar was built in the crater that remained.'

'So whatever happened to Ishtar occurred here as well,' Kirsten murmured.

'Woman, have you no sense at all?' Cob spat, from Ravenwing's back.

'Do you know what happened, Cob?'

The faerie shook his head in disbelief. 'How is it that you are so ignorant? They have dragons on Earth. I have seen them.'

'Dragons!' Kirsten said, and Jeb repeated her words.

'Ai. It was dragons that destroyed Ishtar, although it was called Ichnaarim then. It was a land of the hunter and dragon hide fetched a high price. A fleet of the angry beasts descended without warning, led by their king Morgothal the Stormbringer. They left none alive; such was the power of the dragon in those days. Now, that mighty race has dwindled, alas.' He sighed and his face looked beyond, as if he was caught in a memory of yesteryear.

'I did not know that the Dragon Mountains actually had dragons living there.' Kirsten gazed upward in amazement, as if she expected to see a spout of flame at any moment.

Jeb's eyes followed her line of sight, obviously sharing the same worry.

'Are you deaf, woman? I said that they are dead. All gone,' Cob said. 'Those that were not killed had already passed into another realm and have been seen never more.'

Kirsten's eyes cast downward again; a sudden sadness consumed her, a melancholy at the passing of so great a race that she would never have the opportunity of seeing. She led Ravenwing carefully upward, breathing the free air gladly after the closeness beneath the trees. Jeb shook his head and followed cautiously, uncomfortable with the conversation Kirsten continued to have with a being that he could neither see nor hear.

'Cob, when were there dragons on Earth?' she asked.

The faerie made a face as if to say that he preferred being ignored. 'When I was last there, long, long ago. I take it by your questions that none now reside there.'

Kirsten shook her head. 'Only in legend. It is sad. I wonder what happened to them?'

'Begging your pardon, Milady,' interrupted Jeb, 'but why should you care at their passing? They were killers all.'

Cob jumped up and stamped his feet, causing Ravenwing to splutter in annoyance.

'Ignorant runt!' he fumed. 'They were a proud and noble race, among the wisest of beings. He knows nothing. Why did you bring him along?'

Jeb, unaware of the insult, continued up the path without further comment.

'Why can you not get along?' Kirsten whispered.

Cob seated himself once again and tutted. 'The boy's a fool. If I had my way, I would eat him when we reach the summit. It is the most use we are likely to make of him.'

Thaniel led the company, trudging through the darkness, eating and drinking on the march not stopping until dawn, when by chance Cröedaw spied Exzalander's camp and deemed them but recently departed.

'Gailon, there are two sets of footprints here. She was joined by another it seems.'

Gailon did not respond. He seemed not to hear what had been said; he was both bent and tired, like an old tree, too weathered to go on growing.

'Let us rest a while. Master Gailon looks done in,' said the former Counsellor, who was breathing heavily himself.

'No. We must go on,' Gailon said, as he forced himself up again. 'Ioan, why does she not answer you?'

Ioan shook his head slowly. 'I do not know, Gailon. It is as if her mind is somewhere else, so bent on its purpose that my tiny voice cannot be heard over the roar of her own thoughts.'

'Cröedaw, fly ahead; bring her back.'

Cröedaw nodded and at once, where the Elfin had stood, a blue-black crow flapped its wings and flew off into the forest. The company tramped on in silence, curious as to the danger, but none daring ask Gailon what it might be.

Twenty-Nine

It was mid afternoon when Gailon's company reached the foot of the mountains.

'What is keeping Cröedaw?' Gailon grumbled. 'He should have stopped her by now.'

High in the mountains, Kirsten had prepared a meal for her companions.

'Where are we to look? It could be anywhere and this is just one mountain of many within the range. What was I thinking?'

She stoked the fire, lost in thought, until a flap of wings drew her attention. A crow landed at the fireside and Jeb jumped to his feet as the bird transformed into a man.

'Cröedaw!'

'Milady,' Cröedaw bowed wearily.

Kirsten rushed to help him as he swooned.

'You are weak,' she said. 'Come, eat, rest.'

Cröedaw did not argue with her demand, knowing that he had prevented her from going farther, as she would not leave him.

Her mind was swimming with lost memories; so much had happened and so quickly that she has forgotten Cröedaw's presence at the battle in the swamp. At the time, the crow was as a dream to her, now she realised that Cröedaw had been her feathered friend all along, watching over her. She smiled wryly as she handed the water skin to him.

'Jeb, this is Cröedaw of the Elfin. He is a friend; you may put down your blade.'

Cröedaw nodded to Jeb, but had no words as his focus left him.

'Cröedaw, you are unwell. What possessed you to exhaust yourself further by seeking me?'

He smiled and lay back without a word, feeling that his objective had been achieved. Kirsten covered him with her cloak and looked up at her new companion.

'I like this not. Why did he fly all this way to meet us? Something must be wrong. We need to hurry. Jeb, stay with him. Cob and I will search for the stone. We must be swift.'

Jeb added the last of the wood to the fire and complained to himself at having been left behind.

On a high plateau, the company found Jeb and the unconscious Cröedaw. Ravenwing stood by and shook his mane at their approach. Thaniel and Tom drew their swords on seeing their friend unconscious and with a stranger. Jeb stood, fearlessly facing them, armed with dagger and sword.

'Now now, calm yourself, my friends,' Gailon said. 'If this young man had hurt either Kirsten or Cröedaw, do you really think that Ravenwing would be stood by in such a manner? Put down your swords, all of you.'

Gailon's voice took on a commanding tone that penetrated to the core and all lowered their weapons.

'Now, declare yourself and your business.'

'I'm Jeb. I'm a friend of the princess …'

'I know you!' Tom exclaimed. 'You're the thief who tried to steal my money in Golstur.'

Tom lifted his sword once more and moved to strike, but was met with the token of Tuâth and Shénnin as Jeb presented it.

'I'm a friend. Her Highness set me to watch over Cröedaw as he collapsed and she did not want 'im to be left alone. She herself ventured on.'

'You stole that!'

'I protest. The princess herself gave this to me. The other man who was with you will tell you so.'

Kirsten stopped at the cave's entrance.

'We're not alone, do you not feel it? … Cob?'

She turned and saw the faerie rooted as if petrified by a powerful spell, being unable to move or speak. The air shuddered as a low breathing grew gradually louder. Kirsten planted herself firmly and unsheathed her sword.

'I guess they're not as extinct as you thought they were, Cob,' she said under her breath, wondering why nothing could ever be simple.

Out of the darkness of the cave appeared a huge green head, scaled with yellow and red eyes whose slit pupils shrunk in the last rays of daylight. An enormous clawed foot stepped forward, followed by another. A heavy swish sounded, which Kirsten presumed to be its tail. The creature's nostrils flared, releasing wisps of smoke.

Kirsten's sword arm lowered in sheer awe of the magnificence before her and without knowing why, she bowed low in reverence.

'Mighty Lord,' she began. Her voice seemed quiet in comparison to the dragon's heavy breath. 'I am honoured to make your acquaintance. I was led to believe that your venerable race had abandoned Maldahl altogether. I am pleased to find that this is not so.

'My name is Kirsten and I beg your counsel if you will give it.'

The dragon stared, unblinking at the small warrior woman before him. He sniffed the air for a moment as if there was an odour that displeased him, then slowly his serpentine neck lowered and he bowed back. Kirsten felt her entire body tingle at the encounter.

'I am Morlech the philosopher. I am the last. Once I am gone, we shall be no more. If you have come to slay me, woman, then do so swiftly. There is no need for games.'

His eyes met hers and they seemed to her as wells of despair, telling of agonising loneliness of years uncounted.

'I spoke truly, noble Morlech; I have no desire to kill you. I seek the Anarkhane stones and am told that one may be lost in these mountains. Would you know where I might find it?'

The dragon's eyes suddenly narrowed; he swung his head down until it was level with Kirsten's own and he sniffed at her more closely.

'*YOU!*' he breathed, outraged. His breath knocked her off balance for a moment. 'I know who you are. You show sheer audacity or very little sense showing your face here. Murderer.'

He stepped toward her and she backed away. Raising himself to full height, his breathing quickened and as it did so, his colours changed.

Battle colours, Kirsten presumed. She wanted to speak, to calm the creature, but it felt as though there was a throttlehold on her throat. She breathed hard, trying to focus. The world seemed to turn slower and she saw the flame as it sped toward her.

Dropping the Sword of Taiohãhn, she raised her arms and created a wall of ice that she fought to maintain with each blast of fire that hit. The dragon ceased, realising the futility of his action and Kirsten allowed the wall to melt. Morlech's expression changed from murderous fury, to despair and sadness.

'Have I not suffered enough?' he wailed. 'Now you seek to mock and torment me. Can I not be left in peace?'

Kirsten, soaked through, approached cautiously. 'Mighty Morlech, why do you think me your enemy? I have done nothing to harm you.'

Morlech's rage was so swift that Kirsten was struck down as his claw swept at her. He ripped her weapon belt off, slitting her across the abdomen. She lay bleeding and in pain, reaching for her sword. However, Morlech made no further move against her. He held her weapon belt to his breast, sobbing, and his pain shook the mountain.

Kirsten did not take time to wonder at this new behaviour. She set about healing the wound he had dealt her—dangerous she knew, but being incapacitated by the blow, left her little choice. She let her mind roam in the healing realm of Anarkhane, forgetting for a while her hurt, her quest, and angry dragons.

'Milady? Milady? Come back to us.'

Her eyes slowly opened, as if from a deep sleep and Ioan blinked away tears at her waking. Taking his hand, she stood stiffly, her mind hazy and unfocused. She was aware of voices—Gailon's she thought and another, deeper and more resonant. Her hand reached to her middle to find that her dress was torn, but the wound had healed. Ioan released his hold as Tehd presented her with her sword. She stumbled forward and went to Thaniel's side.

'Glad you could join us,' he said grimly.

'She knew nothing, Morlech,' Gailon pleaded. 'She is innocent in this matter.'

Morlech growled and the ground shook. He held out her dagger, tiny in his great claw. 'INNOCENT! DO YOU TAKE ME FOR A FOOL, APPRENTICE?'

'It was Ardahl who performed the spell; she is unaware of what was done. If you kill her, then Maldahl will fall to Katahl's rule and we will be lost into darkness.'

Morlech sat on his haunches staring at the tiny blade. 'What care I? The darkness took me long ago. I care not if Maldahl falls, apprentice.'

Kirsten felt her spine tingle and a cold sweat broke out across her body. She recalled the boy in the inn who wanted to see the dragon, and Jeb who said that her blade had bit him; perhaps oddest of all was the Trolg, who having claimed the blade, took his own life and that of one of her attackers. She had not pondered such things before; they were of little importance back then, but now, she felt sick. She stepped forward lowering her blade, but Thaniel held her back.

'Please let me be wrong,' she whispered, but she knew in her heart what angered the dragon, why he had stayed when the others of his kind had chosen exile.

She shook herself free, sheathing her sword. 'Why did you not tell me?' she shrieked.

Her anger brought Morlech back from his brooding. His eyes followed as she approached, and he bared his teeth when she reached out to retrieve the dagger.

'Why would Ardahl have done such a dreadful thing, Gailon?' she said, examining the dagger more closely.

'It was for your protection. Your father thought that the strength of a dragon would prove useful to you and he knew that none would remain once you returned to us, so he used majick to enslave one into your blade and he entrusted it to Taiohãhn to await your coming.'

Kirsten shook her head in disbelief. 'Morlech, I am sorry; I never knew. I will release her for you. This should never have been.'

'No.' Gailon said calmly. 'The spell can only be broken when you have succeeded in your task. If you fail to defeat Katahl, then Tehtra will remain trapped forever.'

Ignoring Gailon's words, she placed the dagger on the ground. Closing her eyes, she concentrated on the blade; she felt the cold steel and the strange hilt whose eyes seemed to watch and stare. She gazed back into those eyes and beheld Tehtra the dragon, whose colours glimmered and shifted in the light, making it impossible to tell what colour, if any, she actually was.

'Your Highness,' the dragon said, bowing low.

Kirsten reached out her hand to touch the incredible creature. All watched as the princess addressed nothing but the air and stepped forward, as if to pat a mighty horse; they gasped as an image of the dragon flickered before their eyes.

'Tehtra!' Morlech exclaimed, clambering to his feet. Tears were in his eyes as they reached out to one another, unable to touch, as she was not really there.

Kirsten shook with concentration, but could not release the dragon from the spell.

'Soon my love, soon we may be together once more,' Tehtra said, and her voice was to those who heard it, like the sound of a wind passing through, not quite a voice at all.

Morlech wept and all those who saw him pitied him, for he had dwelt alone for many long years, mourning the loss of his love, unable to leave without her.

Kirsten fell to her knees; beads of perspiration ran down her cheeks, mingling with her own tears. Tehtra was gone. Thaniel ran to the princess and held her steady.

'I am sorry, Morlech,' she said, sagging forward. 'I could not break the spell—to my shame.'

The dragon's eyes closed and he shook his head sadly. He turned and slowly, he walked back into his cave. 'Take what you came for and begone!' he said and sloped off into the darkness.

Gailon turned and his eyes flashed dangerously at Thaniel, seeing him cradle the princess in his arms.

'Take her back to the camp, Thaniel,' he ordered. 'Ioan, Tehd, follow me.'

Cob felt the spell lift and he stomped off down the mountainside, grumbling as he went.

Thaniel sat the princess down and wrapped her cloak about her. Counsellor Jaden had lit a fire and passed around a warm broth that he and Jeb had made. Kirsten stared into the flames, catching a glimpse of past events and she looked away, sickened by the deeds of her forefathers.

'Did you know, Thaniel?' she asked quietly.

Thaniel bowed his head. 'Yes, Gailon told me.'

She could not meet his eyes and turning from him, she sat in silent disgust.

It was little over two hours before Gailon and the others returned. Kirsten had refused conversation with any of them opting to sit staring out into the trees.

Cröedaw was conscious again and sat looking grim, as Thaniel recalled all that had happened.

'Let us be gone from this place at once,' Gailon ordered. He could not be persuaded to rest until they were camped safely in Ánweald, out of sight of the mountains.

As the sun sank into its mighty slumber, the company became suddenly aware of Cob's complaints. Jeb backed away from the angry faerie, fearful of what he might do, but the others seemed to consider him little threat.

Kirsten held her dagger before her eyes. *Tehtra still has some power, is able to exhibit a certain amount of control,* she pondered. *But Katahl has to die before she can be freed.* She sheathed it again, joining the company, as they made ready to leave once more.

'So, did you get the stone?' Kirsten asked coldly, as she walked at Gailon's side.

Gailon did not look at her, but stared at the path ahead.

'No. None of the Anarkhane stones were ever up there. It was the bile I have collected that we need. It can only be found in the abode of dragons, a bi-product from their fire making. It is this substance along with the reunification spell that will amalgamate the shattered gem and so restore the gods' power. You should never have come here.'

'You would rather that I had never found out about Ardahl's darker side, or my father's. I wonder if Katahl really is that bad. At least he does not hide that fact that he is evil.'

'How *dare* you compare my master to him!' Gailon ranted. 'What Ardahl did, he did for the greater good.'

'Tell that to Morlech and Tehtra,' she snapped back at him. 'And I suppose you think that my own father acted for the greater good when he ordered Thomn to massacre the Clan of the Dark Moon!'

Gailon's face turned ashen. 'No, I cannot defend your father's decision. He was frightened for his life and the lives of his family. He was blind to the truth.'

'And what was that?'

'That he could not prevent his or Shénnin's death, that you would be banished was as sure as the sun would rise and set each day. He was a frightened fool to ever trust the Council in such a matter. For even then, they saw a chance to seize power. With the Tûlg Dwellers demise, there would be less resistance to their opposing the monarchy; apart from The Order of Vivienne and Ardahl, the Tûlg Dwellers were the most powerful majick remaining.

'The Council convinced your father that the Tûlg dwellers would be the cause of the downfall of his house. The Order of Vivienne left shortly after the attack on the Vampire Ælves, realising that they could no longer serve him.

'Tuâth never forgave himself for what he had done and neither did Thomn. That is why he was so eager to leave Maldahl to search for you. It was a blessing that he retains no memory of his bloody attack. He suffered and he repented, as did your father.'

'And Ardahl, did he repent?'

'Kirsten, you have to understand that after Ichnaarim was destroyed; the dragons were loathed and hunted. You seem to have a rather romantic view of what are, in their very nature, killers.'

'No more than *we*, Gailon,' she said haughtily. 'They and the Clan of the Dark Moon have as much right to exist in Maldahl as we, and to seek their destruction only aided Katahl. How he must be laughing at us when, over the countless years, *we* have destroyed more of his enemies than he.'

Kirsten turned, joining the others as they traipsed into the heart of the forest.

'You ignorant girl!' Gailon called after her.

She stopped, yet did not turn. She could feel the eyes of the company watching the scene with embarrassed curiosity.

'You remember nothing of your life here,' Gailon continued. 'You know nothing of past events other than what has been told to you. The entire realm is now a barren wasteland to what it was before Katahl's army first rode forth.

'He destroyed the Garamen of the mountains, whose fierce tribal warriors stood alone against him; he killed the Ryeka who were nothing more than peaceful river dwellers; the Daleena, whose population span along the floor of the Freya Valley; the winged race of Ptee Sta, who dwelt in trees between Ealdorbold and the mountains; the Balota, who built wooden houses and platforms across the marshes; the Iyes, great bowman living in a forest that is also no more since Katahl's Trolgs hacked and burnt it to the ground. He fished for the Mo-rye until they were no more; he slaughtered the people of Starigorat, most notably their king, Kryepast, protector of the great fortress;

the King of Starigorat being his own father, whose decapitated head he used as a banner for his bloodthirsty campaign. He brought Golstur to its knees begging for mercy, and he showed none.'

Kirsten walked away, horrified by what Gailon had said. Her body trembled as the wizard paced after her and pulled her roughly about to face him.

'Not all were killed. Many were kept on as slaves. He breeds and experiments on them. And do you know one of the uses he finds for them, Your Highness, who seems to think her betrothed 'not so bad'?'

Kirsten wrenched her arm free, tears stinging her angry eyes. 'HE EATS THEM!' she screamed at him, and ran off into the darkness beneath the trees.

Thirty

The sun rose red over the city of Bashnya and the crystal towers looked like two pinnacles of flame as they greeted the dawn. Richard pulled on the armour that had been given to him and went down to join the Mariners in the piazza. Fahl greeted him, eyeing his fish mail armour with quiet satisfaction.

'The armour you wear was made by the Mo-rye who are alas no more,' he explained. 'It is ancient and very strong. It was entrusted to us long ago, and we have kept it safe. Now, it will serve its purpose in the war against Katahl. Wear it with pride, Richard, for there is no other like it, nor shall be again.'

Richard nodded slowly, overwhelmed by his situation. He sheathed his sword and placed the intricately shaped helmet over his head, resembling some sea creature of the elder days.

The Mariners packed many carts with odd-looking weapons, carts that each had a driver, yet no horse. As they began their procession toward the gate, Richard walked beside Fahl and Walker, wondering how long it would take them to reach Golstur.

At the city gate, Fahl stopped and turned to face the following crowd.

'My friends,' he said, his voice loud and clear, seemed to carry on the mild sea breeze. 'We have dwelt together these many long years. Now the time of parting has come at last. Those of you who wish to fight with us are most welcome, but we know you all too well to think that you would leave your home. We do not reproach you for this, for had it not been for your forefathers' kindness in sailing us out to sea when Katahl attacked Dokee-Gavan, we would have perished. Your ancestors and we watched from the ships, as the town fell and we in our turn helped to rebuild and fortify this city. May Bashnya and its people be forever blessed.'

Fahl smiled, entering the world outside from what had become his haven; it seemed to Richard that the world seemed darker, as they passed over the threshold of the majick city. He walked as if in a dream besides the mysterious giants, thinking about facing Trolgs once more and hoping that he would fare better than the last time he had encountered them.

It was past noon when Fahl ordered a stop, and Richard sat on the sandy ground waiting eagerly for refreshments. He turned to look at the army and startled himself to his feet, unable to believe his eyes.

'Wwhere are they?' he stammered.

'Who?' Fahl said, handing him a draught of clear water.

'THE ARMY, all the mariners,' Richard choked, his knees suddenly weak.

'Did you not hear my speech?' Fahl asked disapprovingly. 'The mariners are fishermen, not warriors. I would not force them to come.'

'B,but your people … the wizards, where are they?'

He looked about him and counted eleven and Walker.

'We are all that remains, though we were never many. Fear not, Richard. It will be enough.'

But Richard *did* fear. He had no desire to die so far away from home. He wanted an *army* behind him, not a group of ancient wizards who had never done battle in all their long lives. He sat drinking the cool water, his hands trembling with shock.

'Richard, if you knew how powerful they are, then you would not doubt as you do now,' Walker said. He seemed more transparent under the bright sunlight.

'In Ánweald, my mistress and I fought Trolgs,' Richard explained. 'I was almost killed, but she brought me back from the brink of death. I have been living on borrowed time and I fear that if there are to be but twelve against those savages, then my time is over. We will *all* perish.'

'Enough,' Fahl said, in a commanding tone. 'Let us march again. We cannot break long if we are to reach the Elfin Woods in two days as planned.'

Richard's goblet disappeared from his hand and flipping his visor down, he rejoined the march.

Kirsten ran on, not hearing the cries behind her. She wanted to be away from them all. The blood thumped in her ears as she remembered the dining table of Katahl and the soulless eyes of his slaves. She had managed to free herself she realised, and yet abandoned them. Her brooding took her to darker realisations when she considered, that by her philosophy, the Trolgs had as much right to exist as she.

'And is that not so?'

The voice seemed to penetrate every pore and the light that suddenly surrounded her, burned; yet, the sensation was not unpleasant.

Cröedaw's keen eyes saw her through the trees and let the companions know that they were gaining on her. However, as they reached Kirsten, she vanished and despite their search, no trace of her could be found.

As Kirsten's sight adjusted, she recognised the Sky Kingdom of Anarkhane and sought the source of the voice she had heard.

'They should be wiped out!' she said indignantly.

'And who are you, daughter, to say whether a race should live or die?'

'I am to be queen!' she snapped, feeling annoyed rather than awed at the abduction.

'Just as your father was king. So, it is your view, therefore, that your rank in society gives you the right to obliterate an entire race of beings if you so wish it.'

Kirsten was confused. The very air in Sky Kingdom mellowed her anger and she fought to reason on what was suddenly so unimportant.

'No,' she said. 'They should be killed because they are ruthless killers without mercy.'

'Rather like yourself it would seem, Exzalander.'

'NO!' Kirsten protested, but all the same, she saw wisdom in the Anarkhane's words.

'It is *your* hate and fear of them that leads you to believe that they should be destroyed, just as it is people's prejudice and fear that drove them to attack Taiohăhn's children and fÿrdracan. Perhaps the Trolgs *should* be slaughtered, perhaps they should never been allowed to exist at all. But are you yet wise enough to make such a presumption? Be careful daughter, lest you become that which you seek to destroy.

'Your task is drawing ever nearer. You must not lose the few allies that you have.'

Kirsten mused over Anarkhane's use of the word daughter, and she supposed herself to be very like a child, as she had spent much time under the higher being's care and tutelage—even if she could not recall it.

'One more thing must I say to you, before you return. Beware your heart. You were joined with the children of Taiohăhn, as should not have been.

They are a passionate and promiscuous race. Do not be ruled by your feelings. Make no further declaration of love.

'You are a warrior—our champion. If you are at last to have the freedom to love, then it is on a path that I have not yet foreseen. You must be stone, therefore, lest strong men crumble who may have achieved greatness.

'Farewell daughter.'

A cold darkness closed in, and she found herself surrounded by familiar faces all of whose names were temporarily lost to her. She was immediately accosted with scores of questions and protestations. Shaking herself, she allowed the world about her to come back into focus again. Thaniel knelt beside her, his blue-green eyes, burning. She reached a hand to his cheek.

'Thaniel?' she ventured.

He nodded and she withdrew her hand, the words of Anarkhane returning to her like the sting of a wasp. Scrambling to her feet, she shook off Thaniel's attention, ignoring the hurt in his eyes.

'The war has started,' she informed them. 'We have been idle long enough. Now we must take Ealdorbold's army and strike down our enemy, lest he destroys us all.

'To Ealdorbold!'

Her voice had changed, as if the last remnants of Kirsten had been swept away on the night air as it had greeted her return to Maldahl. All who heard the command obeyed without question and they marched for many hours before she agreed to let them rest for what remained of the night.

As the others slept, she sat on a rock and stared up at the night sky, contemplating battle.

'May I speak with you, Milady?'

'You should be resting, Thaniel.'

'How can I sleep when my heart is so troubled?'

She turned to face him, her face stern and unyielding.

'You declared that you loved me,' he whispered. 'But now I fear that it is not so, and my heart is breaking. I have never known such feelings before and I beg you to alleviate my fears. Tell me I have been mistaken and consent to be mine.'

'You ask too much of me, Thaniel. Just because one feels a thing does not mean one should act upon it. I *do* love you, it is true, but both our feelings are irrelevant in this matter.'

'Irrelevant! How can you say such a thing? You are *everything* to me. Having declared your love, to now deprive me of it makes my life worthless.' His voice grew louder and Jeb stirred in his sleep.

She grasped him by the wrist and drew him away from the camp.

'Our primary concern is the defeat of Katahl,' she explained. 'If that is achieved then we can continue this conversation, but until such a time I will not see a great warrior struck down because his thoughts were not on battle.'

Thaniel grabbed the princess and drew her into him.

'Your Highness, I am struck down before I ever reach a battlefield. You should never have told me. How can you be so cruel as to deny me that which you offered?'

Her head bowed and she did not break his hold on her.

'Anarkhane has forbidden me to love you, Thaniel. She says that my heart is not to be trusted and that you will perish should I persist in this affair.'

'I will die *without* you.'

She pulled away, hardened suddenly. 'Do not be so melodramatic!' she said.

He seized her again and she struggled against him.

'How has Anarkhane got the right to tell us how to lead our lives?' he said. 'Of course She wants you to concentrate on defeating Katahl. She wants to regain power. All other concerns are secondary to Her. I refuse to be ruled by Her, and you are a *fool* if you listen to Her.'

'Let me go.'

She struggled and he tightened his grip, pulling her closer.

'I have no wish to hurt you, Thaniel, now let me go!'

'No.'

He pressed his lips against hers and she fought hopelessly, before summoning her strength and throwing him back several metres causing him to hit a tree. He lay slumped on the ground and she raced over to him.

'Thaniel?'

As his eyes eased themselves open, he groaned.

'I'm sorry,' she said, 'but you left me no choice.'

'And you leave me none, Milady.'

He threw his body weight onto hers and she toppled backward, where he pinned her, his lips closing in on hers.

'Thaniel, do you not care of the consequences? I do not want to see you killed because love has weakened your fighting spirit. Why will you not see sen ...'

He stopped her mouth with another kiss, and this time her efforts to push him away were half-hearted and then abandoned altogether. The words of Anarkhane melted in the heat of their passion and she returned his kisses violently, as she unbuckled his belt.

She woke as the sun began to rise, her body still tingling from her night's lovemaking. Stroking Thaniel's naked body, she smiled as his glazed eyes opened to greet the coming dawn. Leaning over, she kissed him on the mouth and his whole body responded to her touch. Within a matter of seconds, he was inside her again.

'We have to get back to the camp before they wake,' she sighed, as he moved in and out.

'I want you,' he murmured. His thrusts grew more desperate until her hips moved with his and her hands gripped his back, eager for one last climax before their return.

It was not until they had dressed that she noticed the change in him. He seemed slovenly and slow. His eyes, which at first, she had thought to be showing signs of fatigue, were so glassy that she could clearly see her face in them. His hands did not leave her and eventually she wrenched herself free.

'Come on, Thaniel! We have to get back.'

He followed in silence, yet continued to try to put his hands upon her. As they reached the camp, she suddenly turned.

'Stop that! Do you want everyone to know?'

'I want you,' he said dreamily.

Kirsten grabbed him by the shoulders, shaking him.

'What's the matter with you?' she hissed.

It struck her then that it was not Thaniel who stared back at her; it was an empty shell. His fire and life seemed to have been drained away and all that remained was his desire for her. She slapped him hard, her fear mounting. He gave no reaction and made a clumsy grab for her clothing.

'What have I done?' she whispered.

She heard a twig snap and sensed that Gailon stood behind her.

'THANIEL!' he said, in a commanding voice.

She felt Thaniel's hands drop from her person. A light from the old man's staff placed him into a trance and Kirsten backed away, her eyes meeting the wizard. Tears welled up and she threw herself at Gailon, clutching at him.

'What have I done, Gailon? What have I done?'

He gently patted her back, attempting to calm her.

'Hush my child. Crying will not bring him back. Now listen. I have placed everyone under a sleeping spell and that will give us time to sort this out. No-one need ever know.'

She pulled herself away and wiped her eyes. 'But Gailon, how did *you* know?'

'Cob saw you. He informed me a moment ago. I had suspected that Vampire Ælf blood now flows through your veins and held little hope that he would not be put under your spell.'

'Anarkhane warned me, but I did not know that *this* would happen. What can be done for him?'

Gailon averted his gaze, as if he knew what he was about to say would be painful. 'The spell can be broken if you remove from his memory, his love for you, along with all memory of last night's events.'

'But then he will no longer love me. What we shared he …'

'It is the only way if you wish to save him.'

Kirsten's legs gave way beneath her and she collapsed to the ground, shaking. The intimate moments that they had shared burned into her mind and she cried bitterly.

'Will he ever be able to love me, Gailon?'

The old wizard rested a hand on her shoulder and squeezed it gently.

'That, I do not know.'

She closed her eyes and tears ran down her cheeks as she concluded that what they had shared, he would never know, and most bitter of all was that he would not love her. Clambering to her feet, she placed a hand upon him, and with one simple thought, she took it all away, wishing that she could be so kind to herself, yet knowing the risk of repeating such a mistake was too high.

Thaniel blinked and she realised that Gailon had released him.

'Kirsten, are you quite well?' he asked.

She nodded back at him, unable to smile; her heart was breaking. Unable to issue a reply, she walked back to the camp where her companions were waking.

Thirty-One

Caitul stood upon the wall of Ishtar and gazed out to welcome the dawn. He felt cold, even as the sun's first rays shone across his face. He was always cold now; Katahl's spell gripped ever tighter. Part of him wanted the spell to take hold more quickly, so that he might forget his regret and despair. He tried to recall why he had sworn fealty to the house of Starigorat and found that his memory was hazy. The only clear recollection he had was the day that he had first met the princess. Arrayed in emerald green, her red hair had been piled up, secured with emerald pins. It was like yesterday in his mind. He ached as he thought of her beauty and wondered, as he had often done so, if he had but met her first, if he might have been the man to win her heart. But he considered how the prophecy would have still come to pass and they would have been parted; he would have made the same mistake that his friend had done.

As the sun rose higher, he pulled down his visor; bright light had begun to pain him of late. He bit his lip, remembering his search for her on Earth and how the simple protection spell his lord had cast, aided him in evading the hostiles, but what none of them knew was how he had recognised her ...

Anarkhane plucked him from the darkness, strengthened Katahl's protection spell and for the duration of his search, no man of Earth could harm him. She introduced him to part of Exzalander's soul, allowing him to track her like a bloodhound on the scent.

However, trying to follow Exzalander on Earth had proved problematic. For the most part, he had been non-corporal; Anarkhane had clung to him, fearful that he would be lost to those she called Milesians. Mad She seemed at times, taking to wailing to Herself and reliving some terrible event from Her past, over and over.

He was fearful, for without being able to take hold of Exzalander, he would be unable to return her home. However, his fears were unfounded; Exzalander acted like a beacon to him, drawing him closer and then anchoring him. He was able to touch her; physical contact with the hostiles had been sporadic and he had taken to occupying their bodies in order to gain better access to her.

Such power was lost to him the moment he left Earth behind. He was glad. It had not been a pleasurable feeling having no physical self, and even less so having to share form with another. Such a thing was unnatural...

As Caitul's mind drifted back to Exzalander, he recalled the touch of her lips and her pleading eyes as she had begged for his aid, and he winced with shame for what he had done—left her prisoner to an insane dictator.

His thoughts became tortured between the admission that he should have rescued her, but to do so would mean breaking his oath, which as a man of honour he could not do. He questioned whether it was honour or fear that had made him turn his back on her. To break his oath would mean losing his soul forever. He had a unique perspective on such things, having experienced a fracturing of self. He was unsure if he could face it again, especially knowing that endless torture would be his reward.

He climbed down from the wall and approached the gatehouse. Once Katahl's spell took full effect, he would be lost anyhow.

I should not have abandoned her, he decided, and it was as though he had finally accepted the horrors that would await him.

Inside the gatehouse, the bloodied form of the horse-seller was tied to a chair. The talisman Exzalander had given him lay on the table before him.

How long can I keep it a secret? Caitul thought. *The Wren has seen it; he interrogated the horse-seller quite effectively and informed me of all that he suspected.* The weasel-faced man had relished his discovery and thought of reward from his master.

The horse-seller groaned and his battered head rolled to one side.

'Leave us!' Caitul ordered.

The Wren bowed low, and picking up his long knife, he slipped out of the tiny room. Caitul removed his helmet and bent over the man, his hazel eyes piercing.

'Did you know what it was when she gave it to you?'

The man did not answer, but his bruised eyes rolled upward.

'No, I suppose not,' concluded Caitul. 'You are charged with conspiring against the overlord Katahl. What say you?'

The man's battered face grinned an almost toothless smile. 'I accepted payment for my wares. I did not know Katahl had a law against commerce. If that scared rabbit is who the great ones sent to defeat your master, then I say that we are all doomed.' He breathed heavily, gasping as his broken ribs pained him to speak. 'Still, I would rather follow *her* than that maniacal master of yours any day. So I plead guilty to your charges.'

He spat frothy scarlet blood at Caitul, his wheezing stopped with a loud rasp and he slumped forward, dead. Caitul picked up the talisman and his helmet, walking fiercely from the gatehouse. The Wren, who had waited for him at the door, followed swiftly at his heels.

'Did you kill him?'

Caitul stopped suddenly, the weasel face man almost bumping into him.

'I must report to my master. Take as many Trolgs as you need. Guard the gate, but speak of nothing of what you have learned—to anyone. This news is for Katahl's ears alone and he will flay you while you are yet living if you spread rumour of such things. Do you understand?'

The Wren bowed low. 'I am Katahl's faithful servant, always.'

Caitul nodded stiffly, hiding his loathing for the little man. 'Fetch my horse then,' he said.

The dark knight watched with impatience as the man in green tightened his stirrups then gave him an oily smile. He mounted and rode through the gate without a word, hoping never to see the Wren or Ishtar ever again.

Kirsten kept her distance from her companions during the rest of their ride back to Ealdorbold. Her heart was heavy with regret and loss. It was as though Thaniel had died and the feelings she felt were indeed that of grief—grief that she could not express because nobody could know what had occurred.

Thaniel spoke to Cröedaw mostly throughout the day, seeming oblivious to her and her pain.

'Milady?'

She looked across and tried to smile at Ioan, as his large eyes filled with concern.

'What has happened? Why do we return to the palace when we are all under sentence of death?'

Kirsten's eyes faced forward to the path ahead and her mind spoke her reply.

'I will not let anything happen to you, Ioan. You must trust me. But I need the army that was promised me.'

Gailon's ears pricked up, waiting for the answer then suspicious that she had answered through thought.

'But the Council will not simply hand over control of their army,' Ioan said. 'Not now that we are outlaws.'

'They will have no choice in the matter.'

She spoke with such a sense of finality that it unnerved the company, and Counsellor Jaden stopped as if stricken by that which she had *not* said.

'Report!' Genargh barked at the young guard.

'No sign of them, Counsellor Genargh. All troops sent after them are now missing. May we have your permission to stop further searches, Sir? We've lost five men already.'

Genargh cheeks reddened.

'Request granted,' croaked Daihron. 'But leave two men posted at the entrance.'

The guard bowed. 'High Counsellor,' he said and left abruptly, glad to be away from the remaining ten members of the Council who seemed more terrifying in their growing anticipation.

'AAAaarrgghhh this is not to be borne,' Genargh growled in frustration, knocking over half a goblet of wine. 'How can we just sit here while those traitors roam free within these very walls?'

Daihron struggled to his feet, seeming much aged. 'I do not think we need worry about that. Gailon would not have led them into the catacombs without knowing a way out. They are gone, I am certain of it.'

'Then they could be anywhere,' Jonah huffed.

'Perhaps,' Borin said, 'but I would imagine that their escape would take them beyond the palace walls.'

'Then we should send troops into Ánweald and hunt them down like the vermin they are,' raged Callarn.

'We are under siege, gentlemen, or had you forgotten that?' Vahrn said. 'Would you have us break our defence? If they are gone, then we need not worry. Let us look to ourselves.'

'But what of the refugees from the cities? Should we not throw them out?'

'Valid point, Torhn. Every supply that we have is precious, and it was that *witch* who allowed them in, not us. They should be sent back to their homes.'

Whil stood suddenly, holding the opening of his overcoat. 'Counsellor Ryan, what you suggest is nothing short of murder. Katahl's army would execute them all. Do we not have a responsibility to protect them? Ishtar is officially governed by ourselves, is it not?'

Ryan laughed harshly. 'Counsellors, I had believed Jaden to have left us, but behold, here he speaks through his successor.'

There was a general laugh and Whil sat down again, his eyes fixed firmly on the floor.

'I agree with Whil,' Tristen said. 'They are all now within the walls; we cannot force them out again, therefore let them be put them to good use. All men capable of bearing arms, including the boys, should man the walls in payment for protection.'

Daihron nodded his head and asked them to vote.

'That is settled then. They stay. Now gentlemen, let us bury Gohrn.'

As the company reached Haesburg, Kirsten reined in her horse.

'Wait here,' she ordered. 'This should not take long.'

They protested in unison and she dismounted, removing excess baggage.

'I cannot afford to have you harmed,' she explained. 'It will be safer for all of us if you remain.'

'Are you sure that is the reason, Lady Kirsten?' Jaden asked. 'Or could it be that you wish us to wait here because you do not want us to see what you are about to do?'

Kirsten raised an eyebrow at the renegade counsellor and smiled slyly.

'Perhaps,' she said. 'Now stay here.'

Thaniel spoke to her for the first time since breakfast.

'You cannot order us to remain. You are not our queen, remember?'

She mounted Ravenwing again and kicked him into action. 'Things change, Thaniel,' she called back over her shoulder, as she sped away.

The companions exchanged glances and after a moment of stunned silence, ran after her.

She barely heard the shouts from the walls at her return. The gates opened, despite the guards' efforts to keep them closed. She was as much a part of the palace as its bricks and mortar and so when she commanded the gates to open, they obeyed.

Makeshift tents for the refugees filled the courtyard and obstructed the guards who rushed to meet her. She rode past the tents and on toward the gardens, the palace guard calling after her to halt.

Despite his charge, Ravenwing moved silently toward the funeral party, so they had little warning at her approach.

'You!' Genargh hissed.

'What's this my Lords, a burial for that treacherous snake?'

'Gohrn was a true and loyal member of this Council,' Vahrn's reedy voice piped back at her.'

'SILENCE!' she bellowed.

Her voice echoed about the palace grounds, and time seemed to slow. The guards, having followed her, lowered their weapons, watched and did nothing. They were under her spell, in awe of the warrior in their midst and as the spell worked its majick, they each envisioned themselves doing great deeds on the battlefield under her bloody banner. Their eyes blazed, suddenly hateful of the Council, having kept them from her side.

She raised her hands, muttering soundlessly and the body of Gohrn burst into flame.

'I only wish he were still living to receive this,' she said. 'His death should have been slow and painful. Daihron, you promised me the use of your soldiers. I am going to face the army at Ishtar. Will you stand by your word?'

The old man's eyes fixed upon her and if he was afraid then he did not show it.

'You are charged with treason and are to be imprisoned to await our judgement.'

Her eyes narrowed as she held his gaze.

'Your time is over, old man. Genargh, what say you?'

As she averted her eyes to meet Genargh, High Counsellor Daihron collapsed—dead. The Counsellors' fears grew verbal and many backed away from the old man, as if his sudden death might be catching.

'Y,you killed him!' Genargh spluttered.

'Wrong answer,' she said coldly.

The ground erupted beneath Genargh and roots of trees, long since cut down, wound their way up the man's terrified body and began to drag him beneath the ground. The screams were deafening and several of the Council clapped their hands over their ears. Kirsten waved a hand and the torture stopped; Genargh was buried past the waist, whimpering loudly.

'Borin, I believe that you are the next person to ask,' she said.

'But Borin's mouth did not speak. He stared at the half buried counsellor and fell to his knees.

'Enough!' Counsellor Whil stepped forward, his voice wavering slightly. 'Take the army if you must, but stop this. We know you to be a kindly and just woman. Do you think that this is the proper way to request our aid?'

Kirsten dismounted and drew the Sword of Taiohãhn, holding it to the young man's throat.

'Brave words, Whil, but I have no time for niceties. I tried that and you placed me in prison. Now, while Trolgs destroy my people, you sit and hide, doing *nothing*! Now, there are nine of you. I want a re-vote on whether I should claim my birthright and this time there will no non-decision.'

Whil stared along the blade held to his throat and into the green eyes of the princess.

'But you are making us vote under threat of force,' he protested. 'If we do not relinquish power, then you will kill us.'

The smile that met his words was unnerving, so much so, that he felt no relief even as she placed the sword back into its scabbard.

'I never made any such threat, Whil.' she said. 'You will not know if that is true until *after* you vote.'

'I, I, I wish to announce my resignation from the Council,' squeaked Borin. A strong smell of urine wafted over from his direction.

'Go!' commanded Kirsten.

Scrambling to his feet, he fled.

'Eight of you left. Interesting … I do hope, Counsellor Whil, that you reconsider your last vote. I was most disappointed when I heard that you had stabbed me in the back.'

'What I did, I did for the good of the people,' he said.

'Really! And what is the good of the people, Whil? To sit here and starve as our allies fall, and the chance of defeating Katahl withers into defeat. Now, I will leave you to cast your votes.'

She led Ravenwing away and walked among the Shénnin Guard, who let her through, following silently back to the courtyard.

'People of Maldahl,' she called. 'The time for hiding is through. I march to purge the land of Katahl's vermin. I shall make them rue the day that they dared to set forth from Brëgwela. Those of you who wish to share in this glorious campaign must now fetch supplies. Arm yourselves, for Exzalander rides forth today!'

Her voice was heard in every part of the palace, and those who heard it were filled with joy; they cheered, knowing that their departure could not come soon enough to quench their bloodlust.

The palace had never seemed so alive; people ran to fetch packs and weapons, food and water. As the party entered the great gates, they could feel the change; the very air teemed with excitement. Soldiers, refugees and even members of the court dashed about in preparation, but Gailon saw no sign of the Council or Exzalander.

Food was offered to the newcomers and they sat beside a campfire enquiring as to what had happened.

'It is marvellous indeed. Princess Exzalander has returned and has demanded that the Council hand over power to her. We have been called to arms.'

Gailon put down his mug of ale. 'I must to the Council chamber,' he said urgently.

'Oh they are not there,' the young girl said, with a smile. 'What's left of 'em are in the gardens, that way.' She pointed and bit into her apple.

As the company stood, they saw the Council approach. Whil nodded in greeting.

'Gailon,' he said sheepishly.

Tom toyed with his great double-edged sword, his brow knitting tightly together. 'What's this? No attempt to arrest us? None of you want to call for the guards?'

Whil shook his head. 'No Thomn-the-Cleaverhand, your fate lies in our hands no longer.'

The Council members retreated to the palace, all except for Whil.

'Have you seen the Princess? I have to give her the outcome of our vote.'

Kirsten smiled as she entered Ardahl's Tower; a thin layer of dust had begun to cover everything once again. Breathing deeply, she raised her arms and the room glowed as she soaked up the majick contained there, like water to a sponge. When she opened her eyes once more, the room looked grey and lifeless, each and every object having been drained of its knowledge. Walking to the desk, she opened the book that lay there, catching a glimpse of its empty pages, before it crumbled in her hand. She closed her eyes once more and in an instant, joined her companions in the courtyard.

'Milady!' squeaked Ioan in surprise, as she appeared before them.

Gailon who was looking up at the tower, spun about to confront her.

'What have you done?' he demanded.

'I have made use of the power of Ardahl that lingered.'

'You had no right to take it! The power is Ardahl's!'

'He is dead, Gailon; he does not need it any longer. You would rather that I had let it go to waste?'

Gailon backed away from her, seeming horrified.

'What has happened to you?' he said. 'Do you not see how what you have done is wrong?'

'I am fighting a war,' she replied. 'I am sorry if I am not the innocent little princess that you wanted me to be. I am a warrior and I fight to win, by whatever means necessary.'

Gailon shook his head, his face seeming as ashen as the contents of the tower had been. 'Then how are you any different from Katahl?' he murmured and walked away.

A surge of anger rose within her and an urge to strike him down. Whil distracted her as he knelt before her, taking her hand and kissing it.

'The vote was unanimous,' he said. 'Long live the Queen!'

Kirsten gave a slow smile and all, but her companions, cheered at the news.

Thirty-Two

It was evening before they were ready to depart. Refugees from Golstur and Ishtar joined the soldiers of Ealdorbold, including the elite Shénnin Guard; only a small garrison was to be left to defend the palace. Gailon sat in silence since his frightening revelation, pouring over the book of CODM.

Jaden had gone to the armoury with the intent of going into battle, but on his return the queen informed him that he was to govern in her stead while she went to war. She formerly shook his hand and passed his law of Habeas Corpus. The deed, observed by her companions, gave hope to some that she was herself again. However, there was a coldness to her actions, as if she felt the burden of responsibility too keenly.

As the company gathered at the open gate, former Counsellor Whil approached in full armour and bowed to his queen.

'Your Majesty,' he said humbly, 'permission to join the company?'

Her face did not soften as she ordered him to fall in line. She walked regally over to Gailon, her silver dress shifting like fishes mail followed by the dark of Jared's shadow cloak.

'Gailon, it is time.'

The old man looked up wearily. 'I am not going,' he said. 'You have no need of me. Here, take the book of CODM; it should contain one of the stones. I thought it would be encrusted in the bind, but I have found no sign of it. You, with all you power should have no trouble in locating it, I am sure.'

He held the book to her and instinctively she drew away from it. Gailon's eyebrows arched at her reaction.

'Keep it for me still a while,' she said. 'We *do* have need of you. I want you to protect the others. I must concentrate on the battle at hand, but I cannot do so if I am affeared that they may be harmed. I want you to look after them.'

Gailon sat in silence, confused by her words.

'I know that you hold a low opinion of *me*, but I am asking you not to help me, but your friends. I am going to give you the power that is yours by right. You were Ardahl's successor and so it is only fitting that his majick now pass to you.'

Gailon looked up, his eyes wide and his mouth opened, but she gave him no opportunity to object. A surge of power hit him with such force that he was thrown backward. Thaniel, who had been watching, broke away from the column and drew his sword; he had heard the previous discord between his friends, and hoped that Gailon had been mistaken.

Kirsten felt the tip of a sword in the small of her back and caught his familiar scent.

'I have not harmed him, Thaniel. You may put away your sword.'

Gailon sat up, shaking his head as if waking from a long dream. All weariness had fallen from him, as had countless years. His white hair was now brown flecked with grey, and his blue eyes were sharp and angry.

'Gailon!' Thaniel exclaimed, but could bring himself to say no more.

The wizard sprung to his feet with youthful agility and drew his sword, which usually hung dormant at his side.

'This time you have gone too far, *Your Majesty.*' He circled her, swinging his sword before him.

The column began to break and crowd around to watch the oncoming conflict.

'I have no desire to fight you, Gailon,' the queen said.

He grinned savagely and thrust the point of his blade with precision within an inch of her flesh. 'Draw your weapon, wench!' he demanded, and there sounded a general discord at his words throughout the crowd of onlookers.

She drew the Sword of Taiohãhn and threw it upon the ground.

'PICK IT UP!' he screamed at her.

She retreated, but he ran at her taking another swing, forcing her to roll out of the way.

'Stop playing with me, girl! Pick it up and let us end this!'

She put up her hands. 'I am not playing, Gailon. Please think of what you are doing. You feel disorientated after ...'

'How *dare* you! You think that you have the right to violate me like that. You think that you can do whatever you want and not have to pay the price.'

'Violate? What are you talking about Gailon? I just ...'

'SHUT UP!' he screamed. 'You had no right! You are *so* powerful now that you seek to control and change others if they are not to your liking. You disturb the natural order of things. Is this not the true essence of evil?'

'What?' She backed away. 'How can you say that? You … you're a wizard; your very business is to change the natural order of things!'

'Not like you, I am not much more than a healer. You, you can kill with a thought. Yes, I know what you did to Daihron. So you see this pathetic gesture of surrendering your sword does not impress me in the least.'

Gailon flicked the Sword of Taiohãhn upward with the edge of his foot and caught it, discarding his own blade. At his touch, the cover that Ardahl had created to disguise the blade, fell to the ground and Gailon turned the sword in his hand.

'I expect that you make Taiohãhn proud,' he said, with a growl.

'That is enough,' Thaniel said, as he strode between them, ' I do not know what you hope to achieve by this display, but it ends now. Gailon give Her Majesty back her blade and let us ride out as *friends* into battle.'

Gailon was not listening. He stared into the heart of the largest piece of the broken Anarkhane stone and sank to his knees, trembling.

'NO!' Kirsten shouted, realising the danger. With a swift movement, she ordered the sword back to her hand, leaving Gailon falling forward as it flew to its mistress. The blade tingled in her hand and she sheaved it at once, perceiving the stone's excitement at having been held so near to one of its broken counterparts.

Thaniel helped Gailon to his feet and saw that he was weeping. Kirsten held his gaze for a moment, wanting to say something, but lost for the right words. Turning suddenly, she strode away and with a single command, the column reformed and they rode forth to face the army at Ishtar.

Kirsten avoided her companions, choosing to ride beside the ranks. She felt a pang of guilt at what she had done to Gailon. She had not asked him before imbuing him with Ardahl's power, just as nobody had asked her before giving her the powers that she possessed, she figured. *I'm queen now; I thought that would make him happy,* she thought. *It's all happening too quickly, what does he expect of me? What do any of them expect?*

'Milady?'

She broke away reluctantly from her brooding and saw Tom staring at her from his charger.

'May we set up camp for the night? There is little daylight remaining.'

'Yes Tom.' She gazed up at the rosy sky, frowning. 'Yes, let us rest.'

Thomn-the-Cleaverhand called out and his message was shouted down the line in both directions.

'Tom?' Kirsten said, before he had the chance to ride away. 'Do you ever miss it? Being a police inspector I mean, living on Earth?'

'No. Not any more,' he replied. 'In fact this is the first time I have even thought about that life since ... since the night you conjured us up fish and chips. Do you remember?'

She nodded, smiling sadly; it seemed so long ago to her. So much had happened since then. Now, no trace of childhood or innocence remained to her. She was forever stained.

'Do *you* miss it?' Tom asked.

She halted her horse and looked about her with a melancholy air. 'I miss the years that I never had,' she said.

Kicking Ravenwing, she trotted ahead, leaving the old Captain to ponder what she had meant.

'How fairs she?' Cröedaw asked, as he appeared from the shadows.

'I am unsure; she seems burdened by responsibility and there is a sadness about her that I cannot account for. It makes no sense.'

'Yes it does, Thomn. I fear that it makes perfect sense,' murmured the Elfin.

Kirsten washed and dressed in her black leather, feeling the need to appear less conspicuous. Neatly folding the silver dress, which Bydand had gifted her, she packed it in Ravenwing's saddlebag. She moved like a shadow among the soldiers, at first listening to their talk, but eventually drawn to the night noises of the surrounding forest. She suspected that it was her CODM blood which made her shun crowds and crave the cool night beyond the campfires.

'Milady, you are not well and it grieves me to see you in so much pain.'

Cröedaw was invisible to human eyes in the darkness, but she saw him as plain as if it had been day.

'You are mistaken, Cröedaw,' she said. 'How can Katahl's likeness be in pain? Pain is for the weak.'

'I do not know what happened to you when you were a prisoner in Katahl's fortress. I do know that it must have been terrible. It is understandable that you would have suffered some changes after such an ordeal'

Kirsten walked further into the forest and sat beneath a silver barked tree.

'I was no prisoner, Cröedaw; surely you realised that. You were there in the swamp, I remember; you *saw* me; I was a soldier. I was one of many sent to march on Ishtar to fight *for* him. If the children of Anarkhane had not attacked then I may never have broken free. I was lost you see; I *had* to lose myself to avoid detection and stay alive.

'The first rape was the worst. I wanted to use my majick to destroy them all, but I knew that if I did, then Katahl would know instantly who I was, so I endured attack after attack and it got easier because I shut myself down and left only the warrior.

'The trouble is, I became so good at losing myself that I'm not sure all of me returned.' She smiled bitterly. 'Perhaps part of me is still running free and happy. It's a comfort to me to think that.'

Cröedaw sat beside her, his keen eyes holding hers. His eyes were so birdlike in the darkness that she wondered how she had not realised from the start that he was the crow who had befriended her.

'You should not take Gailon's words too much to heart. He was angry with you; you behaved wrongly, but he is angrier with himself. He blames himself for your capture, and despises himself for not fighting the Council's decision to break from you.

'You see him as a guide, your teacher; you do not know what happened to make it so? Ardahl knew that there was a danger in the spell he performed and so he created what he said was his final measure. He did not know how long you would be gone and he wanted to ensure that there was someone who would remember what had to be done. He cast a spell on Gailon, without his prior knowledge, which would delay his death until he had achieved the task set out for him. That task being to guide and protect you in your quest to retake what is yours and throw down your enemy. Once this is completed, the spell will be lifted and Gailon will be able to die. Gailon was furious with his master for casting such a spell. He had been given no choice; he has continued to age, but has not passed over. Many think that it is *he* who is responsible, but a few of us know better.

'Humans are not made to endure so long. There comes a time when they grow so weary that they welcome their release. What I am trying to say to you is that Gailon is angry with you, yes; you did violate him in a similar fashion to Ardahl, but also you have taken centuries off his age. Just when it seemed possible to him that his end might be near, you have condemned him to remain. Who knows what effect Ardahl's majick will have; he may have endure for centuries. He longed to find the peace that was stolen by the very man whose powers you have forced upon him.'

Kirsten put her head in her hands, not wanting to hear any more. 'How could I have been so selfish, so blind?' She sighed. 'I just wanted this all to be over, for the pain and confusion to stop, and now …'

'I know what happened between you and Thaniel.'

Kirsten returned from her wallowing with a snap. 'What do you mean?'

'Cob told me what occurred last night. I am sorry. I blame myself. I should have warned you.'

Kirsten got to her feet and Cröedaw followed.

'Why would you have reason to warn me?'

'Because I know how you felt about each other. I have always known, before either of you realised yourselves even; it is a gift of my people that I suppose humans do not possess. If I had thought for one moment that he would have acted on his desire then … forgive me.'

The pain she had been repressing burst forth once more and she wept, clinging to the Elfin for comfort. He held her firmly, waiting for the tide to ebb.

'Is there no way I can stop the spell?' she pleaded. 'Am I never to know love again?'

Cröedaw kissed her lightly on the forehead and held her close again.

'I am sorry, Exzalander,' he said. 'I know not enough of the clan's majicks to be of use to you. If the battle is won perhaps you could return to Tûlg and find your answers there.'

'Thank you, Cröedaw; you are a good friend.' She kissed him on the cheek and ran off toward the warmth of the camp, in search of Gailon.

'I am surprised to see you being so sentimental, Cröedaw, especially with a human female.'

'Thaniel! Where did you come from?'

'I was scouting, same as you.'

'Any signs of trouble?'

'Not unless you include my good Elfin friend's sudden intimacy with the Queen of Maldahl.'

'I was simply being a friend, Thaniel.'

'Friend? Interesting. It looked a little more than that when I arrived. Still, what you and Her Majesty get up to is your own affair and certainly no business of mine.' He turned to walk away.

'You are a fool, Thaniel! Your eyes are open and yet they do not see,' Cröedaw called after him, but he was gone.

Kirsten spotted the wizard as he sat alone by his fire on the far edge of the camp. He had his back to her and was hunched over so as Kirsten thought that he might have fallen asleep on his breast.

'What do you want now, woman?' he snapped, leaving the queen to wonder how he knew that it was her.

'I want to say that I'm sorry, Gailon. I know what I did to you was wrong and I have no excuse for my behaviour. I do not ask that you forgive me; I just wanted you to know that I am not so consumed with power that I have forgotten how to feel. I did not ask for any of this. I do not want the power or responsibility and I understand why you are so upset with me. All I can say is that when the time comes, I will release you from your burdens and set you free, if that is what you wish.'

Gailon said nothing. He stared into the flames, remembering the young woman who had sat in Ardahl's tower talking about her betrothed. She had come a long way since then he realised.

'You should take the book of CODM,' he said. 'Even with my new power I am unable to discern where the missing shard is hidden.'

Turning, he held the book to her and observed her pallor as the colour drained.

'I, I would rather that you persevered with you efforts, Gailon,' she struggled. 'I am sure that you will find the answers eventually.'

Gailon's eyebrows arched and as he held the book out to her, she backed away.

'What are you afraid of?' he asked.

'I do not know. I seem to remember that book, as if I had seen it before. I know it sounds strange, but it terrifies me.'

Gailon seemed amused rather than concerned by her reaction and he tossed the book toward her. She did not catch it, but jumped back in alarm, allowing it to crash to the ground at her feet. The pages flickered open and the images within seemed have a life of their own as they leapt from the page. Gailon moved nearer, intrigued by the new development; he saw briefly Troy, screaming in pain, before the pages turned once more.

The gem in the Sword of Taiohãhn began to glow and Kirsten fell to her knees, seeming too weak to retreat from the strange phenomenon. The light consumed her entire being and the gem in the pommel seemed to liquefy and grasp at her quivering body, working its way into her mouth and nostrils, gagging the scream that she wanted to voice, filling her with the strange green light.

Thaniel swung his sword back and forth in annoyance, the image of Exzalander with Cröedaw firmly fixed in his mind's eye. *I never expected that she could love me, but even less so that she would choose Cröedaw,* he thought. *Still, she is a female, and what man could ever fathom the workings of the female heart? It hurts though. When she was captured, the pain was almost unbearable; I realised then how much I love her. I would have been foolish to have presumed such a match, yet there were times when I could have sworn ... bah! I'm just a fool.*

He sheathed his grass-stained sword and went in search of Gailon. *He seems to be the only other person who finds Exzalander quite as frustrating as I,* he considered.

As he approached, he saw the queen doubled over, her eyes wide and mouth fixed open as though she had been petrified by the green glow about her.

'Exzalander!' he yelled, as he ran to her.

Gailon grabbed Thaniel and held him back.

'What are you doing to her, Gailon?' he demanded.

'Not me—The CODM Prophecy. I think we may finally be getting somewhere.'

There was a sound like rushing wind and a low pop and the queen was gone. The book of CODM slammed shut and could not be opened again.

There was a surge of heat and it felt as though Kirsten's bones were splitting. She could not see her surroundings, unaware that she was no longer in Maldahl. Her scream found its voice as the glow subsided and she collapsed to the floor, shaking.

As the pain lessened, her senses began to wake once more and she felt the cold marble beneath her. There was an unnatural silence that grew more eerie as she strained her ears to hear any of the company, a voice—anything.

Her eyes refused to open at first and she could do nothing, but lie still on the cold floor waiting for her body to begin functioning again.

She awoke several hours later and pulled the crisp sheet about her, longing to slumber a while longer. With a start, she remembered what had happened and sat bolt upright. The room in which she lay was bare, except for the bed and a strange side table that appeared to spring up out of the very rock beneath it. Walls, ceiling and floor were all made from white and green marble. She got to her feet and felt for her weapon belt, but it was gone.

Hurrying from the room, she ran down the corridor into the halls beyond. All was the same white and green marble, illuminated by an unseen light source.

'Hello,' she called. Her voice bouncing back at her was her only answer.

At length she came to a platform, opening out into trees that were as green as the veins of the marble within. She could see neither ground nor sky.

'Where am I?' she said to herself.

'It is well you are awake.'

The voice that spoke was male and too resonant to be human. Kirsten turned; the walk had gone and opened out into what appeared to be a throne room. It was a large square space, to the rear of which three steps of marble rose to seat a simple throne, cut from the same marble as seen throughout.

The man seated upon the throne, if man he was, was paler even than the Vampire Ælves had been. He wore an ornate leather jerkin and dark green leather trousers. His boots reached beyond the knees and bore the same crest as the simple silver circlet upon his brow. About his neck, a silver torc was shaped in to the likeness of two stags, one facing the other.

As Kirsten approached, she saw the Sword of Taiohãhn lying across his lap—*His* sword, it seemed clear now; it belonged to Him.

'Taiohãhn?' she ventured.

'Have you forgotten so soon, Exzalander? So little time has passed since last you were here.'

His eyes seemed black at first, but as she lost herself in His gaze, she came to realise that they were the deepest green; she felt like a child lost in a forest, and was unable to tear her gaze away.

'Take the blade, Exzalander. You have need of it still I deem.'

Kirsten did not take the sword from Him, but the weight of her weapon belt was suddenly felt about her waist as the sword was returned to her.

'Why come you to my palace?'

She opened her mouth to speak and felt the cool air touch her tongue and help shape her words. 'I seek the missing Anarkhane stones and am told that the book of CODM contained one of those lost.'

He said no words, but the corners of His mouth lifted into a curious smile that made her heart soar. Here surely sat a god of old; crippled He might have been in Maldahl, but here in His kingdom, He had lost none of His power. She felt the urge to fall to her knees and lower her eyes, yet she did neither; it was as though His will held her there, demanding that she did not waver.

'My Lord ...' Her voice felt nothing more than a strangled whisper, ugly and profane in comparison to the King before her.

'Calm yourself, Exzalander. Must we go through this every time you come to visit?'

He held up a slender hand and suddenly, she felt functional again.

'Walk with me.'

Taiohãhn offered His hand and she took it, trembling slightly. His touch was without warmth and reminded her of new leaves in spring. They walked from the hall along a balcony, which ran beside more of the giant trees and led out into the sea of leaves.

She breathed deeply, the fresh scent hauntingly familiar, yet she could not place it.

'It is a pity that you have no memory of this place. You had some happy times here.'

'I did?'

'Not at first of course. You hated me I think, for not sending you back to Katahl. But as time passed, you began to forget.'

'You mean I stopped loving him?'

'I thought you had. At least until the day you found the heart of my palace. You were so angry.'

'Why? What did I find?'

'Memories, dreams. You saw our first meeting and remembered it. When you were but five years of age, you found the book of my children that I had written as a means for you to travel to me. However, it was too soon and I sent you back. You saw what had been happening to your home and to Katahl; you took my sword and held it to my throat screaming at me. I tried to explain that I had not the power to prevent it, but you would not listen. You demanded to leave, even though your tutelage was not complete. I refused to aid you and thought that I had made you see sense, but you were ever crafty that way.

'Unbeknownst to me, you returned to the heart chamber and stole the shard of the creation gem that I kept there. When the portal opened, I realised too late that you had fled with the stone. I prevented your return to Maldahl, creating a tunnel of fire that separated body from soul; your physical form returned to me, grasping my sword. I can only think that you retained the shard, as I have no power over it, never having wrought a device to keep it bound.

'Your spirit missed Maldahl and remained lost. Anarkhane attempted to retrieve you, but could only confine part of your sprit; between the shard you bore and Anarkhane's power, your soul was wrenched apart. That which you managed to free, finally settled into a body. I watched as a mother died in grief, giving birth to her only child. You missed the woman, who was you intended host, but entered the child, screaming and still clutching the stone. Your mind was lost as your spirit adapted to the confines of the baby's form.

'I know not what happened to the shard. *You* were my link and once you were lost to me, I could see no more. Your body remained with me and I continued to animate it, training your physical form without the presence of your soul. That is why your fighting skill was an instinct to you on your return home and why your progress with majick was slow. Anarkhane taught what was left of your spirit, but once reunited, it took time to adapt to a corporal existence.

'So you see, the stone you seek is no longer here, Exzalander. You stole it long ago.'

'Then it must be on Earth; my father should know what happened to it.'

'You wish to return to Earth?'

'We need that stone, Lord Taiohãhn. I don't see as we have any choice.'

Taiohãhn broke away and leaned on the barrier, surveying His kingdom.

'I can send you there, but I cannot bring you back. My power over Earth diminished long ago; very little evidence of me now remains. You might seek out the Aes Sídhe. I left a portal in their keeping once they were driven underground. There are a few of the Aes Sídhe to be found in the Celtic lands, but they are rare and shy of humans.'

'I will find them, if there are any left to be found, but if not …'

'Then seek the portal alone; find the sídhe that houses it. It will appear as a barrow in the green hills. However, know if you do this, that you risk never returning to Maldahl. If the sídhe no longer exists, you could be trapped forever.'

'Could I not simply transport myself back?'

'It could kill you. The majick that brought you back is now spent. If your power should fail, who would be on hand to save you as my Ælves did? Only when you have reunited the creation gem will you possess the power to achieve such feats without harm to yourself. Promise me that you will not attempt it.'

Kirsten stood as if stone, contemplating His warning, wondering what she would do if she were stuck on Earth. The answer was suddenly clear.

'No Lord Taiohãhn, I can make no such promise. I will make every effort to find the hill people of whom you speak or their sídhe, but if all else fails then I *will* attempt to use my own power to return, rather than give up.'

The Lord of the Forest Realm approached and reaching His hand out, He touched her cheek, smiling.

'Of course, Exzalander, I expected no less. If you had made that promise then I would not have sent you, for fear that you would ne'er return. I know that you will find a way.'

He broke away from her and held His arms on high; the surrounding forest slipped away until they were stood in an opalescent room. Hundreds of spheres of light bobbed about like Christmas baubles, each containing images of the past. The room seemed intolerably bright after the cool greenness of the rest of Taiohãhn's Kingdom.

'This is the heart of my realm, the centre of my power. It is from here that I shall send you back.'

Kirsten was struck by how different the place was from everywhere else that she had seen. It reminded her rather of Anarkhane's Kingdom. She met the eyes of her Lord and found Him gazing sadly back at her, as if guessing her thought.

'Yes Exzalander, this is where Anarkhane's Kingdom joins my own, a small haven from the shadow of evening. She was the heart of me, the centre of my power. She brought light to my kingdom and so allowed the trees to grow. Before, there was only ash, a barren landscape of nothingness. In recompense, I gave Her physical form. I built her from dreams; before that, She had been a being of pure light.'

'And you loved her?'

'How could I not? Alas for my foolishness. For had She remained as She was, Maldahl would not have been lost to us. As She gained physical form, the energy released from the creation left a crystalline deposit.'

'The Anarkhane Stone?'

'Precisely. In Her physical form, She longed for the ability to create life, but was unable. I charged the stone with my own creation majick and made a gift to Her. She loved it over all else. And so it was, after eons trying to convince Her to join with me, that I grew angry. Her attentions were ever focused on the gem and Her creations. I became jealous and began to create the most terrible dreams on Maldahl. The dreams grew more tangible with the passing of time.

'I had hoped to make Anarkhane angry, hoped that She would confront me, but She ignored me. The more terrified of the dreams people became, the more they turned to Her, and the more they adored Her. Finally, I decided the only thing to do was to take the gem back and sever her link to creation.

'She resisted and we fought. It was that argument which resulted in the breaking of the stone, forcing our retreat to our respective kingdoms. The dreams I had set in motion became prophetic as the Old Ones closed in, and they used it as a framework to create a new divine order and so Maldahl was at least preserved.

'This room is the only connection I have to Her.'

'Are you telling me that the situation that I am in now is because you behaved like a jealous child? You created this scenario in your mind and now it has come to pass?'

'Yes. But things could have fared worse, Exzalander.'

'Oh really. That's easy for you to say! You're not the one who has been a pawn in the game that you and Anarkhane have been playing!'

'Exzalander, it was my dreaming that saved Maldahl. The argument with Anarkhane would have occurred anyhow. If I had not weaved my dreams into the fabric of Maldahl and its people, the Old Ones would have destroyed it, wiped out every living thing in order to begin anew.

'I *saved* Maldahl.'

'You're wrong, Taiohãhn. If you and Anarkhane had not interfered to begin with then none of this would have happened.'

'Do you not realise what you are saying? Do you not know who we are? Anarkhane and I created Maldahl from nothing. We gave it form and then we gave it life. **We are gods, Exzalander; the purpose of our very existence is to interfere!**'

Kirsten felt the wave of power as it hit her and she fell to her knees, overwhelmed by His presence. He stared at her for a moment and once He was satisfied that she had learned her place, He pulled her to her feet.

'This conversation is over. We have things to do.'

As He spoke, He released her and she felt normal again—no longer an ant before an eagle.

'I don't understand, Taiohãhn; if you are a god, how is it that you can't bring me back from Earth? How is it that you can't solve Maldahl's problems yourself?'

'You must understand, when I created the stone for Anarkhane, I instilled so much of my divine power into it, that its destruction left me crippled. The little power I have is now bound to my kingdom. As for Earth, I had power there once; I was known by many names; Cernunnos, Beli, Belenos. Anarkhane was Don, Anu, Mother Nature to name but a few. We were different gods, or aspects, to different people. Nobody knew that our essence was one and the same, believing that our personas were separate entities entirely.

'We abandoned Erin after the Milesian invasion, but it was the invasion of the new faith that was to result in our final departure. As the new religion slowly contaminated our faith, the old ways were lost. Now, I am a mere memory there.'

'But there are New Agers on Earth. There are even druids and witches.'

'Not enough. From time to time, a follower truly believes and I catch a glimpse of Earth, but what I see, I wish I had not. Most of my followers are lost, searching for something that they know not. The old ways are forgotten, the rituals and blessings that were handed down through the ages, all gone. Our links are severed and I am content for it to remain so.

'Earth is dying, drowning in its own greed. Let their present gods aid it if they so choose; I am free of it. I am content here in the green wood of my underworld kingdom. I would not wish to sully myself in that poisoned soil, even if it *were* possible. The religions are at war there, each fighting for supremacy and each foolishly allowing their people to turn to violence. There will be nothing left—nothing. I have seen enough to know when to leave well alone. And yet now I am to allow my warrior to go there, unguarded.'

'Will I lose my memory again, Lord Taiohãhn, as I did before?'

'No. You are almost whole again. You will remember everything.'

'What do you mean by almost whole?'

'Part of your spirit remained with Anarkhane. You have only been able to join with it in Her Kingdom. Do not look so concerned; you will be united ere the end. Come now. Let us to the task at hand.'

He raised His arms and the curved wall before her appeared as if water. It was then that she realised that a whole section of the room was a forelócian glæs, leaving the power of Katahl to pale in comparison, and yet she knew that Taiohãhn had access to little of His power, and would continue in His diminished capacity until she achieved her quest. She tried to push the thought from her mind; contemplating such things threatened to overwhelm her. Fortunately, the distorted image of Earth was enough to distract her from her fear.

'Go now my warrior and may your return be swift.'

'Will we meet again, Lord Taiohãhn?'

'We can never be wholly parted; our fates are entwined. I will see you again.'

Kirsten smiled and holding her breath, she stepped forward into the unknown.

Thirty-Three

At the end of the second day out from Bashnya, the Mariners arrived in Elfin country. Richard felt instantly refreshed as he stepped beneath the first trees of the enchanted forest. He hated sand and sun and was glad of the cool damp that greeted them. His armour, though light, had begun to irritate him and he wondered why he could not have put it on as they reached Golstur.

The Mariners blue hue looked stronger still beneath the foliage and Walker was a mere shadow.

'If we continue south,' Fahl said, 'then we should soon reach the dwelling place of the Elfin. This forest used to be vast, but stands now as little more than an oasis with only the desert to protect its borders.'

Richard gazed warily about him, unsure as to the accuracy of Fahl's words. The further they walked, the more convinced he became that their progress was being observed.

'What is it?' Walker asked.

'I do not know. This place is making me uneasy, can you not feel it?'

'I feel nothing, friend; I am only a spirit. Don't worry, the Mariners would have sensed danger if there was any. It is your fear of the unknown that is putting you on edge.'

Richard remained unconvinced. Continuing to look about him, he kept his hand close to the hilt of his sword. Birds sang in the canopy above and the gentle chirping of insects did nought to soothe him. For hours they heard nothing else, until a gentle breeze came sweeping through the trees, carrying a song—a beautiful voice singing about the sea. Richard drew his sword and followed Fahl and the Mariners toward the sound.

The trees opened out to a lake with a sandy shore. Small waves lapped to meet them, as if accompanying the maiden's song. Across the shimmering water of the lake, a huge purple rock jutted from the depths, upon which lounged the song's maker; she was a green haired woman, with a glistening tail instead of legs, naked but for a string of pearls about her ivory throat.

She stopped singing at their approach, smiling pleasantly at them. Richard was transfixed by the stare and his weapon felt heavy in his hand.

'Why come you to this place, strangers?' she said. 'Speak your purpose,'

Richard did not blink. He felt suddenly thirsty and he swallowed, trying to tear his gaze away from her perfect breasts. Moving closer to the waters edge, he failed to hear Fahl's command to stay. He wanted to be nearer the woman, to touch her. His sword fell to the ground and lay partly swallowed by the sand.

As his toes touched the water's edge, the lake seemed to erupt before him. The spray swept across his visor and a wave leapt up, knocking him down. His hand reached out to find his fallen blade as a mighty roar filled the air.

From the lake rose a beast—part horse, part man; its fierce red eyes marked the company as it took huge strides to meet them.

'Stay Kelpie,' Fahl commanded, his voice menacing.

Richard found his sword again, but the sand held it fast, ever sifting and changing so that each time he thought he had a hold on it, it would slip from his grasp.

'Long has it been since I have had some sport,' the Kelpie roared.

'Stay I say,' Fahl said. 'We are here on good purpose.'

The woman swam beneath the water horse's mighty legs and laid her hand on his glistening skin.

'Wait a while,' she sang. ' Do you not see how the lad is dressed in the array of a Mo-rye champion?'

'The Mo-rye are dead Muireann,' the Kelpie said.

'That I know well, but is your curiosity not peaked?'

The touch of the merwoman seemed to calm the enraged beast.

'What business have you here?' he growled.

'We seek the Elfin,' Fahl replied.

'For what purpose?' sang Muireann.

'To ask for their aid. We march against Katahl.'

The merwoman laughed and Richard loosened his hold on his sword again, allowing the sand to drag it deeper.

'Crushed you shall be, as a moth in a gale,' the kelpie said. 'What care we for battles? We are eternal. When you lay dead and your rotting corpses feed the earth, we shall remain. You will need better cause than this for us to allow you to leave here with your lives.'

The sand swallowed the sword and Richard stared blankly at where it had been mere moments before. The Kelpie strode toward them as Muireann dived beneath the water. The Mariners, all of the same mind, raised each of their right hands and the lake began to rise as a wall before them. As the wall got higher, so the lake drained further, until there was nought to be seen but substrate.

The merwoman wailed, her voice no longer enticing; the fish flapped about her, not only fish, but a variety of oddities; a great two headed serpent and a small group of Kappas, glared up at the Mariners through the shield of water, which had been their home.

'You will remain?' questioned Fahl, his voice mocking and judgemental. 'You are nothing more than outcasts now, driven to the brink of extinction, forced to take refuge together under the protection of the Elfins' majick. If you will not help us then we shall leave. *You* are no threat to us. Do not think that we would enter here toothless. If you force us to, then we shall bite.'

The Kelpie, who had been trying to ram his way through the wall of water, stopped and turned to look at his wailing companion.

'They will die ... they'll all die. *Please,*' he begged, 'release the water.'

Richard stared, horrified at the squirming serpent and dying fish. He breathed with relief as the Mariners released the water with a crash. The Kelpie had murder in his eyes and Richard gulped as the beast's fist clenched so tightly that his long nails drew blood from his palm.

'ENOUGH!'

The voice came from the trees and all, including the Kelpie, heeded to its command.

'You seek the Elfin. We have been aware of you since first you stepped over the threshold. Leave our friends in peace and follow us.'

Richard's eyes were straining as he searched the shade of the trees. Arrowheads came into view followed by bows, arms and heads. They were Cröedaw's people, that much was plain.

Fahl spoke softly to Richard as he beckoned him to collect his sword and join them. Richard was about to say that his weapon was lost, but spied it lying at his feet, as if carelessly dropped, not a grain of sand upon it. As he retrieved it, he noticed Muireann crying softly into the breast of the Kelpie, and he could feel nothing but pity for them.

The walk to the Elfin village seemed longer than perhaps it was, due to the silence of the party and Richard's never-ending fear of receiving an arrow in the back.

As they entered the village, Richard saw the many huts with cleverly thatched roofs and small smoking chimneys. His gaze fell upon the group of smiling Elfin that awaited them and he felt his fear lessen.

'Greetings my friends. We rejoice at your coming, for long has it been looked for. I am Ârgrïn, chieftain of the village.'

'We did not realise that we were expected, Chief Ârgrïn,' Fahl said.

Ârgrïn laughed and his voice was as blithe as spring rain. 'Do not all Maldahl's people have their prophecies? My friends, it is long since that we knew a party would travel to us from the sea; one who is spirit and yet doth live, one of the Mo-rye, though they be dead and gone, eleven of the Mariners and yet not, thirteen who are not what they seem, eleven of great power shunned and yet shunning, one who is not of this world and exists in two and one who has helped to turn the tide against the Dark One.'

Richard's head bowed, glad that he had his visor down, yet wondering if they could still see within.

'I am Fahl, Chief Ârgrïn. We are the last remaining wizards of The Order of Vivienne, who left Ealdorbold long ago. This is Walker, Emperor of Bashnya who was separated from body by Exzalander and sent to us in our time of need. This is Richard, a friend and former companion of the princess, who has returned.'

If they were expecting a gasp of astonishment, they did not receive it. A few heads nodded in acknowledgement of the wizard's words.

'Yes, wonderful indeed is that news, though we were already party to it. Our brother Cröedaw sent us word and we have waited for you from that day.'

'Glad are we to have finally made the journey that was foretold to you, Ârgrïn,' Fahl said.

'Come, rest, eat and we shall speak of your proposal.'

'What is there to hear, Ârgrïn?' said an Elfin who stood behind the chieftain. 'They want us to march on Katahl. Thirteen of them and barely a hundred of us. Katahl has *thousands* occupying Golstur and its surrounds; we would be slaughtered.'

Ârgrïn sat cross-legged beside a fire already prepared and gestured for his guests to join him. 'You speak out of turn, Ousan,' he said. 'You are too young to remember the Order of Vivienne. You know not their power.'

Richard ate little, but listened rather to the ancient people as they discussed the attack and Fahl showed them the weapons they had created with the help of Walker. They talked of other things, of times past and civilisations lost; Richard's head fell to his chest and he dreamed at first of terrible beasts, an army of Kelpies bent on destroying all human kind, but then the song of the merwoman carried him off to sweeter things.

He awoke in a bed, still wearing the ancient armour of the Mo-rye. Easing himself into sitting, he removed the helmet, with a huff. At once, he became aware that he was not alone, for as he placed the helmet aside, a small gasp sounded from the other side of the hut. A young Elfin stepped out from the shadows as Richard smoothed back his blonde hair.

'You are human!' the Elfin woman said.

He looked up at her smiling, struck at once by her beauty. 'Yes,' he replied politely. 'What did you think I was?'

The young woman knelt suddenly beside him, her eyes etching his face and her head tilted as if looking at him from a different angle might change his answer.

'Truly, I did not know what you were. Only that you were not of the Mo-rye. How comes it that you wear their armour?'

'Fahl told me that I must wear it always and never take it off. He did not say why, other than it was foretold that I should do so.'

The young woman gave a small cry of dismay and shifted nearer, picking up his helmet. 'Then you should put this back on before anyone else sees,' she told him.

Richard took the helmet, unable to remove his eyes from her, until he placed it back on his head.

'I do not see what difference it makes,' he said, 'surely you can see that I am human anyway.'

'Oh no,' she said, edging closer still. 'In your armour, you are the avenger of the Mo-rye race—nothing more, nothing less, for that is all we see. But do not worry, I will not tell.'

Richard shifted uncomfortably and wondered whether he cared if anyone else knew or not. 'Thank-you,' he said, with a shrug.

She smiled at him and he felt a strange sensation in the pit of his stomach.

'Huçul! Where are you child?'

The girl sprang back from him, muttering, 'I must go.' She headed for the sunlit doorway, but as she reached it, she turned back to him and smiled again before running out into the morning.

There were few Elfin about the village when Richard appeared from his hut, stretching in the morning sun. Fahl waved to him in greeting and beckoned him over to the fire where the Mariners were gathered. He breathed deeply the air, it feeling more like home to him, than the dry, blistering heat of the desert. Seating himself beside Walker, he noticed the fear in the spirit's eyes.

'What has happened?' he whispered.

Walker seemed not to hear him. The Mariner Wizard, Iorich, answered for him.

'He is affeared that he will soon die. His body is in peril and he senses that their connection may shortly be severed.'

'How can we prevent it?' Richard cried in dismay.

'How indeed?' Iorich said, 'His body is not of this world and unless he can reunite himself, I fear that we will lose him. But his purpose is fulfilled, unsure am I to see why he now frets.'

Richard frowned. 'Is that all he is to you? Someone you used to build your city and your weapons? You used his vision of his own world to help you fight a war in ours. *His purpose is served,* how can you be so cold?'

Fahl, who had ceased conversing so that he might listen, interrupted. 'Richard, you distress yourself unnecessarily. If you had lived as long as we, then you would not fear death. Death is simply the next journey that we must all make at the end of the road that we have travelled so long. Each of us has a purpose—a destiny, sometimes only small, or so we think, but every life affects another in some way like the tiny rock that sends ripples across calm waters. When the task is achieved, the life is meaningless until the next journey is made. It is not that we are cold at heart, simply that we see things much clearer than you.'

Richard shook his head stubbornly. 'He does not want to die, then why should he? He might have a greater purpose; who are you to say?'

Whatever Fahl's response was, Richard did not hear. His eye caught sight of Huçul as she stood by listening. Tears streaked her pale, beautiful face; her shining eyes held Richard's and at that moment, he knew that he was no longer a boy.

The thick clouds surrounding had a saline taste that made Kirsten retch. Eventually, the luminescence faded and the darkness set in. She shivered with cold and her eyes struggled to focus. Sitting up slowly, she rubbed at her hands and feet, trying to take her mind of the feeling of sickness from the journey.

She had arrived, but it was dark—very dark. She allowed her night vision to guide her and felt a jolt of recognition when she saw the interior of the old church where Caitul had fought the Trolg, where her life had changed forever. Approaching the door, she found it locked. Whispering a lock spell, she was surprised when it still refused to budge. It took a swift kick and the door crashed open; she saw that wooden beams had been nailed across it, to keep out trespassers. Stepping out into a mid-afternoon sun, she remembered that she was still wearing an array of what would be considered illegal weaponry.

Removing her cloak, she carefully wrapped her sword and dagger into it, creating a makeshift backpack. She then pulled her belt around so that the throwing stars were concealed beneath the package.

Glad was she now that she was travelling in leather gear, feeling that it was not so conspicuous as the gift from the Children of Anarkhane.

A strange sensation filled her as she headed toward the fields that backed onto her old home. She missed Maldahl already. The air was thick with pollution and she could feel it burning her lungs. The cars and the noise filled her with dread and she fought to push her fear to the back of her mind.

What if I never return?

Glad was she when she was stamping across the fields at last, leaving the sound of the traffic behind her. Memories of the past crept up on her and she felt as though she had crossed a bridge of time, recalling Geri joking with her, or having to hide from her father, trying to get the dogs to leave her alone.

Perhaps it was the shock of the journey, or simply that she was so caught up in the past that she was paying no attention to the present, which made her miss the sound of the approaching stranger. A hand clamped across her mouth from behind and a strong arm pulled her into the bushes. She heard her own voice in the past, retaliate to her father saying *"I can look after myself"*, before she finally caught up with reality.

She smiled.

Her attacker was having difficulty trying to loosen her leather trousers; zips did not exist in Maldahl. He held a knife to her throat and growled.

'Take your trousers down, now!'

She laughed and the noise was unnerving to hear, sounding so different from how she used to be, how she had been when such an attack might have actually meant something.

'Stop laughing!' the man hissed, pressing the knife into her skin.

Her blow was quicker than even she herself had expected. Her left hand held the wrist of his weapon-hand and the right backhanded him in the nose. The blade thudded to the ground by her left hip and she jumped, cat-like to her feet, watching him, to anticipate his next move.

Blood gushed from his broken nose and he growled as he reached for his blade. She kicked him lightly in the head, unwilling to cease her sport too soon. He scrambled to his feet and attempted to run, but a simple paralysis spell caused him to fall. Approaching him, she smiled, kneeling on the ground beside him.

'Now tell me,' she said, 'would you prefer death or the chance to live? No need to struggle to speak, I can see straight into your mind.'

She could both smell and taste the fear, yet remained emotionless towards it. He was simply another enemy to be fought, and yet her ties to Earth forced her to be more creative with his fate, for the sake of others.

He chose life.

She was no longer smiling as she unzipped his trousers. With her left hand she levitated his knife and with her right, his member. Concentrating on his penis, she forced as much blood into it as she could, making it stand so erect that she no longer needed to levitate it. She felt the fear increase in him as he realised what it was that she meant to do.

'I give the chance of life,' she said. 'You simply have to make it to a hospital before you bleed to death.'

A split second before she struck, she removed the paralysis spell, allowing his agonised screams to wash over her.

'Here,' she said, dropping the blade by his severed man-hood.

Walking away, she gave no further thought to the attacker, considering only the task ahead of her.

The row of red brick Edwardian terraces looked the same as they had when she had left, except one. The house in which she had grown up was for sale and Kirsten felt a surge of panic as she ran around toward the back door.

What if he has already moved? How will I find him? To her relief, she saw plants still sat on the windowsill, and she breathed again. Pushing down the handle, she unlocked it with a thought, and stepped in.

'Hello,' she called, 'Dad?'

There was no answer and she was accosted suddenly with memories threatening to overwhelm her. Almost eighteen years had been spent there, eighteen carefree years without danger or fear of death. Dropping her weapons, she slumped into her favourite armchair, almost smelling the mug of cocoa that she used to drink. She had forgotten that such things existed and felt scared, suddenly torn, wondering if she closed her eyes and slept now, if it would all have been a dream when she awoke.

'How dare you break in here! GET OUT!'

She jumped to her feet and faced her father; not her real father, she knew that now, but still, she had been his "Little flower" and "petal" for so many years, before …

'Dad?'

He glared back at her. He looked older and greyer than she remembered.

'Dad it's me. It's Kirsten.' But she was Exzalander and had not held Kirsten's form since her escape from Katahl's fortress.

'How dare you! Who are you? A reporter? You've no bloody right! Now fuck off!'

She had to concentrate. Prince Bydand had been right; Kirsten's form was contaminated now; it was so human and she no longer felt the same attachment to it. As her father's eyes changed from fury to fear, she reached up and felt the long cold scar on her cheek, wanting to be rid off Kirsten's form and feel free again.

Her father was shaking his head, as if trying to wake himself.

'No.' he said. His hand groped toward a dining chair and he collapsed into it. 'It can't be!'

Tears were in his eyes as she knelt before him and reaching out, he touched the scar. It seemed a long time that they sat like that, in silence. Eventually, he stroked her hair behind her ears, stood up and went to close the back door. Turning, he flicked the kettle on and proceeded to prepare tea.

'I knew that you would come back,' he said.

She realised that he was not speaking as a father who had missed his daughter, but as a man who knew more than had been presumed.

'How did you know, Dad?'

'Because I knew that you would want what you left behind.'

Her eyes locked on his, but out of respect, she willed herself not to read his mind.

'After I was released from hospital, I begged Lisa to drive me back here. I knew if it was still here then I would see you again. That was the thought that kept me going. Lisa didn't understand.'

She frowned. 'You are still together, aren't you?'

'Yes.' He nodded. 'We don't talk about what happened any more. I thought that was best as there are things I rather she never knew and things that I could never tell her for fear of losing her. I love her, you see.

'I loved you too of course and I was distraught when you left, but I knew, *knew* something like that was going to happen some day. I knew that we were on borrowed time and I had been given the task of looking after you, if only for a while.'

He handed her a cup of black tea and she sipped it thoughtfully.

'Dad, you say you knew I was going to disappear and yet you didn't even warn me. How long have you known?

He sat back on the chair again, shaking his head. 'I didn't know exactly what would happen, just that something was bound to. I have known it since the moment that you were born, ever since you came out of Eleanor screaming "no!" and clutching a green gem in your tiny hand.

'The midwife was too shocked to scream and tried to wrench it from your fingers; it broke in two. You screamed at her, "hand that back!" and for years after I tried to convince myself it had been the shock of my wife's death that had allowed my mind to play tricks on me. But I knew of course it wasn't. The stone exists; it burned the midwife, but even through her screams of pain, she heard what you said. I swore her to silence and every day feared that you would be taken from me. But no-one ever came and you never spoke again, not until it was normal that you should do so.'

'Why did you never tell me?'

He shrugged and swallowed some tea with a heavy gulp. 'What could I have said? You were unaware of what had happened and I wanted you to have a normal, healthy life for as long as possible. How *could* I tell you such a thing? You were a child. You would have been picked on at school and sooner or later, my parenting would have been brought into question. I always held the secret hope that nothing would happen, but that was foolish.'

Kirsten put down her tea and paced. 'You still have the stone?'

He looked pale as he answered. 'Yes, I kept it with some of your mother's things in the attic—out of harm's way.'

She opened the box carefully and took out book after book, none of which seemed to have gathered any dust. She was surprised to see that each was a volume on witchcraft and she flicked through one of them as if to confirm it and her eyes rested upon an engraving of Jack o' the green.

'Taiohãhn,' she whispered, fondly touching the picture.

Her father moved uneasily beside her.

'Your mother was into that stuff you see,' he said. 'I always assumed that she had given birth to a changeling or something, or at least one of her spells had backfired. I told her that I didn't like her messing around with it, but she'd never done any harm before. The house always stank of incense; she would chant and burn candles, but I never saw any magic. I thought it was all nonsense until I saw you clutching the stone that had torn into her belly … and heard you speak. *Then* I believed and I was too frightened to get rid of all this stuff. So you can take it if you want.'

She placed down the book and looked back at her father.

'I have no need of them, just the stone.' She continued to search the box until she saw a small black velvet bag. 'Is this it?' she said, more to herself than to her father. She opened the bag and emptied the contents onto her palm. 'You said that it broke. Where is the other piece?'

There was a silence and she turned to glare at him.

'The midwife kept it,' he confessed. 'It was the price for her silence.'

Her heart sank as she clasped the stone.

'Why doesn't it hurt you?' her father asked nervously.

'Because I am no longer human,' she replied. 'But then I think that you already knew that, did you not? You felt the last bond break as I abandoned Kirsten forever. I need not hold this disguise; it makes no difference any more.' She released the scarred and weatherworn Kirsten for the last time, without regret, and her green eyes met those of the man who had fathered her.

'What is the midwife's name?'

'Mary Rigby,' he whispered, as he stared at the stranger who stood fully as tall as he.

'Is this the reason why you did not believe me when I was accused of conspiring with a murderer?' she asked.

He nodded. 'I suspected that he wasn't human and that he was coming for the stone.'

Exzalander stared long at him, knowing that she would never see him again.

'Thank you, for everything,' she said and embraced him tightly.

He did not return the embrace, but when she released him, she could see that he was crying.

'Goodbye,' she said.

He nodded, blinking away the tears so that they fell like rain down his ageing cheeks.'

Swinging her encloaked sword over her shoulder, she headed toward the hospital, deciding not to look back to her old home. She knew that her father was watching her as she left, and she did not want to wave that final farewell, choosing to push the pain aside.

In the village of the Elfin, Richard fretted that he could not see Huçul amongst the crowd who had gathered to bid farewell. Although he barely knew her, he felt his heart would be steady if she were present. His eyes searched in vain, one last time, before mounting the horse prepared for him and riding out of the village, behind the Elfin warriors and wizards of old.

As the day wore on, the woods began to thin and Walker moved slowly beside Richard, his eyes wide and fearful, no longer seeing his surroundings. Richard could feel his mount moving gracefully through the undergrowth and began to sympathise ever more with Walker's situation. The sensation of touch had been taken away; cold and heat were no more than words to him in his present condition.

Lifting his visor, he spoke. 'I wish there were something that I might do for you, Walker.'

The ghostly figure became aware of his companion and he looked as though he was trying to smile.

'If the princess was here, she would know what to do,' Richard continued. 'She brought Marin back from death and me from the gates of death.'

Walker's eyes closed, as if wearied, and he nodded. 'I am sure that you are right. She had the power to separate me and she could save me, were she here, but she's not; neither do I think that I'll ever get the chance of meeting her again. My time is drawing to a close. I can feel it. It won't be long now.'

Almost as soon as he spoke, he seemed to fade. At first, Richard could not be sure, thinking it a mere trick of the light.

'Walker!' he shouted.

The company halted at the cry, all attention drawn to the spirit's wide-eyed face as it faded into nothingness. Richard reached out, as if to catch him from falling, but there was nothing he could do. Walker was gone.

Fahl met Richard's horror-struck gaze and sadness seemed to fill him. He began to chant a mournful tune, which the other Mariners accompanied, and Richard seemed carried along by a dream-like music, wondering if his own death would be so noted, without tears, but by reverend song.

Stepping into the hospital foyer, Exzalander searched the huge map for the ward that she needed. She passed the signs for oncology, psychiatric, accident and emergency, before arriving at maternity. She heard the sound of crying babies as she stepped up to the reception desk.

'Excuse me; I wonder if you can help. I am looking for a mid-wife by the name of Mary Rigby.'

'Are you trying to be funny?' The woman said, eyeing her up and down with obvious distain.

'No,' she replied, at a loss for anything else to say.

'Well I don't know and I expect she won't want to be found, wherever she is. There are lot of angry parents who might well want to even the score.' The woman peered over her spectacles at the sword concealed in Exzalander's cloak, as if she had guessed what it was.

'Why would people want to even the score? What do you mean?' Exzalander asked.

But the woman threw her another ill-favoured look and turned her back.

'I have no time for these games,' Exzalander whispered, through gritted teeth.

The woman turned, her eyes suddenly fearful. Exzalander had her; she peeled away the layers of her mind as easily as she would the skin from an orange.

'Mary Rigby was dismissed sixteen years since and became known as 'the harbinger of death,' the woman said. 'The case was thrown out of court, due to lack of evidence. The lives of the newborns were simply sucked out of them … it can't have been a coincidence that she brought them all into the world.' The woman breathed heavily, trying to fight Exzalander's intrusion.

'Where does she live?' Exzalander demanded and dug deeper still. However, the woman did not know anything more, nor knew anyone who did.

Exzalander turned on her heel and paced heavily from the room, her boots squeaking against the rubber floor. The woman behind the desk swooned and fell into a faint.

As she approached the foyer, Exzalander saw police everywhere and a prickling sensation was enough warning for her to hide. She dived into the nearest ward and hid in the toilet; closing her eyes, she searched through the minds of others. She saw blood as the man she had castrated was screaming that he had seen her there.

'Damn!' she whispered. 'That's what I get for being merciful.' She crept along the corridor, searching for an alternative exit.

Entering a quiet ward of private rooms, she shook her head, feeling dizzy. Disorientated, she began to feel hot and uncomfortable; her breathing deepened and she was hit with an incapacitating wave of sickness. She stopped, unable to continue and turned back, feeling instantly better. She got a few feet in the opposite direction and was hit by another wave of nausea. Stopping, she took a pace back.

Better.

'What the …?' she whispered, and spotted a police officer at the entrance to the ward. He was facing a nurse and had not seen her. She ducked into the nearest room, pressing herself into the corner, behind the door.

Footsteps came closer and she considered whether she should not simply transport herself away, but she could not. The very thought of it had made her feel nauseous again. She pushed her sword under the bed and concentrated on creating an illusion.

The door opened and the police officer stepped inside. He saw the pretty, dark-haired nurse in front of him and smiled pleasantly.

'Everything okay in here?' he asked.

'Yes,' Exzalander replied, smiling back at him.

The policeman's eyes briefly scanned the room and he winked at her.

'Be nice to him okay; he's one of ours.'

Then he left, his footsteps receding as he continued up the corridor. Exzalander turned and felt a jolt of recognition when she came face to face with the comatose form of Walker. She felt a pang of guilt as she remembered attacking him.

Footsteps headed back and she grabbed for the patient's chart, trying to look busy.

'Oh! Who are you?'

Exzalander turned and smiled at the nurse.

'I'm Clara. I'm from psychiatric,' she said. 'That copper just told me to wait in here while he conducted his search. Apparently, there's some nutter on the loose … yeah, like that's anything new!'

'Yeah well, it's all go in this place,' said the nurse. 'Why were you reading his chart?'

'No reason, just passing the time. I was told he's a copper.'

The woman took the chart from Exzalander and examined the machine to which he was wired.

'Yeah, such a shame. The family agreed to switch off life support.'

'When?'

'Already done; it won't be long now. Sometimes I hate this job y'know? He's got kids an' all.'

'Tragic,' Exzalander said, shaking her head, wondering how long the woman would take.

'What's that?'

The nurse had spotted her sword sticking out from under the bed and Exzalander swiftly decided on a new course of action.

'Sleep,' she commanded, and the woman slumped to the floor. She let her disguise fall and rushed over to Walker, pressing her hands to his head—searching. *He is a policeman; he might know where Mary Rigby is,* she considered, but his mind was far away.

She dragged the nurse out of view of the window and then returned to Walker's side. It was unlike trying to find Thaniel when he'd been injured or even Marin, when she had died. Exzalander did not see Anarkhane's kingdom at all, but Maldahl. She continued to search, trying to contain her excitement at the sight of home, ever conscious of the danger at hand.

'Got you!' she exclaimed at last, and at that moment, her eyes met Richard's and the image was lost before she could be entirely sure at what she had seen. Before her, Walker was wide-eyed and trembling with fear.

'Exzalander?'

She took a step back. 'How did you …?'

'You sent me to Maldahl,' Walker said. 'I learned all about you there. I helped raise an army to march against Katahl at Golstur. Fahl said my purpose was fulfilled; I thought I was going to die. Am I really home?' He wept.

'Yes,' she replied, confused. 'Yes, you are home.' She smiled suddenly, thinking how happy that Tom would be when she told him. 'I must leave now, but this Fahl was wrong. *I* have need of you. I'm looking for a woman called Mary Rigby. Can you help?'

'Mary Rigby? The Harbinger? Now that's a name I haven't heard in a while.'

He laughed long and Exzalander remained patient, understanding how overwhelming it must have felt to be reunited with his body.

'I would have thought it all a dream were it not for your being here,' he said. 'But why are you here? We were told that you were marching on Ishtar.'

'And so I was, but I need to find one of the Anarkhane stones. Do you know of them?'

He nodded, feeling his face with obvious delight. 'Yes, the Mariners taught me of the legend.'

Exzalander raised a solitary eyebrow at his choice of words, but said nothing against it. 'Well, Mary Rigby holds one of the stones,' she explained. 'That is why it is imperative that I find her.'

'Really? Well help me up, I'll take you to her.'

She smiled warmly. 'No. You need your rest. There are police everywhere and they know who you are. I'd never get away if I had you with me, besides, would you not like to see your family?'

Walker fell back onto his pillows, beaming. Exzalander could not help but return the gesture. She looked into his mind and saw the last known abode of Mary. Kissing Walker on the forehead, she stooped to gather her belongings.

'Your great task may be complete,' she said. 'But I would say your *life* is just beginning. Farewell.'

She stepped out into the corridor and smiled to herself, wondering whether it had been Taiohãhn or Anarkhane who had had a hand in her finding Walker. She continued down the corridor, and then swinging open a window, she jumped out onto the soft soil beneath, running off in the direction of the station.

The barriers were open and she boarded a train to central London, trying not to notice the crowds of people, whose soulless eyes desperately avoided each other. It had been a while since she had encountered so many people and yet, despite being squashed amongst them, smelling their mixture of perfume and sweat, she never felt more disconnected in her entire life. In the end, she made herself invisible; she felt it anyhow, but at least making it an actuality, she knew that she could avoid ticket barriers and inspectors.

Before she even disembarked to catch her connecting train, her impatience got the better of her. With each passing mile, she thought of Katahl's advancing army, and she came to a decision. It was time to resort to majick. She was well rested and ever since her encounter with the Clan of the Dark Moon, she felt stronger than ever. Transporting herself to the canal in the north was going to be easier than using a map to try to find her way about. Using the image of Mary that she had taken from the minds of others, she allowed her majick to take her where she needed to be.

The first thing that she noticed when she opened her eyes again was how sunny it seemed, though it was cold, much colder than the stuffiness of London. She waited for the wave of exhaustion to hit her, however, despite feeling tired, the need to collapse into unconsciousness seemed unnecessary. She let out a breath she had been holding, relieved that her decision to use majick had been the right one.

Looking about, she wondered which narrowboat was Mary's. The towpath was muddy after recent rain and dirt splashed up her boots and trousers, making her look more weatherworn than ever.

The nearest narrowboat was old and dirty. Believing it to be derelict, Exzalander almost dismissed it completely, but as she walked near, her sword seemed to sing softly in her ear, indicating that a stone was near. She nimbly hopped onto the boat and it swayed beneath.

'Mary Rigby?' she cried. 'I need to talk with you.'

'Go away or I'll call the police!' came her answer.

Exzalander looked toward the direction of the voice, undeterred by the harsh reply.

'I have come about the stone, Mary. Surely you knew that I would. It was not yours to take and now you must return it to me.'

There was a moment's silence before Mary appeared, carrying a shotgun. 'Get off my boat!' she ordered.

'I can't do that. I need the stone. I cannot return home without it.'

'Who are you?' She scowled and her hands fidgeted nervously with the weapon in her grasp.

'I am the one from whom you took the stone. I asked you then to give it back. Now I am asking again.'

Her eyes looked wide and fearful, but her mouth twisted, defiant. 'Go away! You can't have it. I know who you are *and* why you need it.'

Exzalander doubted that the raving woman knew anything and her patience was wearing thin. She was eager to escape Earth and be in Maldahl once more.

'What guise have you come in this time, eh?' Mary ranted. 'You came as a fairy last time, now as a girl. Go away, Death; you shan't have it!'

'Death? You think that I'm Death?' *It makes sense,* Exzalander thought. *She was so nicknamed, and the children died because of her possession of the stone.* 'I am not Death, Mary, and neither are you. The stone is not of this world and not meant for mortal hands. It has caused you great suffering, I know.'

'You won't have it!' she screeched. Her entire body trembled with both anger and fear.

'I have no time for this, woman!'

Exzalander's impatience resulted in her use of majick and Mary dropped the gun, howling as the hot metal burnt into her flesh. As the shotgun hit the deck, it went off and Exzalander collapsed, not feeling the pain at first, but seeing the blood.

Her blood.

She stared in morbid fascination as the pool of red spread about her. It looked human enough and yet she knew it was not—not anymore.

'But you can't be hurt, not if you're Death …'

'I'm n…ot Death.' Exzalander struggled as the pain hit her in waves of pure agony. She reached for her bloody leg, aware of the bone splinters and torn tissue; she fought to find the peace of Anarkhane's realm, reaching out to the missing piece of her soul, so that she might stem the tide of pain.

Thirty-Four

When Exzalander came to, Mary was bending over her, dabbing her forehead with a cool flannel. She sat up gradually, staring down at her leg. Finding it complete and painless, she let out a sigh of relief.

'I didn't mean to shoot ya. It fell out of me hands and jus' went off.'

'I know,' Exzalander said, sighing at her own stupidity. 'Are we sailing?'

'Yep. I dint want ta hang around after that gunshot. Last thing I need is the police snoopin' 'round.'

'So you were bluffing when you said that you would call them?'

Mary shrugged. 'I've seen your sword. It's got the same stone in't and I know you've got t'other in that bag 'round ya wrist. Why d'ya need another?'

'To stop a war, Mary. The stones were all one once; I need to reunite them to prevent a great evil from taking everything I love.'

'How can the stones bring peace, when all they cause is death?'

Unsteadily, Exzalander rose to her feet, testing her leg for lasting damage. 'Before it was shattered, the stone had the power of creation. It was not meant for human hands.'

'So that man who came for it before, he wasn't Death then? Was he really a fairy' Mary asked.

'I do not know.'

'He said he would protect the stone. He said that he was from … oh I can't remember …'

Exzalander walked to the side of the boat, peering into the water. Her hands felt sticky from her own blood loss. 'Got anywhere I can clean up?' she asked, holding up her bloodstained hands.

Mary directed her inside the cabin and paced in frustration at her own memory loss. Exzalander watched as blood mixed with lather from the soap and went whirling down the plughole.

'Mead! No … Meadha … something Meadha,' Mary said. 'It was so long ago. It sounded Irish though.'

Exzalander thought of Taiohãhn's words and remembered the Aes Sídhe. 'I need to find the man you met. How far can you take me by boat?'

'Not to Ireland, that's for sure; this old wreck aint seaworthy.'

'If you had a proper boat, could you sail us there?'

'Yes, but …'

'That's settled then. Take us to the nearest port town; I will get you a boat, and *you* will give me the stone and take me to Ireland … to look for the faeries.'

The journey to the coast was pleasant, but Mary was strange company. She talked incessantly to herself and Exzalander could feel the pain and loneliness of her existence; it seemed to flow from her as easily as water flows down a stream. *So many lives ruined because of me.* She sat in quiet contemplation, wondering how she might change Mary's life for the better.

The port was filled with all manner of boats and Exzalander caught a flicker of a smile on Mary's lips as she eyed them all.

'Beootieful!' she sighed.

'I'm going to procure a boat,' Exzalander said. 'Do you wish to come?'

Mary sniffed, half smiling. 'I think I'd better, if you're going dressed like that! 'Ere, let me at least get ya a jumper so ya aint so conspicuous.'

It was an hour before they were both ready to leave. Exzalander tied her hair back into a long plait and she wore a burnt orange turtleneck jumper. Exzalander had persuaded Mary to make herself presentable, and the woman's hair was neatly brushed; a clean change of clothing made for a startling transformation.

In the end, it was Mary and not the queen of Maldahl, who found them transportation. She knew what she looking for and they agreed on a price with the captain of a small cargo vessel, by the name of Joe to drop them along with his cargo in Dublin.

Exzalander found that travelling by sea was not as pleasant as the gentle gliding along a canal. Standing on deck with her cloak clasped tightly about her, she waited for the storm in her stomach to spew forth and meet the relatively calm sea.

She clasped the railing so tightly that her knuckles showed white and she listened to the sound of laughter astern, as Mary and Joe became better acquainted. Exzalander took a deep breath, determined not to vomit; staring into the waves, she longed for her torment to end. The deeper she breathed, the more her stomach settled, until it became apparent that the noises she had thought the groans of her own discomfort, were in fact coming from both the air about her and the sea itself. She leaned further over the barrier, trying to make out the sound; convinced that she was in fact hearing voices beneath the waves.

'What are you doing?' Joe barked at her. 'Are you trying to kill yourself? Get down here now! I'll have no deaths on my boat thank-you very much.'

She stepped down from the barrier, all thoughts of sickness forgotten.

'What are ya doin'?' Mary asked.

'I heard voices; someone was calling to me.' She stopped, suddenly aware of Joe staring at her, and waited for his condescension.

There came none. He simply held her gaze for a moment and returned to steering the boat. Mary sat Exzalander down, handing her a flask of tea, which she politely refused.

'Reckon you'll get on well in Ireland, Kirsten,' Joe said, with a wistful smile.

'Why do you say that?'

'Reckon you'll be looking for leprechaun's gold before the day is over.'

Mary beamed up at Joe and his eyes twinkled back to her. It was then that Exzalander perceived the mutual attraction between them, and she was glad.

'Not leprechauns, Joe. I'm seeking the Aes Sídhe.'

'Fairies!' he laughed heartily.

Exzalander said nothing as she waited for him to stop.

'You're serious?'

She nodded, a smile playing upon her lips. 'Well Joe, what do *you* know about 'people of the hills'? You have heard of them certainly.'

'Course I've heard of 'em. I've spent enough time in the 'Emerald Isle' to know a bit about its legends.'

'Perhaps you can help me then. I'm searching for a place called Meadha; do you know it?'

Joe shook his head.

'Sídhe Meadha!' Mary exclaimed suddenly. 'That was where he was from.'

Joe was laughing again. 'Well now, that's different. You'll have to ask in Dublin or take a look in a bookshop. They're supposed to be loads of sídhe all over Ireland. Someone's bound to know about Meadha. So Mary, you tellin' me that you met a fairy then?'

Mary's face coloured. 'No! He said he was from sídhe Meadha, that's all. I dunno what he was.'

The boat rose up onto a wave. Exzalander's stomach lurched and she sank into silence, listening for voices once more.

Unsure how or when it had happened, Exzalander dozed off to sleep to later be awakened by Mary, while Joe was unloading his cargo.

'Come on Kirsten. Time to go. I've got ya something, look.' Mary held out an old battered golf bag, perfect for hiding her sword.

Exzalander struggled to her feet and felt the boat swaying gently beneath her, as the goods were hauled off. She had never been gladder of anything once her feet were back on solid ground. She tried wheeling the golf bag, but it kept veering off to the right. In the end, she thought it best just to carry it.

'Mary, try that tourist information office and see if they can tell ya anything about your sídhe,' shouted Joe, as he waved at her. 'I'll be here at least a couple of hours if you want a ride home again.'

'Thanks Joe,' Mary replied, blushing.

'Tere's no need for no tourist information now. This ol' fellow'll tell ya what ya needin' ta know.'

Exzalander, golf bag on her back, turned so quickly that she almost knocked the man over. She smiled apologetically and put the bag down.

'You know something about sídhe?' she asked sweetly.

'A course I do, udderwise I'dda not said so, would I?'

Exzalander let out a short laugh and he grinned back at her, his blue eyes sparkling as bright as any Elfín.

'I'm looking for sídhe Meadha.'

'Knockma?'

Exzalander frowned, urging the old man to elaborate.

'It's called Knockma; hasn't been called Meadha for a long while now. I'm surprised yud even know its ancient name. Ye'll need ta get yourself ta Tuam and from tere, head west.'

'Tuam?'

'Ai, that's what I said.'

'Thank-you, that's incredibly helpful.'

'No trouble a'tall.' He tipped his hat and bade her good day.

Exzalander stared after him for a moment, convinced that he would disappear before her eyes. However, he shuffled down the road toward the heart of the city. Exzalander ran to Joe, who was unloading the last of the crates.'

'Joe, it's in Tuam,' she called.

Beads of sweat ran down his face and he heaved a sigh as the last crate was loaded onto the waiting truck.

'West,' he gasped. 'Bill here could take ya as far as Mullinger on his barge couldn't ya?'

Bill smiled in reply.

'No trouble at all. Then you'll have to get a train and change at Athenny.'

A tingle of excitement shot up Exzalander's spine at the thought of reaching her goal. She said her farewells to Joe and Mary, happy in the thought that she had brought them together.

Bill was lively company. He joked and told her stories that made her laugh. It was a strange and almost forgotten sound to her. As she stared out at the passing lowland about the Royal Canal, she breathed the fragrant air and began to think of her return as not so welcome. She was returning to war and possibly her own demise; compared to her present location, Maldahl seemed not nearly as inviting as it had.

On reaching Mullinger, she insisted on helping unload the cargo and in return, Bill escorted her to the station, giving her a cheerful farewell.

'*Money*,' she thought glumly, as she stood in line at the station. Guilt stabbed her as she handed over illusionary euros and took her ticket with humble thanks.

She snoozed for a short time as the train trudged along, deciding that she preferred the freedom of horseback. She awoke from a dream about Ravenwing, just as they crossed the Shannon at Athlone. By the time she reached Athenny, she had travelled from east to west in almost a straight line. Stepping onto the platform, she fancied that she could smell a tang of sea air blowing from Galway Bay. She had a long wait before the train to Tuam arrived, and considered whether she should journey to Knockma that night, or rest.

It was the sensation that she was being watched that diverted her attention away from her hunger. She stared at each of the waiting passengers in turn; none of them took any note of her. Her eyes searched the shadows for someone hiding there. Despite finding nobody, she could not shake the feeling. She yawned and stretched, leaning back and noticed a crow in the rafters; her heart jumped.

It took her a moment to realise that there was no possible way that it could be Cröedaw and yet it watched her with a such a keen eye that she had no doubt in her mind that the crow was no mere bird. She smiled up at it, but it made no move. Feeling a pang of hunger once more, she took some food from her bag. Food, which of course had not been packed. The crow croaked and hopped down beside her. Either it was hungry or it sensed her majick.

'Shoo! Whst whst! Go on with ye.' An old woman chased the bird away, although it continued to stare down from the rafters.

'Jeeze girl, are ye bein' aft' comin' a hoodie's bride?'

Exzalander shrugged, not understanding what a hoodie's bride was.

The woman greedily eyed her bread and cheese and Exzalander offered her a share.

'Please, help yourself,' she said politely.

The woman paused, frowning. 'Ye English?'

The woman's eyes stared hard and Exzalander tried to answer truthfully.

'No. I'm ... I spent a lot of time there.'

The woman swept up some food. 'Yer accent's strange. Where did yer spend time?'

'London. Well no ... the outskirts really.'

The woman's mouth was full and her eyes widened with pleasure as she spoke. 'I haven't tasted bread like this since I was a girl. Where did yer get it?'

Exzalander fidgeted. 'A friend packed it for me, for my journey,' she ended awkwardly.

The woman nodded appreciatively, taking another bite. This time Exzalander joined her.

'Nah. That's no London accent yer got there,' the woman said. 'I can't place it. I spent a lot of time in London meself and I got familiar with a lot of accents there and yours ... well, yours is strange, so it is.'

Exzalander shrugged again, feeling uncomfortable with the woman's probing. *Has my voice changed so much since I returned to Maldahl? It appears so,* she thought. 'What did you mean by 'hoodies bride'?' she asked, keen to change the subject.

The woman swallowed her last morsel of food with a satisfied sigh. 'The crow! D'ye not know the legend of the hoodie? The men who take a wife and take crow form ta steal babies.'

Exzalander looked horrified and stared up at the bird, scowling. The woman laughed.

'I was just kiddin' with ye girl. It's just an ol' crow now.'

But Exzalander was convinced that it wasn't and stared at it without blinking.

'So, where ye travellin' te?'

'Tuam,' Exzalander replied, becoming concerned that she might be questioned about what business she had there.

'And you?'

'Ah, I'm not travelling. I'm waiting for my grandson. He's comin' up from Limerick.'

Exzalander smiled good-humouredly, encouraging the woman to tell more of herself, in an effort to steer the conversation away from searching questions. The woman was only too happy to oblige and the time passed more quickly than Exzalander had anticipated.

The train pulled in, less than an hour after the woman had got onto the subject of her grandson. Exzalander was surprised when she was invited to break her journey home, by going to stay with them. She sat smiling, wondering if the woman had decided that she was definitely not English, and now viewed her as a prospective granddaughter-in-law.

She listened politely to all the directions to the woman's shop and smiled a greeting to the flame-haired grandson as he stepped off the train. Bidding them farewell, she took a quick glance to the rafters and saw that the crow was no longer there. She sighed, relieved to be on the train at last. Reaching out to slam the door, she paused as an elegant, long fingered hand grabbed it and she found herself looking into eyes as black as Katahl himself.

'Excuse me,' the man said.

Exzalander turned to seat herself in the compartment and waved warmly to the woman who had forced her disinterested grandson to wave too.

'Are they relatives?' the stranger asked, who had seated himself opposite. Exzalander turned to face him.

'No. We actually only met a couple of hours ago.'

'How nice,' said the man, whose eyes never left her. He had no baggage of any kind, was stylishly dressed in black and darkest purple; his face was startlingly handsome. He smiled at her and Exzalander, realising she was staring, looked immediately out of the window.

'You play golf?' he asked, several minutes later.

'No,' came her quick reply, realising too late his reason for asking was that he had noticed her luggage.

He continued to smile at her and she was glad that the journey was less than twenty miles, feeling uncomfortable under his gaze. She stared fixedly out of the window, pretending not to notice his attentions.

'So, do you plan to stay with the old woman and her grandson on your return?'

Exzalander faced him, feeling a flutter in her stomach.

'No ... I mean, how did you ...?'

'You did not find him handsome, then?'

Her mouth opened, wondering if he had read her mind somehow. She breathed a sigh of relief with the arrival of the ticket inspector. He punched her ticket, smiling. Without even glancing at the man, he left the carriage and continued down the passageway.

'Who *are* you?' she asked involuntarily.

His returning smile was intoxicating. She had only felt that way once before and that was in the presence of the Vampire Ælves. There was majick afoot.

The stranger rose from his seat and sat besides her, sliding her bag toward the door. She let out a little gasp, but his interest was not in the bag, but her. He began to unbraid her hair and she did nothing to prevent him. Her breathing became shallow and she felt control slipping away.

'You are very beautiful,' he whispered, his accent tinged with Irish.

She sighed as he continued to loosen her hair and his gentle touch brushed against her upper throat.

'As if you could marry such a one. You have a wildness in you. I can see it.'

His lips lightly brushed her own and her entire being was on fire, yearning for him. Her hand reached up to his face; her breathing deepened as she urged him to kiss her, and it was sweet. As his tongue met her own, she felt a semblance of her self-control return. The blood of the Vampire Ælves increased her desire, but it began to weave its spell on *him*. Her kiss became more desperate and she rose, sitting astride him, their lips barely parting, his control waning.

'You're ... not human,' he gasped, straining for restraint over his wheeling senses.

'You're one to talk,' she panted, as she unbuttoned his collar. 'You're the crow are you not? The Hoodie?'

'Yes,' he sighed.

'Then you're not a Vampire Ælf?'

He pushed her away suddenly, straining with all his effort against his desire for her. 'How can you know of such beings?'

'The Clan of the Dark Moon saved my life. Their blood runs through my veins.'

She approached him again, but he stood, holding her away at arms length.

'How came you here? There is no way between Maldahl and Earth any longer.'

His hold gave way and her head pressed against his as they strained to keep their lips from meeting once again.

'Taiohãhn sent me in search of the Anarkhane stones.'

He pushed her, turning his back, his body visibly trembling.

'Even were you to find them, you cannot return,' he said.

'Taiohãhn says that the Aes Sídhe can send me back.' Her blood continued to thump and her desire had not lessened by their conversing.

'*You?* Go to Meadha? Fionnbharr will never let you through. He dislikes your kind almost as much as Elfin. Still, you're female; he might find a use for you. His reputation is well-deserved.'

She ignored his comment about Fionnbharr, deciding that it was best not to know what he meant, rather she focused on something else he mentioned.

'You? You're an Elfin! But you said you are a Hoodie.'

He turned; his eyes blazed with both passion and fury. 'The humans here call us that. I am Corvuß of the Elfin race. We lost our women at the rise of Christianity and have been forced to take human wives to bear our children. Few have enough of our blood to build our tribe though. That is why I picked you. Your majick, being strong, I thought you a powerful witch and therefore suitable to bear my children. Had I known that you were my cousin, I would not have … I never … it is forbidden. You are of Taiohãhn and I, Anarkhane. We are not permitted to love; our blood must never mix.'

'I am not a Vampire Ælf,' she said, 'although I am not quite human either. I am a child of both Anarkhane and Taiohãhn. What you say is foolish. There are no such laws on Maldahl, at least not anymore. Indeed I know of an Elfïn who joined the Clan of the Dark Moon.'

It was the wrong thing to say if she had hoped for him to gain control over his desire. It was all the prompting he needed to renew his advance and he threw her back onto the seat, pinning her down with his body. Their kisses reached a passionate frenzy as they fought to prepare themselves for more.

There was no thought of the guard and the world had ceased to exist as their respective majick increased their desire, leaving them with no will, other than to continue with the proposed course of action.

He was still inside her as the train started to slow. They were approaching Tuam.

'This is my … stop,' Exzalander gasped, but there was no will left to fight the sensation of him as he moved in and out.

'No,' he breathed in her ear and time stopped—literally.

The Elfïn felt the power run through him as the world about them came to a halt, frozen while the fire burned in their carriage, the majick increasing their sensation further. Exzalander cried out in ecstasy as his thrusts became harder and faster, each spell working together like one wave striking another, increasing its velocity until both of them were screaming and the carriage shook.

She climaxed, with a final cry, the muscles surrounding his member, contracting. He peaked only moments after and lay breathing heavily against her breast, smiling as the spell was broken. Although her body still tingled with the raptures of mere moments before, a sudden fear grasped her and she pushed him off, sitting up.

He did not have a silly grin on his face, yet she was fearful that the spell had taken him. She cautiously watched him as he began to dress.

'I do not love you,' she said quickly.

Memories of Thaniel plagued her aching heart. He smiled and sat beside her.

'I did not think that you did. Our majick is strong and should not have been allowed to compete against each other, but I will never regret that we let it.'

He touched her face and kissed her forehead; she blushed in response, not knowing what to feel. As she tied her trousers, the train began to move again. She felt a smile reach her lips, realising that if she had been human then it was likely that she would have been married before the day was through. Katahl would have swept across Maldahl without out a care from herself.

Corvuß helped her down from the train and they walked out of the station, without a word. She turned to him and saw that he had such a similar look to Cröedaw, that she wondered why she had not noticed that he was Elfin, at once.

'Do you wish me to show the way to sídhe Meadha?'

'I would be glad of the company, if you've a mind to take me there.'

He smiled and offering his arm, they walked westward, like a courting couple.

'You love a man, do you not? I saw it in your eyes as my spell broke.'

Exzalander nodded sadly, explaining what had happened with Thaniel.

'You must really love him then I think, for most humans desire blind devotion from a companion. You should talk to your clan if you able to return.'

'I intend to, when the time is right.'

The land about them fell into shadow as the sun set, and she felt the warmth of his hand clasp her own.

'Do not reproach yourself for what happened between us,' he said, kissing her fingers. 'You have nothing to be ashamed of.'

She held his hand tightly and her eyes glinted purple as she used her night vision to gaze about her.

'I do not reproach myself for what *we* did, but rather, what I did to him. To be so enslaved by passion … it was wonderful at the time, but to find no release … how could I have done such a thing?'

'You are strange,' he said, as they continued on their way.

'What do you mean?'

'You are not what you seem. No, you are *more* than what you seem. What *do* you carry in that bag of yours?'

'My weapons. I thought it best that they should remain hidden whilst I am here.'

'You are a warrior?'

'Yes.'

'Yes? That is all the answer I am to expect then? After all that we have shared, you still tell me nothing of yourself. You are human and yet have dealings with Taiohãhn himself and his children took it upon themselves to save you from death rather than consume you, as is their wont. You can halt time as the Sídhe do, and yet you are not one of them. You see in the dark as well as I and yet your gaze is not as mine. You spoke of being a child of both Anarkhane and Taiohãhn, what did you mean?'

'I am their creation. Both have tutored me in order to fulfil the purpose for which I was born. My name is Exzalander, Queen Exzalander of Maldahl.'

The Elfin stopped walking and peered into the distance.

'You say that name as if it should mean something to me, Exzalander.'

'I thought that it might. But perhaps you left Maldahl before prophecies were made about me.'

'Prophecies? So you are the instrument of the gods? You return to fight for them.'

'No, I return to fight for my people. They are dying.'

Corvuß returned his eyes to her own, sadly shaking his head.

'Heed my words, Exzalander. Be wary. It has been over two thousand years since I was last in Maldahl and their influence over me has long since dispersed. You, however, are blinded by it. Believe me when I say that whatever gifts of power they have bestowed upon you, they did so for their own selfish reasons; such gifts always have a price. Do not suffer ignorance. Save your people if you will—if you are able, but be ever wary of desirous gods who would destroy a world over nothing more than petty jealousy.'

She bowed her head, not knowing what to make of his words. It was true that Maldahl was almost destroyed because of the god's disagreement; Taiohãhn had admitted as much himself. *But my people and I owe our very existence to them,* she considered. *Does it follow that the gods have the right to play puppeteer over our lives? Taiohãhn said that it does; He is a god after all. They have been good to me, helped me, tutored me, looked after me and yet, would I not have preferred a normal life?*

'I am not asking you to betray them, just to be guarded,' Corvuß said. 'You are nothing more to them than a pawn in their petty game.'

Exzalander threw him an indignant look and retaliated,

'No, not a pawn. I am a warrior—a knight, and thus have more power and am less expendable.'

He grabbed her shoulders and shook her gently, his eyes locked intently on her own.

'That may be, but what happens when the king and queen are threatened? They will move you in place to protect themselves and you will fall. Do not be fooled, Exzalander and despite your feelings for them, I urge you not to speak so highly of them before Fionnbharr. Remember, they abandoned Earth and did not fight the Milesian invaders or the new religion. Without Taiohãhn's support, Fionnbharr was forced underground.'

'But why does Fionnbharr dislike the Elfín?'

'Because we are the creation of Anarkhane. We do not owe our allegiance to the Celtic gods and do not recognise their power or authority.'

'I see. So I am unlikely to get much of a welcome then.'

'That, I do not know.'

Exzalander took her cloak from her bag and wrapped it around her. 'How far have we to go?' she asked.

'About another two miles.'

She shivered slightly, staring up at the heavens, where a new moon had showed its face and the stars came out to greet the two travellers.

'Do you wish to return to Maldahl, Corvuß?'

'No. It is too much a stranger to me now, and I care not for its troubles since She, who we most cherished, abandoned us here. No, I will remain. Here is my home now.'

Exzalander stumbled on the rocky terrain and Corvuß made a grab for her.

'May I ask you something?' she said.

'Of course Exzalander, anything.'

'Why did you resort to majick on the train? Did you never think to woo a woman?'

'On a train?' Corvuß laughed. 'I knew that I did not have much time, as you were getting off at Tuam. I thought that if I could make you desire me, then I could take all the time in the world to woo you.'

'How many wives have you taken?'

'Three in all.'

'And did you love them?'

'Not all of them. One pursued me for months and I thought it best to wed her, as she had threatened to betray me. She bore me two sons, one of whom was suitable to join us. Another human, Nell, I loved dearly and we had thirty happy years together. Humans are so fragile though, their lives so short. Etain was my greatest love. Alas, she was one of the Sídhe. We were lovers, but had not her father's blessing to marry. She was taken from me on our wedding night and I was forced to watch as she was put to death. So you see, my own relationship with the fair-folk is a complicated one.'

'Was she one of Fionnbharr's clan?'

'No. She was of the line of Anyua of Ulster. I've never found a woman to replace her, not in a thousand years.'

'So, why did you suddenly decide on me?'

'I had not for certain. But I told you, there is something untamed about you, something regal, powerful and free. I should have guessed that you were something more than a witch.'

'Do you now regret our meeting, Corvuß?'

'No. Nor shall I, not as long as I live. For in you I felt once more, the passion of Etain; the memories you brought forth are good and I am glad of them.'

'You remind me of my Elfín friend back home,' she observed. 'He too had a love that came to a tragic end and I do not think that he will ever get over the loss. Elfín hearts are no less fragile than humans I deem, perhaps more so, as your lives are long and your memories forever unstained. I am sorry for what you have lost.'

'Do not be. We do not view death in the same way.'

'Now I know you are lying to me. I was there when Cröedaw was forced to kill his love. I felt everything that he felt, and his pain was overwhelming; I shall never forget it.'

'You are right of course,' Corvuß said. 'I did not want your pity; such a thing is ignoble and I prefer to be without it.'

Exzalander linked arms with him once more and squeezed it affectionately.

'You should take it as a compliment,' she said. 'There are those on Maldahl who think me devoid of all feeling. Indeed, I have been accused of being as dark and evil as the power I am trying to overthrow.'

'I cannot believe that.'

She gave a wry smile. 'It is true nevertheless.'

'But you are full of passion and love. How could anyone think such a thing?'

Exzalander shrugged and sighed, her breath hanging in the air before her. 'It is of no matter. Perhaps they are right. I have been swept along, as if on a tide, toward my fate and I have allowed my power to influence my decisions, which were not always for the best.'

She broke away from him and seated herself on a nearby rock. Unpacking her weapons, she removed the orange jumper that Mary had given to her.

'Now I am prepared, should we meet with trouble,' she said, her teeth chattering.

He smiled fiercely back at her, thinking how at home she would have appeared in one of the Celtic clans of old.

Thirty-Five

'**E**xzalander!' Thaniel cried as she disappeared. He fell to his knees, trying to wrench open the Book of CODM. 'Gailon, help me! We have to get her back.'

'Calm yourself, Thaniel, before the camp realises what has happened and you cause a panic.'

'Panic? There is *need* of it. She has gone and you let it happen!'

'I say again, Thaniel, be calm. She is in no danger. She has gone to the kingdom of Taiohãhn, and when she reappears, she will no doubt have the missing stone.'

'And what are we to do in the meantime?'

'We must continue our march and go to battle as our queen ordered. When she returns, we shall reunite the stones we have and defeat Katahl.'

Thaniel held the ancient book to his chest, as if it were a new life in his arms.

'But how do you *know* that she will return?' he asked.

'Faith,' said Gailon, steadily prising the book from his friend's grasp.

However, Thaniel's faith was weak. He had lost her once and his heart remained unhealed. It could not take being broken again.

Luckily, the army was large enough that none questioned the queen's absence, believing her to be riding ahead—or behind.

Gailon informed the close companions what had occurred. Jeb remained suspicious of Gailon's explanation, resorting at first to threats. He stayed close to the wizard, in the hope of learning more, secretly vowing to slit the man's throat if he had done his queen a mischief.

Thaniel avoided Cröedaw for most of the day and remained locked in his prison of gloom.

'Women!' came a voice from the darkness. 'They are ever the wedge that comes between friends. Is it your intention then, to die in battle alone?'

'Leave me be, Cob!' Thaniel ordered. 'You know not of what you speak.'

The faerie laughed wickedly, seeming to enjoy the Thaniel's pain.

'I am sure that I know more about such matters than yourself,' he said. 'I *know* the secrets of Her Majesty's heart.'

He hopped off the log on which he stood, and ran into the trees, leaving Thaniel glaring after him, wondering what he had meant. He jumped to his feet, about to set off after the faerie, when a commotion at the front of the column drew his attention away.

'I must see Princess Exzalander. My reason is most urgent.'

There were cries and screams. The knight's horse snorted as he drew his sword.

'BACK! STAY BACK!' the knight warned. 'I have no desire to harm you, but if you keep me from my purpose, I will have no other choice.'

Tom heard the commotion and ran with Thaniel toward the black knight, sword drawn. On seeing them, the knight lifted his visor, staring in wonder.

'Father?' he ventured, to which Tom made no reaction.

The knight was similar in features to Thaniel, although he had failed to notice. It was the black armour that Thaniel recognised and he made ready to kill the knight of Katahl.

The knight sheathed his sword and dismounted, holding the token of Tuâth high above his head, in symbol of friendship.

'Caitul!' Gailon's voice was heard from the crowd and they parted to let him forward.

'Gailon, where is Her Highness?' Caitul asked. 'I must speak with her immediately.'

'*Her Majesty* will have no desire to speak to an assassin, Caitul. Get you gone. You will find no sport here.'

A cry came from the crowd and Jeb rushed forward slashing at Caitul with his knife. The knight knocked him aside with no more thought than he would a gnat. The crowd roared and Gailon hushed them.

'I will not leave, Master Gailon,' Caitul said. 'I am here to offer my sword to the house of Tuâth and Shénnin, as should have been done long ago. I bring this as a token of my good faith. I intercepted it at Ishtar, where it was to be sent to Lord Katahl. If he had received it, he would have known at once that Exzalander has returned. I present it to you.'

A look of pure hatred burned toward Caitul as Jeb struggled to his feet. He made ready to lunge at the knight again, but Cröedaw held him back.

'You are bound by oath to Katahl,' Gailon said, 'how can we be expected to trust you?'

Caitul's eyes darkened with sorrow. 'I have already betrayed him,' he said. 'Indeed I have done so many times of late, and so my fate is already sealed. But I would wish to spend the time that remains to me, to help Her Majesty's cause, if she will have me.'

Gailon turned and began to walk back through the crowd. 'Follow me. Thomn, Thaniel, you must come too.' He led them away from prying eyes into his tent at the edge of camp.

'What say you, Thaniel?'

'I say we make him stand trial,' Thaniel replied.

'And you, Thomn?'

The old warrior shifted uncomfortably. 'I don't know why you ask me, Gailon. This man's a murderer, that much I do know. Because of him, one of my friends lost his mind and may never recover. I think Thaniel is right.'

'You would condemn your own son, father?'

Tom shook his head, frowning.

'Caitul speaks truly, Thomn-the-Cleaverhand,' Gailon explained. 'He is one of the sons whom you would have left when you agreed to quest for Exzalander, had he not been the first sent to retrieve her. I have no doubt that this was one of the reasons you so readily agreed to such a dangerous mission. He is of your blood too, Thaniel, yet more distant.'

Tom was silent, too shocked to speak.

'This news changes nothing!' Thaniel said. 'He should stand trial.'

'And for what would you have me stand trial?' the knight asked.

'You are a murderer,' Thaniel said.

Caitul removed his gauntlets and unclipped his helmet, placing it as his feet. He ruffled his hair, offering protest. 'The only human life that I have taken on Maldahl was hundreds of years ago. He was a condemned criminal, and Exzalander herself wanted him dead; believe me, he deserved his fate!'

Thaniel sprang to his feet; his hand went to his sword once more. 'You lie!'

'Calm yourself, Thaniel,' Gailon said. 'He does not lie. He was high and noble, First Knight to a once great house. He was not here at its downfall and is but recently returned. He speaks truly.'

'And what of the deaths on Earth? What of those?'

'Thomn, we cannot hold trial for crimes he may have committed on a different world.'

'There is no may about it, Gailon. I was there. I saw the mayhem that he caused.'

'Father, my duty was to protect the princess, now queen seemingly, at all costs. I was in a strange world and the majick that was used to discover Exzalander blinded me to sense; everyone seemed an enemy to me. You yourself have killed in the line of your duty, have you not?'

Tom huffed in stubborn indignation.

'Come now Thomn, you know that you have,' Gailon said. 'The fact remains that the only crime he has committed is to betray Katahl and we cannot very well hold him responsible for *that* now, can we?'

Caitul's head bowed. 'There is one other crime,' he muttered, 'and my honour dictates that I should speak of it. The queen must decide my fate. Now that I am her humble servant, she may do with me what she will.'

'Of what do you speak, Caitul?' Gailon asked.

Caitul could not look up and stared down at his feet as if ashamed to speak. 'I … I kissed the pri … Her Majesty. I touched her royal person …'

Thaniel fumed. 'He should die where he … Death! The sentence should be death. Oh treachery most foul …'

Caitul's head bowed forward further still, so that only his crown of brown hair could be seen. From behind Gailon came a tinkering laugh.

'Death?' Cob said. 'If death be the punishment for such a crime, then half the people present would be found guilty! Tell me when the execution date is to be set and I'll be sure to attend.'

'COB!' Gailon roared, 'BEGONE!' He turned in such anger and fury that the faerie was affeared, seeing for a second time a human majick to outmatch his own. He scampered quickly from the tent.

Thaniel's face was turning purple, as if he had been holding his breath too long. Caitul was looking from one man to another, a puzzled frown on his face.

'Lies! Thaniel said. 'How dare he besmirch her name thus. Gailon … GAILON, WHAT DID HE MEAN?'

The wizard did not answer. He seemed lost in thought and smiled pleasantly to himself.

Thaniel ran enraged from the tent, determined to catch and punish the faerie. Cob hopped and skipped through the trees, his luminescence firefly-like as it bobbed away in the dark.

'Master Gailon?' Caitul said. 'What did the little one mean when he said that half of the people in this tent would be found guilty? There were four of us, five if we include the little one.'

Gailon laughed heartily. 'Three of us are guilty; Thaniel alas, loves her, and she him—yet he knows it not, nor never shall if my advice be heeded. *I* kissed her once, when she was sleeping in my master's tower. I was only a boy, whose head was full of dreams. I had heard that when princesses sleep, a kiss might awaken them ... dear me, I had forgotten. My master, oh how he scolded me, but I did not see as I had done anything so terrible. I was only playing and she would never know. The things we do when we're young, eh? Dear me.'

Thomn appeared to be puzzled and shook his head suddenly.

'Thaniel loves Kirsten? Bloody fool if you ask me.'

'Cob! Stop and explain yourself!' Thaniel ordered.

The faerie hopped up into a tree and smirked down at the angry warrior.

'No! Now leave me be.'

'Cob, you have belied the queen of Maldahl. When she gets to hear about it ...'

'She ent here, is she? She's off with Taiohãhn and even if she was here, she'd do nothing, because I speak the truth!'

'How dare you!'

Cob laughed. 'Oh poor Thaniel. In love, is he? So wounded ... you're a fool! Forget about her. Taiohãhn will be making love to her as we speak.'

'Cob, be quiet,' Cröedaw's voice hissed from the shadows. 'Thaniel, listen not to his babbling. Tonight is the grandest cavalcade of the faerie year. He is banished and so seeks to make sport with your pain in order to lessen his own.'

'And what would you know of my pain? *You,* who carries the queen's favour.'

Thaniel walked away, but Cröedaw pursued.

'Thaniel, you were not to be told. Gailon said it would be dangerous, but I will not lose my friend to such a misunderstanding and I think you have a right to know.'

'I already know! The queen *loves* you.'

'No you fool. Her heart is yours!'

'Leave me be, Cröedaw. Your jest does not amuse.'

'It is true, my friend. Her pain has been as great as yours, perhaps more so, as she knows that which you do not.'

Thaniel sank to the ground, unsure of what he was hearing.

'That you became lovers,' Cröedaw continued. 'You had declared your feelings for each other, but her blood being now tainted with that of the Clan of the Dark Moon, cast a spell, unbeknownst to herself, and you were lost to their majick. The only way you could be saved was to make you forget the night that you spent together and all declarations of feeling.

'She broke her heart that day, Thaniel, and she will never forgive herself. Why do you think that her behaviour changed so? In effort to harden herself against the pain of love, she pushed back all other feeling. She became ruthless.'

'She loves me?' Thaniel whispered.

 Cröedaw smiled and nodded. 'Yes my friend, she does.'

'You should never have told!' chanted Cob, 'I'm going to tell Gailon. What's the point in his knowing? Can't act on it, can he?'

The faerie flitted back to camp and Cröedaw sat beside his friend, who seemed suddenly several years younger.

'Cob's right, Thaniel. Until Exzalander finds a way to prevent the spell, you cannot be together … was I right to tell you?'

Thaniel turned to his friend and his grin gave his answer.

'She *loves* me!' he said and embraced Cröedaw, laughing and crying at the same time.

The desert stretched before the company and Fahl agreed with Ârgrïn, that they should take their final rest before attempting to trek under the blistering sun. Richard patted his horse, lost in thought while it nuzzled at his arm. Several of the Elfïn seemed to be watching him, which made him uneasy. He longed to remove his Mo-rye armour, but remembered the words of Huçul and resisted the temptation.

Fahl had begun to unload the weapon wagon and demonstrated their use to the newcomers. The Elfïn were wary of the crystalline rifles and declared their mistrust of a weapon so governed by majick. Iorich explained its workings and ensured them that once the charge was depleted, they could return to more conventional weapons, but the guns would give them an instant advantage of surprise and reduce the odds against them.

The Elfín reluctantly agreed and accepted a weapon apiece, some being able to double-up and sling a spare over their back, next to their quivers. They had travelled less than thirty miles before they became aware of a distant rumble, a noise that filled them all with dread.

The army at Golstur had left the confines of the city and spewed forth to meet them, like a plague of rats in the distance. They knew of the Elfín's approach and on Nimrïn's signal, they swarmed out to meet their attackers with fierce and savage resistance.

The war had begun.

At the site of Meadha, lying in a deep scar in the ancient hill, Exzalander slept uneasily in the arms or Corvuß, haunted by a nightmare of old, as she dreamed of warriors discharging their weapons across the dunes at their terrible enemy.

Trolgs.

However, this time she understood what was happening. Walker had spoken of an army that marched from the north, on Golstur.

The war had begun.

She screamed out in terror as she saw the first Elfín fall, and awoke shaking with fear and frustration.

'What is it?' Corvuß asked, cradling her gently in his arms.

'I dare not tell you. I have to get back! How long will this Fionnbharr keep me waiting?'

'I hope not long now. Midnight has passed.'

He moved behind and wrapped himself about her, in effort to warm her cold body. His presence was like a huge feather cloak and she settled comfortably against him, trying to put thoughts of her dream from her mind.

Another hour passed that way and Corvuß talked of Maldahl as he remembered it, and of Etain's beauty. Exzalander listened with interest, his musical voice lulling her to a state of calm.

'Corvuß, may I ask you a question?'

'Of course,' the Elfín replied.

'If you were not aware of the prophecy, how did you know about the gods almost destroying Maldahl?'

'Taiohãhn sent one of the Macara Shee here, quite recently in fact. I did not speak to him myself, but a friend—a fellow Elfín informed me of what had happened to Maldahl after I left.'

'But why was he sent?'

Before Corvuß could reply, a man appeared bearing a shotgun. Exzalander and Corvuß sprang to their feet in surprise.

'What are ye doin' here?' the man said. 'Be off with ye! This is private land. Be off!'

The moon cast little light and Exzalander reckoned there was no possible way he could have seen them—heard them maybe. But she questioned what a man would be doing wandering about in the dark, without so much as a torch. *A gamekeeper perhaps?* But her instincts told her different.

'We cannot leave, sir,' she said. 'We await an audience with King Fionnbharr and cannot depart until we have spoken with him.'

The man's husky voice, laughed low. 'Yeh cracked, the both of ye. Now shog off!'

Exzalander threw back her hood and the man scowled at the purple glow in her eyes.

'Enough of these games! I have waited patiently at Fionnbharr's door for hours. Tell him the Queen of Maldahl requests an audience with him.'

The man gave a toothy grin. 'Queen is it now? Well dat's nice for ye. I'm a Roman emperor, don't ye know!'

Exzalander's posture remained composed, apart from her hand, which tapped the hilt of the Sword of Taiohãhn. The man noticed and backed away accordingly.

'Enough!' came a commanding voice and both Exzalander and her companion found themselves suddenly no longer on the hillside in the dead of night, but in a vast cavern surrounded by lights and splendour.

The Aes Sídhe within were unlike the faeries with whom Exzalander had had previous dealings. They were tall, more akin to Elfín in looks and stature.

She knelt low before the elaborately dressed king and queen before her.

'Beannachtaí Exzalander. Táimid tar éis fanacht le fada an lá do do romhainn,' Fionnbharr said. 'Maith dom, tú dócha nach bhfuil focal a thuiscint go bhfuil mé ag rá go bhfuil tú? Ní mór liom labhairt le teanga níos coitianta'

Exzalander lifted her head, her eyes questioning, taking the pause as her turn to speak.

'King Fionnbharr, I am honoured to make your acquaintance.'

The king remained unmoved. 'Methinks that you are no queen, to bow before me thus. Surely a queen would regard me as an equal.'

Exzalander stood, the warmth of the Sídhe filling her with a strange joy. 'I was led to believe, Your Majesty, that you are much *more* than a mere king, and so I treat you with the courtesy and respect that your position deserves. I will of course address you as an equal, if that is your wish.'

A slow smile spread across Fionnbharr's noble face, and he laughed. 'We've been expecting you, Exzalander. Welcome to sídhe Meadha. May I present my queen, Onagh.'

Exzalander bowed her head in greeting to the faerie queen, who was as handsome a female as Exzalander had ever beheld.

A feast was brought forth and the hall filled with singing.

'Corvuß, please eat your fill,' said Fionnbharr. 'Take your ease whilst I talk with your fair companion.'

Fionnbharr offered his hand and led Exzalander away from the joyous throng. Glancing over her shoulder, she saw the faerie clan dragging the reluctant Corvuß into their celebration.

'You said that you awaited my arrival, Fionnbharr. Can it be that you already know the purpose of my visit?'

'Yes I know. You want me to return to you to Maldahl so that you can take the stones back—to make them whole once more.'

He knows about the stones, she thought. *It seems that the Macara Shee who Taiohãhn sent, has been speaking to more than just the Elfín.* 'And will you help me?' she asked.

The king halted and stared out over an underground lake, which glistened in the crystalline cave.

'I wonder that you think I may not. Corvuß has made you distrust us, methinks. He sees conspiracy everywhere … such a pity. I have attempted to help you since your arrival here. I tried to retrieve the stone for you and hold it safe. I have sent many a guardian to watch over you whilst you grew, though you knew it not. It has been many years since I posted Seoul at the docks to wait for you. Glad was he to return home to us.'

Exzalander recalled the old man who had greeted her and gave a wry smile. 'But why? Why would you help me? And how is it you even know of me?' she asked.

'Taiohãhn is a much missed ally. Do I need any other reason?'

'You know Taiohãhn.'

'Yes, but by another name. Long it has been since I last saw Him.'

Exzalander stared at the faerie king, his tall tower-like crown, and his shimmering robes like the sea.

'Politics?' she mused. 'You see in me a chance for you to rise back to power.'

'And yet, though you know my reasons to be selfish, you cannot refuse to accept my help, surely?'

'No King Fionnbharr, I have no choice. But I do not understand how you hope to gain a foothold in Ireland again. Christianity is too strong.'

The king smiled good-naturedly. 'It is only as strong here as we allowed it to be. We permitted the old wells and sacred places of worship to be renamed and the people retained their belief in my kind. I could very easily restore the people's faith in us by taking back the holy wells and stones. I could attack the church from within, to restore the faith. The papal rules are restricting and outdated; the people long for the freedom that we offer. However, I need Taiohãhn's support, especially across the sea. The political situation between the nations is precarious at best. He must establish His support there as I gather mine here, in order to avoid war.'

'Fionnbharr, we live in a multi-cultural society. It is not only Christianity that prevents your return to power. Some of the beliefs and religions are just too strong to be overthrown and to be honest, I think that you underestimate the power of the Catholic faith here.'

The smile remained on Fionnbharr's lips. 'I never said it would be easy, Exzalander, yet do you expect me to continue to fade into nothingness and allow history to forget my very existence? For, when the last believer dies, I will cease to exist. I cannot end like that. I will not.'

Exzalander was lost in contemplation of the king's words.

'So, you create life as a god and the beings that you create can in their turn be your undoing?'

Fionnbharr frowned at her words; she had said something that upset him and his eyes concealed something he was unwilling to divulge.

'It is the way of things, Exzalander,' he said. 'It is the balance of the universe. The more a god's power is exercised, the more precarious His position, and yet, not to use His power, then the god loses it in degrees, until He becomes demigod, then finally mortal. It has ever been this way. Our lives are dictated by the faith that is held in our existence. Without that faith, we return to the stars from whence we were made. All beings from gods to the smallest of worms serve a purpose.'

Exzalander bit her lip, feeling that there was more to what he said than he let on. She had no desire to offend her host by questioning him further, yet remained convinced that the old religions could and would never return.

'You continue to doubt me, ' Fionnbharr said. 'Do not trouble to deny it. I do not require your faith, only that you succeed in your task and then ... well then, time will tell.'

Exzalander bowed her head respectfully.

'Come, you must rest now,' he said. 'This may be the last time that you may do so in safety and comfort, for a while at least. Tomorrow, I will send you home.'

Exzalander slept soundly in the arms of Corvuß—two strangers in the faerie halls, and she dreamt of nothing more than the land, green plains and lush wild country of Ireland.

She awoke late, to find Corvuß was no longer with her. Stretching and yawning, she decided to bathe before seeking out Fionnbharr. As she walked back to the lake, she noticed the Aes Sídhe in the daytime. Here in their hall, it was forever midnight, and yet she knew that above ground, the sun would be high in the sky, shining down on the scarred hill. Whereas the night before the music had been sweet, now she perceived a deep sorrow, for the Aes Sídhe were not free, but imprisoned in their underground cell, unless liberated by Fionnbharr's impossible plan or else they simply ceased to exist.

She stripped and dived down into the dark water below, shuddering as her body reacted to the icy temperature, the shock of which drove all thoughts of pity from her mind.

'Good morning.'

Exzalander wheeled about and saw Corvuß swimming toward her.

She smiled, her teeth chattering. 'I thought you had gone,' she said.

He held out his hands across the water and a wave of warmth hit her.

She smiled lazily. 'Thank you,' she said.

His eyes fixed on her naked shoulders and the top of her breasts as they bobbed in and out of the water.

'My pleasure,' he said. 'You do realise do you not, that if I were to cast my spell again, then you would be unable to prevent your own from retaliating.'

'You wouldn't!'

He smiled mischievously. 'You have no desire then to say a proper farewell to the man that was *almost* your husband?'

'I cannot; you know I cannot.'

His lips met her own for the briefest of moments and he backed away once more.

'I would have been honoured to take you for my bride, Exzalander. Remember, if you ever return and are in need of help, call my name and I will be with you.' He turned and swam to shore, then turning into a crow, flew up to a high ledge, back into the light of the cavern.

She scrambled up the rocks, but there was no sign of him on her ascent. 'Corvuß!' she cried, but only the soft singing of the Aes Sídhe answered her call. Reaching for her trousers, she discovered that they had been replaced with a dress of finest silver gossamer, fit for a faerie queen. She dressed herself, a sense of sadness upon her, and walked off to find Fionnbharr.

'I am ready, King Fionnbharr,' she said. 'I am ready to go home.'

The faerie king nodded. 'All is prepared for you, Exzalander. This way.'

She followed him into a narrow anti-chamber, where stalactites and stalagmites formed so tightly that the way was difficult. Onagh was already waiting for their arrival; behind her was a glass-like sheet of ice embedded into the cave wall. At once, Exzalander recognised what it was—a forelócian glæs, created by Taiohãhn she figured.

'Exzalander come forth. Here we bid you farewell and all our hopes go with you.'

Onagh, who was fully a foot taller than the warrior queen, kissed her cheek and then she and her lord placed each a hand against the ice, turning it to water. Exzalander looked behind her, her eyes piercing the darkness, as if searching for something.

'If you see Corvuß, will you tell him … tell him goodbye.'

Fionnbharr nodded.

'Thank you,' she whispered. Taking a breath, she stepped forward into the gateway she hoped would lead to home.

Thirty-Six

Troy watched from the forelócian glæs in Katahl's tower, as the army of Elfin and Mariners readied their weapons against the oncoming terror.

Katahl's voice echoed from the shadows, mocking. 'Tell me more about this god of yours, Father Troy.'

Troy seemed not to hear, but leaned closer as the first shots were fired. 'There are wizards among the Elfin,' he observed.

Katahl stepped nearer, smiling. 'Fear not, Father, their majick will fail them ere long. Already I can feel them begin to drain. My army will ride over them and rid Maldahl of their impurity. Soon my princess shall be brought home and you shall see us wed.'

Troy turned to face the visage of Maldahl's enemy, with a start.

'Do you not wish to kill her?' he asked.

Katahl's mind lost appetite for battle as there appeared before him, much sweeter meat.

'You love Her Highness?'

Troy's hand moved involuntarily to the cross about his neck and seemed sunken beyond measure. 'No,' he said. 'I did love the girl she was, the innocent, the warrior trying to find her footing in the dark. But she … she betrayed me. She …'

'*What!*' Katahl hissed, realising the enormity of Troy's words.

A fire burned in the priest's head as his mind was thrown open. He fell to his knees and Katahl learned all he desired.

'It cannot be!' Katahl said. 'That woman? But why? *Why* did she not kill me when she had the chance?' He laughed as he remembered the sword throw. 'Is that the best you could do, Taiohãhn? Your warrior lost … the sword! Can it have been? I held it in my grasp and yet knew it not, just as I beheld her and threw her to the dogs. My princess returned to me and I watched as they tore away her purity. She *has* power—that much is certain. Nobody has eluded me thus before and yet, she did not strike. She endured the torture and the conditioning, and then she escaped. She alone of all my enemies was permitted

to walk free. I had her life in my hands and I let her go. I underestimated her
…'

He pressed closer and Troy cried out, but could not resist as Katahl
plundered his mind.

So it was, that Exzalander arrived home unnoticed by Katahl. The sand was
hot beneath her feet and before her was the sound of battle. As she ran toward
the roar with her sword drawn, it was as though she had run into one of her
dreams. The Elfin warriors threw down their weapons as each drained of its
power and their arrows began to fly.

The tall blue wizards sent spells across the desert that hit the Trolg army in
waves, and yet there were so many that Exzalander felt sure that the
overwhelming numbers would eventually over-run the fighters. She could see
the spells as they hit, and each one brought with it death; a hundred or so at
first, then eighty, then less and less again. The Mariner's powers were
weakening. It had taken years to create Bashnya with their majick; now they
used that same power in reverse and the enchantment was strong. They felt
themselves tiring, and although hundreds of Elfin arrows whistled relentlessly
overhead, the enemy pressed closer.

Exzalander's army marched double-time to reach Ishtar and Gailon's fear
grew. The smell of burning reached them long before they met its cause.

Ishtar was empty—a blackened ruin.

'Rook!' Cröedaw whispered. He ran ahead and was lost in the distance.

Cries rang out from the company and the ranks broke as men rushed wildly
into the fallen city, searching for signs of life; for any indication that their
kinsmen and friends did not die in such a way.

Caitul dismounted, staring at the whirl of smoke within.

'I do not understand,' he said grimly.

'Do you not?' The voice was Dahal's, as he stepped out from a cindered
doorway. 'I have been waiting for you, Caitul. My Lord knows of your
treachery and you are too late. He combined his forces and sent them to
destroy your pathetic uprising at Golstur. Your troops are divided, and once
the Elfin fall in the desert, we will wipe you out before we take Ealdorbold.
There is no hope for you … any of you.'

'Listen not to his poison, good people,' yelled Gailon. 'We may yet avenge this place,'

Dahal sneered at Gailon's words, but his eyes did not leave the knight before him.

'Where is the princess? She is to return with me to our master.'

The spell that Gailon had cast over the company, lifted, and all who had stood firm were filled with a sudden madness.'

'She is gone.'

'She has abandoned us!'

'We are to die!'

Dahal smiled, as if the surrounding sorrow fed his very being. Thaniel and Caitul drew their swords. The few who remained standing near, could plainly see that the two warriors were akin.

'No young cous',' Caitul said.

Thaniel nodded in grim understanding and took no further action, while Caitul sprang forward to fight the man who had once been as close a friend to him as friends could be.

The king of the Macara Shee awoke late from their cavalcade. He had found it a disappointment to say the least. They had roamed in search of travellers between Ealdorbold and Ishtar, and as a final resort made ready to enter Golstur.

'Trolgs!' he tutted aloud, and his consort turned in her sleep. 'Ruined our feast … what are they all doing this far south, anyhow?'

A young faerie named Rowan entered the king's chamber and bowed low. 'My Lord King.'

'What is it?' the king asked grumpily, folding his arms. His sleep had done nothing to soothe his spirits.

'Battle is raging overhead, and many of our clan wish to flee, lest we be crushed should our halls not prevail under the thundering advance.'

'What nonsense is this? Of course our halls will not fail. Our majick is stronger than those bloody Trolg feet. Come, help me up. I must address the clan.'

In the Great Hall of the Macara Shee, it was plain for the king to see why a panic had started amongst his people. The sound of thousands of Trolg feet rumbled so deeply, it was like a terrible music that sang of their doom.

'Hear me now,' he projected over the din. 'Those Trolg abominations are all noise. There is no majick in them. We are safe. Come now, you have never reacted in such way before. What care we for wars? We will be here when the battle is done and we shall still be free.'

There seemed to mixed opinions to their king's words. Many cheered or nodded in agreement, but there were also negative protestations.

'No, we won't'

'Yes, free to starve!'

'What of the new power?'

'Now, now,' said the king, trying to calm them. 'One at a time please. Cotyl, what say you?'

'I say, we shall be wiped out, lest we take action to prevent it. The religion that drove those who could escape, back to Maldahl, is here. If it should spread, then where shall we go? Maldahl is our last safe haven. We should have killed the human whilst we had the chance.'

There was a general agreement from the crowd.

'Yes, yes Cotyl, but he was under the protection of Taiohãhn's warrior. What choice did we have, but to set him free?' argued the king.

'The new religion is not our only worry. There may be no humans remaining after this war. Our cavalcade will be fruitless. And how long will it be before Katahl turns to us for new sport?'

'Xylem. We did not give you leave to speak,' the king said. 'Clover, what say you?'

'I wonder that you should ask me, Milord. You know my opinion well. The day you banished my son was the day our fortunes turned against us. Xylem speaks true. Katahl will conquer or destroy. He *does* have majick and can penetrate our hidden realm, even his Trolgs cannot. You should not have banished Cob!'

The king looked thoughtful. 'Let us view this battlefield. Perhaps we may take action to prevent Katahl's power growing. Ready yourselves.'

Clover's eyes met that of her king and she scowled at his approach.

'What I did, Clover, I did for the good of our clan,' he said. 'Never question me again on that regard, lest you find you shall join him in his shame.'

It was plain to see why Caitul had been First Knight to Katahl; his skill with the sword was second to none. Even the warrior of Taiohãhn had not beaten him by skill with sword alone.

Many of the refugees were drawn to the fight. It was as if they needed Caitul to win so that their faith might be restored. Gailon and his company joined the crowd of onlookers; there seemed little else to do, but watch the downfall of a knight of Katahl.

Tehd pointed eagerly in the direction of Golstur. 'Gailon look!' he shouted.

A shaft of white light shot up toward the heavens, causing Ioan to whoop for joy.

'Exzalander! Gailon, she's returned!'

The old wizard's eyes sparkled, as the majick within him grew eager for release. 'Ioan, hold aloft your pendant.' Gailon shouted, reaching up with his ring.

The two gems released the same light into the sky, in answer to their queen's call. And so it was, that few witnessed the final blow that felled Dahal. He held Caitul for a moment skewered on the First Knight's blade.

'You shall die a thousand deaths for breaking your oath,' he rasped.

Caitul pushed Dahal from his blade and watched as the armour fell to the floor, empty.

Exzalander held the sword of Taiohãhn aloft, feeling the will of its master as the beam of light shot up into the sky. Within moments, she saw Ioan and Gailon's answering beacons.

'They're too far away, damn them! If only we had marched a day sooner!' She lowered the blade and turned back to the battle with a sense of growing despair.

A group of Trolgs had broken away and headed straight for her. In her dreams, it had always been at that point, where Katahl appeared and offered his hand, but Katahl was wandering in the past, exploring Troy's mind and learning its secrets.

She felt a surge of adrenaline as the danger pressed closer. Thrusting her sword into the sand, she unclipped her shuriken and stood firm.

'Did you see Lord king?' Rowan asked. 'The light of Anarkhane!'

'Yes I saw it.'

'How comes it that the warrior stands alone?'

'I know not, Rowan. Cob should be with her at least.'

'My Lord king, I do not understand ... why?'

'Do not seek to understand the workings of my mind,' the king cut in. 'COMPANY, LET US TO THE WARRIOR WOMAN!'

Six shuriken struck home and six Trolgs fell, as their companions trampled over them. She had trained so long with the foul creatures that she no longer feared them. As opponents, she knew them better than any other. Her vile imprisonment now worked in her favour. As her last throwing star was spent, she drew her dagger and grasped the sword.

Her despair was gone and she laughed as she slew; the warrior inside her finding place once more, a warrior whose blood was tainted with the children of Taiohãhn; her senses more adept, her reflexes so fast, that no Trolg saw their final blow as it was dealt.

As the last of the Trolg unit fell, she knelt and wiped her weapons, smiling at the approach of the Macara Shee.

'Greetings Lord. What brings you here?' she asked.

The faerie king arched his eyebrows, knowing not how she perceived his presence, when he approached from the rear. Before them, the Trolg army was almost upon the Elfin fighters and Exzalander perceived the horror of their oncoming doom; a sickness rose to her throat then fell abruptly as the battle froze. Arrows hung mid-air, Trolgs suspended mid-attack. Time had been stopped and the majick of the Macara Shee hung like a blue, grey mist between the foes.

'You have changed,' remarked the faerie king.

Exzalander turned to face him, forcing her curious eyes away from the living tableaux of battle.

'Indeed Lord, I have. May I ask once again, what brings you here?'

As she looked upon the tiny faces of his people, the king frowned and she perceived the answer before he uttered any reply.

'I see,' she said. 'You are affeared. You came to discover which way the wind is blowing. Should you pledge allegiance to Katahl? You are shrewd, Lord. I have long since guessed why you banished Cob from your clan. If Katahl wins then you will be his enemy. If I win and you did nought to aid me, then you will be *my* enemy, yet you sent your emissary to me to prevent this.

However, you sent him in disgrace so that you may disassociate yourself from the act should I fail and you are forced to face Katahl. Very clever.'

Clover pushed forward from the crowd. 'Does she speak truly, my Lord King?

The king's mouth twisted awkwardly and then suddenly burst forth into laughter. 'Yes Clover. She speaks the truth. Cob does not know it, but if this woman defeats that upstart, then he will return a hero.'

Clover burst into tears, sinking to the floor.

'Look upon the battle before you, king of the Macara Shee,' Exzalander said. 'See the enemies overwhelming number. Perhaps you care not that Elfin will die. But know this—*I* care. I will care very deeply now I know there were those on hand who may have prevented their fall.'

'We are not warriors,' the king replied.

'I know that. All I need is a little time for my army at Ishtar to get here before it's too late. That is all I ask.'

A slow smile spread out among the host, as they comprehended what she was asking.

'Time? Is that all?' the king said, with a grin. 'I think we may be able to accommodate you. But what if you fail? We will have aided you and Katahl will make it his mission to wipe us out of existence.'

Exzalander shook her head. 'Katahl will seek to destroy you whether or not you helped me. You are a powerfully majick race. All such beings will be erased to prevent any future uprising. Once there is no majick left in Maldahl, he will be all-powerful. Surely you must see that.'

The king's brow furrowed deeply as he carefully considered her words. Exzalander was aware of the profound quiet of the frozen battle and every second that passed by seemed an age to her.

'Very well,' the king said at last. 'We grant you the gift of time.'

A faerie wind began to build and within moments, the host were gone. There was no sign of their passing; it was if they had never been there. The queen turned back to face the desert and the pending battle before her, statue-like, awaiting time to catch them up again.

Caitul removed his helm; his face was so pale that it was almost translucent. He fell to his knees and Tom was beside him in an instant.

'Father …' he looked up smiling, his eyes weary. 'I hoped to see her one last time, before the darkness took me.'

'Are you wounded?' Tom asked.

'No father, but the majick of my broken oath, consumes me from within. I am not long for this world I deem.'

Tom looked up to Gailon, as if begging for his aid. However, Gailon's attention was elsewhere. A black speck flew over the smoking turrets and landed a man at their feet.

'The battle has begun,' Cröedaw said. 'I saw no survivors in Ishtar.'

'I am sorry, my friend,' Thaniel said.

'It may be that they managed to escape. We should hope in that,' offered Gailon.

'Yes you are right of course,' Cröedaw said. 'But little consolation will that be, unless we are able to reach Golstur in time.'

Jeb interrupted. 'We have tarried here too long. You are all complaining that we are so far away from battle and yet make no move to help our queen,' he said, mounting his horse once more.

'Hold Jeb,' Gailon ordered. 'You are brave, but headstrong. Gather as many people back at this point. You shall not ride off alone.'

Jeb nodded and rode off into the city, calling the scattered troops back to their duty.

'I will go with him,' offered the former counsellor.

Ioan pulled suddenly at the old wizard's arm.

'Exzalander says that we are to charge the right flank of Katahl's army.'

Thaniel threw his hands up in the air with a hiss of frustration. 'But surely she saw your signal. She knows that we shall never reach her in time.'

Cob, who was used to being ignored during the day, sat alone on a nearby windowsill, blackened with soot. It was he who first saw his clan's advance and understood what it meant.

'Gailon, Gailon. My Clan!'

Almost immediately there followed screams as the hurricane approached, rounding up the stray army as it swept through the ruined city and settled at the northern gate, where Gailon stepped forward to greet the new arrivals, as nobody else seemed to realise what was happening.

'Greetings King Noch. What brings you to this place?'

Cob jumped down from the window ledge and Clover ran to him, holding him close. He did not argue, either too shocked or overjoyed.

'Greetings, people of Maldahl. We come to take you all to battle. Greetings to you, Cob. You have been much missed. Come join us—all of you.'

Cob still clung to Clover as the faerie wind began to lift Exzalander's army.

The queen watched the frozen battle for signs of life, but there was none. Retrieving her throwing stars from the skulls of the dead Trolgs, she waited. She did not wait long.

The wind rose above the dunes behind the army, and settled to the right flank. Almost immediately, the roar of battle burst forth once more. The Trolgs continued, as if there had been no pause and were taken by surprise as Exzalander's army charged. The reinforcements lifted the spirits of the Elfín, as the Mariners last spells were spent and the tall blue wizards who remained, retreated to the rear of the Elfín—exhausted.

The Trolgs seemed to ignore Exzalander; she had not attacked yet, and was but one warrior. She strained to see her friends on the far side of the battle, but the mass ever entwined and she could make out nothing.

From the dunes, invisible to the enemy, the Macara Shee cut off the retreat back to Golstur. Using their majick, they picked off Trolgs as a last defence. One by one, Trolgs disappeared, but Exzalander had no time to wonder where they were vanishing.

Swords were drawn as the enemy crashed into the Elfín with a battle cry terrible to hear. Richard felt his horse shudder as his sword lashed out. Exzalander's army was little more than an angry mob, incensed with fury and outrage at the atrocities committed upon their families and friends. They had lost all sense of fear and their burning hatred gave them strength.

Whil dragged Caitul up, as he lost his footing in the soft sand. As the desert heat hit them, they tore their helmets off. Tom and Thaniel slew side by side and the blood bathed their faces like war paint. Gailon held Ioan back, explaining his duty was to protect the pendant above all else. Tehd remained with him, sword drawn, lest the fight should head their way. Jeb rode into the thick of battle, hoping to catch a glimpse of his queen. It was then that he beheld the Mo-rye warrior for the first time; he felt as though he had stepped into a dream as legend caught up with time and all that once was, became uncertain. A sharp pain stung his side as an arrow sunk deep into his flesh. He cried out and fell from his horse, which in turn, screamed in terror and ran wildly at the attackers, injuring several before it was hacked down.

Jeb grasped the shaft and swiftly pulled, screaming as it seemed a million fluttering insects were before his eyes. He growled, recalling his dead mother and refused to black out from the pain.

Despite his good intentions, Richard was not a trained soldier and he soon began to tire. The Elfin swords and knives were swift and relentless in comparison and so he became an easier target for the enemy.

The Mo-rye warrior was dragged from his horse and Jeb struggled toward him. A Trolg, who stood fully twice his height, stepped in his path, grinning savagely and brandishing a lethal looking club. Jeb ducked out the way of the first swing and threw his dagger, which sank into chest of his attacker. The Trolg did not fall, however; the attack only served to make him angry. Jeb no longer felt the blood as it poured from his wound. He struck out with his short sword, stabbing repeatedly whilst dodging the colossal swings of his enemy's club, knowing that should it meet its target then he would fall.

Momentarily stunned, Richard hit the ground, waiting for the killer blow while he lay defenceless, yet no blow came, only the sound of clashing steel. He struggled to his feet, his vision blurred at first. His horse was nowhere to be seen, but there, fighting to defend him, stood someone that Richard knew should not be present.

'Huçul!'

She was nimble and deadly, but she looked so delicate and tiny against the towering foe. Richard clasped his sword once more and clambered over to her side, comprehending as he fought, that she had been his warhorse. She, like many of her kindred, was able to change form at will; she had ridden into battle to be with him. He was struck with purpose, knowing he fought for her. Whether he was to live or die, they would be together.

Cröedaw, having spent all his arrows, changed to crow form and flew to the aid of the queen; glad to escape the rising horror within him at the carnage of battle.

Gailon surveyed from the present safety of the dunes, keeping true to his word and protecting, as best he could, those whom the queen loved. But it was becoming difficult to see them as they drove deeper into the melee.

Exzalander ran down the hill to strike at the left flank; her handful of shuriken dealt death to those before her. As she drew out her dagger, Cröedaw landed at her side.

She smiled. 'Timely my friend, timely.'

His bright Elfin eyes glittered as he saw the change in the warrior queen. No trace of Kirsten remained. She was Exzalander and had accepted that, embraced it even,

'Good to see you, my queen,' he said. 'You did not think that I would let you take the left flank alone, did you?'

Exzalander's dagger struck a Trolg's arm. She ducked and swung it behind, embedding it into the leg of another. Rolling backward and upright, she began to slay with the sword of Taiohãhn, as her dagger possessed her attacker. The Elfin knife beside her served as her defence as she attacked.

'Now Cröedaw, you shall see Tehtra at work. None can control that blade, but I.'

Cröedaw laughed as Tehtra's will was done and the Trolg slew its neighbour. The surrounding Trolgs hacked their attacker down and took the dagger from his bleeding corpse. And so Tehtra the dragon defended her mistress in battle, as was foretold. Yet, the dagger had a secondary purpose for which Ardahl had intended and yet Gailon had misinterpreted ...

Morlech the dragon had been ill-tempered since Exzalander's visit. He had caught a glimpse of his beloved Tehtra once more and his depression had lifted. The rage had diminished and a spark of hope had been growing, until he knew that the fire it kindled could be put to good purpose. Slim though it might be, there was still a chance that his mate could be restored. His pride had held him back, debating how a dragon could aid a human. He had been pacing about his cave, even venturing out into the mountains and flying high above the clouds. It was from such a vantage point that he spied the lights in the sky; the trio of Anarkhane stones were like beacons seen by the whole of Maldahl—a call to arms for all. For *all* would be affected by war.

The end was drawing near; the lights marked where his beloved was trapped. If the girl fell in battle, so would his love. If she were to remain alive, then there was a glimmer of hope. There might be a way to free Tehtra. He flew toward the lights, no longer debating what he should do.

Caitul's breath was heavy; his very life force seemed to be ebbing away. He sank to his knees once more and Whil blocked an oncoming blow from a squint-eyed Trolg.

'On your feet, Caitul!' Whil demanded. 'Somewhere before us, our queen fights alone. All we have to do is cleave a path toward her and you shall see her again, ere you depart from this world.'

Caitul grimaced, his breath ever shorter, but his sword remained true as he hacked into the crowd with Whil at his side.

The army was being driven back and yet Richard stayed with Huçul, as she lay beaten and bleeding. She was yet living and he could not bring himself to leave her. Jeb crawled over to them, collapsing nearby. His wound overcoming him at last, he lay and saw from a snail's perspective, the eyes of the fallen— Elfin, men and Trolgs. He wept silently, waiting for his own end to come.

'Come on old man!' Thaniel called, as he felled another Trolg.

'I'll give you old.' Tom said. He swung his sword again and cleaved off his enemy's arm. The Trolg's successor threw the old warrior to the ground and grabbed at him with his great claws. Had Tom not been wearing armour, his lungs would have been punctured in the assault. He pushed at the Trolg, snarling back at him and was relieved to see Thaniel's sword pierce through its gullet. However, Thaniel paid the price for turning his back on the enemy, and a hatchet clipped him across the shoulder blade. He fell, bleeding beside his kinsman.

Trolgs backed away before Exzalander and Cröedaw, having seen what formidable opponents they were. The enemy moved swiftly backward and the faerie host retreated toward Gailon, lest they be trampled. The Elfin, who were now less than half their number, pursued the enemy, meeting with many soldiers of Ealdorbold, in fierce greeting.

Exzalander sprinted over to where Jeb lay, pale and quiet.

'Your Highness, you must help, please!'

She looked up. The voice that had spoken was familiar, yet she could not place it. The strange knight before her lifted his visor, and she met the tear-streaked face of Richard.

'She's dying. Please do something!' he pleaded.

Jeb's hand was cold in hers. She looked over to the Elfin girl at Richard's side, then back to the battle.

'I dare not tarry, Richard,' she said.

'PLEASE!' he wailed.

The words of Gailon rang in her ears and it was at that moment that she finally understood his warning. *If I remain to heal the wounded, I will weaken,* she thought, *and the worst battle still lies before me. Too much depends on me.*

'I cannot,' she said. 'I am sorry.'

She let Jeb's hand fall and backed away, her heart screaming with guilt, which Ioan heard clearly.

'Gailon, we must help the queen,' he said.

Gailon's bright eyes met Ioan's for a moment, and he nodded.

'Your Majesty,' he said to the king of the Macara Shee. 'May we trouble you for another lift?'

The faeries, having left the battle, obliged the old wizard, and as Exzalander turned back to the fight, she came face to face with Gailon.

'Gailon please, can you help them? I must return to the fray. Here, take the stones and the sword. Heal them, then perform the ritual of reunification and let us end this,' she said with a note of finality and ran back to Jeb, snatching up his sword.

'All will be well, Jeb. All will be well,' she whispered, but felt far from certain. 'Come Richard. You are needed on the field. Gailon will heal your friend.'

'I will not leave her,' he replied stubbornly.

'Richard, I was not asking you. It was a royal command. Now ON YOUR FEET!'

Gailon had already begun to heal Huçul, and as the colour returned to her cheeks, she opened her eyes, smiling. Richard smiled back and nodded, running to join Cröedaw and his queen as they returned to the battle.

Exzalander was trying not to think about the stench around her. Blood stained the sand and severed limbs scattered the field. She tried to push the endless screams from her mind and above all, how Gailon on her orders, was helping Jeb and the Elfin girl when she selfishly wanted him to protect Thaniel. She was trying not to worry, but fear spread its icy hand about her body, as she knew that her actions could have a terrible price when the battle was over.

'Cröedaw, see if you can spot Thaniel from the air,' she shouted over the din of battle.

'No, I will not leave your side. We must fight together, besides you should be focused on the battle. You have just lectured young Richard here for the same thing. Did she not, Richard?'

Richard blocked an oncoming blow, ducked beneath his sword and slashed open the opponent.

'Yes she did,' he said, panting.

Exzalander smiled grimly, decapitating another Trolg. 'I am glad to see you well, Richard.'

'I am glad to see you too,' he said, grinning wolfishly. 'Although I feel as though we have not met before. You were wearing a different face when last I saw you. It's difficult to get my head around.'

He might be wearing the same face, she thought, *but he seems to have changed more than I.*

Cob turned to his mother, laughing. 'I want to be angry, yet I'm too happy, mother.'

'I too, my darling boy. It must have been awful for you having to live with humans,' she said sympathetically.

Cob smiled as the clan made another handful of Trolgs disappear.

'I thought so at first, but at times I was glad of their company. Their lives are short, yet so full. Each day is filled with obstacles and challenges they feel they must overcome in order to give their existence meaning. It felt quite exhilarating, and their food is awfully good. '

'My dear boy, they are the food!' his mother laughed.

Cob shook his head. 'I do not think that I could ever eat human flesh again.'

His mother, though concerned, said nothing, assuming her son would embrace their ways once more, given time. However, there were more pressing matters at hand than her son's diet.

'How long does the king want us to leave them down there?' Xylem complained.

'Until they starve to death, I should think,' Cob said.

'And how long will that be? Weeks probably, and our beautiful halls will be ruined, filled with their stinking filth!'

'Then we shall make new halls and leave their corpses to rot,' said the king, as he returned from battle, seeming exhilarated.

The enemy was decreasing, despite the overwhelming strength of numbers. Without their presence, it was clearer to those who remained and how many had fallen.

As the faerie clan imprisoned the last of the Trolgs in their underground halls, a silent, grim stillness set upon those who remained, and they looked on in horror at the level of destruction.

Exzalander glanced from face to face, her heart fluttering with panic as she ran across the body-strewn desert to the main bulk of the allied force.

'Your Majesty?'

She swung about swiftly, hoping to see Thaniel.

'Caitul!'

Whil, who was supporting the knight, set him gently down.

'How came you here, Caitul?' asked the queen 'Did you fight for us?'

'Yes Your Majesty,' Whil answered. 'He broke faith with Katahl and fought in your name.'

Exzalander knelt before him, her eyes searching for blood loss. 'Caitul are you wounded? What ails you?'

The knight's eyes closed involuntarily, he fell forward into her arms and she eased him down onto his back.

'Exzalander,' he wheezed, as he struggled to make his eyes focus. 'You are the most beautiful woman I ever beheld and I have loved you from the moment I first saw you.'

She blinked away her tears and removed one his gauntlets to place his hand in her own. It was so cold, he may have already been dead, but for the fact he had just spoken.

'Caitul …' she spluttered.

He placed his finger to her lips to silence her. She closed her eyes and searched for the plane of Anarkhane, hoping to lead him there.

Nothing but darkness.

'Do not trouble yourself, Milady,' he said. 'There will be no rest, no peace for an oath breaker. I die without honour. I die in shame.'

'No Caitul! There must be something that I can do. I will not accept this. You kept your honour in breaking with Katahl, for fighting for what is right ... Caitul? CAITUL!'

The knight's breathing was still and his eyes stared up at the sky.

Empty.

'Your Majesty, he is gone.' Whil said quietly.

She refused to back away, using her hands to shock him as she had Marin, what seemed like an age ago.

Nothing.

Cröedaw knelt besides her, gently pulling her hands away.

'He is over three hundred years old. Once Katahl's spell was broken, he could no longer cling to life. You *cannot* bring him back. His time is over.'

'No!' she spluttered. 'I will not let him suffer. I must know that he is at peace ... I must ...'

Her tears overcame her and Cröedaw gripped her firmly, drawing her away from Caitul's body. Ioan's voice in her head brought her back from her grief.

'Gailon has performed the ritual, but said to remind you that there is still a stone missing!'

'No ...' she whispered to herself. She wiped her eyes, searching wildly about her, as if the stone might be found lying discarded in the bloodied sand. Her eyes fixed upon a familiar form and she cried out as realisation hit home like a hammer.

'NO!' she screamed, scrambling forward, half crawling before getting her footing. 'It cannot be.'

Cröedaw and Richard saw where she was headed.

'Thaniel!' he cried, as he leapt forward.

Exzalander's heart was pounding in her chest, threatening to break forever should she find him dead. She reached out to him, but even as she did so, there was a blast and the desert faded before her as she was removed from it by majick.

Thirty-Seven

Troy fell to the floor, his mind gone, his soul stolen—an empty, animated shell. Katahl smiled as the priest's soul rejuvenated him, filling a hole that he had been unaware existed. For the first time in as long as he could remember, he felt desire again. His cold eyes returned to the forelócian glæs and he sighed, the hunger for his princess washing through him like a wave.

'I will have her as wife and we will be together, as was foretold,' he said.

As Katahl's eyes turned back to the battle, his sudden fury spewed forth and he screamed with rage.

'Where is my army?' He searched for them, but saw no sign of any living Trolg. 'Where are they?' He fought to centre himself. Such emotion had been forgotten to him for so long that it was difficult to control. As his breathing slowed, he noticed Exzalander kneeling beside none other than Caitul. He watched her tears, feeling jealousy burn and sought for complete calm. His eyes closed, knowing what he needed to do.

There was a rushing sound in his head as he brought her to him, draining his strength. Falling to his knees, he crawled into the shadows, knowing that in his weakened state, he must not be in her presence.

Exzalander appeared in the cold courtyard of the castle of her father—empty, as all had been sent to war.

'No!' she cried. Her voice sounded strangled and it caught in her throat. She ran at the open gate, her heart aching to be near Thaniel again, but as she passed over the threshold, she paused. *Where is the majick barrier?* she thought, forcing herself to focus. *Katahl must have used tremendous power to bring me here and now he is weak and alone. I must find him and end this, with or without the Anarkhane stone.*

'KATAHL!' she raged, her voice echoing slightly off the cold stone walls. 'COME OUT AND FACE ME!'

Nothing.

I have to find him while he is defenceless. Find him and kill him. Gripping Jeb's sword, now her only weapon, she headed toward the throne room. There were not even servants left to prevent her as she passed through the great doors into the chamber.

The room was dim and the fire was not lit. She used her night vision to search every nook.

'KATAHL!'

She silenced herself. *I must use stealth, take him by surprise and not let my anger warn him of my approach.*

'Who are you?'

Exzalander span, Her sword at the ready. 'Lilith!' she said, lowering her weapon. 'It's Kirsten.' She forced Kirsten's image momentarily forth and Lilith's eyes widened with fear.

'I thought you were dead,' she gasped.

Exzalander shook herself at the words. *I must not think of death. Thaniel lies on the battlefield* ... she pushed all such thoughts from her mind. 'Lilith, do you know where Katahl might be hiding?'

The slave shrugged. 'Las' time I saw him, he was heading toward the tower,' she said.

'Can you lead me there?'

Lilith appeared reluctant at first, but relented and beckoned Exzalander to follow.

'Lilith, once you leave me you must gather all the slaves and escape this place. There is no guard and the barrier is down. Head south to Ealdorbold. Ask to speak with Counsellor Jaden. Say that I sent you and he will keep you safe.'

'Safe? Ealdorbold?' she spat. 'The Lord sent his last legion there. He said it was defenceless.'

Exzalander bit her lip thoughtfully for a moment. 'Do you think that you can convince them to follow you and offer a defence?'

Lilith appeared disgusted with the suggestion. 'We're slaves, not soldiers,' she said. 'Besides, when have the people of Ealdorbold lifted a finger to aid us?'

Exzalander hung her head, feeling ashamed, knowing that she had been in a position to help when she had been captive. *How many have died since then?*

'Very well, go where you will. Anarkhane protect you.'

Lilith pointed to the tower's entrance and smiled. It was something that had never been seen on her face before; it was something new and wonderful, which lifted Exzalander's spirits as she dashed up the stairs.

A dim light from the window sent a shaft across the room. In the corner, the forelócian glæs glowed faintly from recent use. She ran over to it and saw the desert beyond Golstur. The explosion she had heard as Katahl took her, suddenly made sense. He had blasted a hole into the faeries' realm, releasing the Trolg prisoners to fight once more. The battle-weary soldiers relief was strangled, when the enemy approached with furious vigour.

A shuffling sound brought her to focus on the target at hand. She held out the blade before her and her eyes shimmered purple as they pierced the darkness. However, it was not Katahl whom she found hiding in the shadows.

'Troy?'

He gave no answer and she took a step closer, sickness rising to her throat, suspecting how Katahl had suddenly learned of her presence in Maldahl. 'Troy, what have you done? You betrayed me. You betrayed us all!'

His eyes were glassy and he seemed not to hear her.

'TROY! WHY? So many have died, Troy, so many … TROY!'

She shook him violently and he gazed past her, walking over to the window.

'He has gone. Troy lives within me now,' Katahl's voice echoed inside her mind.

It was a violation for him to be there and she now understood why Troy had been so angry when she had done the same thing to him.

'Show yourself, Katahl,' she seethed.

'*I think not, my princess. Not yet. How does it feel to be betrayed by one whom you trusted so well? Are you not angry? Do you not wish to punish him for his treachery?*

'*Troy has been teaching me many things, his religion for instance; what a marvellous invention. I have decided to embrace it. The Word will reap devastation worse than any army I could ever muster. But you knew that, did you not? You warned him against such a future. I saw it in his head, just as I saw you after your first kill, as you tried in vain to wash the sin away along with the blood.*

'I cannot decide whether you were more desirable then, or now that you are battle worn. Of course then, you were not wearing your true face. A very clever trick, one no doubt that Taiohãhn taught you.'

Exzalander searched the shadows and when she was certain that he was not in the tower, she approached Troy again. She gazed into his empty eyes for a moment, before cutting off his head and walking from the chamber to continue her search.

'You cannot fool me, my love,' Katahl said. *'That was not anger you felt; that was not revenge. Did you think that you could free him so easily? He is still in me ... still loving you.'*

Exzalander's shock betrayed her and Katahl laughed softly.

'You did not know?'

She did not answer him, but struggled to control her mind, to expel him from it. She breathed hard, trying to centre herself.

'Where is Taiohãhn's sword?' he asked.

She stopped. She was back at the central chamber. Her father's throne was empty and offered no memories of him. Sitting down, she closed her eyes, trying to focus on Katahl, attempting to see through his eyes. When all she saw was the underside of her eyelids, she realised that he was looking through *her* eyes.

'Oh Exzalander, I am in you now. You will not find me unless I allow you to, and I will not do so until I know that you will surrender to me.'

Her eyes snapped open and she huffed in frustration that he had used her trick first.

'And why should I do that?' she spat.

'Because those who are yet living may be saved. I could stop the war. I could spare Shénnin's people.'

'Hah!' she said, and jumped to her feet. 'Katahl, your words are meaningless. You have not even enough strength to face me. Your promise is an empty one.'

She felt a pull on the back of her hair and in an instant she was yanked around and Katahl's lips were on her own. She was startled by her underestimation of him, wondering how he could have regained his strength so quickly. The taste of raw meat hanging on his breath made her stomach turn and she pushed him away. She swung her sword and it disintegrated, falling as ash at her feet. Catching hold of her arm, he pulled her close to him again.

'You cannot fight me, Exzalander. Even as you struggle here, your people are dying. It seems that my power is stronger than yours. I read that in you. You seemed to think that I would be weakened for days by my bringing you here … curious.

'Surrender to me now.'

His majick pulsated through his fingers and across her skin; she began to feel warm and light-headed. Focusing on the feeling, she sent a shockwave of electricity back into him, throwing him across the room. Their subsequent spells struck forth, but cancelled each other out before them.

Katahl smiled, but his handsome features did not show warmth of any kind

'You are more powerful than you realise, my princess,' he said, shooting another spell in her direction.

She dived out of the way and rolled back to standing, sending a sheet of flame to meet him in retaliation. He allowed the flames to wash over him and stepped through the blaze un-singed.

The final battle was being fought. Exzalander had returned to him as foretold. However, there were many versions of the prophecy. In some, she would destroy him and in others, she would rule Maldahl at his side.

Morlech saw the explosion on his descent. Through the hole it created, Trolgs were clambering to the surface to rejoin the battle. Swooping down, the dragon breathed a funnel of flame into the halls of the Macara Shee, destroying them beyond repair. All the Trolgs still trapped there, were nothing more than ashes.

Tom pushed the Trolg from him, temporarily winded. He had been left for dead.

'Thaniel?'

Thaniel lay close by and he had lost a lot of blood. Tom rolled him over, tapping his face and Thaniel blinked up, attempting to smile.

'Thomn? I thought I was dreaming. I saw the queen, but she disappeared,' he mused.

'Can you sit up?' Tom asked.

He helped Thaniel to a sitting position and removed his jerkin.

'That's a nasty gash.'

'Cröedaw!' called Thaniel, at his friend's approach.

'Come and help me bind this,' Tom said gruffly. 'Let us try and stop the bleeding as best we can, until Kirsten can heal you.'

Tom tightly tied a ripped shirt and Thaniel struggled to his feet, closely watching Cröedaw. He had known the Elfin too long to miss even the tiniest facial expression.

'What is it my friend? What has happened?'

Gripping the dagger in his claws, Morlech the dragon, headed for the only human he recognised in the clutter of people.

'Morlech,' Gailon said, as the great dragon landed next to him, sending men running in terror. 'We are grateful for your intervention.'

'I came for Tehtra, no other reason, wizard,' he growled.

Gailon nodded in understanding. 'Yet Morlech, even now, Exzalander has gone to face Katahl alone. She leaves behind the stone of Anarkhane. Just as the moment draws near when Tehtra might be released, all hope is lost, unless I can get it to her.'

The dragon's eyes narrowed and he stooped down. 'Jump on,' he said. 'I will take you to her. A quicker way you will not find.'

Thaniel sprinted over to the dragon and bowed low. 'Morlech, please permit me to accompany you also.'

The dragon stared long into the warrior's eyes and seemed to find something akin to him. He nodded and Thaniel mounted, pulling up Gailon behind him. Morlech's mighty wings beat hard and he lifted off the ground, speeding towards Brëgwela. Those left behind stared after the dragon, hoping that he would be swift.

Huçul ran to Richard and launched herself into his arms. Cröedaw smiled at them warmly.

'So sister,' he said, 'it seems that you are well acquainted with young Richard here.'

She beamed back at him and Richard blushed.

The Mariners, though weak, helped attend the wounded, having to resort to primitive methods as their majick was spent. Eight of their number lay dead; as they had fought, their power had drained the very life force from their bodies.

Once Gailon had tended to him, Jeb was strong enough to stand, but he was disorientated and found it difficult to accept that the battle was over and he was yet living.

Ioan and Tehd sat staring after Morlech, even as he disappeared from sight. Their hands clasped and they leaned into one another, as they sent all their hopes toward Brëgwela.

Tom knelt beside the now empty armour that had once been his son and for the first time in his life, he prayed.

'Why do you resist?' Katahl asked. 'With each moment that passes, you kill more of your people. Do you wish there to be no one left to adore you, to worship you? Perhaps you care nothing now that Thaniel is dead,' he hissed, his eyes flashing dangerously.

Exzalander ran at him screaming, and he blocked her punch with ease.

'Do not speak his name,' she shrieked, continuing to punch and kick at him.

Katahl was centred and calm and read each oncoming blow, as her passion made her attacks predictable.

'And what of poor Caitul?' he mocked. 'You let him die. Now he burns in hell-fire for all eternity.'

She pulled a double punch. One hit, but the other he dodged and managed to grab her wrist again, pulling her closer.

'You could save him the torment, Exzalander. Say you will be mine and I will release him from his curse. I could free Troy also,' he coaxed.

Exzalander collapsed into his arms. His eyes pierced her and she did not move. Her grief was welling up within her, threatening to wholly consume. He had said the words. He had said that Thaniel was dead. *Why live any longer? Why? To stop Katahl's tyranny, to damn the tide of suffering. But what of Troy? Of Caitul? They are suffering too and the only way to release them is to surrender to my enemy. But what then? Rule Maldahl at his side? Perhaps in time, bring light to darkness. Bring Katahl back from the brink of the abyss? No. I would lose myself in his darkness. He will blanket me from everything I have known and loved. But the pain will be gone—lost in sweet oblivion*

'Yes,' she whispered, trance-like.

He let his hands fall and saw that she was still. Helping her up, he led her over to the throne, seating her. His eyes never left her, watching like a patient predator, but she made no move. He could feel her pain and her desire for release. Lifting her face to his, he kissed her again. This time she did not retch; she did not react at all. He seemed not to notice. As he broke away, he walked over to a small leather casket and removed a silver crown of simple design, a crudely shaped green gem, its only decoration.

'How amusing I always found it that there were those who thought that you would reunite the stone of Anarkhane and use it to defeat me. How could you, when all the while I held a shard in my keeping? This was my mother's crown and now I give it to you, my queen.'

Exzalander felt the coldness of Taiohãhn's metal about her forehead and she reached up to touch it—dreamlike. 'The final piece,' she murmured.

'Yes my love. Call it my wedding gift, if you will. Now come.'

He held out his hand to her, as he had done in countless dreams. In each dream, she had taken it; she had succumbed and knew the sweet bliss at a price, for evil followed. She knew that if she took his hand, then a bargain would have been struck—no going back. She would be his; her power would be his and she would obey him, having no will other than *his* will.

The circlet upon her brow pulsated and she reached up to touch it, her hand covering her eyes as she did. Then quite clearly, she heard a laugh.

Her laugh.

It rang out across the throne room and it filled her with new resistance. Two things had at that point occurred. The stone on her brow reacted to the near proximity of its counterparts and she knew that help was near. As her spirits lifted, the wall of grief that she had thrown up, melted enough for Ioan to reach her, telling her that Gailon and Thaniel were coming.

Thaniel's not dead, she thought. *He's here.*

Katahl lowered his hand, his eyes glittering with cold fury. As he moved to send a punishing blow at her, the ceiling cracked and chunks of stone and mortar crashed to the floor followed by spurts of flame.

Dust filled the air and Exzalander could no longer see her enemy. She heard the guttural breathing of Morlech as he climbed into the ruined chamber, and she saw clearly through the smoke, the glow of the Anarkhane stone clutched in Gailon's grasp, as it called to the missing piece upon her head. The metal of the sword had remained and the gem had ornately interwoven about it so that it could still be used as a weapon.

Exzalander ran toward the light, seeing the faces of both Gailon and Thaniel and her heart quickened with gladness.

'Have you any of the bile left, Gailon?' she asked,

He nodded, noticing the circlet upon her head.

'Mmm, dragon flesh,' Katahl said. 'I always wondered what it might taste like. Unfortunately, they were slaughtered. I should know; I helped your father do it. It seems as though we may have missed one though.'

Morlech growled and lashed his tail, but Katahl somersaulted out of the way.

'Thaniel, is that you?' Katahl taunted. 'How would like to die? Come do not be bashful. Speak. I am feeling generous.'

Exzalander gripped the gem-sword, while Gailon searched his pack for the bile. Morlech breathed fire in the direction of Katahl's voice, only to find laughter echoing behind him.

'Morlech, calm yourself or you'll injure us all,' Exzalander said. She swung the new blade and it seemed to sing.

Gailon raised his staff and muttering a spell, the room cleared of smoke and debris. Katahl could be plainly seen, as he leaned against the fireplace, seeming amused.

'Morlech, I have the power to release Tehtra,' he goaded. 'All you have to do is kill Thaniel and she will be free.'

Exzalander's eyes widened and she ran at Katahl with sword swinging. Morlech paused and Thaniel warily drew his sword. The dragon's eyes became slits and he slashed out at Katahl, who disappeared, laughing, reappearing beside Thaniel. His fingers, all daggers, met with Exzalander's blow, as she appeared between them, blocking with the former Sword of Taiohãhn.

Katahl howled in pain and backed away. It was then that Exzalander saw that he was bleeding. *The sword can hurt him,* she realised. *I just have to be quick enough to strike.*

Gailon was mouthing the ritual and made ready with the bile, but Katahl was not beaten yet. His fingers restored, he held on his palm, the dragon dagger.

'Now Morlech, this is Tehtra, very clever how Ardahl trapped her in here. Do you know how easily I could destroy her?'

Morlech stomped toward Katahl, who continued to disappear and reappear at different points in the room. Thaniel shouted for him to calm down, but the dragon would not heed him, His mighty tail lashed, knocking Exzalander to the ground and the sword clattered across the flagstones. Katahl bent and picked it up, a triumphant smile upon his lips. As Morlech turned to face him, he threw the dagger.

Cruelly curved, it was not a weapon made for throwing. Morlech caught it with a snarl, but Katahl used the dragon's shift in concentration to place him under a sleep spell and the mighty beast dropped to the ground, with a crash. Katahl nimbly jumped on top of the slumbering beast and gazed curiously at the glowing weapon in his hand.

'Love is your weakness, Exzalander, where it proved my strength. Through my love for you, I became more powerful and yet I foresee that your love for this whelp will destroy you. You do not believe me? Let us see.'

He swung the blade backward and cast it at Thaniel. Exzalander threw herself between them, trying to catch it. However, the blade, which had always obeyed her commands before, now eluded her grasp, seeming to liquefy between her fingers and yet pierced her flesh like a harpoon of ice. She screamed as it skewered her, pinning her to the ground. Katahl stepped down from the sleeping dragon, smiling.

'I *told* you,' he affirmed. 'I have you to thank, Thaniel, you and Ardahl's upstart. Between you, you brought me the means of destroying my enemy.'

Thaniel fell at Exzalander's side, his body trembling as he reached for her hand.

'You loved her once,' he sobbed.

'I still do. More than *you* ever could. I will not let her die, Thaniel, not completely. She will join with me. I will drain her power and we will rule as one, as was foretold. Or if you wish to believe in other versions of the prophecy, that Exzalander will destroy me then yes, she will. By joining with me, she will create a new Katahl. The old me will be lost forever. Prophecies … they are so very precarious, are they not?'

Thaniel was no longer listening. Exzalander was looking up at him and she was smiling.

'I love you,' he said, choking on his tears.

'I thought that you had forgotten,' she rasped.

He squeezed her hand, holding it close to his chest.

'How could any spell make me forget that I love you? Not even *you* are that powerful, My Queen.' He smiled and the tears streamed down his face, falling onto her hand.

Gailon had stopped muttering. The ritual was complete. Katahl looked over to where the wizard was kneeling.

'Give me the bile, old man!' Katahl ordered.

Gailon looked up and smiled. Katahl frowned, glancing to Exzalander, yet he could see nothing, but Thaniel's back. Exzalander waited until Gailon's voice silenced then she flipped open the flask and drank the dragon bile.

'Get away from her,' Katahl hissed.

He sent Thaniel hurtling across the room, where he fell, unconscious. Pacing over to Exzalander, he tried to retrieve the sword from her dying body. It sank deeper, evading his grasp as her flesh absorbed it. He sent a fire spell at her, but it merely deflected and her body began to pierce the room with a white light.

The light of Anarkhane.

The light of creation, whole once more.

Even at the brink of death, she felt both gods within her. She could feel their power grow and their presence draw near. The commands of both Anarkhane and Taiohãhn reached her ears and channelling the power of the gem, she destroyed Katahl. She did not grant him death, or remove his soul as he had done to Troy; she *uncreated* him. It was as though he simply ceased to exist.

She continued to hear the voices of the gods, but could no longer understand them. The pain was beyond excruciating. She wanted to scream, but no sound ensued. Thaniel was lost from her sight and only the green gem remained as it penetrated every part of her being—tearing, melting, remaking.

A pulling sensation made her search through the crystal glaze of her eyes. Anarkhane and Taiohãhn were present, summoned to Maldahl by the stone's reunification. She was aware of them, their faces fierce and unsmiling. *Why are they not helping?* she thought. *Why are they not taking the pain away?*

The agony and the pulling continued, unrelenting, until she longed for death, to be released from the torture. She began to forget who she was and what had happened to cause the pain. It began to feel as though it had always been there, as if lifetimes had been spent in such torment.

The tugging sensation stopped abruptly and she felt a shove as she was thrust onward into the darkness between worlds. She could not slow down or stop. The gem still twisted and tore inside her, but the pain ebbed and flowed, allowing her mind to wander through the tides of pain—remembering.

The gods had seemed so angry. *They had no reason to be. I rid Maldahl of Katahl. I reunified their gem.*

Corvuß's warning burned hotter than the gem inside her, as realisation struck. She had been nothing but a pawn of the gods. They used her, betrayed her and exiled her. She burned hotter still, the pain and fury combining until she welcomed it. It helped to bring back focus within her changing being. Her mind tuned in on a single thought at last.

Revenge.

She did not know when or how, but she vowed that she would have revenge on the gods who had torn her away from all she held dear.

Epilogue

Troy stood on the threshold of the Underworld palace, looking out into the vast forest. Instinctively, he stepped back, knowing that if he attempted to walk beneath the trees, he might lose his mind forever. *Perhaps I already have,* he thought. *This is no heaven, but it isn't hell, either.*

He remembered Katahl's hands upon him and the darkness that followed. He shuddered, trying to push away Katahl's desires. *Why did she drive me to betray her?* He sighed, knowing that he had nobody to blame but himself. *I missed her so much. I saw her fading, day by day, until she was gone. It was as though Kirsten had been murdered and nobody seemed to care, but me.*

He pondered the quiet sleeping trees for a while. *Perhaps it would be good to lose myself in the forest, to wander until I forget all. But that is too easy. It is not the kind of peace I deserve.*

Turning away from the Taiohãhn's forest, he walked up to the doors of the palace of marble, and pushed. They yielded with a creak and he stepped forward into the unknown.

As he walked through the endless halls of the empty palace, he came to a decision. Somehow, someway, he would find Kirsten again.

The End

Don't miss

King's Gambit

Book II of The CODM prophecy

Coming soon

Bibliography

Ashley, M (editor). *The Giant Book of Myths and Legends* (Parragon Books Service Ltd, Bristol, 1995)

Curran, B. *The Creatures of Celtic Myth* (Cassel & Co, London, 2000)

Ebbutt, ML. *Ancient Britain* (Chancellor Press, London, 1995)

Seligmann, K. *The History of Magic* (Quality Paperback Book Club, New York, 1997)

Skene, WF. *The Four Ancient Books of Wales* (Edmonston and Douglas, Edinburgh, 1868)

Squire, C. *Celtic Myths and Legends* (Lomond Books by Paragon, Bath, 2000)

Stone J R. *Latin for the Illiterati* (Routledge, London, 1996)

Thomas, K. *Religion and the Decline of Magic* (Weidenfeld & Nicholson, London, 1971)

References

The author gratefully acknowledges the use of the following quotations.

Latin mass extracts on page 56 are taken from Psalm 42 and Dis Irae (13th century Latin hymn, believed to have been written by Thomas of Caleno).